# The

# Forbidden Lily

## SHELLEY YOUNG

*Also by Shelley Young*

(Fiction)
THE BLOOD FEUD
THE BLOOD TIE
PLAIN DEALING
THE BLOOD TRAIL
THE RAIN HOUSE
ALL MEN ARE GODS
THE BABISIAN BOX
THE RISE OF THE EIGLEXX
THE BIRTH OF A CORSAI
THE EWA 8: DOMINATION TERMINATED
DOMINANTS & MORTALS

(Nonfiction)
ANYONE CAN WRITE

This is a work of fiction. Names, characters, places, and events are solely fictitious and written from the author's imagination. Any resemblance to actual persons, living or dead or events is entirely coincidental.

Cover design by Maduranga of mnsartstudionew
Edited by Sydney Morgan

Shelley
Fiction
Publishing

www.shelleyfiction.com

*For Birda Williams*

## TABLE OF CONTENTS

# Book One

*"New Orléans is very handsome and well constructed...*
*The magnificence of display is equal to all...*
*The women paint and rouge their face to hide the ravages of time.*
*The Devil has a vast empire here."*
-Sister Madeleine Hachard de Saint-Stanislas - May 1728

# Chapter One
## The Devil

*[Two little birds were sitting, two little birds were sitting on a fence, two little birds were chattering, what they were saying I do not know. A chicken hawk came along the road, pounced on them and ate them up, no one hears them chattering anymore, the two little birds on the fence. —Louisiana Creole song]*

His horse was in full gallop, its hoof striking part of a speckled king snake that Bernard Boisdoré did not see. Everything was a distraction: the feel of the cracked saddle as his horse took on uneven ground, the constant rush of the wind against his face, the warning fear he was traveling too fast.

The six men chasing him gained speed, riding their horses as fiercely as he was and without fear. Only a small distance behind him now, Bernard looked over his shoulder and saw one branch off to his left. Over his other shoulder, he saw another branch off to his right. As he suspected their plan was to force him northeast away from the plantation mansion and toward a swamp infested with alligators, snapping turtles and snakes.

The eternal chill of Death rode in the saddle with him.

"Help me!" Bernard screamed, knowing his screams were hopeless. He was on private property more than a three hour ride from the city. Still he screamed. "Somebody! Anybody!"

Trees were all he saw: small, large and aged. One, in particular, got his attention. Up ahead a live oak blocked the early morning sun, causing the hour to appear like twilight rather than dawn. Its clustered branches looked like gnarled witches' fingers casting conjurations toward the sky. On one of the lower branches, a man lay on his belly with a long rifle aimed in Bernard's direction.

Fire burst out of its barrel as the flint struck the frizzen. Smoke caused by the gunpowder carried in the wind. Bernard's horse whinnied as the iron ball burned through its coat, macerating muscle and nerves. Bernard only had time to kick his feet free of the stirrups as the horse's knees unlocked and its nose dipped toward the earth. Dust flew in the air as Bernard crashed against the ground in the speed of a comet. Flipping arms over legs, gravel scraped one side of his face. Only when he stopped rolling had he been able to gasp, urging his lungs to quickly fill.

Bones had been broken. Surely he knew this even if he couldn't feel it. One more thing was certain. He wasn't ready to die.

In the position he lay in he saw that the riders had stopped their pursuit. To the right of him, through the trees, he saw what looked like a Creole cottage. Getting up had almost been impossible. His right arm hung lower than it should have. There wasn't a part of him that didn't slowly fill with pain. A persistent tinny rang in his ear like the sounds of a plantation bell being rung in warning.

Ambling slowly, but mostly limping tears fell from his eyes.

A quick look was given over his shoulder. The man from the tree was now on his feet waving the barrel of his rifle like Américains did the Américain flag. The other riders and horses pranced in semicircles but stayed where they were. It was then Bernard saw more riders riding furiously toward him, tearing up the Louisiana earth into dry red chunks. Riding in front of the men was the Devil.

Bernard saw the Devil and limped, albeit slowly, to the closest tree. This, at least, placed his enemy behind him. His only pistol had been lost during the first part of the chase. The Yakut his brother had stolen off of a Chinaman was all he had left. Reaching for it, its four-inch blade felt inadequate in his grip.

Leaning to the side of the tree to see where the Devil was now, he felt the barrel of a pistol press against the back of his skull.

"You're dead." The words were spoken calmly and close to a whisper.

Gripping the Yakut tighter, his only thought was living as he licked his lips. "I have money."

"I *am* money," the voice whispered.

"I'll go away. You'll never see me in New Orléans again."

"You're a threat to me now. *Mon ennemi.*"

"Wait," Bernard pleaded, then turned slowly and stared the Devil in his eyes. Unusually tall for a Frenchman, the Devil had waited patiently for the two of them to make eye contact.

Bernard opened his mouth, but no words came out. At that moment it all became clear. *Live by the sword, die by the sword.* A half step was taken when the Devil's pistol fired. Bernard didn't hear the sound it made as a cloud of gun smoke coated him like a transparent cloak. Falling from this cloud, the cool morning breeze licked the wounds on his face as he wondered why he was still alive.

The pistol was dropped from the Devil's hand and a Spanish handheld Flintlock with a folding bayonet pulled from his side. Its seven-inch blade was extended as the Devil whispered in Bernard's ear.

"In every rumor, there's a morsel of truth. You heard plenty about me. Yet you came. I *am* that crazy son of a bitch they say I am."

Bernard had no time to react.

The bayonet was thrust deep into his throat.

# Chapter Two
## The List

*[The higher the monkey climbs, the more it is exposed to danger. –*
*Creole proverb]*

The man known as the Devil to *les* Américains and as *le diable dans Nouvelle-Orléans* to the Orléonois was born Will Henriot Jennings, the only heir of Andreu Arsène Arceneaux Jennings. He stood seven-feet-four inches tall. His muscular frame defied his age. A hereditary pigment disorder caused the hair on his head to turn white while still in the womb and made his skin look similar to the hue of Egyptian bronze. Also, like his father, the irises of his eyes were like clear water, the kind found around tropical islands, and at times like translucent silver when seen in harsh light.

The man lying on the ground at his feet was a stranger to him. The only thing he knew was the man had come to his plantation to kill him.

The blood on the bayonet was wiped away with a handkerchief, and then the weapon shoved into his coat pocket. Will searched Bernard's clothes for clues of his identity. Nothing was in his pockets or underclothes. It was when Will stood again and started to walk away that he turned and lowered again. This time, Bernard's boots were removed. When the right was turned upside down a torn piece of paper fluttered to the ground like a wounded butterfly.

On it, someone had written not only Will's name, but also the names of his children, and one of his three grandchildren, a granddaughter born of a slave who had lived on his plantation years ago.

*Will Henriot Jennings – November 1st, 1754*
*Françoise Marie-Grace Achen – January 10th, 1793*
*Pierre Constance Jennings – November 3rd, 1795*
*Julien Rafael Jennings – June 1st, 1804*
*Désireé Priscilla Jennings – May 10th, 1816*
*All of them have fair to white hair and have extreme height.*

One of the men on the horses dismounted and walked to him. Francis Jessup Achen was half French and half German and was Will's right-hand man. Frances squatted beside him, saw the look on Will's face and reached for the paper. Although realizing what he was looking at, he gave Will a piercing gaze. "What is this?"

Up until that morning, the two of them believed only two others knew that Will was the biological father of Frances' only child, Françoise.

"Will?" Frances asked. He began to shake his head in denial. "This can't be what I think it is."

"It is," Will confirmed. "Someone wants to kill me and all of my children."

"Why the children? You don't even have enemies. I helped you kill them all years ago."

Will turned from him, walked to his horse and mounted. Frances followed closely behind him.

Will stared down at him. "That's why this makes sense."

"How can you say this?"

"Because the men we killed had young sons at the time and now those sons are grown men and call themselves Le Secret Sept."

"Le secr…" Two heavy lines formed on Frances' forehead and on the bridge of his nose. His bushy eyebrows arched as his mouth pulled into a menacing snarl. "Those sons of bitches."

Will waited while Frances mounted, and then he and his men dug the heels of their boots into their horses' flesh, spurring the beasts into motion.

# Chapter Three
## The Enemy

*[The coward lives a long time. – Creole proverb]*

Eleven miles away and later that evening Dr. Louis Guillmard parked his skeleton phaeton beneath one of the numerous trees planted in an abandoned field. A few hours earlier he had sent six of his most trusted slaves to neighboring plantations. The message each of them carried was urgent. The men given those messages in private were to meet him at this precise location at exactly four o'clock. They were meeting for one reason and one reason alone. Neither Daniel Malloy nor Bernard Boisdoré was anywhere to be found.

Nothing had gone as planned. *Nothing.* Daniel and Bernard should have met Dr. Guillmard at noon behind Xavier Beauvais' barn. Everything had been carefully planned. *Everything.* Their absence meant something went wrong and Dr. Guillmard knew exactly what that something was. Daniel and Bernard were dead. And if they were dead it meant the Devil had killed them; and if the Devil had killed them it meant he knew why Daniel and Bernard were on his plantation. Of course, Will did. The answer was quite simple.

In New Orléans, along the river, who can trust the English speaking *nouveaux-arrivés* Américains? They had arrived by the thousands on what used to be French soil and raised their flag of red, white and blue over the *Place d'Armes.* Most of them were taunted by impoverished Creole children who sang an *insulte* whenever they passed on the streets.

*Mericain coquin*
*'Billé en nanquin*
*Violeur de pain*
*Chez Miché d'Aquin.*

As soon as the Américains arrived a large group of families in New Orléans secretly elected seven of the city's most influential men to see to all of their judicial needs not trusting the English-speaking Américains to see things the way that only the Orléonois could or dole to them equal justice. Dr. Guillmard was one of the men they elected. With his careful planning and persuasive manner, he convinced his fellow Orléonois to also choose Vincent Laporte, Juan McGhee, Juan's nephew, Eustace Avila, Edouard Salle, Antoine De La Croix and Jean-Magnon Dupuy. What the Orléonois had no way of knowing was each of these men was the sons of the five men who had murdered Will Jennings' father back in '68.

The Orléonois referred to the seven in the privacy of their homes as Le Secret Sept. The Américains in the city, who feared them greatly, called them by their English name, the Clandestine Seven. There was no one that didn't fear them in some way, except Will Jennings, the same devil of a man who owned large amounts of real estate in and outside of the city. But if the Devil was killed, and his children were killed, then his vast estate would fall into the hands of his next of kin. In this case, the heir would be the wife of Will's eldest son, Pierre. Her name was

Jenna Louise Jennings. Le Secret Sept needed Jenna to be the sole heir of the Jennings' family wealth to ensure their business endeavors at the Port of New Orléans, of which Will and Pierre were prohibiting. But this couldn't happen if Will and any of his children or grandchild were alive.

Dr. Guillmard pulled his watch out of his pocket. In the distance, a horse quickly approached. Jean-Magnon Dupuy stopped to the side of Dr. Guillmard, and, like the doctor, fixated his gaze in the direction he had come from.

"You're late," Dr. Guillmard said. "Did you see any of the others?"

"All of them. I left them behind. I couldn't wait. Were you able to find Daniel and Bernard? I have a family, goddamit!"

Dr. Guillmard drew in his lips and breathed heavily through flared nostrils. "Retain your lunacy, Jean. We *all* have families. What did you think? That joining our little group meant you would be victorious and only that? I'll tell you now. Even in our defeat, you will hold your head up or I'll cut it off, poke it with a stick and hold it up for you."

Standing slightly over five-feet tall, Jean-Magnon dismounted with a jump, removed his hat and crushed it against his heart. His eyes were again fastened on the road he'd left behind. "Maybe all is well. Both men may still be alive."

"They're dead!" Dr. Guillmard spat. "And so are you!" His voice then lowered. "In a few days, all of us will be dead. Maybe sooner."

Jean-Magnon blinked back tears as a team of horses and a single phaeton came into view, approaching at a rapid speed. When the group finally assembled the impromptu meeting began right away.

Vincent Laporte was more eager than the others. "Where are Daniel and Bernard? Have you found them?"

"Dead," Dr. Guillmard answered. "Nowhere to be found. One of you can take your chances looking for them over at the Jennings plantation. That isn't something I'm willing to do."

Edouard Salle looked at his compeers individually. "If Daniel and Bernard are dead, then we are dead."

"What about the other hired hands?" Vincent countered. "Any chance they can get the job done alone?"

Antoine De La Croix tightened his hand on his rein, causing his horse to step forward. "The plan was to kill Will first. He's the most dangerous."

"I think the other hired hands can do it," Jean-Magnon asserted. "All they need is the opportunity."

"No," Dr. Guillmard disagreed. "We only have two killers left and Will Jennings is still alive." His mouth tightened with disgust from the very thought. "Monsieur Jennings is perhaps at this moment roasting our wives over an open flame and boiling our children for supper."

"How dare you!" Antoine challenged.

"I dare!" Dr. Guillmard retorted. "The men in the Jennings *famille* can in no way be considered normal. We are discussing the most notorious family that ever lived in this city. Will Jennings is *insane!* His sons are equally *insane!*"

"What choice do we have, messieurs?" Vincent questioned. "The Devil is ill. Soon he'll be in the grave anyway. Let's kill his sons, daughter and granddaughter and be done with this mess. This is now our only path."

Juan McGhee and his nephew Eustace Avila sat quietly a moment while staring at one another.

"What is it?" Dr. Guillmard asked them.

"Two men were sent to kill Monsieur Jennings when he was least aware," Eustace answered. "By now his sons are also aware. All of us call Will Jennings the Devil but his son Pierre is far more of a devil than his father will ever be. Now if you excuse me, messieurs, I shall take my leave and ready my household. I'm truly sorry it had to end this way."

"We cannot give up!" Jean-Magnon insisted. "We give up and we die."

"We cannot die," Vincent agreed. "We're fathers. We are businessmen who are vital to this city. We can't give up! As soon as our other two killers arrive in the city, we send them after Julien first."

## Chapter Four
# The First Night of Marriage

*[Dear, I love you so, Yes, I love you so, With all my heart, I love you dear, Like a little pig loves mud. – Creole love song]*

Much later that same evening, Julien Rafael Jennings sat at the edge of the bed, his purpose even more evident and eager when he smoothed his hand over the form hidden underneath the coverlet.

The mansion he was in was located in the heart of the Vieux Carré on Rue Dumaine. It belonged to an old friend of his father. The man's name was Charlet Bienvenu. Charlet had traveled through the streets personally to find Julien as soon as he received word that Julien had secretly wed that same day. Wanting to please an old friend, as well as act as a surrogate father over the new bride and groom, Charlet refused to accept no for an answer and carried the couple back to his home. There he gave them his dead wife's boudoir to use for their five day honeymoon. While he and the couple sipped wine and chatted, two of his slave girls were sent up to the room to prepare it with extra linen, fragrant toiletries, water, food and plenty of beverages to drink.

It was the bottle of Château Margaux that Julien reached for from a nearby table. Pouring a single glass, he extended it to his new bride. With his other hand, because he was eager to fulfill his first duty as a husband, he lowered the coverlet part way. Marie-Marie saw the glass and shook her head. In fear that her new husband will snatch away the coverlet entirely, she pulled it slowly up to her neck.

They had been married all of four hours. He had committed a Creole sin and married on impulse. No announcements had been sent. Invitations were completely foregone. None of his friends or family had attended. The only people who had been inside the cathedral with them were spectators curious to know why the son of one of their wealthiest elite stood at the altar beside a woman while facing a priest.

"Take a sip," he encouraged. He had bedded virgins in the past and was quite familiar with their routine. Marie-Marie's reticence was hard for him to decipher. On occasion, he had sensed she had no intentions of sharing the bed with him.

He stood and pulled at his cravat, dropping the cloth to the floor. "I'll blow out the candles."

He removed his tailcoat. As he went about the room removing the rest of his attire, he blew out the lamps only to see the room was now too dark. The bedroom faced the street. Four widely spaced French doors opened onto a private balcony. Julien opened one, partially, then pushed its shutters out toward the street.

The light of night sliced the darkness around him. The smell of the city was instant. Sewage had always been a problem and littered the street. It's sickly sweet stench mingled with the scent of the gardenias and jasmine the servants had attempted to decorate with.

Julien smiled when Marie-Marie saw the darkness and drew in a slow breath of relief. Standing beside the bed again, he offered his hand to her.

She shook her head.

"No, Julien," she pleaded. "A proper woman should stay in bed and lay on her back until it's over."

He studied her a moment, his eyes narrow with disbelief. "If you do not get out of that bed." The threat had been spoken firmly, yet teasingly as well. "I will not be in a marriage where my wife hides behind damask, silk, cotton or any other fabric. I shall see you as God made you."

Her first step out of the bed nearly caused her to tumble. While she recovered, she made certain not to look down at his nudity.

At more than six feet tall, Julien had to lower to encircle his arms around her waist. The full palms of his hands squeezed and caressed her derriere before gripping each cheek and urging her closer against his erection. Lowering more, his mouth pressed against hers.

Earlier in the church, their first kiss had been no more than the pressing of their mouths briefly together. The way he kissed her now when she felt the tip of his tongue slip between her lips, that one touch and she knew this night would not be like anything she'd ever been told. Heat flushed her body. Her eyes became large circles of wonder. The way his tongue filled her mouth alone made her conscientious of the hair that rose on the nape of her neck. Her moan filled his mouth when he sucked the tip of her tongue, drawing it further between his lips until it was nearly consumed.

What was this? She asked herself, aware that she could hardly keep still. A need the kind she hadn't anticipated took possession of her and made her body ache to be kissed and touched more. Leaning on the tips of her toes to reach his mouth, to her surprise, all of her fears slowly began to dissipate.

"Mmm." The deep moan he gave she had felt it in her soul. "Just like that, chérie. Kiss me just like that."

When she realized that she moved her tongue the same way he moved his not to please him, but because she had enjoyed it so, the voice of her childhood priest entered her ears. *Lust is wicked!*

Julien peered at her with wet, parted lips when she suddenly pulled from his embrace. For those few seconds, she had been willing not only to give in to him but to her own desires. This made him more aroused and even more eager. He loved how quickly she had learned to kiss, and how her exploration of his mouth had churned his stomach with anticipation.

Hoping to debunk the myths and old women tales told to young Creole girls about their interpretation of what should occur in a boudoir, his tongue gently touched her lower lip as he gazed into her eyes, and then he began to kiss her more hungrily than before. Nothing escaped his notice, like the way either of her hands reached for him as they should have. As if frightened to touch his bare skin, her trembling fingertips instead traced the contour of his face as her tongue plunged deeper into his mouth. Guiding her hands, he placed them in his hair. Earlier he had loosened the single long braid he usually wore to allow his hair to hang loose because many of his past lovers loved fisting it while in bed.

Marie-Marie felt his hair in her hands and drew back from him again with large eyes this time. The breaths she took were deep and audible. Julien searched deeply into her eyes and saw that Marie-Marie, at least, tonight, would not yield to a wild romp. It was what he had envisaged all evening, but for now, that image would have to wait. Having her as his wife was all he thought about now.

The chemise she wore, with its Sokai embroidery, was quickly pulled over her head. Marie-Marie closed her eyes and chewed her lower lip as his bare hands began rubbing all over her. She experienced a new pleasure that made the skin of her nipples tighten. As if her new husband sensed this, she watched as he lowered and covered one of her small, puffy nipples with his warm, wet mouth. The tugs and sucks made her feel warm, and then as if fire chased the nerves along her spine, and centered between her legs, especially when the nipple he suckled sharpened into a hard point and reached the back of his throat.

What she felt then was nothing less than extraordinary. Rapturous desire quickened inside even the tiniest nerve in her body. If he had been much shorter, she would have thrown her leg on his shoulder to press her sex against him somehow in the hopes of relieving its increasing throbs. It was the thought of this action that made her leg lift slightly. His hand captured the leg and held it up in this position as she was lifted off the floor. It was the feel of the hotness of his manhood as it slipped between her legs the reason she swung her legs behind him until the soles of her feet were flat against the wall.

Take me! The words blared in her brain just as a knock sounded against the door. Both of them looked in the knock's direction panting for breath, and then she was laid gently on the bed. Before he walked away, the tip of his tongue tasted the tip of one of her nipples as his hands parted her thighs very wide. A part of the coverlet was used to cover her.

"Don't even think about moving."

None of his clothing was reached for. As Marie-Marie watched him walk naked toward the door, the desire to run after him, jump high upon his back and fasten her legs around him made her close her eyes.

***

Charlet frightened Julien, so close was the man's face to the door as if he had pressed one eye against it in order to see through the wood. Once he saw Julien on the other side, he stepped back and held a letter high above his head.

Charlet had known the family for many years. He knew how Will and his two sons responded to bad news. Even Julien, who had been the only male who had been born in his family with a happy disposition – *un garçon heureux* – can turn into the devil himself if he felt his family or his life had been threatened.

Charlet thought about this as he whispered in the dimly lit hall. "Hired gunmen have attacked your papa."

Charlet didn't understand why his body fell forward as the door was snatched further open. Fingers bit into the skin of his neck as Julien gripped it, then tightened his grip for a better hold. Before Charlet could unleash the first of many closed fist blows, his feet cleared the floor as his body was rushed further out into the hall.

"He's all right, Julien!" The words came out strangled but were coherent enough for Will's youngest son to release him. Rubbing the skin over his throat, Charlet knew it was better to keep talking rather than stay silent. "He's safe. Don't you realize he must if he's sent his men?"

Julien didn't have the height of his father or brother, still he was tall. Six-feet-and-eight-inches of naked muscled flesh were hard to not stare at as one of the slave girls realized when she stepped out of a nearby room and found herself unable to move.

"Allez!" Charlet hissed at the girl. Looking at a well-crafted man wasn't what caused his anger. It was that the girl was too stupid to notice she was standing too close to the son of the Devil while he was in the midst of being told bad news that infuriated him. The girl had cost him two-hundred dollars. Two-hundred dollars was, for him, too much to lose.

Satisfied when the girl ran down the hall and disappeared down the mansion's stairs, Charlet turned and started to reach his hands out to Julien like any man would when trying to console another. Most Creole men in the city were barely above five feet tall like Charlet was. The shoulders were what he had aimed for, but the height difference had caused Charlet to reach for Julien's waist. *Mon Dieu!* Quickly dropping his hands, he realized how stupid he must appear and wondered if Julien misunderstood his half-made gesture.

Talking was his only way out of this embarrassing moment.

"Your papa killed the man, Jules, and that's when he found the list. I'm afraid it's a duck list. I've heard of these things before, often spoken by the Américains. New Orléans will never be the same now that they have arrived with their uncivilized traditions. Read your papa's letter. If you need me, I'll be down below with a bottle of good wine to drown away my sorrows."

Julien leaned against the wall, lowered his chin and closed his eyes as he rehearsed what he had just heard. His father was not well. It couldn't have been a coincidence that someone would attack now when they believed his father was too weak to defend himself.

He opened the folded piece of paper and read the few sentences written hastily in his father's hand. Seeing the names on the list didn't move him until he reached the last. *Désireé?* His father must have made a mistake. It was then he reread the list and noticed Françoise's name at the top of it. Could the letter be right? Had someone wanted to kill a woman and child?

"Monsieur Julien?"

The voice came from the top of the staircase. It was one Julien recognized. Charlet had mentioned his father had sent his men. Montague was one of them.

Montague didn't come closer and Julien knew why.

"My father, Montague. Is he well?"

"He's good." Montague continued to stay where he was. "Have you read your father's letter?"

"Yes."

Montague gazed knowingly at the two men behind him.

"I can't begin to tell you what happened this morning. You wouldn't believe me if I tried. But what I can tell you is that...is that... shortly after your father killed the first, we soon found another. It's your brother who took the second man's life. I've seen men die before. I doubt there's anyone in the city who can't say the same. But I have never seen anyone killed the way this man was. I think it was the deliberateness of it that sickened me."

Julien took a step closer to the staircase. "Are you trying to tell me that *two* men tried to kill my father on his land?"

Montague still wore his coat and held his hat in his hands. This told Julien how urgent Montague felt this visit was. Instead of allowing the servants to assist him out of his traveling clothes, he had come upstairs first.

"Yes, monsieur." He chose his next words carefully. "And your father fears there are more, as whoever is behind this wants to kill you all, including the petite *mulâtresse* your family is fond of."

"Désireé," Julien whispered. She was only eight years old. Killing a child was unheard of, even if they were of mixed race. New Orléans was filled with mixed race children of every kind, but mostly half Creole. Most bâtards were treated kindly and with respect and rarely mistreated. They owned businesses, and most of them had been freed. Not all, but a majority in the city made provisions for them as well, and these provisions were made public when necessary.

Killing Désireé was the same as killing an eight-year-old child in any family.

"Now that you have his letter, I'll go," Montague warned.

Julien gave a firm nod.

Montague slipped back down the stairs. As Julien watched him go, the letter began to make sense. Leaving Désireé alive and killing him, his father and brother would make her wealthier than anyone else in all of the States of América, as all three of them had made her their sole legal heir.

***

Going back inside the room, he made certain this time to lock the door.

Crossing the room, he peered through the open French door and down at the street. It was impossible for anyone to climb up the balcony. Because of this, he left the shutters and the door as they were.

"Is everything all right, Jules?" Marie-Marie asked from the bed.

He turned and faced her. Leaving tonight was too dangerous. It was better to leave at the first sight of light. Since they would have to stay where they were, he decided to get the night over with and get a good night's rest.

Marie-Marie slid over on the bed to make room for him.

Julien climbed into the bed from the foot of it, and reaching her, drew her back toward its middle. "Everything is fine," he answered.

The smile she gave temporarily made him forget everything else. The kissing began again as they had while standing. Eager fingers gripped locks of his hair. The feel of her naked skin against his, and the heat spreading between her thighs reawakened his desire. The mattress sagged in all the wrong places as he leaned more against her. Teasing the very tip of her nipple had been the same as unlocking a door. A deep arch of her spine was made and followed by a sharp intake of breath. One of his fingers gently slid between her thighs after her knees relaxed even further. Although her sex was searing hot, sleek and wet, the resistance he felt against his fingertip was unlike anything he ever felt before. Taking a moment to explore the feel of her sex, his finger slid between the lips and upward to the hood of knotted, sensitive flesh. Unless his mind was playing tricks on him, other than a very small tangle of gossamer-like threads, it seemed there was no part of her that could be penetrated. Kissing her deeper to take her mind off what he was doing, he pushed gently against the little slender of threads.

"*Veuillez! Cela les blesse!*" She whimpered and clenched her thighs closed from the pain.

"*Calmer, chérie,*" he cooed. Climbing from the bed, because his curiosity was piqued, he again made his way to the door. What he needed was light to see her body up close.

The room beside his was being used by a French couple traveling through the city. The husband and wife were lying on opposite sides of the bed. The man lay on the side closest to the door. He merely watched as a tall naked man stepped into the room and made his way to a low-burning lamp on a table. Beside the lamp candles had been neatly arranged for later use.

Julien grabbed a candle and lit it. By this time, the woman lying with the man sat up, saw his state of undress, then quickly lay back down and rolled onto her side so that her back was to him.

Back in his room, Julien lit three of the lamps, then carried two of them closer to the bed. Marie-Marie sat up.

" No, chérie. Lie down again, mon amour."

He sat one lamp on the bedside table. The other he kept in his hand. Sitting on the bed, he made sure not to burn himself or her or the bed, as he lowered to get a close inspection.

Marie-Marie had a voice as soft as her name.

"*Que faites-vous?*" She asked.

Julien already saw the problem and wanted to put her at ease. "*Je tiens à examiner.* Open your legs wider, chérie."

Marie-Marie stared up at the ceiling, the soles of her feet pressing together as her knees fell further apart. "*Cela peut-il être nuisible?*"

He smiled at her.

She looked down, saw his smile and returned it with one of her own.

"How can it hurt if I'm only looking?" And looking he was. There was no visible opening. Two soft folds of flesh looked as if they had been fused together since birth.

"I heard my mother tell my father how painful it was," she said. "I could hear her from down the hall. My father accused her of exaggerating, and told her that having children had solved the matter. My mother begged him to have affairs. My father told her that no other woman was made like she was, and he was only doing what was his right. It seemed as if I heard her crying inside her boudoir every night."

Julien meditated on this as he set the lamp beside the other on the table. Creole girls were married starting at the age of sixteen until they were twenty-five. Anything older than that, although it did happen on occasion, the young woman was considered a spinster. Marie-Marie wasn't sixteen. She was twenty. The night was possible. If her mother was capable of making love, then she was too.

He was surprised when Marie-Marie twined her arms around his neck and pulled him closer. Julien did what he must; he took his time, slowly increasing her arousal to draw her attention away from her middle.

Marie-Marie was a talker. A woman who talked openly during lovemaking aroused him immensely. *Lentement. Bon. Oui. Lentement.*

When the lips of her sex were parted and the juices laved away with his tongue, she rewarded him with whimpers of pleasure. *Il se sent très bien. Oui. Très bon. Oui. Très bon.*

Waiting until she shivered and rubbed her naked skin against his for want of more, he slid again between her thighs. Bracing his hands on her slim hips, he gave a small thrust. Just as he felt her body begin to yield, Marie-Marie released a piercing scream, tried to clap her knees shut and slapped at him as she tried to crawl away.

Julien held her fast to the bed and leaned more of his weight against her.

"It's all right, chérie," he coaxed. "*S'il vous plaît, permettez-moi de vous aimer.* Give me a little bit more of this honey."

Tears flowed from her eyes as she shook her head fiercely, all of her previous fears returning. In the hopes he wouldn't press the issue, she crawled away from him and hid underneath the coverlet.

Rolling onto his back, he knew he had been so close. He then did what his father or brother wouldn't have in the same situation. He climbed out of the bed, dressed and left the room.

# Chapter Five
## I Do

*[What you don't know is bigger than you. – Creole Proverb]*

The night was still young. A *fais do do* was in full swing. Julien gazed at the clock on the mantle in Charlet's *grande salle*. Half past midnight. Marie-Marie was either sleeping or waiting for him to return. As soon as she saw he had planned on leaving, she had run to the door and called out to him before he reached the stairs. It pleased him to see that his new bride, although fearful of consummating their marriage, wanted him near. Twice while he had stood at the top of the stairs, he thought of going back into the room and sleeping in bed beside her like he would have a sister. Knowing it would be too hard to keep his hands off of her, and wanting her to calm, because only then would she realize he had no intentions of hurting her, he bade her back inside and walked away.

Up until the past few minutes, he had been able to sit in the corner without anyone pestering him. The *salle* was now filled with partygoers who sought attention from anyone near. Leaving the party behind, he was pleased to see one of the servants standing in the door of the dining room to grant the requests of the mansion's guests. His overcoat was brought down. The servant had even tried to help him into it, but he sent her away with a flick of his wrist. Guests nodded and bid him adieu as he made his way out the front door.

A salty, cool breeze rolled its way up the street from the Mississippi. Madam Cosette's brothel was not too far away. As he walked, he remembered the night he first met Marie-Marie. Ill dressed and standing in the rain, it was obvious she had run away from home. Rarely were women seen without a male escort. The reason she was alone was similar to other women who had found the courage to be on the streets of the Vieux Carré alone.

Yellow fever visited New Orléans every year. Her mother was first in the family to die. Days later her father, and then her older sister. The loss of her two brothers within a day apart ended her financial security. It had been the men in her family that had secured work on a plantation in St. Martin. The owner of the small not yet prosperous estate could not afford to pay a white woman for work one of his six slaves could do for free. The options she had were few. With no other family in América, it was either marry in haste or give herself over to the Urseline nuns.

Julien had asked two questions. Are you hungry? Can I take you some place warm? Thanking him for his kindness, she permitted him to lead her to his family's mansion on Rue Royal. The servants were stunned to see he had brought a woman into the house, and more stunned when a bath and food had been ordered up to his mother's old boudoir. From the moment he had laid eyes on her, he knew he would marry her.

Madam Cosette's loomed up ahead. Light spilled out of its tightly closed shutters. Only a *prostituée* at Madam Cosette's could satisfy him on a night like this.

"Who dat?" A young slave girl asked from behind the closed door. That she tried speaking English when this part of the city only spoke French told him Madam Cosette had started taking Américain callers.

Jolie didn't wait for an answer and swung open the door. The sight of Julien smiling in front of her propelled her forward with a smile of her own. "Monsieur!" French was swapped for English. "The mesdemoiselles will be happy when they see you're here. Just so's you know, Madam lets me take a man now and then."

He lowered his face to hers and whispered, "You tell Madam I said to get you off your back or I'll take you out of here."

She giggled at the threat and stepped aside as Julien entered. Taking his overcoat, she continued to smile at him as she led him past the *grande salle* and through the dining room toward the rear of the house. It was there she led him up the dark staircase that led up to Madam Cosette's private *salle*. It was here that only her most distinguished guests were permitted.

Several lamps were lit inside this room. Colored candles also burned. Beside them lay gris-gris. If one had an eye to notice, there were other items in the room that warned that Cosette practiced Louisiana voodoo.

Jolie offered him tobacco, something to drink and even marijuana.

"No, thank you, beautiful." Julien reclined on one of the side chairs.

"I'll get madam for you."

Minutes later Julien stood when he heard the sound of small feet approaching.

"Monsieur Jennings." Like him, Madam Cosette spoke fluent French and not the patois of the Vieux Carré. She stood partially in the door. No attempts were made to step further into the room as her eyes devoured every part of him. The rumors that passed between the gentlemen that thrilled in the lasciviousness of her private quarters hinted she was an illegitimate kin to the *comte de la Châtre*. Everyone who knew her personally knew about her fetish with a book written by a well-known *bel-esprit*.

Madam Cosette bade him to sit. Salutation kisses weren't welcome in her home. She stepped forward then, the silk of her untied sarong sweeping across the rug. Her luminous skin and curves were negligently visible underneath her clothes. Either she was unmindful of her near nakedness or just didn't care.

Sitting in the padded chair that faced him, she pulled forward the deck of well-worn cards resting on the small table in front of her. Next to them a candle of deeper color burned, its flame small and without a flicker. Julien knew she liked reading the lives of the wealthy in the city but never before had she attempted to read his. When suggested to do so, he chose one of the cards from the deck to please her hoping afterwards he would be permitted to entertain one of her girls.

The card was taken carefully from his hand and laid face down.

"Two more, monsieur, if you don't mind."

Julien chose two more.

Each card was partially lifted and peeked at. Turning the cards he chose over one by one, the remaining deck was shuffled and held in front of him. The card he chose was now considered the top card of the deck. All the others were swiftly placed underneath. The fourth card was then laid face up. Eleven more cards were pulled from the top of the deck and arranged in a precise order on the table.

Taking a moment to study the cards, her eyes lifted to his.

Julien sat forward, fearless of the cards or what she might say. Never trust the cards. His father had always told him this. *Choose your own path without the spiritual dabblers in the Vieux Carré persuading you to travel the path they may or may not see.*

The arrangement of the fifteen cards resembled a tree. Two of the cards were positioned sideways.

"Shall I tell you?" She spoke rapidly, her voice beseeching him to say yes. The only movement she made was with her eyes; they darted back and forth as if each of his eyes told her something different.

The pictures on the cards interested him. In one, a man sat in a chair wearing a crown. In another, a naked woman stood with the moon shining brightly on her. There were other images: a serpent, symbols he couldn't make out, and images from a standard deck of cards.

Cosette pointed at the naked woman as if wanting to confirm his suspicion.

"Why not?" Julien finally answered.

"The woman in this card will save what's left of your life. The more you love her, the more her heart will become yours, literally, until it is your own heartbeat beating inside of her. The children she bears will become your future. You cannot avoid this love, as her spirit was designed in another world specifically for her to be your guide."

Julien eased back in his chair.

The expression on Cosette's face was passive as she spoke now in a whisper. "This woman is not the woman you will marry." Another card was pointed to. "*This* is the woman you marry." Her eyes tightened and narrowed as she studied the cards further as if wanting to see deeper into their meaning. "The stars will align in your favor the night you marry. Get an annulment. Leave this woman and find the other. Sickness is what I see. The woman you marry, her family is cursed with sickness." Another card was pointed to. "Grave pain. This one represents her dead relatives. This other tells me she had recent death in her family. If you marry and stay married, death will visit you through your wife."

Her eyes lifted to his, quickly. Slowly her gaze became acute. "Don't you see? The spirit of death is attached to her soul. And if you attach your soul to hers…"

"Enough!" The derision he felt came out sounding like a sharp hiss.

She saw the look in his eyes and sensed no need to tell him anything further. The Jennings men never believed the cards. All of them were far too stubborn.

She sat back the least perturbed by his lack of faith. "What is your desire tonight, monsieur? I can smell your lust. It is very strong this evening."

Julien quizzed her eyes – her every action in the hopes of seeing the truth. "You heard I got married today, didn't you? Someone told you," he accused.

The way she fell back in her chair was as if someone had pushed her against gravity. The flame on the candle leaned dramatically in their direction, then straightened and burned as before.

"Today?" Her eyes were wide.

Julien saw her need to disbelieve what he said and averted his gaze.

She leaned forward and closer to him, her voice urging him to look deep into her eyes. "The cards are always right, monsieur. Maybe that's why you're here instead of why you thought. Who is this woman you married?"

Julien thought of Marie-Marie's family, and how every last one of them were now dead after only being in the city less than six months. Things like these had happened in the past, but he couldn't remember it ever being an entire family and usually only one of the family members. Sickness. Grave Pain. Recent death. He rose to his feet, hating himself for agreeing to hear what the cards said.

"I made a mistake. I shouldn't have come here."

Cosette stood slowly to her feet. "The cards are right."

Julien saw fear in her eyes – fear of him not believing and walking out of the room and something bad happening to him. A growl flew out of his mouth as his hand clasped her throat tighter than he had choked anyone ever in his life. Lowering with her, he forced her to the floor and pushed her face closer to the cards. "You grab 'em, shuffle 'em and read them again. Now!"

Both of her feet pushed desperately against the floor as she struggled to breathe. The chair she had sat on was pushed away with the kicks she made. Her sarong fell off one of her shoulders. As she tried to face him, her right breast became exposed. New fear shone in her enlarged eyes.

Jolie and a servant girl Julien had never seen ran to the door, saw what was happening and became unable to move.

"Read them!" He gritted and released her throat.

Cosette coughed as she collapsed, then lifted quickly onto her knees. While on her knees she grabbed the deck, shuffling them with trembling fingers and hands.

More servants had come to the door, all of them in some disarray of partial dress. Their eyes darted to their madam, then on the candle burning on the table.

"The flame still burns the same," one of them whispered. "Even as she breathes on it."

Julien heard this and stared at the flame. It burned the same way it had when he had come into the room. Pulling her chair closer, Julien lifted Cosette onto it, and then he sat beside her and waited, ignoring those who had gathered to watch.

He watched as she mixed the deck once more, then held it out to him.

Julien lifted the first card and turned it over himself. It was the very same card he had pulled the first time. Laying the card on the table, he chose two more cards like before and saw that he drew them again in the same exact order he had previously.

Snatching the deck from her hand, he turned the deck face up to see what kind of witchery he was dealing with. Half of the deck had a variation of symbols on its face. The other half was standard playing cards.

Turning the deck back upside down, he shuffled the cards himself until he felt satisfied that the cards were thoroughly mixed. With a slow hand, he chose one card and turned it over. The first card he chose was again the same. The need to prove to the others there was no way he could choose the same cards again, he examined the deck a long time and chose two more, carefully. These he didn't turn face up as he laid them on the table. He then chose another card, and like she had, placed all of the others beneath it. Laying the first card down, he then slid one by one the top eleven cards, all of them face down. Only then did he sit back and wait.

He saw the eager way Cosette reached for the cards. Julien could feel the others at the door pressing against each other, desperate to see, to know, but too frightened to come closer. With his eyes intently on the table, he watched as she turned each card over and arranged them the same way she had before.

He began to breathe easier. Most of the cards he had first chosen no longer stared up at him. The man in a chair, the naked woman with the moon behind her, and the serpent were still there. There were two new cards that neither he nor Cosette could stop looking at. One was La Morte (death). Knowing someone wanted him dead made him more uncomfortable than he already was. The other was a woman in a long flowing blue dress. An emblem of some kind was positioned over her breasts.

Julien pointed to it. It was the only card he was interested in. "What is this one?"

"The woman who will guide you out of the darkness, monsieur."

"Is it my wife?"

"Let me read again," she beseeched. "It's the only way you can truly understand."

He contemplated as he stared down at the cards. "Inside this fuckery, you don't only desire the body but also the mind. But you won't have mine. I refuse to believe any of this."

Two half eagles were pulled out of his pocket. One of the gold coins was placed on the table beside the cards, the other flicked to Jolie.

"You have nothing for me here," he said and walked away.

The sight of Charlet's home did little to relieve the stress he felt. During his entire walk, the faces of the cards continually came back to him. Not up for pleasantries or conversations of any kind, he slipped through the home's courtyard undetected and tested the lock of the butler pantry. As soon as it opened, he stepped inside, crossed the dining room and entered the hall. The open doors of the *grand salle* showed couples dancing and female servants bearing silver platters that held beverages for the mansion's guests.

No one tried to stop him.

The up-tempo of a piano and frottoir spilled chords of lust and seduction. It was this reason Charlet's *fais do dos* were widely known.

All of the lamps inside his bedroom had been blown out. The French doors and shutters were tightly closed. The hair rose on the nape of his neck when he heard what sounded close to a whimper come from the farthest corner.

*Sickness. Grave pain. Death had attached itself to your wife's soul.*

It pained him that he was too frightened to call out her name. Hurrying to one of the French doors, he opened it and threw back its shutters, then slowly turned and looked over his shoulder.

Marie-Marie sat on the floor in the area where the whimper had come from. A wooden knife was in her hand. It was unornamented and the kind that servants used for meals. Small traces of blood shone on her bare legs in the moonlight. A small stain of blood was on her gown.

Running to her, he lifted her in his arms and held her tight while kissing her hair.

"What did you do, chérie? Tell me."

The knife fell from her hand as she hugged him tight about the neck. "I don't want my marriage to be like my mother's. I want to be happy. With you."

## Chapter Six
# Pierre & Désireé Jennings

*[Tell me whom you love, and I'll tell you who you are. – Creole Proverb]*

Inside the mansion on the Ashleywood plantation, Pierre Constance Jennings awoke in the small bed inside the study's alcove. He tossed back the coverlets drenched in sweat. Just before waking he had dreamt of killing his wife. It was a dream he had had countless times. What disturbed him this time was he had awakened before he saw his wife buried in the ground.

Careful not to touch the large, smooth wood box on the floor, because of his height he had to lay flat on his stomach to look under the bed. Often Désireé crawled in bed with him during the night, and last night he had been certain she was there.

Désireé lay curled like a kitten, her face pressed against her knees and hidden by a mass of brown curls that turned golden when struck by the sun. From the moment she was born her tiny face was a near replica of his: she had the same twisting flare of his lips and his slender nose. Her soft amber eyes were like radiant sunflowers in full bloom.

Although her mother had been a slave, Désireé was not a slave. The manumission paper that declared her freedom sat in a safe place for now and would be presented to her when she became an adult. As manumitting a child was hard to do since it was hard to prove that children could provide for their own living, several pockets had been lined to acquire it. The same process had taken place when his second daughter had been born.

A small tug was given to her hair. Her eyes squeezed tight as her arms stretched languidly. It was this morning behavior that earned her the nickname *mon chaton* (kitten). Blinking awake, she moved blindly into his arms. Pierre pulled her from under the bed and sat on its edge.

"Why under the bed, *petite?*"

Désireé pulled from him. Her eyes were now alert; a small hand pressed against her chest. "There was a prowler! Last night. On horseback. Near the east *jardin.*"

He knew all about her imagined prowler. Benedicte Debarge was the son of the new overseer. Exceptionally quiet, he rarely spoke unless he had to. Pierre had assigned him the chore of watching Désireé's cottage at night until the business with the hired dogs had been taken care of.

"Find Noémi and have her walk you to your cottage. We leave for town at noon."

She crawled back under the bed to grab her rag doll. He gave a gentle pat to her bottom as she ducked beneath the azure curtains that separated the alcove from the study.

He stood and noticed another child had also hidden in the room. Behind the wing chair in the corner, she watched him intently with blue-green eyes. Abigail was six years old and had wild hair that looked like and was the same hue as a blazing fire. She had been born six months to the day Pierre had married her mother. Abigail was not his biological child. On the night Pierre married, he learned that his new bride was pregnant with another man's child.

Crossing the room, he handled Abigail roughly, shaking her until she whimpered.

"Good morning, Papa." Her small cat-like eyes frantically searched his. Her mouth stayed parted as she neither moved nor took a breath. Pierre could feel her silently begging him to say good morning back or something – anything – along those lines.

A shove was made to the small of her back.

Abigail fell to her knees, her small face looking over her shoulder at him as soon as she hit the floor. Again she waited for him to say something – anything – and then she faced forward and stared at the box.

"Get. Out!"

The expression on his face was all that was needed to get her on her feet. Running quickly through the curtain, she then ran out of the study just as her mother entered it.

***

Pierre followed to make certain she didn't find a new hiding place, then stopped as soon as he saw his wife.

Jenna Louise Jennings had a heart-shaped face, warm brown eyes, a beautifully shaped mouth, and an energetic, lithe frame. She walked into the study like an actress making an introduction on a New Orléans stage.

Pierre gazed at her long and hard, then walked to the desk against the wall and pulled a pistol out of the top drawer.

"Is that any way to greet your wife on a morning such as this?" A demure smile was given. "Oh, Pierre. Do put away your pistol. Bethanie is due to arrive at any moment and the servants are still doing chores. Cook burned the beignets. Semper ruined the gown I've chosen to wear for the evening. But what does any of that matter when your father has the overseers riding across the lawn like unexplored Texas territory? Your father and his paranoia …"

Momentarily consumed in the morning's calamities, she failed to notice he had pulled a second pistol out of the drawer and was now loading it with a paper cartridge. And she was no fool. He could kill her efficiently with one shot. The second pistol was being loaded for Abigail.

Without saying anything further, she lifted the hem of her *bleu* crepe day dress. Leaving the room as quickly as her daughter had, she pulled the doors tightly behind her, then leaned against them and drew in a slow, jagged breath.

House servants in nearby rooms stopped what they were doing and stared at her trembling skirt.

Jenna stepped forward, her hands smoothing down the bodice of her gown. "You ungrateful *nègres!* All of you! I pray for the day I'm permitted to sell only one of you!"

Hands in all direction of her voice rubbed, scrubbed and cleaned harder as she passed them. It was when she reached the formal hall that Abigail rushed out of the *petite salle* with outstretched arms. "A hug for you, Maman!"

Jenna struck the side of the child's face. Unbalanced by the blow, Abigail found herself for the second time that morning lifting herself from the floor. Facing her mother, her small hands pressed against the part of her cheek that stung.

"Why do you keep going near him? Why are you always watching him? You're always in the way! You have been since the day you were born! Had you not been born I would have everything by now. He hates you. And because he hates you, he hates me," she spat, her eyes angry and small as they narrowed more and more.

Abigail winced when her mother tugged her hair, then cried out when two stinging slaps were made to the back of her gown.

"Stay away from him! You get you somewhere. One of you *nègres* come and get this child and do something with her."

The command brought Cook out of the dining room. Cook wasn't her Christian name, but what everyone called her since she managed the outside kitchen and cooked most of the family's meals. Her birth name was Rube, but only the master of the plantation and his sons called her this. Waiting until her madame had made it halfway up the stairs, she stepped closer to her young mademoiselle and drew her into her arms.

"Come with me, mademoiselle," she whispered. "I made *calas*. It's why I came looking for you."

It wasn't the only reason Cook had come into the mansion. She did so every morning, as she was the only servant unafraid of taking the child out of the house without asking permission. Leading Abigail to the outside kitchen, she sat her beside two young slave girls named Mableane and Anne. Three of the children she had taken upon herself to watch daily were now where she could keep an eye on them. There was one more Cook wanted to see if she needed retrieving.

Hurrying back into the mansion, she walked into the west wing and saw that the study's doors were closed. Looking over her shoulder to make sure her madame hadn't come back downstairs, she knocked softly.

When silence answered her knock, she contemplated returning to the kitchen because this child frightened her. On the days she didn't have to look after *it* was the days she had some semblance of peace.

Taking a chance that her monsieur hadn't heard her knocking, she quietly opened the door, then pulled it tightly closed behind her. As she expected, her monsieur was not in the study. Although her madame never dared going into the alcove, Cook feared the small room wasn't safe for the last child she was after.

Believing her monsieur heard her approaching she pushed back the curtain, then stopped and kept still. There were no blankets in the box on the floor. Her Monsieur Pierre was bent over the bed, his arms moving rapidly.

Ashamed that she had witnessed this moment without him being aware, she quickly turned and left the study as silently as she could. *It* was now two years old. On some days, no one in the mansion clasped eyes on it. On many nights Cook prayed *it* died. No one on the plantation that Cook was aware of, except her Monsieur Pierre, wanted *it* given the chance to become a woman.

Back in the alcove, Pierre pinned the diaper tightly together because the child oftentimes tugged at the cloth. Now that she was dry, he stared long into her eyes. The child stared at him with no expression on her face.

Lifting her from the bed, he carried her into the study.

Sitting behind the desk, he lowered and leaned far to hide her underneath it. Once she was in her hiding spot he fastened his eyes on the pistols, then leaned dangerously back in the chair, threatening, momentarily, to turn it over with his bulk. Like his father, he was extremely tall at seven-feet-five inches tall. Thin wasn't a good word to describe him. The muscular frame he possessed was the reason his weight sometimes reached as high as twenty-two stones. When on the streets he was studied carefully, especially by small children.

Lifting one of the pistols he remembered what happened the day before. He had returned to the plantation after being away for more than two weeks to find a real prowler on his land. That particular matter was dealt with quickly, and after it was he had gone inside the mansion to have a bath and something to eat. Once both had been completed Jenna walked into the study. The look on her face told him she hadn't been aware he had returned.

Neither said anything. Not hello or a single word. Since the morning after his wedding, Pierre never spoke to her unless it was necessary. Since the night of his wedding, he had slept each night after in the alcove. Even though both of them hated each other, the sexual magnetism between them couldn't be ignored. And yesterday it had been stronger than ever. When she saw him sitting freshly bathed and smelling of cologne, her mouth parted, slightly, and her chin lifted as her eyes softened.

Pierre saw that she was wearing a cloak, which meant she had come into the study for something before planning on going outside. When she learned he had no intentions to live with her as her husband, she began again her affair with Abigail's father, Chadwick Spencer Speck. It was often that overseers told him how they saw Jenna and Fat Chadwick going into the abandoned barn and not coming out again for hours. He imagined this was the reason she was dressed the way she was.

While he sat and watched, Jenna removed her cloak. Dropping it casually onto a nearby sofa, she turned to leave the room, but not before looking over her shoulder at him longer than it was necessary. Desire burned in her eyes. That she allowed it to show, and during the day, was all the proof he needed that she wanted him at that moment as much as he wanted her.

Rising to his feet, he followed her out into the hall. As she sauntered up the stairs to the second floor, her hips had more sway than usual. As she passed through her boudoir doors, again she glanced over her shoulder. It had been seven years since he'd last stepped foot in her room, and that night had been on their wedding night.

Since no servants were in the room to help her disrobe, she turned her back to him for his assistance. As the buttons and pins were undone on her gown, her hand slid between them. This was the first time she had touched him in any way sexual. The hardness and length of his erection caused her eyes to become large and her breathing to sound as if it was labored. The gown was swiftly lifted over her head. Turning to face him, she reached for his trousers the same moment he reached low behind her to unlace her corset. Quick kisses were given to his stomach as her fingers unbuttoned and pulled cloth to the side. The need to reach his penis became urgent; her hands were trembling.

It sprang free, long in front of her face. Seeing it alone brought her even more excitement. The corset was tugged free and dropped to the floor. The tip of her tongue flicked across the very tip of it.

"Vite, Jenna. Vite."

The way they fell on top of the bed still partially clothed was close to violent. Lifting on her knees, she lifted her rear, then pushed back against him. The moan that slipped out of her mouth as she felt him drive hard inside her and fill every part of her aroused her even more. Handfuls of the coverlet were gripped to brace herself as he moved in a slow, sensual passion she had never experienced. Her body moved with his movements in a slow urgent rock, back and forth.

The pleasure she felt when she became full of him, and the friction she felt each time he pulled all the way out before driving hard inside her again nearly drove her demented.

"Yes, Pierre," she cried when his hands reached forward. With his fingers and thumbs, he clamped down on her nipples, pulling, twisting and making them long. Pulling from him, she quickly rolled onto her back and became twisted in her petticoat. With one firm tug, the petticoat was stripped away and tossed negligibly over his shoulder. Opening her thighs wide, she watched as he lowered his trousers to his knees before climbing on top of her.

Wrapping her arms around his neck, their mouths collided. A whimper was released as soon as their tongues touched.

He pulled back. "Don't dare pretend."

An obscene look came into her eyes as her pantalettes were loosened at the waist, then pulled away. A lift was made of her chemise which now left her more exposed.

Soft moans escaped her lips, their soft sounds real and tangible. As he rolled on top of her, positioning himself between her thighs, she clamped her legs tightly around his waist to feel again what she had before.

A cry tore out of her as he slammed inside of her and began to move at a fast pace. Her mouth became severely parted and her breaths were jagged when she felt what she could only imagine was the building of a climax. Having never felt one before, all she could do was lay still underneath him with eyes of shock. As the sensations inside her climbed and whirled deep inside her, the back of her head pushed hard into the pillow.

I'm going to have my first orgasm! She thought.

Long deep thrusts made her plead and cry out as her knees began to tremble. "Yes! Chad! *Chadddd.*"

Pierre drove inside her once more.

"Chadwick. *Yesssss!*"

Calling out her fat lover's name once was forgivable. Three times was unforgivable.

She stared at him in wonder when he stopped, suddenly, then realizing her mistake she peered up at him in fear.

"I meant Pierre!" She said this in a rush as he climbed off the bed. Getting as close to him as she dared, she watched as he started to adjust his clothes. "Don't stop. It was a mistake. Come back. I was close. So very close."

Running behind him when he began to walk toward the door, she hurled herself on his back. Anger was what she felt as her fist pounded into his spine. When he made a swift turn, her body fell from him and onto the floor.

"My love was never enough," he said. "If it had you would have waited until our wedding night and you wouldn't bring that *salop* you still entertain on my land at my expense."

For a moment, he saw her contempt. It moved him not. He started to turn when she spoke again.

"You loved what you were feeling. I could see you did. You'll come back to me. You'll be knocking on my boudoir door later tonight. I know you will. Sooner or later Désireé will stop climbing in your bed at night, and when that happens, you'll know just how lonely of a man you truly are. So go ahead. Go back downstairs to your precious children. Do you even know why you spend so much time with them? Because you're trying to fill a void that only a wife can fill."

He now leaned forward and stared at the pistols on the desk. The reason he had loaded both was to be prepared if more prowlers came onto his land. The reason he had loaded them in front of her was because he knew she would think it was for other reasons. As he stared at them, he knew she had spoken the truth. The loneliness she spoke of was with him now. It had always been there even before he married. He had married in an attempt to appease it.

He reached forward and grabbed the decanter of bourbon resting at the edge of the desk. Of late it was the only thing that kept him from reminding himself how wealthy he was yet miserable in the life he led.

# Chapter Seven
# The Master of Ashleywood

*[The Devil never sleeps. – Creole proverb]*

Will rarely slept in the mansion anymore. For five years he slept most nights in a Creole cottage nestled between the china and gum trees on his plantation. The house belonged to his paramour. She had been twelve when he had it built, although at that time he had no idea where she was but knew someday he would find her and bring her back. Back then he had no intentions of making her his lover. The thought had never come to him. The reason he built the house was to try and give her a better life, because the one she had many wouldn't have survived without losing their sanity.

Now that he was older being near her meant more to him than anything else. It was this reason as soon as his eyes opened he searched for her, his beloved. It didn't matter that she was lying within inches of him. Rising on one elbow, he wouldn't rest assured until he saw her face.

Unlike other women, his beloved slept with her hair free and loose. It was soft and as dark as plant pitch. Born Alise Bluche, her mother was French, twenty-one years of age and unmarried the evening she gave birth while her father and brothers anxiously watched every minute. As soon as Alise was pushed out of the womb and onto the bed, Élise Bluche's father lifted the infant with the umbilical cord still attached and examined the child. The plantation he owned was isolated and rarely received visitors. Suspecting the child had been fathered by one of his slaves, he yelled and screamed because staring at the child hadn't provided the answers he sought.

With weak and upraised arms, Élise pleaded until her father relented and laid the child in her arms. The servant who attended the birth couldn't stop staring at the child after she cut the cord because she also wondered. Hoping the father wasn't one of the slaves, her eyes examined and studied until she wasn't sure if she was truly seeing the child's real features any longer and only what she imagined. Everyone on the plantation had been questioned and none could attest to ever seeing Élise Bluche with any man at all.

For hours the master of the plantation and his sons threatened to round up all of their male slaves and burn them alive. Élise was slapped and her cheeks squeezed until tears squirted from the corner of her eyes. Even when her father threatened to kill the infant, she refused to name the father.

Days turned into weeks and weeks into months. Hardly a day went by that Élise's father didn't scrutinize over the child's features. When Alise turned one and her skin had yet to darken and her hair looked the same as it had at birth, Élise was pressured even more to reveal the father, as this time her father and brothers believed the child was entirely French and some visitor to their plantation had disrespected their home. It wasn't until Alise was six-years-old when the truth was finally uncovered.

The visitor had come as he always had, driving a cart with two farm horses pulling it rapidly across the yard. As he climbed down from the vehicle, he looked over his shoulder toward the house before making his way across the field. The man was a slave of mixed race. His father was French. His maternal grandfather had been French. Owned by the family whose blood ran through his veins, his father had hired him out to the Bluche plantation for one month. One of the finest carpenters in Cane River, there wasn't a plantation for miles around where he hadn't erected a building of some type. Élise's father was happy to see him. A new corn crib was needed and he had hoped to have it completed before the month was over.

Leading the servant toward the area where the corn crib would sit, the two were in the midst of a lengthy conversation when the servant, Antoine, smiled at his temporary master while assuring him of his work. The smile was all too familiar, as were Antoine's eyes. Élise's father said nothing. Antoine's strong French features were the reason he was readily accepted inside of many homes.

Later that evening Élise's father returned to the house and lifted Alise in his arms. It had been seven years since he last saw Antoine. While sitting at his dining room table, he sat Alise on his lap. Now that he knew who her father was, he found it easier to love his only grandchild.

Two weeks later the hogs became ill. Days after that fever swept through the entire plantation. Élise's father and Antoine died first. Élise's elder brother inherited the plantation the moment their father drew his last breath. He was master all of two days before he too died from fever. Some days later the next oldest brother and five slaves died. Because Élise was the only daughter, and her mother had died years ago, it had been her responsibility to tend to those who were ill. No matter what she did, the slaves kept dying until there were only seven out of twenty-four left. Toward the end Élise also became ill. While lying on her bed, and her muscles trembling with weakness, and sweat pouring from her skin, Alise sat at the head of the bed dotting her mother's brows with a cool cloth as tears fell from her eyes.

Death had been all she'd seen: her pépère, her oncles, many of the slaves. Alise didn't want anyone to wrap her mother in a sheet and carry her to the barn.

Élise had wanted to assure her daughter that she would be well, but her mouth felt dry and the words refused to come out. For a long while, she stared at the ceiling and concentrated on her breathing, wondering if the next was her last. It wasn't until the door opened when she averted her gaze. A white man she had never seen before stepped into her boudoir not once looking at her; his gaze had solely been on Alise. When Élise saw that he held a small pair of manacles in his hands, she tried to scream for her youngest and last surviving brother to come into the room to help her.

All that came out of her mouth was a dry crackle of sound. Gabbing Alise tightly in her arms, she rolled until her daughter was hidden underneath her. Not once did she consider if her daughter could breathe. The only thought that came into her mind was keeping her daughter with her until her brother came into the room and took the stranger away. Hearing footsteps run into the room another dry crackle tore out of her when she realized her brother had come into the room to help the stranger.

At sixteen, his arms were very strong. As if fighting for her own life, Élise kicked, clawed, pulled hair, bit into shoulders and kicked both men wherever she could. Once the two men saw she would willingly kill them both rather than have her daughter taken from her, they attacked her from both sides at the same time.

Alise believed her oncle and the stranger were trying to hurt her mother. Jumping onto the back of her mother's attacker, she sank her small teeth deeply into the stranger's neck and refused to let go. The struggle became more violent and didn't stop until mother and daughter were finally separated. Still Élise fought until her nightgown ripped and hung off her shoulder and exposed her sweaty breasts. Her brother, in an attempt to keep her in the room, wrapped his arms tightly around his sister's middle and dug his feet firmly into the floor.

The strength to save her daughter came out of nowhere. Dragging her brother across the floor, one thought – and one thought only – stayed in her mind, and that was to get her arms around her daughter again. The death of her older brothers now made her the inheritor of the plantation and not her baby brother. If any decisions were to be made, until she drew her last breath only she could make them. It was her brother clutching the back of her nightgown in a way that restricted her movements that brought her down to the floor. Once down, his legs twined around her as he explained that two more slaves had died that morning. With no money to buy new slaves, the crop couldn't be brought in and sold. Selling the last five slaves and Alise would ensure the two of them had enough money to live off of until they could figure something out.

It was unlawful to sell children born from a free woman, especially a white one. The trader knew this, but also knew that slaves with fair skin sold higher than others. Agreeing to take the child, he had offered fifty dollars. Of the six slaves he had taken with him, he sold all but Alise one by one for two-hundred dollars each time he reached a different plantation. As he made the slow trek Alise had attacked him twice with manacled hands. To teach her a lesson, he made the child walk the last three miles to his place of business in the city.

A few hours after returning to the Vieux Carré, he was surprised to see *le diable dans Nouvelle-Orléans* standing at the front door of his business. The sight of *le diable* pleased him because wealthy men never made personal visits to a trader so late in the evening unless it was for a rapid sale. When *le diable* explained he had come for a particular slave girl he was certain was in the trader's possession, with much show and flare the door was pulled opened. The trader's eyes became wide and his heart thumped with sheer bliss when *le diable* laid the equivalent of one-thousand dollars in escudo coins on the table before laying eyes on the girl he had come to purchase.

Eager to hold the soft bag containing them, he looked inside and felt as if he was suddenly wealthy.

"I'm in a hurry," Will explained. "And I don't want to be denied. Write up the bill of sale. I'll find the girl myself."

A few of the trader's overseers stood to assist him in finding her.

Will didn't trust overseers other than his own. Not wanting to frighten the girl, he asked the men to stay inside. The first thing he saw when he stepped through the rear of the building and into the slave pen was an animal cage with what looked like small white arms sticking out of it. The sight of this was so peculiar he thought the darkness of the evening was playing tricks on his eyes. The closer he got the more his eyes narrowed.

The arms were, in fact, white, and human. The cage reeked of animal dung. Lowering in front of it, a child peered back at him. The softest voice spoke to him.

*"Aide-moi, monsieur. J'ai besoin de ma mere."*

Hearing the child speak French as she asked for his help and for her mother, his heart twisted in anguish. The anguish slowly turned to rage. That any trader could treat any child like this sickened him, but treating a Creole child like this gave him visions of murder. As tall and as strong as he was, it was easy to move the cage. Turning it one way and then another, he saw that a lock secured its only door. It was at that moment the trader walked out of the building with a spring in his step and a wide smile on his face as he held a bill of sale up high with his hand. Will stood to full height. The trader whimpered as his body lifted off the ground, then was slammed hard against it.

"You're Irish! Whose child is this?" Pressing a hand against the trader's face to pin his head to the ground, Will searched with his free hand for the key and didn't give up until he found it.

Moving quickly to the cage, he unlocked its door and swung it open. The child tried all she could to move in the small space she had. Reaching inside, he gently tugged until she was free. Once free, she crawled up the front of him, clinging to his neck and refusing to let go. Will could feel the rapid beating of her heart as she pressed her body tightly against his.

The trader had risen to his feet, and taking large steps toward Will, he pleaded. "I know what it looks like, but the child is noir! I purchased her legally. I have the papers to prove it!"

Will stared at the man as if the man had gone mad. It was the look in the man's eyes that caused Will to pull the child away from him and hold her up in the moonlight. The saddest eyes peered down at him. It was only then that he noticed that the child had come from generational mixing of the races making it hard to determine one race over the other. One thing was clear, however. Despite the poor fit of her dress, which was heavily soiled with animal feces from the cage, the child was observably more French than anything else.

"This is New Orléans!" The sound of his voice was close to a roar.

"The family had no other choice," the trader explained. "Most of those on the plantation had died from fever. The surviving heir was within his rights to sell her." The trader knew better than mention that the mother was a Frenchwoman, as this made the sale illegal. Now that New Orléans was under Spanish rule, the laws regarding such matters hadn't changed from when the King of France had governed the land. Children born from free mothers or from white women were not slaves and couldn't be sold.

All of the trader's fears vanished as he took an angry leap forward.

"You cannot steal this child. I own her! When she's of proper age, I deem to sell her for the highest amount and only then!"

During this time in the year of 1780 all that dwelled in New Orléans spoke French as their primary language regardless of what part of the world they had emigrated from. América was at war fighting Britain for their independence. The South was becoming more and more known for its cotton plantations. On these plantations, many slaves lived in huts and not cabins. The huts had earthen floors and roofs made of palmetto fronds or thatch. Will thought about all of these things, and he knew he wasn't leaving the pen without her. Aware of his prejudices against slaves with strong African features, it was his knowledge of *how* they were treated that prevented him from allowing a Creole-looking child like this one to live a similar fate.

With the South needing more slaves to ensure its cotton harvest remained as high as possible, there was no way to be certain the trader wouldn't sell her further Southeast on Américain soil where he would receive a higher sum.

Although Will tended to show favoritism to his slaves of lighter skin, none of the slaves on his plantation were treated as human chattel. An unorthodox system had been put into place by his father. Wages were paid allowing many of his slaves to acquire their freedom. In the South, his plantation was spoken amongst slaves as 'Slaab Heaben.' Because of this his presence at several public auction houses had been banned, as many of the slaves, once they knew he was in attendance, screamed from the top of the lungs, *Massuh Devil, please buy me. I'll be your best nigger.*

"I'll pay you two thousand for the child. In gold."

The trader rubbed his hands vigorously together, then folded and unfolded them as he gazed at the child with pride. "Shall I draw up the bill of sale for you, monsieur?"

"Please do," Will answered, then watched as the trader hurried back through the rear door of the building.

The reason Will had visited the trader that evening was to find the wife of a new slave he had purchased. In Louisiana, the law forbade the splitting apart of slave families. It was a law that wasn't always followed, especially now that the trans-Atlantic slave trade was being threatened and more plantations depended on domestic sales. Depending on the situation, those in power overlooked such matters if it benefited the seller and the buyer. It was a situation that oftentimes Will understood even though like those in the North he saw slavery as a grotesque business that corrupted the hearts of humanity. His wealth had never relied on slavery or the crops his plantation could yield. Had that been different he often wondered if his views on slavery would have been different, but doubted they would be.

One thing was for sure. Never – *ever* – regardless of his financial standing would he sell a family member to be a slave all for the sake of money. If his family had to learn from the Indians how to live off the land, as long as his family was together it was all that mattered. This he firmly believed as he moved through the pen looking for a slave girl named Betsy.

The stench of the child, especially her hair, was hard to ignore. Each step he took, Alise held tighter to him, fearful he would put her down and walk away. At times her small head got in the way, preventing him from seeing the other slaves in the pen. It was just as he was turning to walk the other side of the pen when a male voice whispered from the black bodies surrounding him.

"Massuh? Yous be de Devil?"

"Who's looking for the devil?" He asked, turning slightly to see where the voice had come from.

Large white eyes peered up at him from the black mass.

"I be," a dark male whispered, then looked toward the building to make certain no one inside heard him or saw him having a private conversation with a patron to the pen. "My sistah," he continued to whisper. "Her name be Bessy. I's reckon yous comes fer huh, massuh?"

Will stared at the man and the other slaves shackled closest to him. Some of them were old and lay on the cold ground with no more than a blanket for comfort. A group was huddled together with noticeable fear in their eyes. Will had seen what he was looking at before. An estate auction. These slaves would be sold to the highest bidder to help pay off the debts of their former master.

"And your name?" Will asked.

"I's go by Elda. Been sold *tree* times, massuh. Git lucky de lass time. My fam'ly be on de Houston plantation where's I's git took. He bought me to be wit 'em. Good man he was. I's sorry to see 'em die."

"You have more family here?" Will asked. Those in power would again look the other way as families were torn apart in the hopes that merchants in the city would recover some or all of the money owed to them by Clement Houston.

"Ohs, yes, suh! I's does."

"I's his fam'ly," a voice whispered behind Will.

Within seconds, other small voices claimed the same thing. The pen quickly became energized. Whispers began spilling from every corner, most of them asking if he be De Debbil.

"Oh, massuh. Don't go listenin to dem udders. Deys see you holding dat white chile. And you holdin a child like you does gots thees thanking yous goin ta be a betta massuh dan udders."

Betsy, along with seven others from her family slowly stood to their feet. Two of them were the oldest in the pen. The family hung their heads low and stared at the ground; tears fell from their eyes because it was unusual for wealthy slave owners to purchase slaves they had no use for. Unless older slaves had white protection to buy them if they should find themselves on the auction block, they were seen as a bad investment and passed over.

Alise lifted her head from his shoulders, suddenly, and searching the pen with her eyes, started pointing at different slaves. Will, believing the child knew these servants from wherever she had come from, made motions for each of them to quickly rise. At that moment, the trader stepped out of the building with two new bills of sales, then ran across the pen when he saw more than half of his stock of Negroes standing around the infamous *le diable dans Nouvelle-Orléans*.

Before the man could reach him, Will whispered in Alise's ear. "Who else do you know? I don't want this man seeing you pointing them out."

Her amber eyes peered intently into his.

"*Je ne connais personne ici,*" she whispered.

Will pulled the child from him and stared attentively at her. "If you don't know these slaves why are you pointing them out?"

"*Pouvez-vous les prenez avec vous?*"

"Take them with me?" His eyebrows furrowed. Confusion settled in his mind. It was then he knew this child had been no one's servant. Wherever she had come from someone had taught her strength, courage and the same amount of confidence that any *blanc* man would have. This was further proven when her small face stared deliberately at the trader, pulled into a grimace and her finger pointed accusingly at him.

For the first time in a long time, the Devil threw back his head and roared with laughter.

The trader stood nearby, looking around the pen while watching Will closely at the same time.

Facing the Irishman, he said, "Even our *bâtards* don't take shit from anyone, monsieur. *That...* is the Creole way. This child is Creole. I'm even more convinced of it. I'll take all of those standing along with the two I have already told you I will buy."

"Mr. Jennings, you just can't," the trader said, his eyes imploring. "You just can't. Some of those standing have already been spoken for. It's bad for business. I'll lose my reputation. I can't afford that," he finished with an emphatic plea.

While the trader spoke, several others stood slowly and silently to their feet.

The trader spun around, then barked for his overseers to come out of the building to keep an eye on 'these troublesome niggers.'

"Sit down!" The trader yelled, going to certain slaves, facing them momentarily before moving to another and demanding the same thing.

Alise pointed firmly at the same slaves that sat quickly in fear of being punished. The last slave she pointed out was a young dark male who was unable to rise on his own. When he saw Alise point him out, the face he made was of determination. Using all the strength he could muster, his hands, legs and feet moved with awkward and trembling coordination. Seeing he wasn't going to be able to rise on his own, a few slaves risked punishment to help him to his feet, then peered at the Devil wondering what would happen next. Once standing, and as if he needed to prove he still had some strength left in him, the male trembled severely as he stood as rigidly as possible.

Will saw this and was unable to look away. If the trader hadn't been present, he would have complimented the servant on his strength of mind. While looking at the servant Will saw that the sickness he suffered from would soon take him from this world if it couldn't be cured right away.

"How much do you want for that one?" Will asked.

The dark slave heard this, lowered his head, chewed his lower lip, then lifted his chin again as tears fell from his eyes.

"Can't ask much for him," the trader answered honestly. "He came over from St. Mary Parish. His former owner sold him cheap. Didn't need the money. Just wanted this nigger off his land. Selling him was more profitable than feeding him or fetching a doctor. I was going to keep him and the child you're holding. Once I got him fixed up, I was going to sell him for as much as I can. I can't take less than three hundred. If you can't pay that, I'll have to keep him, monsieur. Business is business."

"You can set your price if you turn your head and sell me the ones who want to go with me and have already been spoken for."

"Can't do it," the trader whispered heatedly. "I just can't!" He begged. "Help me here, Monsieur Jennings. I know you're good for the money, but I'll still have the business after you walk away. Leave me with some of my face left. It'll come in handy when a new customer comes calling."

Will reluctantly agreed.

Bill of sales existed for three of the slaves who were standing, one of which was Betsy's youngest sister, fourteen-year-old Sally. The family wailed loudly on hearing this, as none of them had known that Sally had already been sold. Gathering around her, they hugged her tightly as if only death would pry her from them. As they formed a tight circle, they begged and pleaded with the trader. Sally's mother separated from the group, and holding two inward turned fists in front of her face, she asked the Lord God Almighty to have mercy just this once and she would never ask him anything else.

As the trader had already sent notices for miles around regarding his upcoming auction, he went slowly through his stock, pointing out the women of mixed races and slave boys between the ages of nine and twenty-five and in good form. These he knew would be his best sales when the crowd arrived.

The overseers had hurried out of the building, realizing that something unusual was taking place in the pen. Standing beside Sally's crying family, they threatened to use their whips if the family didn't quiet down and stop stirring up the others. Half of the family vowed to stay behind, hoping whoever had purchased Sally would come back and purchase one or two of them. This way the entire family wouldn't be split apart and at least one person would have someone else in the family with them.

The trader dashed any hopes of this happening. Explaining to Will while the others listened, it was made known that Sally's purchaser was none other than Jean-André Dussault. Jean-André rarely sold female slaves after they were purchased.

Sally's father was old enough and experienced when it came to the mechanizations of slavery to know what his family didn't. Ignoring the looks the overseers gave, he spoke in a low yet firm voice demanding his family, all except Sally, to leave the pen and go off with the Devil as this was the only way to keep the rest of them together. This decision brought their father grief after it was spoken and caused him nearly to collapse.

The arms of his family wrapped lovingly around him. The decision also brought with it more tears, as the family knew once they left the pen none of them would ever see Sally again.

Some of the girls of mixed raced, and the younger boys who the trader saw fit to keep cried when they saw some of their family standing amongst the ones Will proposed to purchase. Hysteria broke forth, of which Will put a swift end to it.

"I didn't come to buy any of you!" He barked. "And I surely don't need any of you. Stay here with your families! By all means. And stop this annoying torment to my ears."

A girl of mixed race who hadn't been chosen quickly hurried past one of the overseers with a small child lifted high in her arms. "I just got my mind right. You're the Devil! You don't have to buy me, monsieur. But if you take this child to Slave Heaven, I'll thank the Lord every day."

This was the first time Will had laid eyes on the girl since coming into the pen. Squinting in the dark, he tried to see her better, because she spoke French as fluently as he did. The child was held high in front of the girls' face. It too was of mixed race. One of its legs was smaller than the other, and one shoulder smaller than it should have been with a slender arm hanging from it. Tonight for reasons he couldn't explain, it was hard for him to leave any behind that wanted to go with him.

"Can you walk with that child a long distance?"

"Oui, monsieur!"

"What's your name?"

"Rube."

"What do you do?"

"I cook, massuh."

"Stand over here with me."

The girl turned and, quickly grabbing the hand of several other children, rushed toward him. By the time she reached him, he had six young slaves standing in front of him.

Will smiled. "Are you sure you're that good of a cook?"

The girl averted her gaze to the dirt underneath her feet.

"Oui." The answer had been spoken softly.

"How old are you?"

"Just on fifteen, monsieur."

"And these children with you?"

"Brothers, sisters and cousins."

Will stared at the girl a long time, and then he leaned close and whispered in a low voice so only she heard him. "Wench, if you aren't any good at cooking, you better be good on your back."

"I know about you," she whispered back. "I'm not scared of you. I know the truth about you. You don't take noir girls to your bed. I'll cook real good for you. And if you promise not to sell any of mine, I'll lay on my back for you too."

For a long time, Rube couldn't look up at him. Although she had tried to speak in a low voice, emotion had swelled inside her, causing her to lift her voice.

"I'm no one's fool, Rube. Let me see your hands."

Seconds passed before her hands were lifted up one by one for him to inspect. Each of her palms was severely calloused.

"Those are field hands. You have never cooked before. Of course you haven't. You're only fourteen."

The children beside her heard this, wailed and went to stand again where they had been before.

"Where you from?" He asked.

"Karlstein," she answered.

"Farm land," Will confirmed.

"Oui, monsieur," she answered in a small voice. "My monsieur died. Half of us were given to his brother back where we from. The other half was given to his brother in Charleston. Me and these children were to be sent there. As soon as he learned our ages, he told the trader to sell us. I heard those men over there this morning. Those he cain't sell here will be taken to Bilocci. The British own Bilocci now. None of us speak Anglais. I see us getting split up and having hard times. Real hard times."

Will stared at the children crying across the pen.

"Get your asses over here," he said and placed a gentle hand on Rube's shoulder.

Before he could finish speaking, grabbing one another by the hand again, the children made a mad dash to him.

"Thank her," he said, nudging his head toward Rube. "Every day."

As Will walked away, Sally followed behind him crying and begging him to take her with him. When this didn't work, she fell on her knees and screamed as if her mind had become addled. One of the overseers dragged her to the animal cage threatening to throw her in it.

"Hush, chile." Her father spoke firmly, his facial features distorted with anguish and emotion that was too hard for him to contain. "Don't cause no need to get stripes on ya back, gal. I taught you better'n dat."

Will had known Clement Houston and his wife Pauline personally. Even when Clement's debts were high and the profits from his crops dwindled each year, he refused to sell a single slave in the hopes of freeing them upon his death.

Will mentioned this to the trader. The trader explained that Pauline had authorized the sale after it was promised that some of the money will be given back to her to relocate with her family in Bilocci – the same city that non-Creoles called Biloxi.

An hour later twenty-eight unshackled slaves walked down the center of the street following behind Will's slow moving coach. As if to prove her worth, Rube carried the smallest child on her hip and marched ahead of the others in a quick gait. The children with her, happy they were together, constantly ran to keep up.

Will had the coach stopped.

"Wench, bring you and those little scamps over here."

The rear of the coach had a baggage department that was empty. Will and his best friend, Frances Achen, who was driving the coach, used rope to make certain none of the children fell off of the coach during the journey. One of the older slaves who had trouble walking, along with the sickly male and one person to tend to them both, were allowed inside the coach with him and Alise.

While these things took place, white residents began to stand outside of their homes to watch. It wasn't Will's purchase of the slaves that increased their agitation. It was the sight of many slaves with dark pigmentation and in no ways bound that caused them to yell that what they saw was nothing more than a spectacle and a bad example. A half hour later when the coach was rolling again, a few white men on horses, and some driving carts, their rifles showing for all to see, followed shouting threats at the slaves that if any of them should get any wild ideas, it will be the last time any of them ever did.

Will had the coach stopped again when he looked out of the curtain and saw the slaves growing fearful of being massacred. Other white men and young boys had left their homes by foot and were taunting them.

Will's tall frame nearly folded in half as he stepped out of the vehicle. Grabbing a Brown Bess that had been situated behind the cushion where he sat, he aimed it over the head of the white man nearest him and pulled the trigger. Screams were made from the ever growing crowd. A few fled at the sound of a rifle fired. The white man Will shot at nearly fell off of his horse as it reared on its hind legs. After the man got his horse to calm down, he rode toward the center of what looked like a frenzied mob.

"I have just purchased Clement Houston's slaves," Will yelled to make sure everyone heard him. "Merchants in this city will receive payment on debts owed to them from these sales. Madame Houston will receive money to relocate with her family in Bilocci. If that is not important to you, then continue what you're doing. But if it does then go back to the comfort of your homes and leave me to my business. Because if you don't stop trying to incite these slaves to run out of fear so one of you can shoot them, I will see who you are and I will return with the most savage Chitimacha Indians I can bribe to come after you men, your sons, your wives and your goddamned children! I *am* the Devil!" He roared. "Now go on and get! I don't need any of your assistance this evening."

A hard gesture was made with the swinging of his free arm.

"*Casse-toi!*" He yelled when the crowd took their time dispersing.

Frances had climbed down from the driver's seat with a rifle, aiming it precisely at the men he decided were moving too slowly.

The police had come when the coach started off again, riding on horses and keeping a respectable distance. Three men. All of them armed with rifles. All three with a whip curled and fastened to their saddle.

The next day the newspaper ran an article claiming *le diable dans Nouvelle-Orléans* had placed the city in grave danger. A week after that he received fines accusing him of breaking several laws and a bill for the escort the city deemed he had been in need of and they had provided.

A week later he rode into town on a farm wagon. Inside it were seven of the slaves he had purchased two weeks before, one of them being Rube. The reason he brought them were to pick out pieces they needed for their new cabins, as Will hadn't wanted to give them what he had or take something from someone else. Lamps, basins, fabrics to make curtains and bedding. Necessary things.

Again residents watched as Will's new slaves climbed out of the rear of the wagon nicely dressed, were clean looking and all were wearing new leather boots. When they saw that he had brought the *blanc* looking slave they had heard so much about and that she had sat up front in the cart with him, tongues began to waggle.

Will ignored them all as he lifted Alise in his arms because he saw she was frightened from the attention. Will hadn't dressed Alise as a slave because he didn't see her as one. In the two weeks since the purchase he listened as she told him and his wife about her mother and family and how she had ended up in a slave pen. The reason he brought her with him was because she had wanted to see the city while he completed the paperwork to have her manumitted. Holding her high in his arms, nobody stopped him as he carried her inside of The Cabildo while his overseer walked with the servants to the market where, for the first time in their lives, they shopped for goods meant for themselves.

A large crowd had gathered by the time Will paid the fines and the escort bill. Those in high positions inside The Cabildo refused his request for manumission. In their eyes, Alise was from somewhere else other than New

Orléans. None of them agreed with giving a child freedom, especially when she had no family in the city.

The crowd watched carefully as the servants climbed in the back of the wagon with their arms loaded with goods that some of the city's residents couldn't afford. Taunts were yelled, as well as horrible names that made the servants lower their gazes. Before climbing in the driver's seat, Will placed Alise on it, then standing away from the wagon so the crowd could easily see him, he turned in a circle, reached for the pistol at his side and fired it into the air.

"*Je m'en fou! Nique ta mere! Connards!* All of you! Now you can send another bill and have more to talk about. Neither I nor my servants did anything offensive. For any of you who believe we did...*casse-toi!*"

The next day a caricature of the devil holding a white-looking slave in his arms ran across the front page of the newspaper. The artist made certain to draw the devil with extreme height. The white-looking child was depicted as being terrified of being eaten alive while the Devil clutched her with twisted arms and sharp talons for fingers. The image had many similarities to Will's facial features. Black wings had been drawn onto its back. A long tail curled around the front of it. Shackled well-dressed slaves watched with gladness as equally well-dressed aristocrats burned in hell's flames close to the devil's feet. The caption below accused *le diable dans Nouvelle-Orléans* as being a threat to society.

Six months later after Will left the plantation on business Alise was stolen off of his plantation by a traveler who had stopped at the mansion for water, food and shelter during his travel to Virginia.

***

Those things happened close to forty years ago. Except for the old slaves he had purchased that late evening, who Death decided not to visit until they were even older in age, the other twenty-six still lived on his plantation and had increased their families over the years, including the one who had been severely ill. Tomas was now married with eight children and had several grandchildren. At the age of fifty-one his family had earned enough to buy all of their freedom. Having learned Creole customs and preferred it over the Américains', he went to Will with an unusual proposition. Instead of moving his family to the city where all of them would have to constantly look for work, he asked Will to lease him a small part of land that hadn't been put to use. It is there where his family now resided. The crops they raised and the services they provided to those along the river permitted them to be accepted amongst the poorer Creoles who would rather do business with someone who spoke French rather than hire an Américain.

Alise had been coming up on her seventh birthday on the day she was stolen. It took Will more than seven years to find her. The day he walked onto the plantation where she had been taken, Alise saw him from across the yard and dropping the gourd of water she had been carrying, outran the overseer who was giving a mean chase behind her. Will shot the overseer when he got too close, lifted Alise in his arms and since then has never traveled back to Virginia.

Will remembered that day as he lay beside her, watching her sleeping. Many changes had occurred since then. América had become an independent country. Spain had ceded Louisiana back to France. France then sold the land to América. On the day Will had gotten her back, never did it enter his mind that the child he had rescued from a slave pen would become his beloved. After his wife Catharine died from yellow fever, leaving him with two small sons to raise on his own, it was Alise who became the most important woman in his life.

Leaning over her once again, he kissed her hair, then climbed out of bed.

At her washbasin, he managed his ablutions without a servant.

Outside the morning was muggy and yellow and smelled strongly of the river.

A choir of crickets chirped harmoniously.

***

As he entered the west wing of the mansion, he came to a standstill. From his position, he could see anyone standing at the study's doors. Abigail was there, and she must have heard him, because she turned and stared at him, then faced forward again and waited. During the moment she had turned to him, Will had seen her eyes. In them had been hope, dread, and disappointment. She wore a pretty little dress and pretty little shoes. Her fiery red hair had been combed prettily around her face.

It took some seconds, but it came eventually: Pierre's bark. It was loud, cruel and belittling.

Lifting her in his arms, it didn't matter to him that Abigail was not his son's true daughter. She was a Jennings, and because she bore the Jennings name he treated her as he did his other granddaughters. While stroking her back while she calmed, he knew the affection he gave was the only affection she received from her family. It disturbed him that he didn't have time to spend with the child as he wished, because if any child, slave or free, needed attention it was Abigail.

"Stop fussing, little one." He spoke softly.

Nothing he had said to his eldest son had been taken heed of. And now with the illness as bad as it was, and Pierre soon to govern the land alone, Will knew Abigail's future would be one of misery.

"Stay away, little one. Find Rube and have her tell you one of her funny stories."

Abigail stared up at him when he placed her on her feet, but only for a moment. Turning from him, her head lowered as she walked in the direction of the outside kitchen like an orphan with no hope of ever finding loving parents. So was the child's life. During most days she spent most hours in the presence of the slaves. Will pitied the child as much as he pitied his youngest granddaughter. It was his youngest granddaughter who had the most dismal future of the three of them.

His eyes searched for his son as he walked into the study.

Pierre had been writing in a book. Lifting his head and seeing his father step into the room, a quill was placed into an inkwell, and the book pushed aside so the open pages could dry.

Will stood directly in front of him.

"She doesn't understand this anger, Pierre. And neither can I. Abigail believe *you* are her father. You *are* her father. You must stop this, Pierre. You're hurting this child far more than if you tied her to a tree and beat her within an inch of her life. I fear her future. I really do."

As soon as his father began to speak, Pierre reached for the decanter at the edge of the desk and poured two glasses of bourbon.

46

The pain Will felt as he watched his son attempt to drink his sorrows away was great. It was then he noticed his youngest granddaughter lying on the rug not too far from the fireplace. A rag doll lay beside her and within reach. The child ignored it and stared up at the ceiling like a child without sight.

Will crossed the room and lifted Gorée Pierette Jennings in his arms. As he had many times before he wondered how God could give the child such a beautiful face and a severely addled mind.

As if she had waited for the comfort of someone's arms, her head pressed against his chest as she closed her eyes. Will knew that many on the plantation prayed the child died because they were frightened of her. Kissing her head, he carried her to the bed in the alcove and laid her on top of it. Beside the bed was a large, smooth wooden crate. It served as Gorée's bed and prison. Like Abigail spent most days amongst the slaves, Gorée spent most part of a day in a box.

Several doctors had examined her. All of them had drawn the same conclusion. Gorée will never walk, talk or learn any form of communication. A diagnosis like this was bad enough for a child of *blanc* race. For a child with noir blood and living in the United States of América, it was nothing less than cruel. The compassion he had shown to children of color that had been born with deformities had prepared him for the day Gorée had been born. He knew, as soon as she was born, that a child like her was lucky to be born in a family like his because no one would love her as much as he and his sons did.

Back in the study, he sat in front of the desk.

Pierre pushed a glass of bourbon toward him. Will wanted to ask why the two of them were drinking so early in the morning. Accepting the glass, he sank back in the chair. "I get frightened when your anger is turned toward me," he began. "But I would be less of a man if I didn't tell you what I'm going to tell you now. Abigail does not deserve the way you treat her."

Pierre lifted his hand to stop his father from saying anything further.

"No," Will argued. "I will not be silent. I'm dying! And this is my death wish to you!" He stopped suddenly and pressed a hand to his chest.

Loosening the cravat around his neck, he pulled it off and dropped it negligibly to the floor. Pierre had always been reticent. His reticence was much agitation to Will at the moment. Whatever Pierre was thinking was being well reserved; no expression shone on his face. Other than twirling the glass between his fingers, he made no other movements and sat far too still for a man his age.

"I'm listening," Pierre finally said.

"Be good to Abigail. Someone has to love Abby other than slaves."

If the tightness in his chest hadn't been as severe as it was, he would have risen to his feet and paced angrily around the room.

"Sooner or later manumission will mean nothing in this country. When Louisiana was governed by France and Spain, any free man was *free*. They had equal rights, Pierre."

Pierre lifted his glass of bourbon, drained it, then poured another.

Will was no longer able to sit and stood.

"In the North free men of color are treated separately – differently from white men. The North has their own Black Laws. Pierre, les noirs are not allowed in many cities and neither can they step foot in many States as a free man." He allowed this to sink in as he thought about it. "The reason for these laws is to preserve the purity of the white race. Exclusion!" He spat the word. "This means that half of the noir population in this city, if they left here, could be apprehended and made slaves although we freed them. Most of them are someone in this city's children!"

He attempted to calm. "According to América, all it takes is one drop of noir blood. It doesn't matter that these children have *blanc* blood or *blanc* skin. Even in the North they are dogs, Pierre. Nothing more. They're paid less wages and only given menial jobs. Unless they have a white benefactor are they given anything better, and even then, if the public should dictate so, the better is taken away from them. This is the government that leads us now. If I hear another Yankie speak so eloquently about the degradation of slavery while most of them up North have learned a quieter and sneakier way of keeping free people of color in bondage, it makes me want to kill every one of them. So what they are not using chains. The chains are still there."

Pierre leaned forward. "Calm down, Papa."

"You don't understand!"

"I do understand. I travel more than you do now. I have eyes."

"Then you see?" Will stepped closer to the desk. "People in the North have kidnapped free people of color and sold them back into slavery. If you hear about it once it means it's happened more than a hundred times. I credit les noir in the North for fighting for the freedom they *thought* they already had, and the Quakers and other noir for setting up schools. If this is how they are treating people of color now, how will they treat them when slavery is forced to end and it's every man for himself? What does that mean for Désireé and Gorée? What does it mean for New Orléans?"

Pierre hurried around the desk and embraced his father before he fell. Will stumbled and fell into his son's arms, then sobbed, unashamed, the tears falling fast and warm.

"I worry," he admitted, staring his son in the eyes. "My worries are killing me, Pierre. Even my father who behaved dementedly knew slavery was wrong. The only way he could fight it was turning this place into what it is today. Oh, how hated we are because of it."

Pierre offered him the handkerchief from his pocket, then assisted his father back into the chair.

Will wiped vigorously at his eyes and cheeks. "I feel as if every inch of this land makes up my skin." The tips of his fingers poked at the sleeve of his coat. "I feel the burden of taking care of it. It seems as if every slave in the South has heard about us now. Slave men, women and children have died trying to get here, Pierre."

"I understand, Papa. I do."

"No, you don't. I will now tell you my death wish."

"I'm listening."

Will nodded because he knew Pierre was truly listening.

Will let out a slow breath and lowered his chin. "What I will say next is cruel, but necessary. You have erred in your treatment of Abigail. In front of her, you have shown affection to Désireé, Gorée, Anne, and Mableane. The damage is done, Pierre. And because the damage is done, Abigail cannot be your heir. If you died and she took control of our estate, she will not value it. Her spending will be defined by the resentment of her past."

"Abigail will never be my heir, Papa."

"Pierre, listen to me. Désireé cannot be your heir either, nor mine, nor Julien's. Not the way things are now. The Américains outnumber the Creole by more than a small number. By death or trickery, either way, one of them will find a way to take from Désireé what should be rightfully hers once you, I and Julien are dead. Leave my granddaughters well off, but as for the heir who will inherit Ashleywood and the plantation Riverside, and who will run our companies here in América and in Europe and France, it must be an heir born from a white woman. Only this way can the child be guaranteed to keep what's his. I don't care where you get this child. You need a son, Pierre. More than one. Jenna cannot be its mother. Too much damage has been done there also. Find a woman, Pierre. Love her and have you some heirs. Promise me."

Taking a swallow of bourbon, Will set the glass down, leaned back and drew in a calming breath.

"I've already thought about this, Papa. I have thought about the same things you have." Pierre lifted his glass to indicate why he drank so much. "I have also thought about having children outside of my marriage. I have even chosen someone to bear me these children."

"Blessa?" Will asked.

"Oui," Pierre answered.

Will grabbed his glass and sat forward. "I have two more requests. I want you to sell our textile company in Europe. With that money – and only that money – I want you to clear the east end of Ashleywood and build more cabins. No less than thirty. And then I want you to purchase as many slaves as you can to fill them. The day slavery ends, I want you to divide the money that's left and give it to every slave we have on this land, so when they leave here they won't die on the streets. I don't care how long this takes. If you must, teach your sons this as well. Promise me."

Pierre folded his hands together and leaned on his elbows. "Papa, I'm going to tell you something I have never told you before."

"What is it, *Fils*?"

"There's a reason I haven't petitioned the church for a divorce."

Will rubbed at the sudden tightness in his chest.

"Before we were married, I confided in Jenna because I trusted her back then. That woman is evil," Pierre seethed. "It is this reason I find it hard to love Abigail."

"What is it?" Will whispered.

"Jenna has shared the confidence I had in her with Chadwick Speck. It is the reason I tolerate his coming here to sleep with my wife."

"What confidence?" Will stressed.

"I have been harboring fugitive slaves on Ashleywood. I have patrollers, Papa. They do nothing else, except search the woods for runaways. We have locations that if a slave can reach it, the people there will see to it that they are brought here by way of the rear swamp. When it's safe to do so, these slaves are taken at night to the port and hidden inside one of our ships. From there they are taken to France."

"How long have you been doing this?" Will asked.

Pierre gave a determined look. "Since I was fifteen."

"Mon Dieu!" Will whispered. "Men who steal free people of color and sell them into slavery are not given harsh sentences. But any man who steals another man's slave will receive no mercy. Why do you keep so many secrets from me?"

"Voir."

Will turned the entire chair in order to look over his shoulder in the direction the voice had come from. Again, a sweet, angelic voice spoke.

"Voir."

The chair overturned as he stood to his feet. With his head leaned far to one side, he watched as Gorée tumbled out of the bed head first. Unable to move, because he couldn't believe what he was seeing, disbelief and fear captivated him as Gorée used her arms to pull her body slowly across the floor.

Turning to face Pierre, Will was at a loss for words.

"Sit, Papa. She doesn't like to be watched."

"She spoke." Will bore an incredulous smile as he sat. "My granddaughter spoke." Tears gushed out of his eyes. A hand pressed against his mouth as if to hold them back.

Pierre also smiled, then reached for the decanter and refilled their glasses.

Will couldn't stop himself from looking over his shoulder. In seconds, Gorée had pulled herself half way across the study's floor. As he was rising, Pierre urged him again to sit. Once he was, Will could hardly keep still. Seeing the child move as quickly as she was, for a moment, he had the urge to throw something at her to get her to stop. The doctors had assured him nothing could be done and that nothing will ever change. Yet Gorée had spoken, and now she was getting around on her own.

"I went into Jenna's boudoir last night," Pierre began. He took a sip of the bourbon, and winced from the memory rather than the bitterness of the drink, then twirled the glass between his thumb and finger.

Will knew his son was only speaking to divert his attention elsewhere.

"While I was in her bed she moaned Chadwick's name in a very sultry voice."

Will reached for the glass, needing a large swallow of the liquor. As he lifted it, he repeated what Pierre said in his mind and stared forward. It was at that moment he looked down. "*Mon Dieu!*" He nearly jumped out of his chair when a mat of hair moved beside his boots.

He looked at Pierre and started to laugh, then laughed even louder when Pierre smiled happily at him.

Gorée continued to crawl until she reached Pierre's boot. When Pierre didn't reach down for her, Will's smile faltered as his eyes questioned his son. To see what Gorée did next, he needed to get out of his chair. Moving around the desk, he watched as the child continued past Pierre's boots and underneath the desk. And then she stopped, suddenly, and pulled herself up into a sitting position, then leaned her head to one side to see if Will was still watching

The smile on Will's face quivered.

Pierre finished what was left in his glass in one gulp.

"She has intelligence," Will said.

"Oui."

"How long have you known this?"

"I knew it from the moment she was born, Papa. And when she looked at me, it was as if she sensed I would be all she had. It's why I never gave up."

"You need to share your secrets sometimes, Pierre."

"I just did, Papa."

"Men in this city want us dead. Have you noticed that our enemy didn't include Jenna's name on the list?"

"I did."

"Never trust this woman, Pierre. If I believed for a moment she had been involved in any of this, I would go upstairs and kill her right now. But I don't think she was involved. Strangely enough, I believe she loves you."

Pierre said nothing.

Will remembered Gorée and peeked under the desk. Gorée had crawled further under it to reach a small blanket. On it were a scattering of small pieces of bread and chocolate squares the same way someone left food for a stray animal they intended to keep. A small piece of chocolate was in her hand, and although she had managed to secure only a part of it in her mouth, her tiny palm held the remaining part against her cheek to ensure she didn't lose it.

*Remarkable*, he thought. If the child got up at that moment and started walking, he knew he would run out of the room. He rose when the door opened. Désireé, now bathed and dressed, saw her pépère and flew across the room to him. Will spun her high into the air and tickled her mercilessly. *Ma fifille. Mon cœur. Mon ange. Ma bichette.* The list went on and on and on; each endearment spoken more heartfelt than the previous.

As soon as she was placed on her feet, she kissed his cheek, walked to her papa and sat beside him on the chair the same way a woman would.

"Voir."

Pierre reached underneath the desk and lifted Gorée on his lap. Désireé kissed her sister on the top of the head, then stared solemnly at her pépère as if telling him to finish the conversation she had interrupted when she walked in the room.

Pierre was looking at him the same way. The three of them looked the way Will believed he did after Catharine had died, a father with two motherless children dressed in the finest clothes money could buy.

"Do you know where these men are that Le Secret Sept has hired?" Pierre asked.

"What I didn't tell you last night was I went over to the Oakes' plantation," Will answered. "Billy Oakes wasn't home, but his mother was. She was more than willing to tell me that it was Le Secret Sept that hired the gunmen. She claims Billy isn't involved. If this were true, Billy would have been there to speak to me himself seeing that their land was in need of much work. I believe it is Billy who is giving the hired dogs all the information they need about us. The lay of the land. Places we visit in the city. I promised her I wouldn't harm him in exchange for the information."

"Your promise means nothing to me," Pierre retorted. "For months Billy Oakes has been spotted on this land. At first, I thought he had somehow learned what I had been up to. Now I'm certain he was watching us to give information to the men who were hired to kill us. And because of this, I'm going to personally take care of Billy Oakes. Have you received any word from Julien? I thought he would have returned from the Vieux Carré by now since he knows how ill you are."

"He got married yesterday."

Pierre stared a long time across the desk.

"To whom?" He finally asked.

"I don't know. Montague says her name is Marie-Marie Bechet."

"I don't know any Bechets with a daughter named Marie-Marie."

"Montague heard that her family had recently arrived in the city by way of France. All of them, other than Marie-Marie, have died from yellow fever. I know my son. For him to marry this woman against our traditions mean he loves her, and that's all that matters to me. Knowing my son, he is on his way home with his new bride so I can meet her."

"I need to delay those plans for now," Pierre said. "Send Montague to find Julien. Tell Montague to bring Julien's wife here where she will be safe. As for Julien, I need him back in the city. He will be easier to find if a hired dog is after him. When these men come after him, there will be no more doubts that I am the new *le diable dans Nouvelle-Orléans.*"

Will nodded in agreement. Although he loved his sons equally, he knew deep down Pierre was just like him. There had been only one time when the two of them had been at odds.

When Pierre was nineteen, he started taking long walks around the plantation at the same hour of day. Will suspected Pierre was doing more than walking and followed without Pierre knowing. The shock he felt when Pierre's walk ended at a newly built cabin in the coopers' quarters on their land. Later Will learned that Pierre had instructed the cabin to be built specifically for the slave girl who resided alone inside it. And it hadn't been a regular sized cabin, but a larger one built close to the size that an overseer would have.

It surprised him further when he learned that Marie-Téa was the servant who lived in this cabin, and how often Pierre visited her. Marie-Téa, by far, was the most beautiful *mulâtresse* that ever lived in New Orléans. Before Pierre had taken up with her, she had daily chores inside the mansion. Shortly after the cabin was built, her chores were reassigned, by Pierre, to the dairy.

The relationship bothered Will. Although he was not disinclined with his son taking a *placée*, this type of arrangement was usually done outside of the plantation. Because Will had his children later in life, he had urged Pierre to marry young and to secure a family as soon as he became twenty-one, which was something most unheard of for Creole men.

Believing that as long as Pierre had a *placée* who lived on the plantation, and that this would prolong his son finding a suitable wife and marrying her, after a year and he saw that Pierre was stalling finding a wife, Will chose one for him. The woman's name was Sabine Mandeville. She was two years Pierre's senior and came from a respectable family in the city. Pierre's refusal to marry the woman had caused Will much embarrassment, as the Mandevilles had looked forward to the union. Will suspected Marie-Téa was the reason for the refusal. When he confronted Pierre, he confessed it was true. At that time, Marie-Téa was carrying their first child.

The morning Marie-Téa gave birth to Désireé, Will sold Marie-Téa to Jean-André Dussault, who had been visiting the plantation that same morning. Knowing that Jean-André would not sell Marie-Téa back to Pierre despite any price offered, he believed he had settled the matter.

Will blamed himself for Pierre's failing marriage. Happenstances occurred where Pierre met Jenna. From first sight, he fell in love with her. When he learned on his wedding night that his new bride was carrying another man's child Will suspected Pierre blamed him for having to choose a bride as young as he was and also so swiftly. He completely turned his back on his marriage and again rekindled his relationship with Marie-Téa.

Jean-André had not known that Pierre was secretly visiting Marie-Téa's cabin. Angry that his servant was being romantically involved with Pierre behind his back, Jean-André neglected Marie-Téa when he learned she was pregnant with Gorée. On and off Marie-Téa suffered from blood burning fevers. Three days before she died, Jean-André relented and sold her to Pierre.

The fever that burned inside of her had taken its hold on Gorée as she was pushed into the world. Minutes after given birth Marie-Téa died.

Will stared at his eldest and youngest granddaughters.

"According to Eleanor Oakes there are two more hired dogs," he said. "One of them is your Américain friend, Siggy Bucket. The other she heard her son say was a demander from the North, but you've heard of him. We both have."

"Who?"

"Knuckles."

"Knuckles Van Troesch?" Pierre's eyes burned with contempt. "It seems no matter how hard I try against it my life emulates yours."

Rising to his feet with both of his daughters, he placed Désireé on her feet and carried Gorée to the door.

"Suzette!" He yelled.

Before the servant girl could answer, he carried Gorée into the alcove and placed her inside of the wooden box.

Suzette ran into the study, dipped at knee at the sight of Will, then hurried into the alcove.

Pierre stepped out of it with the two pistols visibly showing underneath his coat.

"Let's go," he said.

Désireé ran after her father's fast moving feet.

As he stepped into the hall, he saw Abigail peeking from behind a sofa. He had no idea how long she had been there waiting for him.

Standing in front of her, he stared down at her for some time. Before walking away, for a moment – one – he thought about caressing the top of her head. He then reminded himself who her father was and walked away.

Désireé ran to Abigail and gave her a tight hug.

Abigail giggled as she hugged Désireé back.

Abigail then ran to the door behind them. "*Au revoir*, Papa!"
Pierre stopped momentarily and faced her.
*Au revoir, petite.*
The words had formed in his mind but were too difficult to speak.

# Chapter Eight
## Every Dog Has Its Day

*[Never dress in mourning before the dead man is in his coffin. – Creole Proverb]*

Julien hopped down from the rented phaeton, happy to be back inside of the Vieux Carré. Even though Marie-Marie was safely ensconced with his father's men and on her way to Ashleywood, he feared his marriage would be no better than Pierre's.

Earlier that morning Marie-Marie had asked him to take her to church. While there she lit a candle, then slipped into a confessional booth. After coming out of it he noticed tears in her eyes. Kneeling in front of one of the pews, she bowed her head and prayed, her fingers caressing her rosary beads.

Apparently their lovemaking that morning had prompted her decision.

The small cut she had made the night of their wedding hadn't been deep. Because women were taught never to look at their bodies, she had blown out the lamps and closed the French doors and shutters, then sat in the corner, held the knife low and thrust it forward.

Eager just as much as he was to consummate their marriage, that morning she began again where they had left off the night before. Loving what he did to her, she allowed him to position her on her knees the third time. It was shortly after this he saw the change in her.

Before they got on their way to Ashleywood she sat him down and explained that their behavior that morning had been sinful. Good Catholic women shouldn't enjoy lovemaking. The priest had confirmed this during confession after she had confessed the things she had done with her husband that morning. One by one she told him the things a good Catholic woman shouldn't do: touch themselves, look upon their naked flesh, masturbate in any form, or desire sexual contact as it went against their morals and was proof that the desirer was lustful, and how lust was sorely disapproved of by the church. And this part was his favorite. Lovemaking had been created with a purpose, and that purpose was solely procreation. As God was perfect and had created men in his image, it was man's duty to also be perfect.

After he drank two cups of rum, he stared long at her smiling face with an urge to choke her. Maybe if the things she had said had come from someone else he would have been more considerate. For four months Marie-Marie lived in the Jennings mansion without a chaperon and with a single, young man. Not once had she spat any of this nonsense. Neither did she leave his home to reside somewhere else until their marriage took place. Where had her morality been then?

It was true that many women near and far believed the same things she did. The reason he married her was because she *had* lived without a chaperon with him. Believing she saw sex the same way he did, two people enjoying intimate moments together, was the reason he had married her without his family or friends present.

In order to convince him that he too could be happy living a chaste life, she led him inside their room, undressed behind a changing screen and climbed into the bed while wearing a nightgown. Closing her eyes, her hands rested on top of the coverlet while she actually waited for him to climb on top of her.

"Do you love me?" He had asked.

"Oui," she answered with her eyes still closed.

"Then I suggest you climb out of that bed and be prepared to live a life of sin."

Harsh words passed between them and ended with her bursting into tears. Since then she refused to look at him and only spoke to him when she had to. This was not the marriage he wanted. The night before he had due cause to seek an annulment, especially since the marriage hadn't been consummated. Now he was married to this woman for life, as Creoles believed once married only death could end it. The Roman Catholic Church believed this too.

"You're not the man I thought you were," she told him before climbing into the coach with Montague.

Julien lowered his face close to hers.

"Hussy, you have no idea what kind of man you married or the family you have married into. If you ever speak to me in that tone again, I'll slap you to sleep. Permanently."

Those had been their parting words, and Julien felt those words now as he walked the muck-strewn street, stepping high on the flat *banquette*, his carmine and gold embroidered overcoat occasionally slapping the wind.

The good-natured raillery of partygoers blared with high-pitched laughing voices around him. Street lamps trembled with flames similar to women with undulating hips. Two *ivrognes* swayed on their feet as they stepped into the salt musty air. Three women and their chaperons dressed like nuns and priests and on their way to one of the many costume balls given by the *crème de la crème* passed him. The youngest of the trio, a dark-eyed, dark-haired beauty, turned and blew Julien a kiss. He had been ready to turn his life over to Jesus and follow her when he heard his name yelled in the wind.

Grégoire barreled down the *banquette* in his wide stretched gait, his familiar too short jacket squeezing the life out of him. The moonlight gave him the appearance of a hairy boar. Still he was a sight for Julien's newly wedded eyes.

Grégoire didn't stop until he lifted Julien in the air.

"Hell, if I'd known the two of you were going to act like juveniles I would've brought salt water taffy and diapers." Tomas Maison had a voice too soft to belong to a man. His smile was hidden behind a full, well-groomed beard.

He pulled Julien closer, giving him a tight squeeze.

"Julien!"

"Tomas!"

"What is this?" Nel Black yelled. He had stopped during the reunion to lean against a merchant's door to await his turn. "Who wants to be around you sorry bunch of miscreants?"

Julien had no idea Nel had come back from Havana. Nel had gone there after he knifed an Américain and an Irisher inside one of the plenteous saloons on Girod Street. If he was back in the city, it meant his family had been able to pay for his troubles to go away quietly. Nel grabbed him by the waist, his middle equal to Julien's. They jumped together, in sync. A victory dance. And when they landed, Nel, being shorter, struggled to pull Julien down by the crown of his head to vigorously rub his elbow across Julien's fair hair.

"Damn! I've missed you, Blonde Boy!"

They hugged again, this time like proper gentlemen before Julien searched the street for yet another *ami*. One of his friends was missing. Julien found him lounging against a nearby wall, his boot flat on crumbling painted stucco, wood, and brick.

Chrétien Delery Deveraux was not like the others. His father was Jean-Paul Deveraux, his mother, the elegant Eugenie Delery. Chrétien was the only one amongst them, other than Julien, who could boast that his parents were direct descendants from one of the city's oldest families.

His tone was unrehearsed eloquence; pristine. "Julien."

Julien grinned, lifted his arms in surrender, then jumped forward and wrestled Chrétien to the dirt.

Chrétien lunged to his feet. "You sneaky *bâtard!*"

Julien drew a double-barreled howdah from his coat pocket. It's large caliber made it a good hunting pistol.

Tomas and Grégoire whistled.

Julien drew a second howdah from a different pocket.

Nel made a face of pleasure that looked more like a grimace as he took in the pistol's iron work.

Julien winked at him.

Grégoire howled.

"What do you have planned tonight, Jules?" Nel asked, elbowing Chrétien in the ribs.

Chrétien waited patiently to hear the answer, as did the others.

Julien stared down the street in both directions.

Nel nodded with understanding.

"For how long?" Chrétien asked.

"If anyone ask I was with you all night."

Nothing more needed to be said. Over the years, each of them had at least once needed the other to help from being detected after committing a crime. It was because of Julien the reason Nel had made it safely to Havana.

The noise of the Lamp Light Inn met them on the *banquette*. The music magnified as Nel opened its door. Girls, most of them *mulâtresses* and Indians, were dressed in feathers, greeted them as they stepped inside, planting slow kisses on each of their cheeks. "Don't forget to come upstairs, messieurs," they whispered.

The smoky atmosphere gave the appearance of ghosts walking along the ceiling. A four man band with handmade instruments stood on top of a make shift stage made of roped together barrels.

Julien got lost in the band's *tiggidy-tiggidy* beat.

With Nel and Julien together, the men were in for a good night. Grégoire was certain of it. And a good night meant nothing less than a visit upstairs with the *prostituée* nicknamed Merriment.

Once Julien was seated, he searched the room with his eyes until they rested on two men sitting near the back wall.

***

The two men sat quietly watching and waiting for their opportunity.

Knuckles Van Troesch had a way of sensing his victims at first glance. Until now he'd considered it destiny, an awkward awakening of unseen forces joining the living with the soon to be dead. But the man Knuckles watched, and matched perfectly the description given to him by Billy Oakes, made him uneasy.

Julien sat with a pistol visibly resting on his leg and another that bulge his coat.

"I thought Billy said this wasn't the dangerous one?" Knuckles asked, facing Siggy Bucket.

Siggy leaned on his arm closer to the table. "Trust me when I tell you that of the two brothers this one isn't the dangerous one. The one you're looking at, he's the good one. The happy one."

Knuckles' eyes narrowed as he considered this, and then he shook his head. "Look at this one. Really look at him. Other than the men sitting at his table, all I see is refugees, Spaniards, a few Irish. I see two funny looking thieves who look like they came straight from the Caribbean Isles. There's nothing about this brother that makes him fit into a place like this, yet he *does*. I've seen men like these kill for a single Spanish real. So why haven't they gone after this one when I can see he's wearing jewelry, and I can smell he have a pocket full of money from here?"

Siggy began to watch Julien more carefully. This wasn't his first time seeing him in person. Usually, the youngest male heir of the Jennings family was as he was now, enjoying the best that life had to offer. Yet Knuckles was right. The other men in the place were keeping their distance, and Siggy feared there was a reason behind it.

"What do you propose?" He asked.

"Billy said the family has no idea they've been targeted." Knuckles looked over his shoulder and saw that Julien was looking directly at him. "I have a bad feeling about this one," he admitted. "I think the reason he has that pistol on his lap is because he's anxious to cock it."

"There's two of us," Siggy reminded.

Knuckles smiled when he faced Siggy again. The smile slid from his face when he saw Siggy turn completely white.

Slowly Siggy began to lower in his chair; his eyes averted to the door.

"What's gotten into you?" Knuckles sat up when Siggy slid further down in the chair until his head was lower than the table.

"The brother just walked through the door."

The door was behind Knuckles. In order to see it, he had to turn in his chair, as well as look over his shoulder. The man he saw was taller than any man he had ever seen. Long white hair seemed to illuminate as it flowed loosely past his shoulders. The man leaned to whisper into another's man ear. The man he spoke to was the owner. Knuckles had met him on his way in. The owner nodded, then pointed at the table where Knuckles sat. It was then the tall man stood upright and turned his face toward the table.

Even from where he sat, Knuckles could see that the man's face held no expression. It was too dark to see the color of his eyes, but Knuckles could feel them. The heat inside them crossed the room and warmed Knuckles' entire body. Long Hessian boots gripped tightly to the man's calves. One of his hands held something inside his coat that looked too long to be a pistol and too short to be a rifle. When the man reached for the weapon, several patrons turned over chairs as they fled and crawled to a part of the inn they believed safer. The owner fled out of the front door.

There were two ways out of the inn, the front, and rear doors. The rear door was located behind the brother sitting across the room.

Knuckles carefully looked over his shoulder and saw that Julien Jennings was still looking at him. The brothers shouldn't have known that hired gunmen were after them, but somehow he sensed the brothers knew.

Staring down at the table in front of him, he thought of excuses he could give if the brothers approached.

Without warning, Siggy jumped out of his chair and ran in the direction where Julien had sat.

The music coming from the stage still played. This told Knuckles that either the musicians weren't aware that trouble had walked through the door, or they knew the character of the man who looked like the devil dressed in man's clothing.

He glimpsed the front door.

Both brothers were holding each other in a fierce embrace as if they hadn't seen each other in a long while. Knowing now was his time to escape, he jumped out of his chair faster than Siggy had. As he ran he pushed chairs and tables out of his way, chairs that moments ago held bodies in them. Pushing through the rear door, he ran through the courtyard and out onto the street.

If the brothers stepped out of the front door, they would see which direction he ran in. If they had a horse nearby, they would ride after him and catch him before he could get away.

Slipping through the unlocked porte cochère of the house next door, he bumped into empty barrels stacked against the wall. Fearful the noise had given away his position he lowered to the ground and hid behind a large fountain that took up a good portion of the courtyard.

Holding his breath, he listened as the door of the porte cochère creaked open. Taking his chances, he rolled onto his belly and peeked from behind the fountain.

The older brother stood in the door with a rifle held in front of his face as his eyes and the weapon searched the yard.

The younger brother ran to the opening. "I know where Siggy is hiding."

One step backward was all it took for the taller brother to disappear from view.

Thoughts of Siggy being murdered at that moment made his heart pound in his chest. It was then he jumped to his feet and hurried through the porte cochère. When he reached the street, he saw no one.

Breathless and panting, Knuckles was at first unable to move. Dying was what he wanted to avoid. Afraid to go for his horse just in case the brothers were in that area, he pushed off on his right leg as hard as he could and ran fast. The city wasn't one he was familiar with, still he knew if he reached Rue Rampart, and if he went where Billy was waiting, the odds of him being killed was slim. Dark shadows could be seen here and there further down the street, but the shadows were too small to be of importance to him.

The cemetery was where he needed to get. From there he will convince Billy to lead him to the boat the men had arranged to get him and Siggy out of the city after the deed was done.

Knuckles stopped at a house when he reached Rue Rampart and leaned against its wall, then glanced over his shoulder in case he had been followed. Deciding now was the time to get moving again he started to take a step when a pistol pressed against his skull.

"I see you made it," Billy Oakes whispered. "Where's Siggy?"

The pistol lowered.

Knuckles turned and faced the young man. "I think the brothers got to him."

"Both brothers?" Billy's eyes darkened, then darted along the street. "Did you kill the one named Julien?"

Knuckles was staring into Billy's eyes. Billy was looking intently back at him when the boom of a pistol fired, it seemed, at the same moment a plume of blood squirted from Billy's cheek. Billy's face took on a dazed look. His mouth gaped when a second boom tore a hole in the center of his forehead.

Knuckles didn't watch Billy fall. Instead, with an expression of disbelief, he turned in the direction the pistols had fired from just as smoke erupted from a rifle. Searing pain burned the center of his chest. Just as his mouth gaped just as Billy's had, the iron ball from a second shot obliterated his tonsil and blew out the back of his throat.

Pierre heard footsteps running toward him from the corner of Rue Saint Anne. Hurrying to the nearest cottage, he leaned the rifle against it and pulled a hunting knife out of his right boot. Leaning closer to the home's wall, he waited.

A man hurried around the corner carrying a lantern in one hand and a rifle in the other. Only a constable would hurry toward the sound of gunfire. Pierre held his breath as the man ran past him, then started to move faster when he saw two bodies in the street.

Pierre stepped from the side of the house and behind the man.

The man saw a shadow behind him and dropped the lantern. He tried to seize his rifle with his free hand. A deliberate strike of the knife close to the man's neck caused him to fall back on one foot. The rifle was dropped as the constable reached for his throat. Pierre stood behind him, gripped the constable's hair with his left fist, then pulled the knife deeply and slowly across the man's throat, and didn't stop slicing until he knew the constable would die from his wound.

At the same moment he dropped the constable to the ground, Pierre took a large step over the falling body. Since most pistols and rifles were single shots, Pierre took the time needed to pick up the pistols he had dropped after shooting Billy. The pistols were shoved in the pockets of his coat. The rifle was a double barrel, and thankfully it hadn't backfired as most multi-shot rifles were known to do. Retrieving it, he hid it underneath his coat, then hurried down Rue Rampart in the opposite direction.

Siggy had been easy to kill. Hiding behind a carriage parked temporarily against the *banquette*, Pierre also cut his throat.

Julien had been sent back to his friends who would vouch for him the entire night.

Pierre crossed Rue Saint Ann and headed toward Rue Dumaine. Within minutes, he turned south on Rue Saint Phillip, then stopped and stared at a shotgun cottage with a door that looked as if it sat right on top of the *banquette*.

"Who goes there?" A soft voice asked after he knocked.

"Pierre," he answered.

The door was pulled open swiftly.

Blessa Genovese saw him covered in blood and quickly moved to the side to let him in. Moving quickly so he didn't track blood through the house, and because he didn't want Désireé to see him as he was, he hurried toward the rear of the house.

Hurrying behind him, Blessa met him in the courtyard. The two of them worked side-by-side drawing water from the cistern. Every now and then she eyed the blood on his clothes. Never had she seen so much of it at one time.

When enough water had been drawn, Pierre carried the buckets to the kitchen. One of her servants, Suze, stepped out of her bedroom above the kitchen and hurried down. As she boiled the water, Blessa led Pierre inside to prepare her boudoir. Candles were lit. Small towels were arranged over the end of a vanity chair in the corner. Buckets of hot water were then brought in and set at the foot of the tub to adjust the temperature of the water. Once everything was in place Blessa left the room to tell Suze she could go to bed.

Pierre adjusted the water, then reached for his coat to remove it just as Blessa entered the room and a small voice whispered from the corner at the same time.

"Is she gone?"

Désireé peeked from behind the armoire with her rag doll clutched tightly to her chest. The sight of Désireé hastened Blessa's footsteps. Désireé jumped high into the air before the first smack to her derriere could be given. The rag doll was dropped to the floor as two more stinging smacks brought tears into Désireé's eyes.

Blessa lifted the rag doll, handed it to the child, then led her out of the room by the hand. "You are not sleeping with your papa tonight. You are to stay in the room I gave you. Did I not tell you this before he arrived?"

Désireé's face crumpled as she nodded. As she was led through the door, she looked over her shoulder at her papa, wondering why as soon as he had seen her he had turned his back to her.

"I love you, petite," he said.

"Bonne nuit, Papa."

"Bonne nuit, mon chaton."

Blessa closed the door but didn't lock it as she felt there was no need.

Pierre was the first to fully disrobe, as he couldn't get the bloody clothes off soon enough.

Blessa carefully arranged his discarded clothes in the corner. In the morning she will burn them in the fireplace.

As she climbed into the tub with him, Pierre's arms circled around her, holding her tightly against him. She knew Pierre did not love her. Still she knew she would give him the children they discussed that afternoon, if only because she loved him.

Fully turning so she lay on top of him, her palms pressed to both sides of his face as she kissed him.

They both looked at the door as it pushed open slowly. Julien stood inside it breathing heavily. Tears streamed down his face. His eyes were red, his gaze solely on Pierre's.

## Chapter Nine
# Dearly Beloved, Rest In Peace

*[When the foot slips the rest follow. —Creole proverb]*

There was one thing Pierre knew about his father that Julien didn't. His father only told him once, and Pierre had never forgotten it. It was regarding the reason the men of the city called him *le diable dans Nouvelle-Orléans*. According to his father it all began with his grandfather, Andreu Arsène Arceneaux Jennings, the only heir born to Apolline Plessier Jennings.

The family's decline started with Apolline.

She had been orphaned at a young age, quite suddenly and without warning when both of her parents died the same day from cholera. She had been fifteen then and the tragedy of it had made her wealthy. The moment her parents had taken their last breath she became the sole owner of two grandiose plantations, a mansion in the Vieux Carré and many businesses: whaling, glass works, general stores, and the candle shops were only a few. She feared the massive weight of responsibility that suddenly rested on her shoulders, and because of it, three months after her parents died she married Hollis Iverson Jennings. It was from him the family received its Américain name.

Like others before them, Hollis' family was lured to New Orléans in 1724 after hearing the lies of the entrepreneur John Law. They fell for his bamboozlement of tall tales that the city was overbuilt with palatial homes ready for the taking, and that outside of the Vieux Carré was overburdened with unfound riches, so much so that bare-breasted Indian maidens greeted newcomers at the city's gates with small trinkets of gold, silver, diamonds or pearls.

Instead, when his family arrived they found the city as one of the settlers had correctly written about it, *'sans religion, sans justice, sans discipline, sans order et sans police'*. It was filled with the sons of France, of which many, but not all, were either the sons of Paris' societal rejects or Parisian convicts who had been granted clemency. The king had thought it wise to send salt smugglers and prostitutes to settle the city. They along with Caribbean pirates and the Canadian *coureurs du bois* who sold furs, lived in Indian villages and took Indian women as their wives were all there was until John Law's Germans and Swiss poured into the area.

Many in the city suffered from violent fevers, and rampant diseases, and unforeseeable mortal weather. And at best, those who dwelled in the city lived in crude made log cabins that boasted roofs made of bark and palmetto branches. That was – at least – until French architects such as Broutin, Dubreuil, Lafon, Laclott, Guillot, Latour, Pouilly, and also a few free men of color such as Jean-Louis Dolliole continuously began to perfect the city with the building of a convent, a hospital, a town square, sturdy built homes later known as Creole cottages, and unique two story mansions of which boasted a Caribbean influence. It established the city and made it what it was even today. Forever French.

Hollis married Apolline because her father had been a successful merchant from a wealthy family in France. After their marriage, Hollis lived exorbitantly and spent freely. He was blinded to the reality that his wife was a desirable woman to many men. Like her father and grandfather, she inherited her family's strange trait of hair equal to the imagination of straw bleached with lime, and eyes the hue of water interlarded with the sharpness of silver and the faintest hint of blue. His wife made true what was said of Creole women: beautiful, petite, lustrously thick hair and lithe frame. He only made love to her on the rare occasions when his need was very strong, and the mansion was devoid of female houseguests because he didn't want to risk her having a child. If she had a child, it meant she would have an heir. He wanted Apolline's entire fortune to himself.

A week after they married he visited Philadelphia, then the river where her family's glass works brought in astronomical profits. He visited her family's shop in Nantucket to view for himself its large volume of fine oil and candles made from the blubber of sperm and right whales and sold mostly in England. Her plantation Riverside, along the Pee Dee River in Georgetown, was his favorite. Year after year its harvest of rice was a success. Its massive over-furnished mansion consisted of twenty-two rooms of which no comforts had been spared. Although John Law had been a crook in his day, it didn't take Hollis long to realize that the enchanting lifestyle his family had been in search of had been found through his marriage.

She said nothing of his spending, although he was certain her *avocats* kept her well informed. She said nothing when he left the plantation for an entire year at a time then returned for only a few days before leaving again. Because she said nothing, he felt – *almost* – that he had her permission to treat her as he did, and because of this his affairs became numerous. What he didn't know was the reason his wife had kept silent regarding his affairs was because she was having one of her own.

After three years of a marriage she could neither heal nor forgive, she began traveling to Paris, frequently, but Hollis could care less. He was busy yet again. Further north on the Mississippi River he had another plantation built that was much larger and grander than her plantation Riverside; he named it Primrose Valley after his paramour Rose Vali, who lately never left his side. With the building of this plantation, Apolline's family would have full advantage in the market. The Riverside plantation produced rice. Ashleywood, during that time, produced indigo. If he had his way, Primrose Valley would produce cotton.

He had an elaborate smokehouse built, and dovecotes; he purchased only skilled, strong looking slaves. It took three years for the mansion to be completed. All the while his wife had returned from Paris then gone again, but the last time she returned she hadn't returned alone. The man that accompanied her was Baron Andreu Arsène Arceneaux.

When it was told to Hollis months later that his wife had become pregnant during his absence, he left his paramour at Primrose Valley and immediately returned to Ashleywood. His suspicions were proven the morning she gave birth to a son. The babe inherited its mother's strange hue of hair and eyes but had a petit face the same as that of the baron's.

Against his wishes, she named the child Andreu Arsène Arceneaux Jennings, after its father who had died from yellow fever three months before the child was born. Hollis thought the child's name was shameful, and belittling to his ego, but Apolline's friends in the city thought otherwise. They came by carriages bearing gifts and offering Hollis strange looks. One of them was bold enough to confront him. *'Have you looked around the Ashleywood plantation of late, monsieur? Have you noticed that since you have been gone overseers have been hired, and your harvest of indigo has doubled? Have you noticed that your wife is no longer a young girl, but in your absence has become a beautiful woman? Have you noticed that in a short matter of months the Baron had won over the residences of the Vieux Carré with his manner of dress and charm while you, on the other hand, have to continuously work in order for us to even remember your name? Do you think Apolline's papa is truly dead? He isn't. He lives through his avocats that he's left behind. He was a smart man. Very smart, monsieur, and Apolline is fortunate. Where most women must rely on men, because of her papa, she has to rely on no one. And now that she has an heir what do you think will happen next?'*

Hollis realized he wasn't smart enough to know what would happen next. He did know, however, that he hated the child. The babe looked too much like the baron for his liking. From day one his wife gave the child everything she had once been willing to give Hollis: love, affection, and wealth. She went against the grain and had Andreu taught English. By the time Andreu was thirteen, he had been well educated by a barrage of notable French tutors. When he was fifteen Apolline had him deflowered by a scheming *prostituée* that had once been a prisoner of St. Martin-des-Champs and now resided near the barracks in the Vieux Carré. By the time he was sixteen he was definitely a man. She had *garçonnieres* added to each side of the Ashleywood mansion so that her son could live as other young Creole men did, in his own apartment that had a separate roof than that of his *maman*.

After the *garçonnieres* were completed Apolline gave Andreu legal ownership of Ashleywood and Riverside. It was told to Hollis later that his wife had made these changes because she wanted to begin living by the old Creole custom that 'a wife's money remained her money.'

The evening Hollis learned he was no longer master of either of her plantations they quarreled.

"You think your little French bastard is going to be master over what I have governed these past years? Ashleywood and Riverside are mine."

They argued inside his office.

Andreu listened in plain view by the door. Even as a child he never feared this loathsome man his mother had married.

"No, Ollis," she answered. "Primrose Valley is yours. It's the only thing you've built, created and maintained. Everything else, the ships, the general stores, all of my papa's businesses here and abroad were well intact before you came into my life. All you have achieved over the years is Primrose. Andreu and I want nothing to do with the plantation you named after your precious whore. But even as we relinquish it to you, you should never forget that it was my money and Andreu's money that enabled you to build it."

Hollis slumped in the chair behind the desk and pulled forward a decanter of gin. "You think what you're doing is right, don't you? You think you can take away everything I have?"

"Ollis, you brought nothing into this marriage. You gave me nothing, not even a son, although I hear Rose Vali has given you three."

His eyes became wide; his lips twisted. "Are you telling me you want a divorce? That you would rather live in shame – you and your French bastard over there? Is he all you think about? Care about? Woman, I've been good to you. I hardly ever took a hand to you..."

Andreu's sixteen-year-old hands clenched into fists. "If you ever strike my mother I will kill you."

Apolline lifted her hands pleadingly and whispered, "I'll take care of this, Dreu."

She turned and faced her husband. "To spare everyone shame, including Rose, I shall not divorce you, although I should. Only a cruel man would marry a young girl that he despised simply to get his hands on her money."

"Why not?" He countered. "I thought that was what most Creole men were known for? Marrying rich widowers and heiresses so that they can live and flaunt wealth?"

She spoke quietly. "I shouldn't have married you. But I was young and didn't trust any of my father's friends. I should have done as my papa's *avocats* advised and married my own kind. Maybe if I had waited, I could have married the baron, and you could have married Rose."

Hollis gripped the armrest of the chair, dragging its legs a small distance across the floor as he stood to his feet. He gazed at her first, then at her son. "You won't do me dirty. By God. Woman, you won't. I won't allow it. I'll take again what's owed to me one way or another."

Crossing the room to stand closer to him, her eyes narrow and angry, as soon as she reached him, her palm lifted and slapped hard at his face. Hollis held his face, his eyes bewildered. As he stared intently at her, it felt to him as if he was facing a stranger. The Apolline he knew had a genial disposition. The woman standing in front of him with violent eyes filled with determination to ruin him made him realize how much the two of them had grown apart.

Her voice rose. "I've given you Primrose. I think it is payment enough for the shame I've caused you when I had my affair with the baron. But you still owe me, Ollis. You owe me for Rose Vali. And you can repay me by leaving my home at morning light and never coming back."

His laugh was exorbitant. "You conniving little French bitch. Is that how you French think? That you can just tell your husbands' to get and that's it? Well, not us Americans! You think that little slap scared me? How do you expect me to see after the Primrose plantation when you know Rose has no money? She's penniless!"

"Her financial affairs are not my business or my burden."

Andreu rushed forward when he saw Hollis lift the full decanter from the desk.

Hollis' arm swung with hatred and vicious intent. The decanter bashed Apolline's forehead like a mallet made of the hardest substance. The sound it made slowed Andreu's movements. His stomach churned with dread and concern. Unable to move, he watched as the hem of his mother's gown flew up as she fell backward.

Enraged by the sight of his mother lying still on the floor, Andreu tackled Hollis from behind. They wrestled, crashing against the desk. Hollis lifted an angry hand. Again he swung the decanter, this time at the side of Andreu's head near the boy's ear.

Hollis' heart beat fast; he brought a hand to his mouth in disbelief. In a panic, he began to move quickly.

He rushed toward the office door to make certain there were no servants in the hall. He closed the door tightly, then locked it. He rolled Andreu over and saw the empty expression on his wife's face. Her chin rested against her shoulder; her eyes were transfixed on the molding in the ceiling. He expected to find blood everywhere. On the carpet, her clothes, her face.

There was very little blood. Above her left eye was the proof of the horror he had committed. The skin was taut. The wound looked like it was filled with water. It began at the bridge of her nose, spreading across the entire brow so that it looked like her forehead was protruding, and reached as far back as the hairline.

Hollis' heart thumped out of control when her eyes averted to his, slowly; they were mesmerized, wide and fearful. Her chest heaved with each breath. Oh, how he regretted his actions. If he could take it back, he would have at that moment.

Death came not as he supposed, some final gesture or struggle for life; she simply stopped breathing. When? He was not certain. He hadn't realized she was dead until he noticed that the bodice of her gown no longer moved and his wife lay abnormally still.

Andreu gave a small moan and began to stir. Before the boy noticed his mother's still body, Hollis grabbed Andreu from behind, his elbow locking tightly around the boy's throat until there was no longer a struggle between them. He dragged Andreu past the desk toward the door of the *petite salle*, then locked the young man inside. Hollis moved mechanically. To conceal his wife's death, he carried her lifeless body to the nearest marsh. Out of breath and in fear of his life, he slid her into the dark murky water of the swamp. He reported her missing a few days later. The city officials recorded her death as an accident.

The year that followed was unbearable for Andreu. Although Hollis agreeably relinquished what he felt was his hold on Ashleywood and Riverside, nothing could bring back Apolline.

On the night Andreu turned seventeen he coerced several of his servants on Ashleywood to accompany him to the Primrose Valley plantation. They rode during the day, then waited between the trees until the night was dense with darkness. Only then did he and the servants walk through the mansion's front door then up the stairs. The servants with him entered the bedrooms where Hollis' and Rose's children slept. Andreu held in his hand an Italian flintlock pistol. No questions. No remorse. Quietly pushing open the bedroom door, he saw Hollis and Rose asleep in bed. Standing over his stepfather, he aimed the pistol in the same area Hollis had targeted when he swung the decanter at Apolline.

Rose heard the gunfire and awoke with a start. Andreu pulled a knife out of his waist and stabbed her until she stopped making noise. It took nearly a week to clean the rooms and carry Rose and her children to the deepest area of the swamp where no one would ever find them. As for Hollis, Andreu had different plans for his remains. Along with the help of a few servants, Hollis was buried in a hole not far from the slave's cemetery. No marker was made to pinpoint his grave.

When the sun rose Andreu rode to the Vieux Carré for two reasons; to give the servants who had traveled to Primrose with him their freedom, and to report Hollis Iverson Jennings and his second family as missing. Years later when a part of the fields at Primrose were being cleared and made ready to receive new crop, the new overseer and the servants in his charge unearthed a muslin bag. Inside it was a corpse devoid of clothes.

It was then the rumors began.

\*\*\*

Because Andreu had never married, Will never knew his mother. He couldn't remember ever clasping eyes on her, neither did he know her name nor if she was alive or dead. Andreu had mentioned his encounter with the woman only once.

He had visited Paris, by chance, when he was twenty-three years old during the anniversary of King Louis le bien aimé's (Louis the beloved) coronation. Like New Orléans, as this was its true place of birth, the citizens of Paris needed only little reason to celebrate. It mattered not to any of them that the King's popularity had lessened over recent years.

Fireworks were set off at Pont Royal. Bursts of white figments close to the shape of grotesque fleur-de-lis dripped from the dark sky like hot wax down a candlestick. The explosions of the fireworks, at times, seemed to echo from every direction. The sight of so many partygoers crowding the bridge and the quays along both banks of the river altered Andreu's mood.

He had returned to the city to take possession of the inheritance that had eluded him since his real father's death. The cabriolet he had rented stopped to take in a moment of the festivities. After all, he had just gained ownership of the monstrous Arceneaux château (deeply imbedded in the Loire), the chateau's north lying fields, a small village, and a few shops not far from where the cabriolet was stopped at that moment; and he was feeling a little jubilant, because the shops were located on the Pont-au-Change, one of the most lucrative areas of the city.

Tall buildings much different than what he was used to in *Louisiane* flanked him on every side. The air was sweet despite the constant explosion of petards that crackled and leapt across the cobblestones. He was in Paris where his real father and all of his mother's family had been born. The meeting with his paternal grandmother had ended far more pleasant than he had anticipated. The hue of his hair and eyes did little to stop her from recognizing the facial features of her beloved and last surviving son. After kissing him for the thousandth time, and hugging him tightly to a body that seemed delicate enough to break in his hold, she made promises to have him recognized as her living male offspring and assured him he would soon carry his father's title as baron.

And now, while standing where he was, he felt for the first time more French than ever before. Paris was different. Here there were no marshes or bayous or Indians, no overseers or slaves anywhere he looked. There was only the city, which housed the very rich and the very poor. And it was the coronation that had brought both classes together on the right bank of Pont Neuf.

The poorer Frenchmen around him were horribly dressed, yet they smiled as if life was pleasant. On their faces, there was a peace that Andreu could comprehend. It was pride in who they were – pride in the country of their birth. As he began to take in the faces around him, he realized just how much the slaves on his plantation had been stripped of their culture. Their clothing, shoes, the kind of food they ate, the way they wore their hair; all were now different. Showing pride in their homeland was against many laws and punishable.

This thought angered him. He turned to alert the driver it was time to depart when he bumped into Will's mother. Her voice was soft, yet raspy as if the night's chill was slowly snatching it away. She was young and had a plain face that couldn't be described as beautiful. The tatterdemalion clothing she wore hung in some places and gripped her far too tightly in others. Her complexion was flawless. What attracted him was the light hue of her eyes and the smile that warned she had no idea just how poor she was. Because she did not believe this was true, he found that he stopped believing it also the longer she stood in front of him.

'Pardon, monsieur. I didn't see you on account of the noise.'

Within an hour of them meeting he learned she was a chamber maid to the wife of a wealthy baron who had taken up residence at The Hôtel de Condé. Because of her prettiness, her mistress thought no need to dress her properly as the other maids residing in the hotel. That evening, because she had feigned ill, her mistress had given her the night off. The room she slept in possessed no candles and had only a small window that she had to climb on top of furniture to reach.

A wood plank bed, sparse bedding, the floor bare without even the smallest rug, the room had fewer accommodations than the slave cabins on Ashleywood. Andreu thought of none of these things as he removed her clothing and then his, the two of them clinging to one another for hours as they made love inside of that darkened room. One of the things he remembered most about that night was the wind blowing on their entwined naked bodies as they spoke in whispers almost till morning.

As he walked out of the hotel early the next morning, he had the urge to see her again. Creating an opportunity to introduce himself to her employers gave him an invitation to their temporary home. Every chance he got during the night was spent inside her room until the morning they both had overslept.

After she was fired from her job, Andreu had taken her to a different part of the city and found lodging for her there. Days later when he returned, most of her family had also moved into the single room. Throwing them physically out into the streets infuriated her. After she became pregnant, Andreu offered to take her to New Orléans as his wife. When he learned she would rather live in poverty to stay with her family, it changed everything.

'The day you were born I fought her brothers, her father and one of her sisters to get my hands on you and left that house without once looking back. There was no way I was leaving you behind to live in such filth. You should have seen the slaves when we rode onto the plantation the day I returned. You ended up having more than one mother. The servants who worked in the mansion fought between themselves about everything concerning you. I laugh now even as I remember those days.

'I will never marry, but you will some day. The reason I never married is because I didn't want to share the love I had for you with anyone else. When you have children, I want Ashleywood to be a home to them and their children as my mother made it a home for me. Family is everything. *La famille tout est.* Ashleywood will always be here to remind you and yours that wealth has no comparison to blood.'

Andreu was a disturbed man. Will had told Pierre more than once that the same man that loved him immeasurably, hugged and kissed him constantly as a child, tucked him in bed at night, rescued him from childhood nightmares, taught him how to ride, shoot a pistol and run a plantation; the same man that gave him everything he thought to ask for (except a mother), and took him whoring alongside him whenever they visited the Vieux Carré was the same man who had murdered nine men from Biloxi to Baton Rouge and had maimed twice as many.

Still Pierre knew that his father had loved the man he fondly referred to as Andreu. Will had loved the side of his father that others didn't see, like the way he reclined in a chair and smiled after a good meal; the way he was silent with a smug grin on his face whenever they left the home of a good whore or simply the way his father smiled at him whenever he walked into a room. What Will hated most was the way his father died. Because Andreu had never married, and because a trip to the city was sometimes too time-consuming, Andreu often pleasured himself with a few of the slaves on the plantation. The slave quarters on Ashleywood were called The Bottoms because it sat in the plantation's lowest region.

There was one servant woman in particular that he fancied more than the others. A Senegal woman with long, wild tangled hair that fell loosely past her breasts. She had a sweet silk box, his father often said, that kept him constantly depending on her attention. She was the only servant on the plantation who knew how to handle him, and because of this, her life had been easy. It was the leisure she enjoyed most.

Whenever he visited, she plied him with spirits to take the edge of the day off of him. Occasionally she cooked his meals, cut his hair, and massaged his shoulders when they ached. Inside the privacy of her cabin she became the wife he never had. What surprised Will was how much his father relished the woman's affections. When he asked about this his father had replied, '*The first time I went to her I was nineteen. I am now thirty-nine.*' He had said this as if the length of time of their relationship explained everything.

Less than a week later, Will waited patiently for his father on the mansion's front galerie. The last he had seen his father had been three days before. On this day, they were supposed to go into the city. A coach had been parked on the drive for that purpose. When his father failed to appear, Will went looking for him. Believing he had missed his father's return to the plantation and that he was somewhere on the land, he started in the smokehouse, then the dairy; he visited the smithy shop, but the answers were all the same. No one had seen the Master for three days. It was then when Will gazed in the direction of The Bottoms.

When he pushed open the cabin door, the smell was immediate. Nothing in the front part of the cabin appeared out of the ordinary. The room had no windows and was very dim. A heavily scarred table still held the remnants of the light meal the two of them had last shared. Beside a half finished plate of pheasant and corn that had become dry and brittle, a candle had completely burned, then smoldered in its own fat.

His father's clothes lay negligibly piece-by-piece on the floor. His Hessian boots sat neatly near the door. It was inside the small room behind the fireplace where Will found the bodies. They were lying in the bed against the farthest wall, their eyes fixed on one another with absence of life. Will rushed out of the cabin and wretched in the nearby bushes.

It took months before Will learned what happened to his father and the Senegal servant named Tassy. Tassy had given Andreu crushed rosary peas that had been prepared in China and had arrived in the city by way of ship. The poison was mixed in his father's food and drink. A very small portion was enough to kill a man. Hoping he died quickly rather than suffer, she had divided all of the crushed rosary peas she had been given between the two of them. The plan, as it had been told to her, was to kill Andreu. The guilt she felt for allowing someone to talk her into killing the man she loved was the reason she ate the poison along with him.

The crushed red and black berries had been fast acting, upsetting Tassy's and his father's stomachs. What angered Will was the look on his father's and Tassy's faces. Staring eye to eye while lying on the bed facing one another, it was apparent Andreu had been unaware that Tassy had poisoned him. Will believed Tassy died first because one of his father's hands rested on her face and his tears, which had dried after his death, were still visible when the two of them were found.

That his father had died unaware he had been murdered or given a chance to defend himself against his enemies made Will's heart grow instantly cold.

The plan to kill Andreu had been assembled by a few distinguished men that lived in the heart of New Orléans, lesser men who were fearful of residing in the same city with Andreu any longer, men envious of his prestige and wealth, men who couldn't wait any longer for the God spoken of by the priests to strike down and take vengeance on the man they referred to as *le fou*. To get the servant to do as they wished, they convinced her that her family in Virginia would be sold to a band of Indians who lived in the Florida swamps.

The men's names were Narcissi Laporte, Rémy Guillmard, François De La Croix and William Mc Ghee.

Like father, like son, Will was seventeen when he avenged his father's death. He killed Narcissi Laporte in Biloxi. He killed Remy Guillmard on his own plantation while the man swam late in the afternoon sun on a summer day. William McGhee was the easiest to kill. He confessed to everything before falling from a high beam in his barn. It took him a week to die from his injuries. But it was François De La Croix that received the worst of Will's anger because it was told to him that it had been François that had come up with the plan.

Will savored him for last but allowed him to live. Will felt no regret or remorse when he made a verbal contract with a Chickasaw warrior to give him rifles, ammunition, and three young Senegal slave girls if the Indian made an example of François. The warrior did not disappoint. Three days later François was attacked on his plantation. He was found by his servants waddling in his own blood. His hands, feet, penis and tongue had been cut off.

After François' near death from the hands of a Chickasaw warrior, none of Will's enemies dared come forward as witnesses from fear that their families too could become brutalized.

To the Orléonois, who considered Will as their friend, they were as loyal to him as they were to the endearing Lafitte brothers. To those who feared him he had become worse than his father, *le fou*. He was – no doubt – *le diable*.

# Chapter Ten
## Regeneration

*[It's when death comes that you think about your life. –Creole Proverb]*

Earlier in the day, Will told Alise that he would sleep inside the mansion. The reason he gave was he needed to keep an eye on Gorée. This had not been true. Shortly after Pierre and Désireé left the plantation, the pains returned. It was now evening, and although he wanted desperately to sleep the pain kept him awake.

When Rube came to check on him, he made one request.

"Bring the children."

Rube knew her monsieur was ill. Everyone on the plantation did. And like everyone, she believed he would live forever. Gathering the children, she came inside his bedroom and closed the door behind her.

Abigail pulled her hand free and ran to the bed. On Will's suggestion, she climbed up with Rube's help and lay beside him. Will hugged her tightly to his chest. "You are a Jennings. Never forget that your pépère told you this."

Rube also laid Gorée on the bed, then screamed when the child spoke.

"Voir."

With her hand clutched to her chest, she watched in stupefaction as the child rolled toward the edge of the bed. Will grabbed the child's leg just in time. After taking a deep breath, he pulled her closer to him

"Gorée, you will have the best life. This is a promise from your pépère. You are *free*. Don't let anyone tell you differently."

Désireé's face was cupped in his hands and kissed. "Take care of your papa."

Falling back against the pillow he had Rube take the children out of the room.

Rube handed the children to the servants in the hall and returned to the room and held his hand. "Tell me the truth. How are you feeling?"

Will smiled at her. "Have I been good to you, Rube?"

Hearing this she jumped to her feet and hugged him tight.

"Let me get Alise," she pleaded.

"No. Not like this. Sit down, Rube. Talk to me."

Sitting again, she held tightly to his hand.

"I have never known a better man."

"I'm the Devil."

She shook her head. "Not to any of us here."

Will closed his eyes.

"Remember when Sailor stole the overseer's watch?"

Will smiled from the memory.

"Twelve years old he was. The overseer wanted to whip him. When you told him he had his watch back and that you had talked to Sailor, he got real mad."

"Real mad," Will remembered loudly.

A tear fell from Rube's eyes as she smiled.

"The overseer threatened you. Told you if you didn't give him free reign to do his job, he was gone get. And you told him, 'Get on and get then.'"

"I didn't like that man," Will admitted.

"We love you," she whispered. "All of us do. You took me out of that slave pen and been like a father to me. And your wife was good to me. She never complained in the beginning when I used to burn the food. You had me taught how to read and write. What would my life be like right now if it hadn't been for you?"

A sharp pain made him wince. He squeezed her hand tighter. "You were good, Rube," he said after he caught his breath. "A good girl and then a good woman."

She lifted his hand, held it to her breast, then kissed it. When his eyes averted to her, she felt the need to make him laugh. "I have to admit, monsieur. I waited many years for you to come and lay me on my back."

Will laughed silently with his eyes closed tight.

"I know you're going to be all right, monsieur. It's just a bad spell. You don't look sick."

When he lay quietly for a while, and she believed he had fallen asleep, she rose softly to her feet, then left the room.

Will opened his eyes and watched the door close, and then he stared up at the ceiling and prayed. When the pain finally subsided, he fell asleep only to wake hours later to the feeling of his chest being crushed inward by something extremely heavy. Tears fell from the corners of his eyes. Sickness swirled in his stomach.

Gripping his chest and waiting to die, it was as he struggled to breathe when he realized he didn't want to die before seeing Alise's face once more.

Looking toward the French doors along the wall, he saw that the night was pitch black. As late as it was, all of the servants were now sleeping.

As he climbed out of bed the muscles in his chest tightened, then became worse with every step. Twice he stopped as sweat dripped from his face. The hall outside his door was completely dark. Opening his mouth to yell, the pain in his chest stole his breath away. Somehow he had to reach Alise. If he went back in his room, no one would find him until morning.

Reaching Jenna's boudoir, he knocked, then leaned weakly on it and the jamb. The third time he knocked he heard her on the other side of it. The sound of her door being locked was followed by her footsteps leading back to her bed.

The pain became so intense that all he could do was pant. *Alise. Come to me.*

With all the strength he could muster, he made his way to the stairs, making his way slowly down them and into the butler's pantry. In the middle of it, he slumped in a chair in front of the table where meals were placed to cool before serving. The wood was cool against his cheek as he laid his head against it; his arms dangled by his side. He had been there only a few minutes when a servant found him, and fearful of what she saw, ran to the outside kitchen to fetch Cook.

Cook hurried into the butler's pantry. She took a conscious step forward too fearful to call out to him.

His eyes lifted to hers when she leaned low to his face.

"Alise." His voice was small and almost inaudible.

She stood upright and stared at the servant standing in the door. "Run as fast as you can. Bring Madame Ali..."

The servant didn't wait for her to finish and darted out of the room, but it was too late. Will Jennings' head began to slowly lean back on his shoulders. The rest of his body became limp. Rube couldn't bear him falling and grabbed a hold of him. Both of them toppled, then collapsed onto the floor.

She spoke in a sober voice, tears filling her eyes as she stared up at the ceiling. Her voice was a whisper. "Don't be dead, monsieur. Get up, monsieur. Get up."

\*\*\*

Jenna had heard the knocking. It had awakened her out of a deep sleep. Because Pierre and Julien were away from the plantation, and Will had retired early to his room, she had sent Chadwick a letter by the hand of one of the slaves to come to her boudoir that evening.

It had been a long time since she and Chadwick had made love in a bed. Usually, they met in the abandoned barn. It was there where she hid coverlets and pillows to make the hay more comfortable. For the occasion, she had chosen a new nightgown to wear. Chadwick had come precisely when she had told him to, long after the servants had gone to bed.

Chadwick began to undress first because he was as excited as she was to make love on a bed. He tugged at his coat. She had crouched in front of him and removed his boots, tossing them behind her and onto the floor. When he stood, she tugged at his pants. He also began to tug, with some effort, at his waistcoat and boiled shirt. She yanked at his pants, then his undergarments until his flesh was eventually freed. His belly swelled and fell shapelessly over his manhood down to his knees. Staring at Chadwick, she compared his body to Pierre's muscular and fit frame.

Chadwick climbed into her bed and sprawled on his back. In this position his manhood became visible. It was thickly swollen. The gelatinous weight of his body wobbled and physically moved the bed across the floor when he tried to reposition and get more comfortable. Again when he was settled she examined him. Large indentations were where his knees should have been. Above them were large handfuls of flesh that fell both inside and outside of the bend of his knee. His feet were like two loaves of bread with five fat toes sticking out the ends of them. He had large breasts, each of them the size of her head. A large deep groove lay lengthwise across his hairy stomach.

For a moment, she averted her gaze.

*This is what Pierre has reduced me to.*

It was true. If she desired sexual intimacy, Chadwick was the only one she could turn to. Anyone else would get someone killed and she and Abigail sent away from Ashleywood.

Climbing onto the bed, she used her hand to shove his penis inside her. She closed her eyes, and when she did, she thought of Pierre and how he had touched her the day before. So close she had come to an orgasm. It was that same feeling that she was in search of now. Lifting her hips, she pushed her body against his three times when he moaned, and his girth beneath her began to tremble.

As he lay still and breathed hard, she felt disgusted and ashamed. Climbing off of him, his hand reached and tugged her hard against him. "Don't think I don't know what you're thinking. You're going to keep on seeing me, or I'll tell the police everything I know about your husband."

She forced a smile on her face and lay again beside him.

An hour later he was on top of her, grunting heavily with his elbows resting on both sides of her face to keep her pinned beneath him. For a man of his size, the pacing of his hips pushing into hers was very swift. Jenna kept her eyes closed knowing that once he was finished, this would be the last time.

After he groaned and trembled violently, she tried to slide from underneath him. As she stood beside the bed and saw that he had gotten in a comfortable position to sleep, she leaned closer to him and whispered, "You have to go now."

His thick palm slapped the side of her face. Her knees collapsed beneath her as she fell partially onto the bed. A lock of her hair was gripped tightly with his fingers and jerked toward him. "You're trying to get rid of me? What for? No one is coming to this room tonight. I'll stay as long as I want."

She pushed her face close to his. "You're the reason I hate your daughter. Abigail looks just like you. I hate that she's yours."

One of his hands squeezed at her breast until she cried out in pain. Unable to fight him off, she was quickly pulled underneath him.

"You have to go," she pleaded. "You can't stay here."

"I know Pierre is in the city."

"I bought you here to give you money," she lied. "And to tell you, you're going to have to stay away for a while. Le Secret Sept paid men to kill Pierre. One of the killers came onto the plantation. A strange man," she clarified. "Pierre won't do anything to you, but Will and Julien may if they go to Le Secret Sept, and Le Secret Sept tell them it was you who hired the killers. Why wouldn't Le Secret Sept say it was you? Everyone knows about our affair."

He hadn't hired the killers, but she knew he would believe that Pierre and Julien thought he did if Le Secret Sept said this to save themselves. It took an entire minute for him to release her. Still he stayed longer than she had wanted him to and had only left a half hour before Will Jennings knocked on her boudoir door. When she walked to the door and heard his laborious breathing on the other side, she whispered, *Die. Die right now*, then locked the door.

Afraid to leave her room, she sat on the bed and waited to see what will happen next. When she heard loud screams coming from several parts of the mansion at the same time, she had to press a hand to her mouth to stop the laughter from bubbling out of her.

Still she waited.

The knock soon came.

Closing her eyes and taking a deep breath, she then ran to the door and flung it open, then made her face appear as if she had been sleeping. The servant in front of her could barely speak, so overcome was she with emotion. "Madame, it's the Master. Cook sent me to get you."

Jenna trembled with excitement as she rushed back inside her room and grabbed a pelisse out of the armoire. Draping it over her arms, she then hurried downstairs anxious to see her father-in-law's dead body.

A smile split her face when she saw Will Jennings lying dead on his back. He was dead. There was no mistake about it. She said nothing. Did nothing. Servants sat on the floor around him, weeping and sobbing. A few looked in her direction as if she could do something to make their master live again. When it became apparent they would receive no help from her, a few tried to pour brandy down his throat. Two other servants had run forward with the medicine the doctor had left behind during his last visit. Seeing this made her angry. She pressed her hands together and prayed to the Lord to keep her father-in-law dead. She had reached the moment when the prayer should have ended when she was thrust to the side as Alise rushed into the room.

Alise got down on her knees and crouched over him and knew there was nothing anyone could do. He was dead. Her beloved. His heart, which had been failing, had finally given up. She gazed up at the others in disbelief when she saw the smile on Jenna's face. Standing to her feet, and lifting the hem of her nightclothes, she lifted a hand and brought it sharply across Jenna's face. "How dare you stand there and smile. Even as the devil he was more than you would ever be."

Alise then instructed the others on what to do. Some of the servant men were to come and lift the Master from the floor and carry him into the sick room. Alise planned to wash his body herself, but she would need help to dress him. A hand pressed to her mouth because she realized that Will's sons will have to see him like this.

Jenna had pressed herself against the wall. On the inside, she was seething. How dare this strumpet strike her in her own house and in front of the servants. She had a mind to give Alise the length of her tongue but stilled herself. What if one of the servants told Pierre what Alise had said?

Biting down on her lip, she rushed across the room and threw her arms around Will's body. "Father-in-law! Father-in-law! Oh God, no! You can't be dead. This can't be true. It can't be. You were too strong and so good." Licking her fingers without anyone noticing, she smeared spit across her face, then was thankful that real tears came to her eyes. Looking up just as the tears fell, the servants saw her and began to wail all over again.

It was Alise who she needed to convince. Turning her wet face to her, she said, "He can't be dead. He just can't be." And then she pressed her face into Will's chest and sobbed.

Alise instructed the servants to do several things. When they ran off scrambling to prepare water for a bath and to gather some of the male servants, she turned to Jenna and said, "You didn't fool me. You might have fooled them, but not me. I saw Chadwick Speck leaving the plantation not too long ago, and he wasn't leaving by way of the abandoned barn but this mansion. But don't worry. I won't tell Pierre you had your lover inside this house. Him knowing what kind of woman you truly are is not important at the moment. Your day will come. You mark my words. Your day will come. Now get your hands off of my man and get out of my sight before I rip you into pieces and this family has two bodies to bury instead of one."

Jenna ran from the room, fearing her father-in-law had been reincarnated through his strumpet.

\*\*\*

The day that Will Henriot Jennings was buried, people had traveled from near and far to the St. Louis Cathedral located in the Vieux Carré to be in attendance. The reason many of the mourners were there was because they wanted to separate fact from fiction. They wanted to see for themselves if *le diable dans Nouvelle-Orléans* was truly dead, as many didn't want to believe the notices.

Usually, funerals were held inside the family's home, but the family had foregone the usual traditions, as their family held the largest crypt in the St. Louis Cemetery nearby.

Those in the city were surprised when the largest group of slaves followed the funeral carriage down the center of the street. Once the carriage came to a stop, twelve strong looking male slaves carefully pulled the large, wide coffin out of it then carried the coffin on their shoulders inside of the church. When those sitting on pews saw the twelve slaves visibly crying and trying their best to hold back tears, the cathedral drew silent. Behind the servants and the coffin was the eldest son leading the most mournful parade the mourners had ever seen.

Looking dapper in a deep black suit, he escorted his wife who wore a black lace veil that completely covered her face. Often a black handkerchief was poked underneath it. The mourners believed she did this to wipe away what many assumed were tears. Just behind them was their daughter, Abigail.

The younger son followed, and it was the expression on Julien's face that gave the city the evidence they needed that *le diable* was truly dead. Julien was unable to hold back his emotions and had even provoked a few sniffles from a few of the women and men in the crowd. He walked somberly down the aisle, his arms clutched tightly to a woman they all quickly learned was his new bride.

A few in the crowd murmured when Alise walked inside of the cathedral with her chin lifted, and became angry when they saw from the expression on her face that she refused to give them her tears.

Désireé walked closely behind Alise with her head hung low and tears falling from her eyes.

No one said anything when Pierre lifted the child in his arms and sat her on his lap as he sat next to Alise. Jenna kept her chin lifted. Each time someone looked in her direction, she gave Abigail's hand a gentle pat. Abigail didn't notice her mother's touches. As she stared forward, tears streamed down her face as she stared at the coffin knowing that inside it was someone who truly loved her.

"Pépère," she whimpered.

Ashleywood servants filled the back of the church. When the parishioners saw how many more filled the street, many lowered their heads and dabbed at their eyes, because only then did it become apparent that the dead man in the coffin had affected so many lives.

"Pépère!" Abigail screamed with her mouth opened wide and her saliva mingling with her tears. Making her body rigid, she leaned back against the pew with her closed eyes lifted to the ceiling.

Real tears fell from Jenna's eyes. The sound of her daughter's anguish caused a lump to form in her throat. Pressing the handkerchief against her mouth, she reached for Abigail's hand.

Abigail pulled away from her.

"Pépère!" She screamed again. "Don't leave me," she whispered almost as if out of breath.

Julien, who sat behind her, rose to his feet and lifted Abigail in his arms. Rocking her gently, he constantly kissed her hair and held her tightly against him until Abigail calmed. Alise reached a hand back to the child. Only then did tears fall from her eyes.

Désireé was unable to look at the coffin. She didn't want to believe her pépère was inside it, and afterwards would be placed in a stone box inside the cemetery. The very thought of it made her shiver. Burying her head into her papa's chest, she sobbed silently as Père Hoppenjans began the ceremony.

When she could cry no more, she leaned weakly against her papa. To avoid looking at the coffin, she averted her gaze toward the other side of the church. There she saw a little girl wearing a white gown while sitting on her papa's knee. The girl was staring at her, too, and Désireé was certain she had seen the girl before. It was then she remembered that the girl was the youngest daughter of Emile Narcisse Cheval.

Emile Narcisse Cheval was Jenna's father. And the young girl was Jenna's only sister.

Her name was Sarah.

Désireé breathed slowly through parted lips as she stared at Sarah. In her mind, Sarah was the most beautiful child she had ever seen.

Three days later, Pierre read an article in the newspaper.

### 13th of July 1824      New Orléans' Vrais Mensonges

*Six Men Found Dead*

*Le Messieurs Vincent Laporte, Juan McGhee, Eustace Avila, the honorable Edouard Salle, Antoine De La Croix and Jean-Magnon Dupuy were found burned to death in a fire that swept through the Morehead Saloon. The owner, Morgan Heinz, was unsure what the men were doing there. The Saloon had closed around 4 a.m. when the last of its patrons had been forced through its doors. How the fire started is yet unknown. The evidence of a shootout was found in and around the Saloon's front door. Witnesses have yet to come forward.*

# Book Two

*"There were masked balls every night of the carnival at the French Theatre...*

*Tuesdays and Fridays were nights for the subscription balls, where none but the good society were admitted...*

*On Sundays shops are open and singing and playing is common in the streets, for which in New York or Philadelphia one would be in prison..."*

-The Duke of Saxe-Weimar-Eisenach after nine months in New Orléans, 1825 -26-

# Chapter Eleven
## Two Marriages

*[It's the men who make the money; it isn't the money that makes the men. —Creole proverb]*

The Irish girl, Clare, saw them on the street, lowered her baked apple and hurried out of the private quarters of her family's home and into the area that had been turned into a café.

She saw Kate hurrying from behind the counter and flapped a hand at her as if to suggest a beating if the girl kept moving, then walked even faster not caring in the least how foolish she looked to the other patrons in her attempt to reach the table where the brothers sat.

The brothers saw her as soon as she had come into the room and watched her the same way someone would when two carriages collided: anticipation, fear, and dread. It didn't matter how they looked at her. It was attention and Clare would take any kind from Pierre and Julien Jennings.

By the time she reached the table she found she was out of breath, not from exertion, but excitement. Julien's reputation had grown over the years. Diners at the café mentioned him often. At night she dreamed of being in his arms, both of them naked, and him doing things that would cause her knees to tremble. Obsessed was what she was, and she didn't care who knew it. One moment with him was all she wanted, and if their being together was as good as it was in her dreams, maybe he would stop by the café more often to make her knees tremble now and again.

"Well lookie's who's here, eh? The Devils of our great city."

Pierre gave a pert nod. The look in his eyes was as if he had seen lust and pitied her. Clare ignored him, turned to Julien and offered him her hand. The last diner who mentioned him told all who listened how it was the younger Jennings who loved to give delicate kisses on the hand of women he sought to bed.

Pierre's eyebrows rose when he saw this.

Julien stared at the hand, then up at Clare as he took it. The girl gave him a wide smile. The condition of her teeth made him wish she hadn't done that. The hand he held was covered in sweat. Bending over it, he kissed high above and on her sleeve.

When the hand drew back, Pierre reached for his pistol, realized what he was doing, dropped his hand and averted his gaze.

The brothers felt relieved when Clare's mother hurried to the table and clipped the girl on the ear. "Out back wit ya!"

Clare's cheeks reddened as she hurried from the table.

Aggie smiled warmly at the brothers. "You can't fault her none. You both are so good looking. What's a lass to do?"

Julien winked at Aggie. Of all the café's he loved coming to hers best. Other than Ashleywood, no better food could be had in all of New Orléans than Aggie's cooking.

"You always make me feel happy to be in Faubourg Marginy."

"Is that a fact, ay? You keep smiling the way you are, and you're going to have me acting like me daughter."

The giggle she gave put Pierre at ease.

"I hope Clare don't send you away. From the talk in this place, I hear you been making ye claim with all the pretty lasses from New Orléans to Biloxi."

"*Moi?*" Julien asked. His eyebrows arched first in surprise, then shock, then good humor as he smiled. "Aww, no. Those rumors you heard must have been about my brother."

"You!" Aggie teased Pierre with a smile. "Is it the Devil who's making his claims?"

Pierre lifted his right hand slightly, tightened his mouth and shrugged. "You didn't know I have a harem of women on my plantation?"

Julien threw back his head and roared with laughter. Seeing Pierre being playful was a rare occasion, but when he was playful, his humor was never disappointing.

Aggie's high pitch of happiness filled the room. Dishes clanged behind them. Murmurs from tables heightened when she quieted. She slapped a hand on the table, then leaned over it. "My, my. The Devil has a 'arem, does he? Before Clare sees me having too much fun, I best be taking ye orders. What can I get for ya?"

"I need some of your soup, Aggie," Julien said. "A big bowl of it. And a cup of café."

"And you Master Jennings? I knows ye order will be simple being ye have yer own special cook and all at 'ome. I hear about the tables she spreads all the way over here. Is it café then, Master Jennings? With lots of cream and steaming hot?"

"Oui. Café," Pierre answered, "*Ajoutez un peu de* bourbon."

"You need a little extra this morn, I see. 'Erhaps you've been spending the night with the wrong lass? Ay, an 'arem! And how many women do ye 'ouse?"

Pierre lifted both hands while wiggling his fingers. When he smiled, his silver-blue eyes twinkled like a coin catching sunlight. "But I have room left for you, Aggie."

Embarrassed from his attention and the words he'd spoken, she forgot herself for a moment and smacked his hand on the table as if he was an errant child.

Julien turned in his chair and laughed at the new look on Pierre's face.

"I'll give you a hint of our Mick's bourbon," she said softly. "'E keeps plenty of it out back. Back and forth 'e goes all day thinking we're dumb lasses and don't know what e's up to when e's gone half the day. The gormless lout. I'm sure 'e won't notice any of it missing. I'll be back soon with what you ordered."

When the two of them were alone, Julien gave further vent to his laughter as he bent low over the table.

Pierre reclined further in his chair, his smile large enough to make the skin crease in the corner of his eyes.

Julien drew in a breath in an attempt to stop the laughter that still tried to flow. "How were you going to seduce her and kill her at the same time?"

Pierre leaned forward and spoke in a low voice of surprise. "She hit me. It was a reflex. But enough about me. When you leave here you better look over your shoulder. Clare means to have you. I have never seen a girl as forward as her."

Julien had forgotten about Clare. Hearing her name made him look over his shoulder. To his relief, she wasn't in the dining room. "She can't be any more than fourteen!"

"I forgot about that when I reached for my pistol. There was no way I was going to kiss her little sweaty hand."

Julien waved a hand at Pierre to quiet him. The laugh inside him wouldn't abate until it was all out. "I saw that. You haven't changed, Brother. It's good to see you. It's been too long."

"Far too long," Pierre agreed. "How was your trip? How are things with you and Marie-Marie?"

Julien continued to smile. Pierre saw sadness creep into his eyes.

"Why do people get married?" Julien asked. "I guess you can say she's the best sister I never had. It's strange, the people she and I have become. We can laugh together. We can talk together. During the day, she's a little preachy, but she's a good companion. Religion can be a horrible thing. At night, she burns with desire. In the morning she's reciting prayers, begging God to have mercy on her soul. She's not happy. And I'm not either. But it's too late to do anything about it now."

Aggie returned with two cups of café, then walked away. She had been good with her promise. Pierre could taste the bourbon. When he set the cup back down, he gazed intently at Julien. "I need you to have children with Marie-Marie. And soon."

"Ha!" The burst of laughter was short and brief, and then Julien's expression and eyes became sober. "Remember when her family in Paris came to visit?"

"Oui."

One side of Julien's mouth curled upward in disgust. "They're worse than her. Bibles. Prayer. You should have seen their faces when they couldn't find a single cross or an altar inside my home. Now I have three. No meat on Friday. Chicken every Saturday."

"You have always been a bad Catholic."

"It is what it is," Julien asserted. "For nine years she's been trying to have a child, and we haven't seen sight of one yet. Her family has convinced her that I'm to blame. Each time they write and hint at visiting, my answer is no. She's better when they're not around. She's better when I hide the many letters they write."

"Julien," Pierre pleaded.

"You don't have to live with her," Julien argued. "It's a sad day when I have to confess that I'm envious of your marriage. Jenna loves you, Pierre. For sixteen years she's been waiting for you to forgive her. She even ended her affair with Chadwick. Abigail loves you. There's hope for your future. I told Marie-Marie if she shows me another Bible, I will beat her with it. And I meant that."

Again he leaned over the table. "My wife lies on her back and closes her eyes until I'm done, then wonder why I don't sleep with her more often or share a room with her. How do you do it, Pierre? Blessa died nine years ago. I hear the rumors. You aren't seeing anyone. You haven't been seeing anyone. Why are you living like a monk?"

He asked the question then averted his gaze. Their table sat close to the French doors and merely a few feet from the actual street. The branches of cypress, oleander and banana trees offered temporary relief for those traveling and needing a moment out of the sun. On days like this Julien liked to refer to it as wearing the river; the humidity tested even the patience of the priests and nuns.

"These past years I had to travel extensively," Pierre said. "Papa asked me to do something for him before he died. I couldn't rest until I had it all completed. Now that it is, I can focus on my future."

"Good for you."

"Julien, I need you to have sons. I need your sons to help my sons run our companies. Every year in New Orléans hundreds of people die from fever. We have to take that into consideration. We can have ten sons, but it doesn't mean any of them will reach the age of becoming a man. Children. It's what we need. I made a few investments in Europe. They have paid off, Brother. They have paid off very well."

Aggie returned with Julien's soup. He stared into the bowl a long time.

"You always knew best," he finally said. "Maybe I can't have one, Pierre. Nine years is a long time to go without one."

Pierre tried to reach for Julien's hand because he saw in Julien's eyes how badly he wanted children.

Julien stood from his chair and left without saying a further word.

Pierre watched the street as Julien climbed into his coach. When the door had been open, he saw Marie-Marie sitting inside, a prim look on her face. If he had known she was in the vehicle he would have taken a moment to speak to her. But once he saw her face he knew she hadn't wanted this. This made it easy for him to watch the coach ride away without feeling guilty.

He sat back in his chair still watching the street when a battered cart rode furiously in Julien's departure and came to a dusty halt in front of Nowicki's General Store.

None other than Chadwick Spencer Speck climbed down from the driver's seat.

Pierre wondered if Jenna's affair with Chadwick had truly ended.

Rising to his feet, he stepped out onto the street and crossed it hoping to find out.

Josef Nowicki stood behind the counter rolling a barrel into the corner but thought he would lose control over it when the Master of Ashleywood walked unhesitantly into his shop. The abnormally white hair. The dominant squint. What he feared happened. The barrel rolled from his hand and bumped into a display of glass. Broken shards jangled and spilled as it hit the straw strewn floor.

The air inside the shop was stifling. To cool himself, Pierre flicked back the tail of his coat. When Josef saw a pistol strapped to Pierre's hip, he threw his hands up.

"Get low! All of you! Monsieur Jennings is here!"

Chadwick turned, saw Pierre and choked on his spit. He backed into the counter that Josef now hid behind, his hands reaching for both sides. He espied the shop, saw the rear door where plantation owners tethered their horses to receive their loads of credited goods, then ran.

Pierre had only wanted to talk to him and blamed Josef for the lost opportunity. Turning to leave, it was almost as if the woman had come out of nowhere. The color of her hair got his attention. It was close to black, but not quite. Like dark chocolate. And thick. And long as it hung with tight curls. The woman's eyes reminded him of Désireé's — like a jar filled with summer honey that sat under bright sunlight. Her mouth made him think of kissing. Her face was the most beautiful he had ever seen.

As he studied her, she, in turn, studied him, his eyes, mouth, then down the front of him. And then she smiled, her eyes widening with recognition.

"Salut!" Excitement bloomed in the features of her face.

"Salut," he repeated absently, his eyes falling down to her gown. It was made of thin cloth in a color of pale beige and decorated with heavy thread. Rounded breasts filled the uppermost part of the bodice. The sleeves were puffed, the lower half tightly fitted. The slenderness of her neck, the small pearls that decorated her ears. The delicate shape of her hands. His eyes lifted to hers. A smile of intrigue made her expression almost seductive.

Josef Nowicki rushed from behind the counter, and gripping the woman tightly in his arms, he spoke softly in her ear as he led her across the shop and away from Pierre.

## Chapter Twelve
# Désireé's Secret

*[The horse never walks with the ass. – Creole Proverb]*

Désireé's skirt ballooned as she flopped on her heels to examine the squirrel a little closer. It sat beneath a rose bush, a small critter. It couldn't have been more than a few months old. Its eyes were directly on hers. Its fawn-hued fur trembled in pain. It was hard for her to see an injured animal and not feel anything.

The squirrel had collapsed on an ant hill. Quite a few covered the creature, burrowing into the wound on its leg. Brushing the ants away, she laid the squirrel on the soil. No longer covered with ants, it clambered to its feet and hobbled slowly away. On the ground nearby was a small stick. Lifting it, she slammed the kindling on the ant hill until most were dead. Servants nearby were shearing flowers in the *jardin*. Going to one of them, she took their small gourd of water and flushed the ant hill.

"I'll take care of it," Tomas said, stepping closer to her.

"Thank you, Tomas." She handed him the gourd, lifted the basket she had been carrying earlier and stepped into the outside kitchen.

"What you done done to your gown?" 'Done done' was a common phrase used by people of color. Cook dug her fists into her narrow hips.

Désireé settled the basket on top of the table, then stared down the front of her. A very small stain of dirt and water was on the left side of her bodice. "Your eyes never miss anything. It's a little stain." She smiled. "Why are you behaving as if the gown is ruined?"

Cook dropped her fists and tightened her face. "You ain't a child anymore. It ain't the dress I'm worried about. You lose one dress, and Monsieur Pierre buys you twenty to takes its place. I'm worried about the girls. It takes them longer to wash your gowns than anyone else's. And it's this reason that all of us notice every little stain you manage to get on yourself."

Désireé had been approaching the cutting table where Cook stood, but stopped. Lately being in Cook's presence made her feel more like a woman than at any other time. "You're a cook, Rube. A laborer. I appreciate and respect the relationship you had with my pépère, as well as the one you have with my papa and oncle. But what happens in the laundry cabin is not your affair. To insinuate I'm a spoiled child unmindful of the concern of others is hard for me to listen to. And I am a woman. Therefore, your need to upbraid me like a child at every chance needs to come to an end."

Cook said nothing as she grabbed the small bucket of live lobsters, blue crabs, and oysters. Using a large knife, she dismembered limbs and cracked shells. The thoughts that went through her mind were all the things she had done for the family of the woman that stood in front of her. Désireé calling her Rube in front of the kitchen staff, she felt, had been disrespectful and uncalled for. Calling her a laborer nothing more than belittling.

Désireé noticed that when she had entered the kitchen, the servants were all talking at once, shouting orders, giving lesser servants instructions and rehearsing recent events on the plantation that made some of them splutter with laughter.

Now the kitchen was silent. Other than hissing pots with lids on them, and the crackling of burning wood in the hearth, and the sound of utensils and cookware being moved about, not a single word was spoken.

She knew the servants were meditating over each word she had spoken because she had spoken truthfully. In New Orléans once a girl reached the age of sixteen, she was old enough to marry. On the evening of Désireé's 'coming out,' her father had bestowed upon her the manumission papers her pépère had acquired when she was quite young. As an official part of the city's *gens de couleur libres* and because she was very wealthy, she entered the homes of the city's elite with much fanfare. This made her an adult. For this reason, they were now silent. But there was another reason as well. Most believed she was her father's favorite daughter. In their eyes, she had as much power, or perhaps more than their madame.

A few weeks after Will Jennings drew his last breath, Cook learned that Will had listed her in his will and had granted her freedom. Like Tomas, she decided to remain on Ashleywood. A very small lot had been given to her. On it were a small house and two slave cabins. Cook purchased her first slaves at the age of fifty-eight. Unlike other free people of color in the city, the slaves she purchased were not related to her by blood. She had gone to a public auction with one agenda in mind. Buy an entire family. Thinking she didn't have enough money to do this, she hesitated in bidding once she had the chance. But when she heard the prices being offered, she calculated in her mind that she could afford the family she had set her eyes on.

Surrounded by other *gens de couleur libres* and respectable Creole men and women who had also attended the auction, she managed to outbid a few Américains who had wanted to purchase a few members of that same family. Incensed that a black woman was keeping them from purchasing good looking slaves, they had the auction momentarily stopped and demanded Cook not only prove her freedom but how she would support the number of slaves she had aimed to purchase.

Anyone who had ever dined at Ashleywood knew Cook personally. It was this reason that the Creole men in attendance stood behind her, assisting her with the purchase, then provided an escort for her and her new slaves to her small patch of land. To ensure her safety, Pierre had a brick wall built around the property to deter anyone entering it during the night.

As a free woman of color, her duties inside the kitchen were like any laborer who hired themselves out to work. But to the servants, Cook was more than a laborer. Because she had been loved by Will and was still loved now by Will's two sons, her audience with them had earned her a status similar to an overseer. Many of the servants were appreciative of personal favors she had done for them just as much as they were equally appreciative of all Désireé had done for them. So seeing these two women who deserved the same respect as someone white having a disagreement caused the servants in the kitchen to become fearful.

"Very well," Cook said, then lifted her eyes to Désireé. "I will remember my place, mademoiselle, from this day forward."

When the servants saw Cook debase herself by responding like a common slave, although many of them lowered their heads for fear of looking Désireé in the eye, the contempt they felt filled the room.

Désireé not only sensed their anger, she could also see it and feel it. She moved around the table and stood in the center of the room.

"Hate me if you must. All of you. But hate me for the right reasons. I'm aware that Cook has given her life to this plantation, and she has served my family well for many years. I'm glad my pépère gave her her freedom, but freedom means more than not having to answer to the whip and keeping someone else's schedule of chores. It means being responsible for yourself, feeding yourself, and working hard only to earn very little. It means building your own home, which can be costly if you don't own the land you're trying to build on.

"I won't debate with any of you who owes who more, Cook or my family? What I will tell you is this. Cook asked my pépère to buy her and her family at a time when he didn't need to buy any slaves. Before she came here, she labored long hours in the fields of the family whose blood ran also through her veins. My pépère brought her here and taught her and her family how to read and write. She had no cooking skills, but she had aspiration. My pépère sent her to the city to learn how to cook. She didn't buy her freedom with the wages she earned over the years. My pépère gave it to her.

"She didn't build the home she lives in now. My papa did with his lumber, tools and bricks. The land she lives on, my papa allotted it to her. All that she has, *my* family has provided, including her protection of which she still has today. I can go on and on about what freedom truly is, but it's unnecessary as long as I make one thing very clear. *True* freedom is no longer *thinking* like a slave."

She gazed at all of them individually.

"Cook is not my mammy, and I don't have to treat her like one until the day I die. I hope none of you leave this plantation hoping to become someone's mammy or auntie or your men becoming a white man's uncle. That's a slave's way of thinking. Her name is Madame Rube Jennings. You all are mesdemoiselles and mesdames despite what anyone else call you or what they think of you. I didn't disrespect Rube by telling her that I refuse to be treated like a child. I was respecting her as my equal. My papa believes war is coming, and I believe him. If you continue to think like slaves, even when you're free you'll act like one. And if you do, it'll give those you hate more reason to treat you as inferior. Don't only *think* of being free. Think also of how you can become independent women and men or you'll always look to someone who has more to help you instead of you helping yourself. And that… is being a slave without chains."

Turning from the others, she averted her gaze to Cook.

"Rube, as the manager of this kitchen, can you have my basket filled right away, please?"

Tears were falling down Cook's face. It lapped under her chin and pooled underneath her nostrils.

"I want to hear you say it, Rube."

Cook shook her head and lowered her chin more than it already was. The very thought frightened her. For too long she had been taught to address her uppers by mademoiselle, madame, monsieur or master. The fear of losing favor with Monsieur Pierre and Monsieur Julien once they learned she had called Désireé by her Christian name prevented her from saying anything at all.

Lifting the basket, she started to prepare it herself instead of have one of the others to do it.

Désireé gently took the basket from her hand. "Simone, please come fill this basket. Rube has other things to do."

The kitchen stayed silent as Simone filled it.

Once it was handed to Désireé again, she went to the door then turned and faced them. "I have never treated any of you like chattel. If I had one of you would be carrying this basket to my cottage just like one of you would have run to my cottage to fetch it. I pay a decent wage when anyone comes to my cottage to clean it. I know once I walk out of this cabin Cook is going to tell all of you not to listen to anything I said. She's going to say that because she's afraid. Not just of whites, but of all of you. As Cook, she has status – clout. But all of you can have that too. Stop living under a cloud of fear. Rube and I are not better than you are. Buy your freedom as soon as you can and make something of yourselves. Live in such a way that everyone will remember your name. Only then will everyone respect you."

A young slave girl ran up to the door from the yard. "He here! Monsieur Julien!"

Désireé walked out of the kitchen without saying anything further. When no sound came out of it after she had walked some distance, she knew the conversations had resumed, but were being whispered.

Julien's lacquer and leathered coach sped up the long drive underneath the canopy of closely planted live oak trees.

She waved vehemently, unable to contain her glee as soon as she saw it.

Julien alighted as soon as the landau stopped, then assisted Marie-Marie out of it. Servants had gathered around them. A few were removing the luggage tied to the back of it. Désireé watched the servants more than she did her oncle, disturbed by what she saw. Ashleywood was different from other plantations, but it was still a plantation. Whites were treated like gods. People of color were seen as nothing more than the chattel they were, and if the chattel did not exhibit obsequious behavior at all times, it spurred the gods to wrath.

All of the children had dipped at the knee. Marie-Marie only allowed a certain few to come near her. When she rubbed the head of one of them like a pet she had sorely missed, Désireé had the mind to walk to her and slap her. Seeing her oncle not do or say anything about his wife's behavior made her even more disappointed. Instead, he smiled while his hands rested on his hips. Turning slightly he saw her and waved. Marie-Marie saw him wave, then turned to see who he had given his attention to. For several seconds she stared in Désireé's direction as if waiting for Désireé to bow or show some sign of obeisance. Knowing she wouldn't get it, her eyes smoldered as she turned with a stiff back and made her way to mansion where she had a cohort who saw things the same way she did.

Julien knew where Désireé stood was the closest she would come to the mansion and walked to her. Taking a moment to kiss the crown of her head, he then began walking with her across the grass.

"It's good to see you," she said and smiled.

"As it is you," he admitted, then held out his hand to carry her basket. "You looked upset a moment ago. Anything you want to share with me? Or am I correct in assuming that you are not pleased with Marie-Marie's and my behavior?"

Désireé continued to smile. "I know what you think of me, Oncle. I am not trying to start an insurrection. I know that this plantation is better than most when it comes to the slaves on it. A lot is being taught to them…"

"…except independence," Julien finished for her. "That's something they're going to have to learn on their own when the right day comes along."

"I know why my papa keeps Rube in the kitchen. So she could teach the others about fear."

"Fear is necessary, Désireé," he answered. "You can't teach loyalty. If your father gave you your way, you would do more harm than good although your intentions are good. But sooner or later you will learn that regardless of what you do, some will be loyal, some will be jealous of you, and some will never be grateful. That's everywhere in the world. Not just here. Your papa knows that. Fear is the only way to keep balance."

"I hate…"

He stopped walking. "*You* were fortunate. You have never been a slave. You don't know what being one feels like. Why would any of them listen to you? You're just a pampered little rich girl."

She lowered her head and tightened her jaw. "I don't have to be a slave to know what they're feeling. I'm noir. I'm reminded of that every time I leave the plantation. I'm free. Yet still I'm stuck here just like they are."

The two of them began walking again.

"Your papa told me you have refused to get married. You're not stuck here, Desie. You can leave at any time."

"Marry who?" She asked the question politely. "One of the *hommes de couleur*?"

"Surely you don't have a problem marrying a free man of color."

"Not at all, but let me tell you about the free men of color in this city. As long as they have family here, they will never see themselves as equals. I want a man who knows who he is. I want him to have dreams, Oncle, and not be afraid to go after them."

"Perhaps this is why Antoine hasn't asked for your hand. I heard he's interested. His father is also pushing for a marriage between the two of you. But what you said is true. His father is a good man and well respected. Living as you suggest would be the same as disrespecting the father he loves."

"His father has been visiting. As well as a few others. I fear papa will come to me soon and tell me he has accepted a proposal."

Julien stopped walking again. "From your last letter, I suspect that you have fallen in love with someone. Maybe I can help."

She shook her head. Not because she was answering his question, but because she was refusing his assistance. "Since when has a woman been able to marry who she wants?"

"Confide in me, Desie. Maybe I can smooth things over with your father. It will be better than him arranging for you to marry someone you don't want to."

She let out a slow sigh as she stared at the nearby trees. "I wish you could help, but no one can help me. I wish the world were different. Too many women are married off to men they had no intentions of marrying for the convenience of their fathers. I want to marry for love. What's wrong with that? But because I'm noir my options are small in this city. I can only marry a *homme de couleur*. Either that or become a left-handed wife to someone *blanc*."

"You're not going to tell me who this man is?"

The smile she gave made her look even prettier. Julien leaned down and kissed her hair.

"I rather enjoyed your return letters," she said. "I have read each of them quite a few times, especially your last."

Julien smiled knowingly at her and averted his gaze.

"You didn't come right out and say it, but I sensed your visit this time isn't truly to see the family, but someone here. Who is it, Oncle?"

"That is a most inappropriate question, young lady. And I shall also answer inappropriately. I realized from your letters that I was no longer corresponding with a just a young woman, but one who has lost her virtue. Does your papa know?"

"No."

Julien winced. "Desie, what are you doing? Who is he? Is it a slave?"

She tugged on his elbow to initiate the two of them walking again.

"So we shall keep our secrets, shall we?" He asked.

"I can't tell you, Oncle. Not yet."

"Can you imagine what will happen if your papa arranges a marriage for you? Your new husband will learn on his wedding night that his wife is no longer pure."

"I shall tell Papa before that happens." Désireé leaned her head against his arm.

"Have you ever thought of leaving here, changing your name and telling everyone you meet you are *blanc*?"

"Oui." She answered in a soft voice.

"Your papa will miss you. I will miss you, but I will understand. I want you to know that."

"And I will be lonely. And someone I'm not. I will always have to pretend around those who will despise and hate me if the truth was ever discovered. The very thought sickens me. Why can't I be who I am, Oncle? I am French. And I am noir. My maman was born a slave and died a slave. My pépère, who loved me immensely, and who could see beyond the color of my skin, sold my maman on the day I was born as if she was a horse that he tired of. And he loved Alise. My how he loved her. Still he had his prejudices. And if he had those prejudices, what do I have to look forward to away from here?"

"You're looking for perfection, Désireé. There is none nowhere in this world."

"I'll settle for balance, Oncle. And respect for all mankind."

They stopped in the yard in front of Désireé's cottage. Julien stared at it when he saw that Désireé had no intentions of walking any closer to it.

"It's always good to see you, *mon bijou*." Julien handed her the basket. He kissed the crown of her head, then began to walk away.

Désireé watched him for a second or two to make certain he didn't turn around, then walked up onto her galerie. From there she looked in all directions before she walked inside, closed the door behind her and locked it.

Inside her butler's pantry, she set the basket on the table. She pulled a plate and a bowl from the Queen Anne china cabinet she had purchased during her last visit to Paris. Beans, tamales, beignet, crab filled gumbo thickened with rice so the bowl was harder to spill during her journey from the kitchen were spooned onto the plate and bowl.

She placed the plate and bowl on a tray, then walked to her boudoir. When she opened the door, she stopped abruptly. Cyril stood in the double French doors that led to her private galerie. When she had left him, he had been naked, and he still was now as he held tightly to the curtains, hiding behind it as he watched Julien disappear between the trees. He heard her then turned and faced her. "So he's here then? How long is he staying?"

She placed the tray on the bedside table. "I hope a long time. He's a lot of fun." She had been smiling when she said this, but turned to face him and saw fear in his eyes.

"Maybe I should leave," Cyril said. "At least until he's gone. It's bad enough your father is here. The thought of both of them being on the plantation frightens me more than you know."

She gazed at his manhood, then averted her gaze. "Where will you go?"

For months he had been living in hiding in her cottage. If her father learned of this, he would become irate. Cyril was the youngest brother of Billy Oakes, and Billy Oakes, and all of his family, in her father's mind were his enemies. This was separate from the fact that Cyril was penniless, homeless, jobless, white and uneducated. Marriage was impossible, including a plaçage marriage. He was the essential kind of man her papa would want her to avoid.

He crossed the room and folded his arms around her. A kiss was placed near her ear. "I don't want to be away from you. But it can't be safe for me to stay here."

"You *are* safe. My oncle never comes here. And neither do my papa. Both of them are too busy with their lives. I'm expected to go to the mansion if I want to see them, but lately they're never there."

One of her hands slid down his chest. Cyril removed the pin that held the bodice of her gown in place. When it fell slack, he helped her out of it. "I hope you believe me when I tell you I love you."

"I know you love me," she whispered.

"Maybe I should take a chance and speak to your father? If I talk to him man to man, maybe he'll understand."

"No. He wouldn't understand. The moment he learns that his daughter is no longer a virgin, and she has given her virginity to a man who he deems is his enemy, all hell will break loose."

A loud fist pounded on her front door.

Cyril jumped away from her, then closer again to help her redress.

The fist pounded again, this time even louder.

"Hurry," Cyril pleaded.

Désireé ran from the room to the front of her cottage.

Her father pushed through the door as soon as it was unlocked. He stared long into her eyes, then back at the open door. "Why is your door locked?"

Désireé lifted on her toes. Pierre met her the rest of the way. Kisses were planted to both sides of their faces. "I didn't realize I locked it," she lied. "I hurried inside and wanted to change. I have decided to ignore the woman you married and spend some time with Julien in the mansion."

Pierre kissed the crown of her head. "I'm sure Cook will serve her best this evening."

He turned for the door.

"Did you need anything, Papa? It's been a while since you've paid a visit."

Pierre gazed at the front part of her cottage, then at her again. "I have received another proposal from Antoine's father. I know you don't want to marry him, and if I'm honest, I don't want you to either."

"Come sit with me, Papa."

He followed her into the *grand salle*. The two of them sat side by side on a settee.

"The requests are becoming more and more since your coming out. I have even been given proposals for plaçage arrangements, Désireé. I shouldn't be surprised by this. Although you will receive payment for a plaçage arrangement, the hope that any children you have will bind our family to someone else's is the true reward. What I can't understand is the pressure being placed on me to choose. It's political, you understand. I don't mind the pressure so much, but it's making me weary. I cannot go into the city without being stopped and invited into homes. The plantation is receiving more visitors than ever. I do wish it all stops, and the only way it will is if you marry."

Pierre leaned to one side to look into the hall. "You have a servant here?"

Désireé wasn't certain what he had seen and grabbed his hand to divert his attention away from the hall. "I'm not ready to marry, Papa."

"You must marry. I refuse for you to live in this cottage alone all your life."

"I don't plan to, Papa."

"Julius Lavolier has given a proposal for you, Desie. He vows never to take another wife if I accepted a plaçage…"

"Julius Lavolier? Papa, he's one of the wealthiest Creoles in the city. The women in this city will go mad if such an arrangement…"

"Listen," he interrupted gently to quiet her. "Since your coming out men I never suspected have made their intentions known. Apparently many of them have waited for you to come of age. Julius isn't the only wealthy man who has come forward…"

Désireé stood to her feet. "Papa, I don't want to be anyone's second wife. A plaçage? What is it other than me giving myself to a man whenever he wants and giving him children that he would rarely see because he has a respectable family to see to first?"

Pierre smiled as he also stood. "You think that's what I want for you? I want you to be happy, but more importantly, I want you to be protected. Julius can give you those things. The man's infatuated by your mere presence, Desie. He's already put an agreement in writing. You will live on his plantation and become his partner in every sense of the word."

One look in his eyes and she knew he approved of this arrangement.

"He's coming to the plantation tomorrow evening. I'll expect you no later than four. I respect Monsieur Lavolier. He shares many of my same views. As mistress of his plantation, you can make a difference there. His wealth combined with yours will provide all of the protection you shall ever need if anything should ever happen to me. I cannot ask for more than that, Désireé."

"Are you telling me, Papa, that I am to marry Monsieur Lavolier?"

Pierre held her gaze. "I guess I just realized that I am. I will have heirs, Desie. You're a woman now. It's time for you to live as one. Lord knows I have prepared you well enough for such a marriage."

"A plaçage," she corrected.

"This is better than you marrying a free man of color. Maybe there will never be a war, and slavery will continue for another hundred years. The law does not allow you to marry a white man. This arrangement is the only way for you to live a respectable life and have a family as well. Don't you want that?"

"And my children, Papa? Shall I teach my daughters how to become someone's placée?" She turned from him. Tears filled her eyes. "It won't matter if Julius is their father. Everyone will see our children as noir."

"You are my daughter. It is my responsibility to see to your future."

"I want to marry someone I…"

"No," he said, cutting her off. "A chance like Monsieur Lavolier only comes once."

"Papa, I…"

He waited patiently for her to finish.

She lowered her head. She couldn't tell him. Not now.

"Tomorrow," he reminded and walked out the door.

Cyril entered the hall after he had gone and locked the door. Although he now wore trousers, he wore nothing more.

When he hugged her, she drew in a deep breath.

"I couldn't bring myself to tell him."

"I'll talk to him."

Désireé shook her head, pulled from him and walked away. If her father's first night of marriage was a *scandale*, she could see a man like Julius Lavolier making his into something much, much more.

# Chapter Thirteen
## The Stranger

*[Just put a Mulâtresse on horseback, and she'll tell you her mother wasn't a négresse. –*
*Creole proverb]*

Sarah Cheval ate the evening's cold meal alone because her father had forgone eating his supper in the dining room and instead had retired to his bedroom. William Murray had not returned from the city, and of this Sarah was grateful. She could neither stomach her fiancé's attention nor did she encourage it. And if she had her way she will not marry Monsieur Murray as her father had planned.

After she finished eating, she informed the servant she will have café inside of the *petit salle*. She stood from the table and crossed the hall. She was relieved some minutes later when she saw it was Imogen who served her. The trusted servant placed the tray on a small table, then handed her Mademoiselle a single cup.

Sarah took the cup gladly. "Have a seat, Imogen. You must be tired."

Over the years her father had lost nearly everything. When his wife had been alive, it had been she who had kept the plantation going with money from her bank account. When Joséphine died, she left what money that was left to her eldest daughter – her only daughter.

Sarah had not been Joséphine's child, but the result of her father's affair. When she was very young, her papa brought her here to the mansion to live. Joséphine had never forgiven him or his decision to openly claim Sarah as his daughter and the sister to her only child, Jenna.

Imogen reclined in an uncomfortable chair. Within minutes the slave woman was sleeping, her careworn face slack with weariness. All of the remaining slaves on the plantation were also weary. No longer were there enough servants to attend the fields and maintain the grounds.

Sarah finished her café, then stood to her feet. Stopping inside her father's boudoir, she found him half-dressed and sleeping in the center of the bed. An empty decanter lay beside his hand. Empty bottles of spirits sat on the floor near the bed. Drinking was all he thought about now. What little money he did earn, the empty bottles around him was what it was spent on. William volunteered to marry her because he had lost his own plantation and saw Green Lea as another he could claim.

As she pulled her father's boudoir closed, she heard voices coming from down below. Going closer to the staircase, she peered down and saw William slip into the *grand salle*. His idea of a courtship was taking her to his bed before a priest joined them together as man and wife.

Turning swiftly, the skirt of her gown rustled as she hurried inside her boudoir. There was still light left outside. If she hurried, perhaps she could make it to the Ashleywood plantation before dark.

***

Saddling a horse was something she had to learn the same day she returned to Green Lea. All of the servants, except Imogen, Fanny, and Choco, who had full responsibility for the house and kitchen, the remaining servants spent no less than eighteen hours each day in the fields tending to the crop. Menial tasks were sometimes left undone for long periods or seen to after the servants were released from the fields.

Wearing a heavy cloak and bonnet, she mounted the oldest mare in the stable because Sarah wasn't familiar with the two others and refused to ride them until she had gotten a chance to get to know them. As she rode out into the yard, she worried. Although she had urged the mare to travel faster, Trouble shook her head, and her hind legs trembled. A walk was all the horse could muster. By the time Sarah reached the start of the trees, she wondered if she should turn back. Just as she started to pull on the reins to do so, Trouble's legs gathered strength and the old mare began to race. Seeing her move as quickly as she was, Sarah smiled as she remembered riding Trouble when she had been younger.

When she had returned to New Orléans weeks ago one of the first things she heard on the streets was that Pierre Jennings was away from his plantation traveling once again. He must have come back without many in the city knowing about it. And if he was back then surely he would be at Ashleywood. He was the richest man she would ever know. If she asked him for a loan, she was certain he would give it to her. If she had money, she wouldn't have to marry William. If given enough time, she could improve her father's plantation and make it profitable again. She knew she could, even if it meant her and her father working in the fields alongside the ten field hands they had left.

All she needed was a few minutes of Pierre's time to explain her situation. Once he heard it, she prayed he wouldn't refuse. After all, she was family. He not recognizing her at Nowicki's hadn't been surprising. It was close to nine years ago when she left New Orléans. Before that, Pierre had rarely visited her father's plantation known as Green Lea. When he did, it was only on the few occasions when Sarah's father was ill, and Jenna had returned to see about him.

After she had ridden a considerable distance, again Trouble slowed. The area she was in, much farther north of River Road, was nothing more than overgrown trees. The reason no one had come along and cultivated the land was because it was owned by the Jennings family. The story she had heard when she was young was the Jennings' family in France had had favor with the King. When Renaud Plessier had requested land in the new territory, it was to him the King had granted the largest parcel of land, of which the family still had complete control of now close to a hundred years later.

Trouble stopped her sure-footed gait and stood still. Her head lowered, and just as it did, her hind legs weakened just before they locked back into position.

"Are you all right, old girl?" Sarah cooed.

Trouble's head lowered again, and very slowly, the rear part of her body turned slightly and her hind legs buckled beneath her. It was fortunate that the mare's movements had been slow enough for Sarah to dismount without injury. Once her rear part found the ground, the rest of her also collapsed, and Trouble's head lay against the earth.

Taking in the trees around her, Sarah knew it wasn't safe for her or Trouble to stay where they were. On closer examination of the mare, she could see that Trouble had no more strength even to rise. Like the servants, even the horses on Green Lea had become weary from being overworked.

She had no choice but leave Trouble behind, but only temporarily. The good thing was they had reached the Ashleywood estate. Going closer to a nearby tree, she looked for a marker of any kind but couldn't find one. Now determined to get help for her horse, she kept a brisk pace while keeping her eyes opened for runaway slaves, bounty hunters and animals of any kind.

She walked for what seemed an hour when she finally saw what she had been looking for. The tree she had come upon, which was just off to the side of what looked to be a well-worn path, was a visible marker. Plantations used these makers to alert travelers of whose land they were riding upon. This particular marker was the curled letter of a J.

Once she passed the tree, she stopped long enough to take in her surroundings once again, because she was unsure of which direction she should now walk. All Creole mansions faced the river, which she knew should be south of where she stood. Staring in the direction she believed to be south, she continued on. It was some time later when she reached a clearing of recently scythed grass. There were still many trees, but these were all well cared for and appeared to have been groomed. Rounding a separate tightly-knit crop of trees, because she had feared what she would find between them, she fronted what looked like a small yard. On the other side of it and abutted against more trees sat a well-groomed cottage. Its roof was half hidden beneath the tree's limbs. The cottage possessed a small galerie, and three slender Creole-style doors. The abode was much too glorious to have been built for a slave and too far from anything else to belong to an overseer. All of its doors were tightly closed.

Tired from walking and needing to rest, she hoped the cottage was abandoned. Stepping onto its galerie, she unhooked one of the shutters and opened it wide. The door behind it, to her surprise, was unlocked. It creaked as it sprang inward. Inside was very dark.

"Hello?"

Her voice echoed off the nearest wall, which looked to be made of stone. The evening had almost completely fallen. Not enough of the light outside spilled into the room for her to see much. After waiting to see if she heard movement of any kind, she walked closer to a sideboard against a far wall. Here the room was even darker.

Pushing her face closer to the furniture to see it better, she used her hands to feel the objects on top of it, hoping someone had left a few candles behind. Lighting one was going to be a problem, but if she could find a piece of flint and something to strike it against, with enough moss she could get the light to hold long enough to hold a candle wick against it.

The smallest noise trickled into the room causing her to abandon her search and face the open door. Closing it would prevent her from seeing anything in the cottage. Not closing it would give an animal the opportunity to come inside and keep her company. Giving herself only a few seconds to make a decision, she hurried back to the sideboard. Her hands felt along the smooth top of the furniture when this time she heard the unmistakable sound of a horse.

Leaving the sideboard, she stood in front of the door again wondering if she should close and lock it. As she peered out across the yard, she saw a small light move between the trees in the same direction she had come from. Only a stranger would come from that direction, as it bordered the plantation. Closing the door and locking it, she wondered if the cottage had a rear entrance. Moving carefully across the darkened room while leading with her hands, she had only taken a few steps when the horse neighed just outside the door she had come through.

Changing directions, she decided to find a room to hide in until she was given a chance to escape. Feeling along the wall, which was so black it felt as if she was touching heaven, she nearly tumbled forward when the wall gave way. Righting herself, she stepped into an even darker room. Whatever kind it was it appeared empty, as she had managed to take a few steps without bumping into anything. Slowing her pace, she reached her hands farther out in front of her to save herself from falling over a piece of furniture. Soon her hands pressed against something soft and low. Feeling it carefully with her fingers she discerned it was a bed.

Outside, footsteps walked the length of the galerie.

Her lips parted as she breathed slowly to calm her anxiety.

Someone rattled the doorknob she had locked, and then heavy footsteps walked further down the galerie and a different door was opened.

Taking a slow deep breath, she decided to stay where she was and wait.

A small lantern lit up the room she had come from. From its movements, whoever was holding it appeared to be looking for something. The closer the light came in her direction she wondered if the rider had seen her between the trees and had followed her. It would explain why he had reached her so quickly after she had spotted his light.

A sound was made that indicated the lantern had been lowered on top of something. Seconds later an even brighter light burned. With both lights burning, the front part of the cottage was illuminated. Heavy footsteps walked in the opposite direction. Seconds later another bright light burned.

Sarah pressed a hand against her chest, her eyes now wide.

The front part of the cottage was heavily furnished. Although the pieces were outdated, they were of quality. Several settees and richly upholstered side chairs sat comfortably on a wood floor. The floor had been thoroughly swept and also waxed. The wall alongside the fireplace was made of stone and free of cobwebs. Although the room was clean and furnished, something about it gave Sarah the impression that no one used the cottage often. When one of the burning lights started moving closer to her, she began to think of what to say to explain why she was there.

It was then she investigated the room she was in. It, too, was heavily furnished. It had two beds with a narrow space between them. On the bed she believed she had touched a slave woman crouched near its iron headboard gripping a young boy. The woman and child stared at her with wide, frightened eyes.

Seeing them made Sarah take a few steps back until her spine pressed against a wall. It was then she noticed a tall stack of blankets that sat on the floor in one corner. There was a desk and a small table, both covered with numerous ewers and basins. Beside the table was a pile of clothing in various sizes, some of them embellished with threading and trimmed with lace and silk. Standing next to an armoire were three dark male slaves, a slave woman and what looked to be a teenage slave girl. The clothes they wore were so severely torn that it looked as if their bodies had been covered in dirty strips. All five were looking directly at her as if fearful to move and waiting to see what she would do.

The first thought that came to her mind was runaway slaves.

Shielding her face with her arms, she screamed loudly when the rider stepped into the room and held the light in front of her face. The unmistakable sound of a pistol being cocked made her tremble enough to lose most of her strength. It was the feel of the barrel being pressed to her temple that made her whimper. For reasons she couldn't explain, no words would come out of her mouth. Not even a plea to spare her life.

"Who are you? Lower your hands and let me see your face."

Her arms slowly lowered. Her eyes opened. Standing in front of her was none other than Pierre. The sheer sight of him perplexed her. He was the master of a large plantation. Why would he be in a cottage like this when he had overseers to do his bidding? More importantly, why was he threatening to kill her when he had to have noticed the runaway slaves in the room? And runaways they had to have been. Everyone knew that the slaves on Ashleywood were well cared for. None would have dressed in garments not fit for an animal and in boots with so many holes that the toes trapped inside them were visible.

As she stared at Pierre in confusion, he in turn stared at her in equal confusion. The pistol lowered. The lantern was held closer to her face.

"You!"

She knew then that Pierre still hadn't recognized her. She watched as he stared at the slaves in the room, and then the pistol rose again and was aimed at her. His gaze was hard on hers. She sensed he was debating if he should kill her or not. Certain he would pull the trigger, she covered her face and stepped back from him.

The pistol was lowered and shoved in a pocket in his coat.

Pierre examined her clothing. This caused her much embarrassment. Like many of the clothes she owned, the cloak and bonnet she wore needed mending in certain areas. The riding boots on her feet were in need of being blackened; the soles needed repair and the lacing needed to be replaced.

The lantern lowered beside him and then he held out his hand.

She took it, gladly, and was further relieved when he led her out of the room and into the front part of the cottage. A scream tore out of her when she saw more slave men standing in the door of a room beside the fireplace. In their hands were burlap sacks. The looks on their faces were as if they were waiting to be told what to do.

Pierre's long arm circled around her waist. He whispered in her ear. "Calm down before you frighten them."

"Are we safe, massuh?" One of the men asked.

"Yes. Is everyone here?"

"No, massuh. We's waitin for two mo."

"Those in the other room, get them clean, dressed and fed. Do the same thing when the last two arrive. There's been a change of plans. Your escort isn't coming tonight. Bounty hunters are in the area but don't fear. I have a few of my servants watching the cottage. You remember the signal?"

"Yes, suh."

"The bounty hunters have dogs. Did all of you do as you were told?"

"Yes, suh. Ebba lass one of us!"

"Then they won't come here. You'll have to stay here until the area is safe to get you all to the ports. Someone will bring more food in the morning. Keep the doors locked. If you don't follow the rules, I will not protect you. You can't only think about yourselves, but the others who have made long journeys to get here."

"Yes, suh. I unlocked dee doe. I saws her coming. I was 'round back. Saw she was a woman and alone on foot. We's waitin on a gal, you see? And she come troo the right doe. When she didn't give the signal, we stays hid. Den you come."

"As soon as I leave blow out the lamps."

"Yes, suh."

The man stepped forward.

Pierre smiled at him. "You're sure you're not going with them this time, James?"

The man's expression was sober as he shook his head.

"I can't, massuh. Not while Jennie still oba yonda. Beside'n I takes good care of tangs heah. And this house. I's stays heah than go back or to freedom without Jennie."

Pierre's arm unfolded around her. The next thing she knew her hand was gripped and she was being led out of the far door. As she walked, she couldn't stop staring up at him.

Once they were outside she was physically lifted in his arms, and in a mad rush, he cleared the yard to the area where his horse was tethered. The animal was taller, more muscular, healthier and looked stronger than Trouble had ever been.

Pierre mounted, then reached down and lifted her from the ground with both hands. The saddle was large, still Pierre filled it. For her to fit, she had to sit on his lap with the front part of her pressed tightly against the horn and pommel. As high up as she sat from the ground, a fall from the horse would surely leave her maimed. A click of his teeth put the horse in motion. Its long stepped stride startled her. Before she realized it, she clutched Pierre's arm that secured her against him, then leaned against Pierre when the horse picked up speed and ran in a full gallop.

Closing her eyes, she prayed earnestly that she wasn't thrown. When the horse continued in a fast pace, her eyes opened; she peered up at Pierre. He had leaned forward, crushing her weight closer to the horse. Sarah released his arm and clutched the horn of the saddle with both hands. Thankfully, as soon as she did this Pierre leaned away from her and pulled slightly at the rein. No words had been spoken. Still the horse slowed to a trot, then slower still into a walk.

"Please don't take me to the mansion," she pleaded.

Pierre heard this and stared down at her. Twice in one day she had been alone and without a chaperone. This was most unheard of for a woman her age.

Why a woman of any age would be out without a horse or vehicle at this hour of the day troubled him most.

"Please," she begged. The last thing Sarah wanted was to face her sister. Jenna had promised long ago not to lend a single picayune to their father. Other than being allowed twice to attend a Christmas celebration on Ashleywood when she had been younger, Jenna had made it clear that Sarah and her father were unwelcome.

If she wanted Pierre to help her, she would need a private audience with him. The thought of him helping runaway slaves came to her mind at that moment. For the moment, she was unsure how to process this fact. It had never occurred to her that *le diable dans Nouvelle-Orléans,* as powerful and influential as he was, could involve himself with such a crime.

Within minutes they reached a cabin that sat close to the swamp. When Sarah saw it, she knew this was where he had intended to bring her all along. The last part of evening had nearly disappeared making everything she saw strange looking dark shapes. Pierre dismounted, then pulled her down. A yelp came out of her when she was lifted at the waist with strong hands and carried to the cabin. Its door was pushed open, and she was placed on her feet. Turning to face him, she remembered the pistol he had aimed at her.

"Please don't hurt me."

Pierre pushed her further into the cabin and stepped in behind her.

"Who are you?"

"It's me, Pierre. Sarah."

She saw that the name meant nothing to him.

"I'm your wife's sister."

It was hard to see his face clearly, as his back faced what light there was outside. Still she saw him make the tiniest move when it occurred to him who she was.

"Sarah *Isabelle* Cheval?"

"Oui," she answered and smiled because she knew then there was no mistake.

He seemed momentarily stunned, and then he walked out of the cabin.

She stood in the door and stared at him as he mounted the horse.

"Lock the door," he said and rode away.

Remembering him mentioning bounty hunters, she did as she was told. Once she did this, again she found herself standing in total darkness, except this time there was no way of learning who or what was in the cabin with her. Unlocking the door, she pushed it open wide then stepped outside before peering into the cabin. A dark shape lay on the floor in the corner. Beside it were smaller dark shapes. A fireplace was positioned in the middle of the rear wall. The floor was bare and covered with layers of dirt and grime. The cabin looked as if no one had stepped inside of it for many years.

Keeping her eyes on the shapes in the corner, she sat in the door long enough to remove her boots. Pushing them just inside against the wall, she squeezed and rubbed her aching feet. Unsure if her mind was playing tricks on her, she stood again with her eyes on the shapes. She couldn't be certain, but she believed that one of the smaller ones moved. Although it was just as dangerous being outside, she decided to take her chances.

The trees Pierre had ridden her through sat close to the swamp. A narrow bank dropped a bit to reach it. Not wanting to venture too far away from the door, she searched the remaining area with her eyes. The area must have been teeming with frogs and crickets, as these two sounds were constant. The sounds of close to a hundred or more swallowed up the chirps being made from birds nesting high in the trees.

Every now and then a splash could be heard coming from the water. All of these sounds she was familiar with; for this reason they didn't frighten her. All sorts of animals, small and large, lived between the trees, but she didn't think about this. She thought instead of William. The man was thirty-two years her senior. When he sweated, his body smelled like rotting onions. His breath smelled of the teeth rotting in his mouth. In the two weeks she had returned to Green Lea not once had he ordered a bath to be drawn.

Marrying him was unimaginable. The thought of having to lie underneath him and later bearing his children was enough to bring tears to her eyes.

The cabin's door was positioned directly in front of its fireplace. When she saw the fireplace, she imagined herself cooking meals in it. With only a minimal amount of furniture and if she had only a few utensils and the other necessities she needed to survive, she knew she would be happier living inside this cabin than as the wife of William Murray.

Oh, how she didn't trust him. Whenever he was inside the house, he watched her, constantly, and touched her in places he had no business until after they were married. The things he said when no one was around were too vulgar for even her mind to repeat. What she suspected, and hoped wasn't true, was William's plan of bedding her before the marriage as a sure way to seal the deal. Because he knew that if this happened, and especially if she were to become pregnant, her father couldn't change his mind before the wedding took place.

The only reason her father had agreed to the marriage was William's promise of asking his brother for a loan to make repairs, buy provisions and have enough left over to plant new crop. So far the brother had sent no money. And her father, although she loved him dearly, she was not unaware of his ineptitude; he had celebrated the arrangement prematurely, buying bottles of liquor so that he and William could drink themselves into a stupor. William was more than pleased with the celebration. Right away Sarah noticed that he enjoyed drinking as much as her father did. It was when he was drinking did his behavior became coarser than it already was.

There was no money left, and instead of her father or William making plans of improvements, her father asked William every day if he had any news from his brother. Every day William cornered her every chance he got to squeeze her breasts and rear and whisper in her ear. Neither her father nor William seemed concerned that every meal consisted of a small portion of meat, some type of grain and vegetables cooked in a single pot or how the remaining slaves needed medicine, herbs and rest. Merchants in the city were demanding payments and on numerous occasions had petitioned for her father to be arrested.

The weather was in no way cool, still she clutched her cloak tighter around her and sat again inside the cabin door. She was still sitting there it seemed hours later when a small light bounced between the trees as it drew closer. Instead of riding his horse, Pierre drove a small cart. He parked it a distance from the cabin, then climbed down.

Sarah rose to her feet and walked to him.

Pierre saw her, stopped walking and looked around. Then moving forward again, he reached into the cart and lifted a beautiful coverlet and a burlap sack filled to the brim.

"You're being too kind," she said.

"It's dangerous in this area," he said, looking at her.

"I didn't see anything out here. Something is in the cabin."

"Look behind you," he said, holding her gaze.

She turned and saw nothing at first, and then she saw what looked like two eyes staring at her at the base of a tree. As her eyes adjusted to the darkness and the small amount of light filtering from the lantern Pierre had with him, she saw it was an alligator of robust size. Its tail was curled. A small part of the tail was still in the water.

Turning from Pierre, she hurried into the cabin and stood in front of the fireplace to wait for him there.

Pierre dumped the things he brought just inside the door, then disappeared and returned this time with a wide wicker basket covered in cloth. The last trip to the cart was made quickly. As soon as he was inside, the kindling and logs was dropped from his arm, and the door closed fast, then locked.

"Was it getting closer?"

He turned and smiled at her. The lantern in his hand trembled with his laughter. When he quieted, he smiled again. "It seems he brought his friends. If they had gotten any closer, I would be embarrassed of what you would have seen or heard."

This made her smile.

His gaze lowered to her smile and stayed there a while.

Sarah walked closer to him and started to lower to pick up the logs.

"Leave it," he said. "Grab a blanket. Get comfortable."

With the light, she saw what she had been frightened of in the corner: a small pile of folded blankets, and heavy, iron manacles.

"Let me help," she insisted. "You could be in the comfort of your home right now if it wasn't for me."

He started to speak, stopped, then nodded and said what he almost didn't. "I can be inside the mansion, yes. Other than the small part of it that I have claimed for myself, the other parts I find uncomfortable just knowing your sister uses those rooms."

The marriage of Pierre Jennings was a topic William found most interesting. It thrilled him to know that Jenna was pregnant by someone other than her husband on her wedding night. Because he knew this was the reason Sarah believed he disrespected her womanhood the way he did. She had never met or seen a prostitute before, but she suspected that a man like William would respect a prostitute more than he would the sister of a woman he often referred to as a whore.

Pierre had lifted the pieces of wood and was now arranging them in the hearth. As tall as he was, even though he was crouched low on his heels, his head still reached almost as high as her.

"I'm sorry for what happened between you and my sister."

"There's no need for you to apologize. You were too young then to know what was going on. Your father has never apologized, however. I've waited nearly twenty years for him to do so. As soon as he heard I had discovered Jenna's condition, he, you and your mother left New Orléans and didn't return for two years. I paid them a visit a few days later. Your mother sat closely beside your father. Your father refused to remove you from his lap. Their behavior was all the proof I needed."

He stopped and looked at her over his shoulder.

"Still, I'm sorry," she said.

His eyes stared at the parts of her cloak that needed mended.

"From the looks of it, I can say the same thing to you as it appears you have suffered just as much as Abigail has because of it," he said.

A small cloth was pulled out of his pocket. Inside it was moss and thin, dry pieces of bark.

Sarah brought him the lantern.

"Merci," he said without looking at her.

She stepped back from the door when something bumped against it.

"It's perhaps a small animal," he said. "Nothing to fear."

"I'll remember to lock the door when you leave."

He did look at her then. "It's too dangerous to leave you here alone. I can't stop bounty hunters from coming on my land. If one of them found you here alone they may accuse you of a crime you didn't commit."

"You help them often, don't you? Runaways."

He stayed quiet as he lit the fire, then stayed low on his heels as he watched the flames grow higher.

"Can I trust you, Sarah?"

"Oui. Very much so. I was frightened because I didn't realize… I was on my way here by horse when she got ill and collapsed…"

He stood and faced her. "The old draft horse beneath a tree?"

"You saw her?"

"I was meeting with one of my contacts in the area and stumbled upon her. The only reason I got closer was because of the way she laid on the ground."

She took a step closer. "She was still lying down?"

"She's dead, Sarah."

Tears fell from her eyes.

"You didn't kill her," he said. "I've seen the sickness before. Horses get it from dirty stalls. The disease gets into their lungs and strangles them over time."

"Can I sit?"

"Please do."

She walked to the corner where the blankets were and brought them closer to the fire. Pierre emptied the wicker basket, then taking one of the blankets from her, he turned the basket upside down and spread the blanket over it.

"This is the best I can do for the moment."

"And it's most kind," she said, sitting while she held his gaze. "It's shameful the way my father treats his servants. And some of the ones I saw back at your cottage looked as if they had a harder life than those that live on Green Lea. I'm not saying I hate slavery, but I am saying I detest the way some masters treat their servants. Helping those in true need, I find it commendable."

"There's no need for slavery." The tone of his voice gave a clear image of his poignant sentiment on the subject.

She studied his face and eyes carefully. "You own hundreds of slaves."

"Imagine if you will hundreds of men and women working, doing the same chores as my servants for pay. If jobs like these were available on all plantations, América would become flooded with immigrants. Immigrants who arrive now must compete with well trained and skilled slaves, some of them with expertise in their trade after they are combined with their skills from Africa and those here. Except slaves don't get paid. And that, mademoiselle, is the reason the planter can sit high on his throne and boast of his wealth."

Sarah averted her gaze and shook her head. "You don't understand because you're wealthy, monsieur." She faced him again. "My father has never been wealthy. Never could he have been able to afford to hire anyone other than an overseer. The price for supplies, outside services…"

"Do you truly wish to educate me on the business aspects of managing a plantation?"

"No," she answered firmly. "I was merely trying to point out that unlike you, because of the costs necessary to run a plantation, my father has remained in debt without ever seeing a true profit."

"Perhaps your father should have come to me for a job. He knows that my true wealth is made outside of my plantation. But I'll tell you why he hasn't. Because like others it's better to appease his ego and appear in front of his peers as a successful master and lord of a plantation. Because only then will his peers view him as worthy of their company and not like one of the slaves who works his fields."

Sarah stood to her feet. "You cannot be so simpleminded, monsieur."

"Sit your ass down."

Sarah's eyes narrowed and tightened. "Pardon?"

"I said sit your ass down."

She did when he approached very slowly, his eyes now as narrow and tight as her own.

Lowering so they were eye to eye, he said, "Why did you come here? Did you hear there were runaways hiding on my land and you came here to find them? What were you going to do with the information once you had proof? I know all about your father and how badly his finances are ruined. Were you going to use your proof as a ransom to force me to help you both? I'll inform you right now, mademoiselle. I will never give your father neither a picayune nor a peck of corn even if it meant it would save his life."

Sarah sat quietly and held his gaze until he stood again and moved closer to the things he had brought. Only then did she notice the contents that had been in the basket. Jumping to her feet, she couldn't stop staring at the coils of rope, the pieces of long cloths, and the iron spike. All of these items she had seen before and were used to restrain slaves without causing injury, usually when they suffered from sickness or fever or mental unease.

The laugh that spilled out of her was small. Tears fell fast and plenty.

"Do you think I care what you do to me?" She asked. "Go ahead."

To prove her point, she tore the bonnet away from her hair. The pin that had held it in place flew haphazardly across the room and slid across the floor. The cloak was removed and dropped to her feet.

"My boots have already been removed, monsieur. I am now ready. Drive your stake in the floor and secure it. I'll even wait while you do it. How dare you think I came here because I was up to some trickery. My name may be Cheval, but I am not like my sister." She had almost said her father as well but stopped herself just in time.

Pierre remained silent as he gazed at her, and then he reached underneath the rope and lifted a bottle of wine. Inside the burlap sack, he pulled out two glasses that had been wrapped carefully in cloth so that either was damaged during the ride.

A small knife was pulled from his pocket to remove the cork. He poured a good measure of wine into one of the glasses then handed it to her.

"I remembered I put the wine with the rope. It's the only reason I brought the basket inside. The rope is for me to take to the cottage. I refuse for any of the slaves to kill a white man. I don't need rope for you, mademoiselle. You're barely five-feet tall and at most ninety pounds. I do not fear you."

Sarah took the glass and took a large swallow. Standing in front of the fire, she watched the flickering flames. "I came to you for money. My father has arranged for me to marry Monsieur William Murray. I wish to avoid the marriage if I can. I was hoping to borrow enough to improve the plantation…"

"Why would you want to do that, mademoiselle?"

She swallowed more of the wine, then faced him. "I was hoping to turn a profit. I know it will take a while to do so. I have to get rid of Monsieur Murray first. I can't and won't marry him. I just won't. I can make Green Lea a comfortable home for my father, and me, and the slaves again. I know I can if only given the chance."

Pierre poured more wine into her glass. "You're going to need that. Drink." He poured himself a glass of wine and sipped it. "Have you spoken to your sister about your plans?"

"I have written my sister many times over the years. While I lived in Biloxi she sent money on occasion, but not very much. She has never returned any of my letters. She's my sister, but she has never been a sister to me. Joséphine did not give birth to me, monsieur."

"Call me Pierre."

"Then please do call me Sarah."

"I will."

"My father had an affair with my mother. I don't know who she is. I've never met her. She may be dead. I have never received any correspondence from her. No one ever came to Green Lea to inquire about me that I know of. Joséphine hated the sight of me, but Jenna she loved as best as a woman like Joséphine could. I believe Joséphine told Jenna the truth, and for this reason, my sister, because she is still my sister even if Joséphine didn't give birth to me, doesn't believe she owes me any sort of relationship. I'm my father's child, you see? The same father who relied on his wife to support him while she was alive, and then that dependency was laid on Jenna's shoulders after Joséphine died."

"Jenna owns Green Lea, Sarah."

She turned and stared at the fire.

"Joséphine owned the plantation," he continued. "It had been given to her by her father as a wedding gift. When she died, she left it to Jenna. Talk to your sister. I can take you to the mansion as soon as our friends leave. Maybe she'll help."

"Do you think she will? If you do, I will go there now. Friends outside be damned. Please do excuse my language."

Pierre smiled, then gave a small nod. "I truly don't know, Sarah. You may know your sister better in that regard. Our marriage is not the usual one. She manages the house. I handle everything else. Our conversations are strictly business related. It is a most unusual arrangement. I'm too stubborn, and she's too stubborn to change it."

"Do you love her?"

He stared at her.

"I'm sorry," she said and averted her gaze. "That question was too personal. I apologize."

"I don't love her. Can I speak openly with you?"

"Please do."

"The few affairs I've had over the years have taught me one thing. I am *truly* the devil."

"I don't believe that."

He took a swallow of wine. "When the devil reveals to you who he is, listen."

She sat again on the wicker basket, and as he had done to her, she held out her hand. He lowered in front of her and placed his hand in hers. Sarah held his with both hands and gazed intently into his eyes. "I'm sorry about your marriage."

"I'm sorry about yours. I know William Murray. His brother, John, is very wealthy. He owns two plantations in Biloxi. Your father is indebted to John Murray. John had to have approved of William marrying you, I would think. If he did, I can see why. John's son died recently. He now has a plantation some distance from his that he has no way to keep an eye on. If you and William married and moved to Biloxi and take over the second plantation, I can see John willing to expunge some or all of your father's debts. You're young. Your children will be John's relatives. If something happened to him, he has someone to leave his wealth to."

"Help me," she pleaded.

"Your father, Sarah, will make you marry William. I can give you money, of course. If so, you can do with it what you choose."

She lowered her chin and held his hand tighter. "I have no right to ask you what I'm about to. But I have nowhere else to turn. Please, Pierre. Please talk to my sister. Convince her to let us do what's necessary to improve Green Lea. And… and if you can pay my father's debts and give me a loan, I'll be forever indebted to you. I may not ever be able to pay you all of it back, but as much as I can give you from each harvest, I will! I will!"

Pierre used his free hand to pat hers. "Sarah, it will take thousands to bring Green Lea back to the way it used to be. But if that's what you want, I'll do it."

Sarah pulled him back toward her when he tried to stand. Hugging him fiercely, she was too emotional to speak. The relief she felt. If he hadn't been standing in front of her, and if it wouldn't have made her looked arrogant, she would have laughed, right then and there, loudly. Loud enough to disturb the animals outside. She bit down on her lip when she pulled away from him.

"Merci. Merci beaucoup."

"In the morning, you'll talk to your sister."

"Will you be there?"

"No."

She could feel her joy ebbing away like a tide. "If you're there, maybe she'll think kindly toward me."

He rose to his feet. "Have you gone mad? I do not like that woman. I will never be in her debt. As soon as I find someone to replace her, I'm sending her away, and once she's gone, I never want to see her or even hear anything about her ever again. She's the devil. Is it not enough that I've agreed to help you on your terms?"

The transfiguration had been sudden. It stunned her that anyone would agree to give a large sum of money that they had no hopes of it ever being returned, but refuse vehemently the request to sit in a room with his wife during a meeting between sisters.

"Oui. Merci. Merci beaucoup." She spoke in a rush, hoping her sentiment didn't cause him to change his mind. And then she let out a sigh and hung her head. What right had she to ask him of anything? The fact that he was wealthy didn't excuse her behavior. Coming to the plantation had been a selfish thing to do. Women married who they were told to marry, even those from noble families. Had the disgust of marrying a man like William transfigured her?

"Pierre, I'm sorry. I shouldn't have asked anything of you. I can't accept your help. It was wrong of me to behave as I have. In the course of one night, I have killed a horse and exposed a secret you were unwilling to share. I have angered you. And more importantly, you're here instead of in whatever comfort your mansion can provide you." A hand pressed tightly to her mouth. She sat quickly as if her knees had given out. "How many times have I been disgusted by my father's need to lean on others and here I am doing the same at even a grander proportion."

Pierre took a large step toward her when she jumped from the basket and hurried to the fire. With one arm pressed tightly against her stomach she doubled in half. For some reason she thought she could vomit into the fire but it now burned high and its heat prevented her from doing this. The sickness, caused by her disgust in herself, rushed violently from her stomach. The few precious seconds she had wasted to reach the fire left her no more time. The sickness exploded out of her. It hit the wall, the floor, her feet and her gown.

A handkerchief was lowered over her shoulder.

Sarah reached for it without looking at him. She said nothing and was thankful when he didn't say anything either. She continued to stare at the fire a long time, and while she did so she thought of nothing.

A glass lowered over her shoulder. Seeing it made tears fall from her eyes.

"Merci."

She used the wine to rinse her mouth, walked to the corner of the room and was happy to see that there was a small hole in the floor. She spit in it, then used the hem of her gown to wipe her face clean. And then she faced him.

"I can bolt the door behind you. I'll be all right."

"I'm pretty sure you will be. I'm also sure that if I left the rope behind, by the time I came back you'll have the gator and his friends tied up and at your mercy."

The laugh that spilled out of her sounded more like a cough.

"You're not like your father, Sarah. Your father has never worked. But I'm sure if given the chance you will turn Green Lea into a prosperous plantation even if it meant dragging your father into the fields with the slaves."

The reason she laughed now was because deep down she wanted the mood in the cabin to become lighter. Because if it became lighter, and if he laughed too, maybe he would forget about some or all of the trouble she had caused him.

"I see your determination. And I believe it." He pulled one of the blankets forward and got comfortable on top of it. "My daughter – Désireé. I too wanted her to marry someone she may not want to marry. Because of this conversation, and because I can see how truly you do not wish to marry William, I shall tell her in the morning that I have changed my mind. I didn't think about the life she may have while married to this gentleman. I want her to be happy. I think the world will be a better place if more women were happy."

"I shall forever believe that only a man of your height can bestow a vast measure of kindness. What you have shown me tonight is unfamiliar to me."

His head tilted in reconciliation. "Merci. This cabin is not too far from the cottage. I've already told James where I'll be if he needs to find me. But I can't leave now. The less traffic between the trees the less likely one of the bounty hunters will hear or see anything. Later, when it's dark and the bounty hunters have given up for the night, I'll go to the cottage and bring you back water and clean clothing."

"Do you mind if I remove my gown? It has become almost unbearable."

"By all means."

Pierre rose, grabbed the blanket he had sat on, opened it and stretched it wide in front of him.

Sarah not only removed her gown, but she also removed her stays. The bruises were tender where the whalebone had pressed mercilessly against her skin. She folded the pieces, then rolled them together to be cleaned when she returned to Green Lea. Lifting her cloak from the floor, she pulled it over her head so that she was properly covered.

When they sat again, Pierre offered her another glass of wine.

Sarah sipped it and stared at the fire. Life was strange. Earlier it was almost as if something drove her from her plantation to Ashleywood. She wondered what would have happened if she hadn't given in to the fierce urge to get away at that moment and make a stand.

***

Early morning light spilled between the cracks in the wood. Either she was imagining things or she heard something splash in the swamp.

A look over her shoulder revealed that Pierre was no longer in the cabin. As he had promised, clean clothes, a hair brush, pieces of muslin and a small cake of soap sat on top of the overturned basket. Beside it was an ewer of water and a basin for her to use to wash with. Silver and red embers burned in the hearth.

Being able to wash felt glorious after the evening and night she had. The gown he had chosen had embellishments but remained modest. It didn't fit perfectly, but from what she could see when she looked down was better than the gowns she owned, and more appropriate to wear for her meeting with Jenna.

Pierre knocked on the door within minutes of her putting on her boots.

Helping her inside the cart, she sat beside him, and for some reason glanced into the back of it. Emitting a high-pitched scream was the only warning she gave before jumping out of the cart. As she jumped, she realized her scream had been enough. Pierre moved as quickly as she did. Grabbing her by the waist, he jumped out of the cart, running with her for some distance before stopping.

"What did you see?" He asked, still holding her high off the ground.

Laughter burst out of her.

"She laughs," he mumbled and lowered her to the ground.

Sarah watched as he moved closer to cart, then peeked into it. The speckled king snake was one of the deadliest in Louisiana. Reaching for a thin, low-hanging branch, Pierre broke it off and moved back toward the cart.

Sarah wondered how many men in the city could break off a branch the size he held from a tree. Incredible, she thought.

The branch was used to frighten the snake out of the cart and onto the ground, then send it on its way. Because she felt indebted to him so much already, she didn't wait for him to come to her. When the snake was a safe distance away, she hurried back to the cart. Pierre lifted her. She sat, then waited for him to get settled.

During the trip to the mansion she saw nothing but trees, so it surprised her when after some time they were riding across the plantation's rear yard. Pierre rode to the front of the house. From there she was assisted out of it and led inside.

Jenna stood near the staircase talking to a servant when Sarah walked into the house.

Jenna looked at her from head to feet not recognizing her, then at Pierre.

Pierre opened the doors to the *grand salle*. "Jenna, come in please."

Jenna heard this, and then her eyes hardened on Sarah.

Sarah knew at that moment that although Jenna still didn't recognize her, she knew who she was.

109

Sarah watched as Jenna lifted her chin slightly, then gave the most wickedest smile Sarah had ever seen anyone give.

"Riley," Jenna said to a male servant dressed in fine apparel. "Have something brought in for my guest. Sarah, is that you?"

"Oui, Jenna. It's good to see you."

"You seeing me would be a good thing for you, wouldn't it be?"

A servant stepped forward to take Sarah's cloak and bonnet. As the garments were being removed, Sarah couldn't stop looking at her sister. The fixity in Jenna's eyes was acute. In them was a torrent of rage that swelled like an ominous wave. Color had risen in her cheeks. It dawned on her that her sister didn't just want her to know she wasn't welcome in her home, but she wanted her servants to realize this as well. The look on her face caused Sarah to believe that Jenna would rant and yell at any moment, so undignified did she appear.

There was something else that Sarah noticed. The servants no longer bore smiles on their faces. Visible fear had taken its place.

A small bow was made before the servant that held her outer clothing turned and walked away. Pierre didn't enter the *salle* and disappeared down the hall.

Once she and Jenna was seated in the *salle*, Jenna said absolutely nothing. Sitting comfortably in a chair, her piercing eyes accused Sarah of every sin she had ever committed, especially being born. Sarah tried not to think about that.

"I recently learned you own Green Lea," Sarah began. "I'm back, Jen. And I have no intentions of ever leaving New Orléans again. I hope you don't mind, but I have asked Pierre for a loan, and he has agreed to my terms."

The nuance in Jenna's eyes was noticeable.

"I think… I think today would have been better if you answered the letters I've sent over the years," Sarah continued. "I wasn't sure you've gotten them. I have never received anything from you in return. I can see this is an inconvenience, Sister, and I know that our relationship hasn't been as good as it should be. But not on my part, Jen. I swear! I have tried very hard to keep in contact…"

"Do you always talk this much?" Jenna interrupted.

A servant entered the *salle* bearing a silver tray. Soon café was poured into two porcelain cups. Sarah was impressed when a trolley was pulled forward. Inside it were three complete cones of sugar. Three complete cones! But why was she impressed by this when Ashleywood was now a sugar plantation? She imagined her reaction could have been because it had been a while since she'd seen more than a quarter of a cone, of which its owner usually watched carefully over it as if it was a brick of gold. And here her sister lived in a mansion where sugar sat in its own trolley unguarded. Sugar plantation or not, seeing this was impressive.

"How much sugar, mademoiselle?" The servant asked.

Sarah had never been asked this before. The people she knew were stingy with their sugar. Usually, before the cup was handed to her the mistress of the house clipped off a very small amount of sugar and dropped it in.

"It's a simple question," Jenna hissed. Her shapely lips were now thin lines pressed tight against her teeth. "Stop gawking as if you've never seen sugar before."

"Three please," Sarah replied.

Three heaping clips were removed and placed inside her cup.

"Cream, mademoiselle?"

"Please," Sarah answered.

Janna sighed in exasperation. "Where's your manners, *girl?* You're Creole. Have some dignity. You don't say please to a mealy-mouth slave."

Sarah became conscious of her every move as she lifted the cup, brought it to her mouth, took one sip and fell in love with café for the first time. Ignoring her sister, she stared into the cup taking note of its color and consistency. Never had café tasted so splendidly delicious. The brew she was drinking hadn't been made from corn, but what she imagined was real ground café beans. It had been a while since she had pure café and not the blend commonly used by the poor. As she continued to hold the cup, only then did she realize how deprived her childhood had been.

Knowing Jenna will evict her from the mansion as soon as their conversation ended, Sarah decided to take her time. It was then she noticed the room. The wealth inside it made her feel uncertain about how she was dressed or how she looked. The paintings that hung on the wall seemed almost lifelike. Furniture decorated with silver, marble and ormolu shined and twinkled. No parts of the rugs on the floor were faded, and no sides mended to conceal any frays.

When she looked up, she saw pride in Jenna's eyes.

A three tier serving tray was placed on the table alongside two small plates, linen napkins, and what looked like solid gold pieces of cutlery. Surely this was impossible. Plated in gold, yes. Entirely made of gold?

Sarah lifted a fork. Its weight answered her question. Her sister ate off of forks made from solid gold.

"Mon Dieu." The words were spoken like a sigh.

Tamales, beignet, calas, fresh fruit, and a variety of cheese had been neatly arranged on the serving trays.

Sarah reached for one of the plates.

"Anne will serve you," Jenna hissed. This time, the menacing stare she gave looked deadly.

Sarah knew this was the way of things, because in her own home, regardless of how poor or how little they had, the servants always did the serving. Being stupefied by the room was the only excuse she could give for her behavior.

Anne waited patiently to be instructed on what should be put on the plate.

"Everything," Sarah said.

When Anne smiled, Sarah gave a small smile back. It came to her at that moment that the slaves on Ashleywood lived better than she did if any of them were allowed any of its privileges.

Jenna refused the food on the tray and instead enjoyed a cup of café with four clips of sugar!

Sarah began eating, then closed her eyes as the beignet melted against her tongue. "This is New Orléans." Happier moments of her childhood when Joséphine had been alive flooded back.

The calas was equally delicious. By the time she got to the cheese, she sank into the sofa as if she was in heaven. At that moment, she reminded herself that when she returned home watery soup would be served at each of her meals. She thought about her father, the slaves and even William on Green Lea eating so little and pushed the plate away. Once again she was being selfish and only thinking of herself. It seemed of late this had become a routine. The guilt she felt created a puddle of remorse in her stomach. As hungry as she was, she decided not to take another bite. She looked up and saw that Pierre stood in the door. He turned away when their eyes met, leaving the door empty again.

Sarah lowered her head knowing that this meeting would go as she believed it would. Jenna will refuse her help no matter what was said. Still she had to try.

"As I was saying," she began.

"You've said enough," Jenna interrupted. "I received your letters, Sarah. Oh, how long they were. Why you thought pouring your soul on a piece of paper would make you my sister is beyond me. You are not my mother's daughter; therefore, you are *not* my sister. As for Green Lea, our father has run it into the ground..."

Sarah leaned forward in a rush. "Please! Just listen to me. It's all I ask. How you feel about me makes no difference. Not now. I offered you my friendship. You have refused it and I'm willing to accept your refusal. I can see that you want nothing to do with me. But our father resides on Green Lea. I know he hasn't done much to maintain it, and he has most certainly run it into the ground. But I can make it something again..."

"With my husband's money?" Jenna's eyes and face showed just how incredulous she had become. "No, Sarah. You can't make anything of it. The money it will take to rebuild will outdo any profit that will ever come from it."

"If we plant cotton, Jenna, the plantation can prosper. Repairs can be made where they're needed. Since the plantation is yours, you will benefit in the end. We're talking years of profit..."

"That wasn't the agreement."

"Pardon?" Sarah watched as Jenna lowered her cup on the table beside her.

"John Murray has agreed to purchase Green Lea. Now that his son has died and he no longer has any living relatives you have become a precious asset. You are being offered marriage and a home. Stop acting like a child! Surely you can see you are being given what some women will never have. The agreement is Papa will not be turned away and none of the remaining slaves sold. Papa has prolonged the wedding date in the hopes that when John arrives, which should be soon from the last letter I received, he can convince John to also pay off his debts in the city. This opportunity benefits us all. You should be happy to be able to help Papa in his time of need. Marrying William will mean my husband will not have to throw away his money. Papa will not be arrested. What more can you ask for, Sarah?"

Sarah lifted the cup and sipped it nervously, then lowered it and stood to her feet. "Thank you for your hospitality. I'll see myself out."

Jenna sank back in her chair, lifted her café and averted her gaze as she sipped it.

As Sarah stepped out of the *salle* a servant saw her and was quick to fetch her cloak and bonnet. After she donned her bonnet, a different servant stepped forward with a basket covered with nice cloth.

"From our monsieur." She spoke with a soft voice as if she didn't want her madame to hear.

"Merci," Sarah whispered as the smell of fried dumplings, sweets and the scent of fresh fruit permeated her nose. The basket was heavy, which meant it had been packed as tightly as possible.

She gazed at the *salle* door. Inside it was someone of her own flesh. Jenna's rudeness made Sarah heavy with thoughts. Somewhere inside this house she had a niece. Jenna hadn't thought once to the call the child forward so the two of them could meet. All she wanted was her sister out of her house as soon as possible.

Riley stepped forward and gestured toward the front door. When she reached him, he said, "I didn't know how long your stay would be, mademoiselle. I will send someone for the coach. You are most welcome to sit inside or wait outside on the galerie. Perhaps more café and a little more refreshments, mademoiselle?"

"No, thank you. I'll wait on the galerie."

"Oui, mademoiselle."

The front door was pulled open in a grand fashion. Sarah stepped outside holding the basket with both hands. Pierre stood on the drive with his back to her helping a young girl into a cart larger than the one he had used the night before. Sarah felt obligated to thank him again and walked to him.

"Pretty-pretty!" The girl cried and pointed with her finger.

Pierre looked over his shoulder.

"Thank you very much for everything," Sarah said. "Your kindness I will never forget."

"Pretty-pretty!"

"How did it go?" Pierre asked.

All it took was one look into his eyes and she knew he knew the answer. He had known how it would go before she had walked inside his home.

"I was told to marry William. John Murray will arrive shortly, and with him he brings the prospect of paying all of my father's debts."

"Salut," the child said.

Sarah looked past Pierre, saw the girl he had been helping, and smiled. "My. Aren't *you* the pretty one. I thought you were calling me pretty, but I see now you were referring to your pretty dress and your face." It was true. It was apparent by the girl's speech and the way she fidgeted that her mind was addled, but her face was definitely a sight to behold, as was her small gown and the leather boots on her feet. Sarah had never seen a noir child, quadroon or not, dressed as finely as this one. Even the silk ribbons in her hair were a sight to see.

"Your visit is over then?" Pierre asked.

"Oui. I am now waiting for a coach to drive me back to Green Lea."

His eyes fell down the front of her, then back up to her eyes. The look was similar to one he had given the night before. Sarah saw it and averted her gaze.

"I can take you if you don't mind riding in the cart. This is Gorée."

"Hello, Gorée." Sarah gave the girl a second smile.

Gorée smiled back while swinging her legs in anticipation.

"If it's no trouble," Sarah replied. Pierre held out his hand and assisted her up onto the cart. The basket was taken and placed in the rear.

Sarah looked slyly over her shoulder to see what else was there. When she turned again she saw that Pierre had noticed. A small smile was on his face as he climbed up and grabbed the reins.

Sarah looked back at the mansion as the cart pulled off. The front door was tightly closed. Jenna hadn't bothered to say good riddance.

Pierre rode the horses slowly over the road outside of his plantation. Sarah didn't mind the slow pace. If the ride took months, she wouldn't once complain.

"Bird," Gorée said. She sat in between them, kicking her legs and staring at everything around her.

When Pierre didn't offer a reply, Sarah felt compelled to give one. She pointed toward the levee. "Turtle. See it walking?"

Gorée concentrated on the turtle until it could no longer be seen.

"Bird," she said again.

Sarah searched for the bird Gorée was speaking of. There were several, but none stuck out as being more noticeable than the other.

"Bird means to drive fast," Pierre explained. "Some of her words don't mean the same as ours. To understand her you have to understand her way of thinking."

This time the word was spoken very softly. Gorée stared up with imploring eyes. "Bird."

"Stay going. Bird return."

The gentleness of his voice and Sarah knew why Gorée was dressed as prettily as she was. The child was his. This made her stare at him longer than she should have as she tried to understand why someone like him could help runaway slaves. Gorée wasn't being treated like a privileged slave, but like a father would his beloved heir. This was something she had never seen before.

"Her mother was a servant on the Dussault plantation. She died giving birth."

Sarah studied his mouth as he spoke, then chastised herself for her brazen behavior and averted her gaze. "Again I am forcing you to share something you had no intentions of sharing. I'm sorry about that."

He stared down at her a moment, then forward again, keeping the cart at the same pace. "She looks a lot like her mother. Almost entirely. It's hard for me not to look at her and not see her mother's face and my father's eyes."

"These past hours have been very meaningful to me," she said. "I have you to thank for that. Sometimes we can become so enthralled in our own plight it's hard to recognize the plight in others."

"Do continue," he encouraged.

Her tongue licked her lower lip and tasted the sweetness still on it. "Surely I can't be so forward…"

"I encourage it."

Again she stared at him. The more time she spent with him, the more she saw him for the man he was and not the man that the city presented in their conversations.

"You don't smile much, Pierre. You always seem contemplative. My sister isn't happy. I saw it in her eyes. So much luxury, yet she finds no comfort. When we were in the *salle* she liked that I admired the room, but I sensed nothing in it meant anything to her. Not personally, at least. I'm sure if given the chance, she would trade them all for a better relationship with you." She looked up at him. "I saw the way she looked at you when you stepped into the house. The secret in her heart was as exposed as if she had spoken the words aloud. And I'll hope you forgive me for what I'm about to say next, as I mean no harm."

Pierre gazed down at her. "Will you permit me to speak freely afterwards?"

Sarah stared forward. It wasn't because she had seen anything in his eyes. It was because she had found herself staring at his mouth again. "My behavior these past hours have been most inappropriate."

As they rode a small distance in silence, she noticed the way he was looking at her. Her heart skipped a beat.

"Please, don't," she answered softly, then felt troubled when he looked away.

"You were saying?"

"Pierre," she began, but decided not to voice the obvious. "I was going to say that I don't believe my sister is capable of loving me or my father or perhaps anyone. If she did it will veer her attention – attention she wants desperately to give to another." She didn't say him because she realized now that although what she said she believed to be true, it would have been rude to say so.

"I have never meditated on that likelihood," he answered. "I apologize for my behavior last night."

"Please don't apologize," she begged.

"Night," Gorée said and yawned.

The child then studied her for a moment, then sat closer to Pierre as if she was suddenly frightened.

"Wood?" Pierre asked.

Gorée nodded.

Pierre pulled the cart over. Gorée climbed in the back of the cart and lay on top of a thick coverlet. Pierre then put the cart in motion again.

"You don't have to marry William," he said. "I'll pay your father's debts. And I'll give you the money you need."

Sarah shook her head. "It will only anger my sister. John has agreed to purchase Green Lea. She spoke truthfully when she said I was behaving like a child. I can understand her decision. My father will be better off if I married William. What more can I ask than that?"

"Sarah, John Murray is a businessman, and as a successful businessman myself, I'm certain he has no intentions of buying a fledgling plantation for his brother when he and his brother don't get along, and especially when he has a prosperous plantation and no one to run it. If I hated my brother but I found myself suddenly in need of his help, the most money I would loan is the cost to travel to where I needed my brother most. And no more than that, especially when the home he will live in will provide him and his new bride supreme comfort."

"She received a letter…" Sarah began, then realized that Jenna hadn't mentioned who the letter had come from.

*William.* Oh, this man was truly a weasel. Her eyes squeezed tightly together. "My father asks every day has the money come. Jenna believes she's selling Green Lea." No wonder William was pressuring her to bed him before the marriage. It was because he feared her father and Jenna will soon learn the truth. John wasn't buying Green Lea. Her father's debts would not be paid. But if Sarah became pregnant then her father will relent to a speedy marriage to spare her the embarrassment of not being married and having a child.

"Jenna will have no choice but permit you and your father to reside on Green Lea once she learns no one will buy it. Keep your faith, Sarah. You have more meaningful hours to live yet." He smiled at her.

Hours later she stood on the Green Lea galerie and watched as Pierre and Gorée rode through the gate of the plantation. When the cart reached the road Pierre slapped the reins and the cart increased its speed. The last thing Sarah saw was the ribbons in Gorée's hair flying in the breeze.

## Chapter Fourteen
# Roses Have Thorns

*[When a woman lifts her dress, the devil looks at her leg. – Creole Proverb]*

Two evenings later the cottage was as dark as it had been the night she had found it. Sarah rode slowly on Rebel, her father's best horse. Behind her keeping up pace was three of her father's slaves. As she tethered the mare in the same place Pierre had his, the servants with her hurried to the door Sarah had told them about.

Searching the yard, she tried to see if James was about. Seeing no one, she followed the servants to the door and pulled open its shutters. The door that led inside was locked. One by one she checked all three doors and found they were also locked. Going back to the middle one, she knocked and waited, then knocked harder and waited.

"Stay here," she told the others and went around to the back of the cottage where James had said he had seen her approaching. In the back was a door. Sarah tried it and was relieved to find it unlocked. Running back around to the front, she motioned for the servants to come where she was. Once they were with her, she walked in first.

The door led into a bedroom. It was immaculately clean. As she exited it to reach the front part of the cottage, she whispered James' name.

No one answered.

Room by room she searched for James and the slaves she had seen two nights ago. The cottage was empty. The piles of blankets, clothing and ewers were all gone. The cabin had been thoroughly cleaned, the floors waxed. No water had been left behind. No food.

Sarah's heart sank. Not wanting the servants to see her despair, she smiled and told them to get comfortable. Choco, Benjamin and Daniel began to embrace each other and cry as if they had already made it to freedom.

"Remember what I told you. You have to keep quiet. I have to leave for a moment, but in the meantime remember to do everything James tells you if he returns. Do you understand?"

"Yessum!" They answered and started to embrace again.

Sarah hurried out of the cottage. Reaching Rebel, she stared at the cottage and wondered if it was safe to leave them there. Bounty hunters had been in the area those two nights ago. What if Pierre had moved the other slaves to a different location because the bounty hunters were getting close?

As she rode away, she hoped this was very well the case, because deep down she believed her father's servants had reached the cottage in vain and that the others had already gone into the next phase of their journey. By now Green Lea would be in an uproar having realized that three out of thirteen slaves had escaped. It was even possible that either her father or William had sent a notice to the city to put the citizens and police on alert. If she took the slaves back now, each of them would receive a harsh punishment.

Riding hard between the trees, she rode in the direction she believed the mansion would be in. The questions that came to her mind were ignored. The deed had been done. It was too late to change things now. With her heart racing as fast as Rebel was, she prayed she could find Pierre before someone found her servants hiding in the cottage.

As she rounded a tree, she leaned back and pulled slowly on the reins. In the distance, two groups of men on horseback faced one another. A conversation was taking place between them. Sarah didn't see any weapons and didn't need to.

Turning Rebel in a different direction, she rode back a distance, then cut a hard left and rode as fast as she ever had. Before long she passed what looked like a slave row too small for the size of Ashleywood. Certain that she was heading in the right direction she sped past not paying attention to the rows. She had traveled a little farther when she heard the sound of a horse's hooves behind her. Looking once over her shoulder, she leaned back and pulled on the reins, then waited for the lone rider to reach her.

"Are you lost?" The man asked.

Sarah took one look at him and knew exactly who he was.

"Monsieur Julien Jennings?"

"Oui."

"I… I can't tell you who I am. But if you can point me in the direction of your brother. I wish to have words with him in private."

Julien took in her clothing and bonnet, then nodded. "Personal business, is it?"

"Oui. And most urgent."

Julien looked uncertain, but again he nodded.

"Stay here," he said. "I'll get him for you."

"Merci beaucoup."

Julien must have believed it was urgent. Sarah had never seen anyone ride as fast as he did. In seconds he had disappeared. As she waited, she listened to the sound of her own breathing and thought about the cottage. *Please hurry, Pierre.*

Where she waited there wasn't much to see. Through the trees she saw buildings and activity, but couldn't make anything out other than she was surrounded by small groups of slaves diligently working. The shade underneath the tree was nice at least.

*Please hurry, Pierre.*

Rebel got confused when she leaned forward slightly. Holding tightly to the reins she calmed him and kept him still. Pierre's height made it easy to spot him. Both brothers rode side by side through the trees unafraid of losing control of their horses.

Pierre pulled on the reins when he reached her. His brows arched in confusion.

Julien looked at her, then his brother waiting to hear what it was she would say.

"I have three," Sarah said.

"Three what?" Julien asked.

"Where?" Pierre asked, then rode off before she could answer.

Sarah steered Rebel to follow him. Julien kept pace with her.

Pierre saw the group on horseback. The group also saw him. He slowed and changed course. Sarah wasn't certain if she should follow or go to the cottage. Julien pulled up on the opposite side of her preventing her from changing directions. Until they reached the now waiting group he stayed beside her as if steering her along.

Pierre reached the group first and was speaking to the men when Sarah rode up to them.

"Bonjour, mademoiselle," the men said.

"Bonjour, messieurs," Sarah replied.

"Bonjour, monsieur," they said to Julien.

"Bonjour."

"Gentlemen, this is my wife's sister, Mademoiselle Cheval. Mademoiselle, these men are constables from the city."

*Constables!* She had believed they were bounty hunters. The smile on her face froze into place.

"Did you find anything?" Pierre asked.

"Not yet," one of the constables answered. Sarah assumed he was the higher ranking of the three. The man looked in her direction. "Mademoiselle Sarah Cheval, is it?"

"Oui, monsieur."

The man stared at her a moment, then stared back at Pierre. "Since we haven't found anything and the hour is late, can you please permit me and my men to bunk on your plantation for the night?"

"Of course," Pierre answered politely. "Julien, please show the constables to the mansion. And, Constable, I will continue to have my men search every inch of my property. If there are runaways here I can assure you we will find them. In the meantime, my wife will make certain to accommodate you and your men as long as you like. Julien, please also return Mademoiselle Cheval's horse to the stables. Sarah, perhaps now we can be alone and go on the ride we intended?"

"Thank you much, monsieur," the higher ranking constable said, his eyes darting to Sarah, and then onto the men with him.

Sarah dismounted. Julien took a hold of her reins.

"Be careful with him." She had meant for the words to sound as if she was teasing him. Too much emotion had been inside her tone making it sound like a plea.

"Oh, come now," Julien teased eloquently. "I'm not going to hurt him. The last time wasn't my fault."

"Just be careful with him," Pierre said. "You know how she cherishes that animal. I should hate to have to give her another when she's only just gotten attached to this one. Especially after what you did to the last one."

Julien threw back his head and roared.

The constables smiled from the exchange that had been given to make them think Sarah often visited, and then they followed Julien back to the mansion. One of them looked back as Pierre lifted Sarah in the saddle with him. Sarah saw this and thought she would release her bladder. The urge to relieve herself was made stronger when Pierre held her to him like a lover would by leaning his body close to hers and lowering his chin until it rested in her hair. "If the constables find your three, I'll be arrested," he whispered. "Are they at the cottage?"

"I thought the others would be there." She gazed up at him with large eyes.

"Who do they belong to?" His horse moved at a walk through the trees.

"My father."

"Your…? Have you gone mad? Three slaves and *you* are missing from your father's plantation? Take them back, Sarah. Right this minute."

"I can't!"

"You can and you will. This is madness. Have you lost all of your senses? The bounty hunters went to the police. Their dogs found clothing on my land – clothing that proved runaways had come onto my land. Did you come straight here?"

"Oui."

"Then that means the constables saw you in the exact amount of time it would have taken you to lead three slaves from your land to mine. If you had sent them on their own things would have been different. You would have been home. Everyone would have seen you there. Once it was learned they were missing, no one would have accused you of any wrong doing. But *you* brought them. And you, mademoiselle, will also be arrested if your father is angry enough."

"I thought the others would still be here. Where's James?"

"On a ship bound for France along with the others. While you and I were sleeping in the cabin, the servant Jennie that he refused to leave without had waded through the swamp for three miles to reach the cabin. They left my land before you met with your sister in the mansion."

"I know it was a stupid thing I did, but I can't take them back, Pierre. I can't look them in the eyes and speak those words. As acting overseer, William will punish them and will find pleasure in it as he did so because them leaving makes him look bad."

"Sarah, there is a simple solution, and although unpleasant, it will spare four lives, including yours. Give William what he's after, and as acting overseer, he will mete out a less harsh punishment. Have you not figured out by now that William is overjoyed that you have done this? He will use it against you any way he can. Or how upset your father is at the moment? Those slaves were all the value he has left in this world. When all you have is thirteen slaves and a field of crop, you have just stolen more than a thousand dollars I'm sure he feels he can't afford to lose."

"Please tell me something else can be done. Please. Why did you want the constables to think we are having an affair? Surely you thought of a plan to help me!"

"Sarah, I did that so when they reached the mansion none would have the courage to mention *you* were on the plantation. And they won't as long as they are being shown the best hospitality they shall ever receive from *your* sister. If Jenna heard you were on the plantation, as soon as your father told her slaves and you are missing from his land, she will convince him to deal with you severely."

"Please let me down."

Pierre stopped the horse and lowered her to the ground, then dismounted.

Sarah didn't know what to do, but she couldn't keep still. Shaking her hands frantically just above her shoulders, everything she had been holding inside for the past hours spilled out of her.

"John Murray is dead! William got the letter this morning. John's attorney wants William in Biloxi as quickly as possible. He and my father celebrated over the news the way the King of France did at the birth of his first male child. They were jumping. And laughing. And talking loudly. Choco heard them. I heard them. Imogen heard them. We were the only others in the house. William has invited my father to go with him to Biloxi, and of course, he wanted me there as well. The three of us were supposed to leave in three days.

"To get money to travel and keep us until the legalities of John's death is out of the way, William proposed to sell all of the slaves, except one. Imogen. And only because William thought it would please me to see he was allowing me to keep Imogen as my personal maid. I was then sent up to my boudoir to pack and make ready for the journey. I was in my boudoir when I saw Choco, the plantation driver, and another servant running across the yard. And they kept running long after they reached the trees.

"I went downstairs and asked permission to come here and say goodbye to Jenna. William's answer was no. My father told me not to bother. The other slaves in the fields saw those three run off. Surely the others heard what Choco must have said. No one will accuse me. I can say I came here. I didn't steal them. I went after them to convince them to come back. They left thirty minutes before I left the mansion. Rebel and I found them after a ten minute jaunt. If I found them in ten minutes, the bounty hunters would have found them just as easily and made examples out of them.

"They refused to go back, even after I explained this to them, and said they would rather die. They have no food. No blankets. They're scared but more than that they're brave. How could I leave them out there? I know it was stupid to bring them here, but I thought the others were still here and you could get them away. I didn't know what else to do."

She then wept, not just for the three servants she had known all her life, but for herself and every woman who had been in her same situation.

"Sarah. All right," he said gently.

"We are *all* slaves," she said, looking up at him fiercely. "Women are forced to marry and have children by men we will never love, and run households that will never be ours unless our husbands die. And even the best wife must remain quiet while her husband bed other women and have children other than hers. I am my father's most valuable asset at the moment, Pierre. *Me*. Not Choco. Or Daniel. Or Benjamin."

Pierre folded his arms around her and held her as he stared at Julien. Julien had ridden toward them a few minutes before, saw how emotional she was and started approaching by foot. Pierre wasn't certain how much he heard. One look at Julien's face and he knew why he had come.

"Her father's here," Julien said softly. "And her fiancé. They're in a rage, Pierre."

"Did they mention any runaways?" Pierre asked.

"No," Julien said and shook his head.

Sarah heard this and sobbed even more, and then she pulled away and stared up at Pierre. "Why look for runaways when my father needs me most? Please help them. But if you can't, I'll understand."

She turned from him and walked away.

Julien stared at his brother a moment, then followed Sarah to the horses. Once they were mounted he led Sarah back to the mansion.

Pierre watched them go.

## Chapter Fifteen
# One Devil Makes Two

*[Don't call the alligator "big-mouth" till you have crossed the river. – Creole Proverb]*

Gorée had never been to the city.

Pierre watched her from the door as she ran in the courtyard, chasing birds, butterflies, mosquitoes and any and everything with wings. During the night as he slept in the bedroom upstairs, he had tried again to talk himself out of it. Now it was perhaps too late. The message had already been sent. If Sarah had received the message in time, he would know soon enough.

The three runaways were never mentioned during Emil's and William's visit to Ashleywood. As of that morning tickets on a steamboat headed to Biloxi had been purchased. At two o'clock sharp the steamboat was scheduled to pull away from the dock.

Pierre was uncertain if William will board the ship without his fiancé. If he didn't the police would certainly get involved. Not having enough time to plan, all Pierre could hope for was that what he had put together worked. If not there will be much embarrassment and he would lose face amongst his peers. It was something he was willing to risk. From the moment he laid eyes on Sarah, he thought of no one else. Each time he'd seen her after their brief meeting at Nowicki's, his heart beat like a drum in his chest. Several times when he faced her, he had wanted to tell her how beautiful she was. During the night he lay awake for hours imagining her in his arms.

"There you are."

Jenna had spoken behind him. Her voice seemed to him small and contrived.

"The guests will arrive shortly. Are you coming into the *salle* any time soon or shall I greet them alone?"

Pierre turned and faced her. The smile he gave was also contrived. He noticed the small step she made toward him, as well as the hope that had come into her eyes. The hope was there a moment, then gone. Her eyes then studied his, then fell down to his attire and the way he stood. It was then her expression transformed to insinuate she was standing in front of her most dangerous opponent.

The reason he had invited her to the city was because the more people he had around him the least likely he would be accused if the police did come. As he thought about this the smile slid from his face.

"Shall we wait in the *salle* together?" He asked.

She held his gaze for some time.

Pierre stepped forward and offered his elbow. Jenna stared at the offering, then reaching for it very slowly she gripped it with both hands and pressed her cheek against his arm. "Why are you being nice?" She whispered.

He said nothing as he led her into the *salle*, because he wasn't certain what to say. Jenna looked to him how she had before the two of them were married. It was this softer side he had been attracted to in the beginning. Seeing it had an effect on him he thought no longer existed.

The *salle* had been made ready to receive visitors. One of the servants stood ready in one corner holding a large fan. As soon as her madame sat the servant rushed forward and kept the fan in motion to cool her madame and keep away flying insects.

All of the French doors along the wall had been opened. The heat was close to unbearable. The *brise* and other doors had been opened to circulate air throughout the mansion. Servants bustled in an attempt to make last minute preparations, many of them mopping at the sweat on their brows. Pierre stood at the buffet and lifted a carafe of lemonade. Dropping three large pieces of ice into the glasses he poured, he carried the glasses to Jenna, offered her one, then sat beside her.

"Why are you doing this, Pierre? You have never served me a drink in the sixteen years we've been married. I'm having a hard time trusting you. First the invitation. Since we left Ashleywood you have shown nothing other than kindness. I want to know why you're giving me this attention when you never have before."

He took a large swallow of lemonade. Again he saw hope in her eyes. But it was more than hope. What her eyes were asking for was forgiveness, a chance to do things differently between them.

In the beginning of their marriage he had waited for this exact moment. Now he felt nothing. Maybe if it had come sooner he would have felt differently. Too many things had happened between them. Forgiving her now was too hard to do, but the same couldn't be said for Abigail. During the past few years his feelings toward her had changed. His father had been right, of course. Abigail had not been treated kindly by either of her parents. The part he played in Abigail's unhappiness weighed heavy on him more and more as each day passed. It wasn't too late to change things between them. This he believed.

"You have nothing to say?"

"Jenna…"

She adjusted her position in the chair to face him directly, to look dead into his eyes when she said what she had to say next. Those words were kept back when another servant entered the *salle* and behind the servant was the arrival of their first guests. Still Jenna reached for his hand. She spoke in a soft voice so only he heard what she said. "Can we talk later this evening after our guests have gone?"

Pierre had started to answer when her hand suddenly tightened on his and her eyes became wide with alarm. He looked up to see what had caused this reaction. The three individuals who had entered the *salle* were close friends of Jenna's: Bethanie Dussault, her husband Jean-Paul, and her cousin Marie-Claude.

The smile Jenna gave was forced. Normally she thrilled whenever she saw Bethanie, Jean-Paul and Marie-Claude because she considered the three her closest friends.

As Jenna watched them enter, she thought about Pierre's odd behavior She had wanted to know the reason behind it. Now she knew this opportunity was lost, and that the small door that could have bridged her marriage would soon close.

As she returned her guests' kisses of salutation thoughts ran through her mind. Bethanie, Jean-Paul and Marie-Claude would wonder why she sat so closely to Pierre. For sixteen years Jenna had been in a marriage where in the privacy of her home she went one way and her husband another. There were never any kisses or hugs. There was never any hand holding or touching of any kind. Affection between them was nonexistent. Very badly she wanted the separation between them to end, and for the two of them to love each other like they had before they were married.

This had been what she always wanted.

To make Pierre sound more like a devil, and to make these three friends *believe* he was truly the devil, she had told them made up stories about Pierre beating her with his fist and how his anger caused him to throw her around a room every chance he got. Of course, these things had never happened, but she had been much younger when she had told these lies, and each of these three friends had never forgotten them. Each of them still asked her about it every chance they got. Instead of telling them the truth, she had kept the lies going.

Now with Pierre sitting beside her, returning his kindness would make her lose face in front of her friends. Each of them would think her insane to love a man who had repeatedly beat her senseless and hadn't shown a shred of sympathy afterwards.

"It's good to see the two of you this afternoon." Jean-Paul's eyes held a curious gaze as he looked at each of them and how closely they sat, because whenever Pierre and Jenna together everyone in the city knew that Jenna sat on one side of a room and Pierre the other. "It's been a while since the two of you came to the city together."

Jenna's heart raced when Pierre looked at her momentarily. She was still studying his eyes when she felt Bethanie fan herself, then lean forward to examine how closely Pierre sat to the sofa. And then Bethanie leaned closer to her. "Is everything all right?" She whispered.

Pierre heard this and averted his attention to Bethanie.

Marie-Claude also had a fan and was using it to fan herself. "It amazes me how some men can raise their fist to their wives and treat her in an appalling way. Only a devil of a man can do that. What do you think, Jean-Paul? You're a man. I'm curious to hear what it is you have to say."

Jean-Paul averted his gaze toward Jenna at the same moment she looked at him. What he saw in her eyes could have been the reason he changed the subject. "I find it too hot to speak on the matter. When Mallaurie arrives I don't want the two of you cheating at cards."

Jenna continued to stare at Jean-Paul when Pierre looked down on her. Thankfully, the mention of cards had captured Bethanie's interest. She and Marie-Claude became absorbed with the subject as more guests arrived. One of those who entered was Nel. After greeting everyone, he made a cursory glance toward Pierre, then sat amongst the others.

Pierre had seen the look, but couldn't make sense of it or why Nel was sitting instead of trying to speak to him in private. If Nel was in the mansion, it meant Sarah should also be in the mansion. Neither Nel nor Sarah knew of the hiding place that Sarah should have been taking too the moment she arrived.

One of the upstairs bedrooms had a hidden door in its wall. It was positioned behind a bed and beside a large armoire. The armoire was too large for any single man to move it without causing damage to the armoire. This made it a perfect hiding place for the hidden compartment behind it. Six feet wide and eight feet long, it possessed a narrow staircase that led up to the attic. The staircase served as an extra means of escape, as well as ventilation. Once Pierre got Sarah safely inside it she would have to hide there as long as it took for him to make arrangements to send her wherever it was she wanted to go.

Hopefully, William would continue on to Biloxi without her and lay claim on the inheritance that had suddenly changed his circumstances. If he didn't, and if there was a search, then things will get a little more difficult. Because the compartment was trapped between the walls of two rooms, it stayed hot. The window from the attic filtered light through it at all hours making it hard to escape the sun. Pierre's great-great-grandfather had the compartment built as a hiding place for his children and wife to hide in if the city was attacked by Indians. His great-great-grandfather must have planned the compartment as only a temporary solution. Pierre used it to hide runaways. With his mansion so close to the port, it was easier to sneak the slaves out during the night and transport them to one of the waiting ships.

Nel continued to sit and talk to those around him as if he hadn't carried a message to Sarah or helped her get away from her fiancé. After only a few minutes had passed, Pierre became more uncomfortable. The need to see if Sarah was there became urgent.

When he started to rise, Nel smiled at him.

"Since you're up, monsieur. You might as well fix me a drink. Forget the heat. I'll take brandy or bourbon or rum."

Pierre tried to calm when he realized Nel was trying to keep him in the *salle*. Something had gone wrong. This was certain. But he trusted Nel as much as Julien did.

Going to the buffet, he pulled forward a decanter. The other men in the room complained of thirst and needing something more than lemonade. Pierre was pouring several glasses when voices could be heard in the hall.

Jenna rose to her feet when she recognized one of those voices.

Her father and William burst into the room with the police one step behind them.

"Papa?" She said, her eyes showing her concern. "I thought you were leaving this afternoon. Why are you here?"

Emile looked away from her and stared at Pierre. Pierre turned and faced his father-in-law with a glass in each hand. The look of surprise on his face was genuine. He wanted to know what had happened, and if this information had to come from Emile so be it.

Emile saw the look, arched his brows, then narrowed his eyes as he stared at Jenna again. "You helped her, didn't you? Someone had to help her. One minute she was there. The next she was gone!"

"Are you talking about Sarah?" Jenna asked.

William pushed further into the room. The rage inside him made his face darken with a red hue. The women in the room saw this and pressed a hand against their chests. They then began to stare at everyone else in the room unaware of what was going on, but sensing that if the situation wasn't calmed someone may get hurt. In New Orléans similar situations had ended with someone drawing a pistol and firing it.

"You're here!" William accused, staring at Jenna. One of his hands moved slightly. His face became tense, the skin unnaturally tight. Pierre tossed the glasses onto the buffet and hurried across the room.

"You being in the city today of all days is proof enough for me!" William managed to get out. He had taken another step toward Jenna when Pierre pushed the heavyset man hard into the hall.

"You control yourself inside my home, or you'll be sorry," he warned.

The police was quick to intervene.

William had lost his balance and had fallen on his back. Looking up at the servants who stared at him as if he was a stain on the floor they had the urge to mop away made him angrier. Pulling himself to his feet, he adjusted his waistcoat and coat, then tried to calm.

"Monsieur Jennings, is the woman not here?" One of the policemen asked. From the tone of the constable's voice, it became clear to them all that the police had expected to find Sarah there.

Pierre was unsure how to answer. Was Sarah there? Had she come and tried to find somewhere to hide on her own? If so she would soon be discovered. Other than the hidden compartment there was no place that anyone could hide without being seen within seconds of walking into a room.

"Of course she's not here, Constable," Jenna answered. "Feel free to look around if you'd like. We only arrived this morning. No one has come except for those you see in this room with us now."

"She wanted to see you before leaving the city," William accused. "We found her on your plantation that very same evening. It was then you planned this. I'm certain of it. You did it to make a fool of me because you heard about my newfound wealth and correctly assumed that I'm no longer willing to buy Green Lea."

Jenna's eyes hardened. In her hand was the glass of lemonade. Pierre threw up his arm, but it was too late. The lemonade was tossed into William's face. Jenna waited patiently for Pierre to lower his arm, and then she threw the glass at William's chest like someone bringing a broom down on a scurrying rat.

Pierre grabbed William's hand before it could strike, and with his free hand reached for William's throat. The steps he took were rushed. The others watched as Pierre's muscles rippled, and the way William's feet shuffled backwards in a quick gait, and kept shuffling all the way to one of the open doors. William was then rushed through the courtyard and thrust out onto the street through the porte cochère. The way he fell caused him to tumble over backward feet first. Pedestrians and carriages stopped to look at him.

"You despicable old man! You're close to sixty years of age. She's twenty-one. I should think whether she had help or not she would have run away from you."

Nel stood beside Pierre, his hand next to the pocket in Pierre's coat ready to grip the pistol in it and put an iron ball in William if he even thought about retaliating.

One of the policemen had come out with them to maintain order.

Inside, the other constable politely asked Jenna many questions. Jenna spun away from the man and faced her friends. "You are all here and can all stand as witnesses. Let's all of us search this entire house to prove to the police that Sarah is not here."

Nel intentional bumped against Pierre's arm when the two of them entered the room just as Jenna made the suggestion. The two men made eye contact, briefly.

"On an afternoon such as this, us men will need to take a glass of brandy with us while we search," Nel said, hoping to put Pierre at ease.

From there it became a game.

Emile also held a glass. It trembled in his hands as he walked with the group from room to room. If Sarah couldn't be found his life was ruined. William had offered Emile the smaller of the two plantations. An opportunity like this would never come again.

One of the police asked Pierre if it was okay for William to also be involved in the search, as William seeing for himself that Sarah wasn't inside the home was the only way to put the accusations to rest. Pierre agreed. He and Nel stood at the back of the group, neither of them doing any actual searching. Instead, Nel spoke about his recent visit to Havana and the many changes that were happening in Cuba. From the attic to the outside kitchen, slave quarters, the yard and carriage house the group searched.

When they reached the porte cochère and still hadn't found Sarah, William burst into tears. "I'm not leaving this city until I find her. Sarah's still here. I know she is, as well as I know Madame Jennings had something to do with this."

As he walked away, Emile hurried after him still holding the empty glass he had in his hand.

Word spread quickly along the streets that a young woman of twenty-one had run away to avoid marrying a man fifty-six years of age. When it was discovered that the loathsome Américain William Murray was this man, and he was staying at a local home with intentions of staying in the city until his young fiancé was found, the citizens, mostly women and children, who opposed the marriage performed a *chiavari*. Usually, a *chiavari* took place after a widower remarried. Every instrument that made noise of any kind was blown, beat on or banged together. After three days of the constant racket, and to spare the family that had shown him hospitality, William left New Orleans alone.

During those three days the Jennings mansion received more visitors than it had in some time, all of them ready to voice their opinions regarding the marriage of one of their own to the likes of Monsieur Murray. Plenty of food was served, and liquor. There was dancing, and much laughter, of which Jenna smiled but stayed quiet. On the afternoon that she and Pierre had chosen to return to their plantation in the country, citizens stood on their balconies tossing flowers down on the carriage as it rolled down the street.

Pierre stared out the window wondering how long it would take William to return because return he would. The family that had shown him hospitality had also come to the mansion. For hours they spoke of seeing no one more heartbroken or determined, and how the loss of Sarah had affected William greatly.

Pierre stared down when he realized he was being watched. For an entire week the two of them had become more distant than ever. The visitors in the mansion made it easier for the two of them to avoid one another. On several occasions when the mansion had been filled with guests single women and young widowers made their intentions of a possible affair clear to him. The woman he did choose to bear him an heir out of wedlock would have to accept all of his children. There was one such woman that wanted him to return to the city soon so the two of them could spend time alone together.

"I'm no fool," Jenna said, staring up at him. "Christia showed much interest in you. I heard what she told you – for you to return in a fortnight."

She averted her gaze out of the window on her side of the seat. The two of them were inside the carriage alone. Gorée sat up front with the driver taking in the air and all of the sights around her. "If I even suspect you're having an affair with her, I will petition for a divorce. I will do all I can to hurt you like I never have before. Christia is my friend…"

"She is not your friend," he interrupted. "You have no true friends because you turn on all of them for even the smallest infraction or whenever you feel an injustice has been done."

She refused to look at him. "Don't think for a moment that my petition will not be granted. I do have friends – friends who will willingly write letters to support my petition."

"Is Jean-Paul one of those friends, Jenna? I found that conversation between him and Marie-Clause interesting. Why would Marie-Claude say such a thing unless she had been driven? It looked to me that she was offering support to a friend."

"I don't know what you're talking about?"

"You lying bitch of a woman. I spoke to Jean-Paul. He told me everything, how you lied and told him that I have beaten you senseless for years, and how I have physically thrown you across rooms. Why would you tell that lie, Jenna? He's told others! You're not even five feet tall. I'm seven and a half feet. People in the city believe I beat my wife. Now I know why I get strange looks. Now I know why people in the city refuse to do business with me. I'm the devil! But that lie has made me more. I will never love you again. By all means petition for a divorce. I'll also write letters to support your claims. In it I will detail my intention to have an affair with Christia, and if not her then with someone else. But it's time we end this farce. It's time we put this *spurious* marriage to rest."

"How dare you call me out of my name."

Pierre leaned toward her. "Think of it as my father speaking from the grave, because only a bitch of a woman could smile down on the dead body of the man who loved the daughter she refused to."

The hand she swung at him was caught and tossed back to her roughly.

"If I were you, I would tread carefully right now," he warned.

"Don't think for a moment you will send me to Riverside," Jenna said. "New Orléans is my home just as much as it is yours. Why should I have to leave this city because my husband has decided never to love me after something I did when I was a child? The only way I'll divorce you is if you gave me Ashleywood and all that's on it. Isn't it just as much my home as it is yours? If this is true, why have I felt from the very beginning as if I'm nothing more than a temporary visitor?"

"Guilt, madame, is your answer. You have enjoyed the luxury of its mansion more than my own family since our marriage. Désireé won't come near it because of you. Julien and Marie-Marie rarely visit because of you. Don't ever again threaten me with Ashleywood. The very soil," Pierre spat, "and the small particles of water that run through that soil bleed with Jennings blood. Not of one generation, but several. Every blade of grass has the chemistry of Jennings hair inside it. Every activity that occurs on it pulse in tune with the Jennings' heartbeat. If you don't petition the church then I will. Don't let your pride get in the way of what I am willing to offer as a settlement."

"Offer?" She asked, sitting up suddenly and facing him. "What about my many offers, Pierre? How many times have I humiliated myself by giving you hints..." Her hands began to move and gesture intensely with each word she spoke. "...playing this silly game with you knowing you would never give in? How many times have I cried at night hoping for one chance to prove that my love for you is real? I have never met a crueler man than you. But I fought back. Yes. I did. Other women wouldn't have. They would have cowered and accepted whatever their husbands did to them. The reason you hate me is because I fought back. I did what I had to do. How can you blame me for that?"

"You told Chadwick about the runaways! You told him the entire operation step by step! During these past years not only could I have been arrested and tried, but other good people could have also, others who didn't deserve your betrayal."

"You left me no choice! You asked to marry *me*. Our marriage was not prearranged. I'm sorry I didn't tell you that I was carrying another man's child..."

"You should have waited! Why didn't you?"

She let out a loud abrupt sigh then turned from him, suddenly, and gazed out the window. "That is a question you should have asked on our wedding night. Not once in sixteen years have you ever given me a chance to explain. You are not allowed to ask that question now. This war we have waged has always been unfair. It wasn't just me against you. It was me against your entire family and your father's whore. You married me, and because you married me it is your responsibility to take care of my financial needs. I will not go to Riverside with Abigail to fend for myself."

"Who said anything about Abigail? She hates you as much as I do. She'd run like Sarah did to get away from you. You telling Chadwick something I told you in confidence severed my heart into tiny little pieces. Before I learned of that betrayal I thought the two of us had a chance. It has taken me years to put my heart back together again. I have waited sixteen years to hear you say you were sorry..."

"Blame me! It's all you have ever done, Pierre!"

"This ends now. I had affairs, but you did too. In my house! In the bed my money purchased! On the land my family own! You have always had access to any and all the money you needed. I have never come to you once and accused you of anything."

"And I haven't suffered from your hands?" She argued. "Your *bâtard* sleeps under the same roof as me."

"As does yours, madame! As does yours. And there is where your fault lies. Every decision I make you turn it around to convince yourself it was done to hurt you, to anger you. Désireé was born *before* we were married. I sent *my* daughter out of her home just so you will be comfortable when you arrived after the wedding. I will have done the same for Gorée had her health allowed me."

Truth shone in his eyes. She turned away from it unable to look at him.

"Someone told me when I was younger to find good in every bad thing that ever happens to me," Pierre continued. "You telling Chadwick was a blessing. I didn't see that at first. I started leaving money for Chadwick all over the city under your name. I did this on the days the ships harboring runaways left the port, and on that ship was a manifesto with your name on it. Chadwick knew it was me leaving the money. I told him it was me. And pick that money up he did like I knew he would. I have spent the past nine years solidifying my name in this city. If you went to the police now with any information, I shall tell them I knew nothing of it. I shall hint that maybe my dear wife harbored runaways and sold them for money to give to her fat lover. Everyone will believe it. Everyone has known of your affair for years."

Tears fell from her eyes.

"You're worst than the devil," she said.

"I've done what I had to. Too many people rely on me for their financial stability and protection. I couldn't jeopardize you taking that away out of vengeance. I see you crying, chérie, and I'm asking myself are those tears of pain or from the anger you feel now that you know I have outwitted your attempts to gain control of me."

The way she glared at him made Pierre think of firewood crackling in a fire.

"If you believe that then you're a fool."

"Believe me. I am no fool. I'm sure your mind is scheming even now trying to figure out how to hurt me next. I only told you what I've done to stop you from listing it in your petition. You are the fool, Jenna, because it has never occurred to you that had you been someone likeable our marriage could have become a real marriage a long time ago."

Staring long into his eyes was unavoidable. On the night of their wedding the words he had spoken had seemed final. Even now she could see him standing inside the boudoir that had been prepared for them that evening. Him in fine apparel. Her in her nightgown. Flowers had been arranged around the room. Newly married Creole couples were expected to spend their first five days inside the bedroom. It was during those days she had wanted to explain.

The hurt she saw in his eyes that night had frightened her. And then he spoke those words.

*I will never love anyone I cannot trust. I feel more than deceived. I am devastatingly crushed. I thought you and I would have a beautiful life together. You can still have that beautiful life, but without me. To not bring you shame, I won't say anything. You and the child can stay here, but I will never treat you as my wife or your child as my own.*

And then he walked out of the room. The next morning at breakfast she could tell he told his father and his father's whore. Both hardly looked at her, and when they did it was with looks of disgusts. It could have been her imagination but it seemed to her that even the servants had treated her differently. Everyone's behavior that day had been unfair.

It was that morning she decided to hate them all.

Now she could see in his eyes that an apology could have ended it all. How could she have known this when every man she had ever known had done nothing but hurt her? Including her father, forcing her to keep silent because he wanted to get his hands on the Jennings' wealth. Including her grandfather who bounced her on his knee until he became aroused. If it had only happened once she would have gotten over it. But more and more it happened until she finally put a stop to it. Including Chadwick who hasn't once asked about Abigail. Each time he saw Abigail his face pulled into a sneer as he commented how unattractive she was. Chadwick who had saved all of the money she had ever given him and married a Creole woman named Pristine Kelly after Jenna told him she didn't want to see him again. The wealth he had accumulated enabled him to buy land and a build a house. The hard work he had put into the land had helped him lose weight. He and Pristine were now parents to three children and Chadwick proudly took those children everywhere.

Pierre was still staring down at her, his face placid, but his eyes intense. Dislike or disgust, she wasn't certain which was palpable inside them.

Like the night of their marriage she wanted to explain. Everything. But then he said something she could not abide.

"Why are you so evil, Jenna? Tell me," he pleaded. "There has to be a reason. You're not only evil to me, but you're evil to your father. I have my reasons for not helping the man, but he's your father and it disgusts me how you have allowed him to live. The decision he made for Sarah to marry William was of a desperate man. The man is strangling in debt. You have access to my money and your own, still you refused to help him. And you're not just evil to him. You're evil to the very servants who serve you, and you unnecessarily call them vile names. And most of all you're evil to your own daughter, so much so that I feel sorry for her."

*Yawwwww!*

The sound that came out of her mouth was loud and painful to listen to. As she screamed, Jenna heaved up on the cushion using both of her hands. Once on her feet had not her gown restricted her movements she would have jumped higher up the front of him. Using both of her fists, she targeted his face wanting to leave bruises on it. Using her feet and knees, she hoped to hurt him where it would hurt most. How dare he blame her for the life Abigail had when it was his fault.

Pierre's refusal to fight back excited her. With all the strength she could muster she pounded her fists against him until she was tired. Sliding down the front of him she used both fists hammering them against the crotch of his trousers.

Pierre did not feel the carriage slow and pull over. The dreams he had of killing her returned, suddenly. Grabbing her slender neck with both hands, he squeezed it like a cook would an orange for its juice.

The carriage door pulled open.

Jenna's legs kicked wildly underneath her skirt as she felt herself being lifted higher. Her hands gripped his in an effort to pull them from her neck.

Pierre saw a pair of black hands and a small pair of yellow hands desperately pulling at Jenna to release her from his hold. Letting her go, she fell hard to the carriage floor. Gorée got on her knees beside her, tears falling from her eyes as she stared at Pierre over her shoulder.

The servant Patrice stood in the door unable to move. In his twenty-six years of life he had never seen his monsieur ever even hint at harming a woman.

Jenna rolled to one side coughing and panting.

Pierre closed his eyes and drew in a deep breath. Regret. Guilt. Both emotions were very strong. Nothing she said or did could be used as an excuse for his behavior.

Climbing out of the carriage he sucked at the air knowing it couldn't cleanse the way he felt.

"Patrice, take your madame back to the city. Send someone with a horse. I'll ride myself back home."

As soon as Gorée saw Pierre climb out of the carriage she climbed out after him. The brain she had couldn't tell her that she did this because he was her father. What it told her was that this man spoke her language and that he protected her from the people who looked at her funny and pushed at her with their hands to get her away from them. Grabbing the leg of his trousers, she held fast to him while staring in all directions to see if any of the bad people were near.

Patrice nodded, climbed back into the carriage and helped his madame onto the cushion. Jenna was inconsolable. Both of her hands were pressed tightly against her face. Tears fell rapidly underneath them. Climbing back into the driver's seat, Patrice swung the carriage back around and rode off.

Pierre lifted Gorée high in his arms.

She needed to see his face because it looked different to her and she couldn't understand why. Reaching for it, she turned it toward her and studied it a long time. When he gave her a small smile the world she was used to became normal again. She pressed her face against his shoulder and neck but repeatedly lifted it to see his face again.

This was the image Patrice saw when he returned some time later with an extra horse for his monsieur.

"Madame has gone mad, monsieur," he said on finally reaching Pierre. "I fear what will happen while you're away and she's there alone with us all."

Pierre climbed up on the horse. Patrice dismounted and lifted Gorée up to his monsieur.

Gorée had ridden on a horse with Pierre many of times. Once she was settled he stared down at Patrice. "Fetch Frances Achen. Tell him to reside in the mansion as long as she's there."

"Monsieur?" Patrice said.

"Speak, Patrice. Tell me what you think I should hear."

The servant lowered his head. "I heard madame say if it takes her last dying breath she's goin to make you suffer for what you done to her."

***

"Mon Dieu! I'm glad you didn't kill her or hurt her too badly." Alise spoke in a soft voice still disbelieving what she just heard. She tried to envision Jenna and Pierre coming to blows in the back of a carriage and stood to her feet. Too much had been happening lately: the police spending days on the property looking for runaways, the trouble it had taken to sneak Choco and the others off of Ashleywood without anyone other than those involved becoming aware they had been there, Emile having to return to Green Lea without a single picayune in his

133

pocket and only one slave left to see to the entire plantation, William forced to leave the city without Sarah, and Sarah arriving at the plantation a week ago on horseback frightened out of her mind.

"You need to lessen the load on your plate, Pierre. And I think you should start with Jenna."

Julien, Désireé and Pierre stared at her waiting for her to finish.

"Start with Jenna how?" Julien argued.

Each of them wanted to hear Alise's view on the subject.

"Make amends, Pierre."

"No!" Julien yelled. "I don't agree, Alise. Jenna is just as strong willed as he is. Has she not proven this? If the two of them lost control once it can happen again."

"It won't happen again," Pierre insisted.

"Pierre, Julien is right. You lost control and you may lose it again. What would have happened if you killed her? She's a small woman. It can happen. And if it does *everything* you and your father have worked for will be lost. Even if you left everything to Désireé or Julien, Abigail would be pressed by Jenna, Emile, and the city to contest your will. You own too much land that everyone wants their hands on. Land that is sitting idle and uncultivated. Who's to say the court will uphold the will? Thinking they will is the same as taking a chance. I don't trust her. She knows too much. You have to make this right."

"Send her to Riverside!" Julien demanded. "Let her petition for a divorce. How many others had and were denied? A separation will be granted and payment of some kind. Agree to it and be done with it. Be done with her once and for all, Pierre."

The conversation became solely between Alise and Julien, neither willing to back down. Alise brought it to a sudden end.

"Jenna has never mentioned divorce in the past, Julien. For her to do so now may mean she learned something in the city, something she could use in her favor if she does petition for a divorce. How well do any of us in this room truly know this woman? Some believe she loves Pierre, and how she pines for him. I don't know if this is true, but I sometimes believe it is. I will tell you what I know. She's talented enough to get what she wants."

Pierre stood to his feet and walked to the door. No one said anything and only watched, then gazed at one another when he continued out into the yard, climbed on his horse and rode away without saying a single word.

When he reached the mansion he saw that Abigail was waiting for him.

"Where's Maman? I thought she was returning with you."

"She's in the city. If you want you can go to her tomorrow."

For hours she had stood where she was rehearsing the sentence just right believing all along he would curse her with his eyes and walk away like he had so many times before. Hearing him answer was the last thing she had expected. Because she hadn't imagined he would she wasn't certain how to reply, especially when he continued to stand in front of her.

This was the most attention she had ever received from him since as long as she could remember. Hoping to keep it a little longer she took another step down the staircase then lowered her head. Lifting the hem of her gown, she turned to walk up the stairs. Her book was waiting for her inside her boudoir. She had been away from it long enough.

Pierre also found it hard to find words to speak. All he knew was things couldn't stay as they were. As a younger man he hadn't been kind to her. As the man he was now he knew it was possible for things to be different between them if Abigail was willing to try.

"I came in to change," he said as she continued up the stairs. "I need to see to something in the fields."

Abigail heard this as a dismissal. She stopped long enough to give a polite nod.

"Bonjour," she answered softly.

*I'm sorry.* The words were on the tip of his tongue pleading to get out.

"I haven't been a good father to you, Abby."

Again she stopped and stared down at him.

"If you can forgive that maybe we can have supper together."

Confusion rested heavily on her shoulders. The words she should have spoken refused to come out. Pierre Jennings never sat at his dining room table unless the mansion had guests. Meals were eaten inside his study and shared with those he loved, but never with her.

"It'll only be the two of us," he said. "If that's all right with you?"

*Take a step. Why am I standing here silent? Say something!*

It didn't matter that she had waited for this moment for many years. The moment was too unfamiliar to give a reaction. Instead, a voice in her mind told her to run from him and up the stairs.

She stiffened when he began making his way up the staircase toward her. She drew in a deep breath as tears filled her eyes. Abigail stared up at him when his arms circled her waist and pulled her close against him in a hug. The tears were swift, although she tried hard to keep them in.

"I'm so sorry, Abby," he whispered. "I have no excuse to give. I hope someday you can forgive me. If you give me the chance I promise to try to make things right between us."

She pulled away from him because she was used to dealing with her emotions alone. Again he pulled her to him, except this time he lifted her in his arms so she could peer into his eyes. Fearful of looking directly into them she rested her face against his chest. More tears fell when she reminded herself that she had wanted him to do just this for so long.

Pierre sat on the stairs holding her close. The smell of his cologne was pleasant. The tightness of his arms made her realize how small she was and how large and strong he was.

"You are a big man," she said. The sound of his small laugh made her smile. More tears fell when she found the courage to peer up at him. "Why do you hate me, Papa?" She bit her lip and quivered in anguish because she was frightened of the answer he would give.

"I don't hate you, petite. And I don't want to be the devil anymore. I just want to be a man, and a father to *all* of my children."

She gave what she believed was a nod, then hated herself for acting like an invalid child on the day someone other than a servant had finally reached out to her.

It was as if he had read her mind.

"Don't hate yourself, petite. It was never your fault."

This time she couldn't look at him. Rejection from both of her parents had been a constant friend. She couldn't see this friend leaving any time soon, especially right then and there.

"Do you love me?" Her words came out strangled.

"I have for a very long time." He lowered so the two of them were eye to eye. "And I would love to have supper with you."

It was the tears falling from his eyes that ruptured the dam inside her. Shaking terribly, she took a risk by leaning her head toward him. The hug he gave this time was tighter.

"It was good to hear you call me papa again."

She was surprised by the laughter that came out of her. Embarrassed by her tears, she wiped them away with her fingers.

"Can I trust you to handle our supper tonight?"

She gave a definite nod this time.

"I need to go up now. The sooner I return from the fields the more time we'll have to spend together this evening."

She watched as he walked up the stairs and turned toward his bedroom. Gripping the balustrade, she rose to her feet and hurried down the stairs. Unable to control the way she felt, a large smile spread across her face as she ran to the outside kitchen. Reaching its door, she braced the jamb with both hands. Finding Cook with her eyes, she spoke loudly. "My papa is having supper with me this evening. Can you make something special?"

## Chapter Sixteen
# Regret's Cousin is Freedom

*[The crow may be caged, but its thoughts are in the cornfield. – Creole Proverb]*

Pierre climbed down from his horse and tethered it to a tree. The differences in the cabin were subtle but noticeable. For one smoke rose from its chimney. Its door was open. From where he stood he could see a few pieces of furniture inside it.

He stood in the door and peered in only to see that Sarah wasn't there. Alise had seen Sarah arriving on the plantation on the day she had evaded William in the city. True to form, Alise had provided Sarah with the comforts any woman could need, especially after Sarah had refused to sleep anywhere but here.

Servants had carried and set up a rather good sized bed against the far wall. The mattress looked poorly. More moss needed to be added to it to make it sit higher. Pierre noticed the coverlet that decorated it. It was one he recognized from Alise's cottage. A screen was folded and leaned against the wall because leaving it open took up too much space. A rug sat on a now clean floor. A table with two chairs sat in the opposite corner. Cookware, utensils, and toiletries were neatly arranged on top of a small low boy dresser. Pierre looked away from the half hidden chamber pot. At the foot of the bed was a padded stool that could also be used to sit on.

A small fire burned in the hearth. Beside it were gourds of water and dry goods used for cooking, along with herbs. Pierre lifted the bloody cloth that covered a small plate. Underneath were fine cuts of mutton.

He turned when he heard a noise behind him. Sarah crossed the yard closer to the door. Not a single stitch of clothing covered her body. Her head was bent forward as she used a towel to dry her hair. Pierre quickly turned away. "I'm here, Sarah," he said after facing the hearth.

The noise she made was of someone startled.

"If you let me know when you're in the corner I will leave."

Sarah's voice answered him on the far side of the room. Noises were made as objects were pushed around, and then the screen unfolded. Still he waited.

Close to him a drawer was pulled open, and then her feet made a mad dash behind the screen.

"I'm sorry," she said. "I'm used to being alone here. I didn't know you returned. If you can wait outside until I'm decent? But please don't go. I would like to talk to you if it's all right?"

Later after she was dressed and while she cooked he told her most of what happened in the city. He left out the part of tossing William out into the street, but he did mention William appearing as if he was going to attack Jenna.

Sarah finally sat in the chair opposite him. "I'm sorry that my father wasn't allowed to go with him, but I couldn't do it." Her eyes pleaded with him to understand. "That man is vile. The things he would say to me." She shook her head. "I wouldn't have gone to Biloxi as his future bride. He saw me as a possession, a woman given to him to fulfill a debt owed. I know what my life would have been like if I had married him. My father, he didn't want to see that. All he wanted to see was the plantation that was soon to be his to govern."

"He's going to come back, Sarah. What are your plans? I can send you wherever you want to go. I'm certain that going to Biloxi to live with your tante isn't a good decision."

She rose and went back to the hearth to see to the food she was cooking. "Neither Jenna nor my father ever sent enough money during the years I lived with Tante Marianne. The day that my father sent her a letter demanding she send me back to the city because I was to be married..." She hesitated. "He didn't even give her the money for travel expenses. You should have seen her face. Marriage meant stability in her eyes. It didn't matter to her that without me being there she would no longer be able to see to her garden or have help taking what she grew to the city to sell. All of the money she had was used to purchase my ticket. Before I left her house was rented to a family new to the city. Renting a room from a friend she knew was all she could afford afterward. I have no reason to return there even if William suddenly died. I would only become a burden to her."

"I can give you money for you and her. She can travel with you."

"She won't travel with my father. The two of them had a falling out some years ago. I can't leave my father behind, Pierre. Although I feel this way, I know if you gave me any money he would use it to buy tickets to Biloxi to take me to William."

"You can't stay in this cabin, Sarah. Not even my hogs live like this."

She removed the pot from the fire and rested it on the brick to cool. "I was quite taken aback by the servants I've met here so far." She looked over her shoulder at him. "They promised not to tell anyone." She pointed to the mutton. "One of them brought me this." She stood, lifted the plate, and slowly pushed the meaty pieces into the boiling pot. "The first day I came I left the cabin long enough to look for food. I was only so deep between the trees when I ran into a slave carrying buckets of water over his shoulders. I learned from him that Alise had sent him there. The buckets were left inside. When I returned chopped wood, a basket of food and three fish still hanging from their hooks were waiting for me."

The contents of the pot were stirred, and then a lid placed tightly over it.

She sat in the chair. "I know I can't stay here. I wish I could. This past week I have had more peace than I can ever remember having. But my father needs me. I hear that Imogen is still with him. They have little food, but enough to last them a few weeks. I need to go back. I just can't do it right now. Please don't make me. All I need is a little more time if that's all right with you."

"Of course."

Pierre stood to his feet. "I'll send food over to Green Lea. I do have bad news for you, Sarah. When I was in the city I learned that William had all of your father's debts sent to him in Biloxi to be paid in full..."

She jumped to her feet and ran out of the cabin.

Pierre stayed where he was staring at the pot on the fire. He hadn't discovered about the debts until after William had left the city.

He heard his horse whinny and jumped to his feet.

The horse was too tall for Sarah to mount without a stool or someone assisting her. One of her boots, of which Pierre could see clearly was beyond in poor shape, kept fiercely inside the stirrup. Annabelle, a stallion of Arabian and Andalusian mix, continued to take a step forward preventing Sarah from getting a hold of her the way she needed. Pierre pressed his hands to his waist and marveled at the sight he was looking at.

The only way he could make sense of it was Sarah had tried to climb up Annabelle by yanking on the saddle blanket after getting one of her boots stuck in the stirrup. Sarah's entire body was upside down. Her long, dark still wet hair swept at the dirt beneath Annabelle's flank. Her free hand reached for Annabelle's leg while the other refused to let go of the blanket. Her free leg made daring, eager attempts of reaching the saddle. Only the tip of her toe touched it. All of this being done blindly. Gravity had pulled the skirt of her gown, petticoat and chemise over Sarah's face. The *pantalettes* she wore were of the typical fashion, two separate pairs of hoses that fastened at the waist with lace, of which the middle was left open for hygiene reasons.

Annabelle was becoming restless.

Sarah tugged viciously at Pierre's trousers when he neared, threatening to pull them down the waist. He could feel one of the buttons strain.

"I'm stuck!"

The boots she wore were similar to the kind slaves wore. Made of leather, it reached just above the ankle and had a wide width to fit different forms of feet. The boot had turned sideways. A tear had been made in the leather. The tear and the knot of her lace trapped the side piece of the stirrup inside them.

Pierre didn't reach for Sarah. He reached for Annabelle. Usually a temperamental stallion, he could see her patience waning at being tugged and kicked at. If she wasn't calmed soon Annabelle would run in an attempt to rid herself of Sarah. He stroked her mane and allowed Annabelle to muzzle his hand.

"Hold on, Sarah. You're making Annabelle more than anxious."

"I don't want to fall," she pleaded, her free leg now kicking at him to draw him closer and wrap around him.

Pierre held his hand in front of Annabelle and grabbed Sarah's leg with the other after her last attempt to reach him had aimed at his inner thigh. Annabelle felt the jerk and turned her head. Now that he was closer, Pierre could see that Sarah couldn't straighten without breaking or dislocating a bone or two in her leg.

"I have you, Sarah. Release the blanket and try to stay calm. We can't make Annabelle run. You'll get hurt if she does."

Sarah let go of the blanket.

"My foot," she bellowed.

Pierre stroked Annabelle's neck just below her mane until she faced forward and her nose dropped slightly. "I'm going to hold you up then turn you so you can get your foot loose."

"Okay," she said.

Covering her middle with some of the cloth so she wasn't exposed, he then lifted her leg and leaned forward. Sarah gave a soft groan. The iron of the stirrup dug deeper. Pierre flipped her further away from him in an attempt to get the iron free. When her boot finally slipped away, Sarah's hands instinctively reached in front of her to cushion her fall if he suddenly let go. There was no way to stand her upright without reaching for her bodice. When his hand cupped her breast he lifted her higher and grabbed a fistful of her hair. Once this was done he flipped her quickly. Sarah nearly stumbled when her boots found purchase on the ground.

Pierre tried not to smile, but it showed anyway as his hands reached for her waist and tugged her gently toward him. Sarah's entire face had turned red. The areas of her cheeks reddened even more as she stared at him with wide eyes and thought about how she must have looked dangling from a horse, and the way he had to tug her hair to get her on her feet.

This expression stayed on her face as she turned from him swiftly and returned to the cabin. Pierre waited until she was inside then leaned against Annabelle and let loose the laughter inside him. It was muffled by the blanket and saddle.

He stood upright, gave a small shake of his head and fixed his face as he went into the cabin behind her.

Sarah crouched in front of the fire. The lid from the pot had been removed. A wooden spoon stirred its contents.

Pierre squatted behind her close so she could feel his body snug against hers. The spoon was taken from her hand, the lid reached for and placed again over the pot. "I guess now would be inappropriate to tell you how beautiful you are?"

He smiled when her chin lowered, but he knew she was smiling too. Since their first meeting he had wanted to see a sign – any sign that would tell him that she had feelings for him, too. That moment finally came outside. The embarrassment she felt hadn't been because she had gotten stuck on a horse. It was because someone she liked had seen her in an embarrassing predicament.

His arms folded tighter around her. His face nestled close to her hair and neck. "Why are you hiding it from me? I would have let you leave without ever knowing."

The fact that she hadn't pulled from him and how one of her hands cupped gently against his was further proof of her feelings.

She looked up at him. "Jenna."

Pierre heard this and held her gaze before giving a single nod.

"I'm not going to Biloxi. I won't. Can I ask you something?" She asked when her back was to him again.

"Sarah, you can ask me for anything and I'll give it to you."

Her head turned toward her shoulder and closer to his arm.

"I wish you weren't married to my sister," she whispered.

Pierre lowered and kissed her hair. "Whether I'm married to your sister or not – whether she petitions for a divorce or not, I don't care, Sarah."

"Don't say that."

"I wouldn't if I didn't think you needed to know."

She peered up at him. "I'm always asking for something knowing I can never repay you for any of it. But I need your help."

"What is it?"

"Can you help me get Imogen? Once she's here I can write Tante Marianne. She'll help me. She always does. Maybe she has a male friend who can help me leave the city and get away."

"You still want to do that? Leave the city?"

"I can't stay, Pierre, especially not now."

He could see this wasn't true. It showed in her eyes. It showed in the movement of her lips and so many, many other ways. If he had returned and said she could stay in the cabin he knew she would have hugged him in gratitude, as well as would have become happier than she had ever been.

"When you were pulled away from me at Nowicki's it felt as if I lost something of considerable value," he said. "I wish you weren't my sister-in-law, but I cannot help the way I feel about you. If you asked me for a hundred-thousand dollars and my chateau in the Loire, I would gladly give them to you if I knew it meant you would have a happy life."

He helped her up and walked her to one of the chairs. Once she was seated, he turned and left.

***

Abigail leaned on the rear balustrade searching the trees for any sign of him. When she finally saw his massive from riding on his horse it became hard to contain herself. Running out to him would be a childish thing to do. She wanted him to see how well mannered she was, and for him to be proud of her when he noticed.

Pierre handed the horse over to a servant when he reached the house. He saw that Abigail had changed her clothing and had rearranged her hair. Fiery tendrils had pulled away from her bun and strayed wildly away from her face.

"You look radiant," he said. It was true. Life seemed to glow from her. The smile she wore made him smile; it also lifted his spirits.

Supper was served in the formal dining room. Pierre noticed the extra dishes and attributed them to Abigail.

"You will make someone a fine wife," he said. "All of this in just a few hours? Quite impressive."

"I measured the flour for the cake. I hope you like it."

"I shall eat every drop."

She giggled behind her napkin then lowered it.

"If you keep being so formal I will feel the need to display better manners. If I can remember them. It has been too long. Please relax, petite."

She smiled and nodded at him. "I'll be sixteen in a few weeks. I can't wait to sit at the table with you and Maman when guests visit. I have longed for the day."

"Have you thought about your coming out?"

The smile pulled inward until she held her mouth tightly and primly.

"Maman has pushed and pushed. The thought of marrying someone I shall never like displeases me."

"Attend a few cotillions in the city. While there make a list of the men you believe may please you then give me the list. I shall make certain that these gentlemen attend your coming out."

"You will do that for me?"

"Of course. I wouldn't want anyone to have a marriage similar..." He stopped speaking and looked at her.

Abigail seemed to be waiting for him to finish.

"A marriage will either make you happy or very sad, Abigail. I would hate for you to leave this house only to become a part of one equally or more tense than ours have been. Be happy, Abigail. You deserve it more than anyone else."

She jumped from her chair and threw her arms around him. Pierre patted her arm and kissed her hair.

Abigail sat again. An assortment of food sat in front of her, but she had no desire to eat.

"If you do decide to go to the city," he said, "you will learn that your mother and I... had a disagreement. If your mother tells you all that happened and you decide to hate me afterwards still give me the list. And come to me whenever you need to."

"I will, Papa."

Abigail lifted her fork for want of something to do. It was almost as if she couldn't keep silent. Sitting with him alone at the dining room table made her realize what the word wonderful truly meant. She felt that way now. Wonderful. The more she talked the more she noticed how confident she was becoming in telling him whatever came to her mind. When the subjects of books came up and she learned he had read one of her favorites, she felt at that moment what other daughters may have felt the moment they fell in love with their fathers.

After the meal the two of them sat on the rear galerie and talked for hours. She asked him many questions. Sometimes while he answered she barely heard his answer because she had been too busy trying to remember all of the questions she ever had for him. Once the questions ran out and still she wanted to sit with him, and because he also seemed to be enjoying himself, she began to ramble.

"Tell me something funny that happened to you when you were a child," she blurted.

"Oh, that one is simple, but perhaps inappropriate."

"Oh, do please tell. I promise not to tell anyone ever, including Maman."

Pierre gave a mischievous smile. "All right."

She sat closer to him and got comfortable.

"I was trying to impress one of the mansion's guests. Myself and some other boys my age had decided to walk along the levee. Your Oncle Julien was only four at the time. The other boys bade me not to take him with us. I didn't listen. I felt leaving Julien behind was the same as telling him I didn't love him." Pierre laughed suddenly from the memory. "So imagine us walking along the levee with sticks, a group of young rambunctious boys. The closer we got to the mansion and to the young women sitting on the galerie some of the older boys started to jump and flip. When I saw the young girl I was trying to impress I wanted to jump and flip for her."

Abigail's face fell into her hands as she laughed and couldn't stop.

Pierre rubbed at his eye and realized he had tears.

"Well, go on," she pressed.

"I was tall at twelve years old. I needed to get a running jump. I forgot all about your Oncle Julien and that he was even there. So the young girl could see me clearly I took several steps backwards. This way by the time I did the flip it would be at the precise moment. I started running forward and just when I went to throw my body forward your Oncle Julien runs out of the crowd of boys yelling, 'Brother! Brother!' I did do a flip, but not in front of the young girl. To avoid crashing into your oncle I veered to my right, and right over the levee, my body flipping all the way down into the river."

Abigail leaned against him as she lost herself to laughter. When both of them looked up Riley stood at one of the doors just inside the mansion waiting for them to finish before stepping forward.

"Pardon, monsieur. A messenger has just arrived from the city. Madame has sent for Mademoiselle Abigail to go there posthaste."

Abigail narrowed her eyes on Riley hating him for interrupting.

"I don't want to go," she said as soon as Riley walked away.

Pierre rested his hand on hers. "She's going to make you go."

She sat back on the chair. "She doesn't want me to go there because she wants me there. If she's upset with you then all of her friends will visit her. Whenever her friends are around she talks to them about me and you."

Sadness crept into her eyes as she stared at the kitchen and the servants walking in and out of it. "She tells them how she can't figure out how she could have given birth to someone so unattractive and with so many freckles and how no amount of brushing can tame my hair."

Pierre opened his arm so she could rest against him. Abigail rested her head on his chest. For years she had watched him tug Désireé's and Gorée's hair. She felt ashamed that she wanted so badly for him to tug her hair. Just as she lifted a small tug was given to one of her curls.

Tears spilled from her eyes.

"Thank you for this evening, Papa. I shall never forget it."

"I'll be here when you get back."

Abigail shook her head. "She will never stand for that because hating you, she believes, is the only thing that she and I have in common. The real truth is I hate her. I hate her a lot."

She stood to go inside and pack. When she reached the door he called out to her.

"If you want to stay you can stay. Make sure you send her a message telling her so. If you do that she won't wait for you."

"I will," she said, smiled, then hurried inside.

# Chapter Seventeen
## Do or Die

*[Be sure that the candle is lit before you throw away the match. – Creole Proverb]*

While Abigail was upstairs reading her mother's message and preparing for the trip, Pierre tried to talk himself out of going to Sarah's cabin. Nothing could come from this and if it did he was digging himself deeper than he already was. And even while he knew this he mounted a horse in the stables and rode for the distant swamp.

The cabin was dark when he reached it. Not bothering to tether the mare, he went to the cabin and pushed opens its door. Sarah was not inside. The items he wouldn't missed if she took them were no longer in the cabin.

He mounted and rode away heading in the direction of Green Lea, hating himself for having told her the truth. He raced past the cottage. It sat just as dark. Knowing she couldn't be traveling without a light at this time of evening, this was what he looked for, a light of any kind.

It seemed he had traveled a good distance when he thought he saw something. Veering the horse toward it he rode upon a lone man sitting by a fire.

Pierre rode slowly up to him. "This is my land. I can't have you making fires between these woods. If you need lodging, travel southeast and close to the river. My home is there. What is your name?"

"Carlisle Morning, sir. Thank you kindly."

Pierre noticed the man's nag tethered to a tree and the squirrel the man had skinned to cook and eat. "I have fine stables and a good horse man. And plenty of food. You're welcome to stay until your horse is able to travel again. Where are you from?"

"Spanish Texas," Carlisle answered. "Sir, I can't say how thankful I am. If you have work, I'm willing to work for you as repayment for your kindness."

"There's no need. There comes a time in every man's life when he can use the assistance of another man's hand. Putting out your fire right away is all I ask."

Carlisle quickly lowered to the ground, throwing dirt on the flames until they could no longer be seen. He then stood and covered the small area with enough dirt to extinguish the fire entirely and give no chance of it igniting again.

"Southeast," Pierre reminded. "Listen for the sound of the river. When you're close to it, you can't miss my home."

"Thank you!" The man yelled behind him as he rode off.

Pierre started to despair, especially when he traveled a great distance and saw no one else. When he reached the first of the markers, he swung the horse around and rode in a different direction. Sarah couldn't have come this far already, not from the distance of the cabin by foot, especially if there had been an injury caused to her ankle.

There were several paths through the trees. Believing she had to have used one of them, he rode slowly since there was no sense in hurrying this time. Doing so would cause him to have to swing around again and waste time.

For some reason he felt it was better if he looked toward the trees on his left. At times Annabelle was slowed to a walk, and at times he altered his direction slightly. He was coming up onto the end of the path that led to the cottage when something caught the corner of his eye. When he looked in that direction he saw nothing.

Turning Annabelle in this direction, he decided to make sure that what he saw was truly nothing. Just when he thought he had wasted his time he saw something that looked odd at the base of a tree. As he got closer he saw that it was hair, and closer still that the hair was attached to a woman's body. The sight of small white hands rubbing a slightly swollen foot that a lantern was shining light on made him jump off of Annabelle before she fully stopped.

Pierre hurried to her elated he had decided to look even when it seemed nothing was there. He couldn't tell it was Sarah because of the way she sat, but it had to be. No other woman in their right mind would be in this area, especially alone.

Sarah had had her head down, her hands concentrating on the swelling that had gotten worse now that her boot and one of her hoses had been removed. Since her journey began she had heard horses between the trees, and each time she did she hid out of sight hoping the rider wasn't someone dangerous who would cause her harm when they discovered she was alone. Because she was sitting on the ground and was safely behind the last horse she heard, she screamed when suddenly her body was hoisted from the ground. It wasn't until she was high in the air and saw the color of the man's hair when she calmed.

Pierre held her in front of him so they looked each other in the eye.

"Stay." He placed her on the ground, then lowered to look into her eyes again. "Stay."

Tears moistened her eyes.

"Stay, Sarah."

Over and over he repeated the word and held her gaze or some part of her, his voice pleading, his tone painfully beseeching her to do more than what his solitary word implied.

"Please," he finally said when she looked into his eyes again.

"Pierre, I have been in love with you since I saw you walk into your *salle* on Christmas morning when I was five years old. I believed then like I believe now that I had never seen anyone more beautiful. I can't stay. Since Nowicki's all I do is think about you. I love when you're near. I feel different when you're close. But you're my sister's husband. If you weren't, I would stay."

Pierre lifted her again so they were eye to eye.

"Your sister and I are over. The marriage should have ended on its first night."

"Pierre, we can give many excuses…"

"Let me explain."

Sarah found herself still being held in his arms when with one swoop of his arm he grabbed the lantern and left everything else behind.

Only after she sat with him on the saddle and Annabelle walked them through the trees did he begin to speak.

"There's a lady in the Vieux Carré. She reads people's futures with a deck of cards. I have never listened to this woman. Ever. Superstition runs rampant in the city. You know this."

"I do."

"My mother was a devout Catholic. She shunned voodoo and those who practiced it in the city or on local plantations and told me never to listen to any of it when I got older. My mother's words were heavily with me this particular day when the cards were read."

He peered into her eyes thankful that Sarah's eyes showed understanding. Those new to New Orleans didn't understand how heavily the roots and traditions of voodoo were planted inside of a Creole's soul. Sarah, being from the city, would know the importance of the religion in New Orleans whether a person practiced it or not. On too many occasions someone spoke about it, and how their experience either changed their lives for the better or made it worse. Many feared the religion, but others embraced it as a way of New Orleans' life.

"The reading didn't make sense. While she spoke her words were so strange it caused me to listen more intently. When I did start to listen, I don't know if she changed what she had been saying or I was beginning to see the things she said more clearly. She said, 'The decision you make after you find the forbidden lily will change the course of your life.'"

"The forbidden lily?"

"Oui. Listen. She said, 'You won't know who she is until you look for her and can't find her. And I knew it, Sarah. I knew it the moment I reached the cabin and saw how dark it was. And when I couldn't find you. I…" He held her gaze. "I don't want you to do anything you don't want to. I'll never tell you to do that. Let me help you. You can use it. I will never ask anything of you in return."

She continued to hold his gaze. "I went to see Madam Cosette as soon as I returned to the city. I heard people swear by her ability to read the cards."

"Oui. Please continue," Pierre pressed.

"I showed her the letter from my father demanding my return to the city to marry William. She didn't even look at it. Sitting in a chair beside her, she had me to draw a few cards. She laid the cards down, then looked at me for a long while. She said, 'Your future is rife with misery. Your answer is in the tallest tree.'"

Pierre smiled.

Sarah hated that she smiled as well. "She said, 'If you love the tree, your children will be the wealthiest children for many, many years into the future.'"

"Sarah…"

"Pierre, I don't care if my children are wealthy. I have never been wealthy and I have never seen being so as something of importance. You saw me inside your *salle* with Jenna. I thought a slice of cheese and a cup of café with three clips of sugar were the best flavors the world has to offer. It's why you sent me home with more of those treats in a basket."

"Let me give you much more than that."

She closed her eyes and pressed her fingertips gently against his mouth. As soon as Pierre felt her touch, his eyes closed on their own accord.

"My sister looked at me with such hatred. Staying here will cause me equal trouble or more than the trouble I have with William. Jenna will make sure of it if she ever discovers I'm here or how we feel about each other."

"I don't profess to know you well, Sarah, but the woman who was here those nights ago was ready to fight alligators to have what she wanted. Is that your only reason?"

She shook her head. "I'm scared, Pierre. Cosette told me the tree will love me *and* kill me."

He thought about Jenna and how just that afternoon he had wrapped his hands around her throat. "Kill you?"

"For two weeks. And then I will come alive again."

"Did she explain?"

"No. But she gave a warning."

"What?" He urged.

"Heed the tree, because the tree will save my life."

"Heed the tree, Sarah!" The words were repeated emphatically. His eyes searched hers more intently than anyone had ever looked into them.

"My children," he said. "*Your* children. They're one and the same. This is why you ran away. You realized this evening I was the tree."

"Jenna…"

Pierre held her tightly in his arms and rested his chin in her hair. "I have never thought about Cosette or the things she told me when I was nineteen years old. I had forgotten about them. It wasn't until I saw you were gone, and I was racing my horse looking for you when her words came back to me as if she had spoken them yesterday." He hesitated. "I'm not pushing you, Sarah. I'm no longer in any hurry to have children. I have three daughters, of which two will equally inherit a large sum of money. I sat with Abigail tonight and I felt like a new man. Something happened today after I choked your sister…"

"You choked my sister?"

Pierre saw a new look come into her eyes. Unable to tell if his confession had caused him to lose any chance between them, he averted his gaze. His eyes narrowed and his jaw tightened. "Oui. And still I say that after doing so I feel like a new man."

"Is she hurt?"

"Minutes after I choked her, she wreaked havoc on the servants."

Sarah looked away. Choking a woman was cruel. Pierre could have told her a stranger had gotten choked and she knew she would have felt sympathy for the victim. But the image of Jenna being strangled, hard, and her legs kicking, and her face twisted in fear, the same face that Sarah remembered sitting across from her on a chair as if it was her high throne and no one could reach it; laughter erupted out of her.

"I'm sorry," she said, pulling a kerchief from her sleeve and dabbing her eyes. "No, I'm not," she confessed. "I hate her. I have never done anything against her, yet she treats me like I'm her enemy. When I lived with Tante Marianne, if she asked for ten dollars Jenna would only send five. If Tante Marianne was late paying it back, Jenna would send nasty letters."

She looked up at him angry because of the memory. "Tante Marianne was Joséphine's sister. You would think that would make a difference to Jenna. How do you turn your back on your mother's sister? Those nasty letters would make Tante Marianne cry. There were nights we didn't have much to eat." She again looked away from thinking back on the days she spoke about. "One time when Tante Marianne and I were in the city, a man whispered in my ear that he would give me a dollar if I left with him for only a few minutes. I was angry. Not at him, but at myself for salivating over such a small amount. And then I came here and learned that my sister eats off of solid gold cutlery. I guess that makes me sound selfish. It's not my fault that our father had an affair. Tante Marianne never asked much for anything, but when she did she truly needed it. And Jenna never sent it because she knew it would hurt Tante Marianne and me. "

"I can offer no excuses for your sister about why Jenna refused to help. But things can be different for you, Sarah. I don't want you to think that striking women is something I do. Until today I never have. The regret I felt afterwards, I know I will never do it again. It freed me. I don't know how or why. But it did. I felt every need to war or a need to avenge slip right out of me. I knew this was true when I walked inside my home and saw Abigail and felt no anger of any kind."

"As much as I dislike my sister's behavior toward me," Sarah began. "You and I... It's wrong. It just is."

"It is," he readily agreed. "There's no doubt about that. But I have never lived my life for anyone. I don't care what anyone thinks about the decisions I make. If I did I would have treated Abigail better. She has suffered so much. I have a lot to amend between her and me. I should have listened to my father, but I was too angry – too bitter. I felt as if giving in to Abigail was giving in to Jenna. Whether you stay or not, the truth is I will be all right. But what about you? Are you going to be all right, Sarah? If I told your father that I will give him money to rebuild, I doubt he'll listen. Even if I give William the money he will pay out, he won't listen either. Your father doesn't want to work for what he has. In Biloxi an established plantation is waiting for him. Do you think he cares if his daughter is in a loveless, unhappy marriage because of it?"

She sat silently as Pierre rode the rest of the way to the cottage.

"I'm not taking you to the cabin," he explained. "It's safer here, and you'll be more comfortable as well. Jenna never comes to this part of the plantation. She has no interest in the fields or the work to be had in it. The mansion has become her life." He closed his eyes momentarily, then held her gaze intently. "If you do decide to leave, I'll give you whatever you need."

Inside he lit lamps until the rooms glowed with ample light. Afterwards he grabbed a bottle of wine and poured two glasses, then sat with her on a settee. Sarah tried not to study his face but found herself doing so on many occasions. Most of the time they sat was spent quietly, neither of them having much to say. After a few more glasses of wine, he showed her each room and where things were, and how he could change things to her liking if that's what she wanted. The last room he showed her was a larger bedroom with a large bed pushed against the wall.

"Everything you'll need is already here. Except food. I'll bring food myself." He then hurried to an armoire and opened it. "There is clothing in here... But not much. I can have Alise and Désireé go into town and purchase what you need." He gave the room one last look. "I'll be going. Please lock the door behind me."

When he reached the bedroom's door, she called out to him.

"Pierre?"

He swung and faced her.

Sarah walked to him. "I'm stubborn. I know if you walk out that door I'm going to talk myself into walking right out of here."

Pierre knew she was trying to say goodbye and had been trying to do that for some time. Her eyes searched his; her pensive face did little to stop him. Lifting her from the floor, she didn't have time to get used to her body being held upright before she was laid gently on the bed.

Before she could lie fully, Sarah became apprehensive. How was it she was still falling, yet Pierre's broad, tall, muscular frame crawled up her without touching or causing her harm? As large as he was, she was trapped underneath him. With his weight above her and supported by his hands, the pressing of his mouth to hers was similar to a man of thirst with every intention of draining water hidden in a gorge.

The softness and texture of his lips caused her eyes to spring open. The tip of his tongue all but pried her lips apart, then searched for hers. As soon as it touched the tip of hers, her hands swiftly reached for his hair. Running her fingers through it, she gripped it tightly and pressed her face closer to his wanting to taste his very soul. It was at that moment when her tongue was sucked deep into his mouth. The twining of them made her heart race. Heat flushed her body.

One of his hands slipped delicately inside the top of her bodice. His fingertip brushed against her nipple. As he kissed her deeper, his hands slid behind the nape of her neck and unloosened the pin that kept her gown in place. When it became slack, he sucked sensually at her lower lip. One hand again slipped inside her bodice, freeing the cloth and one of her breasts from her stays.

Her left leg curled around his waist as he lowered kissing the length of her neck, taking his time circling his tongue over the skin and suckling until she felt the very center of her thighs become wet with desire. Cupping her breast in the palm of his hand, the squeeze he gave to it puckered its roundness and made her nipple stick out like a sharp point. It was a man of thirst who took the entire top portion of her breast into his mouth and until only a very small part of her aureole could be seen outside his lips, then suckled in the same rhythm a strong hand would when milking a teet for milk. When he began to suck, Sarah drew in an intake of breath as if for the first time. Her hips rubbed against his muscular body hidden underneath his many layers of clothing.

She gave a moaning plea when his other hand searched underneath the many folds of her gown and fingered her wetness. Sarah pushed her hips against his finger needing it inside her to soothe an ache so delicious she thought she would die if it wasn't quickly appeased.

His hands pulled away. His mouth founds hers. Untwining her hands from around his neck as he gave her lower lip one last suck, he staggered off of the bed, breathing heavily as he walked backward to the door while trying to avoid bumping into the furniture against the wall. His eyes were on hers, the want of her so strong inside them Sarah believed he would return.

"Not tonight," he said in a thick voice. "You need to think about it some more. Because once you give it to me, you won't be able to get back what you almost gave just now."

She kept her eyes on the door after he walked away breathing as heavily as he had. Still she could feel his hands caressing her, and his tongue inside her mouth. The scent of his cologne was still in her nose.

Staring around the room, she realized something had happened in her mind. Her eyes darted to objects wondering if his hands had touched them.

"Sarah?"

She jumped from the bed then held her gown to her as she ran to his voice. Outside he had mounted his horse and had come close to the cottage. He didn't smile. Strong desire still shone in his eyes.

"Lock the doors," he said after dropping his eyes where her hands held her gown close against her, and then he rode off.

# Chapter Eighteen
# Coming Into Her Own

*[The frog knows more about the rain than the calendar. – Creole Proverb]*

Abigail stared at the man sitting inside her dining room swallowing large chunks of food, and licking his fingers, and gulping wine, and not once lifting his napkin to wipe his face clean. If she hadn't known any better she had become addled in her thinking, because not once did she feel disgusted toward his behavior. Instead, she felt sorry for him. Never had she seen anyone so hungry.

Again he looked up with apologetic eyes, yet his fork continued to scrape across his plate until there was nothing left. To spare the servants witnessing his behavior, Abigail had sent them from the room. Lifting a lid from a porcelain bowl, she dipped its ladle deep into it and filled a bowl with gumbo until it reached the very top.

"Thank you, ma'am. It's kind of you," he said after the bowl was pushed closer to him. He ate the gumbo slowly, but Abigail could see that he loved the seafood soup more than he had anything else. "You said the man I saw…" The belch that came out of him sounded like something that wasn't of human form had tried to climb out of his throat. Abigail smiled when he looked at her with large eyes.

"Ma'am, I don't have many fancy manners but I do have some, but I reckon it's hard for you to see that just now."

"My father is a good man."

"That he is," he agreed very quickly and had even stopped eating to get this point across.

"He's different from any other man I know. It doesn't matter to him what color a person's skin is. He helps who he can." She spoke softly wondering if she raised her voice if it would startle him and send him fleeing from the mansion because suddenly he looked frightened.

He sipped more of the soup while keeping his eyes on her. "I must say I never met anyone like that before, ma'am. Sometimes skin color doesn't matter. You can be white and poor and treated poorly by your own kind."

"You can?"

The sincere look in her eyes made him smile.

"Yes, ma'am. I wouldn't tell you that if it wasn't true. Just before I ran into your father, I was on the plantation right before this one and a little more north. I think it's called the Dusser…"

"Dussault," she corrected.

"Yes, that's it. Dussert."

"I like your accent."

Carlisle smiled again. "I didn't know I had one. I have to say, I like yours, too."

"You have to forgive me. I rarely speak English. We speak French in these parts, including our servants."

"You don't say!"

Abigail giggled. "Oui. If they can't speak French then how can we speak to them?"

"I don't know any French people personally," he answered. "I think that's the language that Dussert fella was yelling at me. I'm from a working family. In my family you start working when you're young. Only the rich had niggers. For poor white people like me, we had to hire ourselves out. Sometimes finding steady work was hard to do. I thought if I came this way to a bigger city things will be better for me, you see? But that Dussert fella took one look at me and shooed me away."

"It wasn't because you were white," she said.

"It had to be my clothes then." He gazed down the front of him, then back up at her. "I know they need a little mending."

Abigail smiled hoping to put him at ease.

Carlisle liked her smile and the small laughs she gave.

"That wasn't it either," she admitted. "The city here is divided between the Creoles and the Américains."

"Aren't you American? Ain't I in Louisiana?"

"Mon Dieu! Oh, monsieur. S'il vous plaît! Please, don't ever say that to any Creole in these parts. And you might not want to use the word nigger either depending on who you're around. You see, many men here... They... They..."

Carlisle nodded and smiled. "I understand. They have half nigger... I might have trouble not using that word."

She gave him a polite nod. "Well, yes. And you see. Some of their children are skilled in trades or own businesses."

"Niggers here own businesses!"

Sarah pressed her hand against her chest as her eyes went wide. "I do fear for you here, monsieur." She shook her head. "Some of the elite in the city have quadroon and octoroon children whom they love dearly. My father included."

Carlisle sank in his chair, his eyes so large that it changed his facial features and made him look like a new stranger. "I ain't never heard anything like that before. I wouldn't have ever thought that of that kind man..."

Her chair fell backward as she jumped to her feet. "What are you suggesting, sir? That my father is no longer a good man in your eyes? I can't – I won't allow you to disrespect him, especially at his own dining room table. Since he's absent at the moment I am running this house. You can finish your meal in the barn if you're not done already. I'll have one of the servants to make sure you'll have everything you need. And if you mistreat any of my father's servants he'll see to it that you will personally answer to him."

Both of them turned when hands began to clap near the far door.

"Oncle Julien! I forgot you and Tante Marie-Marie were in the house. Please forgive my manners!"

Julien stepped into the room, his hands folding behind his back, his chin lifted and held high. "My name is Julien Rafael Jennings. I've already caught yours, monsieur." He then turned to Abigail and switched from English to French. "Marie-Marie was in the salle when your father came home. She heard the exchange between the two of you. After she told me, we both decided to stay out of sight for a while."

Abigail smiled. "Merci, Oncle."

Julien tugged her hair, and it irritated her the same way it would have if he had been a pestering older brother. For some reason it felt differently when her father did it.

"Are you sure you want this fine young Américain gentleman sleeping in the barn? If so I can show him the way."

"But he said…"

Julien nodded at her. "This one is different, I think." He looked Carlisle over, then shook his head. "Nope. I don't think this one is a Kaintock rooster with his chest puffed out and thinks his farts smells like oleander."

Abigail quickly pulled a kerchief out of the sleeve of her gown and buried her face in it before letting go with her laughter.

Again Julien noticed the way Carlisle smiled at her even though this time the man knew Abigail was laughing at his expense. He wondered how long it would take Abigail to notice the attention Carlisle was giving her.

"The barn," Abigail said, tucking her kerchief back into her sleeve. "Perhaps a night there will make him remember that some things shouldn't be said in this small part of the world." She turned politely to Carlisle and spoke in English. "Good night, sir. My uncle will show you to the barn."

She turned to walk away.

Carlisle nearly knocked over his bowl as he jumped to his feet. Righting it then looking peevishly in Abigail's and Julien's direction he spoke in a small voice. "I just wanted to tell you that I'm sorry for offending you, Miss. And I also wanted to thank you again for your kindness. You and your father's. And you, sir, for showing me to the barn."

Abigail nodded at him and walked away.

## Chapter Nineteen
# I Dare

*[It's by following his friends that a crab lost its hiding place. — Creole Proverb]*

"I'm not going," she said again and this time firmly while staring at Jeanette.

Jeanette gave a distressing look before giving a nod of defeat before leaving the room. All of the servants knew that when Abigail was determined it was hard to dissuade her from any decision she made.

When she was alone Abigail knew the servants would climb the rank of hierarchy until Cook, who wasn't even a slave any longer, would make it her business to come inside her boudoir to convince her to go to the city. Abigail needed everyone in the mansion to know she had decided to refuse her mother's orders and stay home.

Hurrying downstairs, she marched to her father's study. When she saw he wasn't in it she started searching for him room by room. Riley stood in the dining room waiting for the family to arrive for breakfast.

"My father. Where is he?" She asked.

"He and your uncle left the mansion a little while ago, mademoiselle. Your tante is upstairs. Other than that it's just you and the servants in the house. Will you be having breakfast alone, mademoiselle, or will you be waiting for Madame Marie-Marie to join you?"

"I'll wait for my tante, thank you."

She walked out of the house and looked toward the kitchen. Why should she even have to go near it? Knowing this was best she started to descend the galerie steps when she saw Jeanette stepping out of the kitchen with her head held high. Assuming Jeanette had tattled Abigail waved down Lovelace as he passed by on a cart. After he helped her up she told him to take her to Désireé's cottage. Enough was enough.

To her surprise the front door of the cottage was locked. Stepping back from the door, she stared at the cottage in both directions wondering if Désireé had left with her father and Julien. Not giving up just yet, she walked the width of the galerie toward the rear. She was coming up on the *petite salle* when she saw hurried movements inside. Not thinking anything of it she stepped into the room, then pressed a hand tightly against her mouth.

A white man was pulling his trousers up over naked skin. He hadn't been quick enough. Abigail couldn't stop staring toward his middle trying to remember exactly what his penis had looked like. It wasn't until she saw movement on the sofa that she looked in that direction. Désireé was struggling into her gown. She also hadn't been fast enough. Abigail's eyes grew larger as she stared at Désireé's rounded breasts, smooth flat stomach and naked legs.

While turning on her heels she ran from the room as quickly as she could. Behind her she heard a collective, "Get her!" The sound of feet running behind her made her run harder. She had just reached the front of the cottage and was making her way down the steps when she was tackled from behind and knocked to the grass.

"Abby! Abby!" Désireé cried. "Wait! Help me get her up, Cyril."

Abigail heard the name Cyril and her mouth gaped and her eyes grew large again. There was only one man in the entire city that she knew who had the name Cyril and his last name was Oakes.

Cyril reached down to help her up.

Abigail swatted at his hands.

Cyril yanked his hands back.

"Abby, listen," Désireé pleaded.

Abigail stayed lying on her back. "He's Cyril Oakes!"

"*Merde*!" Cyril cried. "Let's tie her up!"

"No," Désireé said. "Abby, you can't tell Papa. You can't tell anyone. I will tell Papa when I think the time is right."

"What were you two doing?" Abigail asked bringing her face closer toward Désireé. "You were both naked. And you were lying on the sofa."

"Mon Dieu!" Désireé cried.

"Let's tie her up," Cyril begged. "She's going to tell. I know she is," he finished looking down at Abigail and looking as if he would reach down and grab her at any moment.

"I'm not tying up my sister."

"She's not…"

"Cyril!" Désireé hissed, taking a step closer to him.

His eyes hardened as he looked away from Désireé and stared at Abigail again. "She's going to tell. I can't leave now, Desie. What about our baby?"

Abigail stood slowly to her feet with her mouth gaped and a stunned expression on her face. Désireé was going to have a baby, and their father knew nothing about it. *And by Cyril Oakes!* Once their father found out Désireé would certainly fall out of his favor. Abigail thought about the plantation and her being made heir over it. Her heart raced this time with excitement as she swung her arms to propel herself away from them as she sprinted across the lawn.

"I told you she's going to tell," Cyril said angrily while turning to Désireé. "You should have let me tie her up until we were able to convince her not to! We could have explained. And now we don't have that chance. What were you thinking?"

Désireé was still looking in the direction Abigail had run in. "I never thought she would be anything like her mother but I guess I was wrong."

"What are we going to do?"

"We're standing in my yard half naked. I think we both should go inside."

"And then?"

Désireé didn't answer. Leaving Cyril behind, she ran as fast as Abigail had, but in the opposite direction. The location she needed to reach was much closer than the mansion. She ran to Alise's cottage.

As Désireé ran away Abigail ran hard through the trees anxious to return to the mansion. Thankful when she saw Lovelace still in the area, she yelled out to him. He turned the cart around and rode swiftly to her. By the time they reached the mansion Abigail couldn't believe her luck. Julien was walking up the rear galerie, which meant he had just come back from the stables. If Julien was back it meant her father was back, and Abigail couldn't wait to tell him that his enemy was on his land and was the father of a child that Désireé would have.

"Oncle! My papa. Where is he?"

Julien saw how fast she was running and watched her curiously. It was then he thought about the Texan in the barn and hurried toward her. "What happened? Where is he?"

"Who?" Abigail asked.

"The Texan?"

"I don't know," she answered in a rush. "Where's my papa?"

Julien knew exactly where Pierre was. The two of them hadn't left the plantation together that morning. It was what they told Riley knowing Riley would tell anyone that asked. The lie would help Pierre, especially after a few servants saw him leave on his horse. Julien didn't expect him to return to the mansion for a while.

"I turned back and came home. He's alone."

"I want to tell you something," she whispered with large eyes.

Jeanette stepped out of the mansion onto the galerie. "Monsieur! I'm glad you're back. Madame isn't doing well. I think you need to come up and look at her."

Julien started to follow Jeanette inside.

Abigail started to follow behind him when she heard her name yelled loudly across the lawn.

"Abigail Jennings!"

Turning in fear, because her name had been spoken firmly, she saw Alise step down from her personal cart beside her personal servant, James. Walking across the lawn as if she was the owner of the plantation, she kept her eyes on Abigail at all times. On the inside Abigail became frightened, but she tried not to show it. Alise was held in high esteem with her father *and* her oncle a hundred times more than Cook ever had been.

Alise stopped walking. "Get over here, child."

Abigail knew that everyone listened to Alise, including her mother. For this reason she flew across the lawn to meet the free woman of color who had always seemed to be in her life.

Alise turned back to her cart before Abigail reached her and climbed back up it without any help from James. As Abigail got closer James gestured for Abigail to climb up. Once Abigail was seated, Alise flicked the reins and put the cart in motion.

"Désireé told me to come after you and bring you back to her place. Why did she tell me to do that?"

"You don't know?"

"I know she's been acting strangely. Do you know anything about that?"

"She was naked! And he was too!"

Alise pulled hard on the reins. The cart stopped abruptly. Abigail threw her hands forward to stop herself from tumbling out of it.

"She has a man at her place?" Alise asked with large eyes.

156

"He was trying to pull up his trousers because he heard me. Désireé was lying on the sofa wearing nothing at all! And then she tried to put on her gown. But I saw everything. And then they chased me and threw me to the ground. And then Cyril Oakes told me that Désireé was having a baby!"

Alise's gaze was sober as she stared at Abigail a long time, and then she lifted her hand and slapped the child across the face. It had been a long time since anyone had slapped Abigail. The blow caught her off guard. Again she had to throw her hands forward to stop herself from falling out of the cart.

"I'm sorry, child." Alise spoke softly. Her expression became soft. "For a moment I thought you were your mother."

Abigail held the side of her face. "You had no right to strike me, Alise. I'll tell my father about this."

"Listen to me, child. And you listen well. You should think about how you treat people."

Abigail waited for her to say more.

"Climb down, child. I need you off my cart now, but before you go I want to remind you of something. My man loved you. He did. When no one else did, he did. And Désireé did. And I did. And your Oncle Julien. And everyone else here, except the two that should have. Now go on back to the mansion and tell your papa whatever you want. I thought this was important. I guess it is. But not the way you think."

Abigail climbed down while staring at Alise. Seeing Alise panic after hearing the news had been what she had expected. Alise's anger seemed misplaced.

James had started walking toward them as soon as he saw the cart stop. He reached it at the moment Abigail placed her feet again against the ground. She watched in anger as James climbed up the cart in a manner to suggest he was the Queen of the plantation's most loyal pet.

"Uppity nigger!" She yelled in English, knowing James didn't speak it. But Alise did speak English and looked over her shoulder at her a long time as the cart rode away. Something in Alise's eyes told Abigail that the insult she had used had been more than a mistake. A troubling feeling in her stomach told her that things would be different between her and Alise, and that couldn't be good. Swinging around she saw that the Texan had not only heard what she yelled; from the look on his face he had seen everything, including the slap.

He gave a small smiled when she faced him. "I was going to ask you later to teach me how to behave around Creole people. But from what I just saw, I think you're in a lot of trouble, Miss. I hate to even think about how much trouble you may be in. I hope you don't mind me asking, but who was that woman?"

"None of your business! And you don't know what you're talking about!"

Carlisle's finger pointed behind her and toward the house.

Abigail took a moment before she turned to look at the mansion because she feared Carlisle had been pointed at her papa. Julien leaned against the galerie balustrade with both hands staring in her direction.

The reason she ran to Julien was to prove to the Texan that he was wrong. Julien waited patiently for her to reach him. "Did I just see and hear what I believe I did? Alise slapped you, and you called James an uppity nigger. Is that about right?"

Abigail took a deep breath and spoke in a rush because she knew once her oncle knew the truth he would make haste to tell her papa. "Désireé had a naked man in her cottage. And *she* was naked. And the man with her is Cyril Oakes. And Désireé is going to have a baby!"

Julien contemplated what he heard from every aspect and angle, and despite how many times he examined it, it ended the same way: Pierre blowing up in a rage. "This is problem," he finally said.

"Papa is going to be upset!"

"I agree. Very angry. Why did Alise slap you?"

"She had no right, Oncle! I told her what I told you and she stared at me, then slapped me, then said, 'Sorry, child. For a moment I thought you were your mother!'"

Julien threw back his head and roared.

Abigail saw that Carlisle was watching and became delighted when he saw the way that Julien laughed.

Julien placed a hand on her shoulder. "I'm thinking we should keep this quiet until we can figure out a way to help Désireé with your papa."

"I think we should tell him as soon as he gets back!"

The look Julien gave her wasn't what she had expected. She had tried to make her tone sound concerned or sad even, but even she had heard too much excitement in it.

"I remember Désireé being real good to you," he said. "Are you sure that's what you want to do?"

She noticed he had laid the responsibility on her then knew she had better think about this a little longer. There was something in his eyes that was similar to Alise's. Believing the two of them knew something about her father that she didn't kept her quiet a little longer.

Julien studied her wondering if she was going to answer correctly or not. Abigail had a big, explosive secret against Désireé, but her telling it would have an equally explosive affect on Abigail. If Pierre ever believed that Abigail could turn against Désireé and Gorée at a later time, it would change everything. And then Julien thought of something else. Désireé had the chance to tell Abigail that Pierre was not her father, but hadn't.

"Do as you wish, petite," he said and walked back in the house.

Abigail watched him go, not seeing Carlisle approaching from behind.

"Can I trouble you for some breakfast, Miss?" He asked.

Abigail startled throwing a hand against her chest. She hadn't expected to hear a voice behind her so closely. As she stared at him a thought came to her mind.

"Please do. You must be hungry."

"I am that, Miss. I suspect it'll be a while longer yet before I'm not. I take it your father hasn't returned?"

"Not yet. Do come inside."

Julien joined them for breakfast.

Carlisle felt as if he was doing all of the talking. He saw that both of his hosts had many things on their minds. As hard as he tried, he couldn't get Abigail to giggle as she had the night before.

After breakfast was over he was happy to hear Abigail make the suggestion of sitting on what he would have called a porch, but she called a galerie. Learning all he could from her seemed important if he wanted to stay in the area.

As they sat he was surprised to see one of the servants come out and offer more coffee. Café, he reminded himself as he accepted the cup. Believing Abigail would do all the talking, he sat a while and waited. When she continued to sit silently he decided to quiz her a little. Each time he asked a question she answered, but her comments were short and curt.

"Why don't I let you do the talking," he suggested and sipped more of the sweetened café and milk it seemed he couldn't get enough of.

"Semper, leave us now," Abigail said to the servant.

Semper nodded and went back in the house.

"I'm real good at problem solving," Carlisle said. "And I know how to keep a secret as well. I'm thinking that's what you're going to tell me seeing you sent your slave girl away."

Abigail frowned slightly. "You speak rather coarse. I'm sorry. I'm not used to it. It's just... It's just you should say servants. It sounds nicer."

Carlisle nodded. "I apologize, Miss. If you can help me – that is if your father doesn't mind – I'm willing to learn."

"You seem nice so I'm going to trust you, although I maybe shouldn't."

Carlisle licked his finger and performed a cross over his face and chest.

Abigail rolled her eyes before she realized she had done so. "We are Catholic here, monsieur. I don't know what that gestures means, but it seems offensive to my religion."

"Miss, I think if you continue to point out my faults alone I will learn a lot." He smiled and brought the cup up to his mouth.

He had an easy way about him. He didn't appear uptight like her father did all the time or the way Julien could suddenly become as he did before breakfast. This made her more curious about Carlisle's Américain culture. "Why did you do that?"

Carlisle slurped the last of the café, then dropped his porcelain cup on a nearby table as if it was made of pewter. Abigail decided not to bring the value of the cup to his attention.

"It means I can't say a word to anyone about anything you're willing to tell me."

She nodded at him. "I'm trusting you to be honest with me mostly, and secondly, not to say anything."

"Alrighty."

She twisted her face.

Carlisle gave a giggle. "That means, 'yes, ma'am.'"

"I told you that my father has children of noir... black blood last night, remember?"

"Yes, ma'am."

"I am my father's only legitimate child. My father also has... another child." She didn't want to mention Gorée because she didn't want to have to explain. "Well, I learned something about one of his noir daughters that will make my father very angry. But it's something he should know and not telling him would be just as bad. What do you think, monsieur? Should I tell him?"

"How much does he love this nigger child?"

"Beaucoup! Very much."

Carlisle leaned toward her. "Then don't tell him. Ain't you heard? I know some men who will kill the bearer of bad news. Haven't you ever read Shakespeare?"

"I have," Abigail answered, remembering the second chapter in Henry IV.

"I told you I was good in solving problems." His hands opened wide, bounced then returned to his lap. It was another gesture she had never seen before.

"I can burden you with one more dilemma?"

"I'm at your disposal, Miss."

"This one is even more important. You can't ever repeat it. To anyone."

"Yes, ma'am."

"My mother wants me to come to the city where she is, but I don't want to go. I think she only wants me there because she's angry with my father. If I don't go I know she's going to be very angry with me. But if I go I will be miserable in her company."

Carlisle stared at the face of this young woman. It was covered in a million freckles so that her true skin color was almost totally hidden behind it. Her hair looked frightening to say the least. Tendrils stuck out wide from her face like the tail of a skunk scared shitless. There wasn't much of a mouth on her, the lips too thin and too small, and not much shape to them. It was her eyes that were the most noticeable. The color of them weren't quite emerald, but not jade either, and somewhere in between. He liked her face because it was different. And he liked the softness of her voice, and her hoity manners, and how even though he could see that she thought him a brute she remained polite even when she corrected him.

"I like you."

Unaware he had spoken out loud, he smiled when her face twisted and the skin behind her cheeks reddened.

"I suspect that your sister know that you know her secret?"

"Yes."

"Since I don't know your family well, I think you should ask your sister for her advice in regards to your mother. This will let her know that everything is all right between the two of you. She'll be so thankful that you came to her, she will readily give you the honest answer you need."

"What if I told you that I hate her sometimes?"

"Oh, that makes a lot of difference, Miss. A lot indeed."

"What if I told you that my father, perhaps, loves her more than me?"

"Then I think you should get over to where she is right away. I thought about what you said last night and your reaction to some of the things I said. What I remember most is that you said your father helps anyone without thinking about the color of their skin. I don't know your father, Miss, and I don't mean to imply that I do. But what I do know is that when he saw me squatting between the trees while burning a fire and trying to cook a squirrel, he paid no attention to my tattered boots or my clothes or my frayed hat sitting on the ground. All he saw was I needed some help and he offered it to me in three seconds after looking at me.

Now if you're telling me that he loves you less when I have sat with you twice and can't fathom a reason why, I think you should ask your sister that question as well."

Abigail rose to her feet. When she saw that Carlisle had also risen because she had, but had no intentions of going with her, her eyes became wide. "You're not coming with me?"

Carlisle smiled. "If you want me to."

Abigail never walked so fast in her life, and although she wanted to get there in a hurry she made no attempt to flag down any of the servants driving vehicles. Carlisle stayed close to her, and for some reason, this bolstered her confidence. As they started to cross the yard to Désireé's cottage, Carlisle stopped walking, suddenly.

"Uh, Miss? Is this your sister's house?"

"Yes."

"And your sister is a nigger?"

"A mulâtresse. Yes."

"And your father built this house for her?"

"Yes."

Carlisle whistled. "This house is better than many of the ones in Spanish Texas where I'm from and white people live in them."

"What do you mean?"

"It's like a mansion. A small one."

"Shall I introduce you to her?"

"Will she mind?"

"No."

"Then all right."

He was curious to see inside the house.

Abigail knocked.

"It's open," a soft voice called out from inside.

Abigail twisted the knob and thought about Cyril and Désireé being naked. She found the two of them sitting inside the *grand salle*.

Carlisle nearly stumbled on his way into it, so busy had he been staring at everything except where he was going. The more steps he took the more he felt like he had entered some strange new world. The wealth inside the house caused his eyes to dart in all direction, and even if he looked in the same place twice he always noticed something else to gawk at. It wasn't until a white hand reached out to him that he pulled himself back to this dimension and gripped it.

The man looked similar to him in a way. There was something about him that made him appear uneducated. He looked slightly or more nervous than Carlisle was, which made Carlisle temporarily uneasy. The woman who continued to sit but waited to greet him made Carlisle stare at her with his mouth slightly parted.

"This is Mr. Carlisle Morning from Spanish Texas," Abigail said.

Carlisle looked in horror as the woman sitting the sofa translated English to French for a white man.

"Bonjour," the white man answered.

"Mr. Morning, this is my *sister*, Mademoiselle Désireé Antoinette Jennings. And this gentleman is a… friend of the family. His name is Monsieur Cyril Oakes."

161

"Oakes?"

"Yes."

"Like an oak tree?"

"Yes."

"And he doesn't speak English?" Carlisle noticed the smile that appeared on Désireé's face. It was strange. Truly strange. When he met their father the night before he had only seen him for a few minutes, still Carlisle could see that face staring back at him now in female form. He also saw it in the brother. The similarities were quite striking. Abigail had none of the same features. A part of his heart twisted when he realized that Abigail looked nothing – *nothing* – like the rest of her family. He wondered what her mother looked like, but even then he already knew why the father loved one sister more than the other.

"In our city Creole is someone who is a white native of *this* city."

"Nice to meet you, Mr. Morning," Désireé said.

Carlisle wanted to hate the woman for some strange reason but made certain he didn't divest any of his personal feelings as he sat when she indicated he should.

Abigail dove directly into the matter. "Maman wants me to come to the city. I don't want to go. Do you think I should?"

Désireé gave a slight glance in Carlisle's direction.

Abigail leaned closer to him. "Show her what you showed me."

Carlisle wasn't sure if his cheeks went red, but they were definitely warm. "What was that now, Miss?"

"The thing you did with your finger that makes you can't repeat things you hear," Abigail said.

"Oh," Carlisle said, smiled, licked his finger and performed the cross. The response he received was equally disturbing as the face Abigail had given him earlier. He watched with curiosity as she leaned toward the others and spoke in rapid French.

"Now that he's done this he can't ever repeat anything he's told to another soul."

"What kind of voodoo is this?" Cyril asked. "Are you telling me that something has bound his tongue?"

"Oui!" Abigail said with assuring eyes.

Carlisle wasn't sure what was happening, but all three were staring at him as if he had just grown horns. "It means I won't say a single word of what I hear to anyone else as long as I live."

Désireé translated in French.

"Mon Dieu!" Cyril said. "What else does he do?"

"All sorts of signs," Abigail answered rapidly.

Carlisle smiled as three pairs of eyes scrutinized him.

"Do you trust this man, Abby? Does he visit the mansion often?" Désireé asked.

"Can he put spells on us?" Cyril asked.

"Papa allowed him to stay with us until his horse is ready to travel. I trust him, Desie." And then she switched to English. "Mr. Morning, can you cast spells too?"

"Spells?" He asked, unsure how their conversation had veered to witches and why they thought he would know anything about spells. "I don't know a single one. But I knew a Mexican witch doctor once – a curandera. She was good at making up healing potions. I watched her make a tea that can cure fevers. Been making it ever since."

Carlisle watched as Abigail and Désireé stared at him as if the horns they saw on his head now had pretty little flowers on them.

"You can heal fevers?" Désireé asked.

"Not all. But some. I use peyote. I never go anywhere without it."

"Can you show one of the servants how to make this healing tea?" Désireé asked. "For that I'm sure my father will pay good money."

Because Carlisle didn't know that fevers were the number one killing disease in the city, he shrugged and smiled.

Both women stared at him still waiting patiently.

"Yes," he answered, then scolded himself for giving a shrug as an answer.

Both gave soft sighs of relief.

"Mr. Morning," Désireé began. "I hope you don't mind me speaking to my sister in French again. The matter is most delicate."

"Not at all," Carlisle said and crossed his arms over his chest in a grand manner, gave a nod, and an even larger smile.

"I think he just cast a spell on us," Cyril said. "Why are his arms like that?"

Désireé leaned forward slightly. "I think this is how Américains behave, but I'm not sure. We've all seen them on the street, but we've never sat down and discussed anything with any of them."

"Pah!" Cyril spat. "Américains!"

"Abby, I think you are too young to defy your mother," Désireé said. "If she wants you in the city I think you should go. If you don't go she will be very upset, and when she's upset she can be very cruel."

"I don't want to go, Desie. Every time she's in front of her friends she says the same things." She looked away when she felt tears fill her eyes. "One of the things she says is she can't believe she has given birth to something so ugly. And her friends laugh then look at me funny. They're always looking at me funny, and they're always calling me 'poor child.' Besides, Papa and I had supper together last night and we sat and talked for hours afterwards and I'm looking forward to it again."

Désireé gave an understanding nod. "Did you discuss this with Papa?"

Abigail gave a solemn glance. "He said I didn't have to go and for me to send Maman a message. But I think she will still be upset."

"Abby, I don't know. Honestly, I don't. I can't see your mother being happy about you staying here to be with Papa instead of her. I have a bad feeling about this."

"Did you tell your father about me?" Cyril asked.

"Carlisle told me I shouldn't mention it."

Cyril stared again at Carlisle. The man was looking around the room noticing everything.

"I hope you don't tell him," Cyril said. "I think I should be the one to tell him."

Both women rose to their feet.

Carlisle also stood and stared forward at the three of them wondering what they were discussing now, then started to listen more carefully although he didn't understand a single word being spoken.

"Now isn't the time!" Désireé urged. "This has to be handled delicately."

"You don't know our papa like we do!" Abigail insisted.

The conversation wrapped up and Carlisle was given a handshake from the white guy and a polite nod from the sister.

Outside he was little happy to be out of the house until he noticed the uncle standing on the galerie to his right.

"Let me explain something to you, *connard!*" Julien belted. "While you're on this plantation you will not accompany my niece or any female family member without an escort! Have I made myself clear?"

"I meant no disrespect, sir. Honestly, I didn't."

"Abby, you get back to the house and stay there. As for you, you uncouth Texan, I'll talk to my brother about you as soon as he returns."

# Chapter Twenty
## Sometimes Blood Means Nothing

*[Cutting off a mule's ears doesn't make it a horse. – Creole Proverb]*

For the first time in a long time Sarah found herself enjoying a meal with someone without feeling a tinge of animosity or tension dominating the atmosphere. Pierre constantly encouraged Gorée to sit and eat. Gorée would smile, nod at him, sit for only a few seconds, then rise again.

Sarah was impressed by Pierre's level of patience, and how he never lifted his voice when he spoke to the child. Gorée, on the other hand, Sarah found her to be interesting: quiet of nature, innately polite, and at all times curious. The one thing that stuck out was Gorée's desire not to be stared at by anyone, including Pierre. Whenever she noticed Sarah watching her, she would stand very still and wait, and only when Sarah looked away Gorée would sneak off in a corner of the room to hide in. On occasion she would peek out from behind a piece of furniture where she had found solace to make certain Pierre was still there.

"Did you sleep well?" Pierre asked, interrupting her thoughts.

After she learned the evening before that Pierre did not feel encumbered by her presence on the plantation, last night was the first time she had slept peacefully. Not once had she awakened to wonder what would happen in the next hour. Green Lea belonged to Jenna; this was also a burden lifted from her shoulder. Her father had sold all of the remaining servants, except Imogen, to a trader; there was nothing she could have done to prevent it, and there was nothing she could do about it now. William would return to the city, and soon, but for some reason this truth didn't worry her at the moment.

She stared down at her food. It had cooled but was still flavorful. "I feel almost like a different person. I find it amazing the difference one day can bring. One little morsel of hope can make one feel able to do anything."

She followed Pierre's eyes across the room. Gorée had discovered an armoire filled with clothing for women, children, and men of all sizes. The gown the child had worn wasn't anywhere to be seen. Gorée now donned a white formal frilly boy's shirt. Lying on her back on the floor, she struggled to pull up a pair of short breeches. Crossing back to the armoire in her new attire that exposed her lower legs and bare feet, she lifted a bonnet overstuffed with lace and placed it on her head.

Sarah was stunned to see that Gorée had undressed herself, including her hose, and had only been wearing her shift and a pair of pantaloons the kind that children wore while she and Pierre had been in the same room and neither of them noticing or hearing it. As if she had to see where Gorée had stripped to near nakedness, Sarah searched the entire floor but saw nothing. When she looked up she saw Pierre was equally stunned and was also searching the floor and had turned in his chair and lowered to see the furthest corner of the room.

Sitting up he stared at the child again. "Gorée!"

Gorée neither turned nor acknowledged she heard anything. Lifting the widest bonnet she saw in the armoire, Pierre snarled at her when she approached him offering it to him.

"I will not," he informed.

"Hot cheese."

"There is no sun in here. I will not."

"I'll wear it, Gorée," Sarah said reaching for it.

"Pierre wear it," Gorée answered.

"She just spoke in a regular manner!" As soon as Sarah realized what she said she stared at Pierre apologetic. "I didn't mean to imply…"

"Pierre?" Gorée pleaded, again reaching the bonnet out to him. When she saw him contemplating she hurried to him and lifted on the tip of her toes. "Pierre. Pierre. Pierre."

Sarah gave a shrill of laughter when Pierre lowered and the bonnet was placed on his head.

"Gorée, I do believe you are misbehaving for Sarah. You cannot call me Pierre. What should you call me?"

For eleven years old Gorée appeared smaller than she should have been. It was apparent that she would not have her father's height. Reaching for the ribbons that dangled from the bonnet on her papa's head, she stared up at the ceiling as she pondered over his question. And then she peered at him and smiled. "Le Diable."

Pierre tightened his mouth and stared at Sarah. Sarah smiled back at him.

"Connard." Gorée spoke the insult in a soft voice unaware she had just called her papa an idiot.

"Mon Dieu!" Pierre spat.

"Fils de salope!" Gorée continued.

Sarah gasped, as this sentiment was more vulgar than the first. Hearing a child like Gorée speak these words was painful to listen to.

"Your sister," Pierre accused looking at Sarah. "She's the only one in the mansion who would refer to me as a son of a bitch."

Gorée continued to repeat other names she had heard Pierre being called. "Mon fils bien-aimé. Fils. Monsieur. Papa."

Sarah smiled warmly at him. The way Gorée spoke without any difference in the inflection of her tone was proof she didn't understand the meaning of any of the words, including papa. "I can't imagine the life she would have without you."

"Now that I'm wearing my bonnet," he began.

Sarah stared at his head. Gorée had tied a knot in the ribbon. It sat to the side of Pierre's cheek like a large hideous button.

They both laughed, shivering in their chairs, she because of what he looked like, he because he could imagine what he looked like.

"Can I show you Ashleywood?" He said.

When she answered yes, Pierre stood and, after finding Gorée's discarded clothes behind a sofa, led her into one of the other rooms. When the two emerged Gorée was once again an elegantly dressed child. She was first out the door, and first to climb into the cart without any assistance. Climbing into the back, she perched on top of a small pile of blankets. This particular cart had boards placed across its width and length preventing Gorée from moving around while the vehicle was in motion.

Pierre was gentle as he assisted Sarah to sit on the driver's seat with him. When he sat he apologized for his size, as there was hardly any room leftover, just enough for her to sit comfortably.

"What if the servants see me then tell my sister I'm here?"

He flicked the reins to put the horse in motion. "There are only a few slaves here who will sell their soul to anyone in the hopes of receiving some sort of favor in return. Eventually, if you stay, everyone will learn you are here, Sarah. Servants who travel with their masters are the ears and eyes for slaves who are stuck permanently on other plantations. They have created their own unique ways of communicating between each other so that what is learned on one plantation is quickly known on another. Any plantation with any connection to mine is privy of most things that goes on here."

"I don't want anyone to know I'm here, Pierre. Perhaps I should go back to the cottage."

"Sarah, I want you to stay here. Forever. It's why I want to show you around. I got an idea last night and want to know what you think about it. As for anyone seeing you, let's not worry about that now."

"You also don't have to worry about the overseers," he said suddenly. "The life they have here with their families is far better than it will be anywhere else. I pay them higher wages. In return they have given me loyalty that is unfound anywhere else."

Sarah watched with intrigue when they reached an area where slaves toiled in the sugar cane fields that stretched as far as her eyes could see.

The plantation had seven storehouses when most had one or two. The smithy shop had a lot of activity in and around it. Its open door allowed her to look in and see the fire burning in the forge. Several male slaves pounded red hot steal with large hammers to create nails, hooks, and door hinges. Another small group was in the process of making a wrought iron gate.

As much wealth as she had seen so far she couldn't understand Jenna's refusal to help their father in any way. That Ashleywood had a smithy shop with enough servants to produce all of the iron works a plantation couldn't live without a little help would have helped their father a long way. It would have prevented him from having to purchase nails and gates from other plantations who gauged their prices to get a higher profit on everything that was produced on their land.

As she and Pierre rode on he explained each area they came to. Because the plantation made a large profit from its coopers – twenty-seven in all – Pierre explained that these servants had been given a prime patch of land behind the dairy. They also had their own overseer and thirteen cabins between them to house their wives and children.

"You seem easier on your slaves than other slave owners I've come across," she mentioned.

"My father learned that from his father. Alise also made changes shortly after she arrived."

The relationship Alise had had with his father was public knowledge. Sarah grew up listening to others speak openly about the quadroon that Will Jennings oftentimes traveled with and treated similarly to a wife. It had been said many times that the merchants in the city often smiled when Alise and Will walked through their shops' doors. The large purchases that were made had kept many of them in business during slower seasons when sales were down. It was also rumored that after Will's wife had died eligible women in the city had openly sought him out in the hopes of marrying him. If the rumors were true, whenever he was introduced to or was in the company of eligible women he politely told them he was unable to marry as his heart would always belong to another.

Everything on Ashleywood was larger, better built and more properly maintained than any plantation she had ever visited. The pigeonnières. The boxed gardens. Separate storehouses held the hogsheads of sugar and barrels of molasses that the plantation produced in mass quantities.

Most of the slaves she saw looked like they were preparing the plantation for harvest. Shirtless, sweaty male slaves chopped wood for the sugar mill, repaired and whitewashed buildings and cleaned ditches. A large group bending and toiling in the vegetable garden sang in French. The song, led by an old male slave in an oversized cotton shirt as he stooped and dug up potatoes sang loudly in a strong voice. The others around him followed his lead singing with fervency about waiting for the sun to go down.

Pierre explained the song they sang. A normal workday on a sugar plantation began at four in the morning and didn't end until the sun went down. Divided in shifts, and with always something for them to do, each servant had half an hour for breakfast and two hours for the midday meal. After the midday meal the servants and the overseers alike carried their own suppers back to the fields and it was there where it was eaten.

Unlike other plantations, other than harvest time and depending on their duties, most of the servants had the evening off. It was during these hours when they tended their own gardens for those who had them. Sarah marveled when she also saw that some of the servants also owned their own small stock of animals.

"They can purchase their own stock here," Pierre said when he saw where she was looking. "We have a merit system in place. The slaves can buy chickens and pigs. The slaves who don't have stock can purchase eggs from their neighbors or a piece of meat. We also have a storehouse where they can purchase other things they may need."

"Where do they get money?" She asked unable to look away from him.

Pierre stared down at her. "They're given wages for the work they perform on the plantation."

"Wages!" The word exploded from her mouth. "This is most unheard of, Pierre!" When he said nothing and only held her gaze she felt compelled to discuss it more. "I have never heard of this happening here or anywhere else for that matter. It's a bad example, Pierre. Surely you know that. If others knew it would start a riot in the city."

"This is why you don't have to worry about any of the servants saying anything. Slaves on other plantations know what goes on here. They keep it amongst themselves for fear of their masters and overseers learning about it. They call Ashleywood 'Slave Heaven.' Heaven, Sarah, because the idea of getting paid for the work they perform is like you said unheard of."

"Pierre," she began facing him more. "Women work many hours and don't get paid for it. I understand what you're trying to say, but it's the way things are."

He leaned closer to her very gently. "Then marry William, Sarah."

She closed her eyes, suddenly, and lowered her head.

"That, Mademoiselle, is what is expected of you. Wrong or right, you marry who your father tells you to marry even if it is a smelly older man."

She opened her eyes and stared out at the distant fields and saw it differently now. Over and over again, each time she saw the lift and swing of a hoe she reminded herself the slave swinging it received a wage.

"My plantation is unique, Sarah. The servants who live here are very aware of this. Strict rules have been put into place. Breaking them has dire consequences. When we have visitors to the plantation the bell is rung. Five rings mean be aware of strangers and behave appropriately."

Sarah couldn't keep still when she reached the slave quarters. It sat like a well thought out town. The number of cabins was too many to count. Dirt lanes had been arranged to look like streets. Smoke lifted from chimneys. Yards sat either in front of or in back of select cabins. The Quarter even had its own guard shack. Male slaves with bands on their arms sat on horses patrolling through the cabins.

Pierre waited for her to take it all in then rode through the center of the Quarter. Sarah saw children underneath an open shelter being taught to read and write. Smaller children played on a patch of grass while several servants watched over them. A small cabin was fashioned to look like a jail. Its door was open. Sarah saw that it was a jail and it had several prisoners. Another building caught her interest.

"What is that building used for?"

"It's our courthouse. All differences between the servants are settled there and all decisions are final. Discord is not tolerated on any level. To prevent it the consequence for the offender is he and his entire family will be held in jail and sold as quickly and as far away as possible. Because I own a plantation in North Carolina it is there where they are first sent then sold."

"Has this happened?"

"It hasn't happened in many years, and I don't believe since I've been born. The servants you saw in the jail just now are being detained for minor occurrences. Alise governs the courthouse. The servants fear her being summoned, because she's only summoned when servants aren't able to settle their differences without her. On the occasions when she had she made examples of the offenders."

"With such freedom surely there's plenty of discord here."

"If you treat a man like a man and a woman like a woman they behave as such. Look around, Sarah. Freedom is not a privilege here. It's a right of being." He stopped the cart and pointed at a servant driving a wagon in the distance.

"His name is Benny," he began. "He purchased freedom for himself, his wife and two small sons from my father when he was twenty-five-years old. I remember the day he and his young family left. So much hope they had. It took all of his money, every picayune, to purchase their freedom. My father gave him more money, not a lot, but enough for Benny and his family to have food and buy what they would need as they traveled to the North. Benny and his family didn't know English but were still able to get by for three years. During that time they learned the language of the Américains and believed that life couldn't have gotten any better for them. Even now he tells the stories to the others.

"Benny was very careful with his manumission papers. While looking for work one day he ran into another free man of color he had seen before. The man told him that he was down on his luck and that he was hungry. Benny led the man to his home and fed him beans and bread. The man left that night very thankful and with a smile. Soon others began showing up at his cabin. Benny never turned any of them away. One night two men and a woman appeared at their door.

"Benny knew they were runaways just by looking at them. He fed them like he had the others. After they ate and had a little more strength they tackled Benny's wife, threatening her with a dinner knife if Benny didn't give them all of his manumission papers. Benny did. Without the manumission papers he knew he and his family was no longer safe. He didn't know how to write. The next morning he went to the house of an abolitionist and told him what had happened. This man quickly sat down and wrote my father a letter, and assured Benny that he would mail it right away.

"He did, but my father was away from the plantation. My mother couldn't speak or read English and had no idea how important the letter was. Benny knew that he had to continue to work to support his family. It was a free state, but if he was stopped and didn't have his papers he knew he could be sold again. A white Southerner stopped him, demanding to see his papers. Benny tried to explain. The man told him to go on home and followed behind him. The next morning the police arrived with the white Southerner who accused Benny and his family of being runaways from *his* plantation.

"A judge decided in the favor of the plantation owner and turned Benny and his family over to the man. Benny's wife was given to another man on the plantation to have children with. She and Benny were forbidden to have any private contact with one another. When the plantation owner died Benny watched as he, his wife and sons were sold to separate plantations. When he arrived on his new plantation he went straight to the master and told him everything that had happened. The master accused Benny of lying and ordered the overseer to give him twenty lashes with the whip in front of all of the other slaves. As he was being whipped his new mistress read from the Bible how slaves should be obedient and how lying was a sin."

"Pierre, please stop."

"I can't stop, Sarah. I'm telling you these things for a reason. I need you to understand. It took Benny six years before he was able to make an escape. He was caught, whipped and returned to his plantation. While he was recovering the plantation master's daughter spoke with Benny and believed his story. She wrote a letter and gave it to a female friend who also knew French. The letter was translated and mailed to my father. My father, of course, had already received the first letter and had sent a returned letter to the first gentleman who had written to him. But this man had no idea what had happened to Benny and the family he had known little about. He wrote my father and told him that Benny and his family must have moved on. My father read that letter and gave it no further thought.

"The second letter he received made him furious. He traveled to Georgia and became more furious when he learned that the matter would have to be settled by a trial. Benny's new master had no intentions of losing a good field hand. My father offered to buy Benny. The negotiation took weeks before an agreement was finally made. My father again gave Benny his freedom. Benny tore up the manumissions papers in front of my father and wept bitterly. My father brought him back here and Benny has been here since. When I was twelve, Benny and I spoke for a long time one day. Just the two of us. With Benny's help we have managed to send three-hundred-and-thirty-eight runaways to Europe where manumission papers aren't needed."

"How does it work?"

"I have property in France. The men and women who live in them are some of the first ones we sent over. They help the others find work, how to speak the language properly, and how to survive, how to stay undetected, as well as give them somewhere to sleep and eat until they get on their feet."

"And my three servants were sent there?"

"Oui."

"I can't thank you enough, Pierre."

The expression on his face was indiscernible.

As the cart was leaving the Quarter, Benny pulled up alongside them.

"Monsieur," he said with the brightest smile. "Mademoiselle."

Sarah saw that one of Benny's ears had been cut off, no doubt received as punishment for running away. Runaways from Green Lea had received the same punishment after they were returned.

"I think you will have a good crop this year, monsieur," Benny said. "I'm sure this will make you mighty happy."

"Not as happy as me hearing you finally settled down and found a wife."

Lines formed on Benny's cheeks as he laughed and smiled widely.

Sarah noticed that Pierre sat comfortably as if he was speaking with a peer of his equal.

Benny looked at Sarah, then averted his gaze.

"That's for the young folks," he finally said.

"We're off now, Benny. Do enjoy your day."

Benny gave a nod, stared at Sarah briefly once again, then rode off.

"What kind of work does he do?"

"He doesn't have regulated chores. Benny has been jailed more than a dozen times since his return. The others know not to bother him. He used to hire himself out in the city until the Américains arrived. For years he saved up to buy land and build a home. He threw away that idea when he learned the Américains was making it hard for free men of color, especially the dark ones, to live with true freedom also here in Louisiana. He's bitter, Sarah. Fillis has recently taken a liking to him. Each time he had been ready to give up on life something good came along. This time that good thing was Fillis. She's good for him. Since they have paired up he hasn't been jailed, and his popularity amongst the servants has increased."

The cart rocked gently as its wheels rolled over small rocks and holes not large enough to affect the horse.

"Have you liked everything you've seen so far, Mademoiselle Cheval?"

His address was spoken in jest, as Creoles considered it impolite to refer to someone by their surname unless speaking about that person to someone else. Asking someone if they heard about Mademoiselle Cheval was acceptable. But now, as the two of them were alone, the proper address would have been a simple mademoiselle, and never as Sarah, as it was far too personal and reserved for only select family members.

"Let's see how I should answer that, Monsieur Jennings." Sarah smiled at him when he laughed freely, then gazed down at her with amusement in his eyes.

She averted her gaze because she had seen a small measure of desire in his and remembered what had transpired between them the night before.

"Your plantation, from what I can see, is self-sufficient. I can't imagine your need for much outside of it. On the contrary, it looks to me like it produces enough to provide subsistence to smaller and not as well equipped plantations nearby. Also, the size of your land and the number of lives on it gives it the ability to be a city of its own. If this is true that will make you this land's president, mayor and head of police, yet I find you to be humble of heart. I have never met anyone like you, Pierre."

"There's a reason for my behavior, Sarah. And there was a reason why my father made the changes he did on Ashleywood. I would love to share it with you."

"I would love to hear it," she said looking up at him, then into the back of the cart. Gorée had fallen asleep on top of a blanket.

The cart veered off of the path onto a smaller one that led under a canopy of trees. Servants in the approaching fields gave jaunty waves as it passed. Each time they did Pierre gave a nod. It was when they were some distance away when he spoke. "I want to show you something first, and I need to get Gorée to Alise."

The area they were in now was referred to as the black trees, which in reality was an outgrowth of trees on the plantation's highest ground where it was less likely to flood. They came upon a sea of green clearing. Alise's cottage was impressive to look at to say the least. Alise sat on the galerie, but stood to her feet when she saw Pierre approaching. As soon as the cart stopped Gorée awoke and sat up to see where she was. On sight of Alise she started to climb out of the cart.

Pierre lifted her and placed her on her feet.

Gorée was running to reach Alise when she fell hands first to the ground. Pierre watched her a few seconds, then said, "Get up, girl. I know you're stronger than that."

Gorée rolled onto her back holding her stomach as she giggled. Sarah watched as a small smile pulled across Pierre's face. Alise waved at him, indicating there was no need for him to worry and that he could move along.

Pierre sat up and slapped the reins. The cart began to roll again.

"I know I asked before, but your affection toward Gorée makes me believe you loved her mother," Sarah said.

He pulled to a stop underneath a tree. Turning to face her, he leaned low, cupped her face and kissed her deeper than he had the night before. There was something about the way he kissed her that made her reach for him and kiss him back with such desire that she pressed herself tighter against him before she realized what she was doing.

Drawing back from each other, then searching the area to see if anyone had seen their behavior, he wagged his finger at her when she faced him again. "Don't do that again. You thought you were leaning against me. No, I was lifting you out of your seat before I realized it."

Not wanting anyone to hear her laughing so heartily, she gave a small one with one of her hands pressed against her mouth.

"Where were you taking me?" She finally asked.

"I have no idea. Further under the tree. I don't know. Anywhere." His face then became sober. "I shouldn't have kissed you. I did it because I was afraid that after I told you everything I may have never gotten the chance again."

He sat upright but held her gaze.

"Her name was Marie-Téa. She was the same age as I was. We were kids. We liked each other. At times I would find her watching me from across the room while she performed chores. There were times when she would look up from doing a chore and find me watching her from across the room. After we became intimate I wanted to do something nice for her, so I had a cabin built for her.

"I knew my father wouldn't approve. To further conceal the relationship from him, I had her chores moved out of the mansion and in the dairy. Shortly after the cabin was built my father found out about us. When she became pregnant he became determined to teach her, me and all the other women servants on this land a lesson. He sold Marie-Téa the morning she gave birth to Désireé. I tried to buy her back, but old man Dussault refused to sell her.

"When she became pregnant with Gorée she became very ill. No one expected her or the child to survive. When Dussault saw how ill she was, and after she had pleaded with him to send for me, he sent one of his servants to the plantation to deliver a letter. I went the following morning, took one look at her and knew she was going to die. By this time Marie-Téa was pregnant with her fourth daughter. Dussault had already written up a bill of sale for Marie-Téa and her daughters that lived on his land. As he handed it to me, he told me that I didn't have to pay him and that the bill of sale was only a formality.

"She lived three days. That second night Marie-Téa slept peacefully. The servant caring for her decided to blow out the lamps and let Marie-Téa sleep. The next morning the servant awoke to Marie-Téa moaning. The servant pulled back the blankets. The way she described it was Gorée just slipped out. As she cut the cord Marie-Téa looked up at the ceiling and died. Gorée was full of fever, her limbs and entire body swollen, and she was barely breathing. The servant thought she was doing Gorée a favor by wrapping her in a blanket to smother her to death. I wasn't sent for until after breakfast.

"As I stood over the bed, I don't know what I heard. I just knew I heard something. The servant had told me as soon as I arrived that both mother and child had died. I drew back the blankets to see if Marie-Téa was still breathing, because sometimes that happened – people are believed to be dead but aren't. I saw the smaller blanket and thought Gorée was dead inside it. I heard it again – something. I could see that Marie-Téa was dead. My curiosity was the reason I opened the blanket. The sound I had heard was Gorée trying to cry. Her face was covered in sweat. Some of the swelling had gone, but not in her face. We had a servant back then, an old woman who had been born in Senegal and was good at healing others. When I reached her cabin, with old trembling hands she lifted Gorée into her arms, stared down at my daughter and spit on her head. 'This one is full of water. If I can't make her dry as the island of Gorée, she won't live. Leave me to my work,' is what she said.

"Five months later she sent for me. As soon as I stepped through the door she waved her hands for me to be quiet, then silently beckoned me closer to where she was. As I got closer I looked inside the basket. Gorée stared back at me. I turned to Alba ready to hear why she sent for me. Some kind of stronghold of fear had taken over here. 'You watch, monsieur,' she said. I watched as Alba moved slowly from one part of the cabin to another. She was very old, her feet shuffling and making lots of noise. Each time Alba stopped she whispered, 'Where she look now?' Gorée was trying to see the noise she heard, but her small head would shake, and her eyes rolled and closed."

Pierre smiled from the memory.

"Alba thought Gorée was possessed by an evil spirit," he explained. "Each time she made a loud noise, Gorée's head would shake, her eyes would roll and close. 'Where those strange eyes look now?' She kept asking. I reached down and lifted Gorée in my arms. I knew it was no longer safe to keep her there. I was trying to think of what to do with my daughter who wasn't like other babies and hadn't realized that Alba had come up behind me to hide. When Alba peeked behind me and saw Gorée looking at her, she screamed."

Sarah tried to suppress her laughter with her hand.

Pierre gave a small laugh beside her.

"The pitch of that scream aroused a fear in me that I can't remember ever having before. I'm embarrassed to say that I startled something wicked."

Sarah imagined someone as tall as Pierre being startled and laughed even more.

"I was so ashamed that she saw me nearly jump out of my skin that it made me angry. 'This be the devil's child. It doesn't cry! She got an evil spirit in her eyes!' Alba screamed at me then lifted a leather pouch from the mantle and started throwing the dust inside it around the room and sprinkled more over the footprints I left behind. The day Marie-Téa returned to my land she begged me to take care of her three little girls. She didn't include Désireé, as she had already heard stories about Désireé from visitors to the Dussault plantation. I guess you can say that Marie-Téa was my placée, so I saw to her daughters' needs as if they were my own. Mableane didn't like learning, but Anne took to it very easily. That's the story, Sarah. All of it."

He looked forward. "I love Gorée because she's Gorée, and I fear for her future. She doesn't know how to cry. When she's hurting she squeezes her eyes closed until the pain goes away. What she does know how to do is laugh. She didn't walk until she was three. She didn't talk until she was five. But she's older now and getting too old for me to take care of her." He stared down at her. "Gorée might outlive us all. If I die, the way América looks now, she will need someone of white blood to protect her in the future."

Sarah started to speak.

He stopped her. "I have more to tell you, and then you can tell me whatever you want. My mother's name was Catharine Bousquet before she married my father. The day she married my father she was twenty-one years old. From the time she was that age until she was forty she gave birth to six babies long before they should have been born into this world. The longest lived only a few hours. According to my father, it was this child's death that nearly made my mother demented. My father also had a hard time dealing with the deaths and stopped visiting my mother's boudoir. He believed God was punishing him for some things he had done in the past.

"He purchased Alise when she was very young. And that story, chérie, is a far different one. It would take me too long to tell you all of it. When Alise was older my father became intimate with her. He loved my mother, but he soon realized he loved Alise more, and because he loved Alise more he began neglecting my mother's needs. Some years later Alise gave birth to my father's first living child. A daughter. After she gave birth Alise and my father became ill. My father's best friend took the child to his own home to look after the child there.

"My father's friend fell in love with the child. Mind you my father and Alise were on my father's plantation in North Carolina at the time, far away from anyone here to notice. The child was very fair with fair hair and soft colored eyes. After my father was well he had to travel to Paris to take care of some business there. By the time he and Alise returned to New Orléans their daughter was a year old. My father took one look at her and didn't want her growing up as someone with noir blood. The friend agreed to keep the child and raise her as his own. This wasn't hard for him to do. Everyone here in the city had known he had been gone and when he returned he had a child. They had already assumed it was his.

"That child was two years old when my mother saw her one day in the city. She looked into the little girl's face and knew it belonged to her husband. She confronted my father and demanded to know who the mother was. She nearly drove my father mad with her questions. When he saw he was hurting her more by not telling her, he felt guilty and told her. My mother didn't believe him. My mother and father reconciled, and again my mother was carrying a child. And so was Alise. My father didn't want to lose a second child to his best friend and made the decision to take my mother and Alise to Biloxi. There he rented a house. And there my mother once again gave birth too soon to a baby that died. A little girl. But when the three of them left Biloxi my mother was draped in new jewelry and fashionable clothes as she rode through the streets with me in her arms.

"My father was ecstatic. He had an heir that everyone believed was white. He and my mother threw parties for an entire year. Losing one child was too much for Alise to bear. Losing me broke her heart. She did not want to give me up. Each time my father visited her cottage she begged him sorely to give me back to her. When he refused, she refused him. She even ran away and was captured by bounty hunters. She was raped. When the men who abused her learned she belonged to my father they were fearful of returning her. One of the men had mercy on her and told my father where he could find her. My father brought her back and promised to never hurt her again.

"He showered her with jewelry and spent most of his time inside her cottage. My mother was happy she had a child but furious she had lost her husband because of it. And then Alise became pregnant again, and my mother became overjoyed again. She wanted my father to take her and Alise back to Biloxi. It was important to my mother that everyone believed she had given birth to healthy heirs. My father agreed, but he didn't tell Alise. Alise lost that child and almost died because of it. It took seven years before she became pregnant again. My mother found out and started padded her gowns so the servants believed *she* was pregnant.

When my father found out about this he confronted my mother and told her he would not give her this child. My mother threatened to kill herself, me and him if he did not give her this child also when it was born. Alise knew none of this. My father didn't tell her for fear she would runaway.

"On the day Alise went into labor my mother took her most trusted servant into her boudoir and confided in her. And then she began to scream and make noises like she did on the days she gave birth to seven dead babies. After Julien was born, my father waited until Alise was sleeping then took the child out of the house and carried him to my mother. When Alise woke and saw that the child was missing she let out one piercing scream. The servants in her cottage believed it was because the child had died. The next morning my father took Alise to France. They stayed there a year. It took that long for him to convince Alise to come back and for my mother to believe that he will go there again and stay forever if she forced him to give her anymore of Alise's children.

"Alise had two more children after that. The first one died at four months old. The second at eighteen months. When I was eleven and Julien only three, Alise and my mother contracted Yellow Fever. My mother died, but Alise got better. My father didn't want anyone to know that Alise was our mother. For this reason he never asked her to come to the mansion and take care of us. He did, however, start taking us to Alise's cottage to visit with her. I would look at this woman and wonder why she hugged us and kissed us like she did, then weep sore when my father took us away. So I asked her one day why she cried so much. She smiled at me but didn't answer.

"I was twelve when I found out the truth. It had been by accident. That day changed my life. It changed who I was and how I saw *everything*. Julien doesn't know he has noir blood running through his veins. We have never told him and we never will. When I confronted my father, he sat me down and told me that once people learned I had noir blood they will treat me differently. And I believed him. You're the only person, other than Alise, who knows the truth. My heritage isn't the reason my plantation is the way it is. My grandfather made the changes long before I was born. I'm asking you, Sarah Isabelle Cheval, if the noir blood in my veins makes a difference to you."

She studied his unusual hair and eyes that were so much like his father's, then his skin. A part of her wanted to refute what he said when she saw that looking at him she couldn't tell. And then she looked away knowing it made no difference. The love she felt, it was still there. The laugh came out of nowhere. She turned and saw the smile he wore. "I know your father hurt Alise. As a child, I visited New York and Philadelphia. I saw things happening there that broke my heart into two. I would agree living in those states are better than being a slave, but you can't ignore what happens. There is no equality. I wish I could say those separations aren't here in New Orléans, but they are. I won't say I don't have my prejudices." She held his gaze. "But I understand. Your father must have been aware of how things were and how they have gotten worse, and for that reason he took the parentage of his children with him to the grave."

"And the reason you laughed, Sarah?"

Again she laughed and held his gaze. "Because I love you, and I only realized now how beautiful love is. How powerful it is," she explained further.

Pierre put the cart in motion. He rode past Désireé's cottage, then stopped in a large open field. Climbing down, he walked to the side she sat on, offered his hand and helped her down. Together they walked through high grass. Facing her, he peered intently into her eyes, then lifted her in his arms until her hip was adjacent to his shoulder.

"I thought about this last night." He pointed down in the grass in several areas. "Your boudoir could go there. A *grand salle* there. You will need your own kitchen." His finger pointed in the distance. "And there beside your boudoir, a nursery. Sarah, with you I can have children that we can teach about Ashleywood. Heirs who will make sure that Ashleywood stay the way it is now long after we're dead or until the North gets their way and end slavery forever. The South is even now trying to recruit the West to employ the doctrines of slavery in the hopes of keeping slavery alive. Without slavery the South won't survive. I need you, Sarah. Be my forbidden lily."

She was turned to face him. Sarah slid further down until they were face to face, and then she nodded knowing more than ever that she would be what he needed her to be. "I understand now the peace that fills this land, and the true meaning behind its beauty."

As they climbed back in the cart another rode in their direction at a fast speed. Sarah sat still. She sensed by the speed of the driver he was coming to tell his master bad news and suspected that the news had something to do with William.

Pierre rode to meet the servant. The two of them stopped.

The servant's name was Hiram. He worked inside the mansion as an apprentice to the butler, Riley.

Hiram sat quietly for a moment staring at Sarah, and then he hung his head and spoke softly. "Can I speak to you alone, monsieur?"

"What is it?" Sarah asked. "Please tell me."

Pierre climbed down from the cart. Hiram saw this and jumped down in a hurry. The two of them walked off some distance. Sarah watched them carefully as Hiram spoke for only a few minutes. When he finished speaking Pierre stood tall and stared down at the servant, and then he nodded.

Hiram climbed back on his cart and rode just as quickly away.

Pierre climbed back into the cart.

"What did he say?" Sarah asked.

Pierre said nothing as he drove them back to the cottage. Inside it he led her to a sofa and made her sit down. Taking her hands in his, he held them for some time.

"Your father. He went to the city today. A merchant accused him of stealing. Your father tried to run. The merchant shot him, Sarah. After your father was shot he fell into the river. They're looking for him."

# Chapter Twenty-One
# Catch Me if You Can

*[Speaking French is no proof of intelligence. – Creole Proverb]*

Emile Cheval was being pulled out of the river at the same moment Pierre and Sarah had stood in the tall grass. As the rope pulled him up, he cursed, screamed and vowed to kill the man who had seen him clinging to floating turf near the bank and close to where a ship had docked.

A small group of policemen inspected his wound and decided to send him to the hospital before taking him to jail. As the wagon carried him there, William Murray walked down the plank of a steamboat and onto the port. The first thing he heard was the news regarding Emile. After finding a carriage for hire he went to the hospital reaching it the same moment Emile did. Emile saw him and knew his luck had just that quickly changed.

William needed Emile to manage his second plantation just as much as he needed Sarah to become his wife and give him children. His resolve to have both had become stronger when he reached Biloxi and learned just how rich he now was. Never had his brother let on how well he had managed his profits. The more William stared at his brother's spending journals he had learned the trick of his brother's success: spend less, don't incur unnecessary debt when possible, and treat the livestock on your plantation as such, livestock. Sarah was young, well formed, beautiful, a hard worker, and had proven that she could survive hard times. This last part was very important to him. The idea of marrying someone of weak constitution was of no benefit to him, especially when such a wife could die before he did. He had seen this happen many times before.

Sarah was different. And there was something else – something new he had added to his mental itinerary. Those minutes he had been inside of the Jennings mansion in the Vieux Carré had given him the desire to live like Pierre. Both of John's homes were nicely outfitted, but the slaves who worked inside them looked like haggard field hands with no vitality. William needed to change this. He wanted his house servants to look like Pierre's house servants did, only then could he live and be seen as the successful man he now was. Paying to get Emile out of the trouble he was in was seen as an incidental expense. While at the hospital Emile's enthusiasm was as strong as his was. William could feel his luck also changing when Emile sent him to the Jennings mansion in the Vieux Carré to speak to Jenna.

When he reached it William made Jenna a generous offer. As he made this offer he had no intentions of fulfilling it, still the offer was made. He would buy Green Lea if she too helped him find Sarah. Jenna readily accepted and told him there was one man in the city who could find anyone, and that man's name was Nel Black.

Nel stood still with inquiring eyes when he saw Jenna and William standing at the room of the door he rented from one of the city's residents. The small amount of cash Pierre had given him to help Sarah escape had long been spent. Down to his last half eagles, he listened eagerly as William offered him one thousand dollars for his help. Nel purposely only looked at William. The fact that Jenna had come with him had already told him what William had wanted. Rising to his feet, he refused the offer and showed them to the door. Why take William's money when Pierre would give his loyalty after hearing what William and his wife was up to?

Outside the closed door bitterness slid down William's throat. And then he remembered Nel being at the mansion the day Sarah had gone missing. Certain Jenna was playing him for a fool and using Nel and Pierre to do her dirty work, he smiled at her and thanked her as they left Nel behind. Later that evening he found three men in a saloon on Girod Street to help him search the Ashleywood plantation for his fiancé. William became overjoyed when a heavy-set man sitting nearby and who had overheard the conversation beckoned William to him and for a small amount of money told William something he needed to know.

"I know that plantation well," Chadwick told him. "I know the owner just as well. You're wrong about Jenna. She never liked her sister and would never help her get away from you. Pierre is your culprit."

William seethed as he remembered the way Pierre had tossed him into the street.

"He has a cottage on his plantation hidden deep between the trees. He hides things of important value to him there. I can tell you and your men how to reach it."

William didn't want to wait until morning. If the men left now they could reach the plantation before night, and once night had fallen they could get inside the cottage and take Sarah, then be back at the port before morning and before Pierre realized she was gone.

While these three men were still on the way to the Ashleywood plantation, Jean-André Dussault was returning from the city and decided to stop at the plantation to inform Pierre the latest news he'd heard about Emile.

Jean-André, much older in years now, looked frail as he sat in the *salle*. He had given Pierre the news, and although he had intended to be back on the road before the sun had completely fallen, he couldn't stop staring at the servant who served him café. Reaching his hands toward her, he beckoned her closer. Pierre nodded at the servant, a gesture which meant she should be obedient.

Anne stepped cautiously toward Jean-André suspicious of the way he had been watching her.

Jean-André's eyes weren't as good as they used to be. When she was close he pulled her with strength Anne didn't believe he still had until their faces nearly touched. When he saw his own features staring back at him, the smile he gave showed the condition his teeth were in. Uncertain how many quadroon *bâtards* he had, he was certain about one thing, and that was Anne was his most beautiful child.

Standing in the corner was another servant. Jean-André had recognized Mableane as soon as he had come into the room. The roundness she had as a child was still visible, as was her plain face. Although dressed similarly, Anne stood out between the two of them. Looking into her eyes, he knew she wasn't some dumb négresse. Intelligence radiated out of her. "How much do you want for this one, monsieur? Name your price. I shall like to have her."

"She's not for sale," Pierre said and smiled at his neighbor.

Anne stared at her monsieur with silent gratitude.

"Why don't we let her decide?" Jean-André bargained. "Would you like that, chérie? You can visit my home, then decide if you would rather live there than here."

Anne did not know that the man smiling at her was her father, and she didn't like the sound of a plantation owner taking her away from Ashleywood. What if this man never brought her back even after she told him she wanted to return? Lowering her head she stayed silent hoping her monsieur would speak for her.

"You like it here, chérie?"

"Oui, monsieur."

"Look at me, chérie."

She peered up.

The old man continued to stare at her as he spoke to her monsieur.

"Pierre, I do believe you are indebted to me. I beg of you to let me leave here with this one to be on loan for one month. At the end of that time I shall return her if she chooses to come back. Do this, monsieur, and I will feel as if your debt has been paid."

"One month," Pierre agreed knowing why Jean-André wanted to take Anne with him.

Anne could hardly keep still.

"Anne, go upstairs and prepare. But hurry. Monsieur Dussault will be leaving shortly."

Anne dipped her knee, then turned and walked out of the room. With her head down she didn't see Julien walking toward her and bumped into him.

Julien braced his hands on her shoulders. "Tears? What is this?"

Anne was unable to talk as she stared up at him.

Julien knew that Anne was disliked by the other in-house servants and led her upstairs to the third floor. There in the small room where tutors from France had traveled to New Orléans to teach him all that he knew, he closed the door knowing none of the servants used this room, as it was deemed a private room to be used solely by the family.

"I don't want to go, m'sieu!" She whispered. "Monsieur Pierre is selling me to Monsieur Dussault."

"Dussault?" Julien had trouble believing this. He knew all too well how the men in the Dussault family behaved on their plantation. Visitors there were given free rein of the slave quarters late at night. Anne wouldn't be an exception. She had been a beautiful child and had become an even more beautiful young woman. Julien leaned closer to her and whispered in a low voice. "Does he know about us? My brother?"

"I don't know," she whispered back, her eyes fearful. "I don't want to go, m'sieu. I don't."

He cupped her face, then kissed her on the mouth. Anne was the reason he had returned to Ashleywood. On a previous visit the two of them had begun an affair. When he returned this time the affair started again exactly where it had left off, except this time with far more passion. Taking her by the hand he led her downstairs hoping no one would see him sneak her out of the mansion. As they reached the hall Pierre stepped into it and faced him.

"Where are your things?" Pierre asked looking at her empty hands. "Monsieur Dussault is ready to travel."

Hearing conversation not too far from where he stood, Jean-André turned the corner and faced the trio. "Are you ready yet, chérie?"

"No, monsieur."

"I'll take her the way she is," Jean-André said. "I'm sure we'll have all that she needs at my place."

Anne was too frightened to look at Julien as she stepped forward. Julien had no intentions of letting her leave the mansion with any man, especially Jean-André. Even if it meant Pierre finding out about their affair it was better than Anne leaving and being stuck on the Dussault plantation the rest of her life. Just as he opened his mouth to speak Jean-André lifted Anne's chin with severely wrinkled fingers.

"You truly don't want to go, do you, chérie?"

"No, monsieur," Anne answered and lowered her chin further than it already was.

"Our debt is settled here, Pierre. You must have been good to this one if she chooses not to leave here with me," he said, turned and walked away.

Pierre followed him to his carriage outside.

As Anne meant to pass Julien, he reached for her hand, his fingers rubbing against hers. Looking over his shoulder to make certain Pierre was no longer there he pulled Anne closer to him and pressed his mouth hungrily against hers. As always Anne was always ready for him. Sliding her hand down the front of him, she gripped the front of his trousers where she knew she affected him most. His manhood hardened against her palm and became very strong. Loving the way she touched him, and the way she made him feel, and the way she needed him as much as he needed her, he forgot others were also inside the mansion. Caressing her derriere, he lifted the back hem of her gown as if he would strip her naked and make love to her there in the hall. Anne sucked his tongue into her mouth. Julien groaned. A sound was made behind them.

Anne pulled from him and fled down the hall, quickly making her way upstairs.

Julien couldn't turn right away without showing whoever was behind him how aroused he was. Adjusting his trousers he instead looked over his shoulder and saw Carlisle Morning staring at him as if in wonder.

"How about you and I having a drink, Mr. Morning? We can sit and talk."

Carlisle cleared his throat and pulled his face back to normal. The things he had seen on this plantation were starting to boggle his mind. "Sir, there's no need for you to waste your time drinking with me. I apologize for standing in this spot. I was hoping to find one of the servants and beg them for a cup of café if it wouldn't have been of any trouble. I do appreciate the kindness everyone here has shown."

"You're saying we don't need to talk, Carlisle?"

"Whatever for, sir? I'm just a stranger passing through that will be forever indebted to this family. Most of the thoughts I have is how to pay y'all back and not how to turn against you."

"Semper!" Julien yelled.

It took a few seconds for Semper to enter the hall.

"Get this gentleman a cup of café and anything else he needs from the kitchen."

Semper dipped her knee and disappeared.

Julien's eyes narrowed on Carlisle. "Stay away from my niece. I'm a crazy man. Don't make me prove that. And I ride fast too. Don't think you'll have any chance of getting away."

Carlisle nodded in agreement. "Sir, I hope you don't mind me being straightforward, but I believe you are crazy." Carlisle looked over his shoulder, then made his eyes grow wide so Julien understood what he was trying to say.

Julien smiled. "She's crazy, too." He knew exactly where Marie-Marie was and didn't need this Texan telling him. Carlisle was the reason Marie-Marie spent more time in the mansion than at Alise's cottage because Julien had needed someone keeping an eye on Carlisle during the moments he sneaked off with Anne.

He turned and ran upstairs in the direction Anne had gone in.

*Unbelievable*, Carlisle thought as he watched Julien disappear, then went back to the *salle* where Marie-Marie and Abigail were.

# Chapter Twenty-Two
# The Smell of Hounds

*[Never let a boy do a man's work. – Creole Proverb]*

Sarah sat at the table staring at the wide bonnet Gorée had placed on Pierre's head earlier that day. It lay on the floor near her foot half on its side with the knot still tied. Pressing her hands together and closing her eyes, she began to pray again that her father was found, and when he was found that he would still be alive. As she knitted her fingers more tightly she heard someone enter the cottage, and then feet began to run in her direction. Believing it was someone bringing news about her father she opened her eyes and rose to her feet.

A male slave ran past her as if he didn't see her, through the open door of the bedroom she was using, and kept running out its rear door, disappearing into the night. The door clanged against the cottage wall, then began to close again at a slow pace. Lifting the hem of her gown, it took her only seconds to realize the slave had been a runaway and only seconds longer to realize a bounty hunter must have been in the area and after him.

Following quickly behind him, she hurried out into the yard then looked in all directions. No one was there, at least that she could see. A branch crackled between the trees. Following where the noise had come from, she thought if she could reach the runaway she could lead him to the cabin and hide him there until Pierre could be found and alerted. She had only taken a few steps when she was tackled from behind and thrown to the ground.

Rolling onto her back, and pressing her hands into her attacker, her eyes became wide when she saw it was the slave that had run through the house. Pressing his finger to his lips, he reached for her wrapping his arm around her neck and pulled her up on her feet. With him now taking the lead the two of them began walking backwards in a rushed gait back toward the cottage wall and into the dark shadow of the ell near its end.

Again Sarah heard branches crackle. Small sounds. And then what sounded like a voice whispering.

"Are bounty hunters after you?" She whispered.

Large white eyes nodded at her in equal fear. "I saws yous in thur," he whispered. "You be Saint Pierre, the keeper of the heavenly gate?"

"No," Sarah whispered and shook her head. Before she could tell him she knew who the keeper of the gate was the slave ran like a cheetah on even ground. His dark silhouette was all she saw before it disappeared between the trees. She knew there was no way she could catch him. Screaming out to him would alarm the bounty hunters and steer them in the right direction.

The night was becoming a sad one, she thought. Turning when she heard the unmistakable sound of a horse, a thought came to her. If she spoke to the bounty hunters and told them she saw a strange looking slave running in the opposite direction maybe the runaway would have a better chance of putting some distance between himself and those after him. She took one step then stopped. Abruptly. Most bounty hunters traveled with bloodhounds. Without dogs leading them with the scent of the runaway in their nostrils, finding a runaway would be the same as walking blindly in the dark. Why didn't she hear any dogs? And stranger still, why was the silence of the night enormously loud? Bounty hunters were always in motion. Stopping for a moment gave a runaway a chance of gaining distance, being paid for each capture the driving force that kept them moving at all times.

As close as she could hear the horse drawing near, dogs should have run past her by now, chasing down the runaway and locking him in their jaws.

Then who was there on horseback during the night riding between the trees as if they were purposely trying to be quiet?

William came to her mind, but Sarah doubted he had anything to do with what she was listening to. Again she heard a voice, this time closer. A whisper so small she couldn't make out any of the words.

Lifting her hem higher she hurried toward the front of the cottage to put distance between her and the voice. As she rounded the front she nearly slipped and fell on her rear when she saw a man on horseback climbing down from his mount. The man heard the noise she made and turned his head in her direction. Recognition shone in his eyes, but Sarah couldn't remember ever seeing this man before.

Jerking her body toward the trees, it wasn't until she was running swiftly across the grass when she realized she had no shoes on her feet. Behind her she heard the man remount his horse then yell at others between the trees. "I found her! I see her! The front of the cottage!"

Sarah tried to run harder even though she knew she couldn't outrun a horse. And that's what she heard, hoofs pounding the earth behind her. While she was staring ahead a dark shadow ran out of the trees with a large boulder of rock held high up in his arms. Sarah kept running as four more dark figures sprang out of the trees like hidden soldiers of war, all of them holding up boulders of various sizes. Horses neighed behind her as their riders pulled hard on their reins. The last thing a white man wanted was an injured horse. Unless they were wealthy, a good horse cost almost as much as a slave.

Sarah looked over her shoulder long enough to see the horsemen turn back to put distance between them and the charging slaves. One of the slaves that had a smaller boulder growled like an animal as he stopped running and hurled his boulder at the one horseman that didn't believe a slave would injure him or his horse. The rein on the horse was tugged as soon as the boulder took flight. The horse's head was still turning when the boulder crashed against the horse and knocked the horse and the rider to the ground.

When the other riders saw this their anger overpowered their need to see about their horse's wellbeing. Turning again, they rode forward furiously creating an arc and charged toward the slaves who dared to hurt white men.

Sarah saw none of this. In her mind she saw an image of William. Once while she slept in her boudoir she had awakened to William standing over her wearing a nightshirt. The front of it was tented from his erection. Pleading with her to permit him to lie in bed with her, he felt the need to humiliate her before he left the room on her insistence. The hem of his nightshirt was lifted high up to his hairy, saggy breasted chest revealing his hard, rounded stomach, his penis and two large hairy thighs that looked like two creases of fat slammed against each other.

One of the slaves caught up with her and grabbed her hand hoping this would make her run faster. Together they reached the trees with far too many sounds closing in around them. Sarah knew if they kept running north they would reach the swamp. And unless the horsemen were willing to travel through it to the other side the swamp was their best chance at getting away.

Running faster than she ever had the sole of her foot split open from something on the ground. Falling to the ground she reached out with both hands just as a horseman rode past her and yanked his horse back around. The slave that had been running with her, believing these men were bounty hunters, had dropped her hand and ran fast in the opposite direction. The rider jumped down from his mount and hurried to her. Sarah was already on her feet. The pain in her foot was too brutal to ignore. Still she ran without once slowing down. A grab made to the back of her gown snatched her backward.

Sarah reached both hands to the nape of her neck and tried to pull the pin away that held her gown in place. The rider fell on top of her as she hit the ground. A groan rushed out of her when his elbow sank into her stomach. As she was yanked to her feet she did nothing to stop the rider from pushing her forward. Without the gown she could run faster, and she could fight her would be abductors. The pin was pulled away. The gown fell slack. The man grabbed more of it in an attempt to keep her near. This helped her out of it. As she lifted the hem, the more he pulled Sarah bent in a way so the gown was tugged over her head.

Another horseman arrived and climbed down from his mount. Sarah tried to see if the other slaves were still nearby. When she saw no one else but two of the three horsemen coming toward her, she began to scream. "I can take you to Saint Pierre! The gates are open and ready!"

The two men surrounded her, yanked her by the arms and did their best to carry her to one of their horses. Sarah pounded with her fists. As she was lifted in the air four shadows sprang out from behind a nearby tree and tackled the two men to the ground. Arms began to swing wildly. Feet began to kick with injurious intent. Sarah crawled away from the melee, and looking around on the ground she saw nothing she could use to beat these men senseless with. All she saw were scattered leaves and dead debris and pebbles too small to do any damage. Falling to her knees she clawed two handfuls of dirt and running forward jumped on one of the rider's backs and smeared both hands of dirt as hard as she could into his eyes.

The man yelled and screamed from the small pieces of grit in the dirt. Sarah didn't stop grinding. With both of her legs fastened tightly around him to keep in place her hands locked over his eyes.

A pistol was fired. A dark figure fell to the ground. With the other horseman's only shot now fired he no weapon left to defend himself with. Sarah rolled away from the man she was on top of, and grabbing two more handfuls of dirt she ran toward the second rider. Dark figures had piled on top of him. The beating they were giving made the man beg for mercy. As the man rolled onto his side to avoid a kick to his head Sarah jumped on top of him knee first pushing the dirt in her hands hard into his eyes as if she wanted to make him permanently blind.

The man tossed her away. Her body rolled with the momentum, and then she sprang to her feet and yelled to the others. "Follow me!"

As she ran all she heard was the sound of their harsh breathing. Run, she told herself. *Run and don't look back.* She looked down and saw how visible she was. The white cotton of her petticoat seemed as if it glowed when the moonlight hit it. Running behind a tree, she pulled it off and tossed it to the ground. This hadn't helped. Her shift was equally white. Removing it would make her even more naked. The thought of being captured and taken to William spurred her into action. Pulling the shift over her head, she then lowered to the ground and grabbed handfuls of dirt to coat her exposed skin.

Looking at her hands she saw how muddy the dirt was. Muddy soil meant the swamp was close. The others saw what she was doing, and willing to do anything for freedom grabbed handfuls of mud and rubbed it on her to help them escape their bondage. Tears burst from Sarah's eyes when she saw this. The sound of hoofs could be heard behind them.

"Go," Sarah stressed. "Straight ahead. Don't stop. Not even for me. Wade the swamp downstream until you reach for the first cabin on the south side of the banks."

They all started to run at the same time. Horse hoofs beat and pounded and got louder and louder. With her arms now free to move, Sarah felt she was running faster as she pumped her arms in rhythm with her feet. Up ahead the swamp could finally be seen. One of the dark figures saw it and took a flying leap inside of it. Sarah didn't know why she thought to do what she did. It could have been her remembering an alligator lying just outside the swamp near the cabin. She also jumped but fell short at the water's edge. Splashes were made around her as the other runaways ran into the water, their legs lifting high in their need of flight.

A horse drew closer behind her. Dashing to her feet she ran and was grabbed around the waist. As she was lifted in the air she saw that all of the slaves had stopped only a mere few feet in the water. It was then she realized that none of them knew how to swim. She was swinging her arms at her abductor when a horse in full gallop and too swiftly to stop dove right into the swamp. The rider on top of it was larger than life and had long white hair, and eyes the color of the moon. Pierre jumped off of Annabelle, ran past Sarah and lifted the second abductor from the ground just as he reached his partner. Lifting him like a log ready to be tossed onto a bonfire, the man hurled through the air over the runaways' heads, and far into the swamp.

The man holding Sarah saw his partner flying in the air, released her, fell onto his back, then tried to crawl away. Pierre's long leg lifted. The knee bent in a determined arch, and then the sole of his Hessian boot squashed down on her abductor like a bug, lifted and stomped again. The man beneath his boot screamed out in pain and tried to roll onto his side and curl himself into a ball.

Sarah saw the second rider running toward Pierre from the swamp. At first she thought he had wanted to avenge his partner, but then she saw the hard-knuckled skin of an alligator swimming fast behind him. "Get out of the water! Get out of the water!"

The dark figures waded until they were able to run, their hands splashing at the water in the hopes of propelling them along. As her would-be abductor ran out of the water Pierre swung his right fist into the man's nose. Sarah and the runaways watched as the rider fell. Pierre lifted him from the ground and over his head, spotted the alligator and tossed the man directly toward it. Once his hands were free they tightened into fists as he leaned forward with bent arms, doubled over and growled like a man demented with rage and ready for the bloodiest war.

The alligator swam away from the man floating on the water's surface.

Sarah was unable to look away. The man was dazed; his feeble attempts to stay afloat made small splashes. The alligator continued to swim further away.

"Eat 'em!" One of the runaways yelled, running closer to the water with his fist shaking in front of him with the same amount of rage Pierre had. "Him right thur! Eat 'em!"

A coat was draped over her shoulder and she was lifted from the ground.

The floating rider became aroused. Seeing he was in water he splashed wildly then started to swim back to shore uncaring that Pierre was still there because he knew it was better to face a man than an alligator.

Pierre lifted her on top of his horse and mounted behind her.

The slaves stared at him. One of them recognized him as the Saint Pierre he had heard about and told the others. They began to hug one another and began to cry and jump up and down.

Pierre steered his horse toward the two horsemen. Both were trying to hold each other up as they made their way back to their horses. "Who sent you here?"

"William!" Sarah yelled as if the name was an insult. "William sent them. They were looking for me. They chased *me*. But your servants kept them from getting a hold of me!"

"If I see you on my land again, I'll release my entire slave population on you to do whatever they will to you. And whatever's left of you, I'll feed personally to the gators."

"We'll be back with the police!" One of them threatened. "When we get back I'm going to point out those darkies over there. I'm going to remember all of their faces!"

The runaways moved closer to Pierre.

The men finally reached their horses, mounted and rode away.

Sarah turned and faced Pierre hugging him tightly against her.

"Where are you slaves from?" Pierre asked, cradling her in his arms and staring at them from over her head.

"Point Coupee," all of them answered.

"One of you will have to go back there to tell the others that the gates of heaven are closed. You should have heard that by now. Which one of you will it be?"

The runaways stared at one another, and then all eyes stared at one of them in particular. The runaway they singled out fell back from them and pleaded with Pierre. "I's helps her! It was me! I's help her. Ax her, monsieur! Tell 'em, mademoiselle! I's helps you!"

"He did!" Sarah wailed. It was the slave that had run through the cottage and had held her hand to help her run faster. "Pierre, please. He helped me more than once. All of them did. They threw boulders at the riders. And they must have injured one because there were three riders and not two. I would be gone by now if they hadn't come out of hiding to help me. Please."

"Listen," Pierre stressed. "The police are watching the ports. My ships are being searched at every port for runaways. The best I can do is hide you here until it's safe to open the gate again."

"I's stay!" One of them said.

"All us wills!" Another answered rapidly. "Juss don't sends us back, massuh!"

"What about the police?" Another asked. "Deys be back comes moanin."

"Someone has to go back," Pierre insisted. "If none of you are returned others will have hope and run here. Too many runaways have yet to be found. I recently attended a meeting in the city held by plantation owners near and far. The alert has gone out. Overseers, bounty hunters, and slave owners are working together like never before. There were mentions of killing the next runaways found to make examples of them."

"I'll go," Sarah said.

"I will," she assured when Pierre looked down on her with an expression she couldn't read.

One of the runaways balled his fist, sobbing as he nodded in her direction.

"We got a little distance to travel," Pierre said. "Let's go. Try and keep up."

***

Pierre stopped at the cabin long enough for her to bolt herself inside, and then he hurried with the runaway slaves to his slave quarters which was known on the plantation as The Bottoms.

Like the first night she had arrived there, there was no light. The water she had left behind when she was there last had soured. Grabbing one of the blankets folded in the armoire she wrapped herself in it and shivered from the coldness that seemed to have crept into her bones. Pierre had told her he would be back as soon as he could. Sarah wanted to believe he would return right away but knew this was impossible. A white man was possibly injured on his plantation. A runaway was possibly dead. Something would have to be done with both of them before the police arrived. And she couldn't be certain of it, but if Pierre meant for her to stay then the proof that she was there needed to be removed from the cottage.

These things would take time, and that time may last all through the night. Sarah didn't believe her would be kidnappers had traveled far. Even if they were familiar with this part of the country it was too dark to travel without proper light and the right provisions.

After making sure that the cabin was bolted again for a third time, she grabbed the coverlet off of the bed then crawled underneath the bed until her spine pressed against the far wall. In this position she could hear everything that happened outside of the cabin on this side. At one point she thought she heard footsteps approaching, but convinced herself this wasn't true when the sounds disappeared as soon as she began to listen more carefully.

As she lay and listened one thing was certain in her mind. She wasn't leaving New Orléans to be the wife of William. She wondered if her father was dead, and if so if his body had been found. The idea of him never being found was too unfathomable to think about. No tears fell from her eyes. She felt nothing, except profound coldness.

As she lay on the floor unaware of how uncomfortable the floor was she kept seeing everything that had happened that night over and over again. The bravery of the runaways made her cognizant of something she heard many times before: if given the chance to organize les noirs could become dangerous. The kind of boulders they used as weapons couldn't have come from Ashleywood. This meant the runaways had carried the boulders with them to reach Saint Pierre. And they had used their only weapons to rescue her. And after the boulders were gone they had used all that they had left: their fists, feet and wit.

She was lying in the same position a long while later when a knock sounded against the door. Crawling out of her hiding place, she walked to the door as quietly as she could.

"It's me, Sarah," Pierre said on the other side of it.

She removed the block of wood that kept intruders from coming in and snatched the door open. She would have run into his arms if they hadn't been filled. Just as she thought everything she had left at the cottage was now in his hands, including her boots.

"Are they safe?" This question seemed most important.

"They're in The Bottoms. I have servants there hiding them where they can't be found."

"And the third rider?"

"Injured. He won't be walking for a while. It was him that led me in the right direction. And then I heard your voice, but couldn't decipher where it came from."

"One of the runaways was shot..."

"He's still alive. He was the reason I was able to ride again in the right direction. It was after I saw him that I figured you were running to the swamp. I think he'll be all right, but he'll have to be quiet or he'll give them all away if the police do come."

"You don't think they will?"

"Going to the police would mean they will have to explain why they were on my land. I told Benny to find seven slaves who look similar to the runaways. As soon as the sun rises I plan on going to The Bottoms and for me and these seven to come up with a story of our own, one that will make these men look like they were up to no good. I know it's wrong to do that, but once the news spread, and I hope it will, I don't want anyone else getting any ideas about coming here, especially when they hear your attackers give their own account of what really happened."

A burlap sack and her boots were placed on top of the table. A bucket of water was set on the floor.

"I'm so scared," she whispered. "I pray no one comes back, Pierre. And I'm afraid about my father, and what's happened to him, and if he's still in the river. I don't think I can handle such news if he is."

One of his hands caressed the side of her face.

"Your father was found, mon chérie. His injuries weren't fatal. My neighbor came to the plantation to tell me about it. He had seen everything. The reason your father jumped into the river was because he realized he'd been running through the streets with the bottle of wine he had stolen still in his hand. Your father had plenty to say as he was pulled up by rope."

Pierre held her closely against him and felt her shivering.

"Let me grab a lantern. I brought one with me."

The door was pulled open again. Sarah watched as he stepped outside, bent low, then stepped in again.

"You're cold and wet. I'll build a fire..."

"No! The smoke! I don't want anyone to see it."

"You need to get warm. And you need to wash. Washing in cold water when you're already cold – I won't permit it."

Sarah watched him bolt the door and start a fire. In the glow of warm light she saw him again riding Annabelle into the swamp, tossing a man over his head and stomping another hard enough to break bone. The pose he made afterwards had told them all he was willing to kill if it meant keeping her safe. She had loved him before this evening, and now she knew she loved him even more.

Lost in her thoughts, she didn't see him approach. Taking her gently by the hand she was bade to sit in one of the chairs. Sarah tried to help him warm some of the water, but he stopped her and waited until she sat again before he measured out what he considered to be a good amount. He spoke with his back to her. "I don't plan on waiting outside while you bathe. I can sit in the corner."

"I don't want you to go," she assured him.

He stood and when he turned and saw her, he saw how frightened and desperate she was. All she wore was a pair of stays, her pantalettes, and a pair of hose. Mud caked her skin and hair.

"I removed my clothing," she explained, staring down the front of her. "It was hard to run in my gown, and my underclothes made it easier for them to see me. I didn't suffer much by their hands. Had it not been for seven runaways searching for Saint Pierre the night would have ended differently. You should have seen them, Pierre. They thought the horsemen were bounty hunters. Still they came out of hiding when I was attacked, unaware that I could help them in any way. All they knew was one of them had seen me in the cottage. This made me someone good in their eyes."

Suddenly it felt as if the night crashed down on her in an inundated wave. Through the blurs of her tears she spoke softly, quietly.

"I have lived my life surrounded by slaves. Tonight I saw seven runaways willing to kill a white man if it meant they could reach Saint Pierre." She turned away from him. "And to think I called out to them for help. I didn't realize how vicious they would fight."

She faced him and reached her hand out to his. Pierre rested his palm in hers. Sarah gripped it tightly with both hands. "You have to stop this, Pierre. You're putting people in danger, and for what? To free only a few at a time? I want to tell you something although I know it can change things between us."

His eyes were calm as they studied hers, fearful of what she would say next.

Sarah lowered her chin, studying her soiled hose. "I didn't help Choco, Benjamin and Daniel because I cared about them. I do care about them. Don't misunderstand. I did it because I *owned* them. The entire time I led them here I wanted them to see and to remember that the woman whom they have served for many years had become their savior. I wanted to make them see that if it wasn't for someone like me looking out for them, they would be lost on their own and couldn't survive."

"Do you hate them? If you do, I need to know why." He asked this question while holding her gaze intently.

"I don't hate les noir." She continued to hold his gaze when she said what she said next. "But there is a *difference*, Pierre, between *noir et blanc*. Surely you must know this is true. It's the reason you want me to give you an heir when you already have one. I'm not saying that *les blancs* is the superior race, but we are a better race of pe…"

He yanked his hand from hers and rose to full height. "Because Alise is my maman I am inferior to you? She is inferior to you?"

She also stood tall. "Pierre, *you're* different. You don't look noir."

Pierre looked away when he realized she believed she had paid him a compliment.

"And neither does my maman," he said. "But it doesn't change the fact that her father was a quadroon. And because of that, mademoiselle, she was sold illegally into slavery. Her own oncle sold her so he could have money to survive on. I – have – *three* – heirs!" He walked toward the door, rested his palm against it, lowered his head and shook it. "I can't leave Gorée a goddamned thing. If she had been *blanc* the chances of someone trying to steal her inheritance would be less. She would have gotten sympathy, and of course plenty of pity, but still she would have been looked after and cared for because she was the same as those who govern this country. I don't *want* more heirs, Sarah. I need them. But not for them to look down on my *visibly* noir children. I need them to *serve* my noir children – to protect them! I thought you understood that."

He turned and faced her. His eyes had darkened, his expression fixed. "You can stay as long as you want. I'll still give you whatever you need. That hasn't changed."

Her eyes also hardened as she gazed at him. "But you don't want me anymore? Is that what you're saying?"

"How can I be with someone who believes men like William is better than I am because he's sans noir blood? I'll help you. Not because I said I would, but because I *want* to help you."

She turned from him and faced the fire. Her arms wrapped around her shoulders as the heat of the fire made her warm. "You're not being fair. I thought you had feelings for me. But I see now all you wanted was to have a *blanc* child."

His laugh made her look over her shoulder. His gaze was piercing as he looked also in her direction.

"I finally see the family resemblance, Sarah. You're more like your sister than you believe. Do you truly think so highly of yourself? I don't need *anything* from you, Sarah. I never have. There are many women in the city who will give me an heir for far less than I'm willing to give you. Alise is my maman, but that doesn't stop Will Jennings from being my father. The way you're talking sounds like you think I'm pretending to be French when the truth is both of my parents are just as French as you are. If my father is *blanc* does that not make me *blanc* too or have I been removed from that race entirely because my maman has noir blood? Will I have been permitted back into the *blanc* race if my maman was Italian or British or Dutch?"

She lowered her gaze and turned away from him.

"Its people like you – who think the same way you do – the reason I fear my children's future."

She faced him again. "I didn't mean to offend you, and I care not about your money. Do with it as you choose. I do not hate les noirs. I never have." She took a step closer to him, her eyes illuminating with renewed vigor. "I have respect for those seven runaways tonight. And Imogen. She has always served my family well. And…"

Pierre bit his lip and lowered his chin. "Please, stop. Telling me a few people out of an entire race is worthy of your respect is painful to listen to."

"You're twisting my words…"

"And these children you and I would have had? How would you feel for them?"

Her eyes danced with repulsion.

"They are my children!" She screamed.

Pierre smiled softly. "Your superiority is at a level I believe surpasses even that of your sister's. Because they're yours that makes the difference? But others… They don't matter?"

The pain she felt from his words, she was unable to look at him any longer. "You see what you want, and hear what you want."

Pierre reached for a glass resting on top of the table and gave it a twirl with his fingers and thumb. "And if one of our children would have been born with dark skin?" His eyes lifted toward hers. "Would that child embarrass you? Would you have sold that child for fifty dollars to save face amongst your peers?"

Her mouth tightened, and then her eyes closed tightly. "You have no right to say that to me! I'm sorry about what happened to your mother. That it happened has made you bitter. You stand there and judge me when you're no different than I am. You hate an entire race of people, and you have given respect to only a few. Had you not hated your own people, you would have forgiven your wife, and you would have a better marriage. And you wouldn't have turned your back on me now. I don't care who your mother is. Hearing who she is didn't change my feelings for you. I loved you for who you are. I can see now that giving myself to you is taking a risk that if I ever displeased you, you would hate me far more than you hate my sister. I wouldn't want you to hate me. Not you. Because I can see that you're a man who's equally filled with wrath as he is with compassion."

As she faced the fire again he reached into the burlap sack and pulled out a bottle of wine. After the wine was poured he held the glass to his mouth and remembered her volunteering to go to Point Coupee even though she knew William had men looking for her. He thought about Choco, Benjamin and Daniel, and how she pleaded for him to help them escape. Of how she was willing to return to her father to help him get back on his feet even after she knew how desperately he had wanted her to marry William.

The glass was lowered.

"I'm not bitter," he said. "There are many things you don't know about me. I don't just help les noirs. I have helped many people in this city, including

Américains. I don't hate your sister because she's the same race as my father. I dislike her because she's a cold-hearted woman. What I can't abide is prejudice. Prejudice kills people for no reason other than the color of a person's skin. Prejudice will someday hurt my daughters. All I want is to prevent that."

Confounded by her thoughts, she studied the blazing fire more intently. "I don't think I'm better than you, Pierre. I think you are better than many of us, especially after I've seen how you govern your plantation."

She closed her eyes, and then she turned and faced him. "I love you because you're willing to risk your own life for others. Not many people are willing to do that. Because you have managed to stay humble instead of use your money as a source of power to rule over others. Because you refuse to be broken by anyone, including the women you love. You refuse to fear anyone. Who's to say that when you were created, you weren't done so perfectly? You are Saint Pierre. Not only to les noirs. I know personally you are also Saint Pierre to less fortunate Creoles in this city. It's why I came to you for a loan. I had already heard. In the past day I've thought about nothing other than living my life with you. I now can't imagine one without you."

The sound of her desire was close to a whimper when he pulled her to him and his mouth crushed feverishly against hers. Wrapping her arms tightly around his neck, she clung to him fiercely kissing him as hungrily as he kissed her. When he drew away she cupped his face and held him near. "Take me," she whispered.

"I will, mon chérie. But in a way you will always remember."

He returned to the hearth and removed what was left of the boiling water from the fire. A basin was pulled out of the bag and hot water poured into it.

Sarah searched the bag to see what else was inside. Grabbing the things she needed, she mixed cold water into the basin, removed her wet clothing, then enjoyed the feel of warm water and soap on her skin. While she had undressed Pierre had crossed the room. An extra coverlet was added to the bed. His boots were removed first. With his back to her, his clothing was also removed and dropped to the floor. As he did this she realized he had changed his attire since they had left the swamp.

Toweling herself dry, she searched the bag again hoping to find a shift or nightgown. One had been neatly folded and laid in the very bottom.

"Leave it, chérie," he said.

His eyes fell to her breasts, and then the junction of her thighs as she walked toward the bed.

The coverlet was lifted to allow her to crawl underneath it. She drew in a deep breath of anticipation.

"Don't be frightened."

"I'm not."

Wanting her to feel and not think he kissed her until her arms closed around him. Deep, arousing, impatient kisses brought them clinging together: their arms constantly moving to change their positions and make their union even more complete. Lying more on top of her, his desire to taste, smell, lick and kiss every inch of her body became crucial. The length of her neck, her throat, the smooth skin of her shoulders. Sarah's impatience became more noticeable when her legs clamped round his waist with bone-crushing strength, unaware of why she was doing this and only that her body, knowing what it was made for, sought to seek nothing less than ethereal pleasure.

So enamored and exhilarated by their kisses, Sarah proved an ardent lover when she struggled against him when he tried to free himself from her hold. Grabbing both of her hands and pinning them above her head, he wanted to show her that there were other parts of her that demanded his attention. Lowering before she could entwine herself around him again, his searing hot mouth sought the roundness of her breasts with every intention of feasting from them for some time.

Sarah mewled with tingling excitement and watching with growing excitement as he changed and distorted the shape of her nipples with mind blowing sucks and greedy tugs that made the very center of her sex ache and throb for equal attention. Watching the hardened, darkest parts of her breasts being pulled between his lips and released after a long pleading suck warm and wet imposed upon her sanity. Whirls of giddy content coursed through her when his mouth lowered between her thighs. From the first touch of his tongue she knew this was something she could not watch, as the feeling was so exquisite all she could do was lie still beneath him and close her eyes.

While her eyes closed Pierre feasted off the taste of her sex that was sweeter than any wine and far more intoxicating than any strong drink. Pierre loved the taste and feel of her delicate flesh, leaving no part of it untouched. A woman unashamed of expressing what she was feeling, he took advantage of the moment she opened her thighs even wider to him, plunging his tongue as deep as he could inside her for more of her heady nectar.

The cry she gave told him just how much she needed him inside her. Not wanting to pull his face from the scorching heat between her thighs just yet, his hands reached for her breasts rolling her nipples between his fingers in such a way he could feel her sex throb with a pulse against his face as it released more of its juices. He could have stayed like this for some time, as the more he stimulated her aroused nipples the more he was able to lave away the sweetest honey. Only when her movements became more desperate, and her whimpers warned she had left the realm of pleasure and was experiencing delicious torment did he lift higher to put her at ease.

The hard nodule at the aperture of her sex teased him like a tiny piece of fruit too small to eat. If her nipples could be milked to release drops of nectar between her thighs, this fruit he rolled against the very tip of his tongue could release a generous bounty. It took only seconds to investigate the fruit with his tongue, then position it for what he needed. Sarah's hip pushed slowly against him as he strengthened his tongue and flicked its tip like a small ball ringing inside an iron bell.

Satisfied when the tiny fruit filled with blood and protruded slightly as it became larger and more sensitive encouraged him even more to flick it just right. Unnerved by her thighs clenching around his head like a well fitted mitt, the need to breathe was far from his mind as he tormented and titillated that little delicate bean until Sarah's head pushed hard against the pillow as she cried out loudly, and as her knees began to tremble and lose their hold of him. The sound of her climax brought him closer to his own. His ever growing desire penetrated him so deeply it felt as if a searing flame had coursed upward and shot up his spine before centering at the nape of his neck.

Lying on top of her, he gave no thought to how squeamish she may be when she tasted herself on his tongue. As his tongue rushed to fill her mouth his hands caressed and squeezed her rear, holding her fast against him as his swollen shaft slipped between her thighs. Unable to wait for them to be completely joined as one, her hips lifted. It took everything within him not to push hard inside her and feel the tightness of her silken walls. He pushed gently until her maidenhead gave way, then stopped. Realizing she had been unaware there would be pain on this first thrust he searched her eyes, then brought her attention back to him with a searing kiss.

Her breathing became as rapid as her heartbeat. Small nibbles were made along his shoulder as he moved slowly. Only then did Sarah notice that the coverlet had fallen from them and onto the floor. She saw the way her legs shivered, and the way his muscular body had her pinned to the mattress. The last of his restraint was being used to hold back from hurting her more.

"Love me." The sound of her voice seemed not her own, so strained and soft it sounded to her own ears.

Pierre's slightly wet lips were parted as he panted and stared intently into her eyes. "You're a *small* woman. I'm a *big* man. I'm not all the way in yet, chérie. I need you to open more for me."

His eyes squeezed closed, and his face became pinched. She knew then that the ache he felt was just as strong as her own. Staying immobile he buried his face into her neck, teasing and suckling, his teeth nibbling in such a way that she felt her sex dampen with new arousal. A pleasurable, deep, breathy groan slipped from his mouth as this wetness allowed him to push deeper inside her.

She pleaded perhaps too loudly and like a wanton woman who had never been churched. The feeling was indescribable: the scorching heat of him, the fullness inside her that now reached almost to the very back of her. Unsure what she should do she stared up at him with large eyes filled with shock. It was when he pulled out of her that she looked down and saw his manhood glistening with her juices. The thrust back inside of her, and this time even deeper, and she knew then exactly what to do. Reaching with her fingers, she gripped handfuls of his hair then gave a vicious tug with locks of his hair toward her as she thrust her hips toward his with the intentions of riding him like she would a horse.

Quickly his head lowered so she couldn't see his face. A small smile had been on it. Although she knew the quiver he made was his attempt not to erupt with laughter, she lifted her hips high from the mattress until he filled her once again. Never had she known that the body could produce such pleasure. The friction of his body against hers nearly drove her mad. Yet deep within she knew there was more to what they were doing.

Pierre unfurled her fingers from his hair and brought them low against his back. While she laced her fingers together his hands repositioned her legs so they were even tighter around him. "You're now ready. Hold on, chérie. Don't let go. I believe this first time will be very violent. *Je tiens à vous sentir ce qu'est l'amour.*"

Sarah heard this and held tightly to him as he instructed, her head falling back against the pillow as his hips moved in such a way that her entire body quaked and rolled to his rhythm. The long, deep strokes he gave felt rapturous, but it was the rapid thrusts that made her nearly demented. Keeping silent wasn't at all possible. Assuring herself that all lovers made the same noises, at times all she could do was pant and feel. Each time she thought she would reach some sort of heart-stuttering release he slowed and with each thrust rolled his hip as if he meant to pierce her very soul with the head of his shaft. The longer he did this deep within she felt her body began to leap as a knot of frenzied tension attempted to shatter into a million pieces.

Pierre lost all thoughts – all – of his life, of any dilemma, of the fate of his daughters or the future of América. The only image he saw – and was quite clear – was of Sarah who smelled of harsh soap and whose skin felt as if it had been rubbed raw with a cake of it. It was the most pleasing smell that ever filled his nostrils. Too soon she had nearly reached her climax. Wanting to savor this moment, and for the both of them to climax together, he slowed until neither of them could hold back any longer. Releasing himself to his budding desire, his hips pushed deeply in a ravishing, rapid rhythm that he could neither stop nor control. Beneath him Sarah bounced her hips against his at the precise moment his joined hers. It took only seconds after that.

Sarah's eyes appeared dazed as the coiled knot of tension peaked, then splintered into a glorious release. Pierre's breathing became rapid and hoarse as their movements began to stutter, jolt and shiver, and her sex gripped him tightly as if to fasten him in place until he released every drop of his seed. Holding her tightly against him as if she had become his very spirit and was trying to escape, with weak arms he rolled off of her.

As he watched her, he knew he loved her more than he had ever loved anyone, and that even his children whom he loved substantially should be mindful of the way they treated her for fear of his retort should any of them treat her unwisely.

Sarah spoke the same three words more than once as they made love again and again throughout the night. *I love you. I love you.*

The next morning he awakened long past the hour anyone should have slept. The bed was empty beside him. Searching the room he saw her near the hearth stoking the fire to get it to burn hotter. Moving to the table her hands moved rapidly doing what he could only imagine was preparing something for them to eat.

Pushing back the coverlet he stepped out of bed and wrapped his arms around her waist as he buried his face in her neck. Sarah's arm reached behind her holding him near. It had been this way the entire night: one touch and the two of them were grinding and heaving to reach another climax.

The feel of his erection against the back of her was all that was necessary. Reaching for the table with both hands, she lay against it and gripped its edges on both sides. Pierre lifted her long enough to remove the shift she wore. After it dropped to the ground Sarah reached impatiently for the edges of the table again, flattening her breasts against its rough top.

Pierre was too tall for her to be in this position. Again he pulled her from the table and lifted her by the waist until the soles of her feet rested in the seat of one of the chairs. Pressing her palms flat against the table for support, Pierre showered her skin with kisses as he took her from behind. With the first thrust Sarah cried out his name and continued to repeat it at times so loudly he was certain that birds outside had heard it and taken flight.

# Chapter Twenty-Three
## Papa Don't Play

*[The parson christens his own child first. – Creole Proverb]*

The police didn't come.

The carriage that drove tranquilly up the drive toward the mansion had been seen from a distance. The slaves that saw it recognized it and began to despair. Word had traveled between them that their monsieur had another woman on the land, and had even taken her on a tour while Gorée sat in the back of the cart. This fact alone meant this woman meant something to him. No one ever rode in the cart with their monsieur and Gorée. Not even Alise. Not even Désireé. All of yester eve many of the servants had discussed the event, all of them ending their discussion with the same words. *I pray he sends the madame away and replace her with this new woman!*

They knew their prayers had gone unanswered when they saw their madame returning from the city. At that moment every last one of them that saw the carriage approaching stopped what they were doing and watched it with heavy hearts. As the servants were used to doing, a few of them darted secretly away from their chores to flee to the mansion to alert the servants there. But this had been unnecessary.

Before the carriage had pulled onto the mansion but was close to it, Anne had a hand pressed against a third story window. Deeply was her chin lowered as she panted and whimpered in ecstasy. Her m'sieu loved taking her in this position. Anne also loved this position as was seen with one of her hands reaching behind her and holding tightly to his hip. On her knees and bent forward with her back to him, she cried out when her m'sieu caressed one of her breasts and squeezed its nipple. When her m'sieu became still behind her she pulled her hips forward then pushed her rounded derriere and sex into him until he filled her again.

"Give it to me, girl," he whispered pleadingly.

Bracing her hands on the mattress, she pushed repeatedly against his erection while giving a deep roll with her hips.

Julien threw back his head, closed his eyes and breathed rapidly up at the ceiling.

"Girl, you're going to hurt me! Give it to me, Anne. Make my heart close to stopping."

It was his squeezing and pulling at her nipple until it was hard and extended, and the feel of him deep inside her that caused her to arch her neck and breathe audibly into the air. At that moment her eyes opened and she saw the carriage turn onto the plantation's drive. The feel of him falling completely out of her as she fell flat onto the bed forced a small sound from her mouth. Not bothering to explain, she jumped out of the bed so quickly Julien lost his balance and tumbled forward. Rolling onto his back he stared at her for only a second. When he saw her bend at the knee to reach her clothes on the floor he too jumped out of the bed as quickly as she had and tried to pull her into his arms.

"Wait, wait, wait!" He pleaded and ground his middle against the back of her so she could feel how hard he still was. Kissing her mouth as soon as it turned upward, his hands lowered and touched her in all of the places he knew so well.

Again Anne pulled away from him and reached for her clothes.

"Madame's coach is on the drive!" She whispered.

Julien released her and hurried to the window to see the carriage for himself. "Damn this woman," he growled in a low voice. "Why didn't my brother choke her harder? Maybe then she would have spent more time in the city."

He turned just as the door of the room flew open and Anne fled out of it.

Julien collapsed onto the bed, drew in a deep breath and closed his eyes. What he and Anne were doing had to stop, and soon. Someone other than Carlisle would soon find out. Still he knew it couldn't stop. Anne was all he thought about. He sought her morning, noon and night, and it wasn't just for a romp. Her very presence made him feel content. The conversations they had weren't only the kind that made him laugh. Anne and Mableane were the only servants in the mansion – or the entire plantation for that matter – who weren't just taught to write and read. Tutors had been brought in to give them a formal education.

With Anne he could talk about literature, and politics, and music, and most importantly, his business ventures. It was there where she was most helpful. No matter how well he believed he had scrutinized a new idea once he related the idea to Anne she saw the things he had missed and brought them quickly to his attention.

He stared down between his legs, then climbed up from the bed and stood to his feet. Lifting his trousers from the floor, he bent slightly to put them on when he straightened and glanced at the door.

Marie-Marie stood inside it, her eyes fixed angrily on his.

"Which one of them is it?" She asked slowly and breathlessly.

"I was taking a nap and pondering a bath," he answered. "You don't know what you're talking about. You're forever accusing me of something."

Stepping into the room, she lifted a decorative vase a low boy dresser and threw it at him. Her aim was accurate. The vase would have hit him in the chest if he hadn't deflected it with the palm of his hand.

"Woman!" His eyes threatened her, warning her not to try that again. "You stop this madness."

"I am not stupid, Julien! Do not treat me as if I am."

He said nothing because he wanted her to go away and take her depressing mood with her. She read his thoughts. Her face crumpled with defeat as she hurried away.

Julien dropped onto the edge of the bed and let out a slow breath. The night before he had seen the need in Marie-Marie's eyes when he had climbed into bed. The reason he had turned his back to her was because he had just left Anne's arms. Falling asleep after his head lay against the pillow had been unavoidable. He was just that exhausted.

I need to stop this, he told himself now.

Marie-Marie's beliefs she had in regards to the boudoir were the same practiced by many other women. Most men didn't have a problem performing their husbandly duties. When amongst these men they never mentioned their wives, but the women they kept on the side who gave them the true pleasure they sought. While they spoke in whispers and bore large smiles their wives sat amongst the women in a separate room pretending as if they led happy lives when deep down they felt like prisoners to their religious beliefs. Many of them knew about their husbands' affairs and the children their husbands had with other women. And this was acceptable because there was nothing that any of these women could do to change it.

Julien refused to believe that God wanted marriage to be like this. Why when married couples got together did the men go in one room and the women in another? Why was it wrong to sit with your wife, and hug her, and kiss her when the right moment came along? Public affection was a sin. Affection was shunned except behind closed doors. As long as the church taught these things he vowed never to step foot into one again unless absolutely necessary. He blamed the church for the many affairs men had because he deeply believed that a loving wife unafraid of intimacy would lessen or bring affairs to a complete end.

Snatching his shirt angrily from the floor, he donned it, then lifted it to his nose and smiled when he realized it had Anne's scent on it.

Downstairs he entered the hall in a slow gait just as Jenna made her way through the front door. Lifting both of her arms she spoke in that wicked voice he detested so much. "I have returned to this circus with its monkeys of all colors and its giant ringleader of whose ass all of you desire to kiss. Well, look who's come to greet me first. Hello, dear brother-in-law. I should have known that you and that deplorable mouse you married would still be here."

"If I start choking you, I won't stop," he confessed. "Choose your words wisely with me."

Delighted with the look that had come onto her face he turned and saw that Marie-Marie had entered the hall to greet her host. From the look on her face she had heard what Jenna had called her and was stunned and hurt by the words.

Julien reached his arm around his wife's waist then led her toward the galerie where the two of them could sit.

Jenna stared at Anne who had come into the hall from the way of the butler pantry. Anne she hated more than any of the other in-house servants. Anne with her pretty face and her round noticeable breasts for a young woman of her size. And most importantly because this creature had been educated as well as Abigail had been educated. For this reason she tormented Anne every chance she got, including in the middle of night. "Where's your mademoiselle?"

Anne bobbed her knee perfectly in greeting. "She has gone to the black hills, madame."

"Fetch her. Posthaste."

"Oui, madame."

There was one good thing that Jenna could say about Anne. She was the most obedient and the most efficient servant in the entire mansion.

"Take my things upstairs," she ordered.

Riley nodded toward the two male servants he had brought inside the mansion to do just that. "It will be wise to advise you, madame, that the mansion has a new guest. A stranger from Spanish Texas by the name of Monsieur Carlisle Alonzo Morning. By permission of the monsieur, Monsieur Morning has the privilege of staying with us until he is prepared to further his journey."

Jenna cut her eyes toward Riley very slowly. "Spanish Texas? Does he even look of the aristocracy? I doubt there is any Texan who will ever meet my standards."

"No, madame," Riley answered honestly. "Not from the looks of him, but he has a pleasant disposition that has made him liked, it seems to me, by everyone here."

Jenna felt threatened by these words because guests with likeable personalities often behaved in a way that made it even more obvious of how much she was disliked in her own home. This was a good enough reason to get rid of this new guest. "Where is he sleeping?"

"Currently in the barn, madame. I do not believe the monsieur is aware of this arrangement. On the chance that you may think it wise to bring him into the mansion, I have prepared one of the guest bedrooms."

"Very well," she answered tiredly. "At supper I shall take full inventory of this Monsieur Morning and if I don't like what I see, regardless of your monsieur's invitation, you *will* find some way to get rid of him. Am I understood?"

"Clearly, madame."

Jenna's expression was peevish as she stared forward momentarily.

Sunlight spilled in from the rear of the mansion and nearly reached the main staircase. Servants stopped what they were doing to greet her in some way. Jenna had hoped to see Pierre in the mansion. On her way back she had imagined him being here in the hall like he usually was as he made his way to somewhere else. She had imagined him giving her a polite greeting while damning her with his eyes, and the exact expression she would have made to counter it with equal vehemence.

During her stay in the city without him she had gone over word for word everything that had been spoken between them.

"Are you all right, madame?" Riley asked. "Perhaps madame would like to sit and have a cool drink?"

She didn't bother replying. None of the servants liked her, and she would not for a moment try and convince herself that they did. Lifting the hem of her gown she started up the staircase to her boudoir. Regardless of the hour she would have a bath and take a few hours to pamper herself before supper.

At the top of the stairs she started making her way toward her room. She had taken only one step before she stopped and stared at Abigail's closed boudoir door. A giggle had come out of it. A very small one, but a giggle nonetheless. Dropping the hem of her gown, her eyes narrowed with gladness. One of the servants must be in Abigail's boudoir doing something they had no business doing from the sound of it. They were also somewhere they shouldn't have been since their mademoiselle wasn't even in the black hills.

Gripping the door, she flung it open and rushed forward. And then she screamed – a loud piercing scream that left her feeling weak, but when she looked at the bed again another scream tore out of her.

Abigail jumped out of the bed adjusting her bodice to cover up her breasts. The stranger did not seem flustered in any way. When Abigail hid behind him the stranger did not chastise her, but lifted his chin and stared at Jenna as if he was ready to defend the child.

"What are you doing in this room? Get you out of here!" Jenna yelled.

Carlisle's hands lifted pleadingly into the air and made a gesture as if asking her to calm down. "Missus, you seem powerfully upset right now, and you have every right to be. I do not want to explain what you just saw if I could avoid it, but I'm willing to do just that rather than you speaking to Mademoiselle Abigail harshly when it's me you should be angry at."

Kindness could be heard in his voice. Genuine kindness. The sound of it sickened her. Listening to it made her consider him a weak man.

"Get! Out!" She spoke firmly, her tone meant to belittle.

"Yes, ma'am," he agreed then lowered his hand, grabbed one of Abigail's wrists and charged hard at Jenna, forcing her to step aside or be knocked over, and kept running with Abigail until both of them flew out of the rear of the mansion.

The sight of Julien made Carlisle more nervous than he already was. Tossing Abigail's wrist in front of him, he yelled, "Run! Hide! And don't come out any time soon!"

Turning he lifted both hands as Julien's more than six foot frame descended the galerie steps in his direction. Carlisle took careful steps back to continue putting distance between the two of them. "I can explain, sir. I only wish we can do so as gentlemen."

Jenna hurried out of the mansion, saw Julien walking down the galerie steps and ran toward him. "This stranger raped Abigail!"

Julien swung around and faced her, stared her in the eyes and said, "Pah! And shame on you for even saying such a thing!"

"I saw it with my own eyes!" She insisted.

Julien saw what looked like true fear in her eyes and stared again at Carlisle. Just behind him Abigail had stopped behind a tree to see what would happen. She too had fear in her eyes, but even from where Julien stood he could see it wasn't for herself, but for Carlisle.

Julien stood nice and tall because right at that moment he noticed Pierre walking from the direction of the stables and in Abigail's direction. Abigail didn't know her papa was behind her. Pierre walked in a leisure gait, which meant he was unaware of what was happening, but soon would be told.

"Carlisle, I think you better start making your way toward me real quick," Julien suggested.

Carlisle saw the look on Julien's face, then looked slowly over his shoulder. Turning forward casual-like, he started walking forward and toward Julien while performing a nervous whistle. The muscles in his legs were trembling so severely it was a wonder that he stayed upright. If his horse had been fit to ride he would have made a run for the stables and used all of his wits to escape the plantation in one piece.

Abigail also looked over her shoulder, saw her papa and also ran toward Julien.

"Oh, no, petite," Julien chastised. "From what I've gotten to know of Monsieur Morning these past days make me wonder if something did transpire between the two of you, and if it did if you were the instigator of it."

"The fault was my own," Carlisle began.

Julien let out an exaggerated breath. "Do not attempt bravery, monsieur. My brother won't attempt to kill her. Perhaps a little beating against her backside. You on the other hand. Hell! Why am I wasting your time? Run. The two of you. Just run. Fast. Like never before."

It was Jenna that ran on his instructions to Pierre. As she ran she was gladdened in the fact that she had married the devil. "A stranger has raped Abigail! A stranger has raped Abigail!" She yelled long before she reached him.

The noise that came out of Carlisle's mouth didn't make sense to him. All he knew was he had never seen anything with seven feet of height move so quickly.

Abigail did not heed Julien's words and stayed hidden behind him. Julien held her close to him with his arms thrown behind him. Carlisle moved closer to Julien hoping this fellow could protect Abigail and save his life at the same time.

The next thing Carlisle knew, he and Julien's head were pried apart in separate directions by massive, strong hands. It was as if the master of the plantation had torn two people who were conjoined at the middle completely in half. Reaching forward, Pierre grabbed Abigail and pulled her to him. "Who hurt you, petite? Tell me!"

"He did, Pierre!" Jenna said, running back to the galerie, because Pierre had outrun her to reach it. "This stranger here!"

Pierre stared at Carlisle, then stared down at Abigail. All he had to do was look once into her eyes and he knew. One of her arms was lifted high into the air while his other hand gave hard smacks against her backside like a broom against a dusty rug.

"Run!" Julien yelled at Carlisle, then doubled over and roared with laughter. "Carlisle, even if you see a gator your chances are better."

Just seeing one of the blows against Abigail's rear sent Carlisle fleeing. Since he'd been a child he was told that running wasn't one of his strongest efforts. Now he knew why. His body was moving and swishing, but he wasn't making much ground. He looked over his shoulder and saw Pierre behind him, closing the gap between them. Julien was running behind Pierre in an attempt to stop him. It was seeing Julien running that made Carlisle aware of how much danger he was truly in. Ducking to the ground he hoped to curl into a ball in the hopes that he would survive what was coming.

Strong hands gripped the ankles of his boots. Carlisle knew he had been snatch up from the ground when his head began swinging dangerously close to the ground. His hands swung out protectively in front of him just as his head was held high above the dirt. It wasn't until he felt suddenly alone and with wind all around him that he realized he was flying through the air. Tucking his knees into his chest and wrapping his arms around them, he hit the ground and couldn't stop rolling. From the corner of his eyes something large was advancing.

"Pierre! Pierre!"

Carlisle had stopped tumbling at the same moment Julien leapt through the air to tackle his brother, except Pierre had been too swift. It was a desperate attempt that Julien made when he reached for his brother's boot as it lifted from the ground. Gripping it he held on tight. All the while he was yelling loud enough for everyone around to hear. "Nothing could have happened! Jenna wasn't in the house but two minutes before she came out yelling rape, and these two were already dressed. It was probably some touching and not more than that. And if that did happen, Abby was the instigator of it."

Carlisle braced his hands in front of his chest and face as more than two-hundred-and-fifty pounds landed on top of him. The wind was knocked out of him, and then more wind was taken out of him when more weight crushed him deeper into the ground as Julien climbed on top of his brother. "Pierre, stopping strangling him like that and shaking him before you break his neck!"

Julien knew he had gotten through to Pierre when he and Pierre began fighting over control of Carlisle's body. If Pierre had still been in a rage there wouldn't have been a struggle, as something more sinister would have happened by then. What Carlisle was experiencing now was Pierre's frustration and nothing more.

Abigail finally reached them. Gripping handfuls of Carlisle's hair, she tugged with all her might. "Please, Papa. Let him go! He didn't even touch me! And I didn't touch him! All I did was shown him my breasts because I thought they were small and wanted his opinion."

Julien heard this, stood to his feet and behind Abigail, then pointed down at her as if to suggest she had confirmed what he had suspected all along.

"Sir, I didn't touch her. I swear it! I know I shouldn't have gone inside her boudoir, and should have run out of it after the door had been closed. But I knew she could trust me. What you heard just now is bad. Yes, sir! That it is – me looking at your little girl and all. But…" He took a moment and stared up at the angry eyes boring into him, and then he lowered his voice hoping only Pierre heard what he said. "I did it with all the right intentions, sir. And if you give me a moment in private, I'll explain what happened from the beginning until the end."

Neither of them saw Jenna reach them from behind.

Abigail heard a noise, and as nervous as she was, wanted to see where it had come from. The slap to her face was a familiar one. As a child she had received many, and when she had been a child she had accepted them. Retaliating against her father hadn't crossed her mind as he smacked her bottom a few times. If anything she had wanted his respect, and it was this reason she had accepted his punishment. But what she felt toward her mother was entirely different. Her mother hadn't slapped her because she had wanted to punish her. Her mother had slapped her because Abigail's confession had embarrassed her.

Abigail reached up and slapped fire to the side of her mother's face. By the time her hand reached down to her side again she was breathing heavily and loudly, staring at her mother as her mother regained her balance and faced her again. And then Abigail was pushed behind her father as Pierre stepped in between them because Jenna had jumped forward with murderous eyes and uplifted hands.

"What are you doing, Pierre? This child just struck me! How dare you stand in front of me! What's gotten into you?"

Pierre didn't reply. Turning to Abigail, he grabbed her hand and held fast to it. "Monsieur, there's no reason for you and I to sit down and have a talk," he said to Carlisle. "You have disrespected my home in the worse way."

"Oh, please, Papa!" Abigail cried. Rapid tears fell from her eyes. "He didn't even know what I was going to do. It was my doing to get him in my boudoir."

"Why, petite?" Pierre pleaded with large eyes, staring down at her in utter confusion.

Abigail saw the hurt in his eyes and lowered her chin. "I heard him and Tante Marie-Marie talking about me. I heard him say I was beautiful. I don't know what came over me. I never heard anyone call me beautiful before."

Pierre saw the pain, fear and embarrassment in her eyes, and the way she trembled as if he would banish her from the plantation and out of his life for good. It donned on him then that only a broken woman who had never experienced a father's love would give herself so willingly to a stranger all because he had called her beautiful.

"Abby, you and I need to talk," he said.

"Please don't send Monsieur Morning away." She spoke in a small voice. "I'll feel bad. He's unable to travel at the moment, Papa. I'll feel terrible if you sent him away because I know it would be my fault if you did."

"What is this madness?" Jenna asked, stepping in between them and staring at each of them individually, her eyes large and her face stunned frozen in confusion. And then her eyes narrowed on the way Pierre held Abigail's hand. "You hate this girl, Pierre. And she hates you. Why are you holding her hand like that? What happened between you two while I was gone?"

"Stop it!" Abigail screamed, then stared at her mother in awe, and with new fear, because if she didn't know any better her mother had suggested something far more sinister than a young girl showing a stranger her breasts. Her suspicion was further proven when her papa turned his head slowly and deliberately to face her mother. Amazement shone in his eyes. And then he bit his lip and forced his eyes closed tightly.

"Sh, petite," he said. "I'll talk to you later. Right now I need to talk to your mother. Go to your room and stay in your boudoir until I send for you."

Abigail nodded, then turned away.

Pierre noticed the way her head hung low as she walked toward the mansion. He could feel every bit of her dejection. Misery gripped his heart like an iron fist. Seeing her like this reminded him of when she had been a child and it had been his anger that had stolen her esteem. At that moment he knew he wouldn't send Carlisle away if only to show Abigail that he cared about her and how she felt.

Jenna also watched her daughter. Twice she had sent for Abigail to come to the city, and twice no one appeared after her summons. She realized only now that Abigail had *chosen* not to come. She also sensed that something had happened between Abigail and Pierre – something that had brought them finally together, and from the looks of it, whatever had happened had forged between them a tight a bond.

*This is betrayal,* she thought. *Brutal betrayal.* First Pierre assaulting her, and then Abigail assaulting her. Abigail had never disrespected her in the past. Ever. This made Jenna wonder if the two of them had made some wicked pact against her. Had Pierre told her what had happened in the carriage? Had he encouraged Abigail to hate her even more?

Her heart beat loud and strong as fear seized it.

"Abigail!"

Abigail turned swiftly after hearing her name called.

Pierre stepped closer to Jenna. "Let her go. You and I need to talk…"

"You turn against me, child?" Jenna yelled because Abigail had made no attempt to return to her. Seeing this as a sure sign that her daughter had turned against her, her anger boiled over. "I'm your mother, but Pierre is not your father, child! Chadwick Spencer Speck is!"

Abigail's eyes flew open as if a dart had pierced her heart, and then she staggered forward. Her chin lifted and her face looked skyward as her eyes rolled to the back of her head and her knees buckled beneath her.

Pierre, Julien and Carlisle had run to reach her. Pierre reached her first. He held her in his arms and stared at Jenna with venomous contempt.

Julien stared down at Abigail, and seeing that she was completely unconscious because she had fainted he seethed with rage and also stared at Jenna.

"Where is your heart?" He asked. "If you only had one the size of a pea you wouldn't have done what you just did," he said and stormed off.

Carlisle was on his knees near Abigail with both hands pressed tightly against his mouth, as if holding back more words from being spoken would wake Abigail up.

***

A little while later Abigail ran through the trees as fast as she could.

Back inside the mansion much yelling was taking place. The servants and Marie-Marie had retreated out of sight. Julien, her mother and father had so far been unable to calm down. Her mother was crying inconsolably. Julien had knocked the contents on top of a table to the floor. Her father had ordered Julien to leave the room and had told him if he couldn't contain himself then he was to leave the plantation and not come back for a while. Her father then told her mother that she needed to leave, too. He told her how evil she was and pleaded with her to tell him why she had said what she had. Her mother had not responded as Abigail thought she would. Seeing her mother throw her arms around her father and stare up at him with sad eyes and ask, "You love her and not me?" had broken what was left of her heart into tiny little pieces.

Abigail didn't wait to hear her papa's answer. *Chadwick Spencer Speck! Chadwick Spencer Speck!* The name kept repeating in her mind. Tears burned her eyes and blurred her vision. Nearly stumbling over a piece of kindling, she righted herself and kept running until she reached Désireé's cottage. Pushing through the front door, it banged hard against the wall. A hanging picture threatened to fall.

Désireé and Cyril heard the clamor and came running out of the *salle*, then stopped when they saw her.

"Did you know?" Abigail whimpered.

Désireé had never saw as much mental and emotional anguish in someone's face as she saw at that moment. Attempting to hurry to her, she stopped and held her hands in front of her when Abigail's fists lifted in the air.

"Did you know!" Abigail screamed.

Tears fell from Désireé's eyes. "What difference does it matter, Abby? We're family are we not?"

Abigail choked as a new bout of tears threatened to spill out of her.

"You knew," she accused. "All these years," she continued, trying her best to hold back her tears. "That's why he loved you and Gorée more. You never loved me. All you did is pity me and nothing more."

"That's not true," Désireé pleaded, stepping forward in a rush when Abigail looked as if she would flee out of the house. "I didn't even know, Abby! I swear I didn't. Surely you can't believe that. I only learned the truth a few years ago. Surely you can remember the times when Cook snuck us into the kitchen to play together."

"Yeah, I remember that," Abigail said, facing forward again. "I remember how your father didn't want you near me so one of the servants had to sneak us around."

"No!" Désireé urged. "Papa didn't care! As long as we were outside of the mansion, he never cared. He was trying to keep me from your mother. He didn't trust her. I swear what I'm telling you is true."

"Why didn't he trust her? Had she ever done anything to you?"

Désireé shook her head. "But your mother did the same thing. She kept you from him and from me every chance she got."

"Maybe because she loved me and didn't like the way he treated me. Maybe she didn't trust him. And maybe because she didn't want you pitying me just as much as I don't want you pitying me."

She turned to leave. Désireé's words stopped her.

"You can believe whatever you want. I'm not going to try and stop you. But I will tell you this. *Our* father and your mother are responsible for this. Not you and me. Don't carry that burden, Abby. It'll kill you if you do."

Désireé turned to walk back inside the *salle*.

Abigail stepped closer to her, then stopped when Cyril's eyes tightened on her. She could feel his silent threat, and then she remembered how he had suggested to tie her up after she had discovered their secret.

"My mother used to call you a pampered bitch! What do you know about anything, Désireé? You're always walking around giving lectures as if you know everything. But what do you know other than your father elevated you and Gorée above everyone, including his own wife?"

Over her shoulder Désireé held Abigail's gaze. "I knew you loved me and you desired to be my sister, but never truly treated me as your sister because I had noir blood. I saw in your eyes that regardless of how my father dressed me, you believed you were better than me. I couldn't understand that as a child. All I wanted to do was play with you, but the older you got the more you pushed me away. And that hurt me, especially when I too got older and realized that others in the city looked at me the same way you did. As if I was something so filthy it would behoove you all simply to touch me. What do you know about my tears, Abby? Have you ever stopped and realized I have cried myself to sleep at night as much as you have?"

Cyril saw tears welling in Désireé's eyes and had started to take a step closer to throw Abigail out of the house. Désireé stopped him by throwing her hand in front of him. Like an obedient pet he stayed where he was.

Abigail saw this and narrowed her eyes on Cyril before staring at Désireé again. "After you found out the truth why do you still call me sister? You saw how he treated me. All those years. What did I ever do to him?" She spat loudly and with much aggression. "These past days he only used me to get back at my mother!"

"Pépère told me you were my sister on the same day you were born. I will never forget those words or the look in his eyes when he spoke them."

"*Your* grandfather! And *your* father. You would be a slave if it hadn't been for your father. A slave! Serving others. Being punished. I hate you. I wish you were never born." As she turned she saw an expensive crystal vase. The sight of it sickened her. Knocking it to the floor, she walked sedately out of the cottage without looking back.

"She's going to go tell him," Cyril said softly as he watched her leave. "Even if it's just to get back at you. I feel sorry for her. I thought she knew. Everyone in the city does," he finished and stared at Désireé.

"It's time for me to go to the mansion," she answered, staring down at the shattered vase on the floor. Her father had purchased the vase during one of their trips to Paris. The vase had been her favorite gift of all the things he had purchased for her in the past. "You don't have to go with me, Cyril," she continued. "You can leave now while you have the chance."

He shook his head. "I should have done it a long time ago. And I'll appreciate it if you stayed behind."

"If you tell him without me being there he'll feel even more betrayed. If you're adamant about being there then we might as well do this together."

***

"You're leaving! Right away! If you don't pack I'll have the servants to pack for you. I want you out of my house first thing in the morning. Anger and bitterness has dwelled inside this mansion long enough and ends now."

"Are you accusing me of bringing it here?" Jenna asked. The two of them were now in his office. Earlier she, Pierre and Julien had ranted at each other in high voices in several of the rooms. Carlisle had stayed near hoping he wouldn't be needed to prevent bloodshed. As the family had unleashed on each other everything they hated about one another, his head tossed from one side to another only in the end to see that all three of them needed a strong drink and a good long hug.

"No. My mother brought it here, and my father stirred it up until it became more deadly than a voodoo curse."

"So I am guiltless of something? I need to hear you say that."

"Why did you do it?" He asked again, then sat forward behind the desk and poured himself a glass of bourbon.

Jenna stared intently at the glass he held.

"We have destroyed this child," he said, sitting back and staring at her. "But while you were away I managed to start something new." He spoke in a low voice.

"No other parents are worse than we have been to Abigail." He looked up. "I need to hear you say this is true."

Jenna pressed a hand against her mouth. Never before had either of them acknowledged what she heard now. The subject had been ignored. A dirty little secret swept underneath the most beautiful rug.

It surprised her when it felt as if a dam released inside her. The lump in her throat was hard to speak over. "You made me treat her the way I have."

"No." He shook his head firmly. "I won't accept that."

The truth spoke softly in her ears. It was as if her soul was telling her its deepest secret. She used her thumb and a part of her hand to wipe away the tears from underneath her nose. "I was happy until I found out I was carrying her. I… I never wanted her to be born. You weren't the only one who hated me because I was carrying her. The morning after we were married I knew you told your family. I thought you would tell others, and I wanted to beat you to it so that I had a chance to explain. The people I confided in told others. From that day forward people started talking badly about me. I lost some of my friends. Men I have known for years looked at me as if I was a whore. From the moment she was born she looked just like Chadwick. Each time I took her into the city people would stare at her like some animal, then look at me as if they knew who her father was. I blamed her, and I blamed you for not protecting me. Had you once just talked to me and allowed me to explain – if you had given me just a little protection people would have been forced to give me a morsel of respect."

Pierre stared across the room. The sight of the alcove was his undoing. Behind its curtain he had given protection to his daughters while ignoring his wife and Abigail. Hearing Jenna speak about her pain made him realize how he hadn't destroyed one life, but two. Because she was right. Had he shown just a little decency toward her those in the city wouldn't have treated her the way they did. Until now he had not known that she had suffered like she had. He hadn't known because he had never been willing to pay attention.

He stood to his feet and coming around the desk, he folded his arms around her. Jenna held fiercely to him as her face pressed against his chest as she sobbed.

"I didn't do right by you. And I'm sorry," he said.

She pulled from him and tried to wipe away the tears, but more kept falling. "I didn't betray you, Pierre. I wanted to tell you so many times before we were married. I was so afraid. I was much younger when I first slept with Carlisle. The same age Abigail is now. After it was over I knew I would never do it again. That was years before you and I met, and when we met I fell swiftly and madly in love with you. How could you not remember that? All the time we spent together before the wedding. Both of our families were worn out from being chaperones."

"I did remember. Each time I did it made the pain worse."

She wanted to tell him what had truly happened before their marriage, and then she remembered that the two of them hadn't learned how to converse with one another without more wounds being inflicted. The last time they tried both of their anger drove them to attempt to kill one another.

She turned to walk away, then stopped, then walking toward him she said, "I was young and foolish. I didn't know that when a woman made love for the first time she lost something she could never gain again. Chadwick heard we were getting married and threatened to tell you, but not before telling me how no man wanted a used woman. I didn't believe him and confided in my mother. My mother slapped me so hard I fell to the floor. When I got on my feet she slapped me again. Her money was running out. Her and my father hoped that uniting both families would cause one of you here to give them a loan. She told my father." Tears rolled down her face as she closed her eyes. "My father has always been a spineless man. He told me on your next visit that he would leave us alone and without a chaperon and that I had better fix this. And then Chadwick came back and promised he would keep quiet if I gave myself to him one last time. I thought if I gave in to him it would give me enough time to sort it all out. And then you went away on business. While you were gone I learned I was pregnant. My mother told my father. He told me if I told you and the wedding was put off he would send me to the convent and leave me and the child there. I thought you and I loved each other so much that you would understand when I told you. But you took one look at me and banished me to the furthest part of your hell."

"You could have told me all of this back then before we were married," he raged.

"Could I?" She challenged. "You came back from your trip and visited. My father left us alone and I tried to kiss you. Do you remember that? You told me to wait until our wedding night."

Pierre sat again behind the desk. "You should have told me. And this!" His hands lifted in the air as if to encompass his entire plantation. "... could have been avoided. All these years wasted. You were thinking about yourself, Jenna. Admit it. You feared being handed over to a convent and took your chances. You knew your parents wanted some of my wealth and you wanted to please them."

Both of them turned when Abigail walked into the room.

"Go away," Jenna said, not wanting Abigail to hear anything Pierre would say next.

Abigail behaved as if her mother wasn't in the room. Her eyes stayed on the man she had believed was her father. "Désireé is carrying a child. The father is Cyril Oakes. He's been living with her at her cottage for some time. Your precious daughter who you love so dearly has betrayed you by taking your enemy as her lover whereas I would have walked into a snake pit if it meant it would have kept you safe."

She turned to walk away feeling nothing inside her heart. Nothing at all. Her mind had already been made. The decision final. She knew what she had to do and no one was going to stop her from doing it.

"Abigail."

She stopped but didn't turn to him.

"I love you."

She kept walking because she still felt nothing and she had decided never to trust him again. She had reached the door when she felt herself lifted in the air. She tried to struggle against him, but he held her tightly to him. "Let me go!"

"No. I won't. I need you to forgive me. You need to forgive me."

He carried her back to the desk and sat behind it with her in his arms. Her feet kicked. Contents on the desk hurled to the floor. Jenna pressed her palms against her face and sobbed when she saw how violently Abigail struggled to get free.

"I hurt you because I wanted to hurt your mother," he confessed. "It was never you, Abby. Never you. And I'm sorry for using you to hurt someone else."

Jenna heard this, lowered her hands, then walked out of the study without Pierre or Abigail noticing.

Abigail tried to bite him. She tried to dig her nails into his skin. The way she whimpered and howled and grunted sounded similar to an injured animal. Pierre folded her against him in a bear hug so she could no longer move. "Don't hate me, petite. We can make this right. All we need to do is give ourselves the chance."

She didn't want to look at him and made her entire body tense until a wail broke out of her and made her weak.

"I'm so sorry," he said. "It wasn't your fault. It never was, petite."

She took a chance and looked into his eyes believing she would see pity in them. What she saw made her head press gently into his body, because in his eyes had been tears, pain and hope.

"I always loved you," she whimpered, her words spoken brokenly.

"I know. And I promise to forever return it." He kissed her hair, and when she looked up again to search his eyes to see if he was telling the truth, he kissed her forehead as tears fell against his cheek. Abigail wrapped her arms tightly around him and held him close. She wished she didn't ever have to let go.

Pierre looked up and saw Julien standing in the study's door and realized he was happy Julien was there if only for the support he knew Julien would give.

"Oh, it's so good to see everyone is still alive!" Julien announced as he entered. Cyril entered the study behind him. "My brother is hot tempered, Monsieur Oakes, so don't expect him to leap over his desk and attack you with his fists. More than likely he'll pull a pistol from one of the drawers and shoot you."

Pierre kept his eyes on Désireé as she brought up the rear and hurried to him.

Cyril visibly trembled as he made his way to the desk.

Julien crossed the room and sat in a chair, then slapped his hands together and chuckled. "Pierre! Here he goes. Listen to this now. You have to listen to every word. I've already gotten a sample of it."

"Monsieur," Cyril began. "My family has always been poor. We worked for other plantations in the area until my father was given a small piece of land. I'm sure you already know all of that, though." Cyril lowered his chin and studied the rug beneath his feet. "We couldn't get that land up and going no matter how hard we tried. And then my father got injured and died and it was up to my older brothers to see about me and my mother. It's why Billy tried to help some men to kill you. I was a little kid, monsieur. I don't think I really understood what was going on. And then Billy died and things only got worse. All I remember thinking was Billy had got done in from trying to do in someone else because he was always doing things like that.

"I don't know. Maybe if I'd been in his shoes I would have done the same thing. My brothers blamed you when we lost our land. Blamed you even more when my maman up and died from we don't even know what from. She just sat on the sofa and died. They blamed you even more when no one would open their doors to us for fear you would find out about it and stop giving them the money you was giving. But I never blamed you, monsieur. Maybe I was just too young and too stupid to understand it all. But when you're poor things don't come easy for you. And they never came easy for me until I met your daughter.

"I was cold, starving and eating garbage left on the street when she found me. She had her driver stop her carriage and then she gave me a few coins. I found out who she was and with a clear conscious I can say that when I snuck on your land I had only come to thank her."

Cyril lifted his eyes to Pierre. "I'm not a fighting man, monsieur. I never was. I don't have anything to offer you for your daughter. And from what I've learned about you, you wouldn't take it even if I had. But if I had money I would have done things right. I would hate to think you will sell her and my child because of me. And that's why I'm standing here now. I can work for you until you feel I've worked off the amount of money you would sell her for. And then I can work for you to earn the money to buy her right."

Pierre gazed at Cyril as if staring at him would confirm if he heard what he thought he just heard.

Julien's roar of laughter was misplaced inside of the room. He laughed until he nearly fell out of his chair, then he jumped to his feet, and still laughing wrapped his arms around Cyril's shoulder and gave him a none too gentle whack on the back. "You're a crazy son of a bitch! With a lot of courage. Do you know that?"

Cyril swallowed audibly, then rubbed his lips back and forth. He gazed quickly at Désireé, then lowered his head again. "I know how to build things, monsieur. You have an old barn I can repair. If that isn't fitting enough I'm willing to work in your fields along with the slaves. I don't have anything, monsieur. No place to go. I have no family with a roof with whom I can find shelter with. I *love* your daughter." He looked up then and gazed first at Pierre, then at Julien. "I do! I mean that. I know neither of you probably believe that but it's true. And now that I'm going to be a father, I will do anything to see that child grow big and strong. I don't care if it's noir!" He spat. "Or look it even. It's *my* child, and *my* blood runs through its veins. This is a nice place to raise a child. As long as that child is here, and he receives not even half of what you've given to Désireé, he'll live a far better life than any other quadroon in this city."

"My daughter is a Jennings!" Pierre's mouth twisted in disgust.

Abigail crawled out of his arms and stood beside the desk, her eyes staring at Désireé.

"She isn't for sale! And neither is her child! And neither is she a slave!"

Cyril's eyes blinked, and then he gazed at Désireé with a look that told all of them he had not known this.

Pierre also stared at Désireé wondering why she had kept this a secret. As he stared at her face, which was so similar to his own, he was reminded of how he had kept unnecessary secrets from his father, and this made him realize just how much she was like him.

He stared at Cyril with resignation. "Do your brothers know you are here? For years I have heard exactly how much both of them wish to kill me."

"No one knew I was here, monsieur. And I haven't left since I got here."

Pierre heard this and stared at Désireé again. "What the hell is wrong with my daughters?" His voice had risen. The question had been asked to no one in particular. He pointed at Abigail. "I can understand why she did what she did today, but you I can't understand, Désireé. This man comes on this plantation to thank you, and not only did you hide him inside your home, but you also give yourself so readily and now you're carrying his child?"

From the corner of his eye he saw Abigail peek further around the desk to see Désireé's reaction. He could feel her anxiousness. Earlier he had taken his hand to her when he learned she had shown her breasts to a stranger. Abigail was paying close attention. She was waiting to see how he would handle this matter, because how he handled it would prove his love once and for all.

In the ensuing silence Pierre had a mind to send Abigail from the room. It would have been the proper thing to do. Until her next birthday she was still underage. And then he stared at Désireé because he realized something. If Cyril had been living at her cottage for some time then it was Cyril he thought he heard in her hall the last time he had visited. Another thing that troubled him was Désireé had confessed to none of this when he had made the decision for her to marry Monsieur Lavolier.

And here he was accusing Jenna for not telling him the exact same thing Désireé, his own child, had refused to tell him.

Désireé found herself falling sideways to the floor as her father jumped to his feet. The slap had been brutal. Pain flared throughout her cheek. One of her eyes felt as if it had crossed on its own accord.

Cyril jumped forward placing himself between Pierre and Désireé. His hand lifted toward Pierre in an attempt to thwart any further abuse.

"Get out of my way," Pierre seethed.

"I'll take it for her," Cyril said, lifting his chin bravely, his eyes glaring.

Abigail stood closer to the end of the desk wondering if Désireé's face stung the way her bottom had earlier.

Désireé stood upright and faced Pierre. "I love him, Papa. What reason can I give other than that? I hadn't been looking for love because God knows I already had it. But this love is different."

"You have no idea what you've done," he said, sitting again in his chair. Jenna's confession came to mind. At the end of it he saw Sarah's smiling face and closed his eyes. "You have no idea what you've done," he repeated.

"I'm sorry, Papa."

"You betrayed me. I would have never thought that of you. This man's brothers told everyone they could that as soon as they got the chance they were going to kill me. And you bring this man on my plantation? You give his brothers an excuse to come here and kill me?"

"I didn't know that, Papa. Honest, I didn't!"

"And if you had would you have come to me then?"

"Yes!" She spoke emphatically, her face tightening with rage. "You mean more to me than anyone. You never shared his brothers' intentions with me."

Cyril lowered his chin, then secretly looked over at Désireé. "Monsieur, my brothers are braggarts. They fear you. They will never come here as they have far too much fear to do so. They found work on a ship. Whenever they're at port they leave a little money for me with one of the merchants. It's not much. Nel Black brings it here to me. I give it to Désireé to do with as she chooses."

"If Nel Black puts your friendship before mine then he is no longer a friend of mine."

"Did I say Nel Black?" Cyril stuttered. He scratched nervously at his hair.

"I'll give you until morning to get off my land. If my daughter wants to go with you, she can. I won't stop her."

"No!" Cyril begged, staring up at Pierre with large eyes, then stared at Désireé pleading with his eyes. "You know I love you, Desie. And I don't want to leave you. Ever." Tears burst from his eyes as he leaned forward. "Stay here. Have my child here where he'll be safe." Ashamed of his sudden emotion he looked up at the ceiling and blinked many times. "Tell him…" He was hardly able to speak; each word was choked and strangled. "Tell my child that his papa loves him and that I didn't leave him because I wanted to. I'll send whatever money I can. Put it up for him." He stared at Pierre and licked tears from his lips. "I'll take you up on your offer for one night, monsieur. Merci beaucoup." He turned with bowed shoulders and hurried toward the door.

Pierre eased back in his chair and closed his eyes. "Come back and have a seat, monsieur."

Cyril turned back uncertain if he had heard correctly and saw Julien beckon him forward. Only then did he approach the desk again very slowly. Julien pulled a chair closer for Cyril to sit on, then whispered in his ear. "If you ever make me cry again I'll kill you."

Abigail stood next to Julien. Julien wrapped his arm around her waist.

"I was moved by your speech," Pierre admitted. "You seem of sincere character, yet it goes without mentioning you used my daughter to better your situation. You can't factor love into a situation like that. The two are separate. Regardless if my daughter offered you the luxury of her home, you had a choice."

"Oui, monsieur," Cyril answered. "I had a choice. But use her, I did not. If anyone would have opened their door to me, I would have accepted. No one did monsieur. I was cold and hungry. And the daughter of the man who everyone wants to make my enemy fed me. The first nights I was here she gave me a blanket and I slept in the corner of her galerie outside her home. And it took many conversations before she allowed me inside her home, and even then I was given a room down the hall. I'm not ashamed for loving her. I see her as an angel, monsieur. A beautiful one, and most intelligent. I would do anything for her. Anything."

Pierre stared at Désireé.

"I won't attempt to make excuses, Papa," she said. "I was wrong for not telling you, and I'm sorry. You taught me how to think for myself…"

"Do you realize you could have been the madame of your own plantation?" He cut in.

"If you believe that, Papa, then you would have made me the heir of yours. But you didn't because of who my mother was. I'm *blanc*, but not enough, not even for you. And because I'm not *blanc* enough, I'm supposed to be forced to marry a free man of color who I don't love or a become the placée of man I don't love? Why can't I love who I choose? The law says I can't marry Cyril. I fell in love with him, and I chose to love him because I am your daughter. Because I am the niece of Julien Rafael Jennings and the granddaughter of Will Henriot Jennings. And the men in my family taught me to ignore old outdated traditions and find a partner I love. Why should I have held back after I found it? What was I waiting for? A priest to sanction what could never be? I won't apologize for that. I could have run off, but I didn't. I'm needed here. And I knew that if you gave Cyril a chance he would be good and loyal to you."

"I don't want to hear anymore of your speech. Leave me. I don't want to look at you," Pierre said.

Cyril stood and faced him. "I promise to serve you loyally, monsieur, if you let me stay. If you don't want me to work for you, I'll find work in the city. I will pay you every cent I receive. I might be afraid of you, but I'm not afraid to work. I'm happy to know my child will belong to no man, and the reason he won't is because of you." He held out his hand firmly for Pierre to shake it.

Pierre took it. "If you ever hurt my daughter, I'll kill you."

"And rightfully so," Cyril agreed with a stubborn expression. "Any man who can turn against the one person that has lifted him out of the mire deserves no mercy."

He had spoken the last words emphatically.

# Chapter Twenty-Four
## Soirée of Sex and Deception

*[You may hide the fire, but what about the smoke? – Creole Proverb]*

Julien volunteered to chaperone Abigail into the city and suggested that Anne go with them, as Abigail might need a servant to see to her in some way. Jenna readily agreed, and now here they were: Julien, Abigail, Anne, Carlisle and Cyril. Carlisle and Cyril were hitching a ride with the intentions of finding work in the city. Abigail wanted to visit a local seamstress. Most girls purchased their coming out gowns from France, but Abigail thought it unnecessary. There were gowns inside her armoires that had been purchased from France or had been made in the city that she had yet to wear. Having so many dresses hadn't been her decision, but her mother's. *If we dress you pretty enough maybe no one will look at your face,* was something her mother had said often while she'd been growing up.

At times Abigail hated she had been born to her mother. Her mother could have been anyone, including a servant on Ashleywood and she believed she would have been happier. Over the past few days she noticed that her mother seemed nicer, however. And not just to her, but to everyone. Instead of anyone accepting it with good grace everyone was suspicious, including her father, including Abigail.

Abigail liked the change that had come over her father. It wasn't a change in his character. It was simply more or less a change in the way he treated her; to others he had always been nice.

"What are you thinking about, Missus?" Carlisle asked.

"The things I shall need before I leave the city," she answered. She held his gaze while she spoke because it was polite to do so, but after the requisite time had elapsed again she looked out the window.

"I'm sure you're excited about your upcoming party. Your father has agreed to your wishes this morning, although your mother didn't approve. The servants seemed pleased, didn't they? Before we left they were running around to prepare the mansion for it. As happy as they were it got me wondering just what kind of birthday party this will be."

Abigail stared down at the skirt of her gown. "It's my coming out party, monsieur. Men will be expected to come. Those who wish to marry me will speak privately with my father. Once a proposal has been accepted, after the wedding I am expecting to leave my home and live with this man. He may wish to move me out of the city. If he's wealthy or from a French-born family, I may be expected to move to France."

Carlisle hoped his face didn't portray what he was feeling. Forcing a smile on his face was all he could do as he tried to lift her spirits despite his surprise in what he heard. "I'm sure there will be plenty, Missus."

"Those who will are only looking for the dowry that comes along with me. I'm sure there are plenty of fathers who are hoping their son is chosen, but these fathers I'm speaking of will not be from the larger plantations. Those fathers will want their sons to marry someone prettier or from France."

"I disagree," Julien said as he sat next to Carlisle on the opposite cushion. "Don't worry, petite. I shall have my eyes open and help your father choose. Only the best man will marry my niece."

Abigail smiled at him. "You have been the best oncle. And I appreciate you."

Julien winked at her and smiled.

They reached the center of town and parked along the street. Cyril had been anxious to reach the city, and after confirming the hour that everyone had agreed to return to this same location he hurried off toward the wharf hoping to find work.

Carlisle parted ways with a smile toward Abigail. He had hoped that he and Cyril could have paired together in their search, but it had been apparent from the time they left the mansion that Cyril had plenty on his mind and had wished to be alone.

The streets were narrow, the houses the sort he had never seen before. Those he passed in this area of the city spoke French just as Abigail had said they would. But he had heard there was an American quarter and that it was located uptown and west of Canal Street.

Canal Street proved broad and boasted a lot of activity. From there he walked quite a few blocks. It was difficult for him to discern by sight who spoke French and who spoke English. Those who spoke to him and had engaged him in brief conversation were pleasant. The son of the man who had stopped to speak to him about the city and the possibility of work stood at the edge of the street and sang this song.

*Kiskadee. Kiskadee.*
*Save a crawfish head for me.*
*Look all around a Frenchman's bed*
*You can't see nothing but crawfish heads.*

The man had heard his son, but didn't stop him and instead smiled at his son after he was done. Carlisle thanked the man and moved on.

Walking a distance of a rectangle of streets he was again in what the Americans called the French Quarter and the Creole referred to as the Vieux Carré. Here he noticed something different. Expecting to be treated as an alien, as there was clearly a war between both cultures, although he couldn't speak French, mentioning Pierre Jennings had been enough. He was ushered inside of cafés and invited inside of several homes for a cool drink and a moment to rest. Before long he had walked clear over to Decatur Street that many of the Creoles had pointed out as Rue Decatur. It was here where ships and boats of all sizes docked. Facing the street were small businesses, of which many served Francophone preferred café.

The reason he had come to this area is because he knew Abigail would be here. She found him before he had her. Calling out his name along the street, he turned, saw her and smiled, then hurried in her direction.

"I didn't find much of what I was looking for, but I did find some pretty lace."

"I am most happy," he exclaimed because he was. Earlier she appeared to be drowning in her thoughts, but now she smiled and seemed possessed by a massive amount of energy. It was hard for him not to reach for her, take her in his arms and swing her around, but he didn't do it in fear of Pierre.

"I do not believe New Orléans is for me," he said.

"What do you mean?" She asked, her reddish gold eyebrows arching in deep concentration. Again he knew that many thoughts had come into her mind.

"I would like to settle somewhere where everyone is like me. Here I find everyone so different."

"If you don't stay how can you marry me?"

The two of them had never spoken along these lines before. Carlisle had kept to himself any emotion he felt. Now knowing that she was attracted to him like he was to her made him smile, and then his eyes searched for Julien. It didn't take him long to find him. A few men stood with him nearby, all of them engaged heavily in conversation. Anne sat alone just inside a shop door sipping café.

"You want me to marry you?" He asked with his eyes on Anne, fascinated in the fact that she sat docile and hadn't once looked in Julien's direction. But then again he assumed this was best, and that Anne and Julien had mastered their skills of keeping their affair a secret from everyone else.

"I do," she answered.

"Everyone will think I married you for your money."

"I don't care. We can marry as soon as you want after my birthday. If you asked my papa he will approve. I don't think there's much he would say no to at the moment."

"Bonjour," Cyril said behind them.

Carlisle turned and faced him and saw that Cyril looked more perplexed than when they had arrived.

"Ask him did he find work," he told Abigail.

There was a brief exchange between the two.

"Only on a ship that docks twice a year," Abigail said. "He didn't want to miss the birth of his child or be away from home so much, so he turned it down. Now he's sad that he has to return to Ashleywood with bad news."

Julien finished his conversation and gestured with a hand that it was time to go.

Anne saw the gesture and rose to her feet.

As they climbed inside the coach none of them saw Pierce Oakes turning in an exasperated circle in the middle of the street certain he had seen his brother standing in this same area a moment ago. Going to a familiar man nearby he explained that his ship had just docked and that he was certain he had seen his brother.

"Oui!" The man exclaimed and pointed toward the Jennings coach that was moving at a swift pace up the street and away from the dock.

"Are you sure?" Pierce asked with a frown. "It looks like I see the Jennings' crest on that vehicle."

"Oui! Julien Jennings was just with your brother, monsieur. I saw both climb inside that carriage with a stranger and a servant girl."

\*\*\*

Carlisle had not spoken to her father. The good thing was he had explained to Abigail that he was waiting until after her party before he did so. Invitations had gone out as far as Biloxi, thanks to her mother. Abigail had expected perhaps one hundred guests to actually arrive. When she saw that the first five carriages that pulled up the drive were from five of the most distinguished families in the city, she began to despair.

Entertainment had been brought in; a nice but small orchestra, a small troupe who performed at the Théâtre d'Orléans and were a favorite. The kitchen's fires had burned high for three days straight. Anne had helped in arranging the decorations, transforming the house to look better than it did at Christmas. Abigail, as the center of attention, had dreamed of such a day like this when she had been a child. Now she knew that quietness and solitude was what she preferred and hoped her nerves didn't get in the way.

The troupes' performance was performed in the rear yard. Abigail fanned constantly at her face in an attempt to cool down and keep flying insects away. Each time she looked in any direction there was always someone watching her, and smiling, and giving subtle hints that a proposal for marriage will arrive soon. Carlisle seemed comfortable. Many found the need to have everything translated to English as hilarious. Whenever he saw her nerves getting the better of her, he took center stage. For this Abigail was grateful, because it temporarily drew the attention away from her giving her time to compose herself once again.

With her father sitting beside her, Abigail noticed that men and women she had known for years were now treating her differently. Every so often her papa would lean toward her, whisper a name, then speak an emphatic no. Just before the performance she had leaned closer to her father and said, "What about Monsieur Morning?" It was hard not to laugh when her papa rolled his eyes and averted his gaze. She held her father's hand in her own and spoke truthfully. "I like him."

"We don't know this man," he whispered back. "By the time we do many of the others will feel offended that we have not given an answer."

"I have until my twenties, Papa. I can get to know him until then."

"No," he corrected. "By then you will not be a virtuous woman. Your behavior toward Monsieur Morning is most inappropriate."

The evening wore on. More than two hundred guests arrived. The dining room stayed open for anyone who wanted to sit and dine on a nine course meal. During this time servants passed hors d'oeuvres in each of the *salles*.

Alise was unable to attend. Three days before she had suffered a fever. Although now better, her appearance was inappropriate. With Yellow Jack as prevalent as it was in the city, everyone would have panicked on sight of her still flushed face and believed she was suffering from the illness although she wasn't. Alise not attending meant Gorée had someone she was familiar with watching her. As Pierre sat and drank with men his own age and older, Jenna secretly watched him from across the room. Conscious of the small medicine bottle sewn in the lining of her gown, she was waiting for the right moment to pour a dose of it into one of his drinks.

Twice she looked up and couldn't find Anne. All day the girl had barely been seen. Rising to her feet she hurried into the butler pantry and yelled at Cook. "Don't think I don't know what you're doing! Get Anne in here now. I want her in the *grand salle* as soon as possible," she threatened.

Cook waited until her employer had gone, then looked at the others. "Where is Anne? I haven't seen her all day."

"Hiding from you and madame," Semper answered. "When you're in here I sees her running out to the kitchen."

Cook hurried out of the house, and sure enough, found Anne and Mableane in the kitchen arranging platters of food. "Madame wants you in the house. Go on, child, before she gets angry!"

Anne had hoped to stay away as much as possible. The Dussaults had arrived as well as the LePrince family. Jean-André's last visit made her fearful of a second proposition. The men of the LePrince family had made it known since she was twelve that if given the chance they would take her as soon as no one was watching.

"I'll help you if you need me to," Mableane whispered.

Pierre was leaning to listen to an older man with a soft voice when he saw movement across the room. Alise stood at the door of the *salle*. Pierre excused himself and hurried to her.

"Gorée's missing."

"What do you mean missing?" He asked.

"She and I fell asleep, Pierre. I woke up and she was no longer in the cottage."

Across the hall Jenna watched the two of them talking and slipped into the sick room. Pulling the medicine bottle out of her gown, she poured half of its contents into a glass then mixed bourbon with it. Carrying the glass carefully, she went out again and saw Julien, Pierre, and Alise standing away from the guests in a corner.

"We're looking for her but can't find her," Alise said, tears falling from her face.

Pierre walked away and found Hiram.

"Get on a horse and get to The Bottoms. Have Curfy gather as many as he need to help look for Gorée. Start at Alise's cottage and search in all directions from there. Do not stop until she's found."

Hiram hurried away from him.

"Where are you going?" Jenna asked.

"Gorée's missing," he said and passed her.

"I'll come with you."

"No. Stay with Abigail."

He used one of the nearby horses and rode slowly to the cabin where Sarah was. Gorée had never gone off on her own in the past. The child knew the plantation perhaps as well as he did. He wondered if she had tried to make her way to Sarah. He had taken her to the cabin the day before and noticed how well she had taken to Sarah. This too had never happened before, Gorée taking to people.

Sarah was surprised to see him. As soon as he saw she was alone he told her Gorée was missing and left right away.

On his way back to the mansion he searched and looked in areas he thought she may be only to discover she wasn't. A thought came to him that made him ride swiftly back to the mansion. Entering the west wing he hurried to the study and flung open its door. This part was empty. Hurrying to the alcove he wrenched back the curtain. The bedding was severely rumpled. Red smears and stains were on the coverlet. The rag doll she had never played with sat on the pillow. He touched one of the stains and saw it was blood. The amount was considerable, but not enough to make him believe it had been left behind by a fatal wound.

He started to leave the room and search the mansion when he stopped and lowered to the floor. The first thing he saw underneath the bed was the coat he usually left in this room. Creamy yellow legs stuck from underneath it. Brown hair fanned across the top of it. More dots of blood trailed to where she lay.

Pierre yanked her by her arm and pulled her to him. Gorée's eyes were squeezed tight. It was the sign she used when in deep distress. A jagged wound tore open her inner right thigh. The bleeding had stopped. Where some of it had dripped near her ankle had started to dry.

He carried her up to the third floor and laid her on a bed then told a servant to hurry and find Jeanette. While he waited Gorée kept her eyes closed.

He kissed her forehead and her hair to let her know he was there. Someone came into the room behind him. "Get Désireé," he said without looking at them. "Tell the others to call off the search."

Minutes later Jeanette hurried into the room.

Pierre stood to give her room to see to the wound. "Do you need help?"

Jeanette was getting ready to answer, but she wanted to finish checking the wound. As she searched higher she pressed a hand tightly against her mouth, and then she stared at him with large eyes.

"How bad is it?" He asked with large eyes.

She shook her head as she stared at him. "I ain't for sure, but I think…. I think something else happened to her."

Pierre lowered beside the bed while he and Jeanette checked to be sure, and then he buried his face in his daughter's hair as he held her tight. "Papa's so, so sorry, baby. I'm so sorry I wasn't there for you," he ended and began to sob.

***

Pierre took a moment inside his bedroom to clean his face and wipe away his tears. Someone had abused his daughter inside his own home and of all rooms the alcove where she slept. He had instructed Jeanette to tell no one.

As he made his way back downstairs one thought went through his mind. One of the men inside his house at that moment was the culprit.

Downstairs he saw Carlisle sitting quietly amongst a group of men.

"Are you interested in my daughter?" Pierre asked.

Carlisle quickly rose to his feet. Knowing that very few people in the home spoke English, he spoke freely. "I am. And, sir, it's not because she's wealthy. I promise you that."

Pierre nodded gently at him. "Let's talk later."

Carlisle nodded at him, and then a slow smile pulled across his face.

Pierre looked at the men who were sitting and smiling at him and accused them all silently in his mind, then walked away.

Jenna met him in the hall.

"Is everything all right? Did you find the child?" She asked.

"Oui."

She handed him the glass she had been holding for some time and had refused to allow out of her sight.

"You look like you can use this," she said softly.

He took the glass and took a generous swallow. She turned away and returned to the *salle*. Pierre entered behind her and sat in the corner. He was polite. He smiled. But what he wanted was to yell for everyone to leave his home.

The party went on for the rest of the evening and into the night. Most of the guests had gone by then. Those who stayed behind would sleep overnight. While he sat and was forced into a variety of conversations, twice Jenna returned with another glass of bourbon and a smile. After his third glass Pierre could barely keep his eyes open. A headache had started to form. An hour later his head felt as if it would burst.

Julien saw him suddenly slump in his chair and hurried to him. He stared deeply into Pierre's eyes and believing him intoxicated helped him to his feet. As soon as he saw how unsteady Pierre was he knew the stairs would be too hard to climb. Just when Pierre looked as if he was going to pass out Julien clutched him tightly with both arms. Riley suddenly appeared. Still Pierre was too heavy for the both of them. A few of the male guests volunteered to help.

Jenna stood close by instructing them where to carry him. "He's been drinking all evening," she assured them. "After a long sleep and a bowl of gumbo he'll feel much better."

The men believed this when Pierre opened his eyes, gave a dazed stare, then accused them all of being fucking savages that he would never ever trust again.

The beds in the downstairs bedrooms were too small for his height.

"The study," Jenna said. "He has a sofa there where he will be comfortable. Someone get Anne."

"There's no need for that," Julien said. "I'll do what's needed."

Once they got Pierre onto the sofa in the study Julien realized he was going to need help after all.

"Riley, go get Anne."

The two of them had a difficult course of it. While Julien struggled to hold his brother in a particular position, Anne struggled to tug off his clothing until only his undergarments were left.

"I'll sit with him," Anne said.

Julien kissed her, then left the room.

Hours later when she could barely keep her eyes opened, she lay on the rug behind the sofa, because here she could hear him if he stirred. She wasn't certain how long she was sleeping when she awoke to a noise. Remembering that her monsieur was near naked she decided to peek from behind the sofa, because she hadn't wanted to interrupt if he was peeing in a chamber pot.

Just as she started to move the sofa bumped against the floor as if it had risen swiftly and settled. Anne stayed where she was a moment and listened. When she realized what she was hearing it was fear that drove her to peek behind the sofa and look up.

A candle burned on top of a nearby table and glowed with adequate light.

Anne looked long enough to see if she had heard correctly, then hid again behind the sofa her heart racing out of her chest. It went on for what seemed hours. Finally after some time had passed the study became quiet. She looked up fearing that her madame was looking down on her over the back of the sofa.

The sofa made a soft shift against the floor. Anne listened while her madame dressed herself, then walked out of the room. Anne waited longer still before coming from behind the sofa. She stared down at her monsieur and became frightened when his eyes opened, blinked, then stared at her.

She hurried out of the room. When she reached the third floor she peeked into the room where she and Julien met in secret. It was empty.

She went to her own room and climbed into bed.

# Chapter Twenty-Five
## Two Accidents

*[It isn't the fine headdress that makes the fine négresse. — Creole Proverb]*

The next morning Julien found her at the cistern. Because of the size of the plantation and the constant need to draw water, his mother had built a cabin around it. This prevented the servants wasting time during the winter and stepping back into the mansion with their clothes dripping wet.

The door was open. Julien had only to see her silhouette and knew it was Anne. He waved an angry hand at the other servants in the yard to send them away from the immediate area. Pulling the door open wider he stepped into the cabin.

Anne nearly dropped the carafe of water she was drawing when she saw a shadow approaching from behind. It took both of her arms wrapping around the carafe and holding it against her gown to stop it from falling. It was one of her madame's favorites and made of porcelain. If she broke it her madame would punish her surely.

Julien stopped where he stood and stared long at her. "Where were you last night?"

Anne's heart raced when she heard this. If she told him the truth and what she had seen nothing good would come of it. The monsieur would hurt the madame. And if she was forced to tell him *everything* she had heard and seen he may even kill her. If he didn't kill her and the madame lived she would stop at nothing to make Anne's life miserable.

He stepped forward, casually. The door was able to close all the way and snapped on its hinges. "Answer me."

She decided to tell the truth but omit some parts. "I was in the study, m'sieu."

"No, you weren't. I went there looking for you. Your monsieur was in the study alone when I was there."

"I went behind the sofa to lie on the rug. I must have been sleeping when you came. I didn't hear you." This was true. She had no idea that Julien had come looking for her. It must have been before her madame had come inside.

"You slept all night in the study?"

"No, m'sieu. I woke up at some time then went to the room on the third floor looking for you. When I saw you weren't there I went to my room."

"Did you sleep with my brother?" To make sure she understood exactly what he was asking, he added, "Did you have sex with my brother?"

Water spilled down the front of her gown as she hurried closer to him.

"No, m'sieu! I wouldn't! I swear!"

"Someone did. And he's very angry. Tell me the truth, Anne. He was drunk. I saw this. Did he force you? What happened? He asked me did I know if anyone had been in the room. I told him you stayed behind to sit with him, but this was before he told me that something happened. He thinks it's *you*. Tell me, Anne. Please tell me."

Anne was breathing rapidly. The carafe slipped from her hand and crashed to the floor. The water inside it splashed upward, wetting her and Julien, but mostly the floor. Anne pressed her hands flat against her mouth. Tears fell from her eyes.

"I promise you I did nothing, m'sieu. I wouldn't! He didn't touch me. I didn't touch him. Not once! I went and lay on the floor behind the sofa when I couldn't keep my eyes open."

"Did anyone come into the room?"

She hesitated.

Julien's eyes grew wide. Before he could stop himself he snatched her against him and shook her. "Tell me! He's with Gorée right now, but as soon as he leaves that room he's going to come looking for you. Semper told her madame that she saw *you* running fast out of the study at around four this morning. My brother claims he remembers being with someone last night, but can't remember who. What happened? Tell me!"

Anne drew in an audible breath. As she did so it sounded like a painful groan. And then she nodded at him. "I did like I told you. I couldn't keep my eyes open. I lay behind the sofa and fell asleep. A noise woke me. I didn't know what it was. I thought he had awakened because the sofa bumped. I thought he was using the chamber pot so I decided to peek behind the sofa first."

Julien released her. "What did you see?"

"It was madame!"

Julien closed his eyes and shook his head.

"It was!" She said thinking he didn't believe her.

"*Merde!*" He seethed.

"I could hear her slapping him to wake him again. I saw her do it. And when he was awake, he…"

Julien's eyes became wide.

Anne nodded at him.

"As soon as she got him awake again the sofa and the noises started again. It went on for a long time. I didn't want them to see me, so I stayed hidden until she finally left, and then I went around the sofa and he opened his eyes and stared at me. I got scared and ran because it wasn't until then that I realized he was still drunk."

Julien hugged her to him. "Oh, Anne. Oh, Anne. *Merde!* I wish you would have said any name but that one."

"I can't tell him, m'sieu. She's going to find some way to punish me if I do."

"Oui, Anne. I wish I never mentioned your name. Jenna will never admit she was in that room or especially to what you said happen. First Gorée and now this. Why did she do that?" He tightened his eyes and balled his fists as if he would turn and walk away, but stayed where he was. "His mind isn't right at the moment. I'll have to talk to him, but first, I need to get you out of here. You're right. Your madame is going to come after you. And my brother may never trust you again. I don't know. I need to think about this for a while. In the meantime, after I hide you, I want you to stay out of sight."

"I need to finish drawing water. If I don't Mableane will get blamed, especially if I go missing. And I broke the carafe."

"I broke it. You hear me? I broke it, and if anyone asks you that's what you're going to tell them just like I will."

She nodded at him. Her face made a severe pinch. "I'm so scared, m'sieu."

"Let me help you draw the water. We need to hurry."

Anne reached for the second carafe that rested on top of a small table.

The broken pieces of porcelain on the floor were large. Julien used his foot to try to push the pieces to one side and out of the way. As the sole of his boot slid across the smooth top of one of the pieces, the piece slid across the water she had spilled earlier. Julien lost his balance and fell backward. His head hit the wall behind him. Anne watched as his eyes became disorientated as his body trembled violently as if he was nailed to the wall, and then his eyes became slack as he fell forward slightly, then slid down to the floor. She looked up where he had hit the wall. A sharp piece of metal stuck out of it dripping with his blood. More of his blood stained the wall making a pattern where the back of his head had touched it on his way down.

Anne jumped forward and fell down beside him. She reached for his waistcoat shaking him hoping to wake him. She screamed when his chest heaved and he began to vomit while he was unconscious. Fisting his waistcoat she tugged with all her might to roll him onto his side, because he had started to choke. "M'sieu," she whimpered. "Please. Wake up."

She shook him gently, then watched as his eyes fluttered open. His breathing was raspy. A gurgle slipped out of his mouth.

She jumped to her feet and pushed open the door, then screamed for help.

Pierre had tried to leave the room twice, and twice Gorée reached for his hand.

"Fire." Her voice was raspy and dry.

*Fire. Fire. Fire.*

She repeated the word close to fifteen times since he had been in the room. Pierre didn't understand the meaning of the word. She had a slight fever, but she wasn't hot enough to cause him dread. He kissed her forehead and stayed close beside her. "Papa's here."

She nodded at him, her small hand holding tighter to his.

"Fire."

"How much laudanum have we given her?" He asked.

Jeanette stepped closer to the bed. "Quite a bit, monsieur. It ain't making her sleep like it should. I thinks her mind is restless. She didn't sleep much during the night."

"Bring me some rum. I think she's in pain."

"Oui, monsieur."

They both turned when Désireé ran into the room. "Oncle Julien is hurt! Come, Papa! Hurry!"

"Don't leave her!" Pierre yelled to Jeanette, then ran out of the room.

When he and Désireé reached the cabin, Alise and several of the servants looked as if they were spilling out of its door. It looked as if they were one mass twisting with desperate motions. Pierre ran harder pushing servants out of his way until he reached his brother.

Julien's right eye twitched as he lay in a semi-conscious state. The front part of his trousers was wet from his bladder having released. Pierre saw some blood, but mostly on the floor was vomit. The nerves in Julien's right arm jumped making the arm tremble in a way it shouldn't have. Anne kneeled in front of him sobbing uncontrollably.

"It's bad," Alise whispered.

Pierre leaned closer.

"He slipped in the water and hit the back of his head against a piece of metal. It went through, Pierre. It looks like it went through his skull." Tears fell from her eyes as her face became pinched and she began to sob harder than Anne was.

"He's going to be okay," Pierre assured her.

"We have to get him out of here," Alise pleaded. "I don't want him to die in here. But I'm too frightened for any of you to move him. He keeps vomiting."

"Let me do it," Pierre said gently.

Alise looked up at him and nodded as more tears fell.

Riley and Hiram helped their master turn Julien sideways then pull him through the door to be lifted.

Once it had traveled over the plantation that Julien had been injured, those who believed they had gifts of healing came quickly on carts bringing with them all of the supplies they thought to grab.

Riley and Hiram helped lift Julien. Once he was high enough Pierre crouched on his knees, lowered underneath him, then rose to full height with Julien over his shoulder. Droplets of blood spilled from the wound in the back of his head as Pierre crossed under the balcony and entered the mansion.

The servants who practiced spiritual cleaning hurried to wherever there was blood drops marking those areas then waited for other servants to bring hot coals from the kitchen and brick dust. After they burned the blood with the coals, they sprinkled the entire area with brick dust to ward off the evil spirit trying to kill their younger monsieur.

Jenna, Abigail, and Carlisle heard Julien had been injured and had hurried to the west wing of the mansion. They were on their way out into the yard when Pierre stepped into the house. Abigail took one look at her oncle and collapsed against Carlisle and wailed.

Jenna quickly went into action clearing the way so Julien could be carried upstairs as quickly as possible. Servants entered the mansion behind her, some of them sprinkling water they had blessed, others waving palmetto leaves to cleanse the air.

Abigail shook and sobbed as she went to the mantle, lifted a candle, lit it and said a prayer.

Anne stayed a step behind Pierre at all times, her hands holding Julien's feet because she believed this made him more comfortable while he was being carried. Marie-Marie saw her husband and pressed a hand against her mouth and sobbed.

Three of the servants who practiced healing were allowed into the room, alongside Marie-Marie, Jenna, Abigail and Alise. Alise knew there wasn't much the three of them could do, except keep him comfortable. One of the healers, Marguerite, thoroughly examined Julien's wound. It was this servant who Pierre had faith in. For years he and his father had sent her to various locations across América and three times to Europe to study medicine beside those who allowed her.

When she reached back a hand another servant handed her a bottle of whisky. Marguerite saturated a piece of cloth and cleaned the wound, then examined it further. "The skull has been broken."

Marie-Marie heard this and whimpered into her open palm.

"Strip him of all clothing and turn him on his stomach."

Anne hurried closer and grabbed one of his boots to remove it. Marie-Marie had already reached for the other.

"You others out," Pierre ordered.

Marie-Marie knew her husband was sleeping with one of the servants, but didn't know who it was. What she did know was Anne was the most reliable servant in the mansion. Because of this she was happy it was Anne who worked beside her to strip Julien of his clothing. Each time he was rolled onto his back his eyes rolled and his right side made small twitches. Pierre didn't like the look of this and pushed himself in between them. He lifted Julien in his arms and kept his face and body downward as Marie-Marie and Anne continued to remove his clothing without further incident.

Anne hurried out of the room and returned minutes later with an arm full of pillows. If Julien was to lie face down she wanted him to be as comfortable as possible.

Sheets were pulled over him.

Marguerite wanted to see his wound better. Using a pair of small shears she cut away the hair above the nape of his neck up to the wound. Covering the cloth she had used earlier with more whiskey she then laid it over the entire area. She didn't know exactly why she did this and was only going by what she felt in her gut.

The others stood around her to also get a better look. The sharp piece of iron had punctured through the scalp and the skull. Marguerite probed the wound with the tip of her finger. Blood and fluid trickled out.

"Anh…"

Leaning over him they saw that Julien appeared semiconscious. The muscles on the right side of his face, which was the same side of the wound, twitched, especially his eye.

"I don't know what to do for him," Marguerite confessed. "Him moving like that makes me think something is going on inside his brain. I'm thinking there should be more blood. Maybe it's spilling inside and unable to come out."

"Anh…"

The others looked at each other unsure of what Julien was trying to say.

Anne knew he was trying to call her name. She got on her hands and knees, crawled underneath the bed and came out on the other side. Marie-Marie saw Anne's eagerness to reach him, and her eyes grew wide. Hurrying to the opposite side of the bed she tried to pull Anne away. As soon as Anne started to scurry Pierre realized what Julien was trying to say. Believing Julien was only making some sort of request, Pierre reached for Marie-Marie and pulled her away from the bed.

Anne didn't care if anyone else was in the room. Fearing he was dying she grabbed his hand, kissed it and stared intently into his eyes so he could see she was there. The others watched as Julien tried to focus his left eye on her.

"It's all right," Anne whispered.

Julien closed his eyes.

"She's sleeping with my husband." Marie-Marie spoke in a cold tone. Her eyes filled with tears.

Anne didn't look up at the others.

The secret that she and Julien had kept for more than a year was now out.

Anne only hoped that her m'sieu lived and that her punishment wouldn't be too severe.

***

"Do something," Marie-Marie spoke like a victim making an appeal to the highest court. "Even this moment she is in the room with him. I want you to get rid of her. Sell her. I don't care. I want her out of this house while I'm here."

Pierre sat behind his desk facing her, Jenna and Alise.

Jenna did not want Anne sold. Julien was terribly ill, and even now no one expected him to survive much longer. When Anne assisted Marguerite and Monsieur Morning, who constantly made a tea from peyote to combat Julien's fevers, the other servants finally had the chance to continue with their chores and the mansion's routine could go on as normal.

"Anne is the best servant I have." Jenna spoke these words directly to Pierre. "You can't sell her. Anne will be too hard to replace. Even when the girl is tired she gets more things done than some of the others. I don't care what she's done. I can't live without her. I just can't. She and Riley alone can run this entire mansion better than a dozen servants."

"Marie-Marie," Pierre began. "I understand your frustration. What's most important at the moment is your husband. I agree with Jenna. Anne takes care of him better than anyone else. I want my brother to live. Don't you? I have no intentions of selling Anne or removing her out of his house or his room for that matter."

Alise heard this and knew she was no longer needed in the room. Rising to her feet she started to walk away.

"What is wrong with all of you?" Marie-Marie asked. "I feel like I'm being betrayed by this entire family. Julien is *my* husband, yet Alise and Anne spend more time with him than I do. I refuse to believe that no one knew what was going on."

Alise stared at Pierre. "I need to go look on Gorée. Excuse me."

Pierre nodded.

"Am I not his wife?" Marie-Marie asked watching with contempt in her eyes as Alise left the room. "I should have time alone with him. I order them out of his room, but Alise does not listen. And she brings Anne in with her. I have never seen such blatant disrespect from les noirs."

Jenna's mouth tightened into a hard line. "I don't like what you're insinuating. I have questioned the others personally. No one knew, Marie-Marie. Not my family *or* the servants. As for Alise not listening to you, you'll have to speak to my husband about it. Alise listens to no one, including me, and my husband seems to believe this behavior is most appropriate."

"The servants are lying to protect her!" Marie-Marie argued. "I know they are! Someone had to know."

"Your husband is sick!"

Marie-Marie didn't like the way Pierre was looking at her or the reprimanding tone he had used. If she didn't know any better it looked as if he was trying to decide whether he should come around the desk and attack her.

"He and Anne were having an affair," Pierre continued. "What difference does it matter who knew or didn't know? My brother is at death's door and you sit there demanding retribution for his sins. No one in this home has betrayed you other than Anne and your husband. Alise is not keeping you from him. She has always taken care of him when he's sick. Should she not do so now when he's obviously dying? You're not asking us to do what's right. You're asking us to get revenge on your husband for sleeping with one of the servants."

Marie-Marie stood to her feet and walked out of the room without looking at either of them.

Jenna also stood to her feet.

"I need to speak with you," he said. "Sit down."

Jenna's smile was radiant. "There's so much to do, Pierre. I'm needed in other areas of the mansion at the moment."

"Sit down. Now," he said firmly.

She sat again.

"What happened between you and I in my study the night of Abigail's coming out?"

"Nothing."

"Did you come into the study that night?"

"Of course not. Why would I? You drank too much…"

Pierre leaned back in his chair and tightened his mouth and his eyes.

Jenna was familiar with the look. It meant he had reached his last rope.

"I purposely didn't drink much after Gorée was injured. I remember you bringing me glasses of bourbon. After the second glass I started getting a headache. After the third I remember feeling ill."

"Everyone was drinking, Pierre," she countered. "It was a celebration. And a successful one. Others became intoxicated as well. Many of our guests ate gumbo before traveling back to their homes the next morning."

"Julien told me that Anne sat with me in the study after she and he had stripped me of my clothes. Years ago when I used to drink heavily it was Anne who helped me to bed. If she was frightened that I would strangle in my sleep she would sleep on the rug behind the sofa during the night. I haven't spoken to Anne yet, but I'm going to ask her if she slept on the rug that night. If she did and she tells me that you came in this room I'm going to be very upset."

Jenna smiled at him. "Why would I have come in here, Pierre? We had a mansion full of guests. I had my hands full making sure everyone had somewhere to sleep…"

"What did you give me?"

"I didn't give…"

"Stop!" He leaned back. His arms rested against the armrest. "I gave you a chance. I knew I should have never trusted you. Too many others told me I shouldn't. But I thought you, Abby and I could do better. I thought we were trying to do better."

He sat forward and reached for a decanter. "I want you to remember we had this talk later, Jenna. What will your excuse be this time? I'm sitting right here. You've had an opportunity to tell me anything you wanted."

"Why would I trust you, Pierre, when you've proven that I can't?"

"Did you come into the study that night?"

"And if I did?"

"Why?"

"Because you're behaving differently. You're not the same. You leave the mansion and don't come back until morning, which means you aren't going very far. This is my home, Pierre. It's not fair for you to force me out of it. You need a male heir. I can give you one. If I gave you one I know you will love him more than all of your children put together, including Gorée."

"Gorée is crazy. My child is insane. But she has nothing on *you*, madame. Do you even realize what you've just confessed to? What is wrong with your brain? Are you crazy? If you saw me trying to mend our relationship why didn't you come and talk to me!"

"Because you're having another affair, Pierre! Only a woman would keep you out of the mansion this much. Is it one of Jean-André's daughters? Is it my best friend, Bethanie? The Dussault plantation is the only one near here. You have to be going there. The last time you were gone this much Gorée was born some months later. Are you, Pierre? Are you sleeping with my best friend? Are you trying to have an heir with someone else so you can finally get rid of me?"

"You are a hard woman to like or love. I will never love you. Ever. I don't care if you're carrying my child or not. If you want to live here you will change. If you ever cross me again. If you so much as speak unruly to a servant. You won't even get Riverside. But you'll leave here. You can go back to Green Lea or do whatever you want. But you will be out of my life. Julien and Marie-Marie will live here until he's well, but I doubt that will ever happen. I'm taking over Primrose. I have too much on my mind to be concerned about your behavior and what deceit you plan next."

"I can help you. You know I can. You can't handle Primrose by yourself. It's almost as large as this plantation. In business we have always worked well together."

"I won't ever trust you again. At this point if you and Abigail left right now I will consider it a blessing. Even now I wonder if sooner or later she will become like you. And if you are carrying, I will never trust that child either. Not as long as you're the mother of it. Loving you is far too hard!" He yelled watching her as she ran from the room.

***

Many mornings later Pierre rolled on his side as he woke; the bottom part of his legs and feet hung out of the foot of the bed. Moss had been added to the mattress to make it more comfortable. But with the bed as small as it was it meant only a part of his body was able to get a good night's rest.

"This bed is sacrilegious, Sarah."

A chair scraped across the floor. The cabin door was opened momentarily. More sunlight poured into the small space and brightened his face. Pierre lifted his arm to shield his eyes.

The smell of food drifted toward him from the hearth. It was early yet. Pierre could tell from the cool temperature next to the wall. Still sharp rays of the sun spilled into the room through the thin curtains over the window. Sarah refused to replace them with heavier ones often complaining of needing the extra light the window provided.

"I'm going to tear this place down after the *maison* is completed so you'll never be tempted to come here again."

"Don't do that." She spoke softly. From where he sat he could hear her fingers rapidly moving. To live in a one room cabin it was ridiculous how busy she stayed. As he pulled himself up he released a small groan and gripped his back.

"I hate this bed."

"Pierre," she cooed, her fingers sounding like they were moving faster than ever.

Slippers sat ready on the floor so all he had to do was slide his feet inside them. Of all the things he hated about the cabin there were a few things that he did enjoy. One of them was walking bare feet. He stretched as he stood to his feet, his curled hands touching the ceiling.

Sarah looked in his direction, loving the muscular contour of his form. The nightshirt he wore barely reached his calves. The way he stood with his chest slightly pushed forward made his manhood visible through the thin fabric. Sarah eyed him there a moment, then looked up at his eyes and smiled. "It's going to rain later today. You know what that means."

"When doesn't it rain in New Orléans?" He crossed to her, folded his arms around her and kissed her neck. It was then he noticed the empty plate at the far end of the table and that the other chair was pushed back. "Was it her that opened the door? Was she here again? Why must you bring her here on the mornings I'm here?" Anger crept into his tone.

Imogen had arrived on the plantation two mornings after Abigail's coming out party – a party no one was permitted to speak of in front of him.

"I wasn't feeling well. She's been my servant for many years, Pierre. She worries."

"She eats here. She sits here for long periods. She didn't sound worried. I don't like when you bring her here while I'm visiting..."

"You visit all of the time now," she said, peering up at him.

Pierre kissed her mouth. "Then I shall stop. It's too personal. I don't want her seeing me undressed or sleeping."

"All right," she said. "I shall tell her not to come back."

Sarah watched him as he pulled from her and sat on one of the chairs. She stood to fix him a plate. As soon as her back was to him she stared at the small fire in the hearth a moment then reached for the pots and skillets warming on the bricks. It frightened her when she saw him like this. She knew he didn't like Imogen. On several occasions she had told Imogen to lessen her visits and Imogen had. It was hard for the servant to know exactly when Pierre would visit or how long he would stay. With everything that was happening on the plantation and in the mansion it was hard for Pierre to make a schedule, and she didn't feel it right to ask him to do so. But Imogen was the only familiar face on the plantation to her. And the more time she spent alone the lonelier she felt.

She slid a plate of food in front of him, and like he had her, she wrapped her arms around his shoulders and kissed his face near his ear. There were many things she loved about him, and most of those things made him different than William. For one Pierre loved cleanliness. While most men smelled of sweat, Pierre smelled of cologne. His hair was always washed and brushed. Even now after sleeping with his hair braided into a single plait it hung down his spine with no need of being unraveled and brushed again.

"When are you coming back?"

It was a question he detested. The reason he answered was because he knew she only asked because he hadn't visited in five days and she had missed him.

"I'm not sure."

Sliding into his lap she sat so she faced him with her middle against his and her legs dangling toward the back of the chair. "Then I better get enough of you now."

She kissed his lips then clung to his neck when he lifted her from the chair. The softness of the mattress pressed into her back. Pierre lifted her nightgown and tossed it over her head, then stared down as he always did of late. She was in the beginning of her pregnancy, but still it was noticeable. Too noticeable. Secretly he wondered if she was suffering from a tumor. "Dr. Marchand should come now and look you over."

"If you think that's best."

An hour later he held Sarah high in his arms at the cabin door. Leaving her near the swamp was always hard to do. Sarah clung to his neck placing tiny kisses against his mouth. She let out a sigh when she was lowered and he crossed the yard. "Stay out of the rain, Pierre."

He mounted his horse, smiled and winked at her.

Sarah saw this and fell in love with him all over again.

Just as Pierre entered the trees, Julien awoke inside the mansion. The room was dark just the way he liked it. Warm coverlets covered him from his neck down to his feet. Pillows were arranged on one side of him to help in stay in a particular position throughout the night. Hating that he was going to have to call for her, he closed his eyes again and drew in a deep breath.

"*Marieee*...Marie?" Since his injury whenever he called for someone he listened afterwards for the sounds of footsteps. His voice wasn't as strong as it used to be and he hated having to make it stronger because it made him cough. If he coughed too much he couldn't breathe. They knew what kind of man he was now. Someone should always be listening. When they weren't it was because *she* had sent them away, and this he hated most of all.

"Marie?" Listening again he relaxed when he heard his door push open and footsteps enter the room. A wedge of light spilled across the floor. Julien didn't like seeing sunlight on the floor in the mornings; it irritated him, although he didn't know why. The man he was now made it hard for him to look to see who entered the room. If he had to say thank you or feel more indebted than he already did he would rather die. It was a wonder he wasn't dead already. The nail in the wall had pierced through his skull and poked a small part of his brain. For weeks a mounting pressure in his head had kept him mostly unconscious. Marie-Marie reminded him often that when he had spoken shortly after his injury he had called for Anne. Julien couldn't remember doing this, and he could understand his wife for being mad if he had.

"Bonjour, m'sieu."

A smiled stretched across his face. Only Anne called him m'sieu. She used the sobriquet whenever they were alone. During the weeks he had lain between life and death an infection had riddled his body with fever. Fluid had gathered in his lungs. The damage done was irreversible. A lot of his motor functions were impaired on his right side. His voice was slightly higher than a whisper. Something as little as turning to see Anne's face took a lot of effort, especially since she was entering the room on his right.

As she rounded the bed she looked over her shoulder to make sure no one had followed her into the room, then climbed onto the bed on her knees and kissed him on the mouth. The very sight of her made him feel better. Each time he looked into her eyes he felt hope for the future.

"Why didn't I marry you?" His speech pattern was slower, and the words sometimes slurred. As always Anne behaved as if she didn't notice any change in him.

"Because it's against the law, m'sieu," she whispered. "I think I'm having a baby."

She searched his eyes intently. Julien saw her fear of the others finding out.

"A baby?" He asked because he wanted to be sure.

"Oui, m'sieu." She grabbed his left hand, because he could move it with no problem, and pressed it flat against her middle.

Julien smiled. Anne saw his smile and smiled at him.

"A baby," Julien repeated. This news excited him. "A baby," he said unable to truly wrap his brain around it. He was going to have a child. "I'll take care of you, Anne. Everything is going to be all right."

She looked again at the door, then down on him. "M'sieu, she's going to be so upset. Even now she's trying to convince madame to move me out of the mansion. The others don't take care of you the way I do."

"You're going nowhere. You'll stay in this house where you belong."

Anne nodded at him, but he could see she had little faith in what he said. Her hand slid underneath the sheets and felt around. "Let me get you up, m'sieu. You've been lying in it long enough."

Anne was better at giving him what little dignity he had left. It was the way she did things that seemed to make it all simpler. Anne never reminded him how much he needed her. Like now. The bed was wet. When wasn't it? The only reason she felt first was to determine how much linen she needed.

As she climbed off of the bed he closed his eyes.

In the corner of the room where the many items he went through in a single day was kept, she stacked clean towels and a change of bed clothes on one arm, then turned to one of the armoires to choose clothes for him to wear. Marie-Marie preferred he stayed in bed, and Julien could understand this decision. Getting him out of bed was easier than getting him back in it. If he was taken downstairs the servants became too busy tending to his needs than those of the house. Julien liked going downstairs. He wished to sit on the galerie everyday if he could even if it rained. The need to see some part of the world that still existed outside his bedroom made him feel a part of it.

Going to parties and even possibly the city may now be all over. Friends had come to see him. They took one look at him and many of them haven't returned. The nerves that control his right eyelid no longer worked like they should. Julien couldn't feel that his right eye now looked smaller. His sight hadn't been altered. It surprised him each time he looked into a mirror and saw his appearance. Some of the muscles in his face had gone slack, but to him he looked closely to the same way he had before. Apparently his friends saw him differently and couldn't associate the way he appeared now to the man he used to be. But what did that matter when he was going to have a child?

Julien heard the door open and knew who it was since the person didn't knock first.

Marie-Marie stood at the foot of the bed and stared at him. Her prim expression made her look like a Puritan preparing to read Bible verses to a sinner. Slowly she looked in Anne's direction. "Get out, girl. I need to speak to my husband."

Anne searched the room to see where she could temporary lay down the bulk that was in her arms. Going to a small sofa she nodded at her madame for approval.

"Hurry up, girl! I don't have all day!"

Anne lowered the items and crossed the room.

Marie-Marie watched her with hate in her eyes and her heart. It made her angry that Anne could get Julien to do things no one else could. It also made her angry that regardless of how hard she tried she couldn't take care of Julien the way Anne did. The girl was needed for now unless Marie-Marie had her way. It was why she had come into the room. For days she had pondered over her decision and now she would voice them while she had the courage.

"Bonjour," Julien said, hoping to deflect her attention long enough for Anne to get away without being berated.

"Don't do that," Marie-Marie pleaded and closed her eyes. "You're only saying good morning to protect her. You shouldn't. Are things not bad enough as they are?"

"Bonjour," he said again.

"Are you wet?"

No. He would not answer this question this morning or any other. Why did any of them feel the need to make him say aloud what they already knew?

"I heard it's going to rain today," he said. "I want to go outside and sit on the galerie."

"So you can catch your death?"

Reminders were now all she gave. The things he had taken for granted before were now ways for him to die. It was hard for him to tell for certain if she truly feared him dying. The looks she gave and the tone of her voice made him feel as if she was punishing him for all the things he had done since they were married.

"Are you wet?"

Julien wanted to yell at her. The only reason he didn't was because yelling made him cough. Taking the few seconds he needed to calm himself, he spoke slowly and deliberately.

"Petition the church for a divorce, Marie-Marie. I've told you already that I won't refuse the church's decision. Neither will I refuse any fair settlement you deem you are entitled to. I've told you before that you don't have to be brave and stay here if you don't want to. No one will speak harshly against you. I'll make sure they won't. Everyone already knows I slept with other women during our marriage. I confess. I did do that to you." The strain that came into his neck made him realize he was holding it up to see her better. Allowing his head to fall against the pillow he began to relax. "I'll accept anything at this moment except you standing there with accusing eyes demanding me to tell you that I have pissed myself yet again."

She turned from him and stared at the French doors. This marriage hadn't been a good one from its very first night. Instead of staying with her that evening he had chosen to leave her alone for hours while he was out doing God knows what. And then he blamed her for trying to help the situation. He silently blamed her for not being a better lover. He blamed her for loving God and being a good Catholic. And now he was a man who suffered from lameness. He peed himself during the night, and in order for her to prove to everyone that she was a good wife she was expected to diaper the very man who slept with one woman after another throughout their entire marriage.

Over the past months she had learned a lot about both brothers. The things Julien had done to her, Pierre had done similarly to Jenna. The amount of wealth they owned seemed to make the brothers believe their behavior was acceptable. Divorce is what Julien mentioned often since his injury. If the two of them divorced then what? For him to suggest such a thing now was far crueler than all the other things he had done against her.

"The wet sheets are making me cold," he said.

She turned abruptly in his direction. "It's a wonder you notice that but can't tell when you need to relieve yourself."

"Merci," he said and closed his eyes.

"Why are you so cruel to me, Julien? Tell me what I've done to deserve it. For years I have tried being the best wife I could. Not once did you appreciate it. All you thought about were the other women you entertained. But this *thing* you have with Anne, why are you making me bear it? With her you get up and get about. When I come into the room you act like an invalid. It makes me angry. It does. Once again I get the least of you while everyone else gets the best. The fact that she is a servant makes this situation intolerable!"

"I'm the same with Anne as I am with you."

She stepped closer to the bed. "You are not! You are not!"

"I very much am. Do you truly stand there and accuse me of lying longer than I want to in my own piss?"

"I can help you, Julien."

"I don't need your pity. You stand there and hate the women I've been with when you don't do what they do. You're so pious. What do you know? You believe like so many that women are only to serve and lie on their backs while their husbands climb on top of them. That isn't a marriage. You have no idea what a wife is. If you did you would be able to see that although I'm lame we can still have a life together. You would have come in here and helped me clean myself up, helped me get into a chair, then removed your clothing and climbed on top of me."

"Sex! Sex! Sex! It's all you think about!"

"No, Marie-Marie. It's not all I think about, and when I was with other women it's not all I did. But sex can bring two people closer together than ever before. In your eyes you're being a good wife by keeping my home clean and that it functions with good organization. A clean house is good to look at. But a beautiful wife is better. No matter how many women I slept with I always ran back to you. I've been waiting, and waiting, and waiting. And now this. I refuse to wait any longer. Now get Anne and leave my room."

"Julien." She stood close to the bed and stared into his eyes. "You're *lame*. That part of your life is over. But I don't mind. Honestly, I don't. And you can't walk."

"I *can* walk, just not like everyone else, and I'm still very much a man."

Marie-Marie stared hard at him, then slapped his face. The blow hurt the palm of her hand. "You are the reason our marriage is the way it is. A good Catholic man wouldn't have dared asked his wife to do anything immoral."

"No," Julien agreed. "A good Catholic man would only make that request to the lovers he keeps on the side."

She studied his eyes as if determining if she would accept what he said as truth or not. "You wasted no time to run off to your whores. And that I shall not forgive you for. You say you have been waiting on me? I have been waiting for you, Julien. How dare you think you can run the streets then return to me with the scent of another woman on you and expect me to lie down for you and receive you between my legs. But those days are over, and I shall do my best to live with the life I'm now forced to have. But you are lame and there's nothing that neither you nor I can do about it."

Julien smiled at her. "What are you waiting for Marie-Marie? My death so you can become an eligible and wealthy widow looking for a new husband? Will you open your legs for him? I've always been honest with you and I'll continue to do so now. I'm leaving my wealth to my children. Not you. I think you should leave my room and go think about that. Anne's carrying my child. Now you know for sure that what you have refused to do someone else is always willing. Even now while I'm *lame*."

She used both hands to slap him this time. She stared down at his face and hair, hated what she saw and slapped him again. "Your brother isn't the devil. You are."

She turned from him and walked away. Before she walked out of the door she looked back at him over her shoulder. A part of her felt remorse for slapping a man who couldn't do much to help himself. This thought was ignored after she reminded herself that Anne was carrying his child. When she stepped out into the hall she looked in both directions, but Anne wasn't there. Good. Now Julien can lie in his piss a little while longer. As she made her way toward the stairs she wondered who she could make an ally with. Surely someone inside this godforsaken mansion had reason to hate Julien as much as she did.

Julien managed to turn his head far enough to see the closed door. As he concentrated on his breathing, he listened. When after some minutes he heard what could have been footsteps his anticipation mounted. The door pushed open silently. Anne stepped into the room carrying a ewer of hot water padded with cloths for her protection.

Julien nudged his head toward the door.

Anne shook her head. No one had been in the hall when she neared. To avoid her mesdames she had taken the servants staircase to the second floor.

The pillows were pulled from underneath him. As he lay flat on his back muscle tremors caused his right side to shake. Anne paid no notice. Grabbing the stack she left on the small sofa, she carried them to him and placed them on his chest. The others saw Anne doing this and started doing it as well. Julien didn't mind. Once the linen was on his chest it was his job to make certain they didn't fall. Doing so helped him with his coordination.

Julien never yelled at the servants who helped him. In the beginning they were all very patient. Now that months had passed many of them were frustrated. Anne got frustrated too at times. It was hard to get something done when it seemed his body struggled against it. And the servants had chores, which meant none of them could spend too long in his room as they were soon needed somewhere else. If he didn't want to be stuck in a bed for the rest of his life he needed to do all he could for himself.

His left arm held the mound against him, but the mound was too high to be held with one arm. To keep it from falling to the floor he would need to use his right arm as well. Dragging it slowly upward, the stack shifted, but he managed to secure it.

The chamber pot was pulled from underneath the bed and positioned on the floor. Some of the hot water in the ewer was poured into a basin and cool water mixed with it. Soap was laid out, his ivory toothbrush, a hand brush, hair wax, powdered cologne, plenty of towels. A rug was pulled closer for him to stand on. A table placed on top of it. Everything was put into place before she turned to him and lowered one side of her bodice to expose one breast.

Anne never gave anyone rules. Through her gestures or actions she made others aware of her intentions and also what she expected of them. Because she was naturally a quiet person it had taken him days once to realize that Anne was purposely not speaking to him.

Anne pulled the coverlets away from him and onto the floor. Each of her movements was fluid. Julien liked watching her agility. She had done the routine enough times to not be fearful of the next steps she needed to take.

Julien reached his left foot for the floor. Apprehension filled him. Nine times out of ten he ended up on the floor. Unless he wanted several servants standing around him while he wore wet bed clothes he would have to wait for Pierre to be found and sent to the room if he fell.

Taking his time, he inched closer to the edge of the bed.

Anne stepped up on the bed frame and grabbed the wooden canopy above to position herself. Reaching for his right hand, she held her position and waited. Julien thought about the child she was carrying and hesitated.

"What if we fall?"

"We haven't fallen in weeks, m'sieu."

Julien reached for her hand. His arm felt way too stiff, and it was hard for him to straighten it out all the way without mind boggling pain. Anne placed his arm around her waist. As Julien struggled to lean toward her, her free arm hooked around his neck and tugged him closer. This made it easier. Slowly his legs began to fall out of the bed. Lowering one of her feet to the floor, once she was standing on her own again she tugged him more viciously.

Julien trembled to stay upright, and then even more once he was on his feet.

Anne moved quickly to remove the nightshirt he wore, tossing it with the coverlets on the floor. Julien concentrated on his breathing. Now would be the worst time to have a spell of coughing. It took him a while, but she didn't complain or rush him. Reaching for the chair with only his left hand was a mistake he constantly made. The chair threatened to turn over. To keep it balanced he reached as fast he was able to with his right. Standing to his feet and gripping both armrests of a chair was a major feat.

Julien stared at a clock resting on top of a table against the far wall. For seventeen minutes he did all he could not to fall while Anne washed and dried him.

Only after he sat on the towel in the chair did Anne permit him to suckle her nipple as long as he wanted before they went on to the next thirteen steps that was needed to get him dressed and ready for the day. His hair was the last step. By the time Anne stood behind the chair to brush it and braid it into a single plait Julien always felt closer to the man he was before, but after more than an hour of standing and exercise he needed to sit a while and rest. This was the reason Anne took her time on this step.

Someone knocked on the door.

Anne hurried to it to unlock it.

The door pushed open and Pierre stepped inside.

Pierre took in the room. It didn't look like a sickroom. Other than the tightly bundled pile of bedding that needed to be carried to the laundry cabin the room was meticulous. Julien sat in a chair wearing trousers, shirt, waistcoat, hose and boots.

"Did you know that your wife is trying to make preparations to take you back to Primrose?"

Julien was too tired to speak and simply stared at Pierre.

"I won't allow it," Pierre said.

Julien could tell it was too soon after his injury to do more than what he was, but if he continued as he was he would talk and walk better someday. He gestured for Pierre to grab a chair and sit beside him.

Anne finished his hair, dipped her knees toward her monsieur as she stood in front of him, then turned to leave the room.

Julien reached a hand toward her.

"Anne," Pierre called, believing Julien needed further seeing to.

Anne turned and hurried back.

"Give me Anne," Julien said.

"Anne, leave us," Pierre said, then waited for Anne to close the door behind her. "I won't give you Anne, Julien. Has she told you yet she's carrying your child?"

"Yes, she has."

"You can have more children. Marie-Marie can give them to you. It's her duty."

"Don't live my life, Pierre. This fascination you have I have never been one with it."

"Because you don't understand."

"What don't I understand? Marie-Marie and I are no more."

"What do you think, Julien? That you can live the rest of your life with Anne!" Pierre rose to his feet.

"Sit down, Pierre. It's too hard for me to continue to look up. If I'm honest I want out of this chair. I'm tired and I want to sit on the galerie."

"I'm not giving you Anne."

"Yes, you are."

"I won't, Julien."

"You're not Papa, Pierre. You are not going to tell me what to do. You will give her to me because it will make me happy. I need her around. I can't have her doing chores. With her I can become better. I know I can. But everyone is always running around. Everyone is always so busy. It's a wonder I don't piss myself more. Give her to me so I can become a better man. Let me have some dignity. I need someone in the room with me at night. Give her to me. I don't know how many days I have left."

"If you give her her freedom she will leave you. She is educated and capable of making a living for herself. She can speak three languages fluently. She will travel. She will live life. Is that what you want?"

"If it makes her happy. If she does you'll be stuck with me, because I have no intentions of leaving Ashleywood."

"And Primrose?"

"I'm giving it to my child after it's born. Unlike you, I don't believe that América will turn its back on all les noirs. Les noirs, the quadroons will have a future in América."

"I refuse to believe you are that ignorant. Apparently you are unaware that France no longer governs Louisiana. New Orléans is already divided. The Creoles are outnumbered by the Américains. Things are destined to get worse, especially if slavery is abolished. The ports in our city are the largest in the South. More men will come and when they come they will not tolerate being neighbors to affluent noir neighbors. Better your marriage with Marie-Marie. Convince her to have a child. Unless Anne's child has a white benefactor the child is going to see some horrendous days by the time it reaches the age we are now."

"I won't. I've made up my mind."

"Stop being stubborn, Julien."

"Stubborn? No. I'm tired of living by everyone's rules, Pierre. I choose to live happy. Anne makes me happy. I'm ready to go downstairs now."

Pierre knew not to argue further. Standing in front of the chair, he lifted Julien over his shoulders. As he carried him downstairs the servants they passed smiled in their direction, most of them telling Julien good morning.

When Pierre stepped out on the galerie he saw that someone had padded the settee with a coverlet and pillows so Julien could be comfortable

He settled Julien down, then rose to his feet and yelled for Anne.

"She's been sent to the laundry cabin, monsieur," Jeanette alerted him after coming to the door.

"The laundry cabin? What for?"

Jeanette looked at Julien, then glanced back up at Pierre. "I don't know, monsieur. She was sent there after she tended to Monsieur Julien."

Pierre walked past her and hurried to the *salle* where Marie-Marie and Jenna sat having café with a few friends and their male escort. He wanted to urge Marie-Marie to sit outside with her husband but stopped himself.

Jenna rose to her feet.

Pierre crossed the room to her, easing her back into the chair. "Don't get up on my account. I thought I would have a word with you and Marie-Marie, but I've changed my mind. Please carry on."

His eyes fell to the middle of her gown where his child grew inside her, then he turned and left the room.

Jenna watched him unaware that those around her were watching her. Only when she turned back to the others did their conversation continued.

Mallaurie leaned closer to her. "Jenna, I'm only saying this as a friend, and because I've seen the changes in you. I also know you are happy about the child you're carrying, and I'm happy for you. I really am. But I don't think you know."

"Know what?" Jenna asked, sipping her café and rehearsing in her mind Pierre crossing the room to bid her to sit down for the sake of the child. When she learned she was pregnant she feared his reaction. The day she told him, he said nothing and only stared at her. It was moments like these when he was unable to stop his emotions from showing, when she became certain that he was looking forward to the birth of this child as much as she was.

"He's building a home here on your land."

Jenna smiled. "Abigail and Carlisle have decided to live on Ashleywood. I didn't like Monsieur Morning at first. But I do believe that his potion of tea helped Julien survive his worst fevers."

Mallaurie shook her head with sadness in her eyes. "Pierre is building two homes, Jenna. Abigail and Carlisle have shown me the location where their home is being built. The other one is farther down the river in the opposite direction, and from what I heard, safely hidden by plenty of trees."

Jenna continued to sip her café making sure that the smile she wore stayed on her face.

"Your sister is here, Jenna. I didn't want to tell you. By the time I heard the news you had just told me about the child and I just couldn't. But now that I've heard about the house he's building for her, and how large it will be…" She looked at the others in the room. "It will be large enough for a large family to live inside it. With your father now living in Biloxi…"

241

"I know about the house," Jenna lied and smiled at all of them. "Why wouldn't I know about the house? It's being built on my land."

"Jenna, he's having an affair with her," Bethanie whispered. "William sent men here to get her back. The men said that Pierre was ready to commit murder rather than let her leave here and that when he finally got his hands on her it was most inappropriate the way he lifted her in his arms and sat her on his horse."

Antoine Dussault had sat in the corner of the room, but now rose and stepped out onto the galerie with his cup of café, because most Creole men refused to sit amongst gossiping women.

Jacqueline Dussault leaned closer over the table toward Jenna. "I don't think what he's doing is right if you ask me. My father hadn't been thinking right when he gave Anne to Pierre. Now my father wants her back, and Pierre refuses to. Everyone knows Anne's my father's child, so why is it right for her to be here serving you when she should be at my mansion serving my family?"

"Jacqueline, you have made that complaint for years," Jenna said. "Pierre is most fair in these matters. If your father truly wanted her back, Pierre would have given her to him. Perhaps your father doesn't truly want her back, and it's *you* who is pushing him to do something. Anne is happy here. Your father even said as much the last time he visited."

Jacqueline's face reddened as she averted her gaze. "I still say it's not right."

Bethanie lifted her cup with both hands and brought it to her mouth. "My papa fell in love with Anne the moment she was born. Don't mind Jacqueline. I believe my papa gave Anne to Pierre because he didn't want her living in our home for fear she would be abused."

"I don't believe that," Jacqueline argued.

"I do," Jenna said. "Some of you know that Anne is educated. Who do you think paid for her education? It was your father who arranged everything, Jacqueline. What I don't understand is why he never forced Mableane to further her education. Oh, that's right. I think Mableane is your uncle's child. Don't mind me. I forgot about that."

Both sisters lowered their cups soundly to the table.

"Perhaps we should not discuss this," Jacqueline said.

Jenna smiled at the woman because she personally knew that Jacqueline's husband was Mableane's father. It's the only reason why Jenna had mentioned it.

Mallaurie waited until the cat battle was over. "Jenna, I have something else to share with you if want to hear it. The only reason I'm mentioning this now is because Jacqueline and Bethanie are the ones who told me in the hopes that I told you in some underhanded way. But you are my true friend, and after I say what I have to say, if they know anything more regarding it they should tell you now."

The sisters lifted their café cups at the same time and took sips while staring at Jenna.

"Tell me everything. Please."

Mallaurie looked at the sisters. "You two know the truth of the matter better than I do. You tell her."

Jacqueline anxiously lowered your cup. "Your papa isn't in Biloxi because William Murray paid his way there. William wants nothing to do with you or your papa. He thinks the two of you had done him dirty."

"Jenna, the rumor is *Pierre* sent your father to Biloxi. He gave him enough money for him and your Tante Marianne to live well off of until they die," Bethanie said softly.

"And it wasn't William who purchased Green Lea from you. It was Pierre. He's given the property to your sister."

"Jenna, why would he do that if she's still here and he's building a house here for her?" Mallaurie asked, then lowered her head. "I wished you and Pierre was doing better in your marriage. It's not right others knowing, and I knew you couldn't have. The last times I visited you seemed so radiant."

"How do any of you know this?" Jenna asked.

"The slave, Guillot, was hired to build this second house. His master..."

"His father," Mallaurie corrected.

"His father's been telling everyone his suspicions. He already knows that Lafon was commissioned to build Abigail's new home."

Marie-Marie lowered her cup and wondered how many tables in the city will discuss her when they learned that Anne would soon give Julien a child.

She excused herself and left the room.

***

Jenna didn't drive a buggy because she didn't want anyone alerting Pierre about it. If a second house was being built on her land she was going to find it. The owner of the slave Guillot knew where the house would be built because he had seen the blueprints. Because of its distance it took more than half an hour for her to reach it. When she did see it Jenna couldn't believe how many servants were working to get the house completed.

Sarah's *maison*, from what Jenna could see, consisted of a house made with twenty vertical posts. Like all Creole homes this house will also face the river. The evaporated wood to block the moisture from the river was arranged nearby. The basement had already been erected. The bricks used to build it Jenna knew had been made at Ashleywood. Abigail's basement would also be made from brick and cypress wood. The ovens to make them had been burning nonstop over the past months. Like Abigail, Sarah's home would also have its own outside kitchen and cistern. The cistern had also been erected. Servants were on top of it in the hopes of the cistern catching its first fall of rain.

Jenna had come by the way of the trees, but now she didn't care who saw her or if they summoned their master. She walked right up to the house, her heart breaking when she saw the care and expertise that had been used so far. Alise and Désireé lived in cottages. For Pierre to build Sarah a house of this size made his feelings for Sarah quite clear.

She stepped around one of the brick posts and stopped. Large glazed vases sat ready to be buried deep in the ground. Once the temperature of the rain water in the soil had cooled it just right, these vases will be filled with butter, cheese and other foods that a home needed to keep cold.

"Jenna?"

Jenna turned and faced him. "My sister? All of this for my sister?"

"Come. Let's talk."

Jenna noticed several servants were silently watching.

243

He led her to a cart that sat on what would be the rear side of the *maison* once it was completed. She didn't stop the tears from falling. Neither did she reach for the kerchief hidden in the sleeve of her cloak. Sarah was somewhere on her land and was having an affair with Pierre.

It surprised her that she didn't feel the need to murder Sarah or him. It surprised her further when she realized that this affair wounded her far deeper than anything else she had ever experienced. As if she had been stunned until she became immobile, all she could do was sit and feel. From what she saw the *maison* would be the same size that sits on large plantations. This told her more than what her friends had tried to. Pierre was in *love* with Sarah.

"It will only be two levels," he said as if reading her thoughts. "The basement and the floor where Sarah and the children will live. No one will be able to see it, Jenna. Its roof won't be higher than the trees."

"Children?" She faced him in disbelief. "Are you telling me she's carrying your child? Are you saying you intend to have more children with her in the future?"

"Yes."

Jenna's entire body went limp. Pierre grabbed her fearing she would slide out of the cart and hurt the child she was carrying.

A roll of thunder crackled overhead.

"How can you do this, Pierre?" She pushed hard at his hand. "Not even the most devilish man would move his wife's sister on his plantation and openly have an affair with her."

"I need to get you back to the mansion and out of the rain."

Jenna tried pleading although she believed she had already lost the war. "Please, don't do this. Even I would never hurt you like this. I always thought that no matter what happened between us, one day you and I would have a real marriage."

Pierre stared down. The pain in her eyes affected him. The woman sitting beside him visibly wounded and visibly despondent was a stranger to him. Turning so he faced her, he reached for her hand. "I love her."

The cry that tore out of her, it pierced his soul. Averting his gaze, he hadn't realized that although their marriage had been fueled with animosity it was still a viable marriage, and somehow their souls had still managed to become one.

"Send her away. Please," Jenna begged. "Be my husband."

The look that came into his eyes made her believe he was considering her request.

"I love her," he said. "I don't trust you. I don't think I ever will. This is wrong. I know it is. I should have divorced you the morning after we were married."

He slapped at the reins, putting the cart into motion.

Jenna stared at the bricks that made up the basement, then gripped her stomach with both hands. "And the child I'm carrying?"

He saw in her eyes there was no other motive behind the question. What she was asking was the fate of the unborn child she already loved. "Where was this woman you're behaving like sixteen years ago!" He roared. "Why hide her? Why!"

Jenna moaned inwardly. The sound didn't come out of her mouth, but was drawn in with a large breath. "My poor child," she said softly.

Again he saw no trickery and real emotion.

"I love the child, Jenna. I tried to convince myself not to, but I couldn't. You must know I will take care of the child when it's born."

The groan that came out of her reached her ears and alerted anyone that heard it how much pain she was in.

"I want us to live amicably, Jenna. Sarah will live on Ashleywood. Her children will live on Ashleywood. If this is something you feel you are unable to tolerate, accommodations can be made for you to live elsewhere. But please don't sit there and behave as if I owe you anything. Not after all we've been through. Even the child you're carry is because of your careful scheming. You're always scheming."

"This is a *scandale*!" Murder shone in her eyes. "No one in the city will ever accept this. You will be ruined! Your businesses will suffer. I'll make sure of it!"

"Hush now, crazy woman, while I provide you with a little education on the matter. Sarah will be accepted. Because to have her, I'm willing to give the Américains and a few of my Creole friends the land they have been after for a long, long, long time, and so much more."

## Chapter Twenty-Six
# The Same People Make the Same Mistakes

*[Doing favors brings sorrow. – Creole proverb]*

Jenna had sat quietly the rest of the way to the mansion. Pierre had studied her often contemplating if he should ignore his desire of Jenna's child also growing up on the plantation. Over the years she had proven just how wily she could become. That she was even carrying his child exposed how far she was willing to go to make certain she got whatever she wanted.

Even though he knew her capabilities, he couldn't send her away. Not now. And it wasn't because she was pregnant. América was in a recession. The price paid for crops were unstable and lower than it had been in many years. For the second year in a row disease had destroyed the crops on Primrose. For another year the plantation will not receive any profits. Instead of the servants bringing in a harvest they were working all hours trying to eradicate the disease and save what little crop they could. After this the focus would be on clearing all of the fields and starting over again. Thankfully Julien had anticipated as much and had set aside the money necessary to do it right.

His plantation Riverside was no different. Going there and she would have nothing other than stress. And there was more to his decision. Despite the things she had done against him in the past, from the first day of their marriage Jenna had taken care of the mansion and the running of it freeing him to see to the land and his other businesses.

She deserved something in return. Giving her a large sum of money and sending her away didn't sit right because he knew as much as she did that Ashleywood had become her home.

The closer his horse walked toward the sugarhouse the more he saw servants at work. A gang of teenage boys were chopping wood. The wood was provided continuously to keep the fires going under the large cast iron sugar kettles. For a short distance three servant women walked alongside his horse carrying water to those working inside the sugarhouse.

Pierre reached the cast iron kettle train just as his head sugar maker performed the strike. Everyone had stopped a moment to watch, and the sugar maker, knowing he had an audience, performed the strike with such precision and charisma that Overseers Langers and Curfy whistled loudly. Some of the slave men clapped when they saw the sugar begin to crystallize. If the strike had not been performed at the proper temperature or at the right consistency, instead of sugar the syrup boiling in the *batterie* kettle would have turned to molasses.

Seeing their master and employer was visiting the sugarhouse, the servants went quickly back to work filling the kettles and grinding more of the cane that sat on high shelves to dry. The process in the sugarhouse began in October and didn't end until January, each procedure done over and over again twenty-four hours a day. Because of this during the months of October through January the slaves worked on one of either three shifts, each of them putting in no less than ten hours of work per day. It was this monotonous routine performed on both Pierre's and Julien's plantation that made Julien and other planters wealthy men. This wasn't true for Pierre. On the day his father died, as the heir of Will Jennings the bulk of his wealth came from the fleet of ships he owned, and the international imports they made, as well as the companies he owned in France, and the chateau and land he had there. More than a thousand men worked for him in some capacity and were paid by his directuers who managed his companies. A company of avocats oversaw the legal aspects. To Pierre, Ashleywood was home. A profitable one, but home nonetheless.

Curfy trotted over to him with a tin of hot punch. Hot punch was served throughout *roulaison* – grinding season. It consisted of boiled cane juice and French brandy.

Pierre dismounted and took the tin from Curfy.

"T'isn't a better sugar maker than Antoine. It's because of him we haven't lost a *batterie* yet." Curfy was the sort of fellow that always smiled – a man who found a way to always be happy. His mirth made even the servants around him to constantly be in good spirits. It was this reason Pierre had hired Curfy to oversee the sugarhouse. Originally from one of the largest plantations in Jamaica, he learned there not only sugar making skills but what not to do to cause a slave insurrection.

Since his arrival the atmosphere in the sugarhouse had been pleasant and peaceful. The servants, elated Curfy had become their overseer, worked diligently for him and were most loyal. They worked hard. In return Curfy worked hard for them oftentimes pleading with Pierre for favors Curfy believed the servants enjoyed. His latest request was instead of eight pigs roasted this Christmas twelve would take its place. Pierre gave in easily. It was decisions like these that made new slaves arriving in New Orleans while they were being examined or when they stood on the auction block to risk the sting of the whip by yelling, 'Mitchie Jennings or *le diable dans Nouvelle-Orléans* take me!'

He lifted the tin toward Antoine and Antoine nodded in thanks while pouring the sugar crystals from the *batterie* into vats to cool. Soon it would be scooped in hogshead barrels and stored for several days while the remaining liquid inside drained from the holes burrowed through the bottom. Pierre sold the liquid as molasses.

"When you finish that, Antoine, stop a minute and have some punch," Pierre said. He brought the tin to his mouth enjoying the hot liquid as it slid down his throat.

"Will do, monsieur. Will do." Antoine grinned. "I'mma make a whole lot of sugar for you dis season, monsieur. Ain't lost a *batterie* since I learnt the trick. With the extra field now growing cane you can be ready for you Madame to troow the biggest party come har-vose."

Pierre finished the drink and handed the empty tin to a nearby servant. "If what you say is true, Antoine, there's a whole ham in it for you and your family."

Antoine nodded, his mouth quivering into what could be interpreted as something close to a smile. And then he studied the floor beneath his feet like all servants did when they wanted something. "'Tis nice of you, monsieur. Cain't deny it."

"But you want something else," Pierre clarified.

Antoine studied one of his boots hard enough to see through it, as well as the silt underneath the sugarhouse's foundation. "My youngin done fixt his eyes on a gal. One from Monsieur Jules' plantation. Saw her last season. Cain't get his mind right 'cause of it. The gal's name be Coffee 'cause she the color of it. My boy'll do right by Monsieur Jules if he'll have him. I'll vouch for the boy. He dun't want to leave his fam'ly, but like I say. The gal dunn bewitched him."

Pierre smiled. "Your son is too good with horses for me to part with. No one can tame or cure horses the way your son can. I'm actually happy he hasn't thought about buying his freedom."

"Yes, sir," Antoine said with his head still bowed. "Constance like it heah. What he won't freedom fo when he live betta heah?"

"That isn't true," Pierre argued. "There are many men of color in the North providing a decent living for themselves and their family."

"Hand to mouth with nothing left," Antoine answered. "Free to work and free to starve. Ain't all like that, but we heah. And we knows what we's got. Constance likes working wit de horses. Earns a good wage and has his own house. All he be lookin fo is to fill dat house wit chilluns."

"Then I think it'll be better for Coffee to come here and give him the children he wants." Primrose was not managed like Ashleywood. It was a plantation like every other. Julien didn't permit his servants being beat with the whip, but he did allow the overseers that managed the plantation to nip an ear or ankle when one of them deemed fit.

Antoine looked up, eyes wide, and then he lowered his head again. "I dun't know what rightly to say, monsieur. Scared if I do say sumpn the real devil will hear it."

"How many young ones you have now?" Pierre asked.

Antoine could no longer hold back his emotion. Curfy, watching this interaction between his best man and employer, nodded at a nearby servant. The servant drew near with a tin of punch and handed it to Antoine. Antoine gripped the tin with both hands, then rubbed a tear from his eye with one of his knuckles. "My youngest, Suzette, dunn give you a nice healthy boy *tree* Sat-tee-dees ago."

"That should make six, am I right?" Pierre asked.

"Yes, sir. The Lawd's been good to me, monsieur. Real good to me. Six grandbabies. Four chilluns. A good woman. All my seed, my mama, my papa, brothers, sisters and all they have living on this land." He shook his head and lowered it again. "I can't axt for mo, monsieur, but you dunn give it to me by saying you'll buy Coffee for my son. And I's tell you right now. Any of mine do anything a'gin ya, I'll take a strap of rawhide to them meself."

Pierre nodded respectfully at the slave. "I hope your family enjoys your ham," he said, then turned to walk away.

"On, no, monsieur," Antoine said, taking a step closer.

Pierre turned and faced him.

"Cain't take the ham and Coffee too. T'aint right. We'll do just fine with the sweet potatoes we got growing, some of the sweet meats we got jarred, and some of the chickens we keep in de coop. It'll be a fine Kiss-miss, monsieur. Better than some whites may have dis year."

"Ham goes well with sweet potatoes, Antoine. It's time you learned that if you haven't already."

Antoine smiled and bobbed his head happily like a horse. "Bless you, monsieur."

Pierre faced Curfy. "Get the new grandfather a jug of brandy."

"Will do, boss. Will do."

As Pierre walked out of the sugarhouse Curfy's voice reached his ears.

"Now don't you go getting drunk tonight, Antoine, then come in here and make a shitload of molasses tomorrow."

Curfy's and the servants' laughter was still carrying on as Pierre mounted his horse. Once he was mounted he gazed across the green lawns at the gristmill, the ice house, the tall white *pigeonnières*, and in the distance, he couldn't see it, but he knew it was there, the hidden cottage where Sarah had found him that night.

Because of Sarah and the children she would bear Pierre felt as if his father was still alive. He prayed that Sarah had a son. As far as her belly had grown even now at this early stage of the pregnancy he knew it would be a large child.

As he rode away he could see his father smiling from the news of Ashleywood having a male heir. *Make it a home, son. There's nothing like home. There's also no other place like Ashleywood. My papa gave this land to me. His maman had given it to him. Her papa had given it to her. And I'm giving it to you. I'm counting on you to fill this place with heirs until our name is known all over the world.*

Pierre had been riding toward the cabin to spend some time with Sarah, but changed directions and headed toward the mansion because an urge deep inside him warned him to go back now and not later.

## Chapter Twenty-Seven
## Sometimes It Hails When It Rains

*[Little by little the bird builds its nest. – Creole Proverb]*

When he reached the rear galerie Julien sat alone. Someone had helped him to lie on the settee. A pillow had been placed under his head. A coverlet was draped over him to keep him warm.

"How long you plan on sitting?" Pierre asked. "I thought Riley would have gotten some help and carried you into the *salle* by now."

"They tried, but I was waiting for you."

Pierre pulled forward a chair and sat close beside him.

Julien studied his face. "What happened? Jenna is in a fit. She got Abigail stirred up along with Marie-Marie. The house servants are running around trying to stay busy, but also trying to avoid the family."

"I'm building a house here for Sarah. Jenna found out about it."

"I've been wondering about you and her. You haven't mentioned her to me at all."

"You have your own problems to think about to have to also worry about mine."

"I saw it in you and her that day long ago when she brought those runaways here. I think I knew it then. I saw you looking at her differently than I've seen you look at any other woman. Are you sure about this? This gets out and it will be the biggest *scandale* this city has known so far."

"She's pregnant."

Julien whistled, then made a face similar to a wince. "That day with Clare the agreement was to find a *stranger*."

"I thought she was a stranger the first day we met. I didn't know who she was."

"And her child? You're thinking about making it your heir?"

"One of them. Hopefully, she and I will have many."

Julien whistled again.

A servant heard the whistle and stepped out onto the galerie.

Julien smiled at her and shook his head.

She went back inside.

"What about you?" Pierre asked. "Have you told Marie-Marie I have given you Anne as of this morning?"

"It was unavoidable. Marie-Marie was the one who sent Anne to the laundry cabin. As soon as she saw her, she confronted me."

"Where is Anne now?"

"Moving her things inside my bedroom and rearranging things."

Pierre pierced his brother with a hard stare. "Don't we have a couple of beautiful marriages? In your room, Julien?"

"I need someone at night. I'm tired of pissing myself and having to try to yell for someone. If Marie-Marie doesn't like it she can return to Primrose. I won't stop her. In the past months she has yet to spend one night in my room. Only the servants. Some of them even slept on the floor." Julien gazed out at the lawn. "You have no idea how sick I am, Pierre. You don't know the headaches I have. I'm drinking laudanum like brandy. Dr. Marchand said if I don't stop I'll start depending on the laudanum every day."

A smiled pulled onto Julien's face as he stared again at Pierre. "I'm too young to depend on laudanum. I'm too young to be a broken man, but I am. I have a child to think about. I can't wait for him to be born."

"Or her."

"It doesn't matter. If me and Anne could make this one we can make more. I refuse to leave this life without leaving something behind."

"If you send Marie-Marie to Primrose it's going to be hard for you to take it from her and give it to an heir."

"I've thought about that," Julien said and closed his eyes. "She can have it. I've decided to petition the church. A divorce won't be granted. A separation will do well enough. We can compromise on a financial settlement at that time. Once it's given she can live her life and I can live mine."

"Are you sure that's what you want?"

"It's what I need. Cosette read the cards to me on my wedding night. She saw it all. She told me to get out of the marriage and if I didn't she saw sickness. She told me someone else will have my children, and those children will save me from financial ruin. She saw Anne. But enough about me. I think you've lost Abigail. She's quite upset. I think she's planning to run off with Carlisle. Maybe you should go in and talk to her."

"If she runs then she runs. I'm sure her mother will be happy about it. Are you ready to go up?"

"Oui. Anne should be finished by now."

Pierre stood in the door and called for Hiram. Riley, knowing what would be asked, came along with the servant. Going upstairs was getting harder to do. Julien was dead weight and his height made it hard to maneuver him through the house without causing him injury. "You better get better on your legs, Julien. I'm young yet, but I'm not that young. It's either that or we're going to have to move your bedroom downstairs."

Julien laughed and winked at Semper who had come to make sure the rugs didn't curl on the floor.

After Pierre got Julien settled in a chair in his room he came downstairs and learned that Abigail, Jenna and Marie-Marie were waiting for him.

Marie-Marie couldn't wait to tell him exactly what she had to say and went first.

"I won't live like this. He has taken Anne into his room. It isn't right. All of you know it isn't. How can any of you allow this disgrace?"

"I agree with you," Pierre said. "Tell Anne to move her things out and we will have one of the servants move your things in instead. And then you can be a wife to him and give him children."

"I won't. The pain he's caused me these past years have taken their toll. He had a good wife but never shown me the respect I deserved. I will not become a servant for such a man now that he's lame."

"Then, madame, there's no reason for you to be here. You have family in France. Send them a letter. I'll pay your way there, as well as give you all the money you'll need to be comfortable there."

"You look here, devil. Primrose is my home. I shall go there…"

"You will not go to Primrose without your husband. And since you have already said you will not give him children you will not own it now or in his death. That land belongs to the Jennings family and only someone with Jennings blood will run it. Even if it means giving the plantation to Anne's child I'll gladly see that that happens rather than give it to you."

"That is not your decision to make. Julien owns Primrose. He shall decide if I can live there or not."

"Write your family, Marie-Marie. Why waste your life here when you can have a glorious one in France?"

She left out of the room in a huff, the skirt of her gown swishing and making lots of noise.

Abigail had sat quietly, but Pierre saw her studying him in a way she hadn't before.

"And you, petite? What do you have to say to me?"

Abigail didn't hesitate. "Are you having an affair with Maman's sister and she's to have your child?"

Pierre glanced at Jenna. For once she wasn't gloating from the discord that surrounded their family. "I am. It is true."

Abigail hung her head. "You're going to give Ashleywood to one of the children Maman's sister gives you?"

"That hasn't been decided."

Jenna had lowered her head but now lifted it.

"I always thought Ashleywood would be mine, Papa. Those in the city will never allow you to give it and your businesses to Désireé. No noir can have that much power. But you had never planned on giving me Ashleywood, did you? Even if Maman wasn't carrying a child now."

"I never planned on giving you Ashleywood and the businesses, Abigail. But like I've been telling you these past months I will see to your wedding and that you're well taken care of."

"I'm always going to be least loved, aren't I? What if Maman or her sister weren't carrying your children? You would have made Désireé your heir, wouldn't you?"

"My plan was to have an affair with someone in the city, have children by her and make them my heir."

Again Jenna lifted her head and stared at him.

"I was going to have many children starting at around this time," Pierre continued. "The more the better. I have been busy these past years setting everything in motion. Once I did find someone your mother was going to be sent to Riverside and me and my paramour was going to raise my children the way my father raised me and Julien here on Ashleywood. That is my decision, Abigail. It was fortuitous when I saw Sarah outside of the city one day. I chose her from the moment I laid eyes on her. Had your mother not betrayed me as many times as she has I wouldn't have a need to make such decisions. But betray me she did even with the child she carries now."

Abigail glanced briefly at her mother because she hadn't known this.

"I no longer wish to live on Ashleywood," she said. "Carlisle heard there's good land in Georgia. I shall like to be married right away, and if you will agree to give us enough money to move there to start a new life."

Jenna looked at her daughter. "You have no family in Georgia. Your family is here. And you have a brother that will be born in only a few months."

"I have seen nothing since I can remember other than two people who have learned very well how to crush a human heart. I don't want to see it anymore. I shall like to go somewhere where I can see how others live because it has to be better than this. Here I am nothing more than the bastard of Chadwick Speck."

"Watch your mouth!" Jenna hissed.

Abigail rose to her feet. "I have nothing further to say. If you both will excuse me."

"You're excused," Pierre said.

Jenna sat up in her chair, her hands gripping the armrests.

"You could have bought land and built my whore of a sister a home there," she said when the door pulled closed.

"My children belong here."

"She is my sister!"

"Jenna, had you treated Sarah like a sister we would not be having this discussion."

"What kind of man are you? You have turned this place into a haven for les noirs! I've watched you do it. You're hated by the men in this city. Had you not befriended the Américain president and those in power here this place would have been burned to the ground long ago. You have made a mockery of the Creole heritage, flaunting your bastard daughter more than any here ever had! Enough, Pierre. I won't allow you to do this."

"Are you the one who plan on stopping me?"

"I'm tired of fighting. I have loved you secretly for many years, Pierre." She hesitated and drew in a breath. "I'm hurt. On the inside. Far more than you know."

"Jenna, I can see it will be uncomfortable. I didn't want you to go, but you do not have to live here…"

"Does not my child deserve his father? Does he not deserve to live on Ashleywood? Is he not a Jennings?"

"Oh, very much so, and because he or she is you will do as I say…"

"Have you forgotten that I know what you did, Pierre? You may have the city accuse me of harboring runaways, but you cannot make them accuse me of killing Leon Boudreaux."

Her words had been meant to frighten him. Leon Boudreaux was a captain in the Américain army. While visiting New Orleans in the winter of 1819 only a month after Jenna and he had been married; while at the banks of the river Boudreaux recognized Will as the man that had killed one of his officers the year before. Approaching Will with the utmost of confidence that his life was in no way in danger, he asked Will his name and the name of his plantation. Will answered not aware that Boudreaux had been a witness to one of his crimes. Boudreaux made the mistake of speaking openly about what he had seen happen to his soldier then told Will of his intentions to locate the sheriff and have Will arrested immediately.

The man turned into the bayonet Pierre had removed from a small scabbard on his side. Jenna had watched in horror as Pierre thrust the bayonet further, twisting it to reach as high up in Boudreaux's chest as possible. The bayonet was then pulled away, and Boudreaux's body pushed over the bank and into the river.

"I have been waiting for you to bring that up for nearly twenty years," Pierre said.

"I'm not threatening you, Pierre." She averted her gaze. "I haven't said anything all these years and I won't say anything now. How do I know you will do right by my child? What assurance do I have? Who would have ever thought that my marrying a man named after the first pope of the Catholic Church that I would have gone through all I've gone through? She's my sister. But if that's what you have decided, so be it. I shall not look behind me anymore. I just wish to go forward, Pierre. If you're planning on moving into the house with her, I shall say nothing about your decision. But this mansion is my home. I only hope that regardless of how many children you have with my sister you will be fair when you do choose an heir."

"That depends on you, Jenna. I want the child to live here. I do. But I can't trust you. When the child is born I would love to raise him the way my papa raised me. I have noticed that you have been different. You have been decent to the servants, to me. I thank you for that."

A tear rolled from the corner of her eye.

Pierre ignored it. Jenna was gifted in the art of producing tears when she felt someone seeing them would provide better impact.

"I thought if you saw me give birth you would love me again."

"You were doing so well, Jenna. Please don't pretend. Not with me. You wanted a child so you would have a reason to petition the court if I sent you away because you sensed I was having an affair."

"How little do you know me." She held his gaze.

"Perhaps as little as you know me."

"I know you quite well, Pierre."

"Good. Then you know that Alise is my mother and that makes your child noir. And if you cross me, I shall tell everyone exactly that and then you can see how it feels to love a child that many will hate without a just cause."

This time real tears fell from her eyes as a hand squashed tightly over her mouth.

"Noir," he repeated. "Like Désireé. Like Goreé. Like me. Like all of my children will be."

"Does anyone know?" She whispered.

He didn't answer.

"Will you protect him, Pierre?"

"With my life."

Before he realized what was happening she leapt out of her chair. The hug was fierce. "My poor Edouard," she whispered against his chest. And then she pulled back and held his gaze with intent. "I dare anyone to ever try and hurt him."

She crossed the room with both of her hands cradling her stomach as if even now she needed to protect Edouard from harm.

Pierre rose to his feet and started to go after her. *Edouard.* The name resounded in the center of his core, an umbilicus uniting him to the fetus in her womb. He knew then that the child would be a boy, and regardless of his dislike for its mother he would love that child with all he had.

# Chapter Twenty-Eight
# Misery Has Come

*[Misery led this black to the woods, Tell my master that I died in the woods. – Irène Thérèse Whitfield, Louisiana French Folk Songs]*

Alise was surprised to see Jenna standing at her door early the next morning.

"Am I needed at the mansion? Is Julien well? Is Pierre?" She stepped swiftly out onto the galerie and looked toward the trees.

Jenna had never studied Alise's facial features in the past. Alise could have been any of the servants on the plantation. Jenna had lumped them into her mind as all being made from the same clay, making them all look the same. Now she stared into Alise's light colored eyes and studied the bone structure of her face, her nose, her mouth. Pierre looked a lot like his father. Jenna didn't see much of Alise in him, but she saw Julien. Before she had decided to come she knew Pierre had spoken the truth. But to see that it *was* true caused a moment of panic inside her.

"Can we talk?" Jenna asked.

Alise studied her for some time, turned toward the house, then back at her again. "Gorée is awake. If you want, you can come back later…"

"I don't mind seeing the child. I actually would like to see her."

Alise's eyebrows rose. Her eyes traveled up and down Jenna. Jenna wore a light cloak. It had rained during the night, but the sun was out now.

Alise pushed her front door open wider.

Jenna stepped inside, her eyes staring at the beauty of Alise' home. She could see now why Will had had an ease about coming here to sleep rather than the mansion.

Gorée sat in the *salle* on a sofa with a table pulled close in front of her. On it was a plate of breakfast treats.

Jenna stared back at Alise. "Do you mind if I go to her?"

"If she doesn't mind."

Jenna approached the child slowly. Gorée had stopped eating and watched her carefully.

Jenna sat beside her.

The child turned and faced her.

Jenna smiled and stared at Alise. "I've never noticed before," she said.

Alise, curious about the visit, sat to hear what it was Jenna had noticed.

"She looks like you," Jenna finally said. "Around the eyes. Similar to Pierre's eyes, but not quite."

"He told you about me?" Alise asked.

Jenna nodded. "That makes you my child's grandmother."

"I was a grandmother to Abby when she allowed me to be."

"Can I ask you something?"

Alise smiled at her as if to assure her. "It won't."

Jenna smiled then lowered her head. "I dreamt last night my child looked like one of the slave children."

Alise's smile pulled wider. "Look at Gorée and Désireé. You never saw their mother. She had more color than me."

Jenna nodded in understanding. "Until yesterday evening I believed my child's grandmother was a French woman named Catharine. I would love to hear about your parents if you don't mind sharing it with me."

"Jenna." Alise spoke politely. "If anyone else had asked me that question I would have been happy to answer. But I know you, and I know what kind of woman you are. It didn't matter that Désireé was born before you married Pierre. Or that Désireé loved her father and wanted to spend time with him. You hated Désireé visiting the mansion because you knew she had noir blood in her veins. The child you're carrying is my *son's* child. My *son*. And you will keep that child away from me now that you know who I am. Me being his *mémère* will make no difference and neither will my love. Now get out of my home."

Jenna stood.

Alise walked her to the door.

Outside on the galerie Jenna turned and faced her. "I always thought Pierre's evilness came from his father. I see now he got it from you as well."

"He will bring the child here to visit me, Jenna. He always does," Alise said and closed the door.

Hiram helped his madame back inside the carriage and drove her back to the mansion. As she climbed out she noticed Pierre waiting for her.

"The servants saw Abigail and Carlisle leave the plantation early this morning. Did you know about this?"

"What do you mean leave?"

"They took one of the coaches, two horses and two servants. Harriet and Dilly."

"Dilly?" She gripped the balustrade and took another step toward him. "Dilly is my driver. Do you suppose they went to the city?"

"Did you give her money?"

"No. She didn't mention going to the city or anything for that matter."

Pierre helped her the rest of the way up the galerie. "They took *your* coach, Jenna. Of all the coaches they took yours." She tried to stop walking. Pierre continued to lead her inside. "I just returned when you arrived on the cart. Where were you?"

Again Jenna tried to stop walking once they were inside the mansion, but Pierre continued to lead her toward the stairs.

"I visited Alise's cottage. Pierre, wait." She faced him growing more and more restive by the second frightened by what he was telling her and his need to take her upstairs. "Why would she take my coach and my driver and Harriet just to go to the city? Surely you have to know something about this. Harriet is no more than a house slave."

"I fear she's run off, Jenna. Lovelace saw Abigail carrying a small valise. Each time Carlisle tried to take it from her, she refused. He saw Harriet keep looking back at the mansion like she wanted to go back, but Abigail convinced her to climb inside. Carlisle secretly gave Antoine a silver pocket watch. I've seen the watch. It was the only thing of value he owned. I think he left it behind because he felt guilty. But if you gave Abby no money and I gave her no money and Carlisle left his pocket watch, I think you need to get upstairs and check your jewelry."

Jenna's eyes grew wide, and then she hurried to the stairs and gripped the balustrade. She held tightly to it with one hand and the hem of her gown clutched in her other. Pierre lifted her by the waist from behind and carried her upstairs. Inside her room she walked straight toward the armoire in the corner. Snatching open its center drawer she pushed the clothing out of the way to reveal the small hidden door in the bottom of it. The small door had been left open. Its deep hidden compartment sat empty.

She turned to tell Pierre this when she saw him standing next to a table against the wall holding what looked like a letter. He was reading it. Jenna hurried to him. He hadn't finished the letter, but he held it back from her so she couldn't read it.

Jenna drew in a breath. The small sound that slipped between her lips sounded as if she was in pain. "Give the letter to me, Pierre. I need to see it."

"I need you to lie down," he said. The letter was quickly folded and stuffed into a pocket in his coat. He tried to lead her to the bed. Jenna refused. She didn't want to lie down. Something was wrong with her chest. She felt as if she couldn't breathe. Pierre must have noticed. He stood behind her and unfastened the back part of her gown.

Jenna stared around her bedroom. She didn't understand why she felt as she did. The floor beneath her seemed unsteady. At any moment she felt as if she would collapse onto it. The gown fell to the floor at her feet. She was thinking about the child she was carrying. A fall could hurt it. Trying her best to stay on her feet she said nothing and stared at the rug as Pierre reached underneath her shift and loosened her stays. It wasn't removed, but her petticoats were. As soon as they lay on top of her gown she was lifted from the mound of cloth now on the floor and held in his arms.

She pressed her head against his chest. Abigail had taken everything, every piece of jewelry and all the cash that had been in the drawer. With five thousand dollars in cash and the value of the jewelry she had stolen she could travel as far as France and still have plenty left over to live on for some time. This thought brought a groan out of her. Keeping her composure became hard to do. She wanted to scream. She wanted to yell Abigail's name in the hopes that her daughter would hear her and come back. And then she thought of the letter that Pierre had hidden in his pocket and she knew. She knew she would never see her daughter again.

"She took everything." The tears fell fast and swift. "Everything. Send someone after them. Alert the police."

It was as if Pierre wasn't listening. When he tried to lay her on the bed she fought him, hitting his hand and kicked with her feet. The speed in which she was lifted and held against him, tightly; the way his hand held the back of her head so she was forced to lean against him made her understand exactly what she was feeling: heartbreak, pain, fear and regret.

The chairs in her boudoir were too small to accommodate him. He sat at the edge of the bed with her on his lap.

"Let her go, Jenna."

"No!" She shook her head until she became dizzy. "You don't understand," she whispered. "There was five-thousand dollars in the armoire. She left none of the jewelry. Not even the pieces my mother had given me. Those pieces have been in my family for many years. You never bought me jewelry after we were married, but I did, because I wanted to look like the wife of a wealthy planter. Pierre, those pieces alone will enable her to get very far."

The remorse in his eyes was too much for her to look at. A moan slipped out of her.

"Jenna, we had many chances to make her life a better one. I won't send anyone after her. It will only hurt her more than she already is."

Jenna drew her arms around him and pressed her head against his middle.

"Once we learn where they have gone we can write to her and let her know she can always come back. But for now, we let them go."

"What did the letter say?"

"She's angry, Jenna. It's not important what she wrote. What's important is what she says when she comes back. Now lay down. You need to rest. I'll get Jeanette to bring you up a toddy."

Jenna drew her hand from him and hid it underneath her shift as he rose to his feet. She said nothing as he crossed the room. As soon as she heard his footsteps in the hall she lifted her hand. Two pieces of paper had been in his pocket. She recognized the largest one as the letter. She opened the smaller one and saw it was a bill of sale for Anne Jennings to Julien Rafael Jennings. Laying this down beside her, she opened the letter.

*I hate you! You never loved me. At least Papa tried, but you never have. It's because of you that things are as they are. Had you tried to love someone other than yourself I know things would be different. Your sister wouldn't have earned the love of your husband, and the children she bears wouldn't inherit all that Papa has. The slaves hate you. No one loves you not even your friends. Your father left the city without telling you goodbye. Because of you, I hardly know my grandfather. Why did you keep me from him? I know the reason, but do you? It's because you're an evil woman. I'm glad Papa never sent you away, because if he had I would have been forced to go with you and my life would be worse than it already is. I feel sorry for the child you're carrying. Whether girl or boy I know you will love it if only because it's Papa's. I also know that you will teach the child to hate and how to be evil and because of this Papa will never give the child Ashleywood. And then what will happen to my brother or sister? Will they be as confused as I am, not understanding the reason their heart beat the way it do? You never saw the beauty of this place. The people here are some of the best souls I have ever met. Had it not been for them I would have taken my life on many occasions. Did you know I used to think about that? I hid rope inside my boudoir when I was twelve years old to hang myself from the galerie during the night while everyone slept. When I looked for the rope it was gone. Someone had taken it. One of the servants. Not seeing that rope made me realize I was loved by someone. This let me know that someone wanted me around. The tears I cried because of you and Papa no one will ever know. I shall never come back to this plantation regardless of how much I love it. I refuse to see your face ever again or watch you dole evil upon good people. My papa isn't the devil. I shall think he will be very upset when he realizes what I've done. I hope someday he'll forgive me. And after these months I've spent with him, I believe he will. He's a good man. Do not send anyone after me as I know you will want to do. Let me be. Let me have some peace, because I know I can have peace with Carlisle. I hope you never change, because when I die I don't want to see you even in heaven.*

Pierre came back into the room because the letter was no longer in his pocket. As soon as he walked in the room he hurried across the room toward the bed. Jenna was in the bed sitting against its headboard sobbing with both hands pressed tightly against her face. In one of her hands was the letter.

Pierre looked down and saw that her shoes were still on her feet. He removed them and dropped them carefully onto the floor. Jenna cried like someone severely broken of spirit. The tears were coming too quickly and choked her and made her tremble.

He couldn't leave her. Not like this. Sitting on the bed he drew her into his arms. Abigail blamed Jenna for everything, but he knew he was equally guilty and the true reason his daughter fled the only home she's ever known to live a life with a man she hardly knew.

"I was a horrible mother," Jenna cried. "I love her. I do. I love my daughter."

Pierre got comfortable on the bed and held Jenna until the tears stopped, and then longer still until she had fallen asleep.

When he stepped outside of her boudoir he saw a silver tray resting on a table beside the door with a toddy on top. Before leaving the boudoir he instructed the servants to look in on her every half hour and to send for him if they needed to.

Climbing on his horse he rode toward the cabin. Dr. Marchand had come to Ashleywood to look on the servants inside the plantation's hospital. Pierre had believed it was fate seeing the young doctor who many in the city didn't trust because of the modern methods he practiced. Pierre had sent him to the cabin to look over Sarah and the child she was carrying.

The reason he wanted Dr. Marchand to look on Sarah was because of the size of her stomach had grown more and more. At the base of her stomach a roundness had formed.

When he reached the cabin and saw Dr. Marchand's cart still parked beside it, he jumped down from his mount and hurried inside. Sarah and Dr. Marchand sat at the table drinking café. Sarah smiled at him. Pierre looked questioningly at Dr. Marchand. "Is she all right?"

"In very good health," Dr. Marchand answered. "Will you wish me to tell you the good news first or the surprising news?"

Pierre stayed where he was studying the pair. When he had walked into the cabin the two of them had been talking in earnest, but now sat smiling at him, their smiles never leaving their faces. It seemed the two of them were in cahoots about something.

Pierre stared at Sarah.

She stood. "Would you like a hot drink?"

"What were you two talking about before I came in?"

"Her servant Imogen," Dr. Marchand answered. "I've looked her over. What Mademoiselle Cheval believed to be tumors are not tumors. It is a protrusion of her bowels caused from heavy lifting."

"Sit," Sarah encouraged and moved closer to the hearth.

"Wine," Pierre said when she lowered to one of the warming pots on the bricks.

"I believe Sarah is much further along in her pregnancy than she believes she is. It's not uncommon for some women to still experience a monthly bleed in the first month. I hope you don't mind me speaking so bluntly, either of you?"

Pierre looked over at Sarah.

"No." She smiled and brought a bottle of wine and two glasses to the table. "I would like to understand. Please carry on, Dr. Marchand." The two of them smiled at one another.

Pierre looked from one to the other.

Dr. Marchand waited until a glass of wine had been poured for him and Pierre then lifted his glass as he still smiled. "Sarah is having twins."

"No!" Pierre sat back from the table in a rush.

"Oui," Dr. Marchand answered.

Sarah's smile turned into a giggle.

Pierre rose to his feet.

"Oh, don't mind me." Dr. Marchand gave a sharp wave of his hand. "I do believe this news deserves some sort of burst of affection. And I shall not deem it inappropriate. I would simply like to enjoy this glass of wine and then I'll be off to the Dussault plantation."

Pierre faced him. "Please do stop at the mansion. I don't believe it's necessary, but I would like you to do so at any chance. Jenna isn't well at the moment. Julien is doing better than you've last seen him, but he can take some looking over as well."

"Then I best be getting to them quickly. I should have arrived on the Dussault plantation some time ago."

No sooner than Dr. Marchand walked out her door, Pierre pulled Sarah into his arms and squeezed her tight. "Two babies?" He kissed her mouth, the tip of her nose, her forehead, and her hair. Sarah squealed with laughter as his hands became playful and his advances caused her to flee from him toward the bed.

"Two babies," he said then kissed her mouth, her neck. She was lifted off of her feet and laid on top of the mattress. And then he jumped up, suddenly, and smiled down at her. "I have to get to the mansion. Stay there. Don't get up. When I get back this is where I want to find you."

"Pierre, this is most unnecessary."

He looked back at her when he reached the door. "I'm going to have three children and one grandchild, and Julien will also have a child all within months of each other. Stay in bed, Sarah. Only get up if you must. This all seems too good to be true and I fear anything happening."

He hurried back to the mansion and hurried even more when he saw Anne struggling with Julien in the hall. Julien was hugging tightly to a table to maintain his balance. Anne had her arms gripped tightly around his waist to keep him upright. What startled Pierre was Julien appeared to have been making his way to Jenna's boudoir. Noises were coming out of it.

Pierre rushed past his brother and didn't stop until he reached her bed. Dr. Marchand had one hand pressed against Jenna's spine. Only her legs were visible on the mattress. The rest of her had fallen toward the floor as she heaved the contents of her stomach.

Reaching her Pierre lifted her up and stared into her eyes. Jenna appeared dazed and if she didn't know he was there.

Dr. Marchand moved out of the way as Pierre laid her back down. She rolled onto her side and curled into a ball, her face buried deep in the mattress.

"She needs to stay in bed," Dr. Marchand said. "I detect no fever. She doesn't appear warm and instead feels cold. I'm not sure what disease has come upon her. I can come back after I visit the Dussault plantation. Maybe by then the disease will have manifested itself by then."

"Merci," Pierre said drawing the coverlets over her. "I'll sit with her until you come back."

Dr. Marchand gathered his things and left the room.

Pierre climbed on the bed beside her, his hand resting on her shoulder. "I'll find her. I'll send someone."

Jenna closed her eyes but didn't say anything.

Pierre left the bed and stood in the hall to call a servant. There he saw Julien still clutching the table and Anne refusing to leave him. Behind them watching from the end of the hall, Marie-Marie stood inside her boudoir door, her eyes glaring.

Pierre stepped forward. "Let me take you back to bed."

"No." Julien spoke firmly, and then he lowered his head and laughed. "If I have to fall and break every bone, I want to try and do it myself."

"How did you get out here in the hall?" Pierre asked.

Julien lifted his chin, a wide grin on his face. "I'm going to have a kid. I need to be able to chase him. Anne and I have been practicing all morning."

Anne smiled shyly up at Pierre.

Pierre saw pride in her eyes. Standing in front of him was a young slave woman who behaved as if her husband, whom everyone believed to be permanently lame, had performed a miracle.

"He shall be bruised for many months, monsieur," Anne said gently. "Twice he's fallen."

"But I got up with only Anne helping me. The girl's a genius. She's tied rope to all of the bed posters. If I pull with my left side I can get myself around."

"No!" Pierre exclaimed.

Julien and Anne laughed because of the look that had come onto Pierre's face.

Marie-Marie stepped closer to them staring at Julien's hands and the way his right leg was positioned stiffly beneath him. "You took two steps. I saw you."

Anne lowered her chin and moved out of the way when Marie-Marie stood behind Julien.

"I can help you back to bed," Marie-Marie said. "I want to," she whispered.

Julien gazed over his shoulder at Anne's middle. "I shall like that, Marie-Marie. Anne, go and rest. You need to get off of your feet. You've been up most of the night."

"Are you certain?" Pierre asked. "You think the two of you can make it back to your bed alone?"

"Oui," Marie-Marie answered before Julien could. "I'm not afraid of falling."

"Take your shoes off," Julien warned. "And I think you better be quick about it or this table shall break underneath me."

Pierre made a gesture with his eyes that he wanted to speak to Anne in private.

Anne walked toward the staircase. Pierre followed behind her. Down below he led her to the butler pantry. "Stay near him," he whispered when they were alone. "I don't trust her. I'm counting on you to look after him. He walked. My brother walked. You used rope?"

Anne smiled and lowered her chin and gazed at the floor. "He has the will, monsieur. He only needed a little help. And he didn't wet himself last night."

"No!"

Anne giggled. Again pride showed on her face.

"Don't worry about how you're to get into his room," Pierre said. "I'll arrange it. But for now do as Julien said. Go and rest, Anne. You look tired."

"Oui." She turned toward the dining room.

"Anne," he said, stopping her. "If you lose that child, I fear what will happen to his mind."

"Oui, monsieur."

# Chapter Twenty-Nine
## Some Tears Fall Like Rain

*[When the big fish fight the shrimps must lie low. – Creole Proverb]*

All of them met at the carriage house. It was here Pierre had told them they would board the coach. Jenna appeared much better. Pierre had refused for her come out of her boudoir, but still on several occasions he had come into the mansion and found her downstairs sitting in the *petite salle*. On sight of him she would avert her gaze and would say nothing when he carried her back upstairs in his arms.

What he hadn't wanted now was for Jenna to see them all climbing inside the coach together. The time for crying was over. It was time for the family to smile and look forward to the future.

Pierre stood at the coach door with his hand extended. "Are you certain you should go?" He asked again. "You're heavy with this child. It's very noticeable in your gown."

Désireé smiled pleasantly at him. "I'm going to tell you like I told Cyril, Papa. I'm going into the city with the rest of you. It'll be a while when I'm able to do so again."

"I think you should stay," Cyril said. Months earlier Pierre had ended Cyril's search of finding work in the city. He was now employed on the plantation. His first chore was to repair the abandoned barn. Other than when he needed an extra hand, Cyril was making the repairs alone. For the most part of the day it was there where he could be found. "You should be lying down and I should be working."

"She's been in the cottage for months," Alise said. "Let her see something different. Let her get a different smell in her nostrils. Woman of color never take to their beds because of carrying a child. Besides, she's promised to sit in the coach for most of our visit. I'll sit with her."

Both men nodded. Cyril climbed inside, and then he and Pierre helped Désireé in as if she was an invalid with legs that didn't work. Désireé laughed from the attention being given to her. "I never thought anyone could be more coddling than Papa!"

After she was settled Pierre lifted Gorée into the coach. The child stayed close to the door refusing to sit unless he or Alise sat beside her. Alise was helped in next. Gorée sat beside her, but only for a few seconds before she was on her feet again.

Anne attempted to climb in unassisted. Pierre quickly reached for her hand and helped her up. Only when she was settled he turned back to Sarah and smiled.

"I don't like that look in your eyes," Sarah said.

The others giggled.

"Oh, Pierre. I hope you haven't changed your mind. I have looked forward to this for two weeks."

"I haven't changed my mind," he assured her. "I just like looking at you and can't help smiling when I do."

She was assisted up. Pierre climbed in behind her. Désireé, Cyril, Anne and Alise sat on one cushion. This left plenty of room for himself, Sarah and Gorée. François closed the door behind him. Minutes later the coach started on its way. Right away the women began giving their list of things they didn't want the men to forget.

Anne smiled as she listened to Désireé, Alise and Sarah plead emphatically about not forgetting to get pins, and particular fabric types, and lace, and thread of all colors. She giggled when Cyril's brows furrowed in concentration as he silently repeated the ever growing list.

"What about you, Anne?" Pierre asked. "Anything in particular you would like to share with me that I am certain to also forget?"

Sarah giggled. "And forget you shall. I'm most certain of it."

Pierre rolled his eyes, then gave an admonishing stare in her direction. "You have recited this list for two weeks even in your sleep. How can I forget?"

She leaned toward him, her expression meant to tease. "If you do I will not be upset. Whatever you do remember to bring back I shall be most grateful."

Désireé, Cyril, Alise, Anne and Sarah roared with laughter when Pierre began to recite a long list in a soft voice that was meant to sound like Sarah's.

"Did I forget anything, mon amour?"

Sarah had an urge to kiss him. Whenever she was with him she found herself his antics. Pierre's sense of humor was often downright silly. It was hard for anyone to watch him when he carried on like this and not lose themselves to laughter. "I forgot to mention heavy fabric."

The *maison* was being built faster now and she had hoped to make pillows for some of the chairs.

Gorée paid attention to none of them. Sitting opposite her papa and next to the window, she had the curtain pulled back so she could watch the trees and the animals she saw darting through bushes and trees as they passed. The wound on her leg had healed but left her with a limp. Pierre wasn't certain if the limp was a medical condition or was Gorée's way of reminding herself of the injury. The limp hadn't stopped her from getting around. She wanted to be outside running with the animals. She wanted to get up close to them and feel what they felt like.

Pierre leaned against her using her as a pillow as he tried to get more comfortable on the cushion. "Give me your feet," he said to Sarah. "Put them up. It will be a while before we reach the city. You might as well try and relax."

She did as she was told. Pierre rested the soles of her boots onto his middle, then closed his eyes. When Gorée tired of the window she snuggled into the small space between the door and her papa and fell asleep.

"Give her to me," Sarah said. "There's plenty of room down here."

Pierre lifted the child. Sarah held the child in her arms and closed her eyes.

Alise and Désireé stared at one another then back at Pierre, Sarah, and Gorée. The sight of the trio looked like a happy family napping during a long journey.

"I like her." Désireé mouthed the words to her *mémère* so as not to wake her papa or for him to hear what it was she said.

"She's good for him," Alise mouthed back, and then she turned to Anne who had stayed silent since entering the coach. "I think you should move out of the mansion, petite. Marie-Marie is determined to keep you and Julien away from each other. No one has used your mother's old cabin in all these years. Maybe you would like to move into it and have a place of your own. I'm sure Cyril and some of the others can get it fixed up for you."

"The cabin at the end of the coopers' quarters?" Cyril asked. "The one you showed me?"

"Oui," Alise answered. "Do you think much has to be done to it?"

"It's very nice," Cyril said looking at Anne. "New doors and shutters. The floor is marvelous and in good condition. And there's a large bedroom. The fireplace can be used on either side of the center wall."

"We can fill it with furniture," Désireé added. "I have a few pieces I can give you. One in particular that should suit you very well."

"And there will be no chores for you to do, petite," Alise said. "Unless Julien sends for you. While we're in the city you should look for things you can use to fix it up. I think it will be better if you were out of the mansion. I thought it the beginning that she would try and hurt him, but not anymore. I think she's truly trying. Think about it."

"The cabin sounds lovely," Anne said.

"I wouldn't be surprised if Marie-Marie has a child," Désireé said. "I think deep down she loves Oncle Julien."

Alise frowned. "Loving him isn't what I'm worried about. If they're going to make it she's going to have to forgive him. And I'm not sure she can do that."

"I'm having a special cart made for him," Pierre said with his eyes still closed and his arms crossed over his chest. "He'll be able to drive it with one hand if necessary. Any man in his condition who can crawl out of bed and use up an hour of his mornings to get downstairs on his own is determined to live life. I don't believe Marie-Marie will stay. She's using this time to take in her situation to make a decision. It's nothing more than that. Julien is not going to release Anne, especially after she has the child. I think Marie-Marie is already aware of this. She has already sent a letter to her family in France."

"Well, no. She wouldn't," Alise agreed. "Not many women who have had husbands like Julien would. Anne has only confounded the matter. No respectable woman of any kind will tolerate her husband openly taking up with another woman under their very nose."

Alise had been looking at Désireé and had turned and saw that Pierre and Sarah were looking at her. "Jenna is no woman," she said when she saw their hurt expressions. "I don't care how much she's changed, Pierre. Don't ever trust that woman. She's like a snake that only a child would try and keep as a pet. She'll let you feed her and give her water and appear as if she's trustworthy. And when you least expect it she'll strike, and when she strikes it's going to be deadly."

"All of you believe she's the devil, but she's not," he countered.

Désireé pressed her mouth tightly together and frowned.

Alise lifted her chin, her face telling everyone in the coach that Pierre could talk until his face turned blue, she would hold fast to her own convictions.

266

"She's not the devil," Sarah said softly. "She's her mother's child. Joséphine didn't know how to show love to anyone. I remember Jenna visiting the mansion before Joséphine died. She stood at the end of the bed and stared at her mother with so much hope. She didn't know I had come into the room with a basin of water. I heard her. I heard the pain in her voice. She asked Joséphine if she loved her then told her to please tell her she did before she died. Joséphine saw me and beckoned me closer as an excuse not to answer."

"Pierre, listen to me, please, and listen well," Alise said. "I know you have your hopes that the child she's carrying is male. Even if that child is born with your disposition Jenna is going to taint that child with her personality. She's going to groom him and trim him like a well-tendered plant. She's going to manipulate that child to do just what she wants. If she's careful and plans things just right that child will do anything he can to please her rather than face his guilt if he doesn't."

"What was Abigail like?" Sarah asked.

"Sweet," Désireé said.

"Strong," Alise said.

"Kind," Anne said softly, then stared surreptitiously at the others to see if they noticed her because a moment ago they had spoken as if she hadn't been sitting in the coach with them.

"And she was becoming just like her mother," Cyril said. "I saw her battling against good and evil in her eyes the few times I saw her."

"Have you heard anything, Papa?" Désireé asked. "Carlisle seemed nice, but what do we truly know about him?"

"He's a chameleon," Cyril offered. "I noticed the way he watched everyone and everything. Abigail was a frightened young woman. I don't think she would have left if he hadn't encouraged her to do it. An Américain down on his luck who stumbled onto great wealth. Excuse me for being blunt, but Abigail is not a pretty woman. I think he saw an opportunity and took advantage of it. I have lived in New Orleans all my life, monsieur, and never have I ever heard anything similar to happen that took place the night of Abigail's coming out. I find it strange that it did after Carlisle Morning visited the city. A quadroon child! Pah! No one would have touched her. One look at the child and they would have seen that she belonged to one of them or even themselves. But a stranger to the city that has lived between the trees for God knows how long, and perhaps hadn't had a female companion..." He looked around and lowered his head. "Forgive my manners. It just sickens me and for that reason I'm getting carried away."

Pierre wanted to sit upright, but couldn't without waking Gorée. When he saw that Sarah noticed his desire to change his position he held up his hand to stop her. She nodded at him, stared down at Gorée and kissed the child's sleeping head, hugging her closer.

"Why didn't you share your suspicions before?" He asked.

"I had no proof, monsieur," Cyril answered readily. "The man behaved most gentleman-like and quickly earned everyone's trust. Each time I saw him he made no errors. Being the man you are I could not bring to you unfounded assumptions against a probable innocent man. After I learn he left the plantation with Abigail and her mother's fortune, I now have no doubts. I think he took

Abigail away because he knew sooner or later we all would see him for the man he truly is if he was forced to stick around."

"Find her, Pierre."

"Find her, Papa."

Alise and Désireé had spoken at the same time.

"This is probably why Abigail delayed so many times the building of the house."

"I'm already doing what I can," he assured.

Sarah spoke softly. "If what's been said is true… I am losing all faith in men."

The conversation stayed its course for some time, each of the others making small mentions of things they remembered about Carlisle until it was unanimously agreed that he was a visitor to the plantation of the worst kind.

The city wasn't as busy as it usually was. During the months of harvest visits to it slowed and only picked up again after harvest was completed. It was the months of January, February and March when the city overflowed with Creoles celebrating the season. Mardi Gras being the one event that everyone looked forward to.

The coach parked as it had the last time it had carried Cyril and Carlisle to the city to find work.

Gorée was still sleeping.

"I'll stay," Sarah whispered. "You all go ahead."

Pierre promised to return to the coach as soon as he could. The mental list he had was given to Anne. She promised to bring everything back without forgetting a single item.

Désireé was apprehensive. The gown she wore fell loosely around her frame, but if anyone studied her long enough she was certain her condition would become noticeable. As hard as she tried Cyril refused to leave her side. Together all of them went store to store to order or buy the things they had come for.

Pierre was first to return to the coach. Gorée was awake and staring out the window.

"Go without me," Sarah encouraged. "I look like I have a watermelon in my gown. I fear that my cloak will not hide it well."

"You need proper clothing, Sarah. Come. Let them talk. What difference does it matter if the city finds out now or later?"

The people in the shops were pleasant. It was hard for Sarah to tell if they realized the affection Pierre was showing her in front of them. After an hour of being on her feet she was tired and wanted to sit some place where she could get comfortable. Pierre walked her back to the coach and lifted her feet on the cushion. The children moved constantly inside her. This made her smile at him.

"Don't forget what you're thinking at this moment," he said. "I will bring back refreshments. When I do I'm going to sit down so you can tell me."

Gorée went with him. Pierre refused to let go of her hand. Often he was stopped by people he knew of all ages. As much as many of them had seen Gorée once or twice in the past it only now occurred to them of who she belonged to. It showed in the way Pierre held her hand and the care he took that she did not make a wrong step into the street. They spoke to him at long lengths constantly looking down at the child. He knew by suppertime he would be mentioned at many dining room tables. His driver, François, had come with him. It took the three of them to carry the food back to the coach.

François ate his on the driver's seat up front alongside Eugene who acted as second driver. The two of them ate ravenously as they shared a small jug of lemonade. They were too absorbed in their conversation to notice Pierce Oakes watching them a short distance away.

Inside, Pierre made certain Gorée was comfortable before he sat in the open door. Sarah sat with the child on the cushion, both of them relishing the tasty treats Pierre had brought back. After they all finished eating Pierre climbed inside with them. It seemed only minutes later when the others returned. They had been followed by the servants of the shopkeepers, their arms laden with packages and bags of all shapes. These items were strapped into the luggage compartment in the rear and on top of the coach.

Cyril and Pierre stood outside of the coach's open door helping the women inside.

Pierce Oakes watched secretly from nearby. He noticed his brother dressed in fine apparel and how he smiled at the Devil's *mulâtresse* as if his brother was being bewitched by her spells. For close to a year he had wondered where his brother had disappeared to and if he was still alive.

Pierce then watched the Devil. When he boarded the coach it leaned heavily on one side from his bulk before becoming level again.

After the coach rolled away, Pierce walked back to the wharf and rented a horse for three days.

***

The tin was large enough for her to fit in with barely any room to spare. The cabin door was bolted. A fire burned in the hearth. Seafood soup simmered on top of a heated brick. Fresh bread and other foods sat covered under cloths on top of the table.

Sarah pressed a palm to her cheek as she watched Pierre undress. A blanket had been spread on the floor beside the tin. The new soap he had purchased in the city had been unwrapped and laid waiting on a piece of muslin. He turned to rest his shirt over the back of a chair when he noticed she was watching. Wearing only his trousers, hose and boots, Sarah spluttered with laughter when he performed a popular dance that was seen at every Creole cotillion.

He then sat in a chair and pulled off his boots. When he stood to remove his trousers, Sarah reached toward him with both hands. "Allow me."

He moved closer to her.

There were eight buttons, some of which couldn't be seen until the front flap of the trousers was pulled down. The underwear he wore was made from the softest cotton. Strings near the top held them up on his waist.

Sarah slowly pulled the string toward her loving the thatch of hair that peeked from behind it. Taking him in her hand she then did something she had wanted to do for some time. Tracing the tip of her tongue over his manhood, she then took him in her mouth. She smiled when he shivered and reached for her. "Let me," she said.

"We can't, Sarah. It's not safe in your condition for us to do anything."

"I just want to hold it and rub it and suck it between my lips. That's all. Just for a little while. And then we can bathe and eat and talk or read before bed."

"If you do that I will lose myself."

She kissed his inner thigh, losing herself in the kisses, then drew her tongue across the head of his shaft before giving a tiny suck. While she did this she couldn't stop touching the length of his manhood, feeling how strong it was, loving how hot it felt as it slid along her palm.

"Sarah…" When he realized she was going to stand up in the tub he reached for her to ensure she didn't fall.

"I can't reach you, Pierre."

He lowered on his knees. Sarah wrapped her arms around his neck and pressed her mouth against his, touching his tongue with hers and drew him into a deep kiss. Pierre rose to his feet afterwards. His underwear was pulled up and tied. One of his hands rubbed anxiously at his mouth as he walked toward the fireplace then back again. "I can't sleep here tonight, Sarah. I won't be able to stop myself."

"Let's bathe," she said staring at the tent in his drawers. Never would she have believed she would hunger for such a sight. With Pierre she had come to know what love truly meant. The way she felt about him, she knew she would feel this way with no other man. It was hard for her to be around him and not touch him in some way.

"You bathe, mon amour. I'll make sure you climb out of the tub safely."

She sighed and averted her gaze.

He lowered and kissed her. And then they bathed. After they were dry but still naked, he laid her on the mattress and buried his face in her sex. Sarah wiggled her upper body closer to him. Pierre felt her movements and lay on the bed. Sarah reached for him with both hands, put as much of him in her mouth as she could and began to suck.

Minutes later he was outside of the cabin on top of his horse staring at the cabin's closed door. The *maison* couldn't be finished soon enough. At least then he wouldn't have to leave her. On the nights where they needed to sleep apart he could go into a different room and still be close to her.

He turned the horse around and rode between the trees. As he drew near the abandoned barn he saw light coming out of it. Pierre rode to its door and peered in. Cyril had his back to him at the barn's far end. A long piece of wood was in his hand. It was placed beside another and hammered into place. "It's late," Pierre said. "Go to the cottage. The work will still be here in the morning."

Cyril turned. Sweat dripped from his forehead. He smiled as he approached the door. "The sooner I finish here the sooner I can start on that cabin in the coopers' quarters."

"Don't worry about that. The servants can take care of it. Besides, I don't think Julien would approve of Anne moving out of the mansion any time soon."

Cyril used the back of his hand to wipe sweat from his brow. "I want to thank you again, monsieur. Because of you, I'm home with my family instead of at sea for months at a time."

"What do you want? A boy or a girl?"

Cyril lowered his head as he demonstrated for Pierre the largest smile he could give. "I don't care, monsieur. Girl. Boy. It makes no difference to me. I've never been happier in my life."

"I hope you have a boy. A grandson can help me out around here."

Cyril giggled. "I would love a son."

"If not this time maybe next times."

Cyril gave a cough of laughter, his feet kicking at the straw on the ground. "You're an honest man. I like that." He looked back to the area where he had been working. "I won't be long. Our trip to the city has tired me out a bit. But there's still a little more I need to do before I call it a night."

"Leave it. I'll see you tomorrow."

"Good night, monsieur."

"You can call me papa now."

Cyril's laughter caused Pierre to smile.

"Good night, Papa."

"Good night, son. I'm glad you're here." He rode the rest of the way to the mansion without stopping. One of the servants took the horse. Inside he went upstairs and knocked on Jenna's boudoir door. A servant opened it. Pierre stepped inside. "Are you well?"

"Oui," Jenna said staring at him but not smiling. "Merci."

Pierre studied her face a moment. "All right. Good night."

Jenna averted her gaze and gaze a small smile. "Good night, Pierre."

Downstairs he stripped out of his clothing and lay on the bed in the alcove. Twice he looked toward the wall where Gorée had slept after she had gotten too large for the box. Now she slept inside her *mémère's* boudoir with all of the doors rigged so Gorée couldn't escape in the night. Alise enjoyed the arrangement. For the first time since she had come to Ashleywood she had one of her family sleeping with her under the same roof.

*** 

The fire in the grate had burned out hours before, and all the lamps and globes had been extinguished. The foggy damp conveyed the wake of morning, the hour before the sun broke slumber bursting through azure perfect skies. And in the darkness Pierre strained to see who was standing over the alcove's bed. He had stayed up late the night before thinking about the future. It appeared as if he had just fallen asleep when someone cowered over him digging their finger into his shoulder. And if he were thinking, if his mind had been at all lucid he would have known then that something was terribly wrong. None of the servants would dare disturb him while he was in the alcove, especially at night.

The dark figure leaned closer.

"Monsieur?" Mableane jumped back, and at first Pierre thought it was in fear of his voice, but she took a step, stopped, then looked at him surprised he hadn't gotten up to follow. It was then he glanced at the clock on the high boy. *Three forty-five.*

Another shadow moved toward the open curtain.

Pierre lifted his head from the pillow.

Anne stood amidst the azure curtains, her arms cradling her shoulders, her eyes filled with fright. "Monsieur… Désireé," she whispered.

The name jumped in his mind. Energy pumped strong in his legs as he jumped out of bed and dressed in no time. Mableane whispered, "Follow me, monsieur."

She guided him quickly down the hall, and being ahead of him she pushed quickly through the mansion's side door and stepped out into the yard. A cold wind pressed against his face, and the chill of it bombarded him with the niggling sensation that something was terribly wrong. He could feel it, that the darkness of the yard was somehow preparing him for it. He turned to Anne. She had yet to get dressed and wore a gown of thin cloth. Her feet were bare and she walked stiffly as if walking to her death.

Pierre stared forward and at Mableane. She rushed across the outer yards guiding him off the main path, and Pierre felt an empty sensation of relief. Whatever it was it couldn't have involved Désireé because the direction that Mableane now led him was to the abandoned barn.

The oversized doors creaked weakly in the wind, a barrier between him and what was waiting for him. At first there was nothing but darkness, but then it looked like something moved in the corner. A small lantern sat on the floor not offering much light.

Darkness conveyed to the dark, and the deep spoke to the deep. His legs shivered and in the hollows of his mind a little girl's voice rang out loud and clear as when she was three years old running down the mansion's staircase. *Papa. Papa.*

He could feel it. There was something in the dark hidden in the opaque corners.

He turned back when a weak light burned behind him. Footsteps were approaching in the pace of racers running a race that had no end.

The bouncing light revealed Alise bending over the barn's floor.

Alise saw him and screamed. "*Vous devez aider mon bébé.*"

"*Notre bébé?*"

"*Oui.*" A penitent tear slid down her cheek. "She's dead. We need to get her and Cyril out of here."

That's when he saw what the room had kept hidden. Blood. It was on Alise. He yanked back his hand and saw it was on his hands.

More people entered the barn, a few of them carrying lanterns. The closer they got the more Pierre saw what he couldn't see before.

'Oh, God! No!" He groaned.

He had thought Alise had been leaning over two burlap sacks. His knees buckled because the sacks weren't sacks, and there weren't two. There were three, the third lying further in the corner.

Désireé's eyes were closed. Her hands were folded across her rounded middle. She lay partly to one side. Blood was everywhere. In her hair, on the straw, on her clothes. Pierre had no idea where it started or where it ended. He tried to lift her when more of it, warm and sticky, gushed in his hands and between his fingers. Laying her back down he wept as he held her tightly in his arms.

When he saw something move beside him, he saw that Cyril's hand was slowly reaching toward Désireé.

"He's alive!" Pierre yelled. "Get a door! Carry him to the mansion!"

More light spilled into the barn along with voices and people running with blankets, buckets of water, baskets of muslin, herbs and medicines.

In the light Pierre saw Pierce Oakes. The kind of small knives used on ships was stuck in his chest. One of Pierce's hands still held it in a position as if he had tried to pull it out but died before he could. The amount of blood down the front of him made it clear that most of his blood had spilled onto the dusty floor around him.

Pierre laid Désireé down and snatched one of the lanterns from a servant's hand. Holding it close to her, he studied her face. He didn't breathe or move while waiting to see if his own child would make any movement. *Show me you're alive, mon chaton.* "Brandy!" He yelled. A bottle was held out to him. Pierre set down the lantern and poured a small measure in Désireé's mouth. He sobbed in relief when she choked weakly.

Alise sank beside him weeping like Pierre had never seen her weep before.

Servants were ripping pieces of muslin, and wherever they saw bleeding bound the area tightly. In the end Désireé looked like a mummy. Cyril's neck was bound tightly. Pierre lifted his daughter and ran beating the cart bearing Cyril back to the mansion.

## Chapter Thirty
# The Smell of Heir

*[A wicked word hurts more than a blow from a stone. – Creole Proverb]*

Four days after Christmas Edouard Pierre Constance Jennings was born at the break of morning just as the sun had started to rise. On the infants head was a thick shock of white hair. His eyes were the color of strong silver. And his skin as white as his mother's.

Lissy, the plantation's best midwife, swore to him that the delivery had been a good one. Pierre had trouble believing this. For hours he had waited in the hall outside of Jenna's boudoir. Every whimper, plea, and scream had gone inside his ears and increased his heart rate. This was the first birth he had been close to. All of his other children had been born while he had been a distance too far to hear anything.

Standing at the foot of the bed now he stared at Jenna. Her body was covered in sweat. The hair closest to her skin was damp and stuck to her face. She had been placed in a clean gown. The linen on the bed had been changed and neatly arranged. Pierre could see her fatigue and that she was still in pain.

He sat in a chair beside the bed. "What can I do?"

It looked as if she was too tired to smile although she tried.

"It's a boy," she whispered. "I knew it would be."

"Monsieur, out you go," Lissy said. "We still have some work here to do."

"Let him see the child," Jenna whispered breathlessly.

One of the servants approached with a tightly wrapped bundle. A tear roll down Pierre's cheek. Edouard looked so much like Will that Pierre couldn't stop crying because he missed his father so. "He would have loved you, baby Edouard."

The child began to whimper. The servant took the child away and carried him to Jenna to nurse. Pierre had a hard time leaving the room.

"He can stay!" Jenna said when she noticed the servants' unease when Pierre continued to sit.

Pierre rose and sat in a chair closer to the bed ignoring the shocked expressions frozen on the servants' faces. Jenna's head rested against the pillow. Pierre jumped to his feet when her breast pulled from Edouard's mouth and the babe tried to find it again.

"He's beautiful," he said.

The rest of the morning was spent in her bedroom. Pierre found himself worrying about everything. If Jenna was truly well. If the babe was hungry. If the babe was still breathing, because this happened a lot. He had heard stories about this many times in the past.

Later Julien and Anne came into the room.

Weeks before the same servant who Pierre had acquisitioned to make Julien an invalid carriage came and asked Pierre if he could also make Julien a wheelchair.

All of the parts needed for both contraptions had been made on the plantation. Because of Julien's height a door had been used for the backside of it, carefully polished and covered with soft fabric overstuffed with Spanish moss to provide the ultimate comfort. The chair worked so well Julien now had two, one to use on each floor.

The bedroom beside Julien's had been remodeled into a large dressing room. A wide door was added to the wall so Julien could enter it with ease. It now held an enormous porcelain tub with one side lower to allow him to get in and out much easier. The invalid carriage was unique in that it could be pushed or drawn by an animal like others, but also had a crank motor attached to allow Julien to get around by himself.

Visitors to the plantation were so impressed with its design that in a short time of receiving it Julien had constant visitors, all of them hoping to see him give a demonstration. Since then Pierre had received ten orders but demanded that none were built right away. Pierre had applied to have the contraption patented. Not trusting the idea wouldn't be stolen by someone once the patent office learned a slave had created the design from his own mind, the patent was put in Pierre's name with the servant's approval. As soon as the patent had been received the ten orders were filled.

A British man visiting the city came to the mansion in haste after he had seen the invalid chair and learned that it had been built on the plantation. After he stepped one foot in the door of the mansion he begged Pierre to go in business with him to start a company to make the chair in his country where it will sell well. Ezra Jennings, his wife, his five children, his two brothers and their three children were given their freedom and had quickly sailed to England. Before the company was up and running orders for one-hundred-and-thirteen chairs had come in solely from the model that sat in front of the shop. As soon as Pierre received this information by way of letter from his partner, Charles Parker, he sent Ezra his first check since arriving in England in the amount of one thousand dollars.

"What's all this ruckus?" Julien teased.

Edouard cried loudly in Jenna's arms, one of his arms flailing in the air.

Pierre lifted the child and handed him to Julien.

"Why is this child ugly like his papa?" Julien asked while staring at the babe.

Anne and Pierre laughed uncontrollably.

Jenna gave Julien a searing look.

Julien saw this and handed the child back to Pierre. "With lungs like that this child is liable of keeping the entire mansion awake."

Edouard calmed as Pierre held him.

"You've got him rotten already," Julien said. "Jenna, you look like you've been up to some macabre mischief. Take a look, Anne. This is what you'll look like soon."

"Julien," Pierre admonished.

"Out of my boudoir, you surly cud!" Jenna hissed.

"I shall be going, too," Pierre announced handing Edouard back to his mother.

Outside, the distant yards were covered in a thin blanket of fog from the nearby river. The air was stingingly crisp, consistent of a northerner's hoary winter. Pierre rode slowly through the trees to Désireé's cottage.

On that fateful night Cyril had fought with his brother to the death. Before this had happened Désireé had walked to the barn shortly after Pierre had left it to bring Cyril a bite to eat and something to drink. What she had wanted was for him to come to the cottage and leave the work until morning. The two of them had sat while he ate, then sat longer as they talked and enjoyed the sun going down. Cyril had given in to her sitting on the hay until he called it quits for the night. He had seen the moment when Pierce had come into the barn. Désireé hadn't because she had fallen asleep. Pierce told Cyril he was disgracing his family by being on the plantation and making a life with the Devil's daughter. At first they had been whispering. Slowly their voices rose. Désireé woke up and stood to her feet. Cyril quickly stood in front of her. It was then the fight began – a fight that almost took all three of their lives. Only two people died that night, Pierce and Désireé's son who was born dead the following morning. The sight of the child brought out many tears from all who looked upon it. It looked full-term, a beautiful child with brown hair. Pierre had his first grandchild buried alongside Will in the cemetery in the city.

Désireé and Gorée sat on the galerie sharing a blanket while Désireé read from a book. Neither saw him approaching until they heard the sound of his boots step up on the galerie.

"*Bonjour*, Papa," Désireé said with a smile. "Say hello to Papa, Gorée."

Gorée's finger moved across the page in the book, and speaking slowly she said, "Say hello to Papa," as if she was reading those words.

"You are reading," Pierre exclaimed.

"Rain bears," Gorée answered.

"She knows you're her papa," Désireé said with a smile.

"Don't ask her what she should call me or you'll hear the most vulgar things come out of her mouth."

Désireé smiled more and averted her gaze, then rose to her feet when she saw Cyril walking quickly in her direction with something in his hands.

"I found it near the barn," he said. Désireé had gone to the edge of the galerie to meet him.

Cyril showed her an injured rabbit.

While the two of them conversed about what they could do to save it, Pierre led Gorée by her hand down the galerie and walked away.

Alise saw them from a window and pulled the front door open before Pierre could reach for it. "It looks like someone is mad at you, Pierre."

Pierre looked down and saw the frown on Gorée's face. He hadn't noticed until now. Not once had he looked at her since leaving Désireé's cottage.

Gorée pulled her hand from his, walked to the sideboard against the wall, lifted a porcelain vase and dropped it to the ground.

"What am I looking at?" Pierre asked.

Gorée kicked the pieces of shattered glass with her boot.

"Am I looking at a fit? She's throwing a fit? Whatever for?"

"She likes being at Désireé's," Alise answered. "It's hard for me to take her away from there."

"Gorée, stop that!" He demanded after another piece of glass was kicked.

She turned and faced him, stuck her tongue out and spit.

Pierre stared at Alise. Alise shrugged.

"She's twelve, Pierre. What did you think? She was going to behave like she was five forever? She's growing. Slowly, but growing. This morning is the first time she's wearing stays."

"I don't want to hear about that, Maman," he scolded.

"She's changing, Pierre. I think you need to pull Mableane out of the mansion and send her here."

"You're saying you need help with Gorée?" He asked in stupefaction.

"I'm running out of things to break. She doesn't want to stay in the cottage. She wants to be outside. She wants to explore. You used to take her out. You don't anymore."

Pierre stared at Gorée. She had waited purposely for him to turn to her before she dropped another vase to the floor. This time a piece of the shattered glass was kicked purposely at him. It lifted high from the floor toward Alise. Alise crossed her arms in front of her face to avoid the piece cutting her. Pierre saw small cuts on Alise's arms. They were healed, but he could see they were recent.

He turned back to Gorée. She ran when he started to walk toward her. Pierre was unaware the child could run so fast. Darting through the open rooms, she ran out of one of the French doors before he could catch her. Running fast down the length of the galerie, Pierre had to make a hard jump over the railing down below to catch her as she tried to flee across the lawn toward Désireé's cottage.

Alise stood outside and watched as Gorée received her first spanking. From the look on the child's face when it was over, she sensed it was an experience that the child didn't want to ever happen again.

Pierre marched her back inside, put her to bed and closed her bedroom door.

"I hear the child was born this morning." Alise set a cup of café in front of him when he sat on a sofa in the *salle*. His gaze was on the hall in the direction of Gorée's boudoir.

"You're happy," Alise said. "You can't live your entire life for Gorée. She'll be all right. I don't want you to feel guilty because you realize she's growing up."

Pierre wiped a hand over his mouth. "Edouard is a beautiful child. I need to figure out something to do with Gorée."

"Mableane handles her well. Send her here. We'll be all right."

He puzzled over this as he sipped the café.

"She'll be fine, Pierre. If I had any fears I would have shared them with you."

"What happened to your arm? They have tiny cuts on them."

"She gets angry sometimes. Thing get broken and kicked."

"Kicked at you?"

"I have Cyril and Désireé. With Mableane we should be all right. I've never seen you happier. Now go on and get. I know you didn't mean to spend so much time here. Sarah's waiting. If she gets any bigger I do believe she will have the babies earlier than she should."

Pierre stared around the front of the cottage. "Where are your servants? Where is James?"

Alise didn't answer. She pulled his cup away. "Get going. There's no need for you to worry about anything happening here."

Pierre looked in on Gorée before he left. She sat at the edge of the bed gripping the mattress tightly in her hands as she held her head heavily bowed.

"Petite?"

She looked up at him, then ran to him, throwing her arms around him. Pierre lifted her in his arms. "Behave. Do not hurt *mémère*. Do you understand?"

She kicked out of his hand, crossed the room to the locked French door, pulled back the curtain and pointed in the direction of Désireé's cottage.

"No." He spoke firmly. It was obvious to him that Désireé and Cyril needed some alone time. After the ordeal they had survived now was the time for them to come closer together. This couldn't happen if Gorée spent too much time there.

He pulled the door closed behind him. When it closed Gorée stuck out her tongue and spit in the direction where he had stood.

Sarah's *maison* was in walking distance, still he rode his horse. Imogen greeted him at the door. Pierre walked past her without saying a word. The servant woman annoyed him like none ever had.

Sarah sat on the rear galerie. Cloth and needle was in her hand. Lately, she sewed constantly. It was a gift she had. Sometimes it was hard for Pierre to believe the end results of what had started off as odd shaped patterns being poked with her ever moving needle.

"How's the child?" She asked, smiling up at him. The garment she was sewing was placed on a table beside her.

Pierre sat in his favorite chair.

Sarah never called for her servants to serve Pierre. She loved doing it herself. She understood his need at times for a little peace and quiet. There was always something happening in the mansion that needed his attention. There were visits to Désireé, Gorée, and Alise that were needed. He had a vast amount of land that he had to oversee. There were visits he needed to make to the city when Frances Achen was unable to travel to the country. At the *maison* she wanted him to have peace and rest, and nothing more than that.

"He's beautiful. His lungs must be large inside his small chest."

Sarah smiled. She didn't bother asking him to take her to the mansion to see her new nephew. Since the *maison* had become completed Jenna made certain to remind Sarah each day who the real madame of the plantation was. If anything was needed from the storehouses Sarah's servants were to go to the mansion to ask permission from Jenna first. As madame of the mansion Jenna wore the key to the in-house pantry around her wrist. The doors to it were kept locked at all times. In it were spices imported from other countries, preserves of all kinds, imported fine oil, the best bottles of spirits that money could buy, and other precious items some of which the mansion produced and others that were shipped in from other countries.

When Sarah's servants went for goods out of the pantry Jenna measured it out herself and made sure it was enough for one day's worth. The same thing happened when Sarah's servants went for chopped wood. Overseer Langers gave them enough for one day. This was how Sarah discovered that Langers was Jenna's hand of power out in the fields. By giving Sarah's servants only small quantities at a time meant her servants had to repeat the routine daily.

The laundry cabin was also an issue. Langers had ordered the servants who handled her laundry to take the garments to the mansion after they were dried and ironed. There Jenna inspected them. By the time Sarah received the items back at the *maison* her gowns had ink spilled down the front of them, linens had hot wax dripped on them, and towels looked as if it had smoldered a few seconds over a hot fire.

Pierre didn't know about any of these things. Sarah refused to tell him. She had decided to deal with all of these issues herself. For now she would permit Jenna to do all she wished. Sarah felt she was often telling the servants how unfortunate it was that they would have to go back for the same things yet again. The servants didn't seem to mind.

Other than Imogen three servants were sent by Overseer Almonester early each morning. Other than Imogen the other servants did not sleep inside the *maison* and were allowed to go home each night. Once when no servants showed up at her outside kitchen Sarah and Imogen went in the kitchen, cooked supper, and carried the food into the *maison* themselves. The dining room was prepared. When Pierre arrived he had enjoyed the meal, and even had seconds never knowing she had spent part of her day preparing it.

Standing to her feet, she was close to the door when Pierre called to her.

"Sarah, sit. Each time I come you're on your feet. Come sit with me."

"Nonsense. You need a drink and I can use one, too."

Pierre sat forward to argue his point when Imogen stepped out of the house with a silver platter. She carried it toward Pierre as if he had requested a beverage, setting the tray on a table beside him. On it was lemonade, a decanter of bourbon, a small silver bucket of ice, and a plate of calas. A napkin was pulled from Imogen's apron. She carefully stretched it over Pierre's lap.

Pierre looked at Sara, then at Imogen.

"Imogen, thank you," Sarah said hastily. "I can handle it from here. Please leave us."

The servant looked surprised on hearing this, then gave a slight nod before returning inside the *maison*.

Sarah readied him a drink.

"I feel like she's always watching and listening. I don't need a servant to place a napkin on my lap."

"She wants you to like her, Pierre. She's tries hard..."

"Why? I don't need her attention, and I hate the way she watches us. At times it looks like she's waiting to see if she needs to come to your defense."

"Life was different at Green Lea, Pierre. Please understand. A lot happened there."

"Whatever it is, you refuse to share it with me." He took the glass and set it on the table.

Sarah kissed his forehead then turned to walk away.

"Don't try and appease me with a kiss each time you feel the need to walk away."

She turned and faced him. "All right, Pierre."

"If you don't want to share your former life with me then tell me that, Sarah. Something is strange about that woman, and whatever it is you refuse to tell me about it."

She sat beside him. "Pierre, I know you think I'm hiding something from you, but I'm not. Green Lea had different rules than here, and the servants that lived there were fearful every single day of feeling the sting of a whip or being sold away. Displeasing their masters came with consequences. It is why Jenna is the way she is. Her mother was the same way. There the servants were given a peck of corn and a small ration of pork each week. Only their masters owned chickens, and although the servants raised and cared for their master's livestock it was rare that any of them got a sample of it."

She could see how weary he was. It showed in his eyes.

"Let me draw you a bath. I can wash your hair if you like. The midday meal should be ready by the time we're finished. You'll feel better by the time you need to head out to the fields."

"As much time as you spend on your feet it's a wonder they haven't swelled."

She pressed her lips against his. "I like taking care of you, Pierre. It makes me happy. I love it here. I love having a life with you."

Pierre lifted her hand and brought it to his lips. "Sit with me. Today we relax. I think we can both use it."

Sarah sat on his lap. Pierre wrapped his arms around her waist. She lounged comfortably against him. Pierre lifted his feet on a smaller chair positioned directly in front of him to make it easier for her to recline.

"I hear Edouard looks an awful lot like you."

"Yes, he does. He reminds me very much of my father."

"And my sister? Is she well?"

"Yes. I do not believe she's going to hand Edouard to a wet nurse anytime soon. I wouldn't be surprised if she has his crib moved inside her boudoir. She is very much attached to the child. Other than me, I've noticed she doesn't like sharing him with anyone else. Have I ever told you that I love you perhaps more than I will love the children you will bear?"

"I just want you to be happy, Pierre. I spend most of my day to do all I can to make sure you are. I feel like you are my entire world. The only thing I fear is losing you."

"You can never do that."

"Don't say that, Pierre. In a year or two things can change. This is a most difficult situation." She hesitated. "You and Jenna might repair your marriage."

Pierre kissed her hair near her ear. "You have my love. All of it. Of that you have never to worry."

Sarah lifted to reach his mouth and the two of them shared a kiss.

"What do you think of the name Charlie?" She asked.

Pierre groaned as if the name had been painful to his ears. "Charlie is too… *feminine.*"

"I've always liked the name Charlie."

"Lucien," he countered. "I like the sound of Lucien. The sound of a man capable of governing his land."

Over the course of the past month they had pondered a variety of names but hadn't been able to agree on any.

"Lucien sounds cleverly wicked," she said.

It didn't take Pierre long to find its incorrigible match.

"Lucien and Alexis."

"Lucien and Alexis sounds far too devilish, Pierre. Like scamps!"

His body convulsed with laughter. "We can name them Pierre and Julien. *Comme le père, comme le fils.* Pierre one and Pierre two."

"The scamps!"

"Yours and mine. Désireé told me the other day that she would have named the child Alexis if it had been a boy."

"How is she?"

"I think she and Cyril have pretty much buried the matter and are moving on with their lives."

"I'm glad to hear that. I've come to see that both of them are vital here. Along with Alise they are most loyal."

Pierre thought about this. There were quite a few more that were also loyal. What he wondered was why Sarah thought it important to notice who was loyal to him and who wasn't. He long suspected that someone was giving her difficulty. Jenna, yes. But someone else as well. If they were he knew Sarah would never tell him.

They sat and talked a bit, then ate their midday meal. Afterwards Sarah got her wish. A bath was drawn. She sat in a chair behind the tub and washed and cut his hair. While they stretched on top of their bed she leaned against the headboard with her thighs wrapped around his chest. It took close to an hour for her to brush his hair dry. Pierre had fallen asleep before she braided it in a single plait. When he woke up it was late in the evening. A silver tray of hot café sat beside the bed along with a cup. Evening clothes were stretched over a chair. His boots were polished and sat next to a chair.

It constantly surprised him how much Sarah got done in one day with only four servants for a *maison* as large as hers.

Before that evening she had never spoken about her past. As he sat at the dining room table that evening she told him about leaving Green Lea as a child and the years she lived with her Tante Marianne. After Pierre listened to all she had to say he understood why she had never told him these things before. Even now some of the memories brought tears to her eyes.

It was common for widowed women or unmarried women to move in with relatives. While in their relatives' home they performed a variety of chores as a way to pay back the financial support they were being given. Most families enjoyed the arrangement, as a widowed female family member often became surrogate mothers to the children in the house.

Tante Marianne hadn't wanted to be a burden on her brother-in-law and his failing plantation. After her husband died she sold the slaves and almost all she had to pay off his debts. She tended her own gardens and often sold the vegetables in town for income. These trips took hours to reach in each direction. With not enough to pay for a room for the night, Tante Marianne would drive her cart and ox back to her home during the night. During one of these trips her Tante Marianne had seen lights traveling in their direction and had hidden Sarah underneath some empty burlap sacks. Sarah had lain under them while she listened to her tante being sexually abused by the three men who had discovered she was riding alone. On two other occasions her tante was robbed by men on horseback. With no money and having sold most of her vegetables, the two of them had eaten rice and potatoes for every meal for three months straight.

Pierre wiped his mouth with a napkin.

"The money you sent her, I can never repay, Pierre. But I'm not here because of the financial support that you provide. If I didn't love you as much as I do, I would have left a long time ago. I'm not frightened of being poor. As long as I can sew I know I can find work. As long as I can build a lean-to I will always have a shelter over my head. I'm resourceful. I've learned how to be. I feel like I'm supposed to be here. And with you."

Later, after the meal was over, Pierre reclined on the sofa in the *salle* while Sarah sewed more clothes for their unborn children. In a tiny corner of each garment she sewed the Jennings crest with silver thread. Pierre was fascinated while he watched her do this. Having done it many times now she no longer had to mark the area first. The crest was sewn by hand and was a perfect resemblance.

She had sewn the same crest on his handkerchiefs and on a few of his waistcoats.

So comfortable had he gotten, he had fallen asleep again and didn't awake until Sarah woke him to come to bed.

***

"Was it a hard thing to do, to come back and see your son on the day he was born?"

Jenna sat up in the center of her bed, her eyes damning him for what she believed yet another betrayal. The day before, she had spent every hour waiting for his return. Every sound she heard in the hall made her stop what she was doing to listen to see if it was him. As much as she needed the servants' assistance none of them knew how frantic she had become waiting for him that if they spoke she felt it hindered her from hearing his approach. By late afternoon when he hadn't returned, her mood became raucous. At times she yelled and seethed, and had even slapped Noémi when she felt the servant was handling her too roughly. Even during the night she had awakened and stared around her dark room hoping to see him sitting nearby. What she wanted to know was what had kept him from visiting the son she had seen clearly he had loved so much the moment he was born.

"I do not answer to you," Pierre said.

Jenna saw anger in his eyes as he spoke. Anger was not what she had anticipated. Anger was too final. She interpreted it as he felt no obligation to Edouard. She averted her gaze because she did not want him to see the tears in her eyes. So certain she had been that if she bore him a son things between them would be different.

"Even with your half-breed children you paid more attention," she accused. "If you cannot be a father to Edouard like you are to them, I shall gladly leave this house and never return."

"What made you think that having a child would make everything right between us?" He asked. "I have never left this house and wanted desperately to return because I knew you were in it. I have a bedroom here on the second floor, but when have I slept in it and not the alcove, a room no longer than my legs can stretch and only a little wider than my arms can reach? In almost twenty years as long as you were content, and had the run of my house, that was all you needed from me. Pray tell. Why are you sitting there behaving as if I have lost your trust?"

When she stayed silent he stood to leave the room.

He had been in the room only a few minutes and had yet to hold Edouard. *He's leaving because he wants to get away from you,* she thought.

Jenna held Edouard high up in her arms. "Please hold this child. I need to see you do that. I want you to love this child, Pierre."

"I love him," he assured as he drew closer to the bed.

Jenna smiled and closed her eyes when Pierre sat beside her and lifted Edouard into his arms, and then his face softened as he held a hand to her face and rested it against her cheek. "I don't want to fight anymore. I want us to be friends, Jenna. As your friend and the mother of my children, I'll give you everything you'll ever want. But I will not be beholden to you as a husband. If Sarah left this plantation today and never came back nothing would change between you and I. Live, *mon ami.*"

A look came into his eyes. Jenna realized his last words were his way of giving her permission to have an affair.

"No more hurting each other." He spoke these words gently. "Can you live with that?"

It was a question she had no intentions of answering at that moment. For twenty-four hours she had waited to see his face and now here he was saying things she wished he hadn't. It was Edouard's future she thought about when she touched the child's hand. "I know I shouldn't hold him as much as I do. If my mother was alive Edouard would have been given to a wet nurse and banished to the third floor."

Pierre smiled down at his son on hearing this. "I think Julien was right. The two of us will make this one rotten."

"We can't," she pleaded. A little base had come into her tone.

Pierre smiled at her in a way he never had before.

Jenna reached for his arm placing her hand gently against it. "With Abigail gone and neither of us knowing where she is, and Edouard being born, I feel like I'm different."

He leaned forward and kissed the crown of her head. "You are different, and I rather like this new person when she's not burning my britches."

She smiled and held his gaze. "You're different too." Since he had come into the room she noticed the difference in his hair, and the crest on his waistcoat, and his boots that looked brand new because of how polished they were. She knew Sarah was the reason for these differences. She averted her gaze. "You look like you have gained a little weight."

"I have and more than a little I'm ashamed to admit."

"I hate her, Pierre. I will always see her as the reason my marriage failed."

"Give it some time, Jenna. This wasn't an act of vengeance. I think both of you are suffering the loss of each other. Who's to say that your sister won't be the very person you will need some day?"

It was hours later when he finally left her room. And for some reason when he did, she felt as if a burden had been lifted off of her. The two of them had talked to each other. She had even laughed heartily when Pierre professed to know how to change Edouard's diaper, then was impressed when his skills proved better than her own. She had told him that he must come back when Edouard's diaper was soiled, and he had laughed as heartily as she had. The mood in the room had changed after that. The longer he sat with her the more she felt as if she was getting to know the man he truly was. Before he left she told him it was all right if Désireé, Gorée and Alise came to see Edouard, but not Sarah. She wanted the others to see him. She was proud of her son and wanted to show him to people she knew would love him as much as she did.

It was close to suppertime when there was a knock at her door. Semper went to the door, opened it, gasped, then pulled it open very wide. Désireé, Gorée and Alise bounced into the room in a happy gait, each of them bearing gifts that Jenna knew they would have been given to Pierre in secret if she hadn't given this invitation. Cyril stepped in behind them carrying a cast iron cocotte. Semper helped him sit it on top of a cloth on a nearby table.

"I want to apologize to you personally," Alise said. "I didn't want to believe that you changed so I said some things that if you ever heard them they may hurt you. But I see now I was wrong. I know now that you have changed. When Pierre told me you were allowing us into your boudoir to see Edouard, I made you this soup. It's just for you. It has everything a woman needs to get better after giving birth."

Jenna nodded and studied Alise's face to see if Edouard bore any similarities to it.

Désireé and Gorée was first to peer into the basket resting on the opposite side of the bed.

"Oh, how he looks like Papa!" Désireé exclaimed.

Alise heard this and rushed closer. Désireé and Gorée moved to the side so their *mémère* could see her first grandson.

Tears fell from Alise's eyes.

"This child looks very much like Will Henriot Jennings." It was hard for her to contain her emotion because staring down at Edouard was the same as if Will was once again alive.

"You can hold him," Jenna said.

Alise readily lifted the child in her arms. One of her tears fell on Edouard's cheek. Désireé used a kerchief to wipe it away. Cyril pulled a chair forward for Alise to sit on. As she sat she knew she would love this child very much. It was when she realized Pierre had come into the room when her tears fell more swiftly. "Your papa," she said and began to sob.

Pierre leaned and kissed her cheek. "I know."

The servants brought in beverages and a light meal for everyone to eat during the entire time of the visit. Alise, Désireé, Cyril and Gorée had sat closely to one another. Jenna was happy when Pierre sat beside her because the others sitting together made her feel like a stranger in her own room. Gorée was fascinated with Edouard. Regardless of who held him, including Jenna, she stood nearby and watched the child silently. During this time Jenna saw Pierre growing restless because of Gorée's behavior. Some minutes later Jenna learned that Pierre hadn't been restless with Gorée, but with her. Taking Gorée by the hand, he sat her in a chair then lifted Edouard from Désireé's hands and placed the baby in Gorée's hands.

"Edouard," he said. "Edouard."

Gorée held the baby carefully. Every so often she would whisper, "Pretty-pretty."

After enough food had been eaten Jenna listened while Désireé and Alise told stories about Will and Pierre that had happened on the plantation. Jenna had never heard the stories before, although most of them had occurred while she lived on Ashleywood. A child was usually involved. Funny stories that made Jenna splutter with laughter. Not because the stories themselves were funny. It was the way Alise recited them and the gestures she used to get her stories across. If a funny part had been omitted Désireé would quickly add it making everyone laugh all over again.

Gorée didn't pay attention to anyone in the room, except Edouard. Now that she was holding him each time Jenna looked in the child's direction she sensed that Gorée's entire concentration was on holding Edouard correctly. When he awakened and started to cry Gorée's eyes became wide, and it looked for a moment that she would cry as well.

"He's hungry," Pierre explained, taking the child from her and handing Edouard to Jenna.

"We should all leave now," Alise said. "You need your rest. We have taken up too much of your time as it is."

"Pierre, can you stay a moment?" Jenna asked.

He closed the door behind the others and returned to the bed.

Jenna leaned against the pillows only then realizing how tired she was. "Can you change his diaper, please?"

By the time Pierre finished changing Edouard's diaper Jenna had fallen asleep. She startled when she felt something touch her nightgown. She looked down and saw that Pierre had opened it to expose her breast then held Edouard against her. He sat beside her on the bed with Edouard in his arms. "Go to sleep. I will watch him."

It surprised her when not only did she go to sleep; she had been sleeping deeply when she awakened to Pierre holding Edouard to the opposite breast. The next time she woke up the sun was rising. The Jennings crib had been brought down from the third-floor nursery. Edouard slept peaceably in it. Pierre was no longer in the room.

Remembering how caring he had been the night before, the fact that he wasn't there now made Jenna hate Sarah even more.

# Chapter Thirty-One
# My Flesh and Blood

*[Bathe other people's children but don't wash behind their ears. – Creole Proverb]*

Three days later Sarah stood in the *grand salle* instructing James where to lay the new rug that had recently arrived. With his and the help of several more servants the room was quickly organized how she had seen it in her mind for months.

Stepping into the hall she hurried inside the dining room. More of the furniture Pierre had ordered from a manufacturer in France had arrived. The *maison*, in her eyes, was looking more like a home rather than a partially decorated shell. Servants were covering the new dining room table with a new tablecloth. Crates of the porcelain plates she had picked out of a catalog and had been finished with a twenty-four karat gold trim sat on the floor.

Servants were unpacking the crates. The dishes were cleaned right there on the floor, dried, then handed to another to arrange on the open shelves of the buffet against the wall. Sarah was admiring the progress when the servants she had sent to the mansion stepped into the room with downcast eyes.

"Madame refused to give us anything, mademoiselle. And Overseer Langers refused to give us wood."

Sarah sighed. The same thing had happened the day before. Leaving the *maison* to go to the outside kitchen, she stepped into it and saw a dismal looking fire burning in the grate. A single pot simmered on top of it. Imogen stirred its contents with a long wooden spoon.

This kitchen was much smaller than the mansion's kitchen. Its brick hearth had separate compartments to cook, as well as to bake and broil. Empty kettles and pots of all sizes rested on the mantle and the brick floor in front of the hearth. Wooden paddles and iron utensils were arranged in various areas unused at all that day. The work table sat clean and new looking. A single orange sat on a small plate at one end with a knife lying beside it. Sarah saw it and knew Imogen was wondering how to turn the orange into something appetizing for the master of the plantation.

Not knowing why she even bothered Sarah moved closer to the cabinets and cupboards to see what or if anything was in them. Both were bare. She turned again to Imogen then approached the servant to see what was cooking in the kettle. Sarah saw what looked like a watery soup that swam with a sparse amount of vegetables and very little meat. The crusty end of a bread loaf had been cubed to top the soup once Imogen deemed it ready to eat. The very sight of the soup reminded Sarah of Green Lea when meals consisted of one kettle dishes.

"Get rid of this," she said. "I don't care what you do with it. I will not serve the master this at his dining room table."

Hurrying out of the kitchen she began to yell and call out until one by one fourteen servants came out of the *maison* and stood in front of her. One of the men held something in his hand that Sarah had every intention of using.

Separating the women from the men she walked toward the now empty carts that had carried her new furniture. With the help of James, she sat in the driver's seat of the smaller cart and had the women climb in behind her. The men followed behind her on the larger cart.

***

Pierre had just left the mansion. Edouard lay in his basket on the floor. Jenna was bringing a cup of café to her lips when she heard noise in the hall. The next thing she knew the noise had gotten closer and Riley had hurried into the room. Sarah pushed past him and entered the *salle* behind him. Jenna's mouth gaped at the size of Sarah's protruding belly. She wore an elegant gown. The boots on Sarah's feet made Jenna envious. She lowered the cup to the table beside her.

Riley gave a nod. Jenna had but to look at his face and knew that Sarah had gone against Riley's wishes of waiting at the front door where Jenna had instructed Riley to keep her if Sarah ever decided to visit.

"Madame." Riley gave another nod, then stepped out of the room.

Sarah didn't wait for Jenna to speak. "I've come with a cart, dear sister. The sooner you and I fill it the sooner I can leave your home and be on my way to the storehouse."

Jenna jumped to her feet. "How dare you come here and demand anything of me! Have you gone mad? You steal my husband and now you're here to take food out of my home so you can provide him with a meal at your measly *maison*?"

"Keep that key around your wrist, dear sister. I have no need of it. The days of my servants walking four kilometers each day for a handful of whatever you decide to share are over."

Sarah hurried out of the room.

Once she stepped into the hall the servants who had come with her fell in step behind her as she made her way to the butler pantry, and then outside.

The mansion's servants that were working in the basement looked in both directions when they saw Sarah enter it. Sarah saw the fear in their eyes. None of them wanted to be forced to go against their madame's wishes.

"I understand," Sarah said softly. "Step out of the way, please."

The servants stepped to one side.

Sarah held her hand behind her. Josiah handed her the ax he'd been carrying and Sarah had told him to bring with them to the mansion. Sarah held it in her hands, and going to the first pantry door raised the ax and gave the door a hard whack above its iron lock.

The mansion's servants scattered in all direction.

Sarah was on her fourth whack when the wood finally splintered. She used the ax to pry the door the rest of the way open, careful not to hurt herself with it. "Grab those empty baskets and sacks in the back of the cart. I have every intention of filling them."

Sarah kept the ax near as she went to the shelves and began pulling vases and jars and wooden boxes to the floor.

"Have you gone mad?" Jenna screeched as she made her way toward the pantry. "I shall tell Pierre how you destroyed this door!"

"Tell him!" Sarah yelled. "I think it's time he knows how Overseer Langers keeps the servants in his charge in fear of him and you! I'll be making my way here every three months and if I find this door locked I'll beat it down again and again. Now out of my way. I have no time to waste on you."

"How can you stand there, Sarah, and behave like you're justified? You're my sister…"

"I was sitting in your *salle* when you told me there was nothing between you and me. But I didn't need to here you say that. I already knew. You owe me nothing, Jenna. And I owe you nothing."

"Is that why you're with him? Is that why you're here on my land sleeping with my husband, giving him children?"

Sarah's shoulders deflated. Anger left her face. "No. It's not. And I'm sorry."

"Sorry?" Jenna said stepping closer. "My son's father sleeps under another roof because of you."

Sarah lifted her head. "That fault lies with you, Jenna. Not me."

The urge to slap Sarah became very strong. The reason she didn't was because she knew all too well the consequences. "Do you truly wish to become my enemy? Because that's what you'll be if you insist on taking even a dust of spice out of this house."

"Maybe you've forgotten, Jenna. You and I come from the same stock. You want to continue being evil? Well, I can become evil as well. I have said nothing to Pierre about how much time he spends in this mansion. Keep doing what you're doing and I'll beg him to never step foot in this house again."

Jenna's eyes hardened. "You stand there with your belly stuck out with my husband's seed and act like you're God almighty."

"No!" Sarah argued. "All I want to do is feed the children in my belly and my servants better than you do your dogs. I didn't come here to fight or argue, dear sister. I know where I stand with you. I've known exactly where I stood with you for as long as I can remember. Even if I had married William your treatment of me wouldn't be at all different than it is now. You've never had to do anything for me, but had you given just a little to Papa and Tante Marianne – only a little – it would have made all of the difference. You have never cared about anyone but yourself. You have lost the love of your father, your tante, and even your daughter. Be careful, Jenna, or you'll lose Pierre once and for all, too. Now get out of my face!"

Sarah didn't watch her leave. The twins weren't sitting high but low against her pelvis. The excitement had been too much. Alexis and Lucien felt as if they were tumbling down a hill inside her stomach. The sooner she could get back to the *maison* to rest the better. "Settle down in there." Sarah closed her eyes and rubbed her stomach. "Maman is not finished yet."

After she came for all she needed and other items that she didn't know had been in the pantry and could use, she waited patiently while the servants carried these things to the cart. The pantry had been so well stocked that when Sarah rode away it looked as if little had been taken out of it although half of the smallest cart was filled with items out of it.

At the storehouse Sarah performed the same feat. Servants ran and scrambled out of her way as she drove her ax into a locked door. If any of the servants other than the ones she had brought with her tried to help, Sarah sent them away. The rest of the smaller cart was filled to the brim. Sarah ordered for it to be driven back to the *maison* and climbed on the larger cart. She wasn't close to halfway being finished yet.

By the time she reached the smokehouse Overseer Langers was waiting for her. As soon as the cart stopped he stared at her peevishly, then made a gesture toward servants that were inside the storehouse and out of her range of view. They stepped out readily filling her cart with an abundance of all the things she had asked for over the past months.

"Mademoiselle," Langers pleaded. "I'll have whatever you need sent over to the *maison*. Just tell me what else you need."

"For you to stay out of my way," Sarah answered. "And the next time I come here I'll pick out my own meats. I don't trust you and from this moment forward I never will."

She slapped the reins and drove to the wood house. Stopping the cart she reached behind her for a jug of orangeat and took a long swig, then handed the jug to the servants to pass around. She climbed down and walked over to a recently chopped pile of wood. "Load it up in my cart. Every piece."

"Yes, mademoiselle," was the answer.

Pierre was at the gristmill when word reached him that Sarah was wielding an ax and driving a cart madly across the plantation. He smiled to himself and started walking out the mill's door when he saw her and the cart approaching. Sarah's hair had fallen from the pinned up hairdo she usually wore and now blew in the wind. Behind her the cart looked like it had been filled with everything a person owned and they were now taking with them to live between the trees.

Pierre stepped back inside the mill and grabbed the glass of orangeat and rum he'd been drinking. Carrying it to her, he waited until she had taken a generous swallow before kissing gently at her lips. "Is there any room on that seat for me?"

She smiled at him and moved over as far as she could.

Pierre ordered a few servants to take sacks of the mill's grains to the *maison* and store it the basement. Back at the *maison* he stood behind her as she slowly climbed the steps up to the galerie. The weight of the twins worried him at times. At the top of the stairs he lifted her in his arms and carried her inside and into her dressing room. The porcelain tub inside it was the largest he could find. Because of the weight of it, the flooring of the dressing room had been reinforced with bricks.

He sat her on the chaise in the corner, then lowered in front of her and removed her boots. Taking each foot in his hand, he started to rub and massaged them when he heard a servant nearby in the hall. Calling out to the servant, Pierre ordered a bath to be drawn.

"Maybe I shouldn't," Sarah confided. "I was told it wasn't good for a woman in my condition to take baths this late in the pregnancy."

"It will make you relax. I'll lift you in and I'll lift you out."

An hour later while Sarah reclined in the tub; she did more than relax. The daily work needed to get the *maison*'s interior completed before the twins were born had finally taken its toll. Her eyes closed on their own accord. The sound of trickling water and the feel of a soft cloth rubbing at her skin only made her sleep more soundly. It wasn't until he lifted her from the tub that she jerked awake.

"I have you, mon amour."

Pierre rubbed her dry as he laid her on the bed. He didn't bother trying to dress her. Pulling the coverlets high up to ensure she stayed warm, he kissed softly at her hair and skin then leaned forward and kissed where his twin sons also slept.

# Chapter Thirty-Two
## A Dream is Only a Dream

*[A bed for two isn't a bed for three. – Creole Proverb]*

Julien refused to get out of bed. The night before, and after his constant persistence did Marie-Marie capitulate and allow him to sleep entirely nude throughout the night. While she had removed his shirt and undergarments her mouth had been held tightly enough for fine lines to distort the shape of them. As long as the parts of him that were now lame were covered in cloth she behaved naturally. Having to look at the loss of muscle in his right leg or his right arm, which now could no longer stretch out fully, brought looks onto her face that told Julien exactly how she felt about him.

As he lay on the bed he thought about Anne.

On the morning Edouard was born Marie-Marie had sent Anne to live in the cabin that had once belonged to Marie-Téa. Jenna agreed as neither woman found it appropriate for Anne to deliver a child inside the mansion. During the nights that Anne had slept in his room with him, she would wake, grab the long jug, and while he slept placed his manhood in it, then slowly poured water over him. Julien would wake up at that moment, relieve himself, and then the two of them would go back to bed. Lately there wasn't a night when he didn't awake on his own, and each time he called Marie-Marie, who slept right beside him, she got up and held a basin for him, then quickly crawled back in bed and turned her back to him.

The frustration he saw in her eyes was becoming more and more noticeable. The thought of living the rest of his life with a wife like her was something he would not bear. And there was something else that bothered him as well. He might be a broken man, but he wasn't completely broken. It was this he wanted to show her. It was also the reason he had demanded to sleep without clothing. Marie-Marie had given no heed to him. Like always she crawled in bed, then put an even greater distance between them before she turned her back to him and fell asleep.

Now he was waiting – waiting for her to come back to the room after she had breakfast. The ropes Anne had tied to the bed were still in place. He wanted to show Marie-Marie that he could get out of bed on his own. Maybe if she saw him do this then she would understand.

It took a long while for the bedroom door to finally push open and for Marie-Marie to step into the room. As soon as she saw he was still in bed, she stopped where she stood and gazed at him with arched eyebrows. Usually while she had breakfast, Julien would get himself out of bed and sit in a chair to wait for her to help him get ready for the day.

"Why are you still in bed?" She asked stepping closer. "Are you not well?"

"I want to show you something," he said. "I just need you to stand there at the foot of the bed, all right?"

She nodded.

Julien smiled.

Using his left hand he tossed back the coverlets.

"What are you doing?" She hissed as soon as she saw his nakedness. "You're inappropriate."

"I'm your husband," Julien said gently although his anger had been kindled.

Knowing if he didn't be quick he would lose her attention, he rolled to her side of the bed, then struggled to reach the rope. Gripping it with his hand he tugged and kicked with his left leg until he was in position. His body moved gradually in her direction. Just before his feet touched the floor, he grabbed the second rope with his right hand.

Marie-Marie screamed when she saw his penis harden and rise above the bed. She screamed again and clutched her throat when the bedroom door flew open and Pierre ran in, his eyes searching to see why she had screamed like she had. Julien bellowed with laughter as Pierre saw what he shouldn't have, did a jump on his feet, then hurried from the door.

"What is the matter with you?" Marie-Marie cried. "Have you gone mad?"

Julien pressed the back of his head against the mattress. "Lie down with me, Marie-Marie. Lay on top of me."

She approached him gently. "Julien, stop this. It isn't right for you to suggest that I should lay with you in an unnatural way for a man and woman to lie together."

"Chérie, husbands and wives lie in this position more than you know. Come here. Just try."

He watched as she stared at his right leg, which was thinner than his left, and then at the bend of his right arm as his hand held tightly to the rope. "It's just an arm and a leg," he said softly.

"Julien, what you're implying I should do is something that only a *prostituée* would do."

It was a partial truth. Husbands who could convince their wives to do more than lie on their backs until it was over were lucky indeed.

"It's your wifely duty, Marie-Marie. What does the church say about your wifely duties?"

"This is vulgar. That you would even debase me by forcing me to have this conversation with you…"

"You are excused, Marie-Marie." Reaching behind him, it took him a while to reach the ropes at the head of the bed. Gripping them in both hands he used his left leg to help pull himself upward. He then reached for a small piece of the coverlet and covered himself. "Send Semper to me, please."

She questioned him with her eyes. Julien saw suspicion settle into her irises. It was her need to leave the room and him the reason she did as he asked.

When Semper came into the room Julien told her to leave through his French door and go to the coopers' quarters to find Anne and bring her back.

Down below Marie-Marie had café with Jenna. Marie-Marie wondered what the world was coming to when Jenna lifted Edouard in her arms and the babe quickly turned its head toward its mother's breast.

"It's unnatural for a woman of your status to nurse their own child. You have plenty of servants in The Bottoms with milk enough for their child and Edouard."

"I love feeding him myself," Jenna tried to explain.

"It's unnatural," Marie-Marie repeated. "This is not the way things are done. And I heard the child crying inside your room in the middle of the night."

"Pierre moved the crib into my boudoir. I'm sorry if Edouard disturbed you."

"Sister-in-law, you are the wife of a wealthy planter. These things are unheard of. Nursing your own child. A child crying in your boudoir. Children are meant to sleep on the third floor. They are meant to have a wet nurse and servants to take care of them. Pardon me for saying so, but you are debasing yourself by doing what you're doing. Surely you must know that keeping this up is the same as you behaving like one of the slaves."

Jenna traced the whirl of white hair on Edouard's crown. No woman of prominence that she knew nursed her own child or tended to the child like she did Edouard. It was time to feed him. Oh, how she hated to run up to her boudoir each time Edouard needed to be fed. How she longed to sit in whatever room she was in and hold Edouard to her breast there. The child seemed always hungry. Already he had gained weight. Jenna feared if she didn't eat more during the day Edouard was going to suck all of her weight away. Unlike when she had Abigail she had lost much weight already. If she lost more she would be smaller than she had been before Edouard was born.

The babe moved his head in tiny motions back and forth, then released a loud wail. Jenna smiled down at him.

"If you'll excuse me, Marie-Marie. I need to feed Edouard and I have no strength at the moment to walk up to my room."

The stunned look in Marie-Marie's eyes made Jenna feel unnatural. Feeding a child in a *salle* while a guest was present was not only considered rude, it was most unheard of.

Pierre stepped into the room and made his way to Edouard. "What's ailing him?"

"He's hungry," Jenna said and started to rise.

Pierre pressed a hand on her shoulder to force her back onto the sofa, then looked at Marie-Marie. "I think Julien needs your help."

"He has Semper helping him this morn…"

Edouard wailed louder.

"Get out of the *salle*, Marie-Marie. My son is hungry."

Marie-Marie rose quickly. This mansion housed nothing other than heathens. None of the family went to mass on Sundays as they should. For a guest to be made to leave the comfort of the *salle* for the sake of a newborn child revealed how uncouth this family was. And to think they called themselves Creole.

Pierre watched as she left the room, then reached behind Jenna's gown to unbutton it. He then crossed the room and informed the servants that no one was to come inside the *salle* again until its door was opened.

"Our behavior at this moment is ridiculous even to me, so why am I enjoying it?" She asked.

"This family is very much Creole, but this family has always made its own rules." Sitting on the sofa beside her, he held Edouard's hand as the child latched onto his mother's breast. "He has a good appetite."

"I will be skin and bones very soon." She smiled. "Thank you. Marie-Marie is right. I have debased myself in the worst way. I have given no chores to any of the servants in regards to him. I love doing it myself. I haven't sent letters to any friends to let them know Edouard has been born. I want to spend this time with him alone."

"When I learned you would nurse Edouard yourself, I also refused to send letters. I told the servants to keep it quiet as well. But I don't think you're debasing yourself. You're being a mother. You love your son. I find nothing wrong with that."

"The crib is still in my boudoir, Pierre," she argued. "Edouard's crying has disturbed Marie-Marie's sleep. If that ever got out my friends will think I have gone mad."

"Let the child sleep in your room if that's what you want. I don't know who started this rule of making children sleep in a part of the house where the child can't be heard."

"I love this baby, Pierre. I never knew I could love anything like I love Edouard. He's still so young, and I have placed him before all of my friends. I feel so guilty about that."

"Don't feel guilty." Pierre held her gaze. "This soft side of you is very appealing." He rose to his feet.

Jenna asked because she needed to know. Pierre's behavior toward her hadn't changed since Sarah's visit. "Does Sarah tell you anything about me?"

He hesitated still holding her gaze. "This isn't easy for her, Jenna. No more than it is for you. I see the guilt and I wonder if sooner or later if it will become too much. Is there anything I should know?"

She thought carefully of what to say. "I hate her."

"I know. And for what it's worth I would understand if you hate me, too. Because I could have done what was right and sent her away, but I chose not to."

She averted her gaze.

"There's nothing I can do to make this right," he said. "I don't want you to go. I want you and Edouard to stay here in this house."

She faced him.

"Even though I don't know if that's the right thing to do," he finished.

He kissed the crown of Edouard's head as he usually did just before he walked away. "I shall be around the mansion for a while longer. I'm waiting for some urgent letters to come from the city. If you need me send for me."

As Pierre walked out of the *salle*, Marie-Marie received a second cup of café while she sat on the galerie waiting for Julien to come out and sit with her. She was halfway finished with the cup when she saw Semper walking back toward the mansion from the outside kitchen. Noémi walked with her, both servants strolling at a leisure pace and absorbed in a conversation.

Marie-Marie rested her cup on the table beside her and stood to her feet. It had only taken a second of watching Semper to know she hadn't been in Julien's bedroom for some time. This meant that Semper had never been called into the room to help Julien get ready for the day and instead as a ploy to get the wench Anne to help in secret.

Hurrying inside the mansion, Marie-Marie formed the words she would use when she flung open Julien's bedroom door and berate the pestering hussy. The words banish and cabin were words she was certain she would use when she reached the second floor. Lifting her hem high she walked in a swift gait to Julien's bedroom. Flinging open its door it took her some seconds before any sound came out of her mouth.

In front of her on top of the bed, Marie-Marie watched in horror as Julien had a strong grip on both ropes at the head of the bed. Anne's naked body was bent in half as she balanced on her knees and pressed her face deeply into the mattress to suppress the whimpers escaping her mouth. Behind her Julien bucked and ground, his manhood poking and prodding, his hips simulating a man riding a horse.

Marie-Marie screamed with all of her might just as Julien went rigid and Anne's head lifted from the mattress as she gave a loud cry. To have seen it all was too much.

Running from the door Marie-Marie ran into Pierre just before she reached the stairs. Marie-Marie pointed toward the bedroom. Pierre ran past her and stood in the door. Marie-Marie watched as he too stared into the room in disbelief, then pulled the door tightly closed. With the door closed in front of him, he yelled, "Anne! You are to come to my study! Immediately!"

"Sell her!" Marie-Marie screamed. "This slave girl has crossed the line. That is the bed I sleep in at night! How dare she! How dare him! There's nothing but madness going on inside this house."

"Pierre!" Julien yelled from within the door. "Anne does not belong to you! Have you forgotten that?"

Pierre had. "This is my house, Julien!"

"Then Anne and I shall return to Primrose!"

Pierre heard this, took a step away from the door, then turned and walked away.

"Do something!" Marie-Marie cried. "This is your house. Make him respect it."

"This is his house, too. He was born inside it just like I was. Do not ask me to fix your marriage when my own became fragmented pieces within its first hours."

"I shall leave this house! If none of you will do anything, I shall leave here right away and return to my family in France."

"Go to your family, Marie-Marie!" Pierre roared. "Maybe if you lift your skirt and appease him instead of acting like a pious saint only when it suits you no one else would!"

Marie-Marie's jaw dropped. No man had any right to speak to any woman as Pierre had just spoken to her. "You are the devil. I can die saying I have laid eyes on him. And your brother is your imp! That injury stole all of his dignity. Before it he had the decency to hide his trollops. Never had he flaunted them so carelessly before me. Is it not bad enough she's carrying his child? To witness what just occurred in my bed, I shall never forgive him. For anyone to expect me to care for an animal as vile as him is unfair. But what should I expect from you when you —

yourself – has taken your own sister-in-law and turned her into nothing more than your whore?"

"Marie-Marie you were not born inside this house; therefore, you have no right to stay underneath its roof as long as you choose. I will gladly give you the money you need to leave my house, enough to never come back. You're no different than any other woman who refused to satisfy their husband and blame others when he searches elsewhere. As for my marriage you can say whatever you will about it. But my wife is downstairs in a state of euphoric bliss over her child. Shit happens between married men and women, and until one of them decides to change their circumstances nothing can ever be done to improve their situation.

"You were near naked and homeless when my brother found you in the rain. You can thank the devil for the wealth you'll now receive. Five-thousand is all you will get. Had you been Anne I would have given more. At least she worked and slaved on this plantation and didn't turn her back on him when he needed her most. So you take your dignity and get out of my face because it means nothing to me."

Marie-Marie yelled for Semper and Jeanette, then hurried inside her boudoir. It took two hours to get a coach ready. While she prepared to leave the mansion Pierre went inside the study and opened the hidden safe. He withdrew cash in the amount of five grand, then sat down and wrote a letter of receipt.

Julien had been made ready for the day. Walking long distances were impossible unless he used crutched. Even then it was hard to keep his balance when his right side was uncooperative. After taking a few slow steps out of his bedroom a few servants watched him silently. He could see in their eyes that they were most eager to help him or would run and get his wheelchair at the least. Julien smiled at them and continued the short distance to Marie-Marie's boudoir at the end of the hall. When he stood inside it he leaned on his left side against the jamb.

"Leave us," he said to the servants who were strapping down the last of the trunks.

The door pulled closed behind them.

"I'm sorry you saw that," he began. "I didn't mean for you to. I heard what you told my brother. If my right leg was working better you would have never known what I had been up to. But my right leg doesn't work, and my wife detests looking at it. I don't blame you for wanting to leave. You deserve better than someone like me. Once you reach your family in France I shall send whatever you need."

Angry tears fell from her eyes.

"You're not going to ask me to stay, Julien?"

"No." He gave an apologetic smile. "Because just like you deserve someone better I deserve a better wife."

The time it took him to turn to make his way to the hall she ran after him, then stood in front of him. "She's a *nègre!* A *nègre* whore! A cunt that's only using you to have a happier and more pleasing life."

"Noémi! Semper! Jeanette! Someone please give this bitch a Bible. Now that hers is packed away she's forgotten what's written in it."

Marie-Marie took each step he did, her mouthing refusing to close. "That's all you're good for. *Nègre* children."

Julien nearly stumbled and had to lean more against the crutch to stay upright. "Don't talk about my unborn child. I'm warning you."

"You can't even walk! I hope your leg shrivels and falls off. And your arm, too! You're despicable! A disgrace of a man. Your *nègre* whore didn't make you this way. You always were. I hate I married you! I hate I ever laid eyes on you!"

"Enough!" Jenna hissed, clutching Edouard tightly to her breast. "What's gotten into you, Marie-Marie? You sound like a wharf wife from the poorest *arrondissement* in Paris."

Marie-Marie breathed heavily as tears rain down her face, then hurried back to her room. Julien spoke softly to the nearby servants to help their madame gather her things and take them to the coach.

"Where is she going?" Jenna asked. "This is foolish! The church will never give her a divorce. At best all she has to look forward to is being another man's secret mistress. She can never marry again until you're dead. And she can never have children without becoming a societal outcast."

Jenna thought about Abigail and hurried to Marie-Marie's room. "Leave her!" She yelled at the servants. They quickly left the room. "Get a hold of yourself, woman!" Jenna yelled at Marie-Marie. "You're young! You will want children some day. You have no money."

Marie-Marie shook her head with determination. "Pierre promised to give me five-thousand dollars. I'm going to France to live with my family there."

"Are you mad? Do you hear yourself? Are you truly saying you would rather live as an adult that will be chaperoned by the men in your family? What kind of life will that be? If you have an affair, or worse, have a child it will shame your family, and then what? You think Julien or Pierre will let you come back then when you have refused to give Julien a child while you were here? You are not that stupid," Jenna hissed. "Julien owns Anne, which means you own Anne. Punish her in the way you see fit and do put away these gaudy looking trunks. I swear, Marie-Marie, your fashion sense is lacking at best. Why do you think you will even be accepted into Paris society looking like you do?"

"I won't sleep with him. I won't."

"Then I shall send in the servants to pick up your trunks and carry them to the coach."

Marie-Marie stared at Jenna because Jenna's voice had lowered and became saddened. "And I don't want to be like you," Marie-Marie said vehemently. "You ask what's wrong with me. I ask what is wrong with you? Your husband is living in sin with your sister on this land!"

The words that came to Jenna's mind she refused to speak. "You're right. You'll be better off taking the money and living with your family in France. Have a safe voyage."

Julien had heard only a little of what Jenna had said. He whispered to Semper to run and get Anne and to meet him out front. As fast as he could he made his way to the stairs. Falling to the floor he gripped one of the banisters and slowly began making his way down the stairs. Pierre saw him and lifted him over his shoulder.

"Take me out on the front galerie," Julien said.

More than half an hour later Marie-Marie exited the mansion's front door dressed in traveling clothes. When she looked to her right she saw Julien sitting in a chair sipping a warm drink while Anne stood docile behind him as if she was hiding.

Marie-Marie knew at that moment she couldn't be leaving soon enough. "I'd rather be a man's mistress than your wife a minute longer."

"A mistress must lift her skirt," Julien retorted. "And do more than lie on her back."

"One day you'll reap what you sow. And your half breed child, too."

As the coach rode away, Marie-Marie refused to look back.

No sooner than the coach rode away the carriage of Frances Achen rode up the drive and parked out front. He alighted from the back of it, then reached back in for the satchel resting on the cushion.

"You're looking quite well, Julien," he said stepping onto the galerie. "You've come a long way since the first days after your injury."

Julien glanced at Anne's belly, then smiled at Frances. "I am that. My brother's inside. I think he's been waiting for you."

Frances stayed all of twenty minutes. After he left Pierre kissed Edouard then left the mansion. At the *maison* he sat down in its study and opened the satchel Frances had given him. Going through each of the documents inside it he was close to the bottom of the stack when he saw a letter from Emile to Sarah.

Carrying it to where she was he handed it to her.

Sarah looked at the letter, saw from whom it was from, then rose to her feet and walked out of the room.

# Chapter Thirty-Three
## Give Me No More Rain

*[Shingles covers everything. – Creole Proverb]*

"Why?" Pierre asked again. "You have less than two weeks before my children are to be born. There should be nothing in the city important enough for you to go there."

"Please," Sarah pleaded. Ever since she learned Pierre was going to the city she spoke of nothing else but going with him.

Pierre gripped the back of the dining room chair. "Tell me now the secret contained in that letter you received from your father."

"There is no secret, Pierre." She held up her hand as if gesturing he should stay where he was. When she returned she handed the letter to him.

Pierre stared first at her then down at the letter. Paragraph after paragraph Emile expressed how important it was for his daughter to travel to Biloxi and become the wife of William. Pierre read the end and stared up at her. "He's in the city?"

"Oui," Sarah answered. "Since you're going to the city I would rather do this now. He needs to know about the babies and that I have no intentions of ever marrying William."

"I can bring him here."

"No, Pierre. He needs to know that he's not welcome here. I don't trust him. You have given him money. If he comes all of us will feel obligated to show him the upmost hospitality. Once that happens he'll keep returning, and when he comes he'll ask for more money."

Pierre gave this some thought, then shook his head. "It's not safe, Sarah. You traveling now."

"If you want we'll stay in the city until after the children are born."

This made him feel slightly better, but not much.

"This needs to end," she said. "He needs to know I'm not a pawn for him to use whenever he's in trouble. And trouble he must be in to want me to go to Biloxi."

Pierre finally agreed. "We'll leave as soon as the servants get your things ready."

After she watched him leave Sarah turned and saw that Imogen had been hiding in the hall waiting for the moment to step forward.

"You must stop this!" Sarah implored. "Why do you do this? Why?"

Imogen lowered her head. "I'm happy here, Mam'selle."

Sarah pressed a hand to her chest touched by the servant's sentiment.

"I know you are," she whispered, "but you are making him nervous. I'm too beginning to see what he's been saying about you for some time. Your constant hiding. Your need to watch the two of us together. What is the reason behind it? Please tell me. This is not Green Lea. No one will hurt you here."

Imogen gave a large smile, and then she visibly became relaxed.

"I's happy heah. Heah deys knows how to laugh. Cain't nobody say what it truly like to be a slave." She gave a shake of her head and closed her eyes. "Summa de tings dey dunn to me I'll neba forgets. I knows what it's like to be used up. But dis moanin I's eats *calas*. Me eats *calas* on a china plate juss like de massuh of dis heah land. Dem out in the world say niggers like me cain't eat *calas*. It be too good for my kinda skin. *Calas* is some rice, some sugar, some yeast, some eggs and some flour made into dumplins and fried. My mama and papa be quadroon. I's a quadroon. And being a quadroon I ain'ts worth a handful of rice, a few spoons of sugar, a pinch of yeast, part of no egg or a few spoons of flour."

She stared at Sarah. "But I's work on a farm to grows those very things. My hands," she said lifting them up. "Look at 'em. I's forty and six. My hands wrinkled like a pore-son eighty-six. Dey bleed. Dey crack. Dey ho-it so bad dey wont bend some times. And de driver say move 'em or get a taste of this whip. Dey ho-it so bad I's couldn't holds me spoon some times. Small chile had to feed me. Dat be my life on Green Lea." Her hands lowered. Her body became tense then slowly relaxed again. "It's juss past Kiss-miss and instead of sweepin and cleanin a big house all by meself, I's sitting in a chair with my Mam'selle befo massuh come talk to you. Heah at the devil's plantation he no devil to me. And Madam Alise is de angel from Heaben. I guess I's watchin 'cause I's scared it's goin to all end."

Sarah smiled and placed a gentle hand on Imogen's shoulder. "You're safe now, Imogen. Stop this hiding," she whispered.

Imogen smiled and nodded at her.

An hour later the coach rode away from the *maison*. Pillows had been taken from the *maison* to make Sarah's journey more comfortable. A low padded stool sat between the cushions to rest her feet on.

Sarah noticed that Pierre's concern for her comfort at times made him anxious to get to the city as quickly as possible. His arm stayed folded around her. On many occasions he rested his hands on the swell of her belly.

"How do you feel? Do we need to stop for a while to rest?"

"No, mon amour," she said cupping one side of his face. "I'm fine. I feel no discomfort." It was true. Other than the occasional bump that startled the twins and made them leap in her stomach, the pillows pampered her feet and legs.

"You'll have to stay in the city until the twins are able to travel."

She knew that Pierre would be forced to come back. The harvest season was ending. There was the management of the books to see to and the final arranging of the last part of his sold crops to ship. Being in the city at times without him didn't bother her. She knew that his mansion had many servants in it.

"I and the children will be fine."

He reached into his pocket and pulled out a jewelry box. "I wanted to give you this Christmas morning. And then I thought it may be better to give it to you on an even more special occasion. I only realized while I was preparing to get ready that any moment should be special enough. Open it."

The jewelry box was hand-painted. Inside a diamond ring sparkled as it captured even the smallest light.

"Whether the Orléonois want to accept our relationship or not is a big issue, mon amour. I'll have to work on their acceptance. I wanted to give you something to wear that each time you look at it you will remember how much I love you. Most Creole men are not expected to marry until they're the age I am now. I wasn't as lucky. I have no intentions of hiding my love for you, Sarah. I must be careful, yes, but I have no intentions of hiding my heirs that you will bear. The Jennings of New Orléans was here from the very beginning. We were with Bienville, and the arrival of *les filles à la cassette*, Bloody O'Reilly, the fires of '78 and '94, French rule, Spanish rule, and now Américain rule. The Jennings are as synonymous as *la famille* Delery, Allain, Forstall, Marigny, de Buys, Bouligny, Deveraux, and Arceneaux. We *are* a part of the *crème de la crème*. My sons, although they will be *batârds,* but because they will be born from a woman without noir blood will be accepted in this city from the day of their birth."

Sarah gazed into his eyes intently. "I love you so much, Pierre. For the rest of my life."

The servants appeared happy and surprised to see him step inside the mansion and further surprised when they saw Sarah enter behind him in her condition.

"Mademoiselle, 'tis good to see you," one of them said. "Your papa said you would come. We tried to tell him there's no way you were coming to the city. He's been waiting for you..."

"He's here?" Pierre asked. "In this house?"

The servant pressed her lips tightly together and nodded. "He's been here for weeks."

"Why wasn't I told about this?" Pierre asked.

"We sent word through Monsieur Achen, monsieur. Did he not tell you?"

Frances was much older now. Pierre remembered how forgetful he had become of late and decided not to press the issue. "I'll speak with Monsieur Achen, Cissy. Bring refreshments to the *salle.*" Pierre took Sarah by the hand leading her into the room. Helping her to get comfortable, he lowered in front of her. "Did you know he was here?"

"No," she said, shaking her head. "Pierre, maybe I shouldn't have come. Why would he be here of all places? I fear he has none of the money left that you've given him."

"Impossible," Pierre seethed. "I gave him more than enough. Only someone..."

"There you are!" Emile accused stepping into the room. When he saw how large her belly was his eyes became almost equal in girth. Sarah had never seen anyone's eyes become larger than his was at the moment. She tried to rise. Pierre pressed her back into the chair.

"Why are you in my home, Emile?"

"No," Emile sang coldly. "Why have you done this? This is my daughter. I didn't believe the rumors. But now I see they are true. Jenna didn't help her escape that day, did she? It was you wasn't it? You're the reason I lost a good friend."

Pierre straightened to full height. "I understand your anger, Emile. Perhaps you and I can sit and talk."

"No," Emile said shaking his head sternly. "This is wrong. And there's nothing you can say that can make this right. My daughter could have lived a respectable life with William. Had I known this would be her end I would have done things differently and forced her to marry William right away."

"Papa," Sarah pleaded. "I'm sorry you had to find out like this. I can't marry Monsieur Murray. I can't. I'm happy."

"Happy?" Emile asked sarcastically. "Happy being your brother-in-law's whore? Who will marry you now, Sarah? You have allowed Pierre to steal away your very future."

"Emile, let's talk," Pierre insisted. "You're here. I'm here. Now is the time. Let's do things differently this time. Let's settle this now, you and I alone and not wait twenty years to discuss it."

Emile lifted his chin. "You've done this to hurt me, didn't you? To get back at me because of what happened between you and Jenna on your wedding night."

"Jenna and I are moving beyond that now."

"Are you?" Emile gave a sardonic squint. "Are you telling this Creole father that you plan on living with both of my daughters as your wives?"

Pierre stepped closer to him gesturing with his hand toward the door. "We can have this conversation in the next room. Sarah needs to rest. You can speak with her afterwards."

"Get your hands away from me!" Emile threatened, and then he stared at Sarah. "I've given you all I could. I may have made some mistakes, but I've done right by you."

"Papa." Sarah spoke softly. "I know my decision is hard for you to understand. I know that marrying William would have made me respectable, but how valuable is respect when you're living a life without happiness?"

Emile's face peered forward like someone straining to look through a dark window. "You're talking like a fool! He is your sister's husband! You're doing this to hurt her, because the two of you have never gotten along. Of all the wrong she's done this is worst! Only a wretch of a woman could stare into her papa's eyes and try to convince him that your decision can be acceptable." He took a few steps closer to her with balled fists. "Jenna is the daughter of my wife. You are a *bâtard!*"

Sarah's expression became stern. "I have made my decision, Papa. It's too late to change it now."

Emile's expression also became stern. "You're talking like someone bewitched by a voodoo spell." He started to walk away, but then he turned and looked solely at her. His facial features became relaxed. "I should have left you in the slaves' quarter." He then turned and stared at Pierre, his eyes dark with murder.

Sarah waved her hand angrily at him. "Enough, Papa! What you're saying is absurd! Are you intoxicated? You must be. But I'll tell you now that I won't fall for anymore of your shenanigans. I will not marry William or anyone else just to ensure that you live a better life. To ensure you have enough liquor to drink yourself into a stupor each day. So tell us why you're here? Is it the money? Is it all gone?"

Pierre had been staring intently into Emile's eyes. Several times he had peered down at Sarah.

Sarah saw the look on his face and tried to rise from the sofa. "Pierre, do not believe him. He's trying to hurt us! To even imply such a thing. How could you, Papa?"

Again Emile had turned to walk away. On hearing this he swung around again hard enough to almost make him unbalanced. "Why do you think I never sold Imogen? You are her daughter."

Pierre stared down at Sarah. Her eyes were wide. She shook her head vigorously.

Finally rising to her feet she held out her hands. "Look at me." She shoved her hands closer to her father's face so he could see them better. "Tante Marianne is my mother. She told me in confidence! This lie you're speaking sickens me."

A tear rolled down Emile's eyes.

Pierre saw this and pressed a hand to his mouth.

"Fifteen thousand," he then offered. "Not for your daughter, but for your silence. Please give our children a chance, Emile. I beg you."

Emile turned his gaze to Pierre. "You are the devil. Your money means nothing to me. Because of you my eldest daughter isn't happy and my younger daughter has become a whore."

Hanging his head in total dejection he took one last look at Sarah's middle, then stormed out of the room.

Pierre turned and saw Sarah's anger, and that she didn't believe what her father had said. He assisted her back onto the sofa, then sat beside her and held her hand. He spoke softly. "Now I understand why Imogen watches us so closely. I thought the two of you were keeping a secret. I see now that she feared your father would tell you as soon as he found out you had wronged him.

Sarah patted gently at his hand. "Pierre, I'm not noir. Imogen is *not* my mother. She and I lost everything on Green Lea. All the people she knew and loved have been sold away. I'm all she has left. It's that she's holding onto. For my father to have stooped so low...."

"Sarah..." He spoke gently. "Why do you think *mulâtresses* are forced to wear tignons in this city? When Spain governed New Orleans visitors to the city couldn't tell someone with noir blood with those that didn't. To maintain the class distinctions the then governor, Esteban Miro, put a law into place that all *mulâtresses* must wear a tignon over their hair, as it was the only way for anyone to be certain if the woman had noir blood."

"Pierre," Sarah pleaded. "Tante Marianne is my maman. She told me herself. She wouldn't lie about something like that. I know she wouldn't. It was she who came for me when she discovered Jenna refused to help us in anyway after Joséphine died."

"Because she loved you like my father loved me," Pierre said softly. "She didn't want you growing up facing prejudices."

"Why are you so ready to believe him?" Her voice had risen. Color had come into her face.

"Because I realize that Imogen's behavior is similar to my mother's when I had been younger."

Sarah started to speak when an image of Imogen running wildly across the plantation each time she returned for a visit came to mind. The other servants had been happy to see her as well, but not like Imogen. The embraces that Imogen would give. The tears that would fill her eyes. Imogen baking an extra cake just for her birthday. And then Sarah remembered the way her father had always behaved toward Imogen. William had wanted to sell Imogen along with the other slaves. It was the first time she had seen her father's boldness. He had refused in a loud voice and in a tone that forced William not to mention selling Imogen again.

Pierre watched with pain in his heart as Sarah lifted her hands and studied them, taking time to inspect the whiteness of her fingers and the soft color of her palms, and then her hands reached for her face.

"Let me help you upstairs," he offered when he saw a change come into her eyes. As if a lantern had been lit in her mind, her soft eye color now seemed to glow brighter.

She looked up at him. "Imogen? No," she said firmly. Her Tante Marianne loved her, but had never hugged or kissed her the way Imogen had. And then she remembered the time when Imogen had been given permission by her father to find work in the city to afford a trip to Biloxi. And the way Imogen dropped the sack she had carried and ran to meet her when she had arrived.

Other things came to her mind, like the way Imogen was becoming more and more excited that soon her mademoiselle would give birth.

But did any of this prove anything?

No. No, it didn't.

"This can't be true, Pierre," she reasoned. "He was upset. And understandably so." And then she peered up and saw how Pierre too looked *blanc*. There was nothing about him that told anyone Alise was his maman, not even the features of his face. Her chest shivered. Her hands trembled. "No."

Pierre gripped her fiercely. "It's okay, Sarah."

Sarah pushed hard away from him. "My father is spiteful. It's why Jenna refused to help him."

Pierre tightened his mouth. "Come upstairs, Sarah. You need to rest and I need to find your father and convince him not to say anything of this to no one."

He didn't wait for Sarah to rise. Lifting her in his arms, he carried her out of the *salle* and upstairs to his bedroom. Because the servants didn't know he would come the French doors were closed and all of the shutters locked. Pierre took a moment to open a few to allow air into the room. Once he was satisfied he walked to Sarah and lowered in front of her. "I'll have refreshments brought up." His hand stroked the side of her face.

She wiped the tears from her face and lifted her chin. "This goddamned city and its secrets." She lowered her head. "You believe him, don't you?"

"Oui."

Her face turned sharply to one side as if she received a blow. "If he tells Jenna she will make my life miserable…"

He hesitated only a second. "You are my lily, Sarah. My personal fleur-de-lis." He held her hand with the ring on it. "Tell me this is true."

She cupped his face in her hands. "I am so hurt. My heart literally hurts right now."

"Why?" He smiled at her. "You're still you. Nothing has changed."

She shook her head. "You misunderstand. I'm hurt because I have been lied to. I have longed to know who my mother is, Pierre. I don't know why Tante Marianne told me she was my mother. Maybe she did it to protect me, although I can't see why. She's Joséphine's sister. A lie like this would damage her if it had gotten out. But if Imogen is truly my mother, I…" Her mouth stayed parted for some time. "I can love her in a different way now."

He kissed her forehead.

Her eyes closed as she sighed. "What if this is why she couldn't stay away even when I told her to? I need to make this up to her. What if she thinks I have known all this time? Oh, God." A hand pressed against her mouth. The collapse she made in the chair was if someone had broken all of her bones. "How hard we worked her. Sunup and sundown. Including me. Never rest. Only work, work, work. I won't be ashamed," she ended emphatically, then stared at him. "I won't. If she is my mother I will accept it. I need to talk to her. I can't wait to return to the plantation."

He stood and, cupping her face with his palms, kissed hard at her hair, then gently on the lips. "Rest. I need to find your papa."

## Chapter Thirty-Four
# The Cost of Betrayal

*[What you lose in the fire, you will find in the ashes. – Creole Proverb]*

Pierre did not return to the mansion that evening or during the night. On several occasions Sarah had contemplated sending one of the servants out looking for him. The reason she didn't was a man had come to the mansion very late in the evening looking for Pierre. A well-dressed man that didn't look like he was from New Orléans. Sarah listened as the man explained he had seen Pierre only a few hours before, then assured the servant at the door that he will go where he last saw Pierre and see if he was still there.

Sarah knew Pierre had business in the city. The man looking for him wasn't surprising. The servants mentioned that men in the city came to the mansion often looking for *le diable dans Nouvelle-Orléans.*

After a sleepless night she woke early and got dressed, then waited for him to return. It was after nine when he finally walked through the bedroom door. It looked as if he had slept in his clothes. When he saw her sitting in a chair a small smile pulled across his face.

Sarah's heart twisted in her chest. Had he stopped loving her since he discovered the truth? She lowered her head because she knew if he had she wouldn't shed a single tear. Time was all she had since he left the afternoon before and during that time she had given everything a lot of thought. No one knew how it felt to be motherless unless they had been motherless themselves. And there was something else she knew now more than ever. She loved herself just as much as she had before her father had told the truth, and if Pierre couldn't accept this, if he took away his love to search for a *blanc* woman then so be it. She was resourceful and she would still be happy with or without him.

"Don't look at me like that," he scolded. Remembering why he had come in the room he crossed to the armoire. Sarah couldn't see what he pulled out of it. Whatever it was it was placed in the lining of his coat before he turned and faced her. "I have to go away for a day. I'll be back as soon as I can. It won't be long. I promise. Have you eaten breakfast?"

"No."

Pierre stood in the door and called for one of the servants. When they reached him, he ordered breakfast brought up to the room then faced her. "You don't look well, Sarah. Are you feeling well? Is it the children?"

She shook her head not sure what was wrong with her. She didn't feel any pain. Just an uneasiness that refused to go away despite the position she sat in. The thought of breakfast didn't sound appealing. "Pierre, can we talk about yesterday?"

He lowered in front of her. As close as he was she knew where he had spent his night. The scent of liquor and tobacco permeated his clothing. "There's nothing to talk about, mon amour. I have to get going. Let me help you to bed first."

"No," she said. "I want to sit here a little while. The air feels good."

He stood quickly, kissed her hair, then walked out the door leaving it open.

Sarah listened as he walked down the hall. The way he left abruptly seemed strange to her. Never had he left her so easily. It was always long kisses and promises to return soon before he could pull himself away.

She stood and walked out into the hall. When she reached the stairs she saw below the same man that had been looking for Pierre the previous evening. The man was standing at the front door. Pierre said something, and then he and the man walked out onto the street, the door closing behind them.

Sarah watched as the servant at the door ran close to another servant and whispered in her ear. Sarah leaned her head to one side when she saw what she believed to be a shadow. Standing inside one of the rooms were five more slaves, all of them listening intently as the girl at the door continued to whisper.

Sarah didn't know any of the servants in this house. She couldn't remember any of their names. "Girl. You there at the door. Come this way a moment."

The other servants startled on hearing her voice, then left the servant she had singled out. The servant came running up the stairs to reach her.

"Oui, mademoiselle?"

"What were you whispering about down there?"

The girl's eyes became large. She spoke softly. "We's a little scared is all, mademoiselle."

"Why?" Sarah asked.

"I cain't be sure. None us could. We juss cain't figure it out. But that man that come this morning and yesterday he be a slave trader and we's all wondering why our monsieur leave wit him in a hurry like he did."

"A trader? Are you sure? A slave trader?"

"Oui, mademoiselle."

"Has he been here before?"

"No, mademoiselle. We's wondering if Monsieur Pierre is selling one of us. And if us made him mad enough to sell us. It t'aint like him to do that…"

*Imogen!*

Sarah pressed a hand to her mouth and her stomach.

"Mademoiselle!" The girl wrapped her arms around Sarah's shoulder. "Maybe you need to rest. Monsieur Pierre will be rightly upset if anything happens to ya."

Sarah drew in a slow breath. "Is there a coach here?"

"Oui. I heard Monsieur Pierre tell Patrice to get a horse ready for him, so the coach is still here."

"Is Patrice the driver here? If he is tell him to get the coach ready. Now. Right away."

"Oh, no, mademoiselle!" The servant pulled Sarah's arm. "I can tell the time has come on you. I had five babies. I cain't let you leave here. Not now. Please."

"Leave go of me," Sarah said and tried to walk away. The girl held her arm and started yelling a variety of names. Sarah turned and slapped the girl's face. "Listen to me! I am not staying in this house. Now you get downstairs and get that coach ready like I told you."

The girl shook her head. "I's more scared of Master Pierre than you, mademoiselle."

Sarah turned from the girl. "Patrice! Which one of you is Patrice!"

Servants had run from separate parts of the mansion and reached her at the bottom of the stairs. A pain settled deep in her middle. Sarah knew if she showed that pain she was never leaving this house.

"Patrice," she asked tightly closing her eyes and taking a long slow breath as the pain subsided.

"He outside, mademoiselle," one of them answered.

"Tell him to get the coach ready. Hurry!"

The servant ran in the direction of the home's rear. Sarah followed behind her, breathing slowly through clenched teeth.

The servant named Patrice had come in the house and now came forward to face Sarah.

"Is the coach ready?" She asked him.

He glanced over Sarah's head. Sarah turned and saw the girl she had slapped gesturing wildly with her hands.

Sarah turned and faced Patrice. "I think I know the servant your master intends to sell. I need to get back and stop him. Please tell me you'll help me."

"Mademoiselle, from the looks of ya, you look like you'll rent a coach if I don't take you myself."

They were wasting time.

"Let us hurry," she said.

"Oh, no, mademoiselle. Please," the girl she slapped pleaded running closer. "Patrice be my man. Please don't make us turn on the master. He good to us. We won'ts no trouble. Please."

"Hitch the coach, Patrice," Sarah ordered. "I'll drive it myself if I have to."

Patrice looked at the other servants. All of them were looking at him, begging him not to do it. "What you all want me to do? If she walks out this house then all us sold."

"I think her time come, Patrice. Look at her!"

Sarah could see that Patrice was sensible and that he had the kind of confidence that most servants lacked. "Patrice, I need to leave now. I know you all are scared, but I am not staying in this house. I don't have time to find a coach to rent..."

"I'll take you, mademoiselle. But I must warn you. In your condition we can't ride too fast. Dossie, you come and go with us. When we gets there I'll explain to Master Pierre myself."

"When you get to the mansion cut to the south path," Sarah said. "My house is there."

Patrice nodded.

It took too many minutes to get the horses hooked up to the carriage, but Sarah could see that Patrice was working as quickly as he could. As soon as he swung open the back door Sarah climbed up and saw that the pillows she had used during her trip to the city had been taken out of the carriage and into the house. Still she climbed up and got as comfortable as she could.

The carriage moved slowly at first, the horses taking their time to maneuver the vehicle through the porte cochère. Sarah wished she had wings to fly. Unless Pierre kept his horse at a walk he would reach the plantation long before they would.

Paranoia spilled down her spine.

*Please, Pierre, don't do it*, she thought

A pain gripped her middle, but she had no time. No time at all. She felt a little easier when the coach began to roll, then picked up speed. She had been stupid. When Pierre left she should have insisted that she was leaving with him. Allowing him to leave alone meant when he reached Ashleywood he would be alone with Imogen. No one would be there to stop him. He could do whatever he wanted. *I won't be ashamed. I need to make this up to her.*

*Oh, God!* She thought. Surely this couldn't be the reason he would sell Imogen, not when Alise also lived at the plantation.

It was hours before the trees outside the coach became familiar. It wasn't long now. They were almost there.

When the coach should have rolled through the Ashleywood entrance it kept straight in the direction of the west fields. It was then she realized she hadn't given Patrice explicit instructions.

Patrice must have realized his mistake, and taking an even longer time than when they had first left, he managed to turn the coach around and head in the right direction. Sarah's heart pounded in her chest when Patrice turned on the south path and the carriage began rolling again. Here the ground was uneven, as the ground hadn't been made level. There had been no need to do so. Sarah hadn't had a need of a coach yet, and when she did she had been with Pierre and taken to the carriage house.

Patrice was unfamiliar with this part of the plantation and ended up driving the carriage behind her *maison* alongside the thick tangle of trees. The wheels of the carriage dipped heavily causing him to slow down at a walking pace.

Sarah sat taller on the seat cushion trying her best to see between the trees and toward the front of her *maison*. As they neared and the ground became rougher she saw an old battered cart waiting on her front lawn. The carriage was now barely rolling. All Sarah had to do was run and she would beat the carriage to the front of her house.

"Stop! Stop! Stop!" She cried.

Patrice heard her and stopped the carriage, then ran to the back door and opened it, peeking in as if he had expected to see her giving birth.

"Help me down," she said.

He grabbed her hands and helped her to the ground.

Once her feet were firmly on the ground she ran. When she skirted the side of the *maison* she looked up, and there, at that moment, she saw the scene that was taking place in front of it. A tear rolled down her cheek, but she had no time to cry. No time. She had to reach Pierre and convince him that still everything could be all right.

She lifted the hem of her gown hating that she had to come all the way around the house then past it to reach where everything was happening. She ran as fast as she could across the heads of the small white flowers that sprinkled the grass, but it wasn't fast enough. She could see the driver of the battered cart sitting close to the trees. The man who had been at the mansion in the city stood up in the front of the cart with a whip curled at his thigh.

Overseers Langers and Almonester carried Imogen kicking and screaming across the grass toward the cart. In the distance Pierre held Désireé and Alise back, because both women were crying and pleading with him not to do what he was doing.

"No!" Sarah yelled.

Imogen was tossed into the back of the cart.

"No," Sarah screamed when manacles were placed on Imogen's wrists. "She's never been chained before!"

Imogen saw the manacles and went wild, bucking and pulling, screaming and pleading. And when her eyes became grotesquely white with fright the stranger showed her the curl of his whip then allowed it to unfurl to the ground.

"Imogen! Imogen!"

Sarah was closer, but not close enough. Imogen heard her voice and turned, and so did Pierre. He pushed roughly at Désireé and Alise, yelling at them to stay where they were.

Imogen's animalistic sobs came to an abrupt end. She knelt tranquilly. Langers fastened a wooden harness around Imogen's neck. Imogen was being brave now. Even from Sarah's vantage a hint of bewilderment shone in Imogen's eyes. Tears rained down her face. Her always-neat hair was wild and her lips kept moving as if she was saying a silent prayer. Langers and Almonester climbed out of the cart. The stranger driving the cart saw Sarah. For a moment he stared at her in confusion, and then as if he sensed the prevention of the sale, he hurried and sat down and slapped at the reins. Imogen lost her balance and fell backward.

"Imogen!" Sarah had reached the cart just as it started to move. Her feet pumped faster. Her hand reached out to grip it the wood only inches from her fingers. She had to save Imogen. Yellow hands lifted over the edge of the cart; it was followed by Imogen's face.

"Sarah!" Imogen cried no longer able to keep her fears at bay. "He'll listen to you! Please tell him to let me stay! Please tell him to let me stay!"

The cart choked with speed, its wheels spinning.

Sarah ran, but the cart moved faster and faster and further and further away from her reach. Sarah stopped running. No air moved in her lungs. Still she managed to yell, "Imogen!"

The wagon rode away fiercely, rocking side by side; twin horses tails could be seen as racing hooves kicked up pieces of the ground. The wheels crunched and whirled.

"*Imooooogen!*"

The cart veered on three wheels as it turned the curve on the path, then disappeared behind the girth of an outcrop of trees.

Imogen was gone.

Sarah's knees trembled. The sky spun dizzily over her head. Images of Imogen hugging her tightly against her breasts and peeking around corners to overhear if she and Pierre were discussing her fate came to mind.

Sarah saw thin clouds merge into one massive curtain. For the first time in her life she felt the need to ask why. "God...?"

Pierre had been racing in her direction. He reached her just as she collapsed, and everything – everything – around her turned black.

*\*\**

When she awoke she didn't know what day it was, but she knew she'd been lying in the same position for some time. Many voices spoke from opposite sides of the bed.

"Come on, Mademoiselle," someone coaxed. "We have one. Now it's time for the other."

Sarah tried to open her eyes. Her eyelids felt heavy and fused together. One side of her face felt stuck against bone. Where had the trader taken Imogen? She had been sixteen when her Tante Marianne confessed she was her mother. Before that day Sarah had mentioned on many occasions when the two of them had talked how she had longed to know who her mother was, and how excited she would be to hold that woman in her arms.

She tried to reach up. Her arm felt strange and heavy. Vigorous hands pressed down on top of her, holding her firmly in place. Bedding had been stuffed underneath her knees for support. She blinked and her eyes opened momentarily. As they closed the image of her naked body lying on top of the bed stayed with her, along with the image of her stomach which had taken on the shape of a crescent.

Why did her body feel stiff, feverish and bruised? Voices continued to prod her.

"Be still, mademoiselle."

"Lay back now, mademoiselle."

"Push, mademoiselle, push."

No matter the pieces of thought or memory that swam through her mind, all of them reverted back to one question. *Where was Imogen?* The confusion of movements and voices escalated the tempest being had in her brain. Like two separate choirs singing in a mournful variety of vocal ranges, and each just as loud, the discord throbbed and swelled. The anxiety of it all was remonstrated by her attempt to lift a hand. Someone seized it. The need to still the room in silence came from deep within. "Leave go of me! Turn me loose."

Water trickled near her ear. The voices continued as a hand dabbed a cool cloth across her brow. Pain came out of nowhere; it started deep in her middle. Like tentacles with an electrifying pulse it traveled through every limb of her body and reached her head. Fearing the loss of her faculties, as there was no part of her that hadn't stiffened until the muscles were beyond tense; to rid herself of it she bore down. The teeth in her mouth ground against each other as the pain wrenched her in two. It was then that her eyes open.

A ceiling circled like a rabid vulture above. A second pain hit at once. An innate urgency to push felt as if the bowels of her soul were slowly tearing from her body. Tightening her body even more she pushed. Enormous pain burned from within.

"Push," five voices screamed at once.

No words could describe the sound that came out of her mouth. A gush of water trickled out of her. It was followed by the melodic drawl of a feeble cat's meow. Like a weak kitten, the cry was soft, tender, helpless and pleasant to those around it. There were exclamations of ten toes, ten fingers and a thatch of angelic white hair.

Alise cried on the sight of the baby. Désireé clasped her hands to her mouth and laughed and cried inconsolably. Mableane and Noémi cuddled in a fierce embrace in the corner. It was here. The second baby had been born and was still alive.

And then – at that moment – the carved Chippendale rosewood bed began to violently shake.

"She's having another seizure," Dr. Marchand announced. Too weary from all that had been endured he had no strength to yell or to feel any kind of excitement. This birth from the beginning had been out of his hands and in the hands of no one else other than the Lord. As he continued to work on his patient he had the confidence of knowing that if the mother now died he had done all that he could. "I'm going to need more water. And more towels. The seizure would have to run its course. She's bleeding heavily and I need to attend to the bleeding first."

The first seizure had been small, but this was one was long and exhausting. The bed continued to make movements. Noémi cried. Désireé wiped dejectedly at the warmth of what had been happy tears.

"Oh, Lord," Noémi cried. "She's dying."

Alise fell to her knees and made the symbol of the cross with her fingers across her forehead and chest. With earnest supplication she mumbled her prayer as she beseeched the Martyr Stephen.

Noémi, unable to face the inevitable any longer, ran from the room to get ready candles that would soon be burned for the dead.

Désireé also ran out of the room. For hours Pierre had paced the hall refusing to leave it until he had received the last and final news. Seeing her papa she gripped his hand and pulled at him. No man, whether respectable or poor, should ever clasp eyes on a woman while in the throes of giving birth. This did little to dissuade him from entering the room. If Désireé sought to pull him inside he knew she wouldn't have done so without a proper reason.

The chaos happening around the bed unnerved him. Little had he imagined that beyond the closed door such a unification of Sarah's apparent indecency spurred little regard for it.

"Papa, you are the powerful *le diable*. Surely you can do something."

"Blasphemy!" He hissed searching his daughter's eyes hoping to see she had not meant what she inferred. Those eyes became wide with disappointment. "Papa?"

Pierre tore himself from her gaze when the Chippendale bed thrashed violently while Sarah had another seizure. As if its tremors had unbalanced his feet, others in the room stopped what they were doing and pressed hands to their mouths when *le diable* collapsed to his knees.

"Don't change her position!" Dr. Marchand yelled. "I'm working on her. Please stay back. I need to make sure if she survives the seizures she won't die in a different way from my inattention."

Like Alise, Pierre's fingers performed the cross from his forehead to chest before entwining in the symbol of prayer. Aloud was his supplication to the Martyr Stephen. "If it will be thy will, Martyr Stephen, please intercede and tell God that *le diable* will gladly give his life for hers."

His words frightened the servants who had been taught from a young age Catholicism. In their eyes it was blasphemous for their monsieur to perceive himself in such a highly position to barter with God. Hearing his words brought the fear of a jealous God striking the room with His vengeance. So it was with no surprise when they noticed no further movement on top of the bed.

Pierre, feeling the shaking had stopped, dared open his eyes and saw his beloved lying sweaty and naked. At that moment he was certain like the others that Sarah Isabelle Cheval was dead.

***

Dr. Marchand stayed at the *maison* six days keeping a constant vigil at the bedside. Herbs were crushed and made into teas. A fever had taken possession of his patient's body. No sooner than it was brought under control it flourished just as rapidly with hell-bent determination. Unfamiliar with the peyote tea that others on the plantation swore saved Julien's life, he refused his patient drinking any and stuck with the practices he knew. Poultices and cool baths were administered with the help of the master of the plantation who had made it clear he would not be removed from the room.

This decision made Dr. Marchand feel as if he had two lives to save. Unsure if the malady had become airborne; his last wish was for the master of the plantation to meet his decline inside this room. Because his patient was in a sound sleep similar to those suffering the last stages of Yellow Jack, purging the illness with calomel and other medicines were futile, as she was unable to swallow at times. Bleeding his patient had been done, but not as long as he wished, as her skin had become pale at the start.

Resorting to other methods to cure her, he ordered servants to burn a continuous fire in the yard, as well as ordered all of the French doors in Sarah's room left open so the miasma caused by the fire could whisk away and destroy the disease that was trying to take her life.

At certain hours of the day Alise, Désireé and Gorée came into the room to burn candles. Dr. Marchand did not dissuade these visits. Secretly he relished in them. A tiny altar had been erected on a nearby dresser. In front of it sat a single prie dieu. As Alise kneeled on top of it her fingers rubbing the beads of a rosary. Dr. Marchand also prayed unaware that Pierre was doing the same.

Whether it was by his ministrations or if one of the many prayers were answered on the seventh day Sarah blinked twice, then opened her eyes. Dr. Marchand and Pierre jumped to their feet. After her eyes became acclimated to the room she sat up like one would when its soul departed in search of heaven.

***

Hours later after she had been bathed and the linen on the bed changed, Alise and two servants, to the dissatisfaction of the others inside the *maison*, bring the babies into the room.

Sarah sat up, took one look at her children, then fell back against the mattress and rolled on her side with her arms holding her body tightly together.

313

SHELLEY YOUNG

Alise and Désireé gazed at one another with raised eyebrows believing Sarah's reaction was her way of refusing the children she had nearly died given birth to. Neither knew that it had been the rushed way in which she sat that caused her muscles to seize up to prevent further activity.

The two of them said nothing. Alise nodded for the servants to take the children away. Désireé peeked onto the other side of the bed. A lone tear squeezed from Sarah's eyes as she rocked slightly in what Désireé believed to be despair.

Sarah became speechless to the pain. It had been foolish of her to move so suddenly, especially after she'd been told it had been a week since she properly used her limbs. As the pain slowly ebbed the rocking gave her a sense of comfort. Behind her closed eyelids, she saw the faces of her children and longed for Alise to keep them near.

Later that evening he came. Sarah kept her chin level as she stared at him. Pillows had been placed around the bed so she sat up more than she lay down. The scent he brought with him was all telling. Harsh liquor. A little earlier she had heard a servant mention their master and how the servants on the plantation now regaled him as *mon maître ivre*. My master the drunkard.

The nimiety of remorse that shone in his eyes was hard for her to look upon, but turning away from them was the same as turning away the many facets of his true character. This man whom she had loved during long days of leisure, refined conversations, childish moments when he tickled her mercilessly, and vowed to love her more than any other had a part of his heart so darkened by the fear of others that he had torn the very life from her. No more will she be charmed and ignorant to the callous behavior she now knew he could exude at his own free will.

It didn't appear as if there was any fight in him. The door was closed behind him. He crossed the width of the room closing each of the French doors. Only then did he face her. The way he walked toward the bed like an errant child approaching his father made her breathe rapidly while tears flowed from her eyes. It was hard for her not to make any sound as he brought a chair closer and sat like someone crippled by pain in every joint. The white parts of his eyes were tinged red. Sarah was uncertain if she was seeing the results of heavy drinking or if he, like her, had cried many tears.

"Sarah…"

She shook her head to quiet him. He said enough already in the way he walked and in the forlorn look in his eyes and in his very appearance.

"Where is she, Pierre? Where's Imogen?"

He folded his hands together, closed his eyes and pressed his face against it. "I can't tell you that, Sarah."

"Do you love me, Pierre?" It had been hard for her to get the words out. So hard was she trying to hold back the tears that her chest kept shivering; her constant need to swallow made it sound like she was gulping water.

"With all my heart, mon amour."

"How could you do it, Pierre? You didn't even give me the chance to tell her I now knew."

314

He rocked slowly from side to side with his face still pressed against his hands. A small breath was taken as he lifted his face and looked at her with lowered eyelids. "I had to send her far from here."

A cry escaped her.

"Sarah, please listen to me. You would have given it away. Imogen would have given it away. The two of you were far too close, far closer than a mademoiselle should be with her servant. You allowed her to live *here* in this house when all the other servants were sent to their cabins each evening. Once the children were born Imogen would have loved them perhaps more than she loved you. The other servants would have become suspicious. If Jenna ever learned the truth – I couldn't risk it. She would have used it against you just to hurt you, to make you suffer. She would have used it against me to force me to make Edouard my heir. And my daughters would have suffered for it. I couldn't risk the court upholding her petition, as he was born from my marriage while our children were born from the daughter of a slave."

"You could have done anything else!"

Sarah realized he was under the influence when he tried to move, suddenly, and swayed. He had to sit still, and then he closed his eyes. Sarah could only imagine he was waiting for the room to stop spinning. Her father had often made this complaint when he drank heavily.

"Something else." His voice was close to a whisper as he repeated her words.

"She loved it here, Pierre. She was happy for the first time in her life. I won't *ever* forgive you for this. Why are you shielding me from Jenna when I see you are far worse than she is?"

"Don't say that," he said holding her gaze.

She averted her gaze and closed her eyes.

Exactly when he left she wasn't certain.

Hours passed by very swiftly. Closing her eyes was sometimes the difference between night and day. Constant footsteps moved around the room throughout the days as they passed. Eyes often peered inside of hers. Cognizant of them, as well as being bathed and dressed, her mind continued to spiral.

During the night she heard her Tante Marianne whimpering and pleading not to be hurt anymore by three strange men. During the day she thought back on servants that had done horrible things on Green Lea. There was good and bad in everyone. This made her believe that every race was the same. At other times she could feel William, and smell his sour oniony scent as he pressed her into a closed door while trying to lift her skirts and make her his wife in body if nothing else. Tears always came to her eyes when she remembered Imogen crying and pleading to stay in what she believed to be slave heaven.

She blinked and continued to stare at the mattress when loud male voices could be heard outside. At first she paid no heed until she heard her father's name mentioned. The stranger's voice continued even when Overseer Almonester tried to get him to slow down.

So far Sarah made out that the man had come all the way from Biloxi. With regret he explained that he was a creditor on official business. Emile Cheval was dead. Five days ago he had gone into a saloon, sat in a chair, and drank long into the night. When the owner of the saloon realized that his best customer hadn't ordered another drink in the past half hour, he walked to where Emile sat and saw that his face had gone white and his heart had stopped.

Almost all of the money Pierre had given her father when he left New Orléans had been stolen away when he put his trust in a man to start a business with him. The man, Buford Dickey, signed a contract to rent a building for a year. Equipment was placed on order and delivered to the new address. All of the things her father needed to become a self-made man were swiftly obtained with ease only for her father to discover that the building, equipment and supplies had been purchased on credit in his name. By then Buford Dickey was nowhere to be found. The man believed he had left Biloxi with the money her father had given him.

The creditor had come to New Orléans with a court order that stated he was the rightful owner of one female slave named Imogen Cheval, Emile's last remaining slave and only asset, and any child born to her, because Emile had listed Imogen as collateral for any debts unpaid on many other business affairs. Almonester, who had come to the *maison* in place of his employer, explained that Imogen was no longer there. It was then the creditor said what he said next.

"We already found Imogen, Mister, and have her in our custody. She'll be sold at the next auction, but God knows not much can be got for her in her condition. The real reason I'm here is because Imogen had a daughter."

"Daughter?" Almonester asked. "I can't say I know who that is. I don't remember Imogen arriving here with anyone. As far as I knew she came here alone. What's her daughter's name?"

"That's the thing, Mister. When asked Imogen refused to give a name. Need I remind you that since Imogen is a slave the law says any child born to her is also a slave? I hear you have a lot of mulattoes on this land. If you look at that court order it says I'm entitled to Imogen and *any* child born to her, as they were the rightful property of Mr. Cheval."

"I can ask Monsieur Cheval's daughter if she knows anything about it."

"Sarah Cheval is here on this land?"

"Monsieur, I know I told you that I can speak in the capacity of my employer, but I think we now need to get him involved."

"Do that, Mister, because I'm not leaving here until I have what's owed to me. Is she here or not, Miss Sarah Cheval? I think a man by the name of William Murray will be interested in hearing this. From what I heard he and Miss Cheval should have been married, but she pulled out of the arrangement at the last minute. I wonder why she did this."

"If you follow me to the plantation mansion…"

"This isn't the mansion?"

There was a hesitation and in that hesitation Sarah knew the man was sizing up the house wondering who resided in it.

"The mansion is further up the road," Almonester said.

"This is the Ashleywood plantation, is it not? I was told to come up this road and knock on the door of the first large house I came upon. I came by horse and cut through the trees for fear of rain and found this one."

"Monsieur, if you come with me I'm sure my employer can clear up this matter rather quickly."

"I hope so. I heard about him, of course. The Devil is what they call him. I'll tell you now that I won't stand for any shenanigans. Maybe you should tell him that when you get him alone. If I have to come back with the police or get permission from the courts to go through every slave here until I find Imogen's daughter, I will."

Footsteps could be heard and then silence.

Sarah stayed as she was. If the man went to the mansion saying the same things he said now, if Jenna heard only a part she would deduce who Imogen was talking about. Jenna would become thrilled from the news, especially after Sarah had beaten her pantry door with an ax. It also meant that Jenna could petition the court in the event of Pierre's death if he listed one of Sarah's children as his beneficiary. As things were now the court would decide in Jenna's favor. The Américains had succeeded in lessening the number of new free people of color in New Orléans. Months ago Julien had petitioned to have Anne manumitted. The petition was denied with no excuse given. The Américains may think little about Faubourg Tremé where many of the *gens de couleur libres* had settled, but awarding a free person of color to inherit a large amount of real estate in the city, as well as making this person the wealthiest in the entire South would not be tolerated.

Sarah rolled onto her back. Weakness made her muscles tremble. Over the past days she wasn't certain how much she had eaten or if she had eaten at all. Her father was dead. Imogen was again to be sold. If Jenna told the stranger that Sarah Cheval was in fact Imogen's daughter the stranger had every right not only taking Sarah with him, but also the children she had given birth to. It didn't matter if Pierre was their father or how wealthy Pierre was. The law was detailed in this matter and had been put into motion just for this reason, so white men couldn't walk on any plantation and take children from it that he believed were his.

Pushing back the coverlets she was reaching a leg over the bed when the door pushed open.

Alise saw her trying to climb out of bed and hurried to where she was.

"They're coming," Sarah whispered. "Hide my children!"

Alise pressed her back into the bed, then leaned close and whispered. "Pierre will kill that man before he allowed him to walk off of this land with his daughters. And after he did that he would put you and the children on a ship to France and gladly hang before he lets anyone get their hands on you and the girls."

"Girls?" Sarah whispered.

Alise smiled prettily as she tugged on the coverlets to cover Sarah up.

"Girls," she repeated. "I'm glad to see you're again in the land of the living. Don't think about them at the moment. Let me get you cleaned up and fed. You need to get your strength up."

"Alise!" Sarah grabbed Alise's hand, fear visible in her eyes.

Alise leaned close and whispered. "It's all right, Sarah. You may have lost faith in him, but I haven't."

It was a short while later when Sarah heard Pierre enter the *maison*. His voice carried down the hall, but Sarah couldn't make out what he was saying. As her heart raced she listened carefully for the sound of his footsteps coming toward her door.

Alise was still inside her boudoir helping her get cleaned up, dressed and the linens changed. As of yet Sarah hadn't seen her daughters, except for the brief moment Alise and Désireé had brought them into the room. Anxious to hear about the stranger and what had happened once he reached the mansion, she tried her best to move faster. It was as a pair of hose was being pulled up her legs when she heard Jenna's voice carry down the hall.

Sarah and Alise recognized the voice and stared a long while at the door in silence.

Sarah then looked at Alise.

Alise shook her head.

"Have faith," she whispered.

Someone knocked.

"A moment, please," Alise yelled out.

Now both of them were hurrying. As soon as she was dressed, Alise helped her sit in a chair. A small blanket was placed over Sarah's lap. A small footstool was pushed underneath her feet. Only when the remaining French doors were opened and the room was once again inspected by Alise was the door opened.

Sarah waited in dread; because once the door had opened she also heard the voice of the stranger. A conversation was taking place down the hall, and then, finally, footsteps were making their way to the rear of the house.

Sarah was unable to move her eyes from the door until she saw exactly who was coming inside her boudoir. Pierre led the way with Jenna a step behind. And behind Jenna was the stranger. He looked nothing like Sarah had envisioned from the sound of his voice. Tall and muscular and dressed in fine clothing, his facial hair meticulously groomed. He put Sarah in the mind of a sheriff.

The man was shown to a settee against the wall. He waited politely for Jenna to sit before he did the same.

"Hello, Miss," he began, nodding his head in Sarah's direction.

"Mademoiselle…" Pierre began.

When he began with a formal address, Sarah's heart raced faster than it already did.

"Mr. Robeson is here inquiring about a servant whom he believes was born to Imogen. Do you know anything about this?"

Sarah saw him pleading with his eyes, hoping she would answer the way he anticipated.

Sarah opened her mouth.

"This is absurd!" Jenna hissed, staring first at Mr. Robeson, then at Pierre. "Imogen had but one child and that child was sold years ago. Why you insist on speaking to my sister regarding this matter when you can see how ill she is warns us all that your greed has encumbered your sense of judgment!"

Mr. Robeson ignored every word while he kept his eyes on Sarah and examined her thoroughly from her head to her feet. Sarah saw the way he was looking at her and understood. He hadn't come for Imogen. He had come for her. She became more certain of this when the two of them ignored everyone else and held each other's gaze as both of them saw the truth staring back at them.

"Jenna, please keep quiet, chérie. I want Mr. Robeson to hear what Sarah has to say about the matter. Maybe then he will be satisfied and take the offer I've given him."

"It's your offer that perplexes me, Mr. Jennings. So easily did you offer a good settlement for a person you and your wife claims doesn't exist. I have laid eyes on Imogen. She's quite fair, and as you know, the lighter the skin the more money could be had for such a slave woman if sold. I feel I have every right to see this woman first. Only then can I see for myself if what you offered is fair."

"Fair?" Pierre's eyes hardened, as did every muscle in his body. A step was taken closer to the settee. "My offer wasn't to replace property you deem yours, but in good faith, monsieur, as it was I who sold Imogen not realizing I had no authority to do so."

"Tell him, Sarah!" Jenna begged, staring with wide eyes at Sarah. "He's already heard it from me and the servants that Imogen arrived here alone."

Sarah found she couldn't breathe.

Pierre calmed and sat in a chair not too far from the settee.

Alise entered the room with a bundled blanket in her arms. The child was given to Sarah. Sarah stared down at the face of her daughter. Through a blur of tears she watched as Désireé entered the room with the second child.

"You'll forgive me, Mr. Robeson," Alise interrupted, "but Mademoiselle Cheval needs to see to her children. It will only take a moment."

The infant in Sarah's arms had a thick head of ghostly white hair. She had the Jennings narrow nose structure and the same flared shape of the mouth like a dove in flight. The coat of arms Sarah had sewn on almost everything, including the small blanket the child had been wrapped in, was tucked underneath the babe's chin. Alise fingered the crest as she stared intently into Sarah's eyes.

"Sarah?" Pierre spoke softly. "I know you're not well. But it is most inappropriate for any of us to be in your boudoir at a time like this."

Sarah looked down at her daughter. The babe looked so much like Pierre that it was startling to see.

"I've known Imogen all my life," Sarah said, lifting her eyes to Mr. Robeson. Her mouth trembled as she spoke. "If she had a daughter, I was never aware of it."

The smallest smile appeared on Mr. Robeson's face. He settled back and got comfortable. "I'm from Biloxi, Miss Cheval. It's amazing what you learn when you put the fear of God in a slave. I find they're more truthful if they fear the taste of a whip. I must admit. Imogen is the only slave gal I wasn't able to anything out of. When she did speak she made the same claims your sister has made. But you see. Mr. Cheval visited here not long ago, and the first person he visited when he returned to Biloxi was Mr. William Murray. According to Mr. Murray, although your father was intoxicated, he made mention of a conversation he had with Mr. Jennings. Imogen was mentioned in that conversation." He leaned forward.

Pierre leaned toward him.

Jenna jumped to her feet. "Pierre! I too feel an urge to slap Mr. Robeson's face for inferring that you and I would pass anyone on this plantation off as *passé blanc*, but let's do calm ourselves."

Mr. Robeson's eyebrows became harsh slants. His eyes hardened the same way someone did when they heard something they considered offensive. His top lip tightened into a sharp line and bared his teeth. Determination masked his face. "Your father is in great debt to Mr. Murray. He wishes to lay claims on any living children Imogen may have."

Sarah rose slowly to her feet. With a confident and unsteady gait she walked to the bed and laid the infant on top of it. And then she swung around, suddenly. At that moment she forgot that anyone else was in the room; her eyes were as tight on Mr. Robeson's as his were on her. Crossing to him, she noticed three things: Mr. Robeson didn't stand when she had although it was the proper thing to do, the noted malevolence in his eyes, and his enmity toward les noirs.

As she stood beside the settee staring at him, he continued to stare at her.

"Did you know my father?" She whispered.

"I did."

The need to make him never forget her name was the reason her arm pulled behind her back before she drew it hard in front of her and slapped the side of his face. The strike had so much energy in it that she was propelled back from it and nearly toppled off of her feet. Mr. Robeson's boots kicked out in front of him as his body slid almost out of the settee and his head bounced against its back cushion.

A shadow had come behind Sarah. She ignored it. Mr. Robeson's eyes were now wide with alarm as they peered up at her in utter shock.

"If you know my father's name then you know mine is Mademoiselle Cheval. Say it! I want to hear you say it!"

No time was given for him to fully take in what she said or to answer. The second slap had been aimed at his left eye. Sarah felt the roundness of it against her palm as she slapped fire to it. Before he could recover a third slap was aimed at his mouth.

"Say my name!" She yelled. "How dare you look at me as if I'm dung stuck to the sole of your boot. How dare you disrespect me with your tone. How dare you think you would come here, cart me away and put me and my children on an auction block. You think I'm pretending to be who I am? No, sir. I am Mademoiselle Sarah Isabelle Cheval, and I will gladly leave here and go with you to Biloxi. And there, sir, I shall ruin you and Monsieur Murray. I will travel far and wide and visit every city I can in the North to let them know that you, sir, would sell any skin color, including white, as well as tell them that no one's family is safe because of your indelible sentiment on slavery."

Mr. Robeson adjusted his attire and stood slowly to his feet.

Pierre grabbed Sarah by her shoulders and moved her gently to one side.

"Mr. Robeson, I find your behavior more than repulsive. That you would even come here with such intendment all because a paper signed by a judge entitles you to recover the debts of your clients disgusts me. I take back my offer, as I see now that even making it caused you to believe it was my intentions to defraud you. My wife and her sister have just learned that their father is dead! I shall tell everyone that instead of being given a moment to grieve they now need to fear being sold by the pound to cover a dead man's death and a wealthy man's sinister desire."

Jenna burst into tears. A kerchief was pulled out of her sleeve and pressed tightly to her face as she sobbed loud enough to wake the child on the bed. Tears rolled down Sarah's face for many reasons as she stared across the room at her sister. Seeing Jenna wail with grief compounded the emotions she already felt. Gasping for breath, Sarah's bodice quivered as the expression on her face forewarned she was on the verge of losing all sanity.

Pierre lowered his head as if he too was close to tears.

Alise rushed across the room when Jenna became so besotted with tears that she almost toppled off of the settee and onto the rug.

Sarah watched as Pierre crossed to the fireplace, gripped its mantle and hung his head. She pressed a hand against her mouth, her tears and sorrow winning its battle to be released. "Poor papa. Poor Imogen. Will this family ever have peace?"

Jenna's legs kicked out from underneath her exposing a portion of her hose. Alise had two hands pressed against Jenna's bodice in the hopes of pinning her to the settee. Jenna's arms flailed wildly; her head thrashed back and forth. Alise's face made a severe pinch.

"Papa's dead!" Jenna screamed loud and painfully. "Oh, Papa! Papa!"

The babe on the bed also began to wail. Sarah lifted her daughter in her arms, rocking the child as she realized that her father would never see or hold his grandchild. When she looked up she saw that Mr. Robeson had been watching with saddened eyes.

Pierre hurried across the room and held Jenna in his arms.

"Burn down the saloon that only thought of money and allowed him to drink himself to death. Oh, Papa! Oh, Papa!" Jenna wailed.

Pierre gave gentle pats to her spine in an attempt to calm her, and then Jenna toppled to the floor.

Sarah saw that Jenna's face was so buried into Pierre's clothes as he held her that she feared Jenna would suffocate. "She can't breathe! Watch her face!" It wasn't until after she spoke these words that she realized she still loved Jenna very deeply. Turning her face toward her right shoulder, she sobbed silently for more reasons than her father's death.

Jenna pulled from Pierre's arms and stared at Sarah. "Our papa is dead." Tears fell swiftly from her eyes. "We shall see him no more." She spoke the words brokenly and in between gasps.

Mr. Robeson hung his head. "I'm sorry I came here. Please do excuse my behavior. I had heard so much of a man who was the devil in living flesh that I had convinced myself that the only way to deal with you all here is with harshness. I was also told by Mr. Murray that once Mrs. Jennings heard the truth, the kind of woman she was she would never abide someone with black blood to be claimed as her family. I see now that nothing I was told was true and you two sisters love each other despite the rumors I've heard. Forgive my manners, and do please help your Missus. Maybe a doctor should be fetched. I'll show myself to the door."

Pierre ignored Mr. Robeson and buried his face in Jenna's hair.

Mr. Robeson saw Pierre's refusal to accept his apology, nodded respectfully and turned to leave the room.

Désireé stepped closer to him. "Mr. Robeson, Imogen was a faithful servant to Madame Jennings and her sister, Mademoiselle Cheval. I'm sure Imogen will be a comfort to them while they grieve the loss of their father. If you can tell us when and where she will be sold."

"Imogen?" Mr. Robeson asked gently, and then his facial expression became grim.

Sarah's mouth opened wide as she breathed heavily through it because she believed Mr. Robeson would say Imogen was also dead.

Mr. Robeson stared at Pierre, who also looked as if he feared what would come out of the man's mouth. Mr. Robeson saw this and drew in a deep breath. "I misled you to believe that Imogen was in my custody. The truth is she's already been sold and is currently on her way by foot to her new master. The details regarding the sale I'm unable to offer, as the sale was a private one. Of course, you being a businessman, Mr. Jennings, I'm sure you can understand that."

Pierre nodded at him.

"Do forgive me," Mr. Robeson said and left before anyone could try and detain him.

Sarah took small breaths as she rocked the babe in her arms. She hadn't realized she had closed her eyes until sometime after her door closed and Jenna spoke softly. "Is that damn beastly Américain gone?"

Pierre turned to Désireé and whispered equally low. "Go out the back and tell the first person you see to watch that bastard until he's off my land, then come back and tell me everything he did."

Désireé handed Alise the second baby and hurried out of the nearest French door.

Alise sat on the settee next to Jenna and smiled. "I've seen you perform in the past, but not nearly as well as you have just now."

Pierre crossed the room to Sarah. Sarah leaned to one side to look past him and watched Jenna. The look on her face and she knew Jenna hadn't been pretending, at least not this time. Regret for the way she had treated their father for many years still showed on her face. Taking a deep breath, Jenna scooted closer to Alise and forced a smile on her face. "He was a determined fellow, was he not?"

Sarah's heart broke more into two when she saw this, because Jenna was pretending now to mask the truth.

"And most sure headed," Alise confirmed not realizing, because everyone on the plantation had become convinced that Jenna had no heart.

Sarah watched as Pierre smiled across the room at Jenna. "I thought when Maman pressed her hands hard into your chest you would come out of your performance."

Alise leaned closer to Jenna and giggled as if they were two young girls caught whilst in the middle of a prank.

Jenna continued to smile. "Her hands were so hard and so heavy I thought it was you. That's why I started bucking wildly. I wanted that uncouth Américain to feel as bad as I could make him."

Pierre threw back his head and gave a quiet laugh.

Sarah stared at Alise.

Alise looked at Jenna as if the two of them had been friends for years instead of enemies. "I started to press my hands over your mouth, but then I realized Mr. Robeson needed to hear you scream some more. I saw the way your tears were breaking him up like brittle kindling."

"The fall to the floor, Jenna," Pierre added. "It convinced me you *weren't* pretending. I thought you had truly gone mad."

Sarah noticed how his words affected Jenna. Looking up, a small glimmer of hope had come into her eyes and then she looked away. It surprised Sarah that no one could see that Jenna was now pretending. How little did they know her sister after all of the years she had lived on this plantation. And it looked to Sarah that Jenna didn't want them to know her as she truly was.

"I wasn't trying to fall," Jenna confessed. "The fall *was* real. The look on my face was real."

Alise and Pierre laughed until tears squeezed from their eyes.

"What do you think he's going to do now, Pierre?" Alise asked.

Pierre smiled at Sarah. "I think Sarah slapped the fear of God into him."

Sarah marveled when she saw Alise throw back her head and bellow the same way Julien did.

Jenna looked across the room and noticed how closely Pierre stood next to Sarah, and the look that had come into his eyes when he last spoke.

She stood to her feet.

Alise saw the expression on Jenna's face and also stood. When Jenna started to walk away Alise gripped Jenna's hand as if to question her, and then she looked over her shoulder at Pierre and Sarah. Her hand fell away as she averted her gaze.

"I forgot," Jenna began, "that all of you are convinced that I'm the only devil here." Tears fell from her eyes as she stared at Sarah. "Don't think I don't know who your mother is. Why do you think I never helped Tante Marianne? Why do you think she sent for you when I stopped giving Papa money? Why do you think I hate you so much? I was the one who found Papa and Tante Marianne in a fierce embrace. Both of them naked. All I knew was what I saw hadn't been right, so I ran and told my mother. My mother, Tante Marianne and my father hated me for telling what I did. Tante Marianne and Papa went away after that, and my mother hated me more. When they returned they brought you back with them. My mother wanted you out of the house. My father purposely brought you to Green Lea so my mother could take care of you financially. My father refused to send you away. Papa told my mother that the day you left that house he would leave too and make a life with Tante Marianne. Because of you I lost the love of my mother. She blamed me until the day she died for her failed marriage, and Papa blamed me for telling her. And then there you were living in my mother's house as if you were the rightful heir to it. Papa forgot about me after you were born and loved you more, because you were Tante Marianne's child, the woman he wished he could have married."

Alise and Pierre gazed at each other silently, because neither had known these things.

Jenna stared soberly at Alise. "My Tante Marianne and my mother never saw each other again. Tante Marianne didn't even come to my mother's funeral. My mother refused to care for Sarah, so my father gave her to Imogen to see after. Imogen was happy to have her, because Sarah reminded her so much of her young daughter that had been sold. My mother sold Imogen's child, because she knew who its father was. The child's name was Meera, and she wasn't my father's only *bâtard*."

Jenna faced Pierre.

"You're just like my father. Every bit!" She yelled. "You could have picked anyone, but you chose your wife's sister just like he did. Why Pierre?" She then looked at Sarah. "And you are just like your mother. You could have married someone else, but you chose to move onto my land and steal my husband and have his children. I hate you now even more than I did before. The only reason I came here is because I know you know Pierre's secret and I didn't want you telling that secret to Mr. Robeson. I don't trust you and I never will. I refuse for you to hurt Edouard to get back at me!"

Pierre hurried to Jenna when she looked ready to collapse.

"I hate her!" She screamed as he lifted her in his arms and held her tightly against him. "She's the reason my mother died of a broken heart. My poor Edouard. She will ruin him just to get revenge against me and for her children to become heirs to Ashleywood."

Sarah hurried across the room following Pierre out of her boudoir and into the hall. "I didn't know, Jenna. Please come back and let's make this right."

Jenna gave a painful scream gripping Pierre tighter and wailing from the top of her lungs. "I hate her! And I hate you! I hate all of you here."

Alise laid the baby on the bed and went after Sarah. With a heavy heart she gripped Sarah by the shoulders and led her back inside the room.

"I didn't know," Sarah said with tearful eyes. "I never knew why she hated me and only that she did."

Alise beckoned two servants into the room to take the children away.

Tears lapped under Sarah's chin as she shook her head. "I want to hold my children. They're all I have now."

"And you will," Alise assured. "But you haven't eaten and you look ready to fall to the floor."

The words must have been true, because Sarah collapsed. Alise and another servant struggled to get her onto the bed. Other servants removed the children from the room. Sarah watched wanting her children near, but knowing that her tears and weakness weren't what they needed she allowed them to be taken away.

Hugging a pillow tightly to her face she cried because her father was dead, and because Imogen had been sold. And because Jenna had a reason to hate her all these years. And because Jenna had spoken truthfully. She was like her mother. Exactly like her mother.

With trembling legs she tried to get out of bed. "I can't stay here. I can't."

Alise pleaded with her to stay quiet.

Servants removed Sarah's shoes. A clean nightgown was pulled out of the armoire and Sarah helped into it. The sooner she got her strength she wanted to leave Ashleywood and return to Green Lea with her children.

Alise pulled up the coverlets to ward off the cool wind coming in through the French doors. Standing beside the bed she stared intently into Sarah's eyes. "I know how you feel. I was here when Pierre showed up. I saw what happened." She pressed a hand on top of Sarah's. "I'm not going to tell you what to do. I'll going to leave that up to you. You are unmarried with two children. Please think about that when you make your decision."

"I shouldn't be here, Alise. I shouldn't have ever come."

"Everyone is to blame, Sarah. Everyone," she stressed. "Your sister and Pierre had a contentious marriage from the start, and neither was willing to make it better. They were young and when you're young you make bad decisions. But some of the decisions they made was downright evil and hurt many people in this family. He is the devil, and she is, too. After everything I've heard that has happened it seems to me you were used many years as a pawn to hurt someone."

Sarah grabbed Alise's hand staring at them as she spoke. "It no longer matters who my mother is. When Tante Marianne told me she was my mother, I hugged her very tightly, but she pushed me away and told me I couldn't tell anyone or she'll lose the respect of her friends. She was kind when she spoke and she was gentle when she pushed away. I saw her fear, and I'm ashamed to say that it affected me. I wanted her to be my mother and not her secret. She did what she could and I thank her for it, but deep down it hurt that I wasn't allowed to call her maman. All my life I have felt like a thief. As a child I felt I had stolen Joséphine's husband and Jenna's father. As a young woman I felt I had stolen Tante Marianne's respect. If I had married William I knew my life would become more miserable than my childhood. But that's not why I did it. Pierre... When he and I were together I wasn't a thief. I could see he saw no fault in me. I can't describe the love we had for each other."

"I know he hurt you, but he still loves you, Sarah."

"And that is why my children and I cannot live here, Alise."

Alise smiled then stood upright, conviction showing in her eyes. "I'm not telling you to have an affair with your sister's husband. What I am telling you is to stay in this house. It's far from the mansion. You can separate your life from theirs. Your daughters are here now. They're born and they deserve the way of life their father can provide. The world makes it hard on children born out of wedlock. Don't let them repeat the childhood you had, Sarah. Give them a chance."

The sound of crying babies approaching the door was the reason they drew apart.

"You still have your milk," Alise said.

Sarah knew this was true. For minutes her breasts felt heavy for a release.

"They have no names," Alise said with a smile as the servants carried the babies to the bed. "We don't know what to call them."

After the babies were laid on the bed the servants were dismissed.

Sarah smiled as she lifted the one closest to her. It had *blanc* hair so white the babe looked an old woman. This thought made Sarah's smile to soften. Alise helped her lower one side of her nightgown. The babe latched on with ease.

"Pierre was so certain you would want to feed them once you had awakened. I felt like a thief each time he and I were in here holding the babies against your breasts."

"I'm glad you did," Sarah said, marveling at the ease in which she had become a mother. Holding the child felt natural. Looking at the child and she knew even if she faced death she would protect her children from anyone and anything. "The other has honey hued hair," she said wondering if the child would also look like Pierre.

"We washed her hair with tea," Alise explained. "A small part of her scalp is irritated. The tea helps."

Alise placed the second child in Sarah's arms.

"They have the same face!"

"They're exactly the same. It's hard for us to tell them apart. Thank goodness you haven't named them yet or we may have gotten them turned around."

Alise lowered the second side of Sarah's gown so she could nurse both twins at the same time.

The one in Sarah's right arm had a yellow piece of cloth tied around her wrist. "I name this one Easter."

"What shall we call this one?" Alise asked fingering the blue cloth on the babe's wrist.

"Estelle," Sarah answered. Imogen had been born Estelle Boré on Easter morning. Joséphine had changed her name to Imogen the day she arrived at Green Lea.

# Chapter Thirty-Five
## Never Defy the Heart

*[What you push away from you today with your foot, you will pick up tomorrow with your hand. – Creole Proverb]*

Pierre did not return to the *maison* that evening.

Lifting the glass of bourbon on the table beside him, he held it to his mouth.

For three-hundred noirs he had been able to give a better life only to turn against the one that had never done anything to anyone and was innocent of any misdeed. Imogen had almost been worked to death on Green Lea. On Ashleywood she lost the woman that loved her. Again he saw her denying Sarah was her daughter. At the time he thought she was lying to stay on Ashleywood.

He swallowed the contents in his glass and quickly refilled it trying not to remember how Imogen fought and pleaded not to be sold. And then he remembered the first time he had decided to make a difference in someone's life. It had been the day he had learned Alise was his mother. He had wanted to go to The Bottoms to spy on the slaves there, because he wanted to know if he looked and behaved the same way they did. Before he could reach it he hid behind a tree near the fields and watched as a male slave with strong African features pleaded and begged for mercy as he was tied half naked to a tree.

Pierre had thought the man would be whipped. The overseer back then had been a Spaniard by the name of Francisco Santiago. Pierre had always seen this overseer as different compared to the others. Santiago was perhaps five-foot-one inches tall with a slim build. Quiet of nature, his expression was always stern, his eyes always looked like he was thinking of every single thing he would do or say next. He performed his job as overseer unconscientiously, perfecting each assignment he was given like a soldier in the midst of a battle and internally driven to win at all costs. Because of this Santiago was praised by Will, especially since Santiago didn't shy away from difficult tasks, but tackled them like challenges of which to prove that he could make anyone or anything yield to his will.

Santiago tied the rope around the tree roughly. After this was done Santiago condemned the slave with his eyes and walked away.

The cries that came out of that servant changed Pierre forever.

*Massuh, please. Don't leave me here. I won'ts fall asleep no mo.*

Every so often a grunt was given.

Pierre drew closer to see what was happening.

The servant had been tied so that he hugged the tree. Every few seconds a muscle twitched in his leg.

Hearing Pierre approaching the servant opened his eyes, saw him, and recognized him as the eldest son of his master. He started to speak, but then his eyes closed suddenly and his head fell back. It was then Pierre saw that the tree was infested with fire ants.

*What did you do?*

*I's goes to sees my boy in de night.*

*Your boy lives on another plantation?*

*He be here. He die two days ago. Buried him the night be'fo. Dens the rain come. Oba-seer don't gives us time to dig the hole deep enough. Says don't worry 'cause deys gone move his little body to the slave cemetery as soon as all de works done. I didn't want my boy to be wet and get froze in de ground where deys bury him. So I's get up. Wanted to put some mo dirt on him and keep him warm. Hole already empty. So I's went looking for him. I couldn't find him. I get back to my cabin be'fo anyone knows I's out. His mama say, 'Well?' I couldn't tell her where's her boy be. Couldn't sleep after that. Just sat in the open door and look at the stars in the sky. Didn't git no's sleep. I gets tired after liffin my ax a time or two when I gets to de fields. Didn't wants to hurt nobody or me, so I's leans it agin the tree and sat aside it and fell asleep. Oba-seer finds me and now heah's I's is.*

*How old was your boy?*

*Almost two yairs. T'weren't feelin well for a day or two. His mama tie him to her back as she worked the field. Thought him sleep when he stopped movin. Whens break time comes she pull him from her back and wailed. I's heard her all the way across the field. Cry like that – I heards it and knew my woman's heart had split open.*

*I'm going to cut you loose.*

*No, massuh! Please, don't do it. Oba-seer get only madder. I's hurtin. Don't want to hurt mo than I's is. I be set free some hours after sundown. I's has to be strong 'til den.*

Pierre pulled the barrel knife that he kept with him at all times and sawed at the rope. As he did this he saw Santiago a little distance away sitting on top of his horse. He had been watching the entire time.

*I don't like that man. My papa says he's needed so no one gets any ideas or start keeping bad habits. What's your name?*

*Gentilly.*

*How old are you?*

*Be's twenty-one.*

*Your cabin is around here?*

*Up yonder.*

*After you put some clothes on I want you to meet my papa.*

Gentilly stood about five-eight. At twelve, Pierre stood more than six feet. Still, Gentilly cocked his head low as he stared into Pierre's eyes from under hooded eyelids.

*You won'ts me to meet yo papa?*

*Oui.*

Gentilly nodded. *My pants oba yonda. Don't's need to go to my cabin.*

Pierre saw that Gentilly was apprehensive at the thought of standing before his master, but also curious.

Will Jennings didn't look at all surprise when his son opened his office door and walked in with a slave with red raised welts on his skin. Pushing the letter away he had been reading he sat back and waited patiently for his son, who did nothing without a purpose, explain the reason he was standing there.

*I want you to give Gentilly a job around the house.*

Will watched as Gentilly's eyes grew wide, then his head bowed deeply as he stared at the floor. *What you think this man can do for me around here? Gentilly works in the fields, Pierre. I don't think we trained him for anything else. At least not yet.*

*I don't want you to use him for his muscles, Papa. I want you to use him for his mind. And I want you to get rid of Santiago.*

Gentilly lifted his head slightly. When he did he didn't look at the master of the plantation, but at the master's son standing beside him.

Will smiled at the sight of this. *Fils, you're too young yet to be behaving like a man...*

*Papa, if you don't want Gentilly around here then give him to me to do with as I wish.*

*This is quite an interesting conversation we're having.* Will's eyes narrowed. *All right. Let's see what shall happen with this. I temporarily grant you ownership of Gentilly.*

Gentilly was the first slave Pierre had freed from bondage, but it wasn't in the same way he had freed others.

\*\*\*

The glass lowered in his hand. His head leaned back against the wall. Upstairs he had a wife that slept alone each night. Between the trees lived the woman that made living worthwhile.

*"Comme le père, comme le fils,"* he said when he saw Julien sitting in his wheelchair not too far away studying him with intense eyes. Until that moment Pierre hadn't known Julien had come into the room.

"Like father, like son," Julien agreed.

Pierre closed his eyes. "Jenna told me I'm just like her father. I'm also like my father. I don't think I can get any worse than that."

Julien wheeled closer. "I'm not sure what you're talking about, Brother."

"I took her. You should have seen her eyes. I sold her the same way Alise's uncle sold her for fifty dollars. I watched them put chains on her and a collar around her neck as if she was an animal. And I let them do it." He stared long into his glass, finished its contents, then poured more. "I watched a man come with every intention of selling Sarah and my daughters on an auction block. I'm looking back over my life and I finally understand why Désireé is so hated. I gave her and Gorée all of my love. To everyone else I said be damned. I behaved as if I had no more love to give and when I did give it..." His head rolled so he could see Julien better. "I gave that love to my wife's sister. I'm not Saint Pierre. I never have been. I'm no better than Mr. Robeson. I am...the Devil, and I, Julien, am the damned."

Julien wheeled a little closer. "Make it right. You can do that."

"I lost Sarah." He swallowed half the glass of bourbon. "I lost my happiness. I created the unhappiness I have around me. I can never blame that on Jenna. I never gave her a chance, Julien. I have hurt that woman, and I hurt Abigail, and I hurt Sarah, and my heart breaks because of it."

"Do you love Jenna?"

"I should have divorced her and maybe all of this could have been avoided."

"Why didn't you?"

"In the beginning I thought some day she and I could love each other like a wife and husband should. When I saw this would never happen I saw how much work she put in alongside everyone else. It didn't feel right to put her out."

Julien reached out with his hand for Pierre's glass.

Pierre gave it to him.

Julien took a large swallow. "What are you going to do?"

Pierre smiled. "I have tasted real love. It's hard going back after that."

Julien nodded because he understood. "I had Frances to resubmit the petition to manumit Anne. No one is going to tell me who I can love. I'm angry.

SHELLEY YOUNG

But I'm not alone. There are others in the city with my same views. And together the things we do and the decisions we make shall keep New Orléans a Creole city the way it has always been since Bienville. I'm hoping they'll stand behind me when I request Anne's freedom this time."

"Chokma," Pierre answered. The word was Chickasaw and meant good.

"Fihna!" Julien added. Another Chickasaw word that meant very. "That's who we are in this city. We're Indians, French, Spaniards, German and African," he ended proudly. "You can't walk in any of our homes and not see a bit of each of those cultures inside it. I already knew what happened today. Jenna told me. I was proud of her – proud she's Creole. When you're Creole you're family. It doesn't matter what that family has done to you. *La famille est tout et tout est la famille.*"

"*La famille est tout,*" Pierre repeated.

Julien's expression was resolute as he gave a firm nod, then maneuvered his wheelchair out of the room.

Pierre didn't watch him leave. Instead his eyes were on Jenna. She stood in the opposite door with Edouard in her arms. The child was sleeping. As Pierre stared at her, he saw from the look in her eyes that she had heard some or all that had been said.

"I knew you hadn't gone to bed yet," she said. "I also know you've been drinking quite a bit. I didn't want to send one of the servants to look in on you for fear you were indecent."

Pierre stared down the front of him, then looked up at her. "I had to make sure I was. I couldn't remember." A smile pulled across his face.

"Are you going to bed?" She asked staring at the decanter beside him with only a drop of bourbon left in it and the glass beside it that was half full.

"Oui."

"All right."

Jenna followed behind him feeling dwarfed by his height and weight. It seemed he took up much of the hall whereas she took up very little. Inside the study she watched as he stretched on the rug in front of the fireplace instead of on the bed.

Semper hurried into the room, no doubt sent by Riley when he saw his master had left the *petite salle.*

"Bring down the basket," Jenna told her. "And a coverlet."

Semper nodded and left the room.

Jenna felt extremely tired. Sitting as far away from the fire as she was the part of the room she sat in felt a little cool. It had started to rain and would go on throughout the night. When Semper returned Jenna lifted the basket and stood to her feet. "Leave the coverlet on the sofa. That will be all."

Again Semper nodded, did as she was told, then pulled the door closed after she walked out of the room.

Jenna wasn't certain how intoxicated Pierre was. Usually Anne sat with him on nights like this. When she had Jenna was confident in Anne's ability to help him during the night if it was needed. Now that Anne saw to Julien, and because Julien needed help during the night she didn't trust anyone else would see to Pierre as well as she could.

Situating the basket closer to the fire so Edouard would stay warm, and not wanting to be too far away from him, she removed her gown and undergarments then lay on the rug in her chemise. Pierre's eyes were closed and he was breathing heavily. She thought about the way he had been treating her lately and shared her blanket with him.

Pierre slept through the night without moving a single muscle. When he awoke early the next morning it was to Edouard sleeping between him and Jenna. The babe suckled at his mother's breast. Jenna had fallen asleep again. The room had cooled. The fire had nearly burned out. As he reached for the coverlet Jenna startled, then looked down at Edouard. She started to rise.

"Don't bother," he said. "By the time one of the servants warmed the bed the sun will be up. Put Edouard on the other side of you."

She pulled Edouard from her breast and turned on her side with her back to Pierre. He leaned over her to see where Edouard was. "Hold him tight."

Her arms tightened around the child.

Pierre pulled her closer to him then covered the three of them well with the coverlet. Within minutes both of them had fallen asleep again. It was a short time later when Riley entered the room in search of the plantation's owners. Seeing both of them resting and how cool the room was he added an adequate amount of logs to the fire. As the room got warmer the deeper Pierre and Jenna fell into a state of sleep.

The next morning Jenna awoke to the feel of Pierre's arms around her and Edouard. She rested more against him and closed her eyes wondering how soon it would be before he made his way between the trees to be with his second family.

She must have fallen back to sleep. She realized this when the sound of giggling woke her. Pierre lay on his back holding Edouard high in his arms. The child drooled as he smiled down at his papa. Pierre lowered and lifted Edouard again. The giggles Edouard gave sounded as if they came from deep within his tiny belly.

"He's a happy boy," Pierre said lowering Edouard to his chest.

Jenna reached up and touched Edouard's foot. "Abigail could have been. I'm the reason she wasn't."

He looked at her. "Are you taking all of the blame?"

"I was horrible to her, Pierre. Horrible. And I was horrible to you. I was horrible to my father," she said closing her eyes. "I didn't want to forgive him. I hated him and loved him at the same time. And now I can never tell him that I did love him or how sorry I am that I never helped the many times he asked."

Pierre pulled her closer and held her in his arms. Jenna laid her head on his massive chest. "I was horrible to everyone then cried myself to sleep at night while asking myself why no one liked me. For as long as I can remember my parents used to tell friends and family that I was a mean child." She looked up at him. "But when they said it I heard pride in their voices. The more I heard them say this the meaner I got. And then I told my mother about my father and Tante Marianne. That's why she slapped me. She told me I was being mean."

"You are mean," he said. "And you're good at it. But I understand why now. Your parents hurt you and you didn't want anyone else to hurt you like that again."

She tried to pull away from him. He pulled her closer.

"I hurt you, Jenna. You said once you were only fighting back. I see now that you believed this was true."

"She's my sister, Pierre. I don't care that you don't love me anymore. I heard what you told Julien last night. Why are you holding me? You never have before. Is this your way of being kind before you tell me you want a divorce?"

Laying Edouard between them, he rolled so he leaned over the child and her, then gripped her face. "You don't want to be mean anymore, Jenna. And I don't want to be the devil anymore."

She refused to look at him. "Then get rid of her!"

"We had our chance, Jenna. And neither of us took it. Even if Sarah decides never to love me again I can't go back. If she decides not to love me, I won't get rid of her."

She pulled away from him and held Edouard tightly in her arms, because she saw something more in his eyes. She was who he wanted to get rid of. Riverside had always been a threat, but it was one she never faced. This was her home. With this thought in mind she stared at each individual piece of furniture unable to imagine never seeing the things inside this home ever again. "Don't be the devil, Pierre."

"I don't want to be. And I promise not to be if you can promise not to be mean anymore."

"I'm numb," she confessed. "So very numb."

"No," he argued. "You're allowing yourself to feel for the first time what everyone else feels. This is our last chance to make things right. I'm even willing to make the first move."

She said nothing as he climbed to his feet and walked out of the room.

*** 

It was cool out, but Jenna decided to take Edouard with them. The sky was part gray, but it didn't look to her like it would rain. The view of the land was clear and remarkably sharp. The cloak and bonnet she wore made her feel too warm, but removing either could bring sickness and death. Often she stared down at Edouard. A blanket covered him completely. She lifted a corner of it. Edouard smiled up at her.

Jenna had seen the plantation many times in the past, but usually in bits and pieces. The fields and slave quarters had never been of interest to her. The routine she kept consisted of her going as far as the weaving cabin. Why it was called the weaving cabin, she wasn't certain. No clothes were woven inside it. Every day of the year, except for holidays and days off, thirteen servant girls sat inside it making clothes for the servants. So good were these women with needle and thread that Pierre allowed them and their male escort to leave the plantation to travel to nearby plantations and offer their services. Jenna also used them for the alterations that were needed for her gowns.

This was the first time she would see the most used parts of the plantation all at once. Pierre had made the suggestion. Suspecting he had a reason behind it she reluctantly went along.

Usually visitors to the plantation, if they so requested, were shown certain areas while other areas were considered off limits. The slave quarters were one of these areas. Jenna had been to The Bottoms on only a few occasions. Not liking what she saw there – in her opinion the servants had far too much privilege – she stayed away from it as much as possible.

As Pierre rode her through it in the buggy she noticed something unusual. As soon as the servants saw the buggy they stopped what they were doing and looked at the moving vehicle with frightened eyes. It wasn't until they had reached its end and a small boy came running from behind a cabin, saw her, stopped and gasped that she realized that what they were frightened of was her.

Jenna turned in the seat to look back at the child and saw his mother fleeing with him across the small clearing that separated the cabin rows as if for her life.

She drew in a silent breath and sat forward. "Why did you bring me here?"

"They need to see you. With me."

She licked slowly at her lips and averted her gaze toward the trees.

The buggy moved at a not too fast pace. While looking in this direction she saw what looked like a dozen or more groups of slave men, women and children performing a variety of chores. Many had begun to lift their hands, saw her and either stopped or continued to wave, but softly.

"You want me to see how hated I am, is that it?" She asked.

He stared at her. "I want them to see *you* with me."

She stared at him a moment, then averted her gaze, smiled and began to truly look at everything around her.

As they rode through the coopers' quarters the same thing happened as it did in The Bottoms. Jenna ignored them this time. Before the evening was over all of them would know that their master had paraded his wife across the plantation.

The race track was the only time that Pierre drew the buggy to a stop. Jenna was relieved. The seat cushion was becoming uncomfortable. When Pierre stood beside her she offered her hand as she usually did so he could assist her out of it. He gestured for her to hold Edouard tighter. Once she did this he lifted her out of the buggy by her waist and set her feet on the ground.

Pierre hadn't looked at her while he did this. His eyes were across the field, his mouth smiling happily as Gentilly made his way toward them.

Jenna loved the race track. It was here where she threw many parties for her friends. The sight of the track alone seduced many of her friends to believe she was indeed the wealthiest woman in the South.

Gentilly's wife had seen her madame holding Edouard from a distance, and lifting the hem of skirt stepped down from the wide galerie of her cabin in a rushed gait.

"You ought to be ashamed of yourself, monsieur, gallivanting around this place with your son while he still so young." Makala then looked over her shoulder and yelled. "Delee! Get on over here, girl. Have your brother ride you back to the big house with the master's child. Stay with him until monsieur and madame return."

"Yessum!" Delee answered.

Jenna stared down at Edouard wondering if she'd done wrong by bringing him with them.

"He's all right," Pierre whispered in her ear. "You kept him completely covered."

"Who's going to feed him?" She questioned. This would be the first time Edouard would be separated from her since he'd been born.

"Delee'll feed him, madame," Gentilly said gently. Jenna could see he was suspicious as to why his monsieur had brought her with him on this visit. "It's why Makala tolds her to come 'stead of one of the udders. She juss dropped her third chile sic months ego."

"Bolon can ride you back to the mansion, Jenna, if you prefer to go back," Pierre suggested.

Jenna gazed at Pierre for only a moment knowing he would be at Gentilly's home for quite some time. Each visit was always the same. And Makala was one of the best cooks. Jenna had enjoyed being out of the mansion, and especially the wind on her face. The prospect of sitting with Gentilly's family while everyone talked, ate and laughed didn't bother her.

"I'll stay," she said.

She wasn't certain if Pierre heard her or not. He and Gentilly just that quickly had become engrossed in conversation.

Delee took Edouard and waited for Bolon as he drove a cart in their direction.

Pierre tugged Jenna by the elbow. The guilt of leaving Edouard behind nearly caused her to change her mind. And then it was too late.

Gentilly and Makala had fourteen children, of which thirteen were still living. Seeing their monsieur visiting their cabin, several of them ran in Pierre's direction. One of them was a long limbed girl who had been holding the reins of a horse. Handing them to a younger stable boy she ran fast toward the slowly growing group and dipped a knee before Pierre and Jenna.

"Bonjour, monsieur! Bon jour, madame."

"If your legs keeps growing your head is going to touch the sky," Pierre teased.

Susie gazed at her father. "Can we show monsieur and madame?"

"What's this?" Pierre asked.

Gentilly smiled with pride.

"You finally gave in?" Pierre asked.

"She's better than the rest."

"Not better than Cabot," Pierre argued.

Gentilly smiled and nodded.

Pierre's face grew sober. "I have to see this."

Taking Jenna by the hand he led her to the wooden benches used for spectators during the races. Cabot was Gentilly's youngest son, as well as the best jockey in the state. Pierre had won plenty of purses at the annual races that occurred on his plantation. The races were one of the events on the plantation that the only servants allowed to attend were those serving in some capacity. Once Jenna was comfortably seated beside him, Pierre folded his hands and leaned forward.

Jenna saw his anticipation and smiled inwardly.

Makala appeared and handed Jenna a pillow to sit on. Jenna nodded at the servant and accepted it.

Makala threw a sly glance at Gentilly. Her madame had *never* thanked any servant. Anything offered was usually accepted with a quick snatch of the hand and a look of disappointment as if to suggest what had taken the servant so long to think of her.

Benita followed behind her mother with a silver platter laden with hot beverages already poured. While Jenna and Pierre sipped café, Gentilly's sons, Hensy and Cabot, and their sister Susie had climbed on prime thoroughbreds that were stabled in this area separate from the other horses. Gentilly stood behind them and gave the long whistle that started the race. Pierre stood when the three children raced forward at a ferocious pace. Cabot was an expert jockey, his small frame allowing him to grip the thoroughbred as if he was a part of its coat. Cabot was in the lead with Hensy behind him and Susie bringing up the rear. Halfway to the finish line Susie closed the distance as she raced to take the lead.

"Allez! Allez! Allez!" Pierre roared, then spun around when she won by at least two heads. "Unbelievable! A girl!" He didn't wait for anyone to answer. Propping his hands on his hips he stared forward as all three children demonstrated jumps and orchestrated prances.

Susie became the center of attention while Pierre, Jenna, Makala and Gentilly dined on cracked crab, corn pudding and roasted potatoes. Jenna knew the history between Pierre and Gentilly. Will had shared it with her shortly after she had given birth to Abigail. Will had given ownership of Gentilly to Pierre when Pierre was twelve. At the time Pierre didn't know exactly what to do with him. For days Gentilly's only chore was to follow Pierre around.

While visiting the stables Pierre learned Gentilly had worked for a short time in one on the last plantation he lived on before coming to Ashleywood. After demonstrating his skills that day Pierre sent him to Europe to learn about horses. Gentilly and his sons still traveled to Europe at times to broaden their education. When Will saw how well Pierre did with Gentilly, he also gave him Gentilly's wife and children.

"We have a secret, Gentilly, and I don't want that secret getting out. At the next races, Susie rides," Pierre announced. Jenna could see that some of the youngest sons didn't like this decision, but the girls seemed thrilled.

"Are you ready to win your first purse, Susie?" Pierre asked.

"Oui, monsieur," she answered.

Pierre smiled then rose to his feet. "We better get going. We'll send Delee back as soon as we get there."

As Pierre stepped outside he looked up. Just that quickly the sky had darkened. Thunder could be heard in the distance. He thought about Sarah as he assisted Jenna into the cart then climbed in beside her. They had gotten only a small distance when the rain started. It fell hard and fast. As much as he kept to the trees the rain wet them just as quickly. Cutting to his right he drove swiftly to the hidden cottage where runaways at one time waited to meet Saint Pierre.

The underground operations of sneaking runaways onto his ships had totally ceased. The runaway slaves that helped Sarah that night still lived on his land, because the risk it took to move them was now far too great.

Throwing one of the doors open he glanced over Jenna's head and saw that many of the things inside the cabin had been stolen. Armoire doors and drawers had been left open. Going room to room he saw that the food that had been stored inside it when Sarah stayed here had also been taken.

Pierre looked up at a cupboard too high to reach even if someone stood on a piece of furniture. In it he found several coarse blankets, two bottles of wine and a few candles. Most of the beds had been stripped along with their pillows. Only the larger pieces of firewood had been left behind because they had been too heavy to carry.

A fire was needed.

Shedding his wet coat he draped it over a chair, then arranged the firewood in the hearth. It was then he realized he didn't have a flint to start it with.

He turned and saw how wet Jenna's cloak was then stared down at his own attire. He hurried to the front of the cabin and opened its door. The rain was falling in sheets. The sky looked like late evening although it was only late in the afternoon.

"We have no fire," she said. "My gown is wet. I'll need to get out of it."

"We have blankets. I'll see if I can find something to start the fire with." Driving to the cabin by the swamp or anywhere for that matter was out of the question. Death was falling from the sky and the only way to avoid it was staying inside and keeping warm.

Jenna helped him search, and as hard as they did nothing was found. She turned to him with fear and apprehension. "I can't get ill, Pierre. Edouard needs me."

"You won't." He grabbed her hand and led her to the sofa. "Take off everything that's wet, then you'll wrap up in a blanket."

Jenna had also wanted to get out of her corset. Pierre unpinned the back of her gown. It was carefully removed and stretched across the kitchen table. The petticoats were removed next. Jenna had every intentions of putting them back on. The more clothing she had on the more she would stay warm. The chemise was lifted over her head and held in her hand while Pierre started untying her corset. Approaching horses could be heard in the yard. Just as Pierre pushed Jenna slightly to the side the door pushed open in front of them.

A slave stood inside it. Over his chest was a piece of animal skin. Rain dripped from his hair and skin. In his hand was a stick with a knife tied tightly to the end of it.

Pierre saw the homemade spear and reached for the pistol at his side and aimed it at the slave. "What are you looking for here? This is private property."

Jenna was pushed behind him with his free hand.

The pants the slave wore looked like they had been worn every day of his life. No shoes were on his feet. Another look into the slave's eyes and Pierre knew he didn't understand French. He then spoke English.

"Are you looking for the gate? Are you looking for Saint Pierre?"

Instead of compliance anger filled the slave's eyes as they became narrow. Pierre had heard at least two horses approaching. As quickly as the slave had come through the door meant he couldn't have been on either of those horses. "I'll ask again. What do you want?"

The slave drew his eyes from Pierre and onto Jenna's dress and petticoats lying on the table. "You kilt my family. And now I'm gone kill you and yours."

Pierre didn't hesitate. He pulled the trigger when the slave took a leaping step closer.

The slave clutched his chest with one hand, dropped the spear, then reached for his chest with his other. A look of shock was in his eyes as he fell to the floor. Pierre handed the unloaded pistol to Jenna to hold, then reached for the second pistol he kept on his waist.

The cabin had four entrances, three in the front and one in the back. Pierre could hear horses circling it and voices. The pieces of conversation he picked up weren't coming from bounty hunters, but more slaves. Aiming the pistol in these areas he walked backward forcing Jenna into the only room in the cottage where the door to enter it was the only one it had.

He nudged her toward the corner. Jenna hurried to it.

This door had no lock. To keep it closed Pierre had to hold it with his hands. Through a crack in the door he watched as four runaways pushed their way into the cottage, then stare down at the dead servant. One of them carried a rifle.

"Someone inside here and they shot Gimme!" One of them yelled.

"Listen to me," Pierre pleaded. "Gimme tried to attack me and my wife. I don't know why you came here, but I can help you. I can give you food and help you hide from whoever you're running from. I've done it before."

The one holding the rifle raised it and aimed it at the door. Pierre noticed the man's eyes. Dementedness is what he saw. It was this same man that spoke.

"You t'aint do nuttin but be white and free!"

"What do you want here?" Pierre asked, taking in the others.

"We needs out the rain!" Another yelled.

"And food!" Another said.

"This is my land," Pierre said. "I don't know where you came from, but it looks to me that the three of you want more than that. I can't have you hurting anyone here. All of you have found the wrong place. This is good land. Blacks here are treated well."

The one with the demented eyes narrowed them even more.

"You's the blacks on this land's massuh?"

Again Pierre didn't hesitate. He had taken in the others and deduced that the one with the demented eyes was the leader of this small rebellion. Another reached for the spear, and after taking his cue from the rifle holder, faced the door ready to attack. The others saw this and also made themselves ready.

Pierre snatched the door open wider, aimed his pistol, and pulled the trigger. The rifle holder fell knee first to the floor.

One of the slaves screamed as Pierre slammed the door closed again. Furniture scraped the floor as someone made an attempt to hide. Pierre stared at Jenna with regret. Both of his pistols had been fired. Two of the slaves were down, but three were still alive and at least two of them were armed.

"Sum bitch!" One of the slaves screamed with rage and heartfelt pain. "We's gone kill ya!"

"Listen!" Pierre yelled. "I don't want any trouble. You're on my property! I have helped slaves all my life. Your fight isn't here! I tried telling you that, but you didn't listen. I need you to get off my land."

"Where you want us to go?" The question was asked like a growl. "Whites own all de land. You kill and sell our families. We ain't having it no mo."

After Pierre heard this he heard silence. Releasing the door as silently as he could, he took off his waistcoat and gave it to Jenna to put on. Its large size made it easy to drape over her shoulders and keep her warm. Pierre had just grabbed the door again when someone on the other side tried to turn it. The knob twisted only a small amount, but enough for the slave to know that it wasn't locked and Pierre was holding it.

"Grab a hold of my waist! Hurry!" Pierre whispered in French. "Don't let go even after I fall."

Jenna hurried behind him and gripped him tight.

On the other side of the door a slave yelled, "Ain't no heaben for you, white man!"

The blast splintered the wood. Buck shots made it past the wood and sprayed Pierre's torso just below his chest. Realizing if he didn't let go of the door another shot would be made, he released it at the same time he realized it wasn't by his will that he was falling, but his injuries. Purposely falling flat, Jenna did exactly as he told her because she knew what he had in mind. The fall of his weight winded her. A sharp pain radiated down the back of her head when she hit the floor.

The slaves pushed hard at what was left of the door. With all the strength Pierre had he pushed his feet against the door to keep them from getting in. Nausea leaked inside him as if his stomach had been blown apart. The more he thought about the pain the more it intensified. His muscles gave no warning and neither had his brain. One second he was keeping the door closed, the next he was unconscious.

Pierre's legs bent awkwardly as the door was forced open. The slaves rushed into the room. One of them stared down on Pierre and spit on him. Jenna buried her face into Pierre's spine when the slaves surrounded her.

"*Veuillex aller,*" she yelled. "*Je viends d'avoir bébé!*"

"You from Biloxi. What she say, Joppy?"

"Sumting about having a baby and for us to go."

"Drag her out so we can split her down the middle with this here knife."

As they attempted to roll Pierre on one side, Jenna clung fiercely to him. The pressure of her arms lifted and squeezed his wound. Pierre became conscious with a wince on his face. As his eyes adjusted and he saw the runaways attempting to roll him to get to Jenna, he punched one of them in nose, breaking it.

The slave screamed, loudly, then fell onto his rump and gently touched the blood running down his face as tears squeezed from his eye. Jenna screamed in pain. Another slave punched wildly. Another aimed the spear at Pierre's side. Pierre could feel his energy slipping. He grabbed the runaway closest to him by the neck and held on tight hoping to squeeze the breath out of the slave until he died.

Jenna screamed when the slave with the spear brought it down. It passed Pierre as he and the other runaways struggled and pierced her leg.

Joppy fell back when Leslie's eyes bulged wide and his nostrils flared, and a tormenting scream was trying to get past Pierre's grip. It was then Joppy saw what was happening. A slave was behind Leslie with a whip in his hand.

Pulling his homemade spear out of the white woman's leg, he aimed it and screamed as he ran toward the slave with the whip.

Gentilly drew back his arm. The whip lashed across the full front of Joppy's body. Gentilly drew the whip back, and in a sideways motion brought the tip of it into Joppy's face. Joppy fell hard to the floor then scrambled into the corner holding his face together.

Gentilly stepped further into the room, and standing in front of the men, he lashed the whip like someone tossing paint from a paint brush. The slaves screamed and tried to hide behind one another.

"What d'you done done!" Gentilly screamed. "Dis be good land! This be Slave Heaven. Why you come here and do this? Dis man be Monsieur Jennings. They's gone kill ya! Kill ya!"

"Him white!" Joppy screamed. "T'aint no good white man ever lived."

"Him not like dem!" Gentilly screamed. "On dis land any man wonts to be free gets free."

Behind him Pierre lost consciousness. As soon as Leslie was able to catch his breath he tackled Gentilly from behind.

Gentilly's oldest son, Cornfield, ran into the room and hit Leslie with the lantern he was holding. The glass broke away from the metal. Fire and oil spilled down Leslie's nape and down his spine. Thrashing across the floor to put it out, he screamed like a mad man and kicked his legs.

Gentilly pushed his son out of the way and drawing back his hand, he made ready to unleash the whip again. "You got three seconds to get out of heah. I should kill you for what you done, but us on dis land be diff'ernt. We knows how's it is! We knows juss how bad it is. Cain't take back what you done done. I feels sorry for ya. Cornfield, Abner, Sosie go finds sumpn we can finish killin dees men wit if dey don't get up and get off this land."

***

Three weeks later Anne gave birth to a baby girl. Slightly early, the newest member of the Jennings family was born March twelfth in the year of 1834.

Jenna had no comment to make when one of the servants told her that Anne had gone into labor in the mansion and Monsieur Julien had instructed her to climb in his bed. For a long time she sat in a chair holding Edouard, tears falling from her eyes. She had just held him to her breast when she heard the cry of a newborn child. Four hours was all it had taken Anne to begin labor and deliver.

The lights in her boudoir burned dimly. The voices outside her doors warned her that everyone was inside the mansion: Alise, Désireé, Mableane and Gorée.

As soon as the baby started to cry it stopped. When it seemed as if the entire mansion had gone silent Jenna wondered if the child had died. Several minutes later Julien giggled with glee. Jenna smiled from the sound of his happiness.

For years she hated this family. There had been a time she had wanted Pierre to die solely so she could dance over his grave. She did not feel like that anymore. Gentilly and his sons had gone looking for their master as soon as it started to rain. There was no doubt in her mind that the runaways would have

339

killed her and made certain Pierre was dead before they left if Gentilly hadn't found them.

Gentilly and his sons had run the runaways off. Although injured they managed to escape to the Dussault plantation. Joppy was shot and killed by Antoine. Leslie and another that went by the name Hansom were taken to the plantation of an established family in the city to await trial.

The smaller group had gotten separated from a much larger group going plantation to plantation burning them down. As they hid in the woods their numbers grew. Before the smaller group had reached Ashleywood they had attacked and killed a nearby plantation owner. His wife and children had gotten away. It was this plantation owner's horses they had stolen.

The larger group was later found, of all places, on Green Lea. All but three of the one-hundred-and-eight runaways captured weren't from Louisiana and had recently been sold on 'trader row' in New Orleans. The revolt started in New Orleans' German Coast. A total of four whites had lost their lives. A total of forty-one runaways were shot and killed, and seventeen more were tried and hung, including Hansom and Leslie. The Dussaults and several other established families discovered during the trial that slaves on their land had aided and helped the runaways by giving them farming tools as weapons and hiding them so they wouldn't get caught. These slaves were also sold.

Often, like she was now, Jenna thought about Gentilly and what he'd done. Love was a powerful thing. Love made men like Gentilly loyal to men who loved them in return. Pierre had given that love when he freed Gentilly and his family and gave them a better life. The Londe family hadn't been as lucky. When the group reached their plantation one of their own slaves turned against his master and helped the runaways kill Gabriel Londe's eldest son with an ax.

As Edouard nursed and fell asleep in the comfort of her arm she thought about hate, because she knew what it bred. For years she hated her father only to realize when it was too late that she loved him. And now her father was dead. Debt hadn't killed him. She had. Pride had prevented her from giving him the money he needed. A little of it would have relieved him from a lot of the pressure he was under. Now it was too late. It was too late for Abigail as well. Pierre had paid good money for three men to find her. Each of them had come back with no information and only apologies. It was as if Abigail and Carlisle had fallen off of the face of the earth.

During the trial Ashleywood was mentioned. The slave, Lovelace Londe, was asked why the group bypassed Ashleywood and burned down the Guillmard plantation. From what she was told, Lovelace hung his head and said, "Monsieur Jennings be a good man. I'm sad to hear what happened to him."

A knock sounded at her door.

She removed Edouard from her breast and laid him in his crib. Opening the door, she faced Jeanette with a somber expression.

Jeanette lowered her head.

"Look at me, girl," she said.

Jeanette looked up.

Jenna gave her a small smile. "They want to come inside?"

"Oui, madame," Jeanette answered and lowered her head again. It was going to take some time for her and the others to get used to their new madame.

"Give me a moment."

"Oui, madame."

Jenna closed the door, pressed her hands against her face and let out a small breath. Smoothing down her gown, she crossed the room to the bed. No mattress in the mansion had ever been long enough to accommodate a male Jennings.

Leaning over the head of it she gave Pierre a gentle shake. Sleeping was what he did mostly. The loudest noises rarely woke him, but a little shake and his eyes always opened. When his eyes were open pain was all he felt. It took Dr. Marchand four hours to remove the buck shots he could find. Eight of them. One of them he couldn't reach and knew he never would without killing Pierre.

Jenna wondered if it was this buck shot that gave Pierre most of his trouble.

The blast of a rifle hadn't killed him. What were killing him were the violent fevers he suffered. After Carlisle had given Julien peyote tea and Pierre had seen its affects, he made arrangements to get his hands on the plant hoping to plant it on his land. It cost him one-hundred-and-twenty dollars to have a crate of the live cactus delivered to Ashleywood. When Dr. Marchand refused to give his patient the tea, Jenna had him removed from the house. She now fed the tea personally to Pierre no less than three times a day.

"Your family is here," she whispered. "Let me wipe you down first."

Pierre watched with lazy eyes as she crossed the room to the table where water waited. She looked tired. Each time he opened his eyes she was there. Looking at her now he knew she stayed at his side even when his eyes were closed.

The basin and a towel was brought closer to the bed and placed on the bedside table. It trickled near his ear and then a cool cloth covered his face wiping away the sweat. Pierre closed his eyes and breathed heavily. At that moment he preferred death than the pain he was in.

At all times a piece of muslin covered with a poultice was kept over his wounds. He pressed his hand against it now hoping to alleviate the nausea.

Jenna stripped away the sheets and the coverlet from on top of him and covered him with clean ones not knowing that it was her need to see him kept clean was one of the reasons he was still alive.

When she started to walk away, he whispered for her to come back.

"Edouard," he whispered.

Jenna squeezed her eyes closed as tears fell from them.

"D-do... right by me," he whispered.

Her fingertips pressed against his lips.

"D-do not fight it. They're my blood. They're Jennings. What I give them let it be. Sarah is to live on Ashleywood, and my daughters are to live here until they're married."

At that moment she wanted nothing more than to put a pillow over his face and smother him. To have kept him alive only for him to turn against her.

Pierre gritted past the pain, and cupping her face gently with one hand, lowered her even closer. When his lips pressed against hers, she closed her eyes as tears fell from them. The first thought that came to her mind was she wanted him out of her bed, but she knew as soon as that happened he would be taken to the *maison* and cared for by Sarah.

When his hand fell away she stared down at his chest and saw it was still moving. Believing he had fallen back to sleep, she whispered, "I have loved you for far too long."

His eyes opened. "And I have loved you, and have given my life for yours."

When his eyes squeezed closed again, and he began to breathe in short quick breaths she walked to the door and pulled it open.

Alise hugged Jenna when she saw how worn she appeared. Jenna made certain to hide the animosity she felt. Since the first day of her marriage, Alise held more clout than she did. If Alise even suspected the animosity Jenna now felt Pierre would be removed from the room.

Désireé gave Jenna a tearful nod. The thought of losing her father was one she couldn't accept. One of her hands held tightly to Gorée's wrist. Now that Anne's baby was here none of them could wait to get back to Pierre.

Gorée saw him on the bed and ran to him. She stopped when she saw his face and how still he lay. "Pierre?"

Jenna started to close the door when she saw Sarah top the staircase, then stop and stare at her.

Both sisters stared at one another.

Sarah lifted her hem and hurried closer. "Please," she pleaded in a choked whisper. "I'm begging you. Please. Let me see him."

Jenna thought about Edouard becoming heir of Ashleywood. She started to turn away when she heard his voice. *Grab a hold of my waist! Don't let go even after I fall.* And then she thought about Pierre's dying wish of Sarah living on Ashleywood for as long as she lived.

"Just let me peek," Sarah pleaded. "He doesn't have to see me."

Pierre believed Sarah came to the mansion each time she could and during each of those visits he had slept through them. He believed this because Jenna had lied to him and told him this. Alise and Désireé knew the truth but hadn't said anything.

Jenna pulled the door open wider.

Sarah stepped closer to it. "Merci, Soeur."

Sarah didn't see Jenna reach for the silver candlestick on a nearby table.

***

It was close to two years later.

Jenna couldn't contain herself. The joy she had seemed as if it would burst from every part of her body. She was uncertain if she should take a moment and stomp like a drunken man at a cotillion or if she should scream from the top of her lungs so that even those on the third floor would hear or if she should continue what she was doing now: running.

The sound of her running brought servants out of rooms to peek out of it and see what was going on.

Jenna had been eager to share her good news. Now that she saw faces she couldn't stop, because she knew what she wanted to do.

It felt good to run like she was; the energy inside her made her feel young again. The letter she had just received was conscious in her hand; she could feel she

342

was holding it far too tightly; her palm hurt, but still she ran until she burst through the mansion's rear door.

Julien had been sitting against the wall in a chair on the galerie. When he heard running feet then saw the way Jenna broke through the door, he gripped the armrest and jumped to his feet as if one of them hadn't been lame. The fall he started to make would have been a bad tumble. For two years he had believed his right leg would become useful again. The nerves in his brain telling him to get up reached only his left side and a very small part of his right. The message to move stopped dead when it reached his right knee. With most of his body moving too quickly to stop, he reached his hands forward onto the small table in front of him.

Jenna grabbed him from behind, holding him so tightly he could feel the swell of her breasts and legs press against the back of him. The sharp end of the table managed to dig into his middle before Jenna, using all the strength she had so she wouldn't fall with him, pulled him back. The chair's cushion caught him just in time. His right leg folded underneath him. The left one kicked out. Sitting awkwardly on the chair he stared up at her face and saw what could only be described as euphoria.

"Woman, I have never felt more lame than at this moment."

The shrill of laughter she gave made him smile with anticipation.

"Why were you running? And why are you looking like that?"

Crumpled pieces of paper were held out to him. Seeing its condition made him realize why one of Jenna's hands had felt like a fist in his side.

"It's from Abigail!"

"Abigail!" He stared at her in disbelief.

"She wants to come for a visit. She's actually on her way."

Julien stared at the papers.

"The letter came by courier," Jenna said. "Some man in a ratted old carriage pulled up in front of the mansion and asked for me by name. Of course the servants were wary because of the sight of him. Julien, I've never seen anyone so poorly dressed. As soon as I faced him, he smiled and handed me that letter. And then he said goodbye, climbed onto the driver seat and rode away."

Anxious to hear what was in the letter, Julien began reading it while she was still talking. It consisted of three pages. Two of the pages Abigail had pleaded to her mother to forgive her. The last page had been written to Pierre telling him how sorry she was. According to the letter, Abigail and Carlisle were married shortly after leaving the plantation and now had a home in Kentucky. Julien noticed that Abigail had offered no details about her life or anything that had happened to her in the past two years other than she was married and where she lived. Stranger still the letter was folded in half and had been sealed with wax instead of being placed in an envelope and mailed.

Jenna started to sit but stopped and smiled at him as if the best thing that could ever happen had happened. "I need to get things in order before she arrives. Do you mind if I give her Marie-Marie's old room? It's of good size and I fear Edouard will be too frightened to sleep that far from me during the night even with Gorée in the room with him."

Julien doubted that. If ever two people lived for one another's company it was Gorée and Edouard.

"Not at all." He smiled hoping she didn't sense his suspicion. From what he read, and hearing how the letter had reached the mansion, Abigail's behavior seemed odd. Too much emphasis had been placed on her departure as if the incident had only happened a day ago instead of two years.

The look on his face must have been convincing. Jenna gave him a hug that felt more like a tight squeeze, then hurried back inside. Adjusting his right side with his left hand, he had just gotten comfortable when Jenna gave a harrowing scream. Julien had been ready to fall to the floor this time as he gripped the armrest and only stopped himself from moving further when several servants began to scream at once. All of the screaming meld together and jerked him to his feet. The sound of high pitched laughter told him there was nothing to be alarmed about. Falling back into the chair, he reached in his breast pocket for his handkerchief to mop his brows. This was too much excitement, but expected excitement.

After harvest, and during the time on the plantation where other chores took precedent, Ashleywood held an annual celebration that only the family and those who lived on it could attend. Julien had returned to Primrose the previous year, along with Anne and their baby girl, and had only arrived back on Ashleywood yesterday.

The voices in the mansion grew louder and louder and seemed to be progressing at a slow pace in his direction. Julien heard two strange voices speaking English, and a female voice, then knew what the fuss was about. He was mulling over the situation when he saw Anne step out of the kitchen and make her way toward him holding a basket in one hand and Jillian Belle Catharine Jennings by the hand with the other. At sixteen months Jill wasn't as sure footed when she tried to run. Seeing him sitting on the galerie gave her the need to reach him. Anne struggled to keep the child upright while also trying not to lose the contents of the basket.

Julien had stopped feeling guilty and sorry for himself a long time ago for the things he couldn't do for his family. Like walking to Jillian and lifting her high in the air. The first time Pierre did this, Jillian, unused to being held so high, became dazed with fear. Now each time Pierre came near she ran and hid behind her parents.

Jillian managed to tug from Anne's grip as the two of them made their way up the galerie steps. Climbing onto her papa's lap, she leaned against him and kicked her legs in content, as if his lap was a chair made especially for her. Anne lowered and kissed him and was lifting when the rear door opened and Abigail hurried out of it.

Abigail had a large smile on her face, and then she saw Anne and looked as if she was confused; her eyes then lowered to Julien. The smile vanished; her face was the perfect remonstration of horror as she stared at the laziness of his right eyelid and the way he sat in a chair like someone feeble. And then her eyes fell to the roundness of Anne's middle where it was safe to assume she was carrying another child.

"Hello, mademoiselle," Anne said.

Not only did Anne's voice sound strange, she looked it as well. The Anne Abigail remembered wore her hair in long plaits. This Anne had her hair fashioned in the latest popular updo and no longer looked a child, but a well-to-do *mulâtresse*.

In the few minutes Abigail had been on the plantation she noticed vast changes since she left. It was hard looking at the child on her oncle's lap, because there was no mistake about who her father was. The color of child's hair and eyes were all telling. Although the child's hair wasn't a strange hue of white, it was fair and close to the color of honey. It was the silvery tint of her eyes that told the world she belonged to the Jennings family.

The reason Abigail stood speechless was the way Julien, Anne and the child were dressed, all three in fine apparel like the lord, mistress and heir of a prosperous plantation.

"No kiss for your oncle?" Julien asked.

Abigail took a hesitant step. It wasn't that she didn't want to hug him. A part of him looked like the man she remembered, except one side of him looked paralyzed, including his face. The left corner of his smile curved higher than the right. Another reason for her hesitation was the three of them made her ashamed of her own attire. The gray dress she wore was plain with no embellishments, and was made of coarse fabric. It was a far cry from the gowns of her youth.

Anger pricked her eyes as Carlisle and his brother stepped out of the house behind her. Abigail didn't look at either of them. In her mind both her husband and brother-in-law could easily see that on this land where even the slaves dressed better than she now did, she had been nothing more than an unwanted bastard, and this was the reason she left all of this wealth behind. For several moments she could neither move nor speak, and then she leaned and gave Julien a delicate hug while she studied his right leg and arm.

"I had an injury," he said. "I fell and hit the back of my head against a piece of sharp iron. What you see is the result of it."

Memories of him loving her as long as she could remember was the reason her arms embraced him tightly. "Can you walk, Oncle?"

"Very slowly. And not a great distance. And not gracefully."

Abigail noticed that his smile was genuine. Happiness is what she saw in his eyes, which was just as confusing as his appearance. The thought of someone as active as he had once been to be reduced to a chair was agonizing for her to accept. How can he be happy living like this?

She looked out into the yard where his finger pointed. A contraption sat close to the galerie. It looked like a one-man carriage made with three wheels.

"Those are my running legs when I'm in the yard." Jillian was lifted in his arm. "This is your *cousine* Jillian. I'm willing the one on the way is a boy. I refuse to live in a mansion filled with girls."

"Oncle, where's Tante Marie-Marie?" Abigail asked, staring at Anne again, then over her shoulder at her husband and brother-in-law. "I have forgotten my manners."

Julien patted affectionately at her hand. Jillian saw this and also gave Abigail's hand a tender pat. "We're legally separated. Marie-Marie lives with her family in France now. If I'm to believe her last letter, she's happy. Anne is free now, Abby. It took a helluva fight to win that victory. Since Jillian was born before Anne was manumitted, to the eyes of the court she's my slave. But this child," his eyes moved quickly toward Anne, "will be *born* free. Anne and I live together on Primrose. You should come visit us some time."

Abigail's eyes and lips tightened at the thought of Anne acting the role of madame over a large plantation.

"If your place is anything like this one we'll like that very much," a male voice said.

Uriah Morning whistled as his hands gripped the galerie railing and his eyes took in the pristine lawn and the layout of the plantation.

Julien purposely didn't give a reply. Not until certain questions were answered would he decide how he would treat Carlisle and his disrespectful looking brother. Convincing a young girl to run away from her family was horrendous on its own. Being an accomplice to stolen money and expensive jewelry was a separate crime. There was no proof Carlisle had been behind what happened to Gorée. To Julien this mattered not. He had decided two years ago never to trust Carlisle again. But more importantly, here was Abigail standing in front of him looking like a poor white cracker when Julien knew the value of what had been stolen should have clothed her better.

"We'll like having you," Anne answered politely. Julien knew she only said this to fill the awkward silence.

The rear door opened again. Edouard had been napping when his sister had arrived. Jenna had gone upstairs to wake him and bring him down.

"Is that my brother!" Abigail wailed switching English for French since her mother didn't speak English. "Mon Dieu! Look at him! He can't be the age of two, yet he's as tall as someone the age of four!"

Edouard was not a shy child. Holding his mother's hand, he stared quizzically at the three strangers as if he could look right into their souls.

"He looks just like Papa!" Abigail said, cupping his small face and smothering it with kisses. "Just like Papa! Look at this white hair and these silvery eyes." It was all she could do from dropping onto her knees and bringing him into her arms. So become with excitement from the sight of him, she looked up and saw her mother beaming down on Edouard with unadulterated pride.

Abigail stiffened as she stood upright.

Jenna lifted the child in her arms, hugging him and kissing him until he giggled.

"For goodness sake, Jenna," Julien pleaded. "Put him down before Pierre sees you."

"Where is Papa?" Abigail asked, her eyes giving her mother a level look of smoldering anger.

"The maison," Jenna answered airily. "Or perhaps the fields. Abby, so much has happened. It will take a while to tell you all of it. Why don't we all go inside? You can get off your feet. You look tired from your trip…"

"I am not tired, Maman," Abigail hissed.

Jenna stared at her daughter and saw three things in her blue-green eyes: jealousy, resentment and rage. With a small smile she hoped to appease Abigail's emotion, if only for a moment. "You don't look tired. I was only trying to be polite."

Uriah elbowed his brother in the side to draw his attention out into the yard, and then he pulled a pipe out of the pocket of his well-worn coat. Securing the bore between his teeth with one hand, he watched the man his brother had told him a lot about. Uriah noticed the cart as much as he did the man. Even the vehicles on this plantation outdid any he'd ever seen. Carlisle had described the wealth of his in-laws, but what he had described did little to justify the oasis Uriah now stood in.

Abigail looked in the same direction and saw what she believed to be two small heads and a girl who could have been Gorée. The sudden exhilaration she felt on seeing her father flitted when she saw he was with his favorite child. From the moment she stepped onto the plantation she had been caught between happiness and disappointment. The dueling emotions were short lived this time. As soon as her father drew closer and realized who stood on his galerie surprise and joy filled his eyes.

"Abby!" Pierre yelled as he stepped down from the cart. "What in the world? When did you get here?"

"Just now," Jenna gushed, stepping closer to the galerie's edge. "I received a letter within minutes of them arriving."

"Wait one moment." Pierre spoke urgently. Reaching into the back of the cart, he lifted Gorée out of it first and placed her on her feet.

"Well, look at that will you?" Uriah drew the unlit pipe from between his teeth, his brows furrowed in confusion. "I have never seen a more finely dressed nigger in all my life."

"Mulâtresse!" Julien corrected. "Don't ever use that word on this land again."

Abigail's face turned as hard as stone as she looked at identical twin girls lifted out of the cart one by one, their small hands then given to Gorée.

Edouard saw his sisters and tried to climb out of his mother's arms. Jenna held him tightly, struggling to keep him on her hip.

Abigail saw her father hurrying toward her and ran to meet him. Pierre lifted her off her feet and swung her high in the air.

Gorée walked past Pierre with her two small charges, up onto the galerie and past Abigail and Carlisle to where Edouard was. Jenna didn't trust Gorée handling all three children at the same time and kept Edouard in her arms against his whimpering protests.

Uriah's mouth gaped as he stared at the twins: the shine of their laced up boots, the fit and fabric of their matching dresses trimmed with lace. Seeing what real money could buy reminded him he was no longer in the small part of Texas where he and his brother were from.

Gorée sat in a chair. Easter and Estelle shared a chair beside her, climbing up onto it at the same time. Pierre lifted Edouard in his arms and placed him on his feet. Abigail watched as he ran to Gorée with opened arms. Gorée giggled loudly as she clasped him to her breasts. Edouard wasn't satisfied until Gorée lifted him on her lap.

Jillian smiled at her cousins, but didn't rise from her papa's lap. After being gone for close to a year, she had no idea that these children were related to her. All she knew was they were children she wished to play with.

Pierre faced Carlisle, giving him a stern look.

"Hello, sir." Carlisle spoke with raised eyebrows as if he was confused by Pierre's behavior.

Abigail quickly stepped forward. "Papa, this is Uriah Morning, Carlisle's younger brother."

"Why don't we go in and sit?" Jenna spoke in a rush. The conversation again had reverted to English. She didn't have to know the language. Tension had crept onto the galerie like a strong wind. "All of us." Abigail had just arrived. She hoped Pierre didn't frighten or anger her to leave again and so soon.

Abigail became embarrassed when Julien rose from his chair. Anne held tightly to him. Jillian, trying to be of help to her mother and father, gripped her father's trousers at the lower part of the leg as if to also hold him up. Abigail wished they could have performed this spectacle after she, her husband and brother-in-law had gone into the house.

"Now there's a well trained slave gal if ever I saw one," Uriah commented. "She even looks like she's happy doing what she's doing. I guess a fine dress like what she's wearing could put any slave in the proper mind of her duties."

"I don't like Américains," Pierre said stepping closer to Uriah. "You speak whatever is in your mind instead of shitting it out in private like a decent man. You don't own this land, and you're not entitled to anything on it. If you disrespect anyone on this property again, you'll regret it."

Carlisle had silently pulled Abigail closer to him.

Jenna's eyes hardened on Uriah. Again the tension had thickened. For the first time in a long time anger filled Pierre's face. It didn't take much to know that Uriah was the culprit, especially since it had been after he had spoken that made Pierre stand rigid. She then stared at Abigail as if to ask why she would bring such a man to the plantation.

Julien had learned how to shoot with his left hand and had whispered to Anne to go get his pistol.

Uriah stood awestruck at Pierre, and then he quickly looked at all of the others before facing Pierre again. "Sir, I honestly meant no disrespect. If I offended any of you, I apologize. I come from a good family, and if you give me a chance I can prove that to you."

Pierre studied Uriah long enough for his appraisal to be considered rude. As he stared intently into Uriah's eyes, he was of the mind that the man had spoken truthfully. Pierre then stared at Carlisle even longer. Gorée came to mind, and Jenna when she had become distressed the day Abigail had fled.

When he spoke, he spoke to both brothers. "You are standing on French soil. I don't care who claims it as their country. When in this house you will behave in the Creole manner. Anything less and both of you will be on your way."

"Papa, please," Abigail begged. "This is the way everyone speaks in Kentucky."

"I've been to Kentucky," Pierre chastised not understanding how she could side with a stranger of who she had known for less than two years rather than with her famille. "No proper man speaks in this manner in front of women and children."

The flush in Abigail's face was noticeable.

"The Creole way, Papa, is to show kindness to visitors to your home regardless of their behavior. If you cannot show this kindness to my husband and brother-in-law then we shall leave here at once."

Pierre saw Jenna studying everyone's faces, her stance pensive, her eyes fearful. Translating what had happened, her response was immediate.

"Oh, please!" Jenna cried, stepping closer to Abigail until she faced her. "You have to understand," she whispered, casting a furtive glance in Uriah's direction. "Things have happened. There's so much I need to explain, as well as so many things I need to tell you. Please, give me that chance, Abby."

"Maman, there's no need to whisper. Carlisle desired to learn French, especially since he knew we would come back here some day. We both taught Uriah. Both of them are now fluent."

Jenna started to look at Uriah, because she had a sneaky suspicion that Uriah knew she didn't speak English and had said the things he said hoping she and the rest of them wouldn't understand.

Uriah didn't notice Jenna or anyone else other than Abigail. Within minutes he had nearly blown their chances. Abigail had told him a lot about her family. What she hadn't told him was some of the people in her family spoke English as well as she did.

***

By the time they were all settled in chairs and on the sofas in the *grand salle*, Abigail's anger filled her heart. She couldn't understand why Gorée was permitted to sit in the room with them. It didn't matter if Gorée sat in a chair in the farthest corner and was surrounded by the children; it was inappropriate for her to be in the room at all.

Jenna studied Abigail's eyes and saw the direction she was looking in. Leaning closer to her, she whispered under her breath. "She's the best child nurse I have. I allow her to sit in the room with me so Edouard can stay near."

Abigail swung her face so she could look her mother in the eye. "When I was his age I wasn't allowed to sit in the same room as adults. No children are, Maman. You act as if what you said excuses your behavior. Even if you have your reasons, why is Anne allowed to sit with my oncle? Do you sit there and tell me it is appropriate for a *mulâtresse* who is having an affair with a married man and the child she had with him to sit amongst guests as if they were a happy family? But most of all I become overwhelmed when I remind myself that you are allowing the twins in this house. I only have to look at them and know who their father is."

Jenna sat still and nonplussed as she realized that Abigail had watched her every action and had judged them as further injustices made against her. Sitting back and more comfortably on the sofa, it occurred to her that she had moved on with her life whereas Abigail, in less than an hour, had been ambushed by not one day, but every day of her past.

"There's a reason behind everything you have seen so far, Abby. I do hope you give me the chance to explain. Perhaps you and I can sit alone together later and talk?"

Abigail had trouble recognizing the woman sitting beside her. Never would her mother have permitted any of what she'd seen so far take place in the past, especially in front of guests. If anything her mother would have done all she could to present the mansion as the most respectful abode in the entire parish. Even her mother's face appeared different. Although it looked the same, it was almost as if light radiated from her eyes and underneath her skin. *Is she happier because I left?*

As she tried to imagine what could have happened to her mother to change her so, she turned slightly and probed her father with angry eyes.

Pierre didn't see the look Abigail was giving. He and Julien were too busy noticing how Uriah and Carlisle appeared to be on their best behavior, and how they now only spoke French as if to please the family. Servants had entered the room with beverages and refreshments. Each time an offer was made to either brother, Uriah nodded and Carlisle verbally thanked the servants with what looked like sincere humility.

Pierre and Julien then looked at one another, both confounded by the behavior they were witnessing. Nothing was said and no gesture was made, still Pierre knew Julien wished to speak to him in private at the earliest convenience.

Later that afternoon Jenna led Uriah to one of the smaller guest bedrooms on what was considered the second floor, as the raised basement was seen as just that. Uriah constantly told her how kind she was and how thankful he was of all of their hospitality. Jenna was none appeased by his fawning mannerism or how he had used many adjectives, as if to unload on her his vocabulary as if she would swallow the words as easily as sweetened cold water on a hot day. Teaching an Américain the Creole language, Jenna felt, was another betrayal committed by Abigail. Still she answered kindly, fearing Uriah would tell Abigail anything she said.

Abigail and Carlisle were then shown to Marie-Marie's old bedroom.

"Why this room?" Abigail asked.

It looked to Jenna as if Abigail had reached her last tether. She watched as Abigail studied the furniture, marking each piece with her eyes as pieces that hadn't belonged to her in the past.

"Abby," Jenna pleaded. "I... I gave Edouard your old room, but only because it was close to mine."

Abigail's nostrils flared, the blue-green tint of her eyes darkened. "And my furniture, Maman? My things?"

Jenna reached gingerly to touch Abigail's hair. Abigail flinched, then pulled away. Fiery red tendrils stuck out like thin branches reaching for a breeze.

"We still haven't been able to talk," Jenna said. "But we will. I promise. Afterwards I'm hoping you'll feel better, and that you'll be comfortable with all of the changes once you understand the reasons behind them. For now just know I am happy to have you back. Very happy."

It was because Abigail wanted to believe this the reason she threw her arms around her mother's waist and buried her face in her mother's neck. Jenna clung to her, squeezing her arms with all the strength she had.

Pulling Abigail away from her with shaking hands, she said, "I love you. I always have. I don't care about the money or the jewelry or anything that happened in the past. All I care about is you staying for a long, long time."

"Merci, Maman," Abigail whispered, choked by the enormity of emotions inside her.

*** 

"You know they're here for a reason, don't you?" This was how Julien started the conversation between him and Pierre. To make certain Carlisle and Uriah didn't overhear or interrupt, the two had gone into Julien's bedroom to discuss what each of them had been holding inside since Uriah and Carlisle had stood on the galerie.

"I know that," Pierre assured. "I also know something more."

"What's that?" Julien asked eagerly.

"Either Abigail or Uriah is the devil."

Julien's eyes became large, especially the left one.

"Have you been paying attention?" Pierre asked.

"Most certainly."

"I don't believe Carlisle had anything to do with Gorée. The same man he presented himself as before they left is the same exact man that has returned. Still I'm sending Gorée to stay with Alise while the brothers are in my home."

"Why do you think Abigail or Uriah is the devil?" This was the part Julien wanted to hear most.

"I think Cyril meant well. As he told us his suspicions we all believed them, but I'm beginning to suspect that Cyril's feelings toward Carlisle are clouded by his prejudice against Américains. The entire time we sat in the *salle*, Carlisle tried to hide it, but at times he couldn't. Watch his eyes, Julien. They constantly watch his brother and Abigail. Every word they speak. Every gesture or move they make. Carlisle watches as if judging the intent behind them."

"Why do you think he's doing that?"

"I don't know. I spoke to him."

"When?" Julien's tone was close to a hiss.

Pierre smiled. "Brother, your days of helping me hunt our enemies are over."

"The hell it is," Julien contended. "But forget about that and tell me what you said to him."

"When he stood beside me to pour glasses of bourbon, I asked him was he behind the missing money and jewelry. You should have seen the look on his face. Julien, the man owns three slaves. He offered to give me one as compensation then explained it was all he had at the time."

"*Merde,*" Julien whispered. "I was ready to hate him."

"After Abigail and Carlisle left two years ago I questioned everyone on the plantation that had spent time with him. All of them said the same thing. They found Carlisle to be none judgmental and an extremely polite man. Even Désireé confessed to this when she and I spoke in private."

"Why do you think they're back?"

"Money of course."

"But the other money..." Julien began.

Pierre's eyes narrowed in thought as he shook his head. "It doesn't make sense. They would have never gotten the true value of the jewelry, but even half would have given them enough to live well. Semper told me that Uriah was the one who brought Jenna the letter earlier today. I know why Jenna hasn't told me this. She fears I'll do or say something that will send Abigail away. This means after Uriah gave her the letter, he rode off of the property, went up the road a spell to give her time to read it, then turned around and drove the three of them back."

"Sounds like desperation."

"Why buy land if you can't build once you buy it?"

"*Merde*," Julien whispered. "Abigail."

"I can't explain the look that was in Carlisle's eyes when I asked him about the money. What I can explain was the fear that came into them after he heard what I said. I want to know why they're here and I want to know right away. I think I can urge it out of both brothers in the morning after I take them on a tour."

"I want to go with you when you do. I'll bring my pistol along just in case. Anne can drive me in one of the buggies."

While Julien and Pierre continued their conversation, Jenna and Abigail were having one of their own. Uriah and Carlisle were upstairs napping. Abigail used this moment to find her mother and have her explain the differences she noticed.

When Jenna saw her daughter walking in her direction, she gave the servants last minute instructions regarding the upcoming celebration. Leading Abigail into Jenna's private *salle*, a servant followed behind them with café and a three-tier serving platter over laden with Abigail's favorite treats.

Jenna spoke first, telling Abigail almost everything that happened on the plantation from the morning Abigail left. She spoke only briefly about the breakdown she experienced, because she hadn't wanted Abigail to feel responsible.

Hearing that both her father and oncle had both nearly died became quite sobering. Abigail listened intently as her mother left out little detail, and saw how emotional her mother became when she spoke about being attacked in the cottage by runaways.

"Your papa and Gentilly saved my life. After he got well, he had the cottage torn down. He had to. It was too far away from anything and had attracted too much attention."

"The two of you are all right now?" Abigail asked when Jenna became silent while sipping her café. "You and Papa?"

"Things are not the same as they used to be, Abigail. It's about half and half, good and bad. I'm not the same as I used to be, either. I've come to see things differently. I react to things now with new eyes."

"Are you happy?" Abigail watched carefully as her mother leaned over the table in a rush and lowered her voice.

"I almost killed Sarah two years ago," she whispered, then sat back again in her chair. Abigail could see that her mother had been happy to share this new bit of information, not because she had been proud of what she'd done, but because it looked at the moment as if she hadn't had anyone to confide in, and getting it out after it had been bottled up had given her a moment of relief.

Averting her gaze, Jenna stared across the room seeing that day again in her mind. "No one saw me grab it. I wish now that they had." She faced Abigail then. "You have to understand how I felt. I had been taking care of him. Had even given him my bed to make certain he was comfortable. Sitting up at all hours of the night. Washing him and stripping the bedding. It's common for women in my position to see after anyone ill, but I can honestly say that before that I never had. Alise was always sent for. She was the one that took that responsibility solely on herself."

She gave a bitter shake of her head, her lips pursing tightly. "I can remember the few days when your father made me feel loved and hated at the same time. I thought... I thought we were on a new path, and he and I would be husband and wife in its proper sense. And then he had awakened the same day Jillian was born. That's when he said it. He mentioned Edouard first, but said nothing after. And then he said if he died Sarah was to remain at the *maison* for as long as she lived. And her children there with her. I got angry. How was I supposed to know, Abby? How?"

Abigail pressed a hand to her mouth when her mother actually hung her head and looked both woman and child filled with remorse.

"I found out later that Sarah had planned on leaving. A letter had been expressed to Tante Marianne, and Tante Marianne expressed one in return. The two of them were going to move to Mobile together where a distant oncle lived." Again her mother looked up, as if searching Abigail's eyes. "Sarah hadn't told anyone, you see? We were all seeing after your father. Not many visits were made to the *maison*. Only the servants closest to her understood what was going on. But she came that day, here, and asked me if she could see your father. That's when I did it. I grabbed the candlestick, you see? The one that belonged to my mother."

Abigail pressed the tips of both hands against her mouth. She knew the candlestick quite well. Five pounds of sterling silver had been used to make it.

"I swung it without looking. She must have known, because she threw up her arm. It hit her close to the back of her head. I regretted it the moment I saw the blood. And the way she fell. She just dropped. I stared down and saw that her eyes were closed, and that she had our father's face. I had never noticed that before the way I did that day. I knew then despite what she'd done, I hadn't truly wanted her to die. I had never called her my sister and meant it in the past, but it's what I felt when I stood there. That she was my sister, and I had almost killed her."

"And then what happened?"

Jenna shook her head repeatedly. "They left your father's side and ran to her. Everyone was screaming. Servants were running around. Alise didn't trust Sarah in the mansion with me. She had servants carry Sarah on top of a door back to the *maison*. One of the servants told your father what happened. I guess he imagined Sarah becoming like your oncle. Bitter tears, Abby. That's what he let out. And then he too was moved to the *maison*. Tante Marianne came right away. She took care of both of them, but before she did that, as soon as she arrived on the plantation the first thing she did was come here."

"To do what?" Abigail demanded.

"To slap me like my mother used to." She gave a faraway stare as she averted her gaze. "And she told me things about my mother and father that I didn't know. After she told me all that she had wanted to say, something happened to me, Abby. This house – it was just like my home on Green Lea, a home of two angry people living together. I chose not to live that way anymore, and I haven't looked back since."

"What does that mean, Maman?"

Jenna tried desperately not to hesitate. The words that formed, to her, made her look desperate, or weak, or like an ignorant woman. "It means your father doesn't want to be married to me anymore, and I have accepted it. For the first time since we've been married I can honestly say we have become friends."

"Maman," Abigail pleaded, as if what she had heard had been painful. "Your husband sleeps in the alcove…"

"The alcove is Gorée's private room now. She goes there when she wants to be alone. She lives here with me and Edouard."

"Do you hear yourself, Maman? Gorée is your husband's noir *bâtard*. She should not be allowed to live in this mansion."

Jenna smiled pleasantly. "Gorée loves your brother. If he even looks like he's coming down with a fever she sleeps on the floor beside his bed. I actually enjoy her company at times."

"How can you say that?"

"Because I refuse not to see things as they are. I don't live in the past anymore, Abby. When I stopped doing that I realized life has a lot to offer."

"He's your husband!"

"He is," Jenna agreed. "Sometimes what you lose, Abby, you can never get back. Your father had every intention of sending Edouard and me away once he got better. I hear it was Sarah that talked him out of it. He didn't want to fight anymore. I didn't want to fight anymore. The three of us have decided to leave things as they are, because you see. They got closer while they were getting better. I used to wonder what would have happened if I had let things be. Back then I wanted to hurt others before they hurt me. I'm glad I'm not like that anymore. Your father, he and I talked, and since that day we have learned how to live together and be happy at the same time."

Abigail stared at her mother, not understanding the things she heard. Memories of the life her parents had together flooded back. She averted her gaze. "You said earlier that Papa was at the *maison*. I take it to mean that he lives with her while you, Edouard and Gorée live here?"

Jenna stirred her café to incorporate the sugar better. Lately anything sweetened made the nausea return. "I guess you think it's foolish of me to be carrying another child?"

Abigail rose to her feet. "How can you live like this, Maman? You tried to kill her and rightfully so. Sarah is your sister. If Papa is spending time at the *maison*, you should leave!"

"And go where? Riverside? And do what? Start a new life? Or shall I live with you and Carlisle? Or alone? This is my home. This is Edouard's home. My friends live in this city. I was born in this city. Why should I have to leave it behind? My marriage is *over*, Abigail. And it has been over long before these past two years. I rather have what I have now than go back to the way things used to be before!"

Abigail sat again and lifted her cup with refined dignity.

Jenna gave a laugh of derision. "You dare sit there dressed in a coarse linen gown and worse than any slave I have ever laid eyes on and judge me?"

Abigail didn't feel like she was judging her mother. What had entered into her mind was how life on the plantation had gone on without her as if she had never existed on it. Feelings she hadn't had for two years now returned, each of them fresh, the wounds once again very deep.

"Tell me about Kentucky," Jenna continued. The spite in her tone was evident to both of them. "You have yet to mention it."

Abigail gulped down the café in her mouth and lowered the cup.

"Carlisle and I purchased land there."

"And the two servants you left here with?"

Abigail lifted her chin and stared brazenly into her mother's eyes. "I sold them, Maman. I needed the money. The land we bought didn't have a home or any buildings. We had to build everything ourselves. We have three slaves for now. Two males and one female. I'm hoping the girl gets pregnant soon. Still it will be some time before her offspring are old enough for chores. I have grand ideas, Maman. Grand ideas. Carlisle doesn't know what I took when I left here."

Jenna lifted her cup and nodded for Abigail to continue.

"I lied and told him I had money in the bank. Carlisle had written Uriah and told him about the land. Uriah came to Kentucky to help us build. When the money ran out, Uriah tried to acquire a loan from the bank assured that I would pay it once payment was due. He even went to the bank to draw funds from the account he believed I had. That was almost a month ago. Can you imagine my embarrassment when he confronted me later that day? He knows I'm the daughter of a wealthy planter, so why was it I had very little to show for it?"

"How much do you need?" Jenna asked.

"I didn't come for money. Carlisle thought it was time to return for a visit. Life is different in Kentucky. Of course it has its wealthy planters just like everywhere else, but most there are not wealthy and live simple lives."

Jenna stood to her feet, pressed a hand to her mouth and turned away, because she'd seen in Abigail's eyes that she hadn't wanted to come back. She had become content living like a peasant rather than have anything to do with the family that could help her. Facing Abigail again Jenna fretted over the right words to use.

"Let me help you. Tell me how much you think you need, Abby, to build faster."

Abigail gazed at her critically. "I must admit, Maman. This new woman you are is strange to me. You have never offered money in the past, and refused to give it to anyone. Gorée and Anne sitting with you in your *salle* as if they are *your* family…"

Jenna pursed her lips tightly together. "Anne is a free woman of color, Abigail, and the woman your oncle has chosen to be with. Everyone had given up on him and expected him to die. He now runs his own plantation. Should I be angry because of who he has chosen to live his life with?"

Abigail's mouth tightened. "They're *nègres*. Nothing more. Treating them any better only confuses them. The Bible says…"

"Shut up!" Jenna threatened, then turned, because now she had reached her last tether. A part of her wanted to resort to the woman she used to be. A slap to the face and harsh words were what she wanted to give. The reason she didn't give in to the urge was because she knew that she had behaved just like Abigail was during the first sixteen years of her marriage. She faced Abigail again and saw that her daughter was staring at her with equal intent.

"The mother you left behind is no more," Jenna declared.

For a long while her lips pressed tightly together. The look in her eyes and the way her shoulders lifted and fell in slow rhythm warned Abigail just how upset her mother had become.

"Don't spout a single scripture to me to prove your point," Jenna continued. "You haven't lived long enough to know what I know. Your father is good to the people on this land. It was because of his goodness Gentilly fought three runaways to save mine. Me! Back then none of the slaves had any love for me, and for good reason. Gentilly saw your father with holes in his stomach and thought he would surely die. The reason he saved my life is because earlier that day your father had ridden me around the plantation. At the time I didn't understand why. What he was doing, child, was putting me in my proper place and letting everyone know it.

"I was near naked and trapped under him. Your father *knew* they would shoot through that door. He didn't run. He didn't push me in front of it like I probably would have done him had I been younger. What he said was hold on. Don't let go. Even if I fall. And then he stood there and allowed runaway slaves to shoot him not knowing if he would live or die. And that isn't all, girl. With the last bit of strength he had he fought those runaways to make sure I suffered no harm."

She closed her eyes and lifted her chin. "That's true love. Not many people will give their life for someone that had once been an enemy. I hurt that man, Abigail. I hurt him! I know because I did it on purpose. That he can look in my face now with only care and concern means something to me. I don't care who doesn't understand the relationship that he and I have now. If I ask for *anything*, he makes certain I have it. Not because of guilt or what's happening between the trees, but because he and I have finally come to respect each other and now only have each other's best interest at heart. Maybe when you become my age, after you've made the mistakes I've made, after you've seen all I have seen, after you have lived many years with hurt and pain, you'll learn that to live for all there is worth to live you have to forgive everyone that has ever hurt you and forget the past. Your father, even this day, suffers from the injuries he got while saving my life. I don't ask him what he does at the *maison*!

"I cannot contemplate over Sarah's decision to be with him. I don't even think about it anymore. If he and I only trusted each other from the beginning, I know things would now be different. But just like your birth I can do nothing to change that now. While he and I hated each other, he found someone who gave him the love he believed I never could. By the time he and I realized we could have a life together, it was too late, Abigail. He loves her! His life at the *maison* is separate from here. But I'll tell you this. Not once has Sarah tried to stop him from coming here. Once when he'd gotten sick she walked here herself and invited me and Edouard to come to the *maison* to be close to him. You think I'm foolish? Think what you want."

"But it doesn't excuse it, Maman. He saved your life, and you're allowing him to live as if he has two wives?"

Jenna smiled as she looked away from Abigail in disgust. "That's what you think? That he shares my bed? Sarah has his heart. It's her bed he sleeps in, and only hers."

Abigail started to speak. Jenna waved her hand angrily in the air.

"I wanted a brother for Edouard. Another son to hold and love. It was nothing more than that. I asked and he gave it to me. He may have Sarah, but he hasn't torn me down because of it. In this house, on this land, in the city, I am the Madame. He made certain everyone knew this, and because of that, instead of being pitied I am respected by more women in this city than you'll ever know."

Abigail lowered her voice. "Don't you hate her?"

A look came into Jenna's eyes. "I think about the truth. If it hadn't been her it would have been someone else – someone without a willingness to work things out peacefully – someone who probably would have made certain he gotten rid of me. And I think about the friendship that he and I have now." Her gaze planted firmly on Abigail. "He *loves* Edouard just like I knew he would. Edouard will be his heir. I'm most certain of it."

Abigail saw that her mother believed this. "And your sister's children?"

Jenna averted her gaze. "Sarah is pregnant again. You may not understand it, but it's true. I'm over it. I'm happy now, Abby. I'm happy because I love *myself* now. I'm happy because my relationships with my friends have also changed, and they love me. Being loved can make you see things differently."

"You're not happy, Maman. You're only trying to convince yourself you are."

Jenna held Abigail's gaze. "Why are you here, Abigail? You *look* like you need money. There's something you aren't telling me. I would appreciate it if you told me what it is."

Abigail neither looked at her mother nor focused her eyes on anything.

"Tell me," Jenna pleaded.

Tears fell down Abigail's face. Her cup was lifted with a trembling hand. She managed to bring it to her lips and take a sip. "A lot has happened," she began. "I can't tell you it all because I'm too ashamed."

"Tell me who's to blame. Is it Carlisle?"

"No." Abigail's voice was close to a whisper.

The plea that came into her eyes gave Jenna hope that the woman she was looking at now was her real daughter.

"He's a good man."

"Tell me," Jenna begged. "I have waited for this moment – to see you again. I wasn't a good mother to you, and I wish that wasn't true. I didn't realize that I loved you until you left. The pain – I can't describe it. Please let's put the past behind us. Please trust me to be a good mother to you now. You said you didn't come for money, but I still want to give it to you. Right now I would give my very life if you would call me maman and mean it."

Abigail rushed out of her chair. Jenna rose to her feet. Both sobbed uncontrollably as they fell into each other's arms.

"I love you so much," Jenna whimpered. "Please forgive me for all that I've done against you."

Abigail was unable to speak. All she could do was hold her mother a long while. "All I can tell you, Maman, is Carlisle came here expecting nothing from you or Papa. If he and I lived under a tree, he would be happy just being with me."

"He is a good man, Abby. Please don't make the same mistakes I did. And Uriah? Is there anything this family needs to know about him?"

Abigail licked away a tear, bit firmly on her lip and shook her head.

"I'm *so* glad you're home," Jenna said.

"Me too," Abigail answered and smiled like she used to during those few months before she left.

\*\*\*

Abigail awoke to a vase of fresh cut flowers and a note from her mother to sleep in as long as she wanted.

Pierre rose early, as did Carlisle and Uriah. The offer of a tour was readily accepted. Anne drove a buggy behind Pierre's cart. Julien kept his eyes open and his pistol ready. The tour lasted a long while. Every part of the plantation they came upon brought questions from Uriah. Seeing Pierre's success made him interested in the secrets behind it. Pierre patiently answered each question. Carlisle sat at leisure in the back of the cart as if he was simply enjoying being alive another day. Each time he saw a servant he remembered from before, he made a habit of waving and giving them a warm smile.

Pierre had learned a lot during the tour, but not the answers he sought. The land Carlisle and Abigail owned hadn't been purchased as Abigail had told Jenna the day before. Carlisle had received a land grant from the President. The brothers' father, Winslow Morning, had fought against Spain and France in Spanish Texas. Because of his bravery under the command of Augustus Magee in the siege of La Bahia wasn't the only reason President Jackson granted Carlisle the land.

"After my father died we were destitute, sir. A friend of my father's was one of the Old Three Hundred. He invited my family to move in with him and his family temporarily until we could get on our feet. My mother, sisters and brothers didn't want to leave the home our father had built for us. I made the decision to go on my own and bring money back as much as I could. I met a soldier there named John Austin. The two of us quickly became friends. I guess you can say I'm like my father. I enlisted with the militia. We received orders to transport canon up the Brazos River."

"You fought in the Battle of Valesco?" Pierre asked.

"Yes, sir. Pretty intense for someone with little militia experience. I was happy to be under the command of John. The group I was assigned to attacked from the north. We made shields out of pieces of cypress. We lost seven men. More than a dozen of us were wounded."

"And you were one of the wounded," Pierre speculated.

"Yes, sir. I can never have children, sir. As much as I loved your daughter from the moment I arrived, I couldn't bring myself to mention this to her. The matter was just too delicate. I came to New Orléans because John told me about it. I wasn't looking for a wife. I just wanted to get out of Texas. As much as I wanted to marry her, I tried hard to dissuade her from marrying me. It's why she stalled on the house you wanted to build. I didn't believe that a wife as young as Abigail would want to stay married to a man who couldn't give her children. I took the coward's way out. Instead of come to you, I told Abigail I was leaving. We talked about it for a long time that night until she finally agreed to let me leave. The next morning I had been on my way to the stables to fetch my horse when she came running out to me. She told me she had permission to go to the city and that she would give me a ride there. I didn't know what she had planned. I purchased my ticket. The steamboat wasn't leaving for some hours so I walked the city to get a last view of it. I had already boarded and the steamboat had left the dock when I saw her approaching on the deck. I'm sorry I have to tell you all this and I hope your love for her doesn't change because of it."

Pierre nodded.

"She told me she wanted to marry me anyway. I was happy and frightened at the same time, because I only realized then that she had run away. But I can take care of her, sir. I know it doesn't look like that now, but it's true. John sent a letter to President Jackson confirming my duties. I think he may have added a little bit on the bravery part, but whatever he wrote made President Jackson agree to the land grant and remuneration. I'm waiting on that money now."

After the tour Pierre spoke with Carlisle alone inside the study.

"Tell me about your brother," he said after a long silence that followed brief trivial conversations.

"He's a hard worker. Most of my family is."

"Are you going to raise crop on your land?"

"Yes, sir, but nothing as grueling as sugar. Bowling Green isn't anything like New Orléans, but agriculture grows well there. Our place is close to the Barren River."

"Carlisle, I'm going to be honest with you."

"Please do, sir, and I'll give it in return."

"Abigail left here with a considerable sum of money. I got the impression yesterday you knew nothing about it."

Carlisle's face became grim. "I told you I would be honest with you, but..."

"It won't change my feelings toward her. I need to understand everything that happened."

Carlisle shifted in the chair to lean over the desk. "Sometimes she can be terribly happy. At other times terribly sad. She's shared a lot with me about her childhood here. I personally think she's trying hard to discover the woman she wants to be. I don't agree with her newly adopted mindset. My brother may be the reason behind that. But overall, she's a good woman."

"I'm glad to hear that."

"When we left here I had every intentions of staying with another militiaman who had relocated to Bowling Green. I had no money. You know that. I had a ring that used to belong to my father. The ruby in it was well intact. I sold it to purchase my ticket and had a little left over. When Abigail found me on deck, she told me her mother had given her a little money here and there over the years and that she had saved it. I know nothing about this money or jewelry you're speaking of. I've never seen it."

"And the two servants you left here with? Where are they now?" Pierre knew the answer. Jenna had shared it with him the day before. What he needed to see was Carlisle's reaction, then hear what he would say afterwards.

Carlisle's eyes became large, and then he sat upright. "I assumed Abigail had sent the servants back here before she boarded the steamboat."

Pierre closed his eyes. Abigail hadn't only stolen five thousand dollars and jewelry. She stole the lives of two good servants who had no idea what was happening to them when they left his land.

He sat back in his chair and stared at Carlisle. In his mind he imagined what those two servants went through that day. The coach hadn't been returned which meant Abigail had either abandoned it for someone to steal or sold it as well. This went well beyond the treachery he thought she was capable of, and he could see in Carlisle's eyes that he had also fitted the pieces together and now had a clear understanding of what had truly happened.

Carlisle couldn't stop staring at him. Pierre had no way to know what he was thinking, as Carlisle's face didn't give it away.

"You have never seen her spend any of this money, have you?" Pierre asked.

Carlisle lowered his head and pressed his hand tight against mouth.

It was that moment Pierre got an even better understanding. He reached forward and pulled closer a decanter and poured two glasses of bourbon. Carlisle readily accepted the glass and took a generous swallow as a tear rolled down his cheek. "The day my brother arrived in Bowling Green he looked like he had no money." His head lowered and his eyes closed tightly. "He's been spending freely since he arrived. A lot of the money he spent went on things we needed on the land. It was my friend that saw them. I trusted Uriah. I trusted Abby. The spending. The betrayal. A month ago I was told that Uriah had gone into the city in an attempt to withdraw funds from a bank account he believed Abby had here."

Pierre nodded that he understood what Carlisle was trying to tell him.

"The reason I'm here, sir, is because I have to get rid of my brother if I want to save my marriage. I thought if we came back here now that our home has been completed, and she saw her family and the love here that I had seen between you all, she'll remember how important family is. I told my brother that if she chose me, I'll be sending his ass back to Texas."

Pierre leaned forward with his glass raised in a toast. "To sending his ass back to Texas."

Carlisle gave a wide smile and clinked his glass against Pierre's. "I'm sorry for the trouble I've caused, sir."

"There are many a poor people who would gladly give their newborns to a well off couple."

"At the moment Abigail claims no desire to have children. Whether we have them or not makes no difference to me. Her time is very precious to me."

"I need you to find out from your brother how much of the jewelry he has left, and then I want it returned. Some of the pieces have been in my wife's family for many years. I'm sure she will bequeath them to Abigail in her death, but Jenna is carrying another child and if it's a girl she may want to divide the jewelry up or even give a piece or two to Edouard's wife when he marries. The jewelry is hers to decide what to do with it."

"By all means, sir. I need you to know that I have not mentioned to Abigail what I know. I didn't want to give my brother an advantage. I told her we came here just to visit."

"I want to help you," Pierre said. "You're a good man. I believed that on the day I told you can marry my daughter, and I believe it even more now. I'll pay to send your brother wherever he wants to go and put enough money in his pocket so he'll never bother the two of you again. I also want to build you and Abigail a decent home in Bowling Green. Instead of you waiting on money from the government, I'm willing to provide you with all you need to get your crop planted as soon as possible. Abigail's letter states you have three slaves."

Carlisle finished what was in his glass.

Pierre saw more tears in the man's eyes and refilled the glass.

"Thank you." Carlisle's voice was strained. "I don't want you to think I came here for money. I know your daughter is dressed poorly, and if I could have done something better for her before we came, I would have. I was desperate, sir."

"Don't worry about that. All of Abigail's clothing is still here. Maybe tomorrow we can go into the city and get you some nice suits. I want you looking your best and comfortable for the celebration."

"Thank you, sir."

***

Carlisle saw Abigail descending the staircase and couldn't move another step. The gown she wore was of deep green silk, the bodice captivating her slender frame with such perfection that Carlisle refused to believe he had seen her look more beautiful than she was at that moment.

"You look beautiful."

Carlisle closed his eyes and lowered his chin, because it hadn't been him that had spoken.

Uriah must have been standing in an area out of Carlisle's range of vision. It also occurred to Carlisle that Uriah couldn't see him either or he wouldn't have dared said what he said.

Abigail smiled at Uriah and gave a polite word of thanks, then hurried down the staircase and ran into Carlisle's arms.

Uriah stepped out of the *salle* into the hall, saw this and walked away.

Carlisle wanted to kiss his wife. No. He wanted to do more than that. He wanted to make love to her. The avidity must have shown in his eyes because Abigail smiled the way she did when she too felt the need of him.

"You're more than beautiful," he said.

"We can go upstairs," she whispered.

Carlisle didn't wait another moment.

In the bedroom given to them he kissed her with hungry passion, his hands reaching for the back of her gown to quickly strip her out of it.

Abigail giggled. As soon as the pin was removed she stepped back from him.

The pain he felt when Abigail preceded to strip out of her dress like a prostitute entertaining a high paying client. This was something he suspected she had learned from his brother. Waiting patiently for her demonstration to end, he again devoured her mouth with deep kisses as he reached this time for her corset. As Abigail removed the rest of her clothing, Carlisle quickly disrobed. The two of them fell back on the bed in laughter. Abigail had small breasts with puffy nipples close to the tint of her hair. White skin. The sprinkling of freckles on her shoulders. Whenever he looked at her nude he envisioned his interpretation of Correggio's painting, "Jupiter and Io."

The two of them made love very slowly, and very intensely. The sound of Abigail's shivering breaths always pushed him further over the edge. Not wanting to appear rude with their absence down below or for anyone to figure out what they'd been up to, they quickly washed and redressed, then walked out of their bedroom arm and arm.

Uriah was waiting for them in the hall.

"Oh, there you are." He spoke matter of fact. "I didn't want to be alone when I met the family for the midday meal."

"Well, here we are," Abigail replied with reddened cheeks.

The three of them walked downstairs together.

As they walked, Abigail clung to Carlisle's arm mindful of how closely Uriah stayed behind them. When he had arrived in Bowling Green she had been enamored with his wild side. She had confided in him the things she had been unable to tell Carlisle. In the beginning she liked him, and then the two of them began having an affair. As soon as it began she had wanted to end it because each time she had been in Uriah's arms she thought only of Carlisle.

Uriah became angry when she told him they must stop their secret meetings. So that he didn't tell Carlisle about the affair or the money and jewelry or anything she had done wrong, she found herself giving in to anything Uriah asked for. The day he confronted her about visiting the bank on her behalf, she sensed that Uriah had been using her all along. When Carlisle mentioned visiting her parents, she jumped at the chance hoping it would put some distance between she and Uriah. She saw now that Uriah had no intentions of backing down. What if someone had heard him tell her how beautiful she looked or saw him standing outside her boudoir?

Uriah entered the formal dining room behind the couple. Right away he realized Abigail was the center of attention. The servants couldn't stop looking in her direction with large smiles on their faces. It was obvious that each of them were happy she had returned home. Mrs. Jennings had been standing next to her husband, but quickly left his side and folded Abigail in her arms.

This was not the behavior Uriah had expected from the family Abigail had told him about in private.

He began to pay close attention, not only to Mrs. Jennings' peculiar behavior but to everyone's behavior. The cripple was already seated at the table and had raised his glass toward Abigail and Carlisle. Mr. Jennings pulled out a chair at the head of the table, waited for Abigail to be seated, gripped Carlisle by the shoulders, kissed both sides of his face, then pulled out the chair beside Abigail for Carlisle to sit in.

Uriah's eyes narrowed as he wondered if this extra show of affection was somehow directed at him.

A male servant dressed in livery pulled out Uriah's chair. Uriah gave the servant a harsh glare, warning the servant with his eyes to get away from him as quickly as possible. So far the only thing he was grateful for was no children were in the room, which meant they wouldn't be dining with them. If anything Uriah had expected hostility. Where was it? Abigail had stolen money and jewelry from her mother, so why was her mother acting as if Abigail hadn't been a thief? The reason he knew about the money and jewelry was because he was in possession of what was left of the money and all of the fine pieces: necklaces, earrings, brooches, rings, ornate pins, all made with finely cut gems: diamonds, onyx, emeralds, pearls, sapphire, rubies and turquoise.

As he unfolded his linen napkin, it was hard for him not to give Abigail his attention as well. The dress she wore made her look nothing less than someone from royalty. Makeup had been applied to her face. The many freckles on her face were totally covered. Rouge had been applied to her cheeks and lips. An Indian necklace adorned her exposed upper chest. Someone had tamed her hair by braiding it, then weaving the braid into a bun. Ringlets of curls fell against her forehead, ears and down past her shoulders.

Uriah noticed that several tablecloths had been layered one on top of the other. Servants entered bearing a single dish on each plate.

"Julien, I'm taking Carlisle into town to get fitted for a wardrobe. Would you like to come with us?"

Uriah stared surreptitiously at Mr. Jennings wondering if the omission of his name had been deliberate.

"There's no need," Jenna said with a smile of pride. "The girls in the weaving cabin had completed the wardrobe they started back when…" A look had come onto her face. She managed to stop it before it could fully formulate, then smiled again. "The girls are getting the clothing ready as we speak. I expect Hiram to have them in Abby's room and put away before evening."

The conversation that followed consisted of a mixture of topics. Uriah wasn't certain if any of the comments he wanted to add would be considered offensive and stayed quiet, mostly. The more any of them noticed his silence, the more he was asked questions directly. This made him feel a little more comfortable. In Kentucky Abigail behaved as the other wives there. Slaves were slaves and treated with partiality. None of their house servants pranced around in clothing similar to whites. Most slave women in Kentucky covered their hair with cloths. For years he had heard about the magnificent lifestyle of the Deep South. He knew now that no one in Bowling Green had come close to reaching the status and wealth of the Jennings family.

After each course was served and eaten the servants arrived and removed the dishes as well as the tablecloth revealing the next one underneath. A tradition amongst the Creoles, he soon learned. The more tablecloths there were represented the home owner's wealth.

With each new tablecloth that surfaced another course was placed on top of it. Uriah had never sat at a table with four drinking receptacles: one for café, another for wine, one for lemonade, water or tea, and a small glass for rum, bourbon, brandy or whisky. Noticing that the Jennings men refused offers of liquor, Uriah followed suit, then scourged Carlisle with his eyes when his brother accepted a small measure of bourbon. The male servant who served him smiled as if he had already known this would be Carlisle's choice.

Uriah had decided by the fifth course that he would allow Carlisle to have this moment. For now Carlisle could entertain his in-laws and lap the luxury they were apparently willing to lavish on him, but when the three of them returned to Bowling Green, Abigail would be his.

By the eighth course Uriah couldn't eat another bite. While the courses had been served he thought he was being polite by finishing everything on his plate. By the time he realized that the others were saving room for the next it had been too late. The sweet dish, if possible, was the most appetizing of them all: homemade ice cream topped with bread pudding, pralines and a sweet sauce. A garnish of sliced bananas had been added to the side of each plate. As stuffed as he was, Uriah found himself scooping another spoonful until the plate looked as if he had licked it clean.

Bourbon and café was served in the *grand salle*. The men sat on one side of the room while Abigail and her mother sat on the other. Anne had mysteriously disappeared after the meal. The children still had yet to make an appearance. It was as if Abigail had read his thoughts.

"I haven't seen Edouard at all today," she said.

"He's between the trees," Jenna answered.

Uriah wondered what was between the trees. One of the things he noticed during the tour was that the beautiful abode owned by the half breed Désireé hadn't been shown to him. He wondered if it was Désireé's home Mrs. Jennings meant by Edouard being between the trees.

Biding his time, he waited patiently for an opportunity to present itself. It came just before everyone retired for bed. Abigail had gone to the butler pantry to speak with Anne. Uriah followed behind her, grabbed her elbow and pulled her into an empty room. Closing its door, he tried to pull her into an embrace. The sudden lift of her hand and the strike of her palm against his face stunned him.

"Have you gone mad?" She whispered with hate in her eyes. "This is my parents' home! Stop this. You must."

The finality in her tone, and the plea for him to release her caused him to avert his gaze.

"I miss you, Abby."

"I told you already, Uriah. It will never happen again. You have my money and my family's jewelry. What else could you want from me?"

He tried to reach for her hair, because the need to touch this new regal woman had become strong. Thoughts of them becoming more than secret lovers and a proper married couple came to his mind. If that happened it would be him receiving the attention Carlisle was getting.

His penis hardened in his trousers. To kiss her lips. To caress her breasts. Doing these things suddenly became urgent. It suddenly felt as if doing these things would make his new ambition true. "Carlisle can't give you children," he whispered. "What do you want him for? I told you he's been going to that nigger girl on his land."

As he lowered to kiss her, she jerked from his hold and crossed the room to put distance between them.

"I don't believe that. I did in the beginning, but not anymore. I think you're only saying it to make me hate him. Carlisle loves me. Not you. So why are you pretending you do? I love him. I shouldn't have ever done with you what I done." Her voice had risen slightly.

Uriah glanced over his shoulder wondering if someone in the hall had heard what she'd said.

"The only reason you're doing this is because you're jealous of him," Abigail accused.

Hearing this made him stare at her again, suddenly.

"You could have left the comfort of your family's home and went with him to the Old Three Hundred colony. You could have become a militiaman, Uriah, and fought in a battle, and also been wounded. I think what he has, you want. I think that's all you're about. I'm almost certain of it. I told you it will be no more and I meant it. I don't care if you tell him my secrets. I told you before that I'm staying with my husband. And if you tell him, and if Carlisle doesn't want me anymore, then I'll stay here with my family because I realize only now that this place is truly my home."

His jaw tightened as she walked further up the room and left out of a second door. Uriah waited giving her time enough to leave the hall. Only then did he open the door. He had taken a step into the hall and saw that Abigail was still there. Carlisle stood close beside her, along with Mr. Jennings. The three of them were talking and smiling about something, and then all three of them laughed.

Trickery was the word that blared through Uriah's mind. All of this. Everything. Carlisle had tricked him into coming. Abigail had tricked him into believing he still had a chance.

Uriah couldn't be certain, but after all he had seen so far, he sensed that neither Mr. nor Mrs. Jennings liked him and were trying to make a fool of him.

***

The day of the celebration had finally arrived.

Uriah was amazed by the sight of it all. The overseers, along with their families, sat with the family on the rear galerie. A bonfire burned in the distant yard between the rear of the mansion and the start of the trees. The slaves on the plantation had dressed in their finest apparel and came from all regions of the property bearing savory dishes it had taken them all night to prepare. Barrels of rum had been brought up from the storehouse and sat on top of tables. For this reason the servants had also brought cups along with them and blankets to spread onto the grass when there was a need to rest. Salt water taffy, sugar coated pralines and thin slices of pineapple were in abundance for the children.

Uriah was introduced to many faces. Names were being spoken. Apparently handshaking wasn't commonly practiced. The women remained seated as they were introduced. While fanning their faces they gave polite nods at him and then only a few words spoken in French as they lifted their hand for him to kiss. The men also nodded at him, but with each other kisses were simulated to each side of the face.

Uriah believed he had met everyone when a clamor occurred in the yard. A slave he would later learn was named James drove a cart teeming with people. Behind the cart was another of equal size and also driven by a male slave.

Pierre stepped into the yard to assist the women out of the rear of both vehicles.

Uriah watched the reaction from the slaves in the yard, which to him seemed to have come about because of the presence of the newcomers. Leaning on one of the galerie's columns, he studied with fascination as the group slowly made their way up the galerie. This time Uriah had no trouble remembering names.

The notorious Désireé captured his attention most. If Abigail was dressed like a princess, Désireé was dressed as Queen. It wasn't so much what she wore. The difference between them was Désireé's countenance: the ease of her smile, the

365

warmth of her soft colored eyes; her entire carriage was of someone well educated and refined. Most noticeable was the amount of confidence she had. It made Abigail appear as if she had none.

The reason Uriah couldn't stop staring at her was because although Désireé was confident, she managed to shadow it demurely with constant politeness. And her face. It was beyond beautiful. And her form. The gown she wore seemed to accentuate it.

My God, he thought, then rubbed a knuckle across his mouth because he feared he would visibly drool. Never had he considered bedding a woman of a different race, but he could see himself doing so with this one.

Désireé and Abigail hugged each other the way only sisters could smiling after the two of them had whispered into each other's ear, then giggled and rocked each other with excitement.

"I'm sorry I hadn't come as soon as I learned you arrived," Désireé said. Her smile became more pleasant. Euphoria made her eyes crinkle at the corners. "I'm having a baby, Abby. It's been difficult. I have been firmly told to stay off my feet and that I would only be allowed out today for the celebration."

While she spoke, the man Uriah believed to be Cyril pulled up one of the chairs. Two small pillows were reached for. One was placed on the seat, the other propped against the back. Pierre had pulled forward a small stool. Both men looked as if they were forcing Désireé to sit and sit quickly.

Abigail squealed with laughter, then averted her gaze to her mother. "The men in this family! Even those that are married into it!"

Married? Uriah examined Cyril more closely wondering if the laws in New Orléans allowed white men to marry women of color. Only after Désireé was seated was he introduced to the new arrivals.

Mableane and Gorée saw to the children. In Uriah's mind, Edouard, Easter, Estelle and Jillian looked like pampered turkeys made pretty and festive for a Christmas table. Too much pomp had been added to their apparel.

Mère Alise was chanted from the old and young alike on the lawn when Alise stepped forward.

The Jennings brother hugged this woman tightly, planting heartfelt kisses on the crown of her head. Jenna patted an empty chair beside her for Alise to sit on. A beautiful blanket had been draped over the back of it. The servant named Noémi stood ready with a fan. After Alise was seated, Abigail and Carlisle took turns hugging the woman and speaking softly in her ear. Alise returned their affection with a smile that Uriah deemed made her look beautiful and concealed her true age.

Uriah wondered who Alise was. What he was trying to figure out was her relationship to the family. If she was one of them then why didn't she live in the mansion? This was the first time he had seen her since he arrived.

The woman named Sarah was even harder to figure out. The end of the galerie, just before it wrapped around the side of the house, had been previously prepared for her arrival. The swell of her middle was proof she was having a child. No man had traveled with her other than the servant that drove the cart. While everyone else talked, laughed and leaned closely to someone in conversation, Sarah sat silent and alone and stayed in her designated area. And then Uriah noticed something. Whenever Pierre thought no one was watching he would glance in

Sarah's direction, wait for her to notice him, and then he would either smile or wink. It was only at these moments when Sarah's eyes twinkled with the affection she seemed to be trying to keep hidden.

It was at that moment he noticed something else, and that was Julien's behavior. For someone crippled he seemed not to notice. Often his voice carried across the galerie. The things he said kept the others in a fit of laughter. To make things worse he was most animated. Not only did he swing his good arm when he spoke, the lame one also moved stiffly and not as high. At times the small blanket over his lap would fall to the floor. It would lay there until his half breed daughter noticed and tried to put it back. Sometimes Julien took it from the child's hands absentmindedly. At other times he smiled with the kind of affection that no white man should give to a black child. Pride also showed in his eyes each time the child toddled back to the other children. A half breed and she was dressed as finely as the other children.

Anne also was an oddity to him. The gown she wore was made of soft cloth and heavily embroidered. A nigger. And here she was not only dressed like a respectable woman, but like a wealthy one as well. Jewelry hung around her neck. Ribbons and flowers adorned her hair. Money wasted is how he saw it and no one on the galerie seemed to care.

Taking his eyes off of her, he stared at Désireé again watching her interaction with Cyril.

He stopped watching the couple and noticed how closely Abigail and Carlisle sat together. Carlisle had a glass of bourbon in his hand. Abigail held a glass of Moët. The suit Carlisle wore was of deep colors; lawn hued trousers, white shirt, a matching lawn hued waistcoat with brass buttons down the front; the coat was burgundy with attention given to its cuffs. In a manner of a day Carlisle had also been transformed by this family's wealth.

This time when one of the servants offered Uriah a glass of liquor he accepted it. The rum was the best he had ever tasted, and this made him angrier than he was. No one should live with this much luxury. No one. And the thought of his brother now living with it alongside Abigail made Uriah feel so violent that if he had been a demented man he would have attacked everyone on the galerie for no reason at all.

The glass in his hand was drank swiftly and another needed just when to everyone's pleasure, Anne and Abigail recited someone named Goethe's *The Sorrows of Young Werther*. The others sat even more silent on the end part and the mention of a woman named Charlotte.

"What talent!" Cyril declared when the women had finished.

Uriah rolled his eyes. He knew a yokel when he saw one. Cyril was unrefined although to Uriah the man was trying his best not to show it. And no one was calling Cyril out on it either.

Each time Uriah stared at Abigail, even if he waited a long time, Abigail continued to talk and laugh ignoring him completely. What made him angry was her behavior hadn't been an act. She had truly forgotten he was there.

Bitch, he thought as he lifted his glass yet again.

***

Evening was falling when the plantation's musicians, many with homemade instruments and several with instruments purchased by the master of the plantation, had arranged themselves some distance from the galerie and struck the first chord of the song "Alcée Leblanc. »

Julien approved by lifting his glass of Moët high into the air. "Now we're getting there! The evening has finally begun!"

Anne pushed his wheelchair closer to the railing.

"Let us hear you now when you all start to sing!" Julien instructed the servants nearest him in the yard.

Alise swung her fan sharply in Abigail's direction. Abigail's eyes grew wide.

"Oh, come now, Abby," Jenna pleaded. "You have a beautiful voice."

Uriah could see that Abigail was frightened of this new attention.

Carlisle led her to the center of the galerie as if it was a stage for her to perform on.

Gorée clapped. The children saw this and also started clapping.

There were a few giggles.

Abigail looked shyly at Carlisle, then opened her mouth and sang in a sweet small voice at the start of the song. Carlisle had moved closer toward the children and kicked with crazy legs a popular dance seen at cotillions in Texas.

Jenna openly laughed at the sight of him. At this moment, she felt closer to her daughter than she ever had.

*Alcée Leblanc*
*Mo di toi, chère,*
*To trop capon*
*Pou payé ménage!*
*C'est qui di ça,*
*Ca que di toi chère,*
*Alcée Leblanc*

This song was quickly followed by another Creole favorite. At the start of "Mo Ché Cousin," almost everyone present on the galerie sang some part of it. As others clapped and laughed when the song ended, Pierre again looked in Sarah's direction.

Small children in the yard lifted homemade noise makers running wildly across the lawn in the hopes of spreading the merriment and keeping it going.

"Nice singing, sweetheart," Carlisle complimented.

Dipping her knee like a respectable woman, Abigail stood beside him. The two of them then moved closer to the railing beside Julien and Anne.

Pierre and Jenna, Désireé and Cyril, Alise, including the overseers and their wives also moved closer to the railing.

Uriah wondered what was happening and turned and faced the yard.

A roar of excitement was made when the musicians with sabar drums beat the harsh rhythm that had been learned long ago in their country of Senegal.

Uriah heard this and became confused. The sound he was listening to was foreign and stranger to him than the French songs he'd heard and similar to when a tribe of Indians gathered before heading out to war.

"What's happening?" He asked.

One of the overseers' wives – he believed her name was Obrionne – answered him readily.

"They're going to dance for us." Much excitement could be heard in her voice.

*Slaves dancing to this music?*

Uriah looked down the end of the galerie and saw Pierre pull Abigail closer to him, both of them smiling and waiting with anticipation. Looking again toward the yard, Uriah noticed a group of slave women removing their shoes and hose.

The bare-footed women stood in the center of the yard with the skirt of their dresses pulled tightly against their bodies and held in place with their hand pressed purposefully against their middles. In the positions they held, and with the pulling of the skirts, the definition of their legs was visible. Madness was what Uriah saw. The women looked to him like savages straight out of the Congo.

The beat of the drums changed and with it the servant women used their hips to move with the drums' rhythm, as if it were their own hips that produced the maddening percussions. Occasionally they stamped a foot as they swayed from side to side and faster to the mounting drums' beat. Their hips moved with the need of ridding the center of their core of some sort of infernal passion.

"What are they doing?" He asked.

"The servants call it 'the buck,'" Obrionne answered without looking at him.

*The buck*, he repeated. "I take it this is another Louisiana custom that the men in this city allow where others in America would never consider it."

"Aw, well," Obrionne answered. "Ashleywood has always governed itself like no other plantation."

"You mean this only happens here?" Carlisle clarified.

"Every year," Obrionne confirmed. "Since Monsieur Andreu Jennings returned from Paris. He claims to have gotten the idea there. But don't be deceived. Some of the dancing that could be found in Congo Square is considered far more entertaining."

The dancers suddenly lifted on the tip of their toes. Fanning their legs open and closed, their middles bucked feverishly with each pound of a palm against the drums. The looks on the servant women's faces were of severe concentration. Uriah believed he was watching nothing less that some voodoo incantation.

Just as he lifted his cup of rum the drummers changed the tempo to a stuttering thump as a large group of male servants, who had removed their shoes and shirts, picked up small sticks and twigs from the ground. Raising them in the air like spears, they created two lines while making small bounces with their feet. It looked to Uriah as if their feet barely lifted from the ground, yet the line propelled like a well-trained chorus.

Slave children held up necklaces of beads and shells that tinkled as they shook them, dancing on the side lines and watching the dancers as if learning the movements they would dance some day when they were older. A small break in the drums stopped the procession. The dancing women lifted the hem of their dresses higher then kicked their legs high off the ground. The drums beat again and this time the procession of slave men moved in the opposite direction.

It was this point when the other musicians joined in with fiddles, and with bugles made with animal horns, and a few made of brass. A young male servant wearing a cloth of decorated muslin jumped from the opposite side of the bonfire where he had been hiding for this moment. As soon as he was out in the open the noise in the yard and on the galerie magnified.

The lone dancer wore a crown made of dried braided tree leaves.

Uriah snickered at the spectacle and sipped the rum happy that the atmosphere had become something familiar to him. Blacks acting silly.

The servants smiled and threw their hands in the air while clearing a way for the crown wearer. The smile of pleasure on the dancer's face made those on the galerie laugh loudly from seeing it. The dancer removed his crown and held it high earning him roars of amusement and excitement from those around. Shuffling his feet in marching steps, he made his way closer to the galerie.

Pierre and Abigail leaned their heads closer talking rapidly and pointing further out into the distance.

The dancer held the crown higher then shimmied it in the direction of the galerie.

"Don't pick Carlisle!" Julien warned. "Y'all are too intelligent for that!"

"No cheating!" Désireé shouted. "Someone's already been chosen. You know that, Oncle."

Obrionne offered Uriah an explanation. "Each year the servants choose someone in the family to present the crown to. The person chosen has to wear the crown for the rest of the festivities."

Uriah said nothing back as he watched the servant tease the family with the crown, shaking it and making its dried fringes shimmy and dance in the wind. It veered toward Abigail, Cyril, Désireé, Julien and Pierre. For a long time it danced before Alise until those on the galerie gave whoops of laughter.

"Who is she?" He asked.

Obrionne studied him a moment, her expression becoming sober. He sensed she was deciding if she should answer or not.

"She was the paramour of the father of my husband's employer."

Uriah turned slightly and stared at Pierre and Julien.

Obrionne leaned closer to him and lowered her voice. "She doesn't look it, but she's noir. Black," she emphasized.

Uriah studied Alise's face, not believing what he heard.

"She is," Orbionne insisted. "And the former master of this plantation refused to marry one of his own kind and treated her better than he had his wife when she'd been alive."

Uriah stared at Obrionne, his eyes tightening. "If this is true why do the brothers allow her to live here?"

Obrionne gave him a conspiratorial smile. "This place is Slave Heaven. Haven't you heard?" She looked away from him. "The only reason I stay is because my husband is treated well and he likes it here."

The dancer returned to Alise to tease her more with his crown. Her hands waved back and forth in front of her face. When this didn't work she hid her face behind her fan until the servant moved further along.

Jenna's desire to be awarded the crown was obvious. With her eyes dazed upon it, she watched its every move shimmy before her face. For a moment Uriah believed she would snatch it and be done with this game. The servants in the yard laughed on seeing her reaction. This moment was clearly the highlight of their evening.

He then watched as Cyril circled his arms tighter around Désireé's shoulder and bellow when four new male dancers wearing straw hats formed a line. The first removed his hat staggering and dancing like a drunkard, threatening to tip over and off his feet. If he swayed too closely to the onlookers in the yard they collectively pushed at him with their hands until he was in the center again.

Abigail leaned closer to her father and whispered. Uriah, anxious to know what the two were earnestly discussing, leaned closer to Obrionne and whispered, "What are those two doing over there?"

Overseer Almonester pulled back from the galerie having heard the question. "They're deciding the best dancers of the evening, monsieur. They usually give the winners something afterwards."

"And the purpose of rewarding slaves for doing something they want to?" Uriah asked.

"Fun and leisure, monsieur. Have some rum. Enjoy the moment."

Uriah burned Almonester with his gaze, because he had seen clearly in Almonester's eyes his attempt at censoring him from saying anything further.

Reaching the galerie, the staggering servant shuffled his feet and bucked like the women dancers. The women servants on the grass shamelessly tittered into the palms of their hands.

"More babies are born from the servant girls after this celebration."

Uriah noticed then that Overseer Langers had also been watching him and listening, because it had been him that made this comment.

"It's likely if you pay attention, you might learn something. Tonight is the first night of mating season. Just like the master of this estate will choose a dancer of the night, so will those slaves girls out on the grass. I usually turn a blind eye since it leads to my employer increasing his stock."

"No, thank you," Uriah answered holding Langer's gaze. "My brother owns three slaves. There will be no weddings for slaves on his plantation. Ain't no celebration going to be needed either. All me and my brother will have to do is point to the barn to send one of our nigger boys and our nigger girl to it. She'll do what we tell her and she'll keep doing it until her belly is full."

Overseer Curfy stared at Uriah a long time.

The servants holding sticks bounced the line across the grass clearly enjoying themselves.

The second hat dancer used his hat like a tambourine. It twirled in the air was caught and slid underneath each leg, then lifted again as he shuffled and bucked low to the ground and in circles.

A third dancer stepped from the line holding his hat high in the air. Staggering like a drunkard the same as the first, his feet shuffling better than the others had. It looked as if he glided on air as he reached the galerie, and then his legs lifted high one after the other as he bucked to the beat of the drums.

The last of the hat dancers was tall with bulging biceps and was perhaps the biggest slave Uriah had ever fastened his eyes on. As soon as he stepped forward the servants on the grass began to chant, Ho! Ho! Ho! Ho!

Removing his hat and crouching low to the ground, he twirled the hat like an animal tamer being controlled by a ferocious beast. Swaying into an upright position, the hat was slammed down as if striking a talisman against the earth to break it apart. His arms then arched as his knees locked and his body rolled like a snake. The movement became stiff; his middle bucking in a way that it looked as if he would soon break in half. Pinning one arm behind his back, one leg then kicked back and forth propelling him closer to the galerie. It was there that, like the women dancers, he fanned his legs and bucked at the hips with an expression on his face that his movements will make the entire world shake on his command.

The crown wearer danced around all four hat dancers. The musicians beat and played their instruments in a stammering, climatic chord. The crown wearer removed the crown from his head once again, and raising it high, he again started his teasing with the family. Moving along the width of the galerie, he teased Anne with the crown. Julien roared as Anne pleaded with her hands not to be chosen. The dancer then moved to Jenna rattling the crown in a circle, stopping momentarily at all of the other family members. One last beat of the drums brought the music to an abrupt end and the crown was presented to Pierre.

The overseers and family clapped heartily on seeing this.

"State your boon! State your boon!" The slaves chanted.

Pierre reached for the crown as it was delicately handed to him. He raised it above his head to show everyone and all around that he accepted its entitlement, and placing it on his head he performed his rendition of the servants' dance.

Abigail pressed one hand to her chest and another to her temple as she reared back with laughter. Never had she seen her father so playful.

Jenna smiled at Pierre. She too had never seen him at this level of leisure. A quick look was given over her shoulder. Satisfied to notice that Sarah wasn't watching the master of the estate, she turned again to Pierre and clapped her hands. "Mighty fine dancing, Husband!"

Pierre smiled and nodded warmly at her, because he knew the words hadn't been meant for him. The only reason Jenna allowed Easter and Estelle to visit the mansion was her way of keeping him at it rather than between the trees. Sarah was not permitted in the mansion for any reason. The galerie was as far as she was allowed to get, and solely on occasions like this one.

Pierre pulled Abigail closer to him. "In honor of my daughter's return she shall pick the best dancers of the evening," he announced.

Abigail openly blushed. "I choose Jubilee as the best hat dancer."

Jubilee was the last of the hat dancers.

Uriah stared at Jubilee, then hard at Abigail for choosing this dancer.

Jeannette stepped from the rear of the galerie. For the past hours she and Noémi had refilled glasses, shooed away flies with fans, and heeded to the requests of everyone on the galerie. Lifting a gift wrapped in burlap and tied with a small piece of rope, she handed it gracefully to her Madame Abigail.

Abigail handed the gift to Jubilee.

Inside the sack was a small jug of rum, an entire cake, and sugar coated pralines wrapped in muslin.

"Merci, Maddy-mo-zel," Jubilee said, nodding his head deeply as he took the gift.

Uriah looked out in the yard when the servants became suspiciously silent.

"I choose Uncle Neto as the best line dancer," Abigail said.

"Good choice," Pierre said beside her.

"And Delee as the best bucker."

Delee gave a high-pitched screamed. This was the first time she'd ever won as best. She lifted the hem of her skirt and beat Uncle Neto to the galerie. Both were handed muslin bundles that contained the same items that Jubilee received. A dip was given with her knee, and much thanks spoken before Delee ran back out into the yard. Two of her three children jumped around her happy she had won the gift. Her father, Gentilly, patted her proudly on the back because of her win.

Pierre stared briefly over his shoulder at Sarah. Moments like these were hard for her, because Imogen was no longer here to be a part of them. For years he had been trying to find her, but like Abigail had in the beginning it seemed as if Imogen had fallen off of the face of the earth. As the crown wearer it was customary to award one servant or all of them a boon.

"You have all worked well this past season," he began. "As many of you may have heard our country is suffering another recession at this time. The price of crops has dropped considerably yet the expenses for harvest has increased more than it had in some time. With the help of all of the overseers, all of you have maintained these grounds and produced more hogsheads of sugar more than any other plantation in this entire region. You have worked safely at your chores with lesser of you becoming injured from the sugar process that you all know is dangerous to perform. For your efforts..." He hesitated. "My boon to you *all*," he stressed. "There will be no chores tomorrow. You shall use tomorrow as you choose. Now let us get back to enjoying the rest of this evening."

Soon the musicians were playing again, except this time everyone on the galerie danced to the music. Uriah had wanted badly to dance with Désireé, but she and Sarah had stayed seated and simply watched everyone else having fun. When there had been a break in the music, and then it started up again he had gathered enough nerve to approach Abigail. In his eyes the opportunity had seemed perfect. Carlisle and Julien weren't paying anyone else any attention as the two of them grew deeper in a private conversation. Just as Uriah leaned to get Abigail's attention, Pierre gently pulled his daughter closer to him.

As the slow beat of the music played, everyone on the galerie stopped what they were doing and watched as father and daughter danced just as slowly while smiling at each other. When the song ended and the beat changed to something more upbeat, Abigail sat beside Carlisle, and Pierre reached for Jenna. And then something happened that Uriah had least expected.

The cripple was lifted from his chair, and while leaning on a crutch that had been brought to him by one of the servants, he wiggled his hips at a manic pace as he danced with Anne.

Everyone who watched Julien, including many of the servants in the yard, laughed until tears fell from their eyes.

Uriah reached for another glass of rum hating every person his eyes rested upon.

***

It was traditional amongst the Creole to serve a cold meal at the close of the day. It didn't necessarily mean cold food dishes, and more or less, not as savory ones as the courses served during the midday meal.

The family sat inside the dining room alongside the overseers and their wives. Sitting to Pierre's right was Alise. This chair, Uriah assumed, was one of preference.

Servants ladled and forked food onto gold trimmed china plates.

Almonester waved a servant away from offering him any more food. Although this was the last meal, the selections were far too savory for his appetite. Lifting his glass to quench his thirst, he received Uriah's attention when he spoke. "It seems all of the servants showed up this afternoon. Only those infirmed or were needed elsewhere weren't present from the looks of it. I shall say as I have many times over the years. This plantation has seen much good fortunes one after another considering the number of slaves that reside on it."

"Perhaps Mr. Jennings will tell his secret," Uriah said, lowering his glass. "Behavior most unorthodox I have witnessed this very evening. Yet everyone present seems to be at peace with it."

Abigail lifted a glass of claret. "I rather enjoyed the dancing this evening. It gives the servants a chance to express themselves..." She stopped speaking when she noticed the dark glare that came into Uriah's eyes.

"Express themselves?" He asked as he drew his eyes from hers and glared at the others. "I have never seen half naked slave women dancing around with unmistakable immoral intentions as I have seen take place here."

Alise rose to her feet.

Pierre and the other men also stood.

"Please sit, Alise," Pierre said.

"I shall not," she answered politely with a smile.

Pierre nodded to say it wouldn't be seen as disrespectful if she left the room.

Alise nodded in return and stared at the others pleasantly. "Bonne nuit. To all of you."

Uriah remembered word for word what Overseer Langers had said on the galerie. Wanting the others to believe he had mentally analyzed the dancing and had drawn his own conclusion, he reared back in his chair and sat up tall. His hand reached for the glass of rum in front of him. "With as many servants as is on this plantation, the birth rate of newborn slaves enables you, Mr. Jennings, from having to buy slaves from other men. Slaves, of which, must be broken in when they arrive, and taught. I see this dancing as a means to get your slaves to procreate. Privileges like these, as well as giving healthy slaves a day off, are the reason we have slave insurrections occurring across our country."

The shattering of glass in the hall followed by running feet caused Pierre to rise swiftly from his chair. Riley also heard the clamor and shooed his hands at the servants waiting near the sideboard. As they meant to hurry through the door,

Gorée burst through it, knocking some of them to the floor. "Pardon! Pardon!" She sang without looking back, a smile on her face as she ran to Pierre's chair. "Papa!"

Pierre heard the word and couldn't move. Only when she was close did he lift her in his arms and hug her tight as he stared into her eyes.

"Pierre!" Jenna hissed. Fingers pressed to the center of her forehead as she was want to do when she was sorely vexed. Gorée sitting quietly in a room at an informal sitting was one thing. Interrupting a meal shared with guests inside her dining room was entirely different. And Gorée calling him papa. And Pierre staring at the child as if he could cry. "Please!" She pleaded.

Mableane and Alise hurried through the door, saw what was happening and waited patiently to get Gorée back within their reach.

"Good night, *bon enfant*," Pierre said, then kissed her hair, placed her on her feet, then pushed her gently toward Alise and Mableane.

Uriah watched the exchange with stupefied amusement.

Gorée ran from him and around the table and hugged Désireé in her chair.

"*Bonne nuit*," Désireé whispered.

"I apologize, everyone," Alise said gently when Gorée finally reached her and held out her hand. "It won't happen again," she assured.

Jenna made slapping motions with the back of her hand hoping to be rid of the interruption immediately. And then she stared long and hard at Pierre.

Uriah couldn't believe what he had seen and stared unabashedly at Abigail giving her plenty of time to read his thoughts. A smile pulled across his face. He waited patiently for Abigail to notice him, because he wanted her to know that he now knew that her father had a half breed, mind addled child. This fact was then added to the arsenal he would use against her when they were next alone.

Abigail finally noticed him and was unable to look away from Uriah's gaze.

Jenna saw this and lifted her glass while she silently watched Uriah and Abigail, hoping the new suspicion that came into her mind wasn't true.

"What were you saying?" Pierre asked, knowing the more Uriah spoke the more the man was apt to let details of his true character slip.

"Oh, yes!" Uriah exclaimed, suddenly feeling better than he had the entire day. "I was saying that such behavior can lead to a revolt at any time."

"I find your comment most absurd," Julien commented.

Désireé had waited patiently to join the conversation. Seizing the moment, she spoke softly. "The dancing you saw, Monsieur Morning, is traditional African dancing. The slaves came to this land with it. It has no significance to mating. My great-grandfather thought it necessary for the slaves on this land to keep some of their culture. Apparently other Creoles in the city felt the same way, as you can find public display of similar dancing in Congo Square. This dancing is the way they express celebration…"

Uriah waved his hand, his eyes intense as he looked in her direction. Twice on the galerie he had tried to get her attention, and twice she had noticed him and quickly looked away. She was far too uppity for his liking. It was time someone put her in her proper place. "Pardon my manners for speaking…"

"She wasn't finished speaking," Julien interrupted. "We do things differently here, Monsieur Morning. You will respect everyone at this table as my brother's guests, regardless if it's apparent who their parents are."

Uriah smiled with large eyes as he stared around the table, then pinpointed his eyes on Désireé. "Please do continue, *girl.*"

"Mon Dieu!" Julien spat, averting his gaze from Uriah and casting them on Anne. "Get my pistol!"

Cyril took a moment to take in Uriah. It was the first time that evening he paid him any notice. Men like Uriah, newcomers to New Orléans – couldn't understand that most Creoles tolerated any man, woman or child with Creole blood running through their veins. The city had too many men like Uriah now, unwilling to adapt to the Creole way of living.

Reaching underneath the table, he soothed a hand over Désireé's skirt to comfort her from Uriah's insult.

Jenna thrilled inwardly when Pierre folded his hands together and leaned on his elbows on top of the table. The gesture meant his patience had dwindled. She cared not about Uriah calling Désireé a girl. It was Abigail she wanted Pierre to defend. For the past minutes Abigail had chewed her lip and stared deeply into her plate. Jenna sensed Uriah was the reason for her sudden unhappiness.

"You're speaking to my daughter," Pierre began.

Jenna thought she would shatter the glass in her hand, so tightly did she grip it on hearing this.

"Her name is Désireé if you've forgotten. The proper address for you, monsieur, is to refer to her mademoiselle. But you *cannot* call her 'girl' while you're on this plantation. She is a free woman of color. As a free woman of color she deserves the same respect and rights as those of any free man."

Uriah looked away from Abigail. For once he was the center of attention and he meant to use it to his advantage. "My apologies. I heard mention once that when America took over this city there were recorded in the city's records three thousand slaves and more than seventeen hundred free people of color. A rather high number, don't you think?" He leaned back in his chair. "That number is higher than any other city in America. What I don't understand is why this city? What is so special here?"

"The people," Pierre interrupted, because he knew the next comment out of Uriah's mouth would have been in reference to Julien's relationship with Anne. "*Creole* people, Uriah. If you don't believe that ask President Jackson. During América's war against the British it was he who came to this city to defend it. Alongside him, the same men who helped him to become victorious were Creole men like myself and a large number of our free men of color. These men of color were ready to take an iron ball like the rest of us. When France and Spain governed New Orléans any slave manumitted had equal rights as everyone else.

"Here we have plaçage marriages. My daughters Désireé and Gorée were born from my placée. As their father it was my duty to educate them and provide for their financial futures. Many of us men in these arrangements manumitted our children, and many of those children, along with their mothers, live fortunate lives. More importantly they are a part *of* the city. When Creole people in this city see a quadroon or octoroon, we recognize them as the children of our peers. And no one here wants to hurt his friend or neighbor just as much as they don't want their friends and neighbors hurting them by treating their children unfairly."

"That's very interesting and all," Uriah began, "but I refuse to believe that other plantations are ran like yours."

Pierre forked some of his food, chewed, then got comfortable as he licked his tongue across the front part of his teeth. "Each man governs their plantation as he sees fit, this is true. You don't approve of my family's way of living?"

A confident smile spread across Uriah's face.

"Uriah, maybe you've had too much rum," Carlisle said. "Monsieur Jennings has explained the differences between our cultures and his. Who are we to say which is better than the other?"

Uriah leapt to his feet, disturbing the table. "You can sit there all gussied up and acting sididdy if you want! But at least tell the truth!"

"Sit down, Monsieur Morning, and tell us all what this truth is," Pierre said.

Embarrassed that others had witnessed the anger he had toward his brother, he sat again. "Americans *fought* for this land. Soon Texas will be incorporated into it. Men like my brother were injured. Some lost their lives all for the sake of independence and to make this country great. What I find wrong here is that you all think you're better than Americans, including your half breed children of whom you dress so prettily. You have no regard for American culture, yet you're on American soil. I find that most offensive, Mr. Jennings. You sit there and act like Americans are bad people. If you believe this then why did you allow my brother to marry your daughter?"

When no one said anything and stared at him with silent eyes, his angered increased. It suddenly felt as if he was sitting amongst alien beings with no comprehension of the things he said.

"You live here in this fine house," he continued. "You live on well tendered land. Hell, you even own your own race track. You let your slaves perform voodoo incantations right before your very eyes, and then you wonder why they turn against you the first chance they get. It's because of who they are! They were savages when we found them. The tamed ones you see now is because we taught them how to control themselves."

Carlisle squeezed his eyes closed and drew in a breath.

"Monsieur Morning," Jenna began. "I find you to be the *most* uncivilized man I have *ever* laid eyes on. Even still I have treated you kindly, have I not? You sit at my table and accuse my family of slandering Américains. I have heard no such slander. Even if we do feel the way you say we do, our manners – our very culture – prevents us from revealing those personal feelings in the presence of our guests. All you have seen thus far is our way of living and nothing more than that. If our way of living offends you, I do not apologize for it. We will not stop our habits or routines because you are visiting *our* home."

Uriah lifted his glass of rum. He didn't know what it was, but there was something about this woman he had hated from the very moment he laid eyes on her. "And this is appropriate?" The glass gestured toward Désireé first, and then harder still toward Anne. "You have white guests sitting at your table, Missus. Forcing guests like me to share a meal with blacks is the same as slander. I don't care how you look at it."

Jenna looked at Pierre, then down the table at each person sitting at it. What she saw were people who loved her children – people who got along peacefully and cared about each other.

"I don't care what the North is doing or saying," Uriah continued. "People of color will *never* run this country, including the half breeds. America may be divided on its views on slavery, but we're united in our views on other matters. No brown race of any kind will *ever* be allowed to become politicians or vote or run for any government office. It is people of color who bring this country down, them and their unorthodox beliefs. As a country we must not allow strange doctrine to be incorporated in our governing decisions. The day that happens, only then will you see true division, and if divided we become a weak country and subject to becoming overpowered by other foreign empires."

"Some of what my brother says is true," Carlisle intervened. "But he speaks for himself and not for me. In Texas I have seen Americans, Mexicans and Indians work together for the good of the country. The way things are here, I have seen nothing like it. I make no judgments toward it in one way or the other. I have seen for myself that men of all color must learn from each other, especially when you find yourself in a vast wilderness like many of us have been before. Whites have helped Indians learn how to farm. Mexicans have shown Whites the many dangers of the land. Indians have taught Whites and Mexicans the power of healing. War is cruel. When the last shot is fired and you're standing in the smoke looking at the blood that has been shed, it makes you wonder why you were fighting at all. I hope to never see anything like that ever again. And to sit here now and listen to a conversation of verbal war of whose beliefs are better than the other disgusts me, because it's conversations like these that lead to war."

"A bigger war is coming," Julien said. "And it's fueled by what all war is fueled by. Greed," he said, shifting his eyes to Uriah. "You have many prejudices, sir. Many prejudices. You haven't given me one kind look since you've arrived. You see I'm lame and look at me as if you're better. Each time I walk you look as if you're offended. Yesterday morning you accidentally touched my cup, then dropped it as if you had touched the cup of a diseased man. This is my home, yet I have seen you behave as if you're more entitled inside of it because you can walk.

"You want to know why Creoles in this city don't like Américains? Because Américains have no respect for *any* culture other than their own. Even those of other *blancs*, solely because those *blancs* are different than they are. The King of France sold you Louisiane, Uriah. America didn't fight or conquer it. After the purchase, you entered this city with puffed out chests as if you had built each of its buildings. You didn't ask. You demanded we speak English. You looked at our 'half breed' children and refused to live amongst them, then stared down at us because many of us provided for all of our children despite who their mother was. America won their independence from Britain and since has behaved as if they have conquered the entire world. You have no couth and I hope there is judgment for men like you in the afterlife."

"Gentlemen, please!" Jenna hissed.

Pierre pressed his hand on top of hers to silent her.

"Mr. Morning," he began, "your views are similar to the rest of the world and those views are welcome in this house. Just don't become offended if my brother and I don't agree with the way you see things. It's not what you're saying, Uriah. Real men must learn to amicably disagree. Until then they're only boys. You're a guest in my home, but you weren't invited to the celebration you saw today. What exactly offended you this evening? Have you even asked yourself that? I've watched you from the moment you stepped foot into my home. If you were Indian your name will be Kicking Mule. You're stubborn like a mule, and I've noticed that you mentally kick against anything you dislike. You hate anyone who looks like they're better than you are, including your own brother. I have seen you give him looks the way no man should ever give his brother. The way he's dressed right now is burning your butt, because it means he's closer to achieving his goals. My question to you is what are *your* goals? I don't hate all Américains. Every race of people has good and bad, including my own. I have never held my hand like a fist to anyone in need. Had you come here with your own goals and shared them with me, I would have tried to help you achieve them. The reason you haven't done so, even after you saw exactly how wealthy I am, is because you have none. I can look at you and tell you don't want to work for anything. All you want is what other people have. And you want what your brother has. Respect. Vigor. Determination. I'm even willing to wager that anything you do have in your possession someone else gave it to you instead of you earning it on your own."

Uriah gripped his glass tighter as his eyes darkened and narrowed into slits.

"Oh, oui, monsieur," Pierre chided, as if Uriah had denied everything he said. "Don't look at me as if what I said isn't true. I've met plenty of men like you. They talk a lot, you see. Even the words they speak aren't their own, but words they heard someone else speak. They talk words of war, because war appeases them. It means they can get rid of the groups of people they hate most. Only then can they feel accomplished at doing...*anything*."

"Anne, forget my pistol. Pierre, I think you just fired a fatal shot." Julien roared with laughter causing his body to lean closer to the table.

Jenna studied Uriah's eyes, recognizing what she saw in them. Beckoning Riley to her, she whispered in his ear to have Edouard taken out of the house immediately and taken to Alise's cottage. She didn't want Edouard listening to loud voices later that evening, as she believed would happen from the look on Uriah's face.

When she faced forward again, she saw Uriah studying her with equal regards. *He's going to retaliate*, she thought. She knew this because once it was what she would have done. Having the last word was of high importance for people with Uriah's countenance.

"My brother is young yet," Carlisle said. "He'll find his way. All he needs is time."

"Speak for yourself!" Uriah hissed.

Carlisle looked momentarily stunned. In his mind he believed he was coming to Uriah's defense. Regardless of what his brother had done against him, the two of them were still blood. And he loved him.

"Jealous of you?" Uriah's face twisted into a sneer. "What do you have for me to be jealous about? That measly hut you now call a house? That little bit of money you're expecting from the government? Or maybe I'm jealous because you can't give your wife a child. You were always a stupid man, befriending any and everyone you came in contact with." He stopped himself from saying more. "I got plenty. I got stuff you don't even know I have. I have no reason to be jealous of you."

"I wish no one talks anymore," Abigail said.

"I agree," Jenna said.

"I got plenty," Uriah repeated staring down at his plate.

***

The bedroom that had been given to him had been meant to impress him. At least this was what he believed as he sat in a chair and waited. Before he left he would make certain each of them knew how he felt about this room. The things Pierre had said had been bad enough, and after the meal things had seemed to calm down. The family continued to be polite. The men had sat on the galerie and smoked tobacco and behaved as if nothing had happened. Uriah had decided to let the entire matter die, because as swiftly as everyone's tempers had flared they had quelled. He had reconfirmed this thought when Jenna had the servants serve the sweet dish he had liked along with café with plenty of sugar.

*Let it die*, he had told himself when not minutes later two things happened that made him change his mind. Everyone had gone to bed to retire. Hoping to sneak a bottle of Moët inside his bedroom, he stepped through the French doors and onto the galerie. Not wanting the family to see what he was up to, he quietly began making his way to the stairs that led down into the yard. From there he would walk to the butler pantry, and if no one was there he would head over to the kitchen knowing the servants were still inside it cleaning and preparing for tomorrow's meals. If there was one thing he noticed was the slaves didn't refuse him any request.

He had reached another room and saw its French doors were still open. Peeking in to see if anyone was inside, he quickly pulled back when he saw Jenna and Abigail sitting together on a sofa and engrossed in conversation.

"I don't like him, Abby. Find a way to get rid of him. Convince Carlisle if you must. That man has too much anger in his eyes. I get the feeling if anyone angers him, he'll turn against them, including you, including his brother."

"I liked him in the beginning," Abigail admitted. "The people in Bowling Green are different, Maman. So ready was I to adapt to their way of doing things. When I was around other women I behaved as they did. I think I did this because I wanted them to accept me."

"I understand, Abby. And why you would even feel this way."

"I saw the way Carlisle looked at me when I yelled at my servants in front of our guests. Those looks made me feel as if he betrayed me, but Uriah was different. I soon found myself trying to please him. Oh, Maman. I have been married less than two years and already I've made so many mistakes. I think you're right. I think it's time for Uriah to go. Only then can Carlisle and I be truly happy."

"Your papa and I want to visit as soon as we can."

"Oh, Maman! I shall love that."

"Your papa has big plans. All he talks about is the fancy house he wants to build for you and Carlisle. Apparently he and Carlisle have already discussed it. Your papa doesn't want either of you to wait for Carlisle's money to come. While in Bowling Green your papa says he'll open accounts for you and Carlisle to buy anything you need. I hear you live close to a river?"

"We do."

"Your papa wants to give you and Carlisle your own boat to transport your crops."

Uriah peeked into the room when it became silent. Jenna and Abigail were hugging. Turning back, he walked to his bedroom and pulled the doors closed. A fancy boat, a fancy house, a line of credit at every store. These were the things he was thinking about when his door pushed open sometime later and Carlisle stepped through it.

"I bring you here and you embarrass me like this!" Carlisle accused. "I don't care if you didn't like who you had to share your supper with. This is not your house! And for you to have spoken so openly amongst people you barely know shows what kind of fool you truly are."

"I'll apologize in the morning," Uriah conceded.

"Do that. Posthaste! And stay away from Abigail. It's over. She's chosen me and has refused for you to return to Bowling Green with us. As much as I hated to hear him say it, Pierre read you like a new law written by a competent judge to a repeat offender. I didn't want to believe it and hoped you didn't, but now I know you did. She told me about the money and the jewelry and where you have it hid. Well, I'm telling you now. You're not going to get your hands on the rest of it. Mama would have laid into you with a strip of rawhide had she known you had taken money from a young lady. From this moment forward you'll get nothing from me. If I were you, I would get along with the people here and maybe then Pierre would have mercy on you and send you wherever you want to go."

"You son of a bitch," Uriah snarled, stepping back from his brother so he could see all of him at the same time. "You weren't thinking about sending me back when I sweated alongside you, helping you build your house. Now that they have promised you better a life, you're trying to get rid of me?"

"Who told you about that?"

"You were gonna keep it from me, wasn't you? I helped you build that shack you currently live in!"

"And you slept with my wife. I say that makes us even."

"You think you're going to get rid of me and take what's mine?"

"It wasn't yours to take. I've already talked to Pierre. He's sending someone in the morning to recover the jewelry. You're just gonna have to work for what you want."

"War changed you, Lyle! The man you are now I'm ashamed of."

"Likewise," Carlisle retorted. "I'm going to amicably disagree with you so that makes me no longer a boy. And you can call me Mr. Morning if the two of us ever lay eyes on each other again after we leave here."

***

The room was now ready for the family to see what he'd done to it. He would have done more, but the noise would have woken someone and he hadn't wanted that to happen. This family had turned his brother against him and for that they were going to pay. Already he had gone downstairs and helped himself to plenty of the family's silver. The burlap sack he had hidden the goods in now sat hidden behind a rose bush on the side of the house.

The other thing he had wanted to do was get inside Pierre's study, but the door had been locked. It didn't matter. He'll get plenty for the silver pieces, then head to California where men like him could make something of themselves.

Leaving the room through its French doors, he pulled it closed silently behind him. Now it was time to complete his plan and that was none other than killing Edouard. Abigail loved the child. Jenna praised him. Pierre was most proud of him. He had to kill Edouard because everyone loved the child, including the slaves, and Uriah wanted to hurt everyone. The pain the family will feel after they discovered the child dead would remind them to never make a fool of someone like him ever again.

Earlier in the evening he heard Riley mention that Edouard had been sent between the trees to Alise's cottage. Uriah would kill her too or anyone else if they tried to get in his way. All he had to do was find the cottage, and he knew exactly which direction it was in because it was the only area Pierre hadn't taken him in, and the same direction the carts had come from at the start of the celebration.

After running across the open space of the lawn, he then kept to the trees. In his pocket was a bread knife he had taken out of the pantry and a muslin cloth to stick in Edouard's mouth to keep him quiet while he died. The burlap sack was heavy, but didn't slow him down.

He walked many minutes in darkness without seeing much. Believing he had gotten lost and was perhaps walking away from the estate, he started south toward the river. It was just when he was certain he had gone in the wrong direction he noticed the trees would soon come to an end.

The house he saw was even more magnificent than Carlisle had described when he mentioned Désireé's cottage. This was no cottage. It was a house of huge proportion. The first floor was a raised basement. The second stretched wide underneath a Spanish tiled roof. The house had its own carriage house, outside kitchen and cistern.

Wondering whose property he had come on and if they were Creole, he stared at one of the doors of the basement and wondered if it was locked. Looking behind him to make certain no one was there, he hurried across the lawn and came upon a pair of stairs that led to the home's doors.

A child's wagon sat next to it. The family crest painted on it was more than familiar. Taking a step back, because only then he realized he was still on the Jennings property, he wondered who the house belonged to.

Alise swiftly came to mind. During the celebration everyone had treated her with high respect. Staring again at the wagon, he believed it to be Edouard's and understood why Jenna and Pierre would allow the child to sleep in such a house.

A macabre unease to injure this family came into his eyes as he hid the sack behind some brush then made his way up the stairs. Gripping the knife in his pocket, he pulled it out and made it ready. Alise couldn't have lived in the house alone. Maybe she had her own slaves, and from what Uriah had seen, these slaves may take it upon themselves to protect her.

The galerie was wide and well furnished. The floor beneath him still looked new. Not a single board creaked from his weight. Walking softly, he stopped at the first French doors he came upon. Inside was a *petite salle*. On the opposite side of the room an open door revealed what looked like a nursery. A lamp burned in the room casting its glow against a wall that had been painted with the face of a smiling alligator, the image the kind that only a child could look at with fascination.

Inside the *salle* a servant sat sleeping on a chair. Her leather boots had been removed and sat upright on the floor. Uriah reached for the door to test it. The lock refused to budge and gave an unexpected click. The noise was alarmingly loud in the night's stillness. Stepping away from the door, he leaned against the wall wondering if the servant had heard it. Seconds later the door opened. The servant stepped out with a yawn. From her behavior she hadn't expected to see anyone.

Uriah held the knife against her throat and covered her mouth. Forcing her inside, he turned her around so her back was to him. Leading her forward, he walked inside of the nursery.

Edouard wasn't in the room. Matching twin beds were pushed against both walls. Uriah saw the twins and whispered in the servant's ear. "Edouard? Where's Edouard?"

The servant looked up at him with large eyes, then shook her head.

Staring down at the twins he realized the house belonged to Sarah. Sarah didn't have a man. If she had she would have brought him with her to mansion. Earlier he had noticed that the twins had the same hair as the family. He stared at the hair now and wondered who Sarah's husband was.

And then it came to him. The way Pierre kept staring at Sarah and winking. The way she had been forced to sit in the corner and hadn't been allowed to eat dinner with the family.

Pulling the servant back into the *salle*, he gripped her mouth tighter and pulled the end of his knife against her throat. For only a second she struggled. Allowing her to drop to the floor, he watched as a large amount of blood spilled from her wound. In an attempt to stop it she gripped her neck with both hands, and then her hands fell by her side and her eyes closed.

Energy coursed through him as he saw a third door that led into a hall. Stepping silently into it, he marveled at the home's interior. Sarah's boudoir was enormous. The moonlight spilling into the triple set of French doors made it easy to see. Pierre slept soundly on his back. Sarah lay to his side with her face buried in his chest. Uriah's eyes fell to the swell of Sarah's belly and saw what her gown had hidden earlier. She was carrying another child.

Killing Pierre would be a challenge. As tall as he was, his feet hung out at the end of the bed. Unsure if Pierre would wake before he reached him, he stepped quietly from the door and gave himself a moment to think. Finding Edouard may be too hard. The land was larger than he believed it was and had far too many trees.

As glorious as this home was, the mansion was much larger, yet here was Pierre sleeping in one of its bedrooms as if he did so all the time. He and Sarah were sleeping as if they were happy and at peace. Well, not any more.

Walking softly back to the nursery, a new thought came to him. When he stepped into the *salle*, he stared at the servant and saw she hadn't moved. Stepping around her, he entered the nursery. If one of the children woke and cried out, he couldn't be certain Pierre wouldn't wake up. Tucking the knife in his pocket, a thought of the river came to him. Drowning one would be easier. Drowning both would hurt Pierre forever.

The twin in the bed he stood over was lifted carefully in his arms. Not yet two years old, she didn't wake and only sighed in her sleep. Lifting the second was just as easy. A fidget was made, and then she slept again once her head rested against his shoulder. Remembering the silver, he decided to take them out into the yard, kill them, then be on his way.

He walked out of the nursery into the *salle* and out the door. He started to walk across the galerie when a noise was made behind him. He looked over his shoulder as the servant jumped up and ran into the hall.

Uriah ran fast down the galerie, down its stairs and headed toward the trees on the east side of the house. The twins had awakened, their small heads lifting. Behind him not a single sound was made. It didn't take long to reach the river. Climbing the levee with two small children while out of breath became a struggle.

On the other side, he lost his balance. With strong arms he held the twins against him. The river was high from seasonal rains.

"Easter! Estelle!"

The names were being yelled behind him.

"Easter! Estelle! Say papa! Say papa so I can find you!"

Uriah heard the dread in Pierre's tone but had no time to be glad over it. Just as he reached a tangle of trees, he lost his balance when he tripped over a piece of debris. When he saw that the fall would land him in the river he dropped the twins and reached out with both hands. The momentum propelled him into the river as easily as a boat.

Uriah couldn't swim well. The sight of the river looked calm and still. It wasn't until he was in that he realized that underneath the surface was a strong, ferocious current. And it was this current that was bent on racing him downstream.

Thrashing with his arms and legs, he began to panic when he couldn't feel the riverbed beneath his feet. The water was cold and rushed up his nostrils like two fingers trying to stop his breathing. From the corner of one eye he saw one of the twins. The river tried hard to claim her. Her hands reached into the water, and then she couldn't be seen.

Pierre will never find his children. Uriah would make certain of this. He would kill them both if it was the last thing he did.

Fighting the currents, he spotted a pirogue. Reaching with his hands, he kicked with his feet in an attempt to grab tall grass before he could be swept past it. Clutching the coarse blades, he struggled with the tangle of grass roots beneath his feet. Using them to propel himself forward, he pulled at the grass as if they were ropes until he reached the pirogue. Climbing inside, he grabbed the single oar, then dropped it when he saw a white sleeping gown attempting to float past him.

"Easter! Estelle! Say papa!"

Uriah worked swiftly. Reaching into the grass where the gown had gotten tangled, he grabbed the twin lifting her hard because she felt heavy. It was when she lifted that he realized what she had reached into the water for. Her small hands held tightly to her sister.

Currents tugged at the front part of the pirogue turning it sideways. Uriah lost his balance falling into the pirogue on his back to the sound of a crack. Now out of the water, the first twin wailed.

"I hear you!" Pierre yelled. "I hear you! Say papa! Say papa!"

Gripping the oar again, he moved the pirogue with the currents until the rest of the boat pulled onto the river. The plan was to reach the other side, drown the twins, then leave their bodies where Pierre could find them.

"No! No! No!"

Uriah looked over his shoulder. Pierre ran swiftly along the levee, then down the bank with every intention of diving in. The pirogue reached the center of the river, then spun, rocked, and nearly tipped over. The currents moved them faster. Uriah used the oar to keep the pirogue upright. Ahead he saw that the river curved into a wide bend.

One of the twins screamed.

Uriah turned. Water pooled inside the pirogue. Seeing it and he wondered if the crack he heard had damaged its bottom. Water reached up to the ankles of his boots. The second twin lay with her head just above it, her eyes dazed from the amount of water she had swallowed. The other twin slapped the water hoping her angry hand would stop it from rising higher.

The currents shifted the pirogue, spinning it once again to turn with its new direction causing the bottom of the pirogue to splinter then break apart.

# Chapter Thirty-Six
## Good Things Never Last Forever

*[When the Devil goes to mass he hides his tail. – Creole Proverb]*

Julien was determined to get inside the *maison*. Hiram had come along with him. For three days Pierre had barricaded himself inside it. Sarah was currently at the mansion. Jenna was also there holding Edouard tightly to her chest and refusing to put him down.

Three nights before Maissy had pretended as if she was dead because she feared Uriah would see she was alive and cut deeper the next time. As soon as she saw him walk out the *salle* door a voice inside her told her to get up and run. Fearing that screaming would shoot more blood out of her neck, she ran quietly and fast into Sarah's boudoir.

When she reached the bed, she used her fists to beat on the sleeping forms of her master and mademoiselle. Sarah and Pierre had awakened at the same time and jumped at the sight of her. Sarah screamed because of how much blood there was. Pierre had taken a moment to try and stop the bleeding unaware his children had been in danger. When Maissy realized neither would know what happened until she told them, she yelled loudly that Uriah had taken the twins out of the house.

Jenna had stood over Maissy's bed the day the servant had repeated again everything that had happened. According to Maissy, she hadn't known anyone was outside. When she opened the door, Uriah had put a knife to her neck and forced her into the nursery. As he stared down at the twins, he kept shaking her and asking her where was Edouard.

Maissy told them all how she had seen disappointment in Uriah's eyes after he saw the twins, and how he had been getting more and more violent each time he spoke Edouard's name.

Jenna heard this and knew. Oh, she knew. Uriah had wanted to take Edouard, because he had seen how much everyone had loved him. Guilt was also what she felt. Unbearable guilt. And fear. She had known there was something evil about Uriah. It was the reason she had gotten Edouard out of the house. Never had she thought Uriah's anger would be directed at a child. The most she suspected was him getting into an altercation with one of the men. Still for the past three days she agonized if anyone would accuse her for not warning anyone else about what she had suspected.

Julien climbed out of the invalid chair and reached for the banister. Hiram gave him the support he needed. Eight minutes later he reached the top of the stairs dripping with sweat. Needing to sit, he flopped into the closest chair to catch his breath.

"Bang on that door and you tell him if he doesn't open it, we'll crash it down."

Hiram nodded at Julien, turned swiftly, faced the door, lifted his hand as if he was going to bang against it, then lowered it and gave a polite knock.

"What the hell you doing!" Julien berated. "Beat that goddamn door down! You let him hear you and that we mean business."

Hiram banged with both fists.

"Kick it!" Julien instructed when either door still hadn't opened.

Hiram gave a single kick.

"Go find something and come back," Julien said while leaning forward with his left arm gripping the armrest. His mouth stayed open as he breathed heavily through it.

Hiram returned with a pick ax. The glass of the door shattered. Once the rest of the glass was knocked clear, Hiram reached inside and unlocked the door. As tired as Julien was, he staggered to his feet. Hiram grabbed him by the waist and helped him walk better. The room they were in was the same room Uriah had used to commit his crimes.

Going room to room, Hiram dragged Julien more than Julien walked. Finally reaching a room that had its door closed, they stepped into the darkened room, and then both of them came to a standstill as they stared across it. The shutters and doors and curtains had all been tightly closed. Pierre was in the corner, the chair he sat in large enough to support his frame.

"Leave me and go to the mansion. Don't let Sarah hear anything you say. Find Semper, Jeanette and Noémi on the quiet and bring them back. At least with them …" He hesitated. Sudden tears filled his eyes. "… my brother would have some dignity."

Hiram was unable to tear his gaze away from the corner. "What about the madame? Should I tell her?" His face became pinched.

Julien saw Hiram was on the verge of losing control.

"I need you," he said, then reached for the jamb of the door and held tightly to it. "Don't say anything to anyone. We're going to keep this quiet for now. Just bring the girls back."

"You'll be all right alone, monsieur?"

"Get going," Julien instructed.

Hiram nodded, stared quickly in the corner again, then hurried and left the room.

Julien stared at his brother. When he had heard about the twins no tears had come to him. It wasn't because he hadn't loved them. It had been because things like these happened all of the time. Murder. Theft. Rape. It happened to the best of people. On many occasions the perpetrators were never caught and tried. When these things happened there was nothing anyone could do to change the situation. The best way to handle it was to forget it right away and move on with your life.

At that moment he was unable to stop the tears rolling down his face. Never had he seen his brother like this. Pierre's head was leaned to one side. No movement could be seen coming from the back of the chair.

Julien thought about Edouard growing up without a father, and Désireé, and Gorée, and Jenna, and Sarah. Pierre's death would change them all.

Needing to get closer for a better inspection, he dropped to the floor and pulled himself closer. When he finally reached a point where Pierre's back was no longer to him and he could see his face, he saw that hair had grown on his brother's face because he hadn't shaved. The look in his eyes was as if the last thing Pierre had seen was the real devil and he couldn't get the sight of what the devil looked like out of his mind.

The vulnerability Julien felt. The courage he once had, it was now gone. It wasn't until then that he realized that he would take this death harder than anything he had ever experienced in his life. Reaching for his brother's leg, a noise escaped his mouth when Pierre's head became upright, and his eyes gazed down on him.

Julien screamed in fear. After he screamed a second time he realized he wasn't witnessing a ghost, but that his brother was still alive.

He collapsed onto his back and gulped air. "I thought you were dead."

When he opened his eyes again, he saw tears fall from Pierre's eyes. The expression on Pierre's face had yet to alter and was frightening to look at.

"Get your ass up!" Julien demanded. "We need you! None of us can lose you now!"

"I saw it. The pirogue broke apart at the river's bend. One of my little girls was clinging to the side of it. Uriah kept going under. No one survives the river here. You know that."

"They're dead." Julien spoke the words because they had to be said out loud. "Dead!" He repeated. "And no one can ever replace them. But you have other children who are not dead. And neither are you. I didn't survive a piece of iron cracking my skull to watch you give up now. Now get your ass up and remember who we are. We're Creole and in New Orléans, a city plagued with disease, fire, foreigners, crime, and floods… a man is never promised tomorrow. He is only responsible for today. It is the way the Orléonois has lived. And it is the way we shall die. We suffer, but New Orléans has always healed itself in time. And in the meantime *laissez les bon temps rouler!*"

# Chapter Thirty-Seven
# To Heir is Human

*[When the birds scream overhead a storm wind is coming. – Creole Proverb]*

Pierre ran with such fierceness he was uncertain if the knot in his side was because he was winded or if his nerves were getting the better of him. When he reached the outer yard he stopped to catch his breath. No longer was he as young as he used to be.

While breathing in the crisp air he asked himself yet again why he was running. The letter had assured him that everyone was in good health, but in the recess of his mind a tender voice whispered the correspondence of yesteryear, a time when he had been at his lowest point. Although the letter expressed this was not a repeat of that day, he had suffered so many tragedies after the death of his twins that he now expected some form of sorrow to present itself at every chance.

Starting again at a slower pace, he had come around Désireé's cottage when he heard the pattering of feet running in his direction. Knowing who the feet belonged to, he stopped again just as his daughters came in sight. Two were tall for their ages. A third was much shorter than her sisters had been when they had been her age. One had hair the same hue as his; silver blonde, and eyes of an indeterminate color and closer to blue, but not quite.

Another had hair as dark as her mother's and piercing amber eyes. Her slender nose and well-shaped mouth gave her, at all hours of the day, a pensive appearance, as well as made her look older than she truly was. Fearing her older sister would outrun her, Sade clung to Jurney's gown to keep her close as the two of them ran to meet him.

The third had been faster and was in the lead, reaching him first. The sight of her reminded Pierre of the daughters he had lost. If they had still been living they would have been nine years old.

Alexandrine was he and Jenna's child. Lifting her in his arms, he gave a swift kiss to her platinum blonde hair, then readily lifted the others and kissed them as well.

"Papa's here! Papa's here!" They yelled.

"*Les coquins. Les vilains!*"

"Papa, I am no rogue!" After saying this Sade threw back her head and laughed from the very thought. "Only Américains can be so."

"Américains are nice aren't they, Papa?" Jurney contended, then leaned close to him and took his hand.

"Dreadful, disgusting people," he declared. "You are only to like your brother-in-law Carlisle. And you are never to marry one of them. And if you have to do business with them keep both of your eyes open. Never forget that."

Affected by his presence after a long absence, it was hard for his three daughters not to smile and giggle for no reason.

"I told you Edouard said *les Américains* are *vilains*."

"That's not exactly what I said."

Pierre turned to the masculine voice that had come up behind him and smiled when he saw his own face peering back at him. Standing beside Edouard was seven-year-old Andreu.

"What he said was les Américains are connards!" Andreu corrected.

"Exactly that," Edouard confirmed and gave a wide smile that told them all he was happy to see his father.

Edouard was dressed in a brocade suit of a salmon hue and heavily threaded with gold. Anyone looking at him could only accurately assume that this child of nine years was not only the son of someone exceedingly wealthy but expected to achieve many goals by the time he reached adulthood. A silk hat sat on his head. Gloves covered his hands. Tailored tasseled Hessian boots climbed up his legs. Already standing five and a half feet tall, he looked a boy five or more years his senior.

Andreu had deep brown hair and piercing hazel eyes. The suit he wore was made of velvet in a bright hue of turquoise. His brown felt hat was held down by his side in his hand. A natural scholar when it came to his studies, Andreu believed his intelligence made him the equal age of his older brother. The name he'd been given matched his personality. He was Pierre's only child who questioned authority and used foul language every chance he got.

Pierre pulled his sons to him and hugged them. Andreu giggled. Edouard was always too serious to giggle when affection was shown.

"Why aren't you on a horse?" Edouard asked.

"It threw a shoe," Pierre answered.

"All of us have been at the *maison* since morning waiting for you, as we knew you would go there directly."

There was no jealousy in his tone. Edouard loved all of his sisters and brother, and was very protective over the younger ones, especially when his cousins visited from Primrose.

"Were you in a hurry to see the babies?" Alexandrine asked.

*Babies?*

Pierre stared at Edouard.

Edouard gave the smile he only used when he knew a secret.

"We have twins!" Sade yelled.

As the oldest, Pierre always turned to Edouard for answers.

"Boys or girls?" He asked.

"I have two more brothers," Edouard answered, trying his best to keep a cool disposition although Pierre could see that Edouard was delighted about this news.

Pierre began running again.

His daughters squealed with laughter as they tried to keep up with his long-legged gait. Edouard's personality prevented him from running unless it was absolutely necessary. He would walk, then slip inside the *maison* and behave as if he'd been there from the beginning. Andreu stared at Edouard a long while, then left his side to run and catch up with the others.

When Pierre reached the *maison* his heart nearly burst with joy when he heard his sons crying behind a pair of doors. He couldn't stop until he was in the same room with them.

Despite her sons' loud pleas, Sarah lay half asleep. Feeling a dark shadow as it fell over her, her eyes opened. When she saw Pierre leaning over her, and after he had pressed a kiss against her forehead, she smiled and attempted to sit up.

"Sons? Twins? How long have you known?" He asked.

"We wanted it to be a secret," Sarah answered.

"We?" He asked.

Sarah stared across the room at Alise and Gorée sitting against the wall.

Pierre turned to them, and approaching, looked down into the faces of his sons. Alise bade him to sit beside her then offered him the twin she held. "Things have surely turned around haven't they?"

Pierre stared at his sons in disbelief, then emitted a charitable laugh. The strong Jennings' trait had reared its head again. Silver-blonde hair, fierce silver-blue eyes, lips like tiny doves in flight. "How is this possible?" He asked, staring at everyone individually. "I didn't think any of my children could look as much like me than Désireé and Edouard."

Alise carefully took the child from Gorée's arms. "Such a good nurse you've turned out to be."

Gorée grinned, and staring at the others, slapped her hands awkwardly together. It was something new she did when she was extremely happy.

Alise also laid this child in Pierre's arms.

"Identical," Pierre said.

Andreu ran into the room breathless. Some minutes later Edouard entered the room as if it were his own. He smiled broadly at Sarah and Alise in greeting. Gorée saw him and slapped her hands together again. Edouard stood beside her and tugged playfully at her hair. "You're doing it wrong. But don't worry. I'll show you again later."

"We tie thread around their wrists," Sarah said.

"They already have names, Papa," Edouard added. "I wrote them in the family Bible as soon as I learned what they were."

"What are their names?"

To this Alise laughed pleasantly.

"Must you even ask, Pierre?" She asked.

Sarah gave a wide smile. "Lucien and Alexis."

"They have lots of names, Papa. Just like me," Sade said. "This one with the yellow thread is Lucien Will Henriot. That one is Alexis Constance Arsène."

There was a knock at Sarah's boudoir door. A servant hurried forward. She bobbed a knee, quickly, then whispered, "Sorry to disturb you, monsieur. There's a strange slave woman in the yard. She claims *you* sent for her, but I ain't never seen her before, and she don't look like one of ours."

Pierre stared at Sarah when he answered. "Bring her around back. Have her enter the room through the galerie."

"Pierre, this is inappropriate," Alise chastised. "So many in a woman's boudoir so soon after…" She stopped as if saying anything further was too delicate for the many ears around her. Standing to her feet, she beckoned each of the children with her hands, of which not a single one knew that the woman they called Mère Alise was their grandmother.

"All of you out. Your papa is here to stay now. He'll meet you in the *grand salle* when he's ready. Come on. Let's give your mother and tante some much needed rest."

Edouard took Gorée by the hand. "You and I have much to talk about," he whispered. Gorée's eyes became wide. Mableane stepped into the room stopping momentarily to speak in a low voice to the two who constantly got into mischief whenever they could. "Mind yourselves you two. And if you go outside, stay close. I don't want to have to go looking for you."

Standing in front of her monsieur, she lifted Lucien from his arms. Alise beckoned the servant in the door to come forward and take the other child from the room. When the children were gone, Alise closed the door tightly behind her.

Pierre walked closer to the bed. "When I came back from Havana I made a stop in Biloxi. There I bought you a new servant. Someone to help you with the children."

"I have enough help, Pierre…" Sarah stopped speaking when the servant woman who had been shown to the rear of the *maison* now stood in it, and from the looks of her, she had run all the way there.

"Stay in bed, chérie," Pierre said, pressing a hand in her direction when Sarah attempted to climb out.

Sarah's arms trembled as she held them open. Imogen saw the gesture and ran past Pierre, flinging herself into Sarah's arms.

Both women wept bitterly on each other's neck.

***

On the other side of town, and very close to the river, inside of the new brothel owned and founded by Madam Cosette LaRègle in the year of 1826, and in a room separated from her many male customers who had come solely for pleasure and knew that no pleasure could be found like the pleasure had at her new location, were two nine year old identical twin girls ever mindful of the men's presence in the house but hadn't a care. One stood in front of a window holding the hand of her sister that had trouble breathing when she walked long distances or played too hard.

They watched as the rain fell gently on live oak trees unaware that a man named Pierre Constance Jennings, the eldest heir of Will Henriot Arceneaux Jennings, who himself was the only heir of Andreu Arsène Arceneaux Jennings, was at that moment meeting his newborn sons for the first time. They had no idea that a servant named Imogen was reuniting with her old mademoiselle whose name was Sarah Isabelle Cheval after a nine year separation, or how Sarah had given birth to seven children who were named Easter, Estelle, Andreu, Sade, Jurney, Lucien and Alexis, and believed that only five of them were alive.

They were unaware of a man named Julien Rafael Jennings, who at that moment sat on the galerie of the Primrose mansion with his placée, Anne, and their three sons: Rafael, Honoré and Isadore; and their two daughters Jillian and Manette while servants served warm beverages and beignet.

They were unaware of a woman named Jenna Jennings who at that moment threw back her head in laughter at something Alise Bluche said while two of Jenna's children, Edouard and Alexandrine, sat not too far behind her. Or of her daughter Abigail, who alongside her husband, Carlisle, the two of them now known as the King and Queen of Bowling Green because of their expansive mansion, cattle farm and dairy, were at that moment riding together across their estate the least bit worried that children will never be in their future.

Neither were they aware that the woman they believed was their tante was not their tante, and that it had been this woman who had given them the names Marthe and Mathilde, or how this woman had read in the cards that she should be at the bend of the great river on the opposite side of the bank of an extremely wealthy man as soon as she heard about a battle between two foreign groups of people west of that same river.

The morning that one of her customers arrived and told her about the Battle of Alamo, and that it was happening at that moment in Texas between the Américains and the Mexicans, she packed her boat with things she thought she would need, and then she and Roberto, her strong, tall, dark, muscular slave, climbed inside it and made their way slowly up the river.

The cards had told her to kill a serpent, and if she did so, she could pluck from its mouth two pieces of fruit that would bring her great wealth. For three days she and Roberto camped inside of the boat at the river's bend where a stand of trees prevented them from being carried away by the currents. It had been while Roberto was checking a fishing line when he saw a pirogue break apart and a man and two small children become victims to currents that desperately tried to take their lives.

Roberto noticed the children's hair and knew who they belonged to, as everyone in the city knew that anyone with silver hair belonged to the infamous Jennings *famille*. When he saw that the white man with them had on a poor looking coat and looked like an Américain, he yelled to Cosette. "The serpent is a man! And he has arrived!"

Turning, he was stunned to see that Cosette had already drawn the same conclusion. Pulling the boat out of the trees, she and Roberto worked together to save the children first. By the time they pulled Uriah out of the river he looked close to dead.

Roberto stared at the man in awe. For three days he and Cosette had been looking for an actual serpent, and although plenty lived in the area not one had been seen so far.

"Get us to land," Cosette said. "Hurry! I must do it before midnight."

Roberto steered the boat to the first sight of a bank and got them to it.

The children by this time were covered in a blanket and coughing up water.

"Make sure you keep them covered. I'll see to them in a minute," she said, drawing a cutlass out of the supplies she brought. After Roberto made certain the sleeping twins were completely covered, he held Uriah's head over the side of the boat as Cosette sliced the man's throat. She then cut out his tongue and wrapped it tightly in a piece of muslin, then secured the piece of cloth with a thin piece of rope. Next she cut off his penis and followed the same routine.

"You can get rid of him now, Roberto."

Roberto was quick to throw the body overboard.

As the twin girls stood in the window waiting for their tante to return, neither knew that at that moment Cosette had reached a powerful bokor who lived in the countryside, and on her person was the tongue and penis she had kept wrapped in muslin for nine years for this very day.

After laying the pieces of muslin in front of the bokor, she watched as he waved his hand over the cloth while it was still tightly wrapped with string. As his palm hovered above the pieces, his fingers violently twitched. When this happened, his rheumy eyes opened and settled on Cosette. Using his free hand to draw back the still trembling hand, he smiled at her. "What you brung be gud. What can I do for you, maddum?"

"I'm having horrible dreams. In them something very bad happens to me, but I can't see what it is. I need you to cast a spell of protection over me."

"Sit," he said.

The bokor didn't sit in a chair, but on the ground in front of his meager cabin. Loose chickens walked the ground aimlessly as if they were blind behind him.

Cosette caught a glimpse of these chickens as Roberto helped her sit on the ground in front of the bokor.

"Give me your hands, maddum."

Cosette held out her hands.

The bokor began to make a continuous noise that sounded like an unbroken grunt as he read the lines in her palms a long time. And then he pressed her palms tightly together so they were aligned. While holding them with one hand, he reached toward his side for a piece of string that dangled at his waist. On the end of it was an old chicken foot. Binding the string loosely around her hands, he then watched the direction in which the foot swayed. After he saw this, the string was pulled away.

Cosette knew there should have been more and leaned closer to him. "The spell has been cast?"

"Wat chu' do? Tell me de trooth."

She studied him a moment. "I have something that belongs to a wealthy man in the city. Do you think that's why I'm dreaming? Does he come for me?"

The bokor stood to his feet, then walked inside his home. Returning after a few minutes, he sat again in front of her. In his hand he held an ancient wooden cup. Inside it were chicken bones. A single shake was made, and then the bones dropped to the ground.

After reading them a while, the bokor's rheumy eyes stared unseeingly at her. A leather bag was pulled from his side. His old, wrinkled and ashy-gray fingers reached inside it. Without giving any warning dust was blown into Cosette's face.

Cosette fell back into the arms of Roberto, her arms flailing open and wide. Her chest heaved until it looked like it would burst through her gown. The dust stung painfully at her eyes. Roberto watched as the fullness of her chest looked as if something was trying to crawl out of her and escape through her widely parted mouth. When not even a single breath or sound was made, Roberto dropped her from his arms and scooted away from her.

Roberto had never dabbled with the religion Cosette practiced, and had been too fearful to watch the many rituals she performed. Now he knew why he feared her religion, because what he was looking at was something too spiritually dark for a man like him to witness. Something dark had possessed her, and this darkness had nothing to do with voodoo. Just like Cosette collected women who can entertain men, she also collected conjuring and root working rituals of Hoodoo.

Only when she was able to release the breath that suddenly filled her, her eyes opened. Even after she blinked several times, darkness surrounded her.

"You can take 'er e-way now," the bokor said with his eyes still staring forward as if no one was in front of him.

Roberto watched as Cosette fingered the ground aimlessly like the chickens, as if she was under a powerful spell. Small grunts slipped from her mouth as the fullness of her skirt pulled taut and threatened to rip.

Crouching in front of the bokor, Roberto spoke softly with fear in his tone. "Why her don't talk?"

"'Cause her cain't. Not right now. Later on she'll be all right."

Roberto looked at Cosette again. Cosette no longer fingered the ground. She gripped her neck with large eyes as if she couldn't breathe. "Whatchu do to her?"

"What she possess belong to de Debbil, but him ain't alone. Him have sons and daughters now, and they will rule a lot of the money in dis city. Him also have two women born from the same root. For now dem live in peace. De Debbil come for yo maddum soon, and dem him house will be a war of the roses."

"And what you done, you protect her from de Debbil?"

The boker spoke forcefully. "De dark neba choose yo maddum. But her choose de dark. Now I give her to de dark for de dark to do whateba it wants to her."

"And what she stole?"

"What she stole be de Debbil's forbidden lily."
"

# AUTHOR NOTE & ACKNOWLEDGMENTS

New Orleans is rich in history. From its fledgling beginnings, and its transfers from one country to another until it became a part of the U.S., people during that time that lived in the city saw it as nothing less than home.

Many influences made New Orleans different than other cities during the Antebellum South. One of them was its large population of free people of color. Shortly after the Louisiana Purchase, the population grew rapidly, and those arriving saw just how different the city was. Free men of color had been members of the militia for decades. Manumitted slaves weren't forced to leave the State they were made free in, and notations on manumission documents supported this. Mulâtresses such as Eulalie de Mandéville and Rosette Rochon amassed estates upon their deaths equivalent to a million dollars in today's time. It was common not only to see quadroon and octoroon women walking down the street with their mixed raced children, all of them dressed in fine apparel, but noticeably black women also walking in fine apparel while holding the hand of their mixed race child. Some of these women of color also had nice homes in the city built by Creole men they had entered a plaçage marriage with. Those in the city spoke predominantly French, practiced Roman Catholicism; enslaved blacks were allowed to practice African traditions in Congo Square, and the leniency of its class of free people of color in regards to education, skills and respect were hard for many newcomers to accept.

Back then the term Creole did not only refer to people of French descent. In fact, natives to the city who were German, Irish and Polish also called themselves Creole to separate themselves from the newcomers they wanted nothing to do with.

To further explain the differences, an Irish Creole man by the name of Eugene McCarty, who was well respected in the city and had a brother in politics, never married a woman of his own race. Instead, he continued his relationship with his placée, Eulalie, for almost fifty years then bequeathed to her and their five children his entire inheritance upon his death.

The truth is many Creoles, whether in secret or publically, loved their mixed raced children and made financial provisions, educated, and protected their children from injustices that many other blacks experienced in other parts of America. By 1855, nearly 85% of black Creoles were classified as doctors, clerks, teachers and skilled workers. These professions could also be boasted in other parts of America, but never in one centralized location.

Cultural confrontations occurred between the Creoles and Americans almost as soon as the Americans arrived, because Creoles didn't want change in their city. To Creoles, New Orleans was their city, their way of life. Americans wanted Creoles to speak English. Taking down the flag of France and replacing it with the American one was considered an outrage by Creoles. It became a territorial war. Creoles wanted the streets of New Orleans to remain French, and considered Americans as uncouth. Many Creoles, until their deaths, did not permit English spoken in their homes. Renowned Creole, Bernard Marigny, instead of selling a large amount of land into plots to Americans sold these plots to French-speaking citizens only, including free people of color, of which today is known as

Faubourg Marigny and Faubourg Tremé. Canal Street became the dividing line, and no respectable Creole crossed it, because beyond Canal Street was considered the American sector.

New Orleans, from its architecture, cuisine, music and so much more, its Creole influences have survived, and can be seen in the city even today.

This book is about love, and how dysfunctional the Jennings family is. Most importantly, it's about pain and heartbreak, and how these two emotions can inhibit the mind. I truly hoped you enjoyed this first novel in the Jennings family saga.

I need to thank a few people. First and foremost, my mother, Willie Mae, for taking her children to Louisiana each time she could afford it. I 'bleed' Louisiana, and often use it as a backdrop in my novels. I also want to thank my great-grandmother, Birda, my grandmother, Bertha, and my grandmother, Linnie, all of whom lived lives so very differently than the way women live today.

I thank God for his many blessings, and providing me with the gift of storytelling.

I thank the Historic New Orleans Collection for their vast documentations and records of the city.

I thank my son, Anthony, and my sister, Ravena, whose encouragement for this particular novel spanned over many years! As well as my husband, Bobby, for his nonstop, undying support.

I thank my editor, Sydney Morgan. You're a godsend!I thank Kyle and Azize for reading parts of this novel and providing their feedback.

Last but not least, the many readers of my previous books that have been more than loyal and a great support.

Thank you,
Shelley

# ABOUT THE AUTHOR

Shelley Young is a wife, mother and grandmother. From an early age she wanted to become an author, but put her dreams on hold to focus on her family. While working first as a nurse and later as a Customer Service Representative, she spent her spare time writing stories she believed the world would love. Her debut novel, The Blood Feud, became an Amazon international best seller and earned her radio and magazine interviews. She is the author of other Amazon international best sellers, and now as a full-time novelist devotes her time writing as many bestselling suspense-thrillers, mysteries, historical, romance and sci-fi novels as she can. She currently resides in California with her husband and can be contacted on her website www.shelleyfiction.com.

**BONUS CHAPTERS PART ONE**

# THE BABISIAN BOX
(Book One of The Battle of Eiglexx series)

# PROLOGUE

*June 18th, 1952*
*High in the wilderness mountain of Idaho*

The sound of his breathing. The sound of his feet tramping ground. Everything unnaturally still despite a fierce wind as chilly as Wilkes Land, Antarctica.

Sergeant Cooley led his team across scorched, brittle dirt and through trees that had bright, white branches of electrical static shivering across their bark. The trees weren't the only things strange. Once Cooley neared the mysterious object, he asked himself had he run of his own will or had he been lured.

Stumbling to the ground, the rifle flew from his hands. Making a reach for it, he saw he'd gripped handfuls of black-crusted iron, all of them with thumbprints as if God had touched them. Looking up, he saw more rocks falling from the ship like beads of sweat down a chilled glass, except these rocks vibrated.

Gripping his Springfield and drawing it to him, he waved his hand to get the others' attention and stop them from advancing.

Private Yates threw himself on the ground, crawling toward Cooley with fear in his eyes. "What is it? It doesn't look Russian." His gaze on what could have only been some kind of transport ship large enough to drop thousands of troops on the ground. "Is this real? This can't be real."

Chatfield and the others also threw themselves to the ground and crawled closer.

"It's a goddamn German bunker!" Chatfield whispered with certainty. The expression on his face told Cooley no one could convince the young man otherwise.

The ship did look similar but at a much larger scale. It had an opening high up its center wider than the fields of Fort Hood where testing had taken place for destroyer tanks during the war.

Here it was broad daylight, but sunlight was unable to penetrate the darkness in the ship's opening. Cooley thought he saw something move in the darkness. When he realized he did urine snaked down his leg.

It was that moment the ground hummed. The soldiers stumbled and fell over each other as they tried to flee. The ground shifted and cracked like a mirror. Deep lines. Complicated webs. The fissures transformed into gaping chasms. Coming to his senses, Cooley screamed. "Pull back!"

Only able to crawl, the soldiers became blocked as trees toppled and lost their place on Earth. The ground then rumbled. Violently. More chasms were created. The 'things' crawling out of the opening touched ground and advanced at a rapid speed.

Private Menlo lost his grip on the ground, skidding on his belly and became lost in a chasm. Private Turnbull reached wildly for anything to grab when he began to slide. Before he could fall into the chasm the 'things' surrounded him. After that Turnbull could no longer be seen. Cooley abandoned his troop. Clawing and pushing against the ground with his feet, the rocks God had touched slid underneath him like a rolling river. The ground opened. Cooley fell with his hands stretched in front of him and his feet suspended behind him into a chasm ten feet wide.

A tree snapped, knocking Yates into the chasm like a baseball struck hard by a bat.

Chatfield cowered in the curve of a tree trunk. Short bursts of screams faded away as everyone in his unit disappeared. His fingers trembled in front of his face as dozens of the 'things' flew at him like metal to a magnet.

The cold wind snatched Chatfield's scream away as his body sailed through the air.

# CHAPTER 1

*Present Day*
*October 17th, 2022*

"Who'd think three of us will save the world?"

The words were spoken in a whisper and were out before she realized she would say them. It happened at times, the mysterious voice so similar to her own, speaking through her things that always came true. Parapsychologists called it 'intrinsic knowledge,' the ability of knowing something without a physical explanation. Psychotherapists had once misdiagnosed her as having persecutory delusions. Now older, she had been given an accurate diagnosis, and although it had a name, doctors around the world believed there was no known name that truly described her abilities. There was one thing the doctors agreed on. When Ericka Elise Martin spoke, shut up and pay attention regardless of how strange her words appeared.

'Three people' and 'save the world' were the words she focused on, but neither caused any alarm. The words were simply more pieces of a never-ending puzzle. More riddles to solve because often than not the words she spoke didn't have transparent meanings.

She gave a guarded look at the man standing beside her unaware he had come closer after having gone off to look around. Somewhere not far from where they stood a family of five were lost in the forest. After a diligent search turned up nothing she had been asked to help in a second search in the hopes of finding clues as to what happened to them.

Farzad Emir's aviator sunglasses prevented Ericka from seeing his eyes, but still she knew they were trained intently on her. His arms were crossed over his chest. The hard muscles of his arms threatened to tear apart the seams of his jacket sleeves.

"I count seven," he said not moving or averting his gaze. "Including you and me that makes nine. What do you mean three of us will save the world?"

Avoiding relationships had become a hard rule. One touch or the smell of cologne or perfume, one word spoken out of their mouths, one look into their eyes and most times than not Ericka saw what people didn't want her to see. The triggers were never the same and often occurred when she least expected it. Like kindred spirits, strangers attached themselves to her without knowing why. Farzad hadn't been any different. From the moment they met he had become her shadow. Experience taught her that no one ever presented themselves as they truly were. This included her parents.

Disappointment was something she hadn't gotten used to. Avoiding it meant keeping to herself at all times like she did now.

"I meant the nine of us is someone's imagination of a highly skilled team," she said.

Not far from the Bell helicopter Farzad had flown to get them there, a military Mi-17 touched ground, its rotors sending cold currents in sonar waves.

The mission was simple: find and rescue. What she'd whispered had been strange on its own. Farzad's attire kicked strange up another notch: three-piece suit, expensive leather shoes, two long necklaces, the many gold and silver rings on his fingers, the watch on his wrist, the even-tone of his skin like rattan except closer to beige than bronze, the meticulously trimmed six o'clock shadow, the shapely mouth like a heart drawn flat, the top lip more prominent than the bottom. He looked more like he had come to provide lavish entertainment, but her senses told her there was something dangerous about him.

No one had been there to greet them. A small cabin sat behind them, but neither had bothered to go in and check it out. As if thinking the same thing, Ericka and Farzad looked at the mountain covered with a strange-looking forest. Ericka heard nothing and didn't have any new visions, but still she knew that what she was looking at had something to do with the words she had spoken.

The rotors on the Mi-17 increased. Each chopped, blended and whipped the atmosphere. Seven people struggled out of it bowels, then doubled in half or were forced to the ground as the helicopter lifted and flew away while the seven were still close.

"One of them almost came near the tail rotor blade." Farzad's words were spoken in curiosity as he and Ericka watched the pilot lose control. The Mi-17 leaned hard on one side, its cockpit and landing skid threatening to crash against the ground. Farzad dropped his arms.

The Mi-17 made an abrupt recovery. Within seconds it looked no more than a spider running across an invisible web.

"You're a fearless woman," he said. "That just scared the shit out of me. What do you think that was all about?"

Ericka didn't know and didn't answer. She saw no areas of dirt, including on the airstrip, which was more than strange, but not as much as the grass. It grew everywhere she looked in the darkest shade of green she'd ever seen. Beyond the grass, spruce trees of every kind grew almost on top of each other and so closely together that from this vantage the forest appeared impenetrable.

"Why are we here?" she asked herself in a whisper. No family in their right mind would enter what she saw even if they did believe diamonds were somewhere inside.

Ace Diamond Xiang reached them first. He stood no more than five-feet-five, had Japanese features, although his file listed him as Hmong. Dark skin, a thick helmet of black, spiky hair, full lips; he appeared a pretty boy with the eyes of a man twice his age. He, too, stopped to stare at the forest.

Grath Carver looked nothing like his file photo. Ripped muscles Ericka was sure he was proud of hung out of the sleeves of his tightly fitted black Tee. Dark hair. Sunburned skin. A shoulder and waist holster stuffed with large caliber pistols. His attire meticulous. His appearance like someone who had gone through extreme measures to present himself as a Hollywood version of a bad ass cop. He stood a distance back while performing a visual investigation that Ericka assumed he needed before he would join himself to anyone there.

Langdon Lincoln had dressed appropriately, although the bright yellow cap pulled snug onto her head was definitely overkill. Large round breasts protruded out of her thin long-sleeved red sweater like pillows a sleepy head could sink into. The boots she wore looked like they gave her the ability to run fast, climb a mountain, and kick ass all at the same time.

"And the strange keeps coming," Ericka whispered.

Billie Boston looked exactly like her file photo, and Ericka wished like hell that Billie hadn't. Petite in stature with a round face, homely features, short hair purposely hacked, her overall appearance a schizophrenic hobo. A sweater hung loosely over her shoulders by a single button holding on by a thread. The closer Billie got the more she became uncertain, her eyes darting around at everyone, except Ericka and Farzad, as if she waited for a well-deserved beating.

Ericka slid her gaze surreptitiously toward Farzad to see if he'd noticed. He leaned in close.

"I'm getting the impression it's already been decided that we're the outsiders," Ericka whispered.

"I'm getting the impression Billie Boston assaulted a homeless person for that sweater," Farzad whispered back.

Ericka hated that she laughed, because laughing at someone was cruel.

James Burton appeared next, looking like the model soldier. Medium brown skin. Handsome features. One look at his face and Ericka determined he lived, worked and ate the Army's code of conduct.

Two more soldiers brought up the rear, both carrying special-made rifles far too large for a search and rescue mission. Ericka hadn't been given files on these soldiers like she had the others. All she knew were their names: Paul Szwedko and Jeff Bagley. The two of them had been assigned the sole duty of protecting the group.

She was staring at these two men when the whispering voice inside her decided to speak again. "We're unable to communicate with our satellites."

Farzad held her gaze the same way he had before.

"In space," she clarified when he continued to stare at her. "The space satellites are down."

"I don't remember hearing that on the news. Which ones?"

"All of them," she answered and walked away.

Sergeant Szwedko saw Ericka and bypassed everyone else to reach her. "I'm expecting pandemonium in the Pentagon and on every Air Force Base in America. You got something you want to tell me?"

His smile quickly put her at ease. It was a joke she got often, people blaming her for everything that happened in the world. This was their second time meeting and like before she sensed he was a friendly – a name she gave to anyone she sensed would stay friendly toward her regardless of what happened.

"I didn't catch it all," he said. "The pilot mentioned the loss of communication with our satellites. No contact whatsoever. We currently have no eyes into space. Before he dropped, he was told to make it back fast."

"Yeah," she agreed.

His eyebrow rose and then he relaxed the rifle in his hand.

"I'm not surprised by the news," he admitted. "I knew a little about the problem before I got here. Failures have been happening for weeks. Infantry on my Base are on standby and ready to be sent to California in preparation for the worse. I'm surprised I'm even here. Harvey Gabriel must have more pull than I'd imagined. I'm surprised you're here. I was sure I would get here and be told you were needed somewhere else."

"I've been purposely unreachable," she said. "When I feel I'm supposed to be somewhere, I let nothing or no one stop me from getting there."

He leaned closer and lowered his voice. "I'm glad to hear that. Not many soldiers can brag of doing a mission with the great Ericka Martin."

The smile she gave was one she hadn't given in a while. "I get that a lot. Wait until we're knee-deep in it, then tell me how you feel."

He gave agreeing nods because he believed the mission would have more negative results than favorable. "We'll let whatever's happening with the satellites work themselves out while we focus on the reason we're here."

He caught sight of Bagley and hurried away.

A shadow moved closer to Ericka's shoulder. She didn't need to turn to know it was Farzad. "Are you purposely becoming my shadow?"

The way he threw back his head, as if dodging a punch, then laughed brought a half giggle out of her.

"I wanted to be nosy and find out what the two of you were talking about, especially after you mentioned our satellites going out."

"You have an interest in outer space?"

"I have an interest in our country becoming involved in a surprise attack by our enemies. I used to be a soldier. Infantry. It's one of the reasons I was included on the team."

She held up her hands in the direction of his face and waited for his approval. "Do you mind?"

Szwedko had been readable from the moment Ericka laid eyes on him. For two hours she had been alone with Farzad and had seen very little about him.

"It won't hurt," she promised. "I'm usually not curious about people, but I find myself very curious about you."

The heart-shape of his mouth flared into a smile. "I like your come on line."

It was her turn to laugh. She even threw back her head like he had without realizing it.

Faces were too personal to touch. Her palms reached for his shoulders. He leaned closer so she could reach them.

She touched him, drew back her hands and searched his eyes. What she'd seen had been a small glimpse of his future. In the vision he hadn't been alone. A woman lay underneath him, preventing Ericka from seeing what the woman looked like, but Ericka had seen the woman's hands and had recognized them. Sweat covered Farzad's body. He and the woman were kissing in the dark on top of an unmade bed.

Farzad held her gaze happy she couldn't see his eyes behind his sunglasses and see that he was studying more than her face. And then he held up his hands. "May I?"

Another joke she was used to.

"Sure," she said.

He ignored the uncertainty in her tone and cupped both sides of her face. "More beautiful than art. I've never been more curious about anyone. I hope I haven't made you uncomfortable by staying as close to you as I have."

He turned and walked away.

Ericka watched him go. One thought burned in her mind.

If she was the woman in the vision something had been wrong with her hands.

# CHAPTER 2

The man sitting at a computer desk facing six separate monitors went by many names depending on who asked him.

Turning up the volume, he leaned closer. For weeks the monitors had been tuned to ABC, CNN, BBC, CCTV, Aaj Tak and Africa News and only now he saw what he'd been waiting for. CNN jumped before the others. That they did, in his eyes, made them the broadcasting leader of the world.

*The U.S. Space Command has confirmed the outage of their last space satellite. SANDRA, America's space satellite that replaced GEMINI four years ago, has suddenly stopped communicating. General Advisor Connor Shaw has assured that America is not under any form of threat whether global, intergalactic or otherwise. He has also confirmed what our government has suspected for some time. Russia has also lost their eyes on space. At this time no explanation has been given as to why these anomalies are occurring. The LEO has been scheduled for liftoff in the hopes that astronauts from NASA can get the SANDRA up and running again. Secretary of Defense Ashland Donner has issued a statement that no one should be alarmed. Before the outages everything in space looked as it should, reporting that there, in his words, are no other anomalies to report. Secretary of Defense Donner has promised to give a press conference, but only if one becomes necessary.*

"Great-grandfather?"

The man turned and saw one of his grandson's children standing in the door. All of his children and their offspring were hard to look at, except Zizi. That she looked more human the reason they had sent her rather than someone else.

"We have a problem," she whispered.

This he already knew. He knew it as soon as she had come to the door.

He made a gesture with his hand to send her along, then pulled a cell phone out of his drawer and phoned a residence in San Antonio, Texas.

\*\*

President Bleeker sat at the end of the table in a low chair that made him looked dwarfed by the many people around him. Secretary of Defense Ashland Donner also sat silently and looked bored while gazing at images being shown to them on the wall of the darkened Situations Room.

The images were of asteroids and meteors, pictures they had all seen before, and the last images captured by SANDRA before she went down. The news being given was also the same as it had been before. England's Minister of Defense was holding on the phone. That call should have been more important, but his decision to take it now rather than later had been overridden by America's commander-in-chief.

"There's just no way." Once again Jonah Yaeger from the NORAD/USNORTHCOM command center reiterated what he'd been saying all along. His voice spoke clearly and confidently out of the conference system that sat in the center of the conference table. "Our satellites are more advanced than ever. Had anything been coming our way we would have seen it days or weeks before now. An invasion is unrealistic..."

"It is not unrealistic," President Bleeker cut in, then sat closer to the table, rested his elbows on top of it and folded his fingers. "I'm not convinced by the edicts I've reviewed. An invasion at any time should be seen as always imminent."

"Sir?" Jonah Yaeger's tone faltered when he tried to maintain the President's calm. "Astronauts from ISS have already made contact with SANDRA. The news reported the LEO hasn't lifted yet, but only because we wanted a little extra time. What eyes we do have supports..."

"Stop talking," President Bleeker threatened, then leaned back into his chair because most of the people sitting around him didn't know what he and Yaeger and only a few others with the highest level of clearance did. Choosing his words carefully, he spoke in a low harsh tone. "That you are playing this all down to nothing convinces me you are the most ignorant man of our species or you have sided with a long-standing potential enemy. This can't be a coincidence. Russia becoming blind the same moment we are. What are you not telling me, Jonah?"

"Sir..." Yaeger hesitated as he also grappled for the right words, because openly discussing aliens when those in the room weren't certain of their existence would be the worst mistake he could ever make. "The words I'm speaking are the best I can offer of my certainty about the matter. We've always had failures, even more so once we redesigned our technology. I'm sure there's a logical explanation..."

"There is no logical explanation!"

The roar of the President's voice caused others to sit up straight and pay closer attention to a private conversation that had long become suspicious. This wouldn't be the first, secrets spoken openly about but now shared and only understood between those that should have knowledge of them. The difference with this conversation is it wasn't about political issues or contributions or embarrassing matters made public through the media. The conversation was about space, and this was the first time that space was being discussed so heatedly for most of them.

"Let's get it out in the open once and for all. Code Blue Bethesda...," the President began.

"Blue Bethesda?" Donner sat taller and stared at the President as if pain moved slowly throughout his body. "Are you saying from your perspective the outage of the satellites is cause enough to put Blue Bethesda into operation?"

After he asked the question he looked around the table to see if he was the only one concerned.

President Bleeker studied the faces peering at him and spoke as gently as he could. "You all need to know and now's the time. Former Presidents from as far back as Truman in 1952 have signed favorable executive and administrative orders in regards to technological weapons development for all of our military branches. With those orders Blue Bethesda was organized. I fear we are now facing the possibility of following Blue Bethesda protocols for the sake of our country."

"An alien invasion." Donner spoke the words, but didn't want to believe them. For years hypothetical scenarios had been spoken of and disproved by mathematical and science geniuses from every corner of the globe. This morning when he'd walked out of his home his thoughts had been about buying a gift for his wife. Their wedding anniversary was only two days away. Now the thought that there was a possibility of an invasion, he saw, had changed the room's atmosphere. Making phone calls were all he could think about, and the response he would get when he said what no one truly expected to hear.

The awkward silence around him became unbearable the more he sat. Doomsday refused to plant seed in his brain.

"Jonah, is PACAF and SAC in the air?" the President asked.

"They are," Yaeger affirmed.

More people in the room felt a sudden unease as the conversation happening between their President and the commander of America's most important space observation program pulled more into the light.

412

Those sitting at the table drew closer to someone. Whispered conversations began, and those conversations were solely about family and loved ones.

"Prepare the EWAs," the President said. "All of them."

Secretary of Energy, Ernesto Peña, stopped chewing the end of his pen and lowered it diplomatically. Not wanting to be the voice of panic he decided to become the voice of reason. "I estimate less than five EWAs becoming available immediately, the remaining becoming available over the next two weeks. The natural resources to operate them were contracted through private and publically owned energy companies. Firing up the EWAs will drive false spikes on the stock market. After the threat is over those spikes will crash. We're talking large companies such as CleanAire Corporation in full collapse."

"Do it," President Bleeker said firmly. "If former presidents can bail out the auto industry I can certainly bail out our energy industry. I'll take full responsibility for the fallout. I also want everyone in this room flown to FEMA as soon as possible."

"This can't be happening," John Johnson spoke up. "I mean, come on, guys. We're talking about an alien invasion."

The Secretary of Homeland Security, Shawn Coleman, reared back in his chair. "You sound as if you're certain Code Blue Bethesda is necessary, President Bleeker. If it is what are we going to tell the public? How will we tell the public?" He looked around the table, waiting patiently for an answer.

"We tell them the truth," the President began. "It's a truth that most of you here don't even know about. America discovered extraterrestrial life on our soil in 1952. Unlike the many myths, these life forms didn't expire once they became exposed to our atmosphere. Many of the same extraterrestrials that were discovered in 1952 are still alive, and since then have given birth to more of their species here on Earth. Since 1952 these life forms have been secluded to Blue Trees Mountain."

Chairs squeaked. Body positions changed. A few objects were repositioned on the long, polished wood conference table. Silence became as dense as space.

"Why was this kept a secret from the public?" Donner asked.

President Bleeker shared the answer. "I'm just as surprised as all of you are. All of you know I've just gotten in office. I only learned of this species a few months ago."

"But the truth hasn't been told since 1952," Coleman debated. "What you're asking us to do, Mr. President, is cause panic on the street.

CNN has already reported the space satellites outages. Firing up the EWAs. PACAF and SAC in the sky. Cabinet members being whisked to safety…"

"A nightmare," Donner concluded. "Of mass proportion when Yaeger is advising we have no proof to support your…suspicion, President Bleeker." A stalwart expression appeared on his face. He had decided not to believe it, because he didn't want to believe it.

"At least the public will be aware," the President refuted. "Like you all are now aware. The type of attack we may be facing… I'll gladly go down in history as the most ignorant President we ever had if what we warn the people of America about turns out not to be true. We have no eyes in space. What better time for them to come when we're not looking and unprepared. Any news from Camp Blue Trees? General Felt, I expected you here with us and not where you."

A strong voice lifted from the conference system.

"My intentions had been to be there, President Bleeker," General Felt assured. "Nothing unusual is taking place here. Even still, I stand behind your call."

"I just want to be clear," John Johnson said, leaning closer to the table and folding his arms on top of it. "Alien life forms exist here in America, specifically in Blue Trees Mountain and, General Felt, you're not seeing any strange activities although the loss of our satellites supports President Bleeker's suspicion?"

"That's exactly what I'm saying," General Felt answered. "And I'm also saying that perhaps Blue Bethesda should go live. I'll do what I'll have to here. The EWAs will make a difference if President Bleeker's suspicion rings true. We fire them up then wait and see what happens. If nothing we lie to the public like we've always done."

"My Lord," House Speaker Nina Calloway whispered. "Telling us at a time like this doesn't leave much time, does it?"

"I strongly feel like we're jumping the gun here. My command center knows about space. It's us here that have watched it many years. If there was something we'd have seen it. Twenty-four hours," Yaeger begged. "If our astronauts can't get SANDRA up and running by then I, too, stand by the President's call."

The President sat forward. "We don't wait. I'm initiating Blue Bethesda in the meantime."

"How certain are you, you can have SANDRA up and having sight by tomorrow?" Johnson asked.

"I'm not," Yaeger answered honestly. "But considering what we've seen before she went down and what we'll face on the ground if all of this is nothing it's worth every try."

"Your decision, Mr. President?" Peña asked. "Once the start of the EWAs has been initiated there's no going back."

"How long before they'll be ready to fire?" the President asked.

"Two – three days tops depending on cooperation from our contractors."

"Can the EWAs defend us from this species?" Calloway asked.

"In theory, yes," General Felt answered.

"How powerful is this species?" Calloway asked.

"We don't know," President Bleeker responded. "We'll wait twenty-four hours before we alert the public, because truthfully speaking, warning them now the only difference we'll see is America killing ourselves before the species arrive. That former Presidents since '52 have kept such a secret from our population is beyond me regardless of what the payoff has been. Let's just hope this is only a false alarm and our former leaders have made the right decisions in regards to our welfare and future."

General Felt continued to listen carefully to the President as he sat in his office at Camp Blue Trees. He stayed connected to the conference until its very end. Only then did he hang up and stare blankly across his desk at three photos that hung on the wall. Rushing to his feet, he hurried out of his office and into the main hall. He took the elevator down to one of the Camp's lower levels, then stepped out of it and hurried inside of the command room.

He had lied when he told those attending the conference that there had been no change in Blue Trees Mountain, and for good reason.

"Anything?" he asked.

Three soldiers stared at him over their shoulders with distressed faces and tightened mouths.

"Anything!" he roared in what they called his McEnroe voice.

"We have more trouble," Sergeant Pakuk answered. "Maybe you want to come closer and take a look?"

General Felt stepped closer when suddenly all three soldiers turned and faced the monitors in front of them. John soon saw the same things they did. The helmet dashcams of the soldiers that had been sent to escort Ericka and her team to safety all had mangled, sharp teeth in them that dripped with blood before the teeth made another dive for the blood sources.

"Everyone on the team we sent are dead, sir," Pakuk said.

"Then why are you sitting there?" John questioned.

"Sampson..."

"You get out there," General Felt demanded. "I don't care about the others, but make sure the three that I mentioned from the team make it back here alive."

Sergeant Pakuk Nukusuk rose to his feet and crossed the room. Already suited, he grabbed a large rifle from the wall and ran through the command room's door.

# CHAPTER 3

"Do you think we'll find them?" The question came from Billie and was spoken as Ericka walked through the cabin door. Ericka saw the question for what it was: an invitation for anyone to talk to her, because just that quickly Billie had become faceless. Ericka noticed that the others purposely avoided talking to Billie and kept their distance from her.

The nine had chosen the cabin to go over the rescue plan.

The cabin seemed smaller on the inside than it appeared on the outside. A small open kitchen sat against one wall. The rest of the cabin formed a reception area. As promised, Harvey Gabriel had supplies brought up in advance and left on the floor alongside a number of light-weight sleds for each of them to pull.

A secondhand clock on the wall read 5:18. Since the hour was closer to two, James looked behind the clock then alerted everyone the battery was a relic and of a brand that could no longer be purchased on the market. A rusted aluminum tea kettle sat on a single burner operated by propane. Ceramic owls with large eyes hung on the wall above. Someone had left an afghan on the seat of a red, leather chair. A strong scent of rotting wood, mold and dust warned the cabin had sat abandoned many years.

"Did you see that forest out there?" James had decided to take on Billie's unspoken request since no one else had. "They couldn't have gotten too far in that."

"Why this team?" Ericka asked, then stopped herself from looking at Farzad. He sank into the chair next to hers and got far too comfortable. One of his arms hung over the back of her chair. She knew from his closeness that the others would believe the two of them had known each other long before today.

Farzad sensed that Ericka wanted to look at him and was pleased she didn't. She had taken him off guard the moment they met. The photo in her file was of a ten-year-old girl. Other than her name the only other information the file contained was an Army brief on the subject of clairvoyance. The last thing he expected to see was a beautiful woman.

A daisy sat above one of her ears. She wore her hair natural. Wild curly locks framed her face. A gentle breeze from the open, sun-filled door pushed a tendril close to full lips that were painted a matte shade of a red plum. Nut-brown skin smelled of lotion as fragrant as perfume. Her eyes were black pools that would ripple if poked with a fingertip. Although she looked in her twenties, the expression she wore was of someone determined to make a difference in the world.

He chose to sit next to her because the others had annoyed him within minutes of shaking their hands. If he had to guess, the other seven were far too overly self-centered. Like Ericka, he also wondered why this team had been assembled: a cop, three soldiers, two wilderness women and an Asian kid who looked around as if this was his first time out of the city. This seemed more than a rescue mission. He wondered if anyone other than him and Ericka had drawn this same conclusion. Another thing that bothered him was the hasty retreat of the Mi-17.

Sergeant Szwedko stood at the end of the table with both hands pressed against it. "Before we get into that, Ericka, I think it'll be better if I introduce you to everyone."

"Didn't everyone receive a file on me?" Her eyes traveled around the table.

"Not exactly," Szwedko answered.

Grath Carver laughed. "What I received could have been pasted on a postcard."

"I didn't get anything," Ace said.

"Neither did I," Langdon and Billie chimed in.

Private First Class Bagley started around the table, placing a single card from a deck in front of everyone except Ericka. The atmosphere quickly became that of a classroom.

"Can any of you tell me without looking what card you have?" Szwedko asked.

"Is there a reason she doesn't have a card?" Grath asked, nudging his head toward Ericka.

Szwedko ignored the question and asked one of his own. "Do any of you want to take a guess?"

"If it was a new deck, depending on the number of shuffles the odds are increased by fifty-two," Ace said.

"What if I told you Ericka can guess what cards you have?" Szwedko asked.

"If she's a mathematician I'll buy that she can probably guess one of ours," Ace answered. "But not all of us. It's impossible."

"She's not a mathematician, Ace," Szwedko said. "Clairvoyance," he continued, changing the subject and raising his voice as if the cabin stretched farther and was filled with students, and he wanted those in the back to hear him. "Studies indicate those claiming to have this gift can predict a future occurrence after seeing a vision, or having a dream, or touching something, smelling something, hearing something. Ericka falls out of every study known to man. From the age of six she's been studied by experts around the world. Many names have been applied to her gift. Some of you may be familiar with them. Extrasensory perception also known as ESP. An esper. A precog. A retrocog. A psychic. There are many names. Ericka is one of only thirty-two people in the entire world who falls under each of the categories I mentioned. She also holds the highest number of public and private validations, and is the only winner of the Randolph Award."

Ace stared at Ericka with tight eyes.

"Are you saying she knows which card each of us has without looking at it?" Langdon couldn't stop staring at Ace's expression.

"Do any of you wish to volunteer?" Szwedko asked.

"I will," Ace answered.

Szwedko made a gesture for Ace to stand.

Ace rose then shoved his hands in his pockets.

"Do you think this is necessary?" Ericka stared at Ace, then at everyone else.

"I'm actually curious," Farzad admitted.

No one else said anything. Ericka knew then they had all become curious. Szwedko was playing the group and for some reason he wanted her to play along with him. Only because she considered him a friendly did she stand, then walk around the table and stand behind Ace.

Ace smiled and waited, his eyes looking down on the card, and then at the others. After a few seconds and nothing happened, he looked over his shoulder into her eyes.

A part of his past filled Ericka's eyes like smoke trapped behind glass. Her neck snapped back. Chair legs scraped the floor as a few people got nervous and couldn't keep still. It all happened very quickly.

She returned to her chair, pulling it closer to the table by the seat before sitting again.

Szwedko's eyebrows rose.

Ericka gave a small shake of her head.

Ace saw this and stared at Szwedko. "What just happened?"

"Apparently, Ericka saw something too personal to share with everyone."

"I don't believe in clairvoyance," Ace asserted, holding Ericka's gaze. "The Randolph winner? I don't buy that. Many people claim they have the gift, but can only give vague details or descriptions that hint at the truth. If you saw something then prove it."

Being called a fraud was something she didn't take kindly to. The more she held his gaze the more she saw. If he didn't care, she decided she wouldn't either. "You spent last night with two women. *Beautiful* women. You cried this morning after you discovered they were no longer in your apartment and had taken the money out of your wallet, and had stolen your favorite watch. The wallet is made of red leather and has some kind of stitching on the front. You stared into the wallet a long time, and then you said, 'I thought they were really into me,' and cried some more until you said, 'Fuck it.' And then you prepared to come here only to realize you had spent so much time crying you no longer had time to take a shower."

Bagley gaped at Ace in pity. "Shit. Bummer."

"Anyone else?" Szwedko asked.

Ace stared at Ericka, refusing to look away, because he saw that she'd seen more than she'd let on. No one had been in his apartment after the women left. What the women had done had been too embarrassing for him to share with anyone else. The more he looked at Ericka, the more he wondered how any human being could see such detail about someone else's life.

Farzad stared at the others then raised his hand.

Szwedko couldn't hold his excitement that someone else was willing to have something personal about them shared with the group.

"I don't want to do him," Ericka said. "Pick someone else."

Farzad leaned closer. "Why not? I didn't sleep with two women last night."

Ericka turned and studied his eyes, then stared down at his hand before touching her pinky to his. She kept it there a while, then closed her eyes and drew in a deep breath. "You've never slept with a woman before. It's against your...reli... No. Not religion. A *law* you live by. The law requires that you are only allowed to sleep with..." She opened her eyes, remembering what she'd seen about him when they'd been outside.

*Everything's connected.*

The voice came to her suddenly. She stared at the others, then at the owls hanging on the walls, the single burning stove, the red chair, and had a feeling of déjà vu. This moment. It was almost as if she had lived it before.

*You don't know what you are*, the voice inside her warned.

She pressed a hand to her chest and breast the same way she had the last time the voices had said the same thing. All of her medical reports proved she was human. She reminded herself of this as memories of the time she'd spent inside an asylum flooded back.

*I'm human*, she silently told herself. *I'm just like everyone else.* It was the second affirmation she didn't and couldn't believe, because she wasn't like everyone else. The voices inside her never stayed silent. Her eyes never stopped seeing.

"Go on," Farzad encouraged softly, leaning closer to her.

After looking around and noticing everyone giving her a curious stare, Ericka gave a small smile. "The woman you marry," she finished, then looked down and saw that Farzad wasn't wearing a wedding ring.

"This can't be real," Billie said, then smiled as if everyone was playing a joke. "The two of them know each other."

"We met only today," Farzad assured everyone.

"Is what she said true?" Langdon asked.

"Very true," Farzad said, keeping his eyes on Ericka.

"She's the real thing," Ace finally said and sat again.

"I don't know which of you to feel sorry for," Grath said, his eyes darting from Farzad's to Ace's while his mouth pulled into a sneer.

"It doesn't matter." Ericka leaned back in her chair. Anger crept into her eyes. "The person you feel sorry for most is yourself. You've never been married although you want to be, but women just don't like you. You used to have a girlfriend. Her name was Carlyle..."

Grath sat tall in his seat, confusion showing on his face. "What?" he asked.

Ericka talked over him. "The *last* girlfriend you had loved telling people she was named after the hotel her parents conceived her in. You hit her at the dinner table on Thanksgiving Day in front of her parents. She refused to press charges. She and her family refuse to have any contact with you. You were able to keep your job, but you've been drinking since, not because you feel bad about what you did, but because you can't figure out how to get even with Carlyle without jeopardizing your career."

Grath stood to his feet, his eyes on Szwedko, accusing him of telling Ericka these things, but then he looked at Ace and took his seat again.

Ace studied the hardened expression on Grath's face, then stared at Ericka. "How do you do it? And what does this have to do with the cards?"

"I don't know how I do it," Ericka answered. "And it has nothing to do with the cards. It's a new deck. If I touch them, I might see something about Bagley since he's handled each card the most. But I don't see everything. I don't know everything. For some reason I can read a lot about one person and see very little about someone else."

"But you can see something about all of us?" Langdon questioned.

"I usually see something about every person I meet, but nine times out of ten it's something vague." She stared at Ace. "The more I'm around someone and watch their behavior the more I see." Ericka eyed Billie. "Your boyfriend didn't leave you. He left the house and went to work like he always did. The police were waiting for him. His trial is over and he's been sent to prison. He hasn't contacted you because he's ashamed to tell you where he is and what he did to get there." She stared at James. "The kid's yours." She stared at Ace. "Your father is a professional gambler. You were named after the suits he loves best." She stared at Grath. "I don't like *anything* I see about you." She turned to Farzad. "You have never met your mother. You often wonder what she looks like."

She glanced around the table. "I can't explain what makes me the way I am. If I could shut it off, I would. If I had mentioned something insignificant the rest of you would have asked questions, and I wanted to avoid that. Lots of questions coming at me from a group make me feel like a freak. Sharing something personal lets you know I'm real. People usually stay away from me. It's okay if you want to stay away from me, too. I'm used to it. I'm used to being alone."

Billie captured Ericka's attention. "Thank you," she whispered.

"Now that you know about Ericka, let's get back to the mission," Szwedko said. "Two weeks. We do what we can and then we leave this place, return to our lives, and put this place behind us."

Farzad leaned closer and whispered in Ericka's ear. "Are you all right?"

Ericka heard him, but couldn't stop staring at Szwedko.

*Run!*

A sword edged with diamonds lifted in the air. A gray tongue as thick as an arm became severed and leaked blood similar to tree sap.

She stood to her feet and waited to see more, because if she did she had no intentions of staying where she was.

"Ericka?" Szwedko whispered as he stood upright and stared at her with apprehension.

For reasons she couldn't explain, she stared at Farzad after Szwedko had spoken. The vision she saw was his hand cupping her naked breast as tears rolled down her cheek. In the corner, not too far from where he stood, two tentacles red in color and with pointed ends stretched across the floor to reach her.

She pressed a hand to her mouth and closed her eyes. The same vision repeated itself, but this time she saw more. She and Farzad were in a room with cement floor and walls. A strange-looking bed sat in one corner. *I'll keep you safe no matter the cost*, Farzad assured.

She opened her eyes and saw that the others were staring at her. One by one she looked into their eyes. She stared into the corner where there was nothing, then fell back from the table.

Farzad stood and grabbed her hand. Szwedko also came around the table.

Langdon and Billie sat up in their chairs. James looked tense, his eyes taut and holding her gaze.

Ericka saw an image of the fuel line on Farzad's helicopter. It sat in the red.

"Sit down," Farzad whispered.

Szwedko walked back to the end of the table. "Ace might not look like much, but he's a five time champion of the Marsden Award. His I.Q. is one-hundred-and-ninety. He earned his first Ph.D. at the age of twelve. There's not a subject he doesn't know something about. If we come across any forest plants or animals that none of us are familiar with, we're hoping he can tell us what it is and if it's dangerous. I'm actually glad he's with us. Blue Trees Mountain is one of the least altered wildernesses in America. Don't be surprised if we see things out there we won't see anywhere else. So let's suit up and get moving. The sooner we find the Gabriel family the better chance they have surviving whatever it is that's kept them from coming out of those trees."

# CHAPTER 4

"Are you sure that's what you saw?" Szwedko and Ericka stood away from the others. "Ruined cities all over the world? Military jets falling from the sky?"

"When I looked in the corner I saw the *world*," Ericka stressed again, hoping this time he believed her.

"How many jets?"

"Hundreds. The sky was full of 'em. And they were falling, but none of them were damaged or smoking or anything like that. Just dropping like flies. And the cities, they were in complete ruin worse than any war photos you've ever seen. And the thing I saw you kill wasn't a snake. It was something that wasn't human, and it's waiting for us in the wilderness."

Szwedko's eyes focused heavily on hers. Fear. He sensed it in her body language and the alarmed look in her eyes. He had read every report he'd been given on her. According to those reports everything she saw in visions eventually came true.

"I'm telling you something is *wrong* with this place," she said. "Look at the trees. I can even see they're different. And there are people out there in the wilderness. You told them to run. You were trying to help them. The loss of our space satellites. Jets falling from the sky. Ruined cities. And there's something else. The helicopter outside has no fuel, which means we're stuck here until someone comes for us."

He rubbed vigorously at his mouth. She saw his need to doubt everything he'd heard.

"Radios don't work out here," he said. "We knew this coming in."

He grabbed her hand and led her to Farzad.

Farzad saw them approaching and stopped digging in his supplies for clothes to change into.

"Are you black on fuel?" Szwedko asked.

"Of course." Farzad stared from Szwedko to Ericka. "Are we calling this off already?"

"Show me how much fuel you have," Szwedko said.

The three of them walked out of the cabin to the Bell. Farzad quickly climbed in, put the headset over his ears, and fired it up. Szwedko and

Ericka leaned over him. The fuel needle refused to lift out of the red zone just like she'd seen in her vision.

"That can't be right." Farzad tapped the meter with his finger. "I would have noticed on the way here."

Szwedko stared at Ericka.

Farzad stared at Szwedko and Ericka. "I checked the BuNo myself before I left. There has to be juice in this helo."

"Radio headquarters," Szwedko began.

Ericka gripped Szwedko's arm, then pulled out of the helicopter and stared around at the trees. "I'm getting a strange feeling like we should be here and not to leave."

"But what you said!" Szwedko spoke heatedly.

Ericka faced him. "I know what I said and I'm telling you being here is going to be better than being down there. I'm staying."

Farzad cut the engine when both of them climbed out, then he climbed out after them.

"If you saw that many jets, Ericka, it means a lot of Bases are following procedures for an impending attack."

"You didn't see the cities the way I saw them," she argued. "My gut is telling me to stay here and stick to the mission. I'm asking you to trust me on this. Never try and change the future. Bad things happen whenever someone tries."

"Shit!" Szwedko raged.

Ericka touched his shoulder. "Most of us are safer here. None of us will be safe out of this mountain."

He stared at her a long while. "How certain are you of that?"

"Just as much as everything else."

Szwedko thought for a moment about his family and friends on the ground, and how what Ericka saw would affect them. With no radio and no fuel in the helo, he had no way of communicating with anyone other than those at the cabin.

Ericka turned and walked away. Halfway to the cabin she saw that just that quickly Szwedko no longer believed what she'd told him. And she couldn't blame him. It was hard for her to believe herself.

Farzad stepped inside of the cabin with her, then followed her to the other side where the last of the supplies had been left.

The others were either on the other side of the cabin going through backpacks, boxes and their portions of supplies or were outside looking to see where the best place was to start.

Farzad removed the aviator sunglasses and held her gaze. "What were you two talking about back at the Bell?"

She lowered to go through the supplies, because suddenly it became urgent to have as much as she needed before going inside the forest. She even grabbed more than she needed, and changes of clothing in various sizes. *What the hell am I doing?*

Farzad lowered beside her. His voice softened. "Talk to me, Ericka. What was Szwedko talking about?"

"I don't think Szwedko believed something I told him. I'm sure you won't either."

His hand pressed on top of hers, stopping her from filling a box with more supplies. "I have never been with a woman. No one knew that. I have never met my mother. I think about her all the time. If you saw that I'll believe whatever it is you have to say."

She studied his eyes, then bit down on her lip. "I think something will soon happen in cities all over the world. And I think something not human is waiting for us in the forest."

He gave a nod that was hardly noticeable. "Not human. An animal?"

She took a chance, because what she saw was too large to keep to herself but too frightening to share with everyone else. "Aliens. And I know how crazy it sounds. And even though I saw what I saw, I'm getting a strong feeling it will be safer in the forest than in the city."

He held her gaze a moment longer, then stared back at the door. Szwedko stood outside it, checking his rifle and making certain it was fully loaded. "I think he does believe you."

Ericka gazed over her shoulder. Szwedko stared at her, racked the slide on his rifle, then walked away.

Farzad stood and walked away. She saw it very clearly.

She stood to her feet. "You're one of the three!"

When he turned she saw he was confused.

"What I said earlier about three people saving the world. You're one of the three," she repeated, then lowered again and finished what she'd been doing.

Farzad stood where he was a long time.

# CHAPTER 5

Farzad's three-piece suit had been switched to Army fatigues. The all-terrain boots on his feet revealed they had been worn on many occasions. Again sunglasses covered his eyes, and Ericka knew why he continued to wear them. His eyes were the palest shade of blue. In the cabin he squinted harshly against the sunlight after he'd taken them off.

Langdon and Billie stood close together sharing a map, their fingers pointing out several areas of the forest, then down again.

Szwedko sipped bottled water, his eyes constantly finding Ericka's.

Bagley waited patiently as he watched Langdon and Billie. James leaned against three black cases tied down to a single sled. Inside them were I.V. bags of glucose and needles to hydrate anyone they found.

Strapped to each sled were enough medical supplies to share with more than a dozen people.

As Ericka watched everyone, she knew Szwedko hadn't shared with them the things she saw.

The cabin now sat empty. Everyone had their sleds. Ace left his a few feet away and lowered to the grass, his fingers brushing across it like carpet.

Ericka pulled her sled closer when Farzad also fingered the grass. Ace heard her approaching, stared at her, then out at everyone else. "Look at this grass. Really look at it."

It didn't look like grass and more like lettuce. Each blade grew thick and closely together just like the trees.

Not far from them, Grath also lowered to the grass, pushing his fingers through it.

Langdon and Billie stopped studying the map, saw that the others had lowered to the ground, and stepped closer to Grath. A small conversation took place and then everyone drew closer together.

"I agree with James. Neither family could have gotten far in that," Billie said, nudging her head toward the forest. "It looks far too wild and uninhabited."

"It's on you, Ericka," Szwedko said. "I think you should point us in the right direction."

Ericka already knew where she was going. Even now the area pulled on her to get there in a rush. She stood and looked southeast, pointing in its direction. "I'm going over there."

"We all are," Szwedko corrected. He held her gaze. "Are you ready?" He looked down at the grass, indicating he also thought it looked beyond strange.

When they reached the trees, the trees were tightly together just like they'd appeared from the cabin. To get inside the forest, one by one each team member climbed over tree roots while using both hands and using their legs and feet. Each of them made sure they kept their sleds with them. One step inside the forest and sunlight almost disappeared with barely enough penetrating the treetops, giving the impression of early evening.

Ericka stopped walking and stared farther south, then walked in that direction.

Farzad saw her change directions and followed. To get on the other side of the trees that the two of them came to, Farzad had to lift her to reach the top of the root that grew above ground.

Ericka used her feet to climb up. Climbing down the other side was what she had expected, but once she reached the top, the other side of the root was buried into a higher floor in the forest. It looked almost as if the ground had once shifted and had never righted itself. All she had to do was stand and walk, but not before she pulled her sled up behind her. While she did this the others talked below. Soon hands reached for the top of the root. Bodies climbed over. Once they were all standing, they stared ahead of them, then turned and stared behind them.

Behind them lay a painstaking maze of upraised roots. In front of them grass carpeted the forest floor.

"Guys, this is... fucked up," Ace concluded in a tone of awe. "I mean. There's hardly any sunlight." He stared at them to see if anyone was catching on to what he said. "Grass shouldn't grow here, especially not like this."

Ericka walked ahead, pulling her sled. The others saw Szwedko and Bagley following her, then also followed. After several steps the grass could no longer be seen, but it could still be felt.

"Oh, man," Ace complained, staring down and watching each step he took.

Above the grass grew a garden of never-ending, knee-high fern.

"This is beyond fucked up," he said.

"And I thought the grass was strange," Langdon said.

Ericka kept walking, only the uppermost part of her sled visible through the fern.

"Keep walking," Szwedko said when Langdon and Billie paused to take in everything they saw.

Farzad pulled in front of everyone and walked beside Ericka. "You have to admit it's kind of beautiful. Strange, but beautiful."

And it was. Beautiful and wild.

It took almost an hour to walk out of the ferns. It stopped abruptly in front of tree seedlings in various stages of growth. In between the seedlings mature trees had grown high into the sky.

"I just saw something that meets my qualification of being highly suspicious," Ace said.

Szwedko and Bagley kept a tight perimeter, both of them staring up at the trees.

"Like why we haven't seen any birds?" James asked.

"That and the silence," Billie answered as she attempted to look past the treetops to see the sky but couldn't. "The more I walk the more I feel I've stepped into a cave with a disappearing door."

"There's no moss," Langdon said, her eyes darting from tree to tree in search of moss to prove herself wrong.

"There's nothing dead on the ground either," Billie said. "Not even leaves."

The others looked down in search of anything that can be classified as no longer living, except Ace.

"Are you guys stupid or something?" he asked. "Are you telling me none of you noticed that three trees are growing out of each other over there?"

Eyes darted to see the spectacle, and when they saw it they all stood silently.

A single tree grew out of the ground. A second tree grew out of it just above the roots. A third tree began halfway up, its roots wrapped around the trunk until all three trees became one. Branches didn't grow out from the trunk until very high up, branches wide enough for three people to sit side by side and still have room left over. The leaves were overly large on all three trees, lustrously green and thick and wide enough to fold around a person like a blanket.

"Guys, for this forest to grow like it has I'm talking advance metabolic growth," Ace said. "And for that growth to reach as far as the cabin, something is feeding this forest from underneath *and* above ground."

He started to point to another tree when James walked a short distance away and stopped; his eyes tight and narrow as he stared ahead.

Szwedko took a step closer to him.

"You saw something?" he whispered.

"A blue glow," James answered. "Saw it from the corner of my eye, but can't find it now."

Grath stepped closer. "Small or large?"

James shook his head. "Don't know, and I don't think we've been told everything about this place."

Up until that moment Bagley had taken every step with his rifle braced against his shoulder and aimed. It now lowered. "What do you mean they didn't tell us everything?"

Szwedko's eyes were narrow in thought. "This forest isn't what we were told we would find. The last search team didn't mention any of what we're looking at."

"Maybe the forest on the other side looks different," Bagley suggested.

A sound similar to a startled cougar echoed between the trees.

A crackle sounded on everyone's left and in the direction James claimed to have seen the blue glow.

Szwedko and Bagley raised their rifles and aimed. Their reaction released a collection of crackles, it seemed, from all directions. What frightened everyone was the crackles didn't sound like dead twigs or branches snapping, but more like dry brittle bones grinding against each other.

"Ericka," Szwedko said. "Are you picking anything up on this?"

Their eyes met.

"You didn't believe me back at the cabin," Ericka said.

Szwedko tightened his hold on his weapon.

"What did she tell you earlier?" Bagley asked, his weapon visibly trembling as the crackling noises closed in. "What the hell are we listening to?"

Ericka's shoulders deflated. Her chin lowered. A cool breeze closed in around her. On her left, crackles sounded as the creature's outer plates shifted and reset. A three-toed foot pressed heavily against the ground. For seconds she saw darkness, and then a small fire burning. Sitting in front of the fire sat a black, teenage boy hugging his legs. The floor of the forest covered his face and had lines running through it like those on a map. Something positioned just above his forehead refused to pull into focus.

She reached a hand out to the side of her as she struggled to keep the image in her mind, forcing it to stay where it was.

"Side pocket! Side pocket!" Szwedko yelled.

James reached into Szwedko's side pocket and drew out a small notebook.

"Get the pen, too," Szwedko said, "and put both in her hand."

"What am I looking at?" Ace stared at Ericka. She stood still and as if she no longer drew breath, like a statue of someone long forgotten that had been erected between the trees.

"Sh!" Farzad warned as his hand passed slowly in front of Ace's face to get his attention. And then Farzad stared at Ericka and began to nod. "Okay. Okay," he whispered to no one. "I see now why they brought you here."

"What is she doing?" James screamed when Ericka began drawing a map while her eyes were still closed. "Make her stop!"

"I've read every report the government has on her," Szwedko said. "She's never been wrong in the past. Ever. Let's hope she has some good news."

Ericka's lips parted. A sliver of air could be heard coming from between them.

"Oh, shit!" Ace fell back from her. "Is she possessed? I know about demon possession. I know some of everything!"

Ericka's eyes opened; her mouth slowly closed. She held the map out to Langdon.

Langdon refused to reach for it.

"Guys, I'm getting really scared," Billie cried, her face pinched in a pained expression as she continued to search where the crackling noises were coming from. Whatever was moving, there were now many of them, causing the crackles to sound like many bones popping into place one after the other and in a domino effect.

Langdon heard the noises getting closer and took a cautious step closer to Ericka, snatched the notebook, then took a quick step back.

"Talk to us, Ericka!" Szwedko yelled, his rifle aiming up, down, in one direction, and then another. "What are we listening to? What did you see just now?"

Ericka's shoulders and chest rose and fell in a rapid rhythm.

Farzad lowered in front of her and held her gaze.

"Tell us what you saw," he said softly, gently.

Ericka's mouth tightened. "I think the light James saw was them trying to see him better."

James turned in a circle nonstop, aiming a pistol up at the trees.

"I think they want the black boxes. I saw one of the boxes fly into the air. I think we should give the boxes to them instead of them taking the boxes from us."

"Them?" Bagley asked. "What are they?"

Ericka hesitated. "Aliens."

"Did she say aliens?" Ace asked.

Bagley kept his eyes on her, waiting, the word aliens not registering.

"Is it people, Ericka?" Grath pressed. "The Gabriels?"

Farzad stayed lowered in front of her, and held her gaze.

"Wait," Ericka warned and closed her eyes. They were closed for only a second when she snapped them open. Her eyes became wide. "I just saw what they look like! And it's real! I'm talking aliens! Aliens! Aliens!"

The pitch of her voice sent them all running. All of the sleds pulled behind them, except the one that contained the black boxes. Through the trees. Darting through outreaching branches. Over tree roots that grew above ground. And grass that cushioned their feet. Arms pushing wildly at anything in the way. Hard breaths. Loud pants. The sound of nine sleds swishing like skis on ice. At times the team separated. At other times the team joined together. At all times one person ran ahead.

And then everyone stopped when they noticed Ericka had come to an abrupt halt. Seeing this, everyone hurried to where she was.

"Listen to me," Ericka said in between breaths, and then her eyes got large. "Oh, no! This is not what I expected! I'm seeing only bits and pieces. We're running but some of them are outrunning us." She looked up at the trees.

"Why did we stop?" Bagley asked.

"Something is traveling over the trees," Ericka whispered. "It moves fast. One of them dropped to the forest floor ahead of us. It's waiting for us."

"How do we get out?" Billie screamed at the top of her lungs.

James grabbed Billie and gave her a violent shake. "Shut up! Did you not hear what we all just heard? We're outnumbered. Didn't you hear large butterfly wings clapping together as we ran? We need to stay quiet." He looked at Ericka, jagged breaths exhaling from his lungs. Fear in his eyes.

Szwedko searched the trees frustrated he couldn't see anything.

"I don't know what's waiting up ahead," Ericka said. "It hid behind a tree. Langdon needs to take us to the location on the map."

"Fuck that! We go back!" Ace whispered heatedly, staring at the others, waiting for someone to side with him.

"We can't go back," Ericka warned. "Something is back at the cabin. They have been watching us since we arrived. If we go back we'll startle it and all of us are dead. You don't even want to see what I saw if we go back."

"This can't be real," Billie said. "She's talking about aliens! There has to be a logical explanation."

The others stared at each other uncertain what to believe.

They were still staring at each other when a branch leaned far to one side as something crashed into it. The object broke apart, then rolled onto the ground. It was one of the black boxes. Claw marks had torn it apart until it was hardly recognizable. The case was now empty.

"What are we waiting for?" Ace screamed.

"Ericka!" Szwedko yelled.

"I'm not moving until Langdon does," Ericka answered.

Ace ran forward and pushed Langdon like a wrestler his opponent off the mat.

# CHAPTER 6

Billie's behavior left Farzad in awe. Twice the woman had to be restrained. Although she cried she was smart enough to do it silently. This told him that everyone now believed what Ericka said.

Szwedko looked over his shoulders, then pointed his rifle at nothing. "Something is moving. It almost looks like the *trees* are moving." Because that's what he saw, the entire forest taking each step they took.

"I was thinking the same thing," James said. Aliens didn't exist, he continued to tell himself, but until any of them saw what could make the noises they all heard he could only imagine what the enemy looked like.

Bagley kept his eyes on the trees.

Ace often stared at the others and wondered if he should risk going back to the cabin alone. The cabin couldn't have been worse than out here. Every step he took he saw something more and more wrong with the forest, and although he didn't want to believe it, only something alien could be the cause of it.

Langdon gripped the notebook like a GPS system. Her eyes constantly glanced at it. What she feared was reading it wrong. The lines on it curved constantly. An 'X' had been drawn at the top. In her mind X marked the place of safety.

"How're you doing with that map?" Bagley whispered.

"I don't know." She took careful steps as she looked down and up, down and up. "Let me concentrate."

Farzad stole a glance at Ericka and saw that she was already looking at him. As soon as their eyes met she stopped as if she'd been waiting for them to make eye contact.

Szwedko reached Ericka's side. "Langdon, bring the notebook."

The others realized the others had stopped, then hurried back until they formed a single group.

"Does she need an antenna to see more shit?" Ace asked, staring around.

Farzad reached for Ericka's hand, because she suddenly began to breathe heavily. She held his gaze, her eyes wide. She gave a small shake of her head.

A crackle sounded behind them.

James and Grath aimed pistols in that direction.

Langdon held up the map, then pointed in a different direction than they'd been heading in. "I can't read this map, but if I had to choose which way to go it'll be that way. The trees are planted differently there."

Ericka squeezed Farzad's hand and gave a slight nod. He knew then she had seen this moment happening and had stopped everyone so it could take place.

"Is that the right direction, Ericka?" Szwedko asked.

"Yes."

"How can you be sure?" James asked.

Billie pushed closer to Ericka. "I'm a better guide. Tell me where we need to go and I'll get us out of here."

"Stay calm, little woman," Farzad warned. "Now is not the time to lose your head."

"I'm curious to know why it has to be Langdon," James said.

"That's a good damn question," Ace reiterated.

"There's a kid alive somewhere near here," Ericka said. "Langdon finds the kid. Langdon needs to lead us out because I heard what she told him when she finds him."

"What?" James asked.

"The others scattered and are dead," Ericka answered.

"Langdon," Szwedko encouraged. "Get us out of here. Hurry."

"I say we go that way," Langdon said. "It's the way I'd go if I'd been alone."

She didn't wait for anyone to agree with her. She lowered the notebook and hurried in the direction she mentioned.

Ace saw Farzad holding Ericka's hand, then ran to catch up with Langdon to hold hers.

Langdon snatched her hand away without looking at him.

Ace stopped walking a moment, then walked alongside Grath, wondering if Grath would be offended if he held his hand.

If Langdon felt any fear, it couldn't be seen. Szwedko watched as she searched between the trees with hard, acute gazes. Each step she took was done as if sneaking up on a finish line. This woman had strength and for his sake he hoped the others had an equal amount as well.

Grath looked over his shoulder. For minutes he sensed something following. The crackle he heard had been small, but this time much closer than any of the others.

Another crackle.

"There's a clearing up ahead!" Langdon shouted with excitement.

Ericka squeezed Farzad's hand. He stared down at her. She held his gaze then gave another small shake of her head.

The trees up ahead came to a sudden end. The closer the team got they saw more and more of a row of dilapidated, dark wood cabins. One of the roofs had caved in.

Ace and Grath heard it at the same time, another crackle. Ace didn't turn to see what it was and kept his pace. Grath stayed where he was.

"Keep walking!" Ericka hissed in warning, but she didn't stop walking. She'd learned long ago that some of the things she saw no one could stop them from happening. "Don't look. Come on. Keep walking," she said.

Grath felt as if he had to look. Not once had any of them seen anything. He knew from experience it was hard to kill the enemy when you didn't know who the enemy was or what the enemy looked like.

Where he stood was just outside a break in the trees. He took a moment to search again. Now that they were out of the forest it surprised him to see what they had trekked through. In front of him looked more like a sea than a forest, with many waves that reached different heights. Most of the tree roots grew above ground, twisting above the dirt as tightly as string around a ball. Some of the leaves hung low and were bluish in color, giving an appearance of thickly woven spider webs or scattered condensations of fog.

His eyes narrowed on one of these areas, then locked on one in particular. In the center of it he saw a white and pink head of alien proportion. A chin was nonexistent. The head was larger at the crown, then narrowed at the ears and formed with the neck and chest. It had eyes larger than humans' that rested flat against a skull that had no skin or protective covering. What could have been cheeks but looked closer to gills flared underneath the eyes and close to a fleshy slit shaped like a Y. Intricately shaped bones marked the area below similar to the way Native Americans painted their faces for war. It wasn't until the smell of a decomposing corpse permeated his nostrils did he realize that whatever he was looking at perched on long arms and smaller legs, its face only an inch from his.

Bagley looked over his shoulder, saw what was standing face to face with Grath, aimed his rifle and squeezed the trigger while running toward it. The fear he felt rushed out of his mouth in both a yell and a groan.

The fleshy part of the creature's face opened. *Ka ka ka ka ka.* The noise started slow then became faster than the buzz of a chainsaw without losing its sound.

"Shit! Shit! Shit!" Ace screamed, his feet moving under him in no particular direction.

Szwedko had been waiting for this moment – the chance to see something to shoot at. Now that he saw it – for a moment – he had forgotten he was a soldier. It wasn't until the creature's body began to swell when he took calculated shots. With the rifle scope against his eye, he took large advancing steps, aiming only for the head.

Langdon's jaw opened wide enough for something to crawl out of it as she lowered to the ground with equally large eyes.

Ericka screamed with her mouth opened wide and her hands waving frantically in front of her face, because the creature she was looking at was different from the one she saw in her vision. *There's more than one kind of them!*

Farzad stood next to her, covering his mouth with both hands.

The creature's body made slow movements. With each move its many bones popped, making a sound similar to tubes pulled away from pressured gas. As its torso lowered to the ground its outer shell of a million bones rubbed against each other, causing the crackling noises they'd heard. Once on all fours its jaw lowered all the way to the ground. Its mouth became a cavernous hole a foot wide. A rope like tongue with fleshy barbed hooks darted out in instantaneous speed.

James unloaded his pistol, watching in awe as the rounds bounced off the creature's bones with no effect. He ejected the empty magazine, slammed in another, and kept shooting while frustration released out of him in piercing screams.

The sound of a thousand butterfly wings clapped together out of the forest. The ground underneath everyone gave small vibrations as heavier creatures ran in their direction. The last shot was fired when behind the smaller creature the trees parted on both sides. What stepped out sent the team running in separation directions. All except Billie. Crouched on the ground with her hands trembling in front of her face, she became paralyzed by what she saw. The thing in front of her couldn't be real. None of this is real is what she told herself as, "Ah! Ah! Ah!" rushed out of her mouth.

Bagley ran in an arc to reach her, his rifle aimed and firing.

"No!" Ericka tried to run after him. Farzad wrapped his arms around Ericka's waist and held her back. Her feet kicked as she continued to scream. "No! No! No!"

Szwedko saw his team scatter and remembered Ericka's warning.

"Follow Langdon!" he yelled. "Fall back! Fall back!"

Ace hugged the tree he was behind with his eyes closed, tears streaming down his face. Grath saw what was behind Ace, reached him, grabbed him by the hand, and fled across the clearing toward Langdon without realizing he was dragging Ace on the ground.

James, Szwedko and Bagley laid down fire.

Farzad yanked Langdon up from the ground with his free hand. "Get us out of here."

Langdon stumbled to her feet then looked left and right, then over Farzad's shoulder at the trees. Her eyes became wide.

Farzad turned to see what could have frightened her even more.

The bones on the larger creature were hard and smooth and burned in a blue glow. The glow turned the bones into mirrors that reflected the forest. As the creature took a step, it looked as if the forest moved with it, but the team saw that this wasn't true. Each individual bone had become one solid mirror, reflecting the forest in a three-hundred-and-sixty degree angle, causing the creature to almost totally disappear. Four three-toed webbed muscular black hands and feet with razor sharp nails sliced through grass. A head slowly emerged out of the creature's center where a stomach should have been. Four eyes encased in bone sat far on both sides of a hanging face. In the center of the eyes, overlapping bone separated, creating wing-like sounds as the creature's jaw opened wide.

Langdon ran not knowing where she was running to.

Billie clawed the ground as she tried to scramble to her feet.

Bagley ran closer to her, firing his weapon.

The smaller creature pounced.

The sound of a cougar's yowl was made as two muscular, red tentacles shot from between its legs and coiled around Billie like snakes fastening tightly to prey. Billie's eyes grew wide as her body curled and lifted high into the air as the tentacles tightened. Bagley saw this and fell back. A rope-like tongue with large barbed hooks darted out of the larger creature's mouth and coiled around Bagley's body with the strength of a boa constrictor. As the larger creature retreated into the forest, it pulled Bagley behind it on the ground. The last thing the team saw were Bagley's hands dragging on the ground before disappearing between the trees.

"Come on!" Szwedko yelled as he ran past Ericka and Farzad, hoping he could catch sight of Langdon and where she had gone.

The smaller creature didn't take Billie with it. Her body now lay on the grass. The creature pressed its face against Billie's as it peered deeply into Billie's dead eyes, then it gave a single bounding leap toward the trees and disappeared.

Farzad looked to his left.

Everyone was gone except Ericka. She stared at him breathing hard, patiently waiting.

"Did you know that would happen?"

"What I saw hasn't happened yet."

"Can you get us out of here?"

"I need to get on the other side of the mountain. Can you come with me?"

"What about the others?"

"I didn't see them where we're going. I can't change what I see. Please don't question it."

"Did you see me with you?"

"Yes." She hesitated. "I saw you protecting me."

BONUS CHAPTERS PART TWO

# THE BLOOD FEUD

## (Book One of the Dardian Dreshaj novels)

# CHAPTER ONE

It was the eleventh hour.

Three hours into a twelve-hour shift, ER Nurse Michaela Cosenza held up a syringe of Demerol toward the light at the same time she saw what appeared to be the naked buttocks of an elderly man fleeing across the room.

"What the hell!"

She snapped her head toward the image and saw that the naked buttocks was being chased by a tall, black male nurse.

Nurse Alvin Canton reached the waiting room door just when eighty-one-year-old Albert Foat did. At first Mr. Foat hadn't seen Alvin, but when he did he let out a high-pitched shriek, then blurted, "Gah-gah!" He knew he was outweighed in battle and much shorter than Alvin's six-foot frame, but still grabbed for the door. He managed to thrust it open, revealing behind it the crowded waiting area.

Not only was the waiting room filled to bursting with its usual number of heart patients, influenza sufferers, the elderly, crying babies and asthma patients in desperation, all breathing in a cocktail of vomit, antiseptic cleaners and vending machine coffee-scented air. Bill Clinton, a believable Marilyn Monroe, the Tin-Man and hordes of vampires watched with amusement as a naked Mr. Foat took on the physically fit male nurse, both of them wrestling for control of the door.

Mr. Foat had no chance of escaping into the night as was his plan, but this hadn't stopped him from putting forth his best effort. He forced his entire body to go rigid and planted his feet firmly on the floor. Alvin tried to counterbalance Mr. Foat's weight, which caused Mr. Foat's body to begin rocking back and forth. And so did his penis. It swung up and down, up and down as if it too was in battle. It was Michaela's gasp that caused Alvin to glance down. He saw what was swinging madly at him and had enough. He tried holding Mr. Foat away from him, but Mr. Foat made a lunge toward him and gripped him in a wrestler's hold.

Alvin managed to untangle himself. "Mr. Foat, stop this madness!"

Mr. Foat returned with, "G-yah! G-yah!"

"Michaela! Is this your patient?" Alvin yelled.

Another nurse appeared from behind a curtain, blinked at what was going on, then stood stupefied, her eyes telling Alvin he was on his own with this one. But she did offer, "Michaela!" as if Michaela possessed the cure-all to calm Mr. Foat down.

A nurse stuck her head out from behind a curtain. "Mr. Foat, come away from that door! Haven't we told you over and over you can't walk around like this? You must stay in bed until the doctor has a chance to see you."

Mr. Foat was now rocking vigorously, as if to shake Alvin senseless. He then closed his eyes and yelled, "June! June!"

Michaela dropped the syringe in her medication cart's drawer and slammed it shut, then hurried toward Mr. Foat. His eyes opened and widened when he saw her; she knew what would happen next. Although he was nearing eighty-two he pulled away from Alvin with great strength, shuffling across the linoleum like a toddler imitating a locomotive picking up speed. And then he was off, his gait unsteady.

"Catch him before he falls!" Alvin yelled.

Michaela reached out toward him, but he slipped through her fingers like something oily and made his way to the counter that used to be the old ER admittance desk. He gripped it tightly, then held on for dear life. "June! June!"

Alvin slammed the waiting room door, closing out the instant roar of laughter behind it. "There is most definitely a full moon tonight," he said as he slipped back behind a curtain to hang an IV.

Michaela grabbed Mr. Foat gently by the shoulders. "Come with me, Mr. Foat. Your bed is over there."

"Where's June? You're not June! She was just here. What the hell did you and all these people do to her?"

His family assured the staff there was no such person in his past, but Michaela wasn't so certain.

"June! Where the hell are you?"

She whispered in his ear, hoping the staff didn't hear what she said. "Mr. Foat, June is looking for you."

His brown rheumy eyes squinted as his mouth gaped open. "What? Speak up. I can't hear you."

"June!" Eva, the ER clerk, said loudly. "June is over there!"

Mr. Foat's chin lowered to his chest, his arms hung limp by his side. He climbed on his gurney unassisted. Michaela pulled the blankets over him and saw that the gown he'd worn earlier had been tossed in the trash. As she bent to retrieve it she heard a groan. She straightened and saw that Mr. Foat had just that quickly fallen asleep. She gazed at the curtain behind his bed and knew then that the groan had come from behind it.

She lifted the bed's safety rails hoping this time Mr. Foat couldn't escape. She tossed the gown in a hamper outside his curtain, then crossed the room to wash her hands. As she dried them she gazed at the curtain beside Mr. Foat's and saw an orderly slipping from behind it. The patient behind the curtain was Carlo Mancini. She decided to check on Mr. Mancini to make sure he wasn't in any more pain. As she neared the curtain a woman tapped her from behind. "Nurse?"

Michaela had forgotten about the Demerol. She hurried to her medication cart, double checked the dosage in the syringe, then followed the woman behind a different curtain to give the patient there the injection. Ridding herself of the syringe, Michaela hurried toward Carlo Mancini's curtain.

She ripped it back, took one look at the bed and screamed louder and more maniacally than Mr. Foat had for June.

Mr. Foat's head was first to come through the side of the curtain, and then the rest of his naked body followed. "Gal, what the hell you do to this feller's chest?"

# CHAPTER TWO

**H**omicide Detective Jesse Richards was last to arrive.

The hospital's residential neighbors were out in full mass. Some of them still in trick-or-treat get-ups, some in pajamas and robes. One of them held a sign that read 'no room for NY mobsters here.' The sign was turned over. The other side read 'a crime like this need to stay in NY.'

News vans claimed every inch of the curb, and would remain there until they captured live footage of the body being loaded inside the coroner's van.

A small drive for unloading patients sat in front of the ER entrance doors. Jesse recognized the many unmarked Crown Victorias and Dodge Chargers crammed tightly together. There wasn't much left of the drive's asphalt; still he had no intentions of parking anywhere else. Pressing down on the gas, he pulled as close as he could, door to door, to a Vic similar to his.

At that moment a black Chevrolet Tahoe turned the corner and parked in a red zone, the last part of the street that hadn't been staked. Jesse was certain the two men, dressed in grey suits, climbing out were federal agents.

An officer manning the yellow crime-scene tape lifted it high enough for him to stoop underneath. More officers inside recognized him and gestured for him to head toward them. One of them handed him a pair of blue nitrile gloves to wear. The officer's name was Studebaker.

"It's gotta be him. The piece of shit. They're all in the back waiting for you."

Forensics agents were everywhere making notations, documenting, drawing sketches, taking hordes of pictures, video recording and removing anything they felt could be used later as physical evidence.

His partner of seventeen years readily stepped away from an

officer and headed his way. "You're not going to believe this," Edwards said. "Hell, I almost didn't believe it myself. Half the fucking world is out looking for this scuzzbag. Twice he was featured on 'America's Most Wanted,' but neither airing resulted in anything concrete. From what I've heard, the FBI exhausted all their leads."

"They're here. They just showed up."

"It's him, Jess," Edwards said, trying to disguise a smile. "Vito fucking *Russo*. And someone offed him here – inside this hospital in *our* jurisdiction. Wait 'till you see him."

Edwards led him deeper into the examining area. All other patients had been removed. There were more agents, officers.

Against a wall, in the middle of the room, a narrow bed was trapped between two curtains. The man lying on top of it was beyond dead. Gray toes. Large purple bruises underneath his legs where what was left of his blood had settled. The blunt end of a scalpel was sticking out of his chest.

A forensic agent was standing beside the bed waiting for him.

Jesse took in the crime scene. There was something totally wrong with what he was looking at. Where was the blood? A small amount was contained to the bed. The floor underneath still looked cleaned and polished. The walls were free of blood stains and spotless. At first sight it looked like Vito Russo had committed suicide by sticking a scalpel in his chest and had somehow managed to keep the scene of his death as contained as possible while he laid there and barely bled. That is until Jesse got closer. It became obvious that someone had given Vito a little help in entering the afterlife. Vito Russo had a large perfect smile where there shouldn't have been one. A hamper sat perpendicular to the bed. It was filled to bursting, its lid tightly closed.

"Our killer?" Jesse asked Edwards.

"They found everything exactly like this."

The agent pointed toward the too large smile. "I think your killer is left handed. He started on the left side of the neck just below the ear. The first cut severed the carotid artery, but your killer didn't stop there. He continued here making sure to cut deep enough. It looks to me like he sliced through the vocal cords, but the M.E. will have to confirm this."

"He didn't have a chance to scream?" Jesse asked.

"The scuzzbag never had the chance." Edwards answered, glancing over his shoulder at the sound of footsteps. Jamison, their lieutenant, sidled up to the bed.

Jamison said, "Judge Wendell was interrupted while dining at the Vagabond. Everyone is anxious to get to work on this if you haven't noticed. What have you got?" The question was directed at both detectives.

Edwards spoke up. "His medical records have already been bagged and tagged. I got a chance to get a peek at them. One of the nurses gave him a strong sedative and a killer amount of pain medication. It could be that more than one person was trying to do him in. My guess is he never even realized what was happening to him."

"Why didn't one of the doctors phone the police as soon as he arrived?" Jesse asked.

"None of them recognized him. He was going by the alias Carlo Mancini," Jamison answered.

Jesse glanced down at the grey yet pleasant expression on Vito Russo's face. The vic couldn't have known he was dying or the expression would have been different. There wasn't much he knew about him, except for what he'd seen on television. He was the ex-don of the Manzara crime family in New York. During the 80s and 90s he was mentioned on the news often. Murder, extortion, but mainly he was remembered for operating one of the largest prostitution rings in Manhattan.

After one of his best girls leapt from the minor leagues to the majors by becoming a madam and taking two other of his best girls with her, Russo sent out a few of his button men to make an example of her. The woman, Jennifer Pettis, was twenty-two at the time, a teenage runaway with a thousand-dollar-a-day drug habit. She was porking an up-and-coming senator when Russo's goons burst through her bedroom and riddled them both with bullets. An investigation proved that Russo knew Senator Jim Bannock would be there, and that it was Senator Bannock who had given Jennifer the balls to leave his organization for a small slice of the pie. Russo, who had helped pitch the senator into the limelight, ordered the senator be whacked, too.

Not only did the DA get the murder charges to stick, Russo couldn't believe it when indictments were also handed down for one hundred and thirteen prostitution-related crimes. And this is where things get sketchy. A reliable tip believed to have come from a nearby precinct alerted him of exactly when the cops were coming for him. Russo went on the lam. That was eighteen years ago. Every image that Jesse remembered of him was of a much younger man wearing tailored suits and dark sunglasses, who was always surrounded by a horde of inhumanly beautiful babes.

The man on the bed was twenty pounds underweight and almost bald, and other than being dead appeared to have been living well.

"Why was he here?"

"Leukemia," Edwards answered. "Diagnosed a year ago. At his last visit his doctor gave him only months to live."

Agent Morales was examining the neck wound again when his head suddenly lifted. "Someone definitely wanted him dead sooner."

Jesse leaned closer to Russo's neck. "Now that's a clean cut."

"Better than a surgeon's hand." Morales gave a smile of pride. "The cleanest I've ever seen, if I may say so. It almost looks like surgery. No blood splatter. It's amazing there's no trajectory. We checked. Not a single drop of blood hit the walls or the floor, none of the furniture."

"But you're gonna keep looking, right?" Derision crept into Edwards' tone.

"Because our killer took his time,    " Jesse answered, ignoring Edwards' question. He turned Russo's head and caused aimless eyes to avert across the room, the pleasant expression mocking Jesse as he gazed at it. "Too much time."

"Someone had to see something," Edwards insisted. "The problem is, so far, all of the staff is saying they saw nothing unusual."

On Russo's chest the killer had carved the word 'besa,' then plunged in the scalpel so it stuck out like an exclamation point.

"Besa means kiss in Spanish," Edwards speculated.

"Something tells me it means something else," Jesse said. "Fingerprints?"

"Not a single one that will lead to anything. Someone wiped down the bed, at least the exposed areas where we should have found prints. Not even on the bedside table. The top of it was also wiped clean. As for the hamper, it came from a new shipment that hasn't yet made its way to the floor, except this one."

"You're telling me our killer took the time to clean?"

"Exactly that."

Jesse gazed around the room and noticed for the first time that most of the people inside it were looking busy, but weren't actually doing much. And now he knew why.

"Who found him?"

"The nurse who took care of him since he arrived."

"Where is she?" Jesse asked.

"The nurse's lounge," Jamison answered. "I commandeered it to use for questioning. Pattison and Trigg are questioning the other staff, but I told them to hold off questioning her until you got here. Get answers on this one. As soon as you can. The next time a camera and microphone is shoved in my face, I want to have something more than a goddamned, unconvincing smile. "

No one knew anything. Security guards, nurses, doctors, housekeeping; none of them saw anything unusual except a patient named Foat who had run around naked.

Nurse Cosenza sat visibly trembling at the table nearest the corner, her hands constantly flicking back her hair. A nervous reaction. Jesse had seen it time and time again. Edwards had been asked to stay near the door and observe. Jesse hadn't wanted to frighten her more than she already was. Half of his department believed she was the killer. Jesse wasn't so sure.

Michaela sat up in attention as he approached, her eyes widening.

Jesse smiled and sat down. "You like coffee? How about a cup?" He reared back in his chair and glanced over his shoulder. "Coffee. Two cups. Lots of sugar and cream in both."

Within seconds two vending machine cups were placed on the table.

Jesse pushed one of them forward with his fingertip. "Long night?"

Michaela nodded at him and lifted the cup with shaky fingers.

"I hear ER was chaotic tonight. A patient by the name of Foat ran around naked twice. I hear he's a regular, just like Mr. Mancini."

"I never met Mr. Mancini before today."

It made sense. The patient known to the hospital as Mancini should have been admitted as soon as he arrived. The hospital had booked a bed for him on one of the upper floors well in advance. Why he had been in ER was still a mystery at this point. Whenever he asked, none of the staff seemed to know the answer.

"Did he look familiar?"

She shook her head.

He leaned forward. "Tell me what happened, Ms. Cosenza. Everything."

Michaela sat the cup on the table. "Mr. Foat had been worse than ever. He kept removing his gown. The man's like Houdini. One minute there. The next minute gone. I must have chased him from every corner of the ER tonight."

"How close was his waiting area to the victim's?"

"Right beside it."

"While you were chasing him did you see anything unusual?"

She shook her head.

All of the other nurses and doctors had said the same thing. None of them had seen anyone go behind the curtain, except Nurse Cosenza.

"Mr. Mancini was very quiet – didn't say much." A tear came to her eye. Very slowly she licked off more of her lipstick. "He just laid there and asked for more and more pain meds. His chart said it was okay, you know?"

There was something in her voice that alarmed him. She knew something – something she wasn't telling.

"Something had to happen, Ms. Cosenza. You saw what Mr. Mancini looks like now, didn't you?"

"I didn't do it!" she screamed, and then she leaned back in her chair and flicked him off, and then she flicked off the officers huddled in the doorway.

A loud sigh escaped her lips. "I know what you're all thinking. That it was me."

Jesse shot back with an equal amount of frustration. "He was your patient."

This winded her. Slightly.

The next thing he said he knew would push her back into her corner. "You were the only one *seen* going behind his curtain."

Her chin lowered.

"One of the nurses was quick to tell us that you have family in New York – that you're Italian and that you often brag of having family and friends linked to the mafia."

Her head lifted sharply; her eyes were huge.

"What the hell does that have to do with anything? I'm Italian, okay! So what, I'm from New York. Mr. Mancini knew what was going to happen to him! He wasn't in pain. I can tell. And he wasn't a drug addict either. I can tell that, too. He *wanted* to be overmedicated. I know he did. He knew someone was coming after him and didn't want to feel what they were going to do to him. He wanted to see who was coming. He kept telling me not to close the curtains. He kept asking me when we were moving him upstairs where it was safe."

"Did anyone hear him ask for pain meds?"

More tears fell. Her head shook.

Jesse traced a finger over his lips. He believed her, but still he knew she knew something more.

"Did you close the curtains?"

"Yes, but only after he had fallen asleep!"

"Why?"

"He refused to be covered with blankets. You saw him. He wasn't wearing much. All of the patients who passed his bed kept staring at him. In nursing school you're taught to preserve patient dignity."

"Where do you suppose the killer got hold of the scalpel?"

"Behind the curtain next to Mancini's bed."

"Was anyone in that room?"

She shook her head. "It hadn't been cleaned after the last patient. It sat empty for a long time."

Jesse sat forward. He was finally getting somewhere. The killer could have been hiding behind those curtains waiting for his opportunity.

"Did you leave the curtains in that examining area drawn or closed?"

"Closed. It was a mess. There was blood on the bed, the floor. The patient was given an emergency trach. Housekeeping was called to clean it, but they never showed up. I don't know why."

"Tell me about the groan."

Russo couldn't have groaned. The wound on his neck and the expression on his face proved it. Jesse suspected the killer made the noise as he plunged the scalpel in as far as it could go.

"I thought he was in pain." She tried to lift the coffee, but now her fingers were trembling uncontrollably, and then her head lifted high above her shoulders like someone had kicked her in the rear. "An orderly!" she blurted loudly. "After I heard the groan. I had gone to wash my hands. When I gazed back I saw an orderly step from behind Mr. Mancini's curtain." She leaned forward in a rush. "He was walking toward the waiting room. He was slightly shorter than you, but not by much. He was wearing gloves. I couldn't see his hair, because he wore a green paper protection hat. I saw his face, but it was covered."

"What do you mean covered?"

"He was wearing a mask. And he must have been wearing protection goggles, because I don't remember seeing his eyes. I think he saw me, but I can't be sure. I thought it was Anthony Cook, because he works on the oncology unit. I thought he had come to transport Mr. Mancini upstairs, because Mr. Mancini was to be admitted."

Jesse ravenously munched on a handful of Skittles as he stood beside the hospital's security team.

Anthony Cook, the orderly assigned to transport Carlo Mancini to the Oncology Unit, had never left his floor. His whereabouts at the time of the murder were verified by the staff working that evening. This excluded him as a suspect. There were still a few other ER doctors that needed to be questioned, but Jesse was certain that none of them had anything to do with the murder.

He popped more Skittles in his mouth.

Edwards stood closer to the security feed monitors, his eyes telling the security tech to get on with it. Edwards was coughing continuously, but was unfazed by the looks given to him by the others in the room. He had been coughing for days. Tonight it seemed worse.

"Are you all right?" Jesse asked.

"I'm good. I'll do even better once we get on with this. By the time this techie brings up anything, our killer could be long gone."

The technician rolled his eyes and continued working with the feed to get it to the right hour they needed. If they could get a glimpse of the security feed recorded in the ER, they may have the opportunity to see their killer in the flesh.

The tech began manipulating more buttons, then began to play the feed slowly.

"That's the parking lot," Edwards said. "We need to see inside the examining area."

"Ain't going to be able to do that. Cameras are not allowed in the examining areas."

"What about the waiting room?" Jesse asked, pitching the empty Skittles bag in a nearby trashcan. "As close to the examining rooms door as possible."

The room became silent when the killer suddenly appeared onscreen. He emerged into the waiting area a few seconds before Nurse Cosenza screamed. He was wearing hospital scrubs, all of his skin covered so his nationality wasn't clear. He wore latex gloves and a green paper hat so that his hair color wasn't visible. His face was covered in a mask, his eyes shielded behind a pair of safety eyewear as Nurse Cosenza had suspected. What made both detectives alarmed was the killer didn't walk out of the hospital, but turned into a hallway that led toward the chapel and other offices.

"The son of a bitch is still here," Edwards said.

*Nurse Cosenza.*

Jesse ran back to ER only to discover that Nurse Cosenza had been given the rest of the night off.

I hope you enjoyed the bonus chapters. To see all of Shelley Young's books that are on the market, check out her website at www.shelleyfiction.com.

Made in the USA
San Bernardino, CA
07 May 2020